THE FIRES OF FREEDOM

THE EMBERS OF HOPE

BY

SALLY LAITY & DIANNA CRAWFORD

COMPLETE AND UNABRIDGED

Since 1948, The Book Club You Can Trust

Library of Congress Cataloging-in-Publication Data

Laity, Sally.
  Fires of freedom / Sally Laity and Dianna Crawford.
      p.   cm. —(Freedom's holy light ; v. 4)
   ISBN 0-8423-1353-2 (alk. paper)
    1. United States—History—Colonial period, ca. 1600-1775—Fiction.
2. United States—History—Revolution, 1775-1783—Fiction.   3. Man-woman
relationships—United States—Fiction.   I. Crawford, Dianna.   II. Title.
III. Series: Laity, Sally. Freedom's holy light ; v. 4.
PS3562.A37F57   1996
813'.54—dc20   96-3590

Printed in the United States of America

01   00   99   98   97   96
 6   5   4   3   2   1

First Combined Hardcover Edition for Christian Family Book Club: 1997

The Fires of Freedom

*To our husbands, Don and Byron, for the continued love and support
that makes our writing possible. And to our families, with love.
May God's richest blessings be their portion.*

The authors gratefully acknowledge the generous assistance provided by

    Philip Bergen, Librarian
    The Boston Historical Society
    Boston, Massachusetts

who helped us gather necessary period data and maps, shared extensive knowledge of various settings, and forwarded biographical information on prominent figures who played a part in colonial America's fascinating history.

1

Autumn 1774

Abigail Preston looked up at the fluff of cloud that had momentarily dimmed the afternoon sunshine. Could it be possible? Had that been her own voice, mere seconds ago, accepting a marriage proposal—for a wedding barely two months away? And even more incredible, a marriage that would bind her forever to a man who had wandered across her path quite by chance on a stormy night last winter—and then come calling on precious few occasions since? Did she even truly know Benjamin Haynes, this dashing postrider and courier for the patriots who held her so close that she could scarcely breathe?

Abigail felt her heart skip a beat against the relentless pounding of his. She eased herself gently away and searched his face, taking in the tender smile that softened the square-ness of his jaw. It was hard to believe, but she thought she saw love shining in his light brown eyes. His boyishly handsome face looked ever so appealing, so hopeful.

Since meeting Ben, she had admitted to herself that she would one day welcome the idea of marriage again for the sake of herself and her children. But to be truthful, she had also expected their relationship to develop slowly and naturally over time.

"It'll be wonderful, you'll see! I can't wait for my parents to

meet you!" Ben's enthusiasm made its way into her consciousness and over her mounting fears. His arms held her gently
in place while he spoke. "It'll be the first Christmas my whole
family has been together in ages. And who knows, possibly the
only one for many years to come, when we'll be able to gather
at my parents' farm."

"I—"

"Christmas?" Cassandra repeated eagerly from her seat in
the garden dirt at their feet. "I love Christmas." She tugged
on the sleeve of Ben's doeskin jacket, still gripping the furry
lamb he had given her a little while ago. "Is your farm like
Gramma's or like Mister Spooler's over yonder?"

Abigail relished the interruption, the few seconds' reprieve
from having to respond to Ben. She looked down at her
daughter's angelic face, those big eyes glowing beneath her
honey blonde hair. So innocent, yet she had endured so
much for a child of three. She and her little brother could
sure use a father—especially one as gentle and kind as Ben.

Glancing back at Ben, who had stopped to hug Cassie, Abby
knew her heart had been drawn to him the day they first met.
Her dreams had been filled with him throughout the long
absences when he was busy delivering missives and coded
messages. And when he appeared today, interrupting her
work in the garden, she had barely been able to speak for the
joy that filled her heart. She didn't want to hurt him—never
that. But everything was happening so fast. Too fast. She
needed time to think, to sort out her thoughts. Time to pray
for guidance.

"My folks have a big horse farm, sweetheart," Ben was
explaining to Cassandra.

"They do? With baby horses, too?"

"Yep. Lots of them." He kissed her on the forehead. "You'll
see them real soon."

Cassandra skipped happily around them, flaxen hair and
muslin dress billowing in the breeze.

Ben turned again to Abigail, his expression pleading. "If we wed at Christmas, my love, every Christmas thereafter would have a double blessing, don't you think?"

His words were so persuading. She could envision a festive Christmas wedding, and at the very thought of it, she began to smile.

Ben grinned. "Then, after the holidays, you and the children could remain with my parents."

Abigail felt the knot of fear rising again. "Stay there? In Rhode Island?" *With strangers?* she all but added. And his parents' home had to be far, far different from this unassuming Massachusetts farm. She glanced at the weathered sheds and outbuildings nestled around the plain wooden house. This had been her home since the day she had married Raymond Preston and for all the lonely days since his drowning. She had tried so hard to fit in here as a new bride not even fifteen, to be accepted by Ma Preston and Bertha, Ray's sister. What if Ben's family didn't take to her either? What then?

"I realize my responsibilities as courier take me away most of the time," Ben went on, oblivious to her misgivings. "But the farm is on my main route of travel, so I'd be with you at least once a week—or pretty near so. Having you in Rhode Island would simplify a lot of things for us, believe me."

Abigail had harbored a multitude of daydreams and fantasies over the past few months—dreams of her charming Prince Ben riding in to whisk her and her children away from their lonely existence. But now all her marvelous dreams seemed to be dissolving under the light of reality—and fear. She rubbed a gritty hand over her temples, a grim reminder that she was standing in the garden, her work boots and homespun skirt caked with mud, as a young man proclaimed his love. He even offered her a kingdom, of sorts—but one he would only be able to share with her a day here, a day there. Trying to think of something to say, she toyed with the edge of her long apron, rolling it nervously in her fingers.

"Or I could try to find a larger apartment in Cambridge, where I'm headquartered." Ben whisked a smudge of dirt from her nose with his thumb. "But that might be impossible.

So many people are leaving Boston Town, now that it's been blockaded by the British. And once folks learn about the Continental Congress's decision to no longer abide by the decrees of Parliament, they just might start pouring out of there while General Gage is still allowing it."

He paused and shook his head. "You know, it wouldn't surprise me if the British tried holding the entire town hostage, the way they did my sister-in-law, Susannah. Or worse. I truly believe that the farm in Rhode Island is a safer, better place for you and the children. Truly."

Abigail's mind raced, trying to make some sense out of everything Ben was saying—not the least of which was the disturbing news that the Colonies had banded together in an agreement to defy England. She said the first thing that came to her mind. "Christmas is only five or six weeks away."

"Only?" Ben's tone was light and teasing as he stroked her cheek with the back of his fingers. "To me it seems an eternity. I've thought of nothing but you for so long."

His words tugged at her heart. He really was dear—and so charming. Any woman would be fortunate to have his attention. Timidly, she reached up to touch his face, only then aware that she still held the bottle of French perfume he had brought her. The sight of so elegant a gift only served to heighten her apprehensions. Surely such a well-spoken and traveled young man had to have sophisticated relatives. She slid the exquisite bottle into her apron pocket. "Just hearing you speak of your family, I'm afraid I—I would shame you."

"How can you say that?" he asked, drawing her close again.

But she would not be put off. She moved out of his arms and took a step back, embarrassment warming her face as she assessed the soft deerskin of his jacket, the finely crafted leather boots beneath his store-bought woolen trousers. "Look at me. Really look at me. Have you ever seen anyone in your family wearing homespun—and even worse, faded homespun with patches?" She indicated a neatly mended tear in the skirt. "How could I expect to be at ease among people who'll be talking about worldly things and wearing fine, fashionable clothes?"

He let out a relieved breath. "Is that all?"

"No, I'm afraid it isn't all. I have nothing to bring to this marriage, either. No household goods, no dowry, nothing. Your family could not possibly approve of me."

"My dearest Abby," Ben said, turning her palm up and bestowing a kiss, "if all I wanted was a wealthy wife, I would be out courting the daughter of some rich merchant. But I love you, do you hear? Only you. And as for clothes, I wouldn't care if you wore your work apron to the wedding." When she tried to interrupt, he placed his finger against her lips. "But if it'll help you feel more comfortable, we'll have some *suitable* clothes made for you. Surely there's a competent seamstress in Millers Falls."

Abigail could barely speak over the realization that someone so truly wonderful could love and court someone so lowly as she. "Yes, there is," she admitted. "Spinster Franklin, two doors down from the bakery."

"Then give this to her as a deposit." He pulled some money from his pocket, and without so much as even counting it, pressed it into her hand. "Have the woman make you a special dress for our wedding and two others besides—and a couple of outfits for Corbin and Cassandra, too."

Opening her fingers, Abigail gazed down at more money than she had ever seen at one time. "I . . . I can't take all this, Ben. It's far too much."

"It's only a fraction of what I intend for you to have in the future." He smiled down at Cassie. "What's your favorite color in the whole world, princess?" Ben asked, giving her nose a tap.

"Pink. It's the prettiest."

"Then pink it is, just for you, when I marry your mama. What do you think of that?"

"Oh, goodie! Pink, pink, pink!" Her face alight, she skipped a circle around them in the garden.

Abigail, having watched the exchange with a smile, was

amazed that Ben could get beyond her little girl's shyness. She and Cassie's little brother, Corbin, were the only people who had ever done so. Refusing the money for the dresses would surely rob Cassandra's joy . . . and Ben's also.

Still, this endeavor could prove to be a very expensive one, of that she was more than certain. She worked up courage enough to meet Ben's gaze. "Would you mind awfully if I were to purchase the goods with this money but sew my own new dresses, instead of wasting funds on a seamstress?"

Ben moved close and slipped an arm around her waist. "Not at all. As you wish . . . except for your wedding dress, that is. I would like that to be my gift to you. Order one as fancy as you want—and fancy slippers to match."

"For me, too?" Cassandra coaxed, her eyes wide and shining. "Please?"

"Yes, little one," Ben said. "New shoes for you and Corbin, too. I want all of you to look every inch as beautiful and *acceptable*," he added with a kiss on Abigail's cheek, "as you truly are."

"But—"

"No buts. I've had very few opportunities during my years as a postrider to spend more than a pittance of my earnings. It will give me the greatest pleasure to put some of my savings to good use." His eyes mirrored her own smile, then took on a teasing spark. "Now, m'lady, are there any other obstacles I must surmount?"

Abby only shook her head.

"Good. Then let's wipe away these worry lines." He brushed a strand of hair from her brow, then sprinkled her forehead with kisses.

"Me, too," Cassie cried, scrunching her expression into a comical scowl.

Abigail's heart swelled with love as Ben gave her daughter a loud smooch.

"Then it's agreed. I'll come for the three of you a few days before Christmas."

A shiver of fear, tinged with exhilaration, raced through

Abigail. She took a deep breath and nodded. "This will be such an adventure. I've never been farther from Millers Falls than the Connecticut River."

Ben grabbed her in a hearty hug. "Ah, my sweet, sweet Abby," he breathed. "The adventure is just beginning." Taking her hand, he turned her toward the house.

At the sight of the dwelling, Abby's shaky confidence dwindled. "Would you mind telling Ma Preston about us?"

2

Ben's spirit soared as he walked Abigail and Cassandra to the house to relate their grand plans to Abby's mother-in-law and guardian, Ma Preston. For weeks he had clung desperately to the hope of convincing Abby to marry him. He had prayed all during the ride from Cambridge that she would hear him out and accept his proposal. Things were definitely looking up.

Perhaps Dan was right. Dan was forever talking about the power of prayer and trusting the Lord. In the past Ben had not had much use for his brother's preacher talk, but lately he'd begun to believe it for himself. He had to admit he had witnessed some incredible miracles with his own eyes over the past couple of days. Just yesterday, Dan's wife, Susannah, had been allowed to leave Boston after having been kept under virtual house arrest for almost a year by British Lieutenant Alex Fontaine. She had appeared at Ben's rooming house in Cambridge even as Ben, Dan, and several others were at prayer, seeking God's guidance regarding a rescue attempt! That could only be the hand of God at work on their behalf.

And now, wonder of wonders, the fair Abigail had generously overlooked a tactless blunder Ben had committed on an unfortunate past visit and had agreed to become his wife! That had to be the Lord's doing also. His heart was near to bursting with joy. Swinging a glance her way, he was overcome by her fresh, wholesome beauty and the breathtaking sparkle in her turquoise eyes. He made a silent vow never to do anything that would cause it to dim.

Ben hugged her a little closer as they walked, revelling in the feel of her slender, soft form against his side. "I just know you're going to love the farm in Rhode Island. It sprawls over rolling green landscape, acres and acres of it, all measured off in fenced sections for the horses."

"Sounds lovely, doesn't it, Cassie?" She gazed down at her daughter, skipping contentedly beside them.

"Mm-hmm! 'Specially the baby horses!"

Ben chuckled and swept the three-year-old up into his other arm. "And," he went on, "the seaport of Providence is just four miles away. It's always busy and exciting. Ships sail in from faraway places loaded with all sorts of fancy things. . . . That is," he added, not bothering to disguise his bitter tone, "if the British navy doesn't stop them along the way and confiscate the goods first."

Abigail slid her arm around Ben and gave an empathetic squeeze. The move surprised and delighted him, and his love for her grew all the more.

Climbing the steps to the door of the two-story house, they could hear Ma Preston's gravelly voice and Bertha's boisterous one carrying from the front parlor. Ben felt Abby stiffen and hesitate as she peered anxiously up at him.

Ben lowered Cassandra to her feet and turned to Abigail. What a sweet, fragile thing she was, living with this pair of overloud females. No wonder Abby and her little girl seemed to draw into themselves when Ma and Bertha were around. And recalling Bertha's zealous attempts to maul him every time he came to the farm, Ben knew he would forever thank the Lord for sending along Wesley Nelson, right in the nick of time. Wes, a boatman on the Connecticut River, somehow managed to divert Bertie's attention long enough to marry her!

"Is there anyone else, sweetheart, who I should go to and ask for your hand? Your father, perhaps?"

She shook her head. "My folks are both dead. I was living

on my uncle's place a few miles from here when Ray started to come calling. Soon after we married, Uncle John sold his poor farmstead and moved on to the Mohawk Valley. I have a grandaunt in Millers Falls, but we've never been close."

Ben nodded, gave her an encouraging smile, then ushered his girls through the kitchen and into the hall.

"Now, that would be a sight to see, that would!" Bertha's voice had no difficulty reaching them from the front room. A loud bellow of laughter followed, accompanied by the stomp of a heavy boot.

Becoming a little nervous himself, Ben gave Abigail's hand a squeeze as they entered the parlor. Ben noticed that the room was as tidy and clean as he had seen it on other occasions. He knew, too, that it was largely Abigail's responsibility to keep it that way while the others tended the farm and the livestock.

Ma Preston, in a shapeless work dress and an overlarge sweater that was obviously a castoff from her late husband, sat in a wooden rocking chair, mending a sock on her darning spool. Straggly wisps of thinning gray hair had worked themselves out of her mobcap. Bertha's solid form occupied one end of the threadbare settee, and her big strapping husband sprawled on the other two-thirds of it, his head in her lap, his long legs dangling over the arm.

Ma glanced up as the threesome came in. "I see ya found our Abby right quick."

"Yes," little Cassandra said, proudly clutching the toy lamb Ben had brought her. Her free hand maintained its grip on his pant leg. "And he gave me this kitty and Mama some stuff that smells like flowers—and he's gonna marry us."

The remnants of a smile vanished as Ma's jaw dropped open. "What did you say?"

Wes sat up, and Bertha jerked her braid-wrapped head around and gawked at Ben in stunned silence.

"I . . . um . . . he . . ." The child shot a glance at Ben, then bit her lip and stepped behind the protection of his leg.

"That's right." Ben put an arm around Abigail and pulled

her close. "Abby has done me the supreme honor of agreeing to become my wife." From the corner of his eye he could see her color heighten as she raised her chin. "We wanted you all to know."

At that moment, Corbin toddled into the parlor, tugging the string of the toy stage wagon Ben had given him. "My Ben!" he cried, his face brightening in two-year-old delight. He reached up to him. "Come play?"

Ben felt his heart surge as he bent to embrace the towhead. "Not just now, buddy. Maybe later we can play. But for now, play with your sister, while we grown-ups have a talk." He turned the child toward Cassie. "There's a good lad."

Having eyed Abigail since getting the news, Bertha took possession of Wesley's elbow and cleared her throat. "We're just—just plumb pleased. Ain't we, sugar pie? Plumb pleased."

"Sure enough." He jumped up and grabbed Ben's hand, shaking it for all it was worth. "Congratulations, fella."

Upon closer scrutiny, Ben realized that Wesley Nelson's exuberance went a step or two beyond merely "plumb pleased." The man could only be making plans for the Preston property—property he now wouldn't have to share. But before he had time to mull this revelation over in his mind, Ma's wary demeanor caught his eye.

"Seems a mite strange to me," she said, cocking her head toward Abby, "that the wind started blowin' in that direction all of a sudden." She shifted her gaze from Abigail to Bertha, then finally settled upon Ben, as if awaiting an explanation.

"Well, yes, I suppose it does," Ben answered hesitantly. Amazing that the woman still believed he had actually been interested in her horse of a daughter. Ben had endured Bertha's numerous attempts to corner him, and on more than one occasion he had felt relieved to escape with his life. "But the truth is," he explained gently, "since the first day I met Abigail, I've thought of little else. I love her very much." He smiled into Abby's eyes. "And I'm looking forward to making a home for her and the little ones. In Rhode Island," he added to assure Ma that he wasn't interested in her farm.

"Horsefeathers!" the older woman spat, her voice even harsher than usual. "I'll hear no more such nonsense. The gal has a home—a fine home, too. Right here with us. I'll not abide any talk of you taking her and my Ray's boy away. It ain't fittin'. This is where they belong, and this is where they'll be staying." She tapped a gnarled finger on the arm of the rocker in emphasis.

Bertha snorted and gave a stout nod as Wesley retook his seat.

Ben felt Abigail withdraw into herself like a fragile flower closing against the frost, and he caught her trembling hand in his. The need to stand up for her fortified him. He met Ma's squinty blue eyes, which at the moment were blazing with fire. "I don't understand, Ma. I thought you liked me, that you'd be pleased to hear our news."

"I do like ya, boy. That ain't the point. That ain't the point a'tall. I gave birth to a gaggle of hardy gals, but had me but one son. And my Ray had only the one. I'm not about to let ya take what's mine away." The angry lines in the old woman's face softened as a wily smile tweaked her mouth. "'Course, if'n you was to stop traipsing all over the countryside and hitch that fine horse of yours to our plow and live here with the rest of us, now that'd be somethin' else altogether." She relaxed into the chair and began to rock in nonchalance, but her knuckles retained a whiteness from the strength of her grip on the armrests.

Some life that would be, Ben thought, ignoring Bertha's smug expression. He couldn't imagine himself under Ma's thumb the way Abigail had been all this time. Part of the reason he wanted to marry Abby so quickly was to take her out of here. She deserved a better life than this.

"But then," Ma continued after the slight pause, "I'm not so all-fired sure I want that, neither. Her marrying you would be like killing off my Ray all over again, like buryin' him a second time. And I don't need none of that."

Ben felt Abigail sag against him. He'd have to be the strength for them both. Even as he tried to encourage her with a tighter hug, he looked Ma square in the eye. "Mistress Preston, Abby is a grown woman. A widow. And she is free to do as she wishes."

"Is that a fact, now?" Ma leveled back, red spots appearing in her plump cheeks. "I say it ain't. The gal's been my responsibility since the day my boy married up with that pitiful, penniless orphan and brought her onto my property. She's my ward, and so are them kids of hers. And no court in the land'll see it any different."

"Well, Ma," Wesley said with a nervous laugh, "even if you did wanna take it to court, you know all them judges General Gage appointed have hightailed it to Boston to hide behind them troops of his."

The older woman's scorching glare wiped the grin from the big man's face, and a strained silence filled the room.

Ben could not believe the turn things had taken—and right after all the other recent miracles. He thought not only of Susannah's release but of his other relatives, hunted by the British. But miraculously, all of them were still free and were even entertaining thoughts of traveling to Rhode Island for Christmas. He had thought that God was at last smiling on his family. Was he wrong?

Someone tugged at his coat. He looked down at Cassandra's worried face. "Aren't we gonna go see the baby horses?"

Her eyes were the exact shade of Abigail's, and the pleading in them wrenched his heart. He gave her head a comforting pat. Then with renewed determination, he took a step toward Ma to have this out once and for all.

"Hey," Bertha said, getting up and going to the window. "There's a rider coming. Handsome one, too. I'm gonna find out who he is." Barreling past everyone, she bolted toward the door and wrenched it open.

"Good afternoon, my good woman," a man said from the front yard. "The horse at your rail belongs to Ben Haynes. Would he, perchance, happen to be here?"

Having recognized at once the British accent, Ben snatched Abigail's hand and rushed outside with her in tow to meet his brother-in-law Ted Harrington. "I'm here, Ted. But how did you get here so fast? I only just arrived a short time ago!"

"I've come straight through, in hopes of catching you. I've brought dire news. Dan has been arrested."

"Oh, no . . ." Ben rubbed a hand over his face as he felt his blood turning cold. "Don't tell me he was stupid enough to try going back into Boston."

Ted ran a hand through his hair and replaced the three-cornered hat he held in one hand. "No. We can but assume the British had Susannah and Felicia followed after their release. At least a dozen soldiers burst into your room at the boardinghouse."

Having had firsthand experience with lobsterbacks and their ruthless searches, Ben had no trouble whatsoever picturing that incident. "How did *you* escape? And what about Robby? And Yancy Curtis?"

With the hike of an eyebrow, Ted gave a shrug. "Well, you know Dan. As he's done before, he sacrificed himself again so the rest of us could get away." He paused, and profound sadness dulled the smoky blue of his eyes. "I'm terribly sorry, Ben."

As if only now aware of the things he was saying in the presence of strangers, Ted whisked off his hat again. "I beg your pardon, mistress," he said to Abigail, his accent all the more prominent in the polite tone of his voice. "You must forgive my unexpected intrusion."

Suddenly Ben realized his own lack of manners. "I'm sorry, Abby. This is Ted Harrington, my sister Jane's husband. Ted's sister, Susannah, is married to my older brother, Dan." He shrugged. "It's a bit complicated until you get used to it." He turned back to Ted. "I'd like you to meet Mistress Abigail Preston. This beautiful woman," he added with a grin, "to my very great joy, has agreed to become my wife."

"You don't say!"

Abby offered a wavering smile as she raised her shy gaze to Ted and dipped in a slight curtsy. "Pleased to meet you."

"And I you," Ted replied. "I can tell you unequivocally that contrary to all the rumors, you'll find Ben to be quite the decent sort."

Her eyes grew wide. "Rumors?"

As if she hadn't been hard enough to convince, Ben thought, branding Ted with a scowl. "He's jesting, my love, merely jesting," he assured her, then took on a menacing tone. "Aren't you, Ted?"

His brother-in-law shrugged, his smile full of mischief.

But the reason for Ted's visit made its way once more to the fore, overshadowing Abigail's sweet charms. There was much, much more Ben needed to learn at the moment. "What about Yancy and Robby? Did they manage to escape, too?" He tipped his head toward Abby. "Robby MacKinnon is another one of my brothers-in-law," he explained, "and Yancy Curtis is a sailor who has befriended all of us at one time or another." He returned his attention to Ted, anxious for his reply.

"I'm afraid I can't provide any definite news of Robby. The last I saw of the Scotsman was about an hour after your departure. Quite frankly, it's possible he has been captured. I saw him through the window of your room as he was returning from the mughouse with our breakfast. He dropped the tray rather suddenly and yelled out a warning, then turned and took off running. That's when a dozen or more king's men came from between two buildings. The officer in charge issued an order for two of his men to go after Robby, and the rest made a beeline straight to your rooming house."

"With Susannah and Felicia still celebrating their reunion with their husbands."

"Quite right. And with broadsides of Yancy's smuggling charges plastered throughout Boston and Robby and me being sought for desertion, the hangman's noose was nigh upon us."

"Even if there had been a back way out of there, the

lobsterbacks would've had it covered," Ben grated. "Well, fire and brimstone, man! What happened?"

Abigail moved nearer and took Ben's hand in both of hers. She stroked it comfortingly, though Ben knew she could not possibly know the seriousness of the situation.

Ted sank down onto a porch step. He leaned his elbows on his knees, his hands dangling as he stared ahead. "I tried desperately to open the window, even started to send a chair crashing through the glass. But Dan stopped me. 'Let the soldiers think it's just me and my family here,' he said. He pointed to the hatch which led up to the attic and told Yancy and me to hide there. There was no reasoning with him that he, too, was in danger of arrest. He just shoved Yance and me to safety. 'They only *suspect* me,' he said. 'They have no hard evidence. You two would be hanged for sure.'"

Ben listened to the grim tale without a word, wondering if he would have shown Dan's courage in the face of the lion. Immensely proud of his older brother, he nevertheless felt his own newly found faith sinking by the moment.

Ted's voice became quieter, his tone defeated. "In the attic, Yancy and I lay listening to the whole sorry episode. Susannah and Felicia's pleas, Dan's babies crying, the soldiers banging furniture around. Once again Dan sacrificed everything for me. I still can't believe he did it . . . or that I allowed him to, for that matter."

Ben lowered himself and sat on another step, tugging Abigail's hand for her to do likewise. He reached over to give Ted's shoulder a pat. "Well, don't be so hard on yourself, Ted. If the situation had been reversed, I'm sure you would have done the same for him. Before these dangerous days have passed, we'll likely all be called upon to make hard sacrifices."

"Perhaps," Ted conceded. "But that hardly makes me feel better about it."

"What about Yancy, then? Where did he go? Do you know?"

"He said he'd wait for you in Cambridge, that his friend the wheelwright would know where to find him."

Ben rose, assisted Abby, then hurried over to his horse. He

unhooked one of his saddlebags and brought it to Ted. "I'd appreciate it if you'd distribute these flyers in the villages on your way back to the Green Mountains. And tell folks up there in the New Hampshire Grants to keep spreading the word about all the decisions made by the Continental Congress— particularly the one about arming themselves and strengthening their local militias."

When Abigail gave a low gasp at his last remark, Ben realized how preoccupied he had been with proposing marriage to her. He had barely mentioned the monumental decisions made by the first-ever gathering of the Colonies. He removed a flyer from the pouch Ted held, then looked at his brother-in-law. "I've got to return to Boston, but tell everyone there's no turning back now. The die has been cast, and from now on, we'll all have to pull together."

Ted gave a grave nod and strode toward his horse, and Ben handed Abigail the flyer listing the results of the meeting held by the colony representatives. "Give this to Bertha's husband when you go inside." Then seeing that Ted was mounted and ready to leave, he hastened to the hitching post. "Did Yancy mention anything about a plan to break Dan out?"

"No, nothing at all," Ted answered, obviously surprised by the question. "Godspeed," he murmured. Then, tipping his hat at Abigail, he spurred his horse and galloped away.

Ben turned to Abby. As his eyes filled with the sight of her, his heart swelled, and he drew her close. She trembled in his arms, but said nothing. With a gentle smile, he cupped her face in his hands. "I know all of this sounds pretty awful, my love, but please try not to worry. Nothing is going to stop me from coming back for you as we planned. You see to getting those clothes made. I'll deal with everything else—including that mother-in-law of yours."

"But—"

"I'll make everything right. I promise. Please trust me. I have to go now." With a swift kiss on her soft lips and a last warm embrace, he smiled and swung up into Rebel's saddle. "I love you." He swallowed a great lump in his throat at the sheen of tears that filled her eyes, but just as quickly, she blinked and lowered her lashes.

Ma Preston and the others stood in the doorway talking among themselves. Ben knew they were as staunchly patriotic as he and would never divulge anything they had just over-heard. Nonetheless, the old woman looked as stubborn as ever. "Trust me, Abby," he said again for her hearing alone. Then he nudged his mount forward.

Abigail chased after him a little way. "I love you too, Ben Haynes. Please be careful. I'll be praying night and day for your safe return."

As Ben crested the rise east of the Preston farm, Abby's parting words were more unsettling than comforting. Only a short while ago he had been thanking God for the safe return of both Susannah and Yancy's wife, Felicia, who had been with Susannah since before the birth of her new daughter. When he'd left Cambridge, Ben had trusted the Lord for the safety of everyone he left behind in his rented room. He had even foolishly trusted that God was giving Abigail to him.

Now look at the mess everything had turned into—in just one day! Dan and Susannah were always so trusting of God and his providence. Well, perhaps after this, *they* wouldn't be so gullible either.

3

Susannah Haynes peeked for the hundredth time into the basket of food she had brought to the South Battery. Somewhere within these bleak walls, her husband was being held prisoner by the military. The very thought was almost more than she could bear. When would Samuel Quincy return to the waiting room with permission for her to visit Dan? It seemed like forever since the lawyer had gone behind closed doors to see the head officer and learn the precise charges against Dan. She would have preferred asking help from the lawyer's brother, Josiah Quincy, or even John Adams. But Josiah Quincy had sailed to England for the cause of the Colonies, and John Adams hadn't returned from the meeting of the First Continental Congress. She had been forced to place her hope in Samuel Quincy instead, though he was known to be quite conservative in his dealings with her old countrymen, the British.

This truly was a cold and dreary place, she decided, allowing her gaze to wander over the cluttered front desk and other stark furnishings. The official portrait of His Royal Highness, King George III, did little to hide the peeling paint and cracked walls. But no doubt poor Dan had it far worse wherever he was being held, and his capture was all her fault. How could she have assumed she and Felicia and the children could simply walk out of her house—after being under constant surveillance for nearly a year—without being followed?

Had Alex Fontaine's supposed "change of heart" been a mere ploy? Was the quest for revenge still uppermost in the lieutenant's twisted mind, even though he had sailed home to England just before her release? He and her brother, Ted, following their dream of a military life, had been such fast friends when they first arrived in the Colonies. Now, a scant four years later, that friendship seemed part of another life. Alex had felt personally betrayed by Ted's defection.

Susannah felt no less betrayed herself. Throughout the months she had lived under Alex's vengeful thumb, she actually believed all things were working together for everyone's good. Now she felt like a Judas goat, having led her beloved Dan like a lamb to the slaughter. How could the Lord allow this to happen to his faithful servants? It was all so unfair.

With a heavy sigh, Susannah glanced once more at the closed office door, then settled back against the hard bench. Despite everything, she could not bring herself to believe God had forsaken them. There had to be some reason for the way this had all turned out, and she would cling to that hope until her dying breath . . . or at least as long as she could.

The door suddenly opened, startling her.

"Private," a commanding voice said from inside, "escort this man and his companion to Haynes's cell."

"Yes, sir!" A freckle-faced soldier emerged from the cramped room, followed by her lawyer, Samuel Quincy.

Forty years of age and with a pleasant face and slightly pudgy build, the attorney approached Susannah, a smile of reassurance in his shrewd eyes.

She rose and accompanied them down the hall, their footsteps echoing from one end of the dark corridor to the other. "May I ask why they are holding Dan?" she asked the lawyer.

"It's best we discuss that later, mistress," Quincy answered, indicating more with the flick of an eye in the soldier's direction than he had with his words.

With an understanding nod, Susannah refrained from further conversation. Considering the length of time the lawyer had spent discussing the matter with the officer in charge, she feared the outlook must indeed be dreadful.

At the end of the long passageway, the soldier inserted a brass key into the lock of a heavy door. He opened it and gestured for them to go inside.

Led into the dank recesses of a second passageway between rows of barred cubicles, Susannah felt the color drain from her face. Her Dan, in a horrid place like this! How could she bear the knowledge! But she must not cry. She must not. He would need her strength.

As she followed Quincy and the uniformed man, she spotted one jailed soldier lying on a cot, staring at her. She pulled her light shawl more securely about her shoulders. Her eyes searched for a glimpse of Dan.

She saw him rise. "Susannah!"

It was all she could do to endure the interminable seconds it took for the private to unlock his cell door. "Oh, Dan!" She flew into her husband's arms, disregarding the attorney's presence, as well as the ominous click of the lock behind them.

He wrapped her in a snug embrace, his pulse throbbing against her cheek. He kissed the top of her head. "Why did you come to this place?"

"How could I not? I'm only sorry they would not permit me to come yesterday." Easing back a little, Susannah took stock of her husband, noting the new worry lines beside his dark sable eyes, the stubble on his jaw. "How are you, my love?"

"A bit ill prepared to receive guests," he said wryly, "but nevertheless, profoundly glad to see you. To be truthful, I've been more worried about you. Are you and the children well and safe, or did they drag you back to Boston?"

"We're fine. We'll talk of that later, I promise." With an attempt to smile, Susannah gestured toward the lawyer. "I've hired Samuel Quincy to represent you, sweetheart. Mr. Quincy, this is my husband, Dan." She stepped aside while the two men shook hands.

"Reverend Haynes." The lawyer inclined his head.

"Mr. Quincy finally secured permission for me to visit you," Susannah said.

"I'm most grateful to you, sir." Dan gripped the older man's hand. "And honored as well . . . I recognize you from the Boston Massacre trial. If anyone can help me, Mr. Quincy, it's you."

"Well, then, we had better get down to business."

❦ ❦

Daniel Haynes was already quite certain why he had been placed under military arrest, but he asked the question nonetheless.

Samuel Quincy answered without hesitation. "You are to be tried for aiding and abetting the desertion of a Crown officer, one Theodore Harrington, from the royal armies of His Majesty, King George the Third."

Dan gave a nod of resignation. Hearing Susannah's quick intake of breath, he purposely refrained from looking at her. "And have they told you when my trial will be?"

"There's no definite date as yet, I'm afraid." The older man's expression was sympathetic. "They must wait for the arrival of Lieutenant Fontaine, the key witness. He's taken leave until after the first of the year."

Susannah sprang up from the rickety cot where she had been sitting and came to Dan's side. "Are you saying my husband is to be left in this horrid place until Alex deigns to arrange passage back here from England?"

"Precisely." Samuel Quincy shrugged. "He's the accuser, the sole person with evidence to convict Dan. I did make it clear, however, that due to the prolonged wait, your husband is not to be denied visitors. And the army is more than willing to comply, considering the state of unrest in the city."

"I'm most grateful for your efforts on behalf of my husband and me, Mr. Quincy," she said.

But Dan noticed that the trepidation clouding her blue-gray eyes did not lessen, and the worry lines in her forehead did not ease. He was more than aware that Susannah had endured countless months of inner pain while he had been in hiding, and the knowledge filled him with remorse.

"Alex may believe he has what he considers 'evidence' against Dan," he heard her say, her trembling hands belying the conviction in her voice. "But in truth, he is relying merely on strong suspicions. I hardly think it fair for Dan to be held here indefinitely."

The lawyer smiled in benign comfort. "I understand how you feel, mistress. But we must do what we can within due process." He turned to Dan. "Before I can take the first step, Reverend, I need you to relate the entire story which resulted in your arrest. Be as truthful and thorough as possible. I assure you that nothing you say to me here will go any further than this room, but I must know everything so I can be prepared for any accusations they throw at you."

Dan nodded in agreement. "Come and sit, sweetheart," he told Susannah, guiding her to the cot. As he did, the attorney checked up and down the corridor beyond the cell. He indicated that Dan should continue.

"On the sixteenth of December," Dan began quietly, "the night of the town's now infamous 'tea party,' I returned home quite late in the evening, only to learn from my wife that Lieutenant Fontaine had been there looking for her brother, Ted. Upon discovering my absence, Alex immediately concluded that I had assisted in Ted's desertion. This, of course, was untrue."

"You had absolutely no hand in the matter?" Quincy asked.

"None. But to make matters worse, my own sister Jane—who had been engaged to marry Fontaine—had run off with Ted. Alex was furious."

"Quite livid," Susannah added. "Almost to the point of irrationality."

"Needless to say," Dan continued, "the man decided that the lot of us had conspired together against him." He glanced toward the empty hallway to see if a guard might be eavesdropping, then lowered his voice even more. "If I had told the lieutenant where I really was that night, I'd have been arrested as one of the 'Mohawks' who had thrown the tea party!"

"And by exonerating yourself of the one charge," Quincy concluded, "you'd find yourself implicated in one equally serious."

"Right. I had no choice but to become a fugitive."

"I understand, Reverend." Quincy kneaded his jowls in thought. "Have you had any contact whatsoever with either the deserter, Lieutenant Harrington, or your sister since the incident in question?"

"Actually, yes, I have. Not long after I got home that night, a man sent by Jane and Ted came to let us know where they were and that they were unharmed. That's when I decided to help them escape Boston for the interior. Having been a postrider, you see, I'm acquainted with a fair number of sympathizers who would be more than willing to help us. And with Jane and Ted being family, it didn't seem right to ask someone else to take on the risk of assisting them."

"Yes, I see your point. Given the same extraordinary circumstances, I'd have done no less myself." Quincy looked from Dan to Susannah and back. "As far as you know, does this Lieutenant Fontaine have even the slightest proof which could link you to Harrington's escape?"

"If he had, I'm sure he or his cohorts would have tracked us down long ago. No doubt Susannah has told you how they kept her here in Boston all this time, all but under lock and key, refusing permission for her and the children to leave the city. Their intention was to use her as bait to trap one of us."

Quincy gave a knowing smirk. "Yes. And that will work in our favor, see if it doesn't. Tell me, Daniel, when the officers here questioned you, what precisely did you say to them?"

"No one has questioned me yet. I haven't seen anyone but the guards who dumped me here."

"Splendid! Then, with the assistance of your lovely wife, I'll prepare a statement this very day and bring it back for you to sign. When I give it to the officer in charge, I will most adamantly insist on being present whenever you are interrogated. That should keep them watching their backs, since they know General Gage is less than anxious to incite your friends and neighbors, not to mention your congregation at Long Lane Church. At the moment, he can't afford an incident which could jeopardize the fragile peace in Boston."

"Just one more thing, sir." Dan met the older man's astute gaze. "As a minister of the gospel, I have certain responsibilities to my congregation and to my heavenly Father. Were I to be asked specific questions, I would find it impossible to lie."

"Not to worry, young man," he said with a careless toss of his head. "Just follow my instructions and leave the rest to me." He shook Dan's hand warmly. "Now, I suppose the two of you would appreciate a few moments alone. I'll return shortly. Guard!"

The heavy outer door protested on its hinges as a uniformed man came and let the lawyer out of the cell.

As soon as the men left, Dan turned to Susannah with a smile and pulled her into his arms. The fragrance of her hair was a welcome relief from the harsh smells of the jail. He was glad she had left her hair uncoiled, tied instead with a velvet ribbon at her neck. And the fact that she had on the gown he loved best was not lost on him either. He tipped up her face and kissed her deeply, ending the kiss only with reluctance. "At last, my love. I've wanted to do this since the second I looked up and saw you coming."

"I know the feeling," she breathed, still in his embrace. "I had thought at long last our separation was over."

Dan felt the heavy weight of truth in her words, knowing that same emptiness whenever they were apart. "It seems I've brought you nothing but unhappiness these past months, though I'd rather cut out my own heart than hurt you."

She pressed her fingers to his mouth. "Don't ever say such a thing, Daniel Haynes—or even think it. The times we've been together, whether months or moments, have been the only true happiness I have ever known. I'm praying that soon all of this will be behind us."

Dan stroked her cheeks with the tips of his fingers, drinking in the sight of her. Her beauty was far more than the mere outward appearance of her creamy skin and her eyes the color of a summer sky. Susannah's loveliness came from deep within, from her boundless faith and peace with God. The first time he ever laid eyes on her, she had seemed a bright contrast to the dreary barrenness of winter, and here in this bleak, lonely dungeon she was the very breath of Eden. He had been truly blessed the day God brought this spirited English lass across his path . . . and had drawn his wandering heart to thoughts of hearth and home. "How are the children, sweetheart? Where are they?"

Susannah inched back and smiled up at him. "Julia and Miles are just fine. They're with Felicia right now, in Cambridge. You needn't worry after them at all."

"What of Yancy and the others? Is there any news of them?"

"Yes, actually. Ted is on his way back to Jane even as we speak, and Yancy is in hiding at the wheelwright's. And just this morning we received word that Robby is en route to your parents' farm in Rhode Island."

Dan sighed in relief. "Good. Now, I'd like you and the children to go be with my parents, too, so—"

"How can you ask that of me?" she cut in.

"Please, Susannah, listen to me." He looked deep into her eyes. "If there's one thing I don't want, it's for you and the children to be trapped in Boston again. I have no idea how long I'm going to be detained here."

She gazed up at him momentarily, then shook her head, a flush settling over her cheeks as if her defiance contained a measure of inner guilt. "I cannot leave you here alone at the mercy of the military. Don't ask me to do that. The only way I can bear this is to be here for you, to be able to see you, to bring you food. I've decided to move back into our house on Milk Street."

Dan's spirits plummeted. It took several seconds before he could respond. "That's not wise, Susannah. I need to know my family is safe. As volatile as tempers here in Boston are, they can only worsen from this point on. There are bound to be protests, brawls, perhaps even military action in the streets—" But as he spoke, Dan could see that his words were falling on deaf ears. His proud beauty had already made up her mind.

"The Lord kept me safe here before, sweetheart. He has everyone at the church looking after me. Why, even the soldiers posted at the gate saw to our comfort."

"But, darling, please . . . think about the children. They'd be far better off in Rhode Island, away from all this turmoil. Would you put them at risk again? Needlessly, this time?"

"I've not done that." She smiled gently. "They're in good hands. Felicia is wonderful with them, and they adore her. She has assured me that she'll keep them safe in Cambridge as long as necessary, and I'll check on them every day or so. She's such a dear sort. She's been quite like a sister to me."

Dan shook his head. For all her attempts at comforting him, there was no getting away from the reality that he would worry about her constantly all the while he was in prison.

Susannah raised on tiptoe and kissed him lightly. "We're in God's hands, my dearest Dan, the lot of us. He's never let us down before, nor has he allowed anything to bring us to harm. Surely we can trust him as much during this trial of our faith. Isn't that what you've always said?"

He could see no point in arguing with such logic, particularly when his wife was throwing his own words back in his face. Dan tugged Susannah close and buried his face in her hair. Like it or not, he had no recourse but to trust the Lord to look after his dear treasures until Samuel Quincy secured his release—if that was possible. And until then, he would have to content himself with praying fervently for everyone he loved. He exhaled in frustration. This was so much harder than being the one making the decisions.

The outer door squeaked open, and a guard stuck his head in. "You'll have to be leaving now, miss."

So soon? Dan thought desperately. *After so few minutes of privacy?* Reluctant to let go of Susannah, Dan felt her nod and draw gently away as the young man came with the key.

"I'll come again on the morrow," she promised as she turned to leave.

"Regardless of what Sam Quincy said," Dan blurted angrily, "do you actually believe they're going to allow you to walk in here anytime you please?" His fingers coiled in frustration.

Susannah merely smiled. She took his hand and mollified him with a kiss. A curious sparkle lit the softness of her eyes as she lowered her voice to a whisper. "You'd be amazed how much influence a woman bearing fresh-baked cookies can wield."

4

The sun was nearing its highest point when Ben arrived in Cambridge, and the first aggravating sight to meet his eyes was a party of redcoats heading back toward Boston. But he did derive comfort in recognizing some local militiamen watching the mounted soldiers from various positions nearby. Lobsterbacks rarely ventured beyond the Boston Neck anymore without their every movement being monitored.

"Don't hurry back," a sneering bystander yelled in their wake.

"Hear! Hear!" came a second call from the opposite side of the street. "March yourselves back to that hole you crawled out of!"

Ben clenched his teeth to keep from blurting out a few choice sentiments of his own as the patrol passed. Soon enough, when the colony militias rallied in strength, he could help put the British in their place. And he could hardly wait for that day to come.

Turning at the next corner, he rode around to the back of Sean Burns's wheelwright shop and hitched Rebel out of sight. Then he strode to the main door, where he could see the good-natured tradesman hard at work inside.

"Greetings, Benjamin," the Scot called with a wave of his muscled arm. "Go right on up. I'll follow directly."

"Will do." Ben mounted the side stairs, brushing at some of the dust he had acquired on his journey from Millers Falls.

Halfway up, he heard Yancy bellow from inside the dwelling. A baby wailed. With all the racket, Ben conceded, it was fortunate he wasn't a redcoat sneaking up on Yancy. Ben could see no point in knocking, so he walked right on in.

"Over my dead body, I'll tell ye, and that's that!" the red-haired sailor yelled. One freckled finger jabbed at the air as he loomed over his wife.

Felicia Curtis, not the least disturbed by the outburst, remained completely composed in the rocking chair as she comforted Dan and Susannah's baby daughter, Julia Rose. She gave Ben a hint of a smile as he came in. Across the room, out of harm's way, Sean's wife, Maggie, stood holding Julia's brother, Miles.

Ben slammed the door, drawing Yancy's attention.

"Young Ben!" the redhead blurted, rushing over to him. "You've come just in time, mate. I need ye to talk some sense into me wife. She'll not harken to a word I say!" He flopped onto a kitchen chair in frustration.

Ben rolled his eyes. He hadn't ridden all those hours and miles just to settle a marital dispute. "Where's Robby? Anyone hear from him yet?" he asked instead.

Yancy's scowl eased. "Aye. The lad's probably in Rhode Island by now . . . with a wife who knows her place, I might add." He shot a glare toward the winsome brunette who wore his ring—and who was expending great effort to maintain a straight face.

The seaman had definitely met his match in that spunky, dark-haired woman, Ben had to admit. He was also aware that the two were deeply in love. "What about Dan? Where's he locked up?"

"One of them choice suites at South Battery," Yancy replied. "Ye know them well."

"I figured as much." Ben rubbed his nose absently. "Not an easy place to break someone out of, but if a small boat could be maneuvered under those cannons—"

"Hold on there, laddie. There's a wee matter to consider

before doing something rash . . . that fleet of royal tubs floatin' in the bay surrounding the fortress."

"And thank Providence," Felicia piped in, "we received some very hopeful news from Boston a few minutes ago. So any heroics the two of you might concoct will be quite unnecessary." She dipped her finger into a jar of honey at her side and offered it to the babe. "Dearest, why don't you tell Ben about it—in a soft voice, of course, so you don't frighten little Julia again."

Yancy grimaced and turned his attention to Ben. "According to Susannah, the lawyer she found is pretty sure he can get Dan off. He says the Crown has no actual proof. But the bad news is that they refuse to release him until that scoundrel, Fontaine, sails over from England to testify, and as ye know, the blackguard went home for Christmas. He won't be back till February, at the earliest. And in the meantime," Yancy added, shifting his gaze back to his wife as he continued, "don't ye agree with me that Felicia should take Dan's wee ones and go to your parents' farm, where it's safe?"

"Where is Susannah?"

"The fool girl's gone back to Boston to be near Dan."

Ben's mouth gaped open. "Are you telling me my sister-in-law actually returned to Boston?"

"Not only has she done so, but she plans to stay there."

"So you see, Ben," Felicia answered evenly, "I can't possibly see any fairness in depriving Susannah of the company of her children in this trying time."

Suddenly Ben understood his friend Yancy's plight. He directed his attention to Felicia. "And now you feel it's your Christian duty to go and stay with her again, is that what you're saying?"

She nodded.

"Which makes all the chances your husband and hers both took in coming back here for naught—no, worse. Now Dan has been incarcerated."

Yancy slammed a fist down on the table, rattling the bowl of dried flowers in its center. "Me very words!"

Julia Rose let out another shriek, and Miles wriggled from Mrs. Burns's grip and bolted in Ben's direction, giving Yancy a wide berth. "Uncle Ben!"

As he plunked the boy on his knee, Ben shook his head in wonder at this latest turn of events.

"Well," Felicia said in a defensive tone of voice, "it would put things in a better light if you knew that Susannah is no longer under any restraints and can leave Boston at will."

"Oh, aye," Yancy groused. "They've already blocked the bay. Now they'll plug the Boston Neck tighter than a cork in a bottle. The whole town'll be held prisoner."

She waved a hand in the air. "Now, dearest, that possibility is months away. By the time Parliament votes in a decree, Dan will be free. And besides, Yancy, my love," she added, her tone becoming syrupy sweet, "it's not as if you're going to be sitting here waiting for me, now is it?" Raising her chin, she focused on Ben. "A few of his old shipmates came this morning, announcing a plot to smuggle gunpowder into the colony. I ask you—tea was bad enough, but gunpowder? The whole idea is too dangerous even to consider. Much too dangerous."

Ben only barely managed not to laugh aloud. He had been down this road before with Yancy and Felicia. And it would end up exactly the same way this time. She would go stay with Susannah, and Yancy would hightail it off on another smuggling venture. "Mistress Burns," he said, turning his attention to the lady of the house, who had yet to move her broad form from the safe corner she had been occupying since his arrival, "does that happen to be fresh coffee I smell?"

"To be sure, and I'll gladly pour you some, laddie." Obviously relieved for the change of subject, Maggie Burns smiled, and the button nose on her round face pinkened. She took down a cup and moved at once to the hearth to fill it, then brought it to Ben at the table. "You must be tired after your long ride."

"Yes, and thank you," he said as she retreated to a chair in the sitting room and took up her knitting. Ben tousled Miles's light brown hair. "So, buddy, have you learned how to whistle yet?"

"Mm-hmm. Listen." The tot puckered his mouth and blew, but not a note came forth. He tried again.

"Say, how far did ye get, Ben, before Harrington caught up to ye?" Yancy asked.

"A good seventy miles." *Where I left another unsettled argument behind me,* his sullen thoughts reminded him. Relaxing against the chair back, Ben sipped the coffee and studied his sea-going friend and his wife. Maybe all wasn't smooth sailing with the pair all the time, but at least they were together and had each other to fight with, to worry over, to love. If Ma Preston had anything to say about it, he and Abigail would never have that.

Miles finally managed a sound somewhat akin to a whistle. "There! Hear it?" he asked. His chest puffed out with pride as he turned his beaming face to Ben.

"Sure did, buddy." Nuzzling the boy close, Ben thought of a towhead named Corbin, who quite probably at this moment was playing with his toy stage wagon. And sweet little Cassandra no doubt had not stopped hugging her "kitty." Ben had begun to consider those two dear little ones as good as his, but now he had to wonder if they ever would be.

5

"I bid you good evening, gentlemen," Susannah told two church elders as she accompanied them to the front door of her home. "It was so kind of you to look in on Felicia and me now that we've returned to Boston. I don't know how we shall ever repay you."

"No need for that, Missy Haynes," Mr. Simms said. He plucked his coat from a peg and tugged it on. "Old McKnight and me talked it over. Won't put neither of us out to stop in of an evening to see that you and your little ones are well." He set his wool hat atop his head, then nodded to his friend.

"It's like the reverend told us right before we came here," Elder McKnight affirmed. "There's no such thing as doing too much praying for one another."

"I can just imagine how thankful Dan was for your visit in that dreadful place." Aware of the contrast between the fine furnishings in their home and the pathetic surroundings her husband had at the South Battery, Susannah could scarcely manage a smile.

"Aye, it's that, no doubt about it," Elder Simms replied, stroking his dark, curly beard. He raised the latch, but opened the door only a fraction. "The reverend said that with friends and neighbors popping in to see him most every day and you bearing gifts of food each morning, he can't recall havin' so much company in his life, much less eatin' so well."

Elder McKnight straightened his short, muscular frame

and leaned nearer with a satisfied grin. "You can rest assured, mistress, we left your husband in very high spirits. That is, thanks to Samuel Quincy's optimism and the Good Lord, of course."

"Indeed." Susannah placed a hand on the man's sleeve and lowered her voice. "Mr. Quincy informed me that he's met with the very individuals who helped Ted and Jane escape that evening. Not one of them has ever been under suspicion or even questioned by the authorities."

Felicia stepped out of the nearby parlor, a tray of teacups in hand. She slid her free arm around Susannah's waist. "I don't mean to speak out of turn, Susannah. But it might not be wise to repeat things of that nature. You wouldn't want to put your church members at risk if they were to find themselves facing the authorities and their awkward questions."

"Oh! Quite right!" Susannah's hand flew to her throat. "Please do forgive me, gentlemen. I hadn't given the matter the slightest thought."

"Don't you worry over the likes of us, missy," Elder Simms said kindly. "Neither of us heard a thing, there's such a fierce wind blowing." Nudging his pal, he opened the door, and the two walked out into the still night.

Susannah nodded when they waved from the walk, then she closed the door, immediately throwing her arms around Felicia. The teacups teetered, and both women fought to keep them from toppling over the side. "Thank you, dear friend," Susannah said when they had saved the china. "One of my greatest faults has always been talking too freely. I shall be much more careful from now on."

"I was almost afraid to mention it," Felicia replied. "You know I care about you and Dan. I wouldn't want to hurt you for the world."

"Well, I'm grateful you cared enough to correct me! After all, it was the silence of the Rhode Island colonists after the *Gaspee* was set ablaze and the silence of the townsmen after the Boston Harbor affair which kept all the involved parties safe. I pray it will work in Dan's favor also."

"And Yancy's." A sad smile clouded Felicia's fine features, making her brown-black eyes all the darker. "But I'm afraid that unless God Almighty makes that husband of mine invisible, his smuggling activities will catch up with him one of these days."

"Oh yes. He's always been the adventurous sort—"

"Aren't we all," a third voice answered.

Susannah and Felicia both jumped at the man's voice, and one china cup smashed to the plank floor, scattering fragments in a dozen directions.

"Ben!" Susannah cried in exasperation. "Can't you ever knock on a door—or at the very least, call out once you've entered? You frightened us to death! And tracked in half the mud of Boston on your boots, I might add." Her hands on her hips, she glared pointedly down at the trail he had left.

His grin did contain a touch of guilt as he assessed the mess he had made of the hall. But not for long. "Thought you two could use a little excitement to brighten up your humdrum existence, so I waded in at Windmill Point."

"I declare." Felicia's smile was barely in check as she shook her head. "You and Yancy do love taking chances. One day the redcoats are going to catch you sneaking into Boston."

"Is that so?" Ben teased.

She sniffed and raised her chin, but her smile broke free. "I don't suppose my wandering husband has come with you," she said hopefully as she stooped and began gathering the china pieces.

"Not this time. He left for Salem at first light. He says they'll sail at eventide."

Felicia's hand paused above one broken chunk, and her smile wilted at the corners.

"I'm sorry, dear," Susannah said at once, kneeling to bestow a comforting hug.

Her friend's eyes glistened. "Well, it's not as if I wasn't expecting it any day." She blinked away the tears while capturing the last remaining pieces, then started to get up.

Ben assisted her. "Yance told me to tell you both that if he doesn't get back before then, he'll see you at Christmas in Rhode Island. And I'm with him. It's time we all went home and spent some time together."

"As wonderful as that sounds," Susannah mused, leaning back against the highboy, "surely you know Dan has not the slightest hope of being released until well after December. Everything rests with Alex."

"I wouldn't be too certain about that."

Susannah thought she detected a calculating inflection in her brother-in-law's voice. But it vanished with his grin.

"And as for you ladies," he went on, "as Yancy pointed out, you're no longer tied to the mast. So whether or not Dan can go, it's about time the children get to meet their grandparents."

Susannah felt torn. She was fully aware of how eager Dan's parents were to see their oldest son's children at long last. And they had to be suffering as greatly as she over the heartache of his imprisonment. But leaving him alone in that bleak cell for Christmas while the lot of them went off to have a carefree time was quite impossible to consider. She turned to Felicia. "Yes, do go. And perhaps you wouldn't mind taking little Miles along. Our firstborn might be a great comfort to Dan's parents in this sorrowful time."

With a snort, Ben shifted his weight to his other leg. "If I am able to rally the right crew, you'll all be going—and that includes Dan."

"Please don't say such things, Ben," Susannah said, going to him. "It's dangerous. And it could so easily jeopardize any chance he has of being exonerated."

He did not respond.

"Come into the kitchen, and I'll fix you something hot. Felicia and I were about to finish the pot of tea we made a little while ago anyway. And perhaps you might take off those soggy boots?" She grimaced at them.

"They are pretty bad," he confessed. "I hadn't realized. But the British have added more patrols along the wharves, so I quite literally had to wade ashore at Windmill Point and walk the rest of the way."

"Honestly," Felicia said. "Between you and Yancy and all the careless risks you take, it's a wonder the rest of us get any sleep at all for worrying."

The scamp scratched his cheek with a look of wide-eyed innocence, as if he never did anything dangerous.

Felicia chuckled at his impudence and turned toward the stairs. "The truth is, I'm exhausted. I think I'll check on the little ones, then go to bed. Have a pleasant visit." Her smile included them both before it sobered. "Just one thing, Ben. Don't hinder God's efforts where Dan is concerned. With all the prayers being offered up on his behalf, I'm sure the Lord's plan has already been set in motion—whether or not we can see it." She handed the tray of china to Susannah, then took a fold of her emerald linen skirt in her fingers and turned toward the walnut staircase. "Good night."

Susannah led Ben past the dining room and into the kitchen, where the glow from the hearth added a warm homey feel. She went at once to stoke up the fire beneath the kettle of soup they'd had for supper. Out of the corner of her eye she noted Ben's dour expression as he took a seat and yanked off his boots.

"Don't you women ever stop to think that God's busy enough without being expected to handle your every problem?" he asked bitterly as the first boot clunked to the floor. "There's a whole big world out there beyond Milk Street, you know." A second clunk punctuated his words. He sighed and leaned back in one of the dark-wood chairs.

Susannah glanced up from stirring the pot. "Something other than Dan is troubling you, isn't it? The last time I saw you, you were overjoyed at the prospect of going to see your Abigail. Did your visit go other than you had hoped?"

"My Abigail," he said with a scornful laugh. "If only."

His glum demeanor precluded any more questions, but somehow Susannah knew he would elaborate if she kept her silence.

"The very thing that drew her to me will keep her from me, isn't that a joke? So you see, God isn't always sitting there awaiting our beck and call."

She watched his fingertips drum impatiently on the table-top. How unfortunate that mere days after he had begun to trust the Lord, things had gone awry for him. And not only for him, she realized. Misfortune had befallen so many of the people she loved. She was striving hard to maintain her own faith, but it seemed left up to her to bolster Ben's faltering belief. Susannah gave the soup one last stir, then went to the sideboard and took down a bowl. "You've told us Abigail is shy. Was she too shy to accept your courtship?"

"No. That she did gladly." He ran a hand through the restless waves of light brown hair at his temples, then met Susannah's gaze with a small smile. "I even managed to convince her to marry me at Christmas. But her mother-in-law! She's another concern entirely," he sighed. "The old bat refuses to give her consent."

"How perfectly awful."

"Yes. There's the matter of Abby's son, Corbin, the one and only grandson. Ma Preston's not about to give him up."

"I'm sure that would be a hard thing for anyone to do." She ladled soup into the bowl and carried it to the table with some bread and butter, then collected utensils from the cupboard.

Ben smiled his thanks. "Abigail loves her children very much. She would never leave Corbin behind—not that I would ask such a thing of her."

"Of course not. I could never give up little Miles."

"Well, there you have it." He dipped his spoon into the hot liquid and raised it to his mouth. "If you had ever met Ma Preston, you'd know what we're up against." After a tentative sampling, he gulped the remainder from the spoon.

Susannah poured herself a cup of tea and sat opposite him. "From what you're saying, you consider this Preston woman Abigail's legal guardian. But are you quite sure that's the case?"

"Abby would never find the courage to challenge Ma," Ben

said with a wave of a hand. "So it wouldn't make much difference one way or the other."

"Is that what she's told you?"

"She didn't have to. Ma is a stone fortress. Abby's the opposite. I can draw my own conclusions."

"I see." Susannah patted his hand. "Well, don't count it all a loss so soon. Things may appear hopeless at the moment, but as someone once said, 'It's always darkest just before the dawn.' Trust God to give Abigail to you. If she's the woman he has for you, it will surely come to pass. Dan and I have known such happiness—"

"You'll forgive me, Sue, but I can't see that God's been looking out for you two a whole lot either."

His words hit hard. *Dear Lord,* she prayed, *you have to know how desperately I'm trying not to feel that way myself. Help me to say the right thing.* She took a deep breath before replying. "I cannot believe that our heavenly Father is toying with our lives any more than an earthly father would. He loves us. There's some reason known only to God—and a good one, I'm sure—that Dan is in jail at this time."

"You don't say. Mind letting me in on it?" Ben asked facetiously.

Susannah laughed, but more from awkwardness than anything. "I've not the foggiest notion. Nevertheless, I know he's supposed to be there. And I beg you not to do anything irrational, such as trying to break him out without the direct leading of the Lord."

Ben's expression hardened as he stood and glowered down at her. "This happens to be my only brother we're talking about."

She got up and stretched to her fullest height, leveling her gaze to his. "And he's my only husband, and my children's only father."

Ben inhaled and averted his eyes. After a moment he relaxed his stance and reclaimed his seat. "Aw, Susannah, I'm not the kind of person who can wait and do nothing, you know that."

"Then go see Sam Quincy," she said quietly. "Talk to him. You might discover that many of your worries are unfounded."

Ben appeared to consider the suggestion. "Where is the man's office?"

With a smile Susannah sank to her chair and placed her hand over Ben's. "You'll probably have the best luck finding him at Faneuil Hall. Of late, most of the town leaders have congregated there in the mornings."

"Fine." His countenance softened to near normal, and he grinned. "And since I've managed to sneak into the city, I might just as well report to the Committee of Correspondence in person for a change."

❧ ❧

The following morning, while Ben walked along the wharf on his way to Faneuil Hall, he noted some obvious peculiarities since his last daytime visit. There was no activity whatsoever on the water, far different from the way things were before the blockade. Ships of all sizes were moored along the entire length of Long Wharf, and vessels from the increased British fleet were lying at anchor. But on shore it was the opposite. With shipping at a standstill, the lack of business and trade sent an unusual number of townsmen out of their shops to mill about in the streets.

British military presence had also increased, he noted. In addition to the familiar Fourteenth and Twenty-ninth Regiments, which had been patrolling Boston over the past several years, Ben spied insignias from New York's Tenth and Eighteenth, plus some from the Forty-seventh, a regiment he did not know. A dozen or more marines swaggered along the docks as well—reinforcements, he assumed. So much for any realistic hope of breaking Dan out of jail.

The eight o'clock bell tolled from Faneuil Hall, and he picked up his pace.

The imposing structure, with its grasshopper weather vane, housed an arcaded market on the ground floor and a great assembly hall above. Nearing the building, Ben detected a murmur of excitement from a gathering of men standing near the door. He threaded his way through them. "Excuse me," he said, tapping someone's shoulder. "Has something happened?"

The fellow's head turned, revealing a weathered face and pronounced chin. "Sure has, lad. Sam Adams and the delegation got back from the congress last eve. Supposed to make an appearance this morning."

"Splendid." Knowing he had better find Quincy fairly quickly, Ben strode inside and took the stiff climb upstairs.

The lawyer sat at a long table with several others, conversing congenially over coffee, but Ben couldn't afford to waste time in being overly polite. "I beg your pardon, Mr. Quincy," he said, cutting into another's remarks. "I'm Ben Haynes. I wonder if I might have a word with you."

The lawyer's eyebrows rose, and he gave a pleasant nod. "You must be Pastor Daniel's brother," he said astutely. "Pull up a chair and join us."

It wasn't what Ben was hoping for, exactly, but he knew he was among fellow patriots. He snagged an empty chair from the next table while the attorney motioned to the bony older man nearest the coffeepot to pour some for Ben.

"So you're the reverend's brother, eh?" the old fellow said, passing a full cup to him.

"Do you know Dan?" Ben took a seat.

"Met him once or twice. And those of us who haven't still know the name."

The others nodded in agreement.

"We were just discussing him, in fact," Quincy added.

Seeing the optimistic expressions around the table, Ben felt an unexplained ray of hope.

A blustery gentleman directly across from him grinned. "You've got nothing to worry about concerning that brother of yours, young man. General Gage knows there's a town full of colonists watching every move he and his motley crew make."

"Well, now," a pudgy fellow occupying the end of the table droned, "I wouldn't count my eggs just yet."

Watching the man as he rolled a quill around in his beefy fingers, Ben felt a twinge of apprehension.

"By now," the man continued, "the general has to know all about our big meeting in Philadelphia and about the decrees. He won't chance a trial here. Wouldn't surprise me if he made good on those threats and took young Haynes out of here right quick and sailed him off to England to their courts. None of us would know the outcome till it was too late."

Ben felt alarm mounting inside and tried to quiet it. This possibility hadn't entered his mind. He shot a glance at the lawyer.

Quincy merely shrugged. "Don't listen to him, lad. Gage knows the riot he would have on his hands if he carted one of our citizens out of the colony for trial. And as your brother's lawyer, they'd be obliged to inform me regarding any such foolhardy intent. Such an incident would be just the spark needed to light the fuse in this powder keg of a town. Put your mind at rest. Their only recourse is to bring Lieutenant Fontaine here to testify."

A few of Ben's own bitter memories of military arrest by Alex Fontaine rose like bile. When Ben was finally released, he was prohibited from entering the city of Boston again. But that hadn't prevented him from using the cover of darkness to return when duty called, regardless of the danger—or the ravaging effects of salt water on his good boots. "That snake Fontaine knows nothing for certain, not even in which direction Ted escaped. I figured that out when I was occupying a cell at South Battery myself, being interrogated by the man day and night. And *if* Fontaine never discovered *where* Ted went, it's easy to calculate he didn't learn who escorted Ted either!"

Quincy clasped Ben's shoulder. "Excellent reasoning, my boy! And that's why we have nothing to fear regarding Dan."

"Except for one thing," Ben grated. "That scoundrel is not an honorable man. He's not above paying someone to testify."

The blustery man across from him snorted. "Nobody around here would be brave enough to take the blackguard's money. My friends down at the ropewalks would bust his head open."

A chuckle of assent circled the group.

Ben wasn't so easily appeased. "Maybe it's time the town brewed up something a little stronger than tea. Lobster stew would be far more satisfying."

The heavyset man pounded the table. "A boy after my own heart!"

"Prudence," the lawyer interjected, "is the better part of valor . . . particularly when the minister prefers to be exonerated rather than rescued. Give due process a chance."

Another blasted reasonable man, Ben groused to himself.

A cheer from outside Faneuil Hall broke forth.

"Sam Adams, no doubt," Quincy said, rising. "This should be interesting. He just returned from Philadelphia last night."

Chairs scraped back as the group stood and headed for the entrance.

It was fortunate for the patriots, Ben concluded, that their most hailed leader was far less reasonable than Samuel Quincy. He and the other delegates departed from the convention with every nose-thumbing decree they sought. With that satisfaction uppermost in his mind, Ben caught up with Quincy at the head of the stairs. "Sir, would you mind if I asked you a few questions regarding a more personal matter? I know a young woman in dire need of legal advice."

"Another time, my boy," he said, brushing past him. "Didn't you hear? Adams is back."

6

Abigail paused in washing the stack of dinner dishes and baking pans and closed her eyes with a heartfelt sigh. *Dear heavenly Father, please, oh, please, don't let any harm come to Ben. Take care of him now, wherever he may be.* But after an entire week without a single word from her betrothed, the prayer provided little comfort. When Ben left, he had seemed fully intent upon breaking his older brother out of an army prison. For all she knew, he could be in a cell now himself . . . or even worse. He might have been shot in the attempted rescue, and his bloodied, lifeless body laid to its eternal rest.

She shuddered and opened her eyes, forcing herself to concentrate on the sermon she'd heard at church this past Sunday. What had the preacher said about trusting instead of worrying? Could a person "take no thought" regarding everyday matters and truly believe that the Almighty knew what each of his children needed? Was it true that merely by seeking first the kingdom of God and his righteousness, everything else would fall into place? It was a lovely promise, but Abby had problems putting it to practical use. If only Ben would come—or send word that he was safe. Surely he must know she would worry about him.

"Girl!" Ma said from the back door, startling Abigail. "A statue you ain't. Stop that infernal mooning, and get them dishes done. No sense actin' the fool. That scoundrel ain't coming back."

Abby's heart froze. She turned to her mother-in-law. "You think he's been arrested or killed trying to break his brother out of jail, is that it?"

"Him? Pshaw!" the older woman snorted. "It's braggin' talk, that is. The upstart just ain't coming back, that's the sum of it. Time ya faced up to the truth. Once I told him he wouldn't be in for a piece of the pie, he's the type what'll be looking around for better pickings. Anyways, travelin' men ain't to be trusted any more than sailors. Wouldn't put it past him to have a wench pining after him in every town 'twixt here and Philadelphia."

The callous remark made Abby cringe. She clamped her lips tight to hold back a biting retort, then thought of the stash of money he had given her for a trousseau. "But Ben asked me to marry him. Why, he gave me—" She caught herself and said no more.

"Hmph. Asking is a far cry from marrying, you know," Ma interrupted, stabbing a bony finger into the air. "Use your head, girl. If that young man comes from some fancy horse farm down on the coast and has a cash-payin' job besides, what would he be wantin' with a nobody like you?"

Her words stung Abby deeply. What if Ma was right? Not too long ago Ben had suggested she meet him on the sly, without Ma or anyone else knowing about it. Only after she had balked did he return with a promise of marriage. But regardless, she couldn't believe Ben would betray her that way. Ma had no basis for saying what she had. Abby reached for the sticky mixing bowl and resumed her chores.

Ma Preston wiped her hands on her work apron and moved to the table, where she grabbed a handful of Abby's cookies still warm from the oven. She stuffed a whole one into her mouth and talked around it, her words muffled. "And don't never forget, all the sniffing he was doin' around here in the first place was after my Bertie, not you. Right up till he showed up and found out she got herself that big, strapping Wes for a husband. That was when all suddenlike he took notice of you. 'Course—" she eyed Abby up and down—"I suppose second choice is better'n none."

It was all Abigail could do to clench her teeth around a disrespectful barb of her own. She scrubbed furiously at the crusted baking sheet. Ma would never believe a man would willingly choose someone over her precious Bertha, though anyone in his right mind could see that Ben constantly tried to ward off the overzealous girl in her attempts to hog-tie and marry him. The satisfaction of that knowledge dispelled some of Abby's anger. With a secret smile, she rinsed the soapsuds from the pan and set it on the sideboard to drain.

A wailing Cassandra slammed the door as she came in from the backyard. "Mama, look. Look at my pretty kitty," she sobbed, tears streaking her face. "Corbin threw it into a mud puddle."

As Abby dried her hands and bent to comfort her little girl, Corbin walked smugly inside, hands in his pockets, angelic halo all but glowing above his head.

"Ah, there's Granny's little man," Ma crooned, scooping him into her arms and giving him a cookie.

"Is my kitty all spoiled, Mama?" Cassie whined, turning her stuffed lamb over to peer more closely at it.

"No, sweetheart. We'll see about making it clean again, all right?" She glared bitterly at Ma's back. Her son she would deal with later, when the three of them were upstairs in their bedchamber. Taking the toy, she began wiping it with a soapy cloth.

"Can I please have a cookie?"

"Of course, sweetie." Abby looked down at her own wet hands. "Ask Grandma for one."

Ma Preston, obviously having overheard, stopped swinging her grandson playfully around and grunted as she thrust a cookie at Cassie without a glance. Then she went back to coddling Corbin.

Cassandra munched the treat and gravitated back to Abigail. She took hold of Abby's skirt and clutched it comfortingly while the lamb's coat was being scrubbed.

Abby was thankful Cassie didn't seem to mind her less-than-exalted—in fact, barely tolerated—position in the family. Timid to begin with, the little girl was made all the more frightened by the loud booming voices of the household. But in truth, Abigail couldn't fault Ma entirely for preferring Corbin. Except for the boy's blonde hair, which ran in Abby's side of the family, he was the spitting image of his daddy. And, thank heaven, he also had Raymond's temperament, open and happy, instead of the typical Preston bossiness.

Ray, now that she thought about it, had been a lot like Ben. Not only did Ben not look down on her, he had unselfishly given her money for new gowns so she wouldn't feel so ashamed of her appearance. *And no man would give a woman a small fortune for no reason.*

He is coming back for me. He is. A man in his position had many duties and important responsibilities. Once they had been dealt with, he would come for her, just as he said.

The bottle of French perfume he had given her remained, as always, in her pocket, tangible proof that he really had asked her to marry him. Even as she moved against the sideboard, washing Cassie's toy, Abby could feel it close to herself.

Ben promised he would deal with Ma. But could he? Chancing a glance at her mother-in-law, Abigail couldn't help wondering how on earth anyone—even Ben Haynes—could rescue her from the formidable older woman.

Until he actually managed that incredible feat, Abby knew she needed to bolster her shaky faith in him. Besides, he had left her with a new responsibility of her own . . . that of acquiring some pretty, new clothes. And she wasn't about to let him down.

Abby didn't need anyone to tell her to keep Ben's generosity to herself. If Ma had the slightest inkling about the cache of money hidden behind a drawer in Abby's wardrobe, the old woman was sure to confiscate it.

The stuffed animal now appeared relatively clean, so Abby

smiled and gave it to Cassandra. "Here you are, honey. Go set it in the sunshine to dry."

"Oh, it's all better!" her daughter cried. "Thank you, Mama." She ran happily outside again.

As the child left, a plan began to formulate in Abby's mind. After chores, she would go to her room and find an even safer place to hide her little fortune. She'd wait for whatever miracle it took to provide an opportunity to go into Millers Falls by herself and purchase new fabric. And then she'd sew in secret. Ma would never even know about it.

Just, please, God . . . let Ben be alive.

7

Ben scarcely noticed autumn's splendor all around him as Rebel's hooves clattered over the bustling streets of the "red-brick city," Philadelphia. The opportunity of speaking to Samuel Quincy had come and gone. It was a keen disappointment to have the lawyer put him off until later, when Ben so desperately needed his advice regarding Abigail's legal position. And *later* never came. Wealthy patriot leader John Hancock had dispatched Ben on an urgent mission to the port authorities in Philadelphia. But even as he smoldered inwardly, Ben knew the matter could not be helped. If Hancock's ship was not rerouted before weighing anchor, it would surely face seizure of its cargo in Boston. He guided his horse along the straight, wide streets of the town toward the warehouses and wharves. Beyond the docks a virtual woodland of tall masts sliced the sky, stirring lightly on the dark currents of the Delaware River.

A commotion just ahead soured the normally congenial atmosphere of the City of Brotherly Love. A merchant waved a fist in the doorway of a public house. "I'll have this pigsty closed down if you don't keep that drunken rabble of yours from harassing my wagoners!"

Apparently some shopkeepers here weren't abiding by the boycott. And if that was the case, this hotbed of Tories would not have their precious warehouses or ships for long—despite the redcoats posted on every corner and the protection their presence afforded. The thought of spurring his mount directly at the nearest pair of lobsterbacks made Ben smile. How he would have loved scattering them like a couple of sorry chickens. But, he concluded, such sport would not be "prudent," to use Quincy's repugnant term. After all, Ben had been able to move about in Philadelphia with relative ease up to this point. There was no merit in jeopardizing that freedom.

"Ben! Ben Haynes! Is that you?"

The familiar voice hailing him went with an equally familiar face—a former college mate of Dan's from Princeton, whom Ben knew through his own family connections. Ben veered his horse over to the hatless young man standing near a loading freight wagon, his sleeves rolled up to his elbows. "Well, if it isn't Morgan Thomas."

"I daresay." Morgan laid aside a tally sheet and straightened to his six-foot height, a devilish grin widening his mouth. "What brings you to our fair city?"

Ben clasped Morgan's proffered hand and shook it. "An errand. I see your father has put his crown prince to work."

"Ah, yes." An impish gleam sparked in his blue eyes, one that looked particularly at home with his perpetually mocking expression. "Even we princes must dirty our hands now and again. Say, it's been some time since you've been around. Just in from Boston?"

"Yes, as a matter of fact, I am."

"Well, step down, man. We've a lot of news to catch up on. How are Dan and the fair Susannah? Things going better with them now? Has Dan gotten back home?"

Wondering where to start with answers, Ben swung down. "You don't want to know," he said in a flat tone.

"Why? What's happened? Don't tell me your brother's been arrested. Or is something amiss with Susannah? I swear, if that king's puppet Fontaine has harmed a single hair on that lovely head of hers, I'll—" His expression turned deadly. "I should have gone to Boston months ago!"

Ben recalled the close relationship Morgan and Susannah

had once known. The man had been her escort at a holiday ball a few Christmases back. "Susannah is fine," he said. "But you're right about Dan. He's being detained at Boston's South Battery for trial when Alex Fontaine comes back from England."

"No!" Tally book forgotten, Morgan grabbed Ben's shoulders. "Well, why are we wasting time? Let's go get him out of there."

Ben shrugged out of the young man's grip. "Hold on, friend. If it had been up to me, Dan wouldn't have spent a night in that rat hole. But he wants more than anything to be exonerated so he may continue his ministry in Boston. If by some chance they do manage to convict him, though, I'd be more than happy to have your help—if you mean what you say."

"I do. I'm quite serious. I—" Morgan glanced toward the double warehouse doors and the older man who had just exited. "Uh-oh, here comes my father. Be careful what you say in front of him."

The sight of Waldon Thomas brought back additional recollections of that long ago Christmas ball. The man's adamant loyalty to Great Britain equalled that of Ben's own merchant cousins, who also resided in the city, and the ties between the two families remained strong. Ben's mother had given him and his father strict orders on their every visit to leave all inflammatory politics at home. "Politics change with the wind," she would say. "Family is forever." He plastered on a dutiful smile and stretched out his hand. "Good day, Mr. Thomas. A pleasure to see you again."

A smile of recognition lit the distinguished man's face as he shook Ben's hand. "Why, aren't you one of Sophia's boys? The younger one, I believe." Thick graying eyebrows winged up at the edges.

"That's right, sir. Ben."

"Yes. Benjamin. Well, this is a rare treat." Slight remnants of a British accent colored his speech. "We haven't seen any of your family—not even your mother or Jane—since that young officer your sister was so fond of got transferred to Boston. No doubt they've wed by now."

So, Waldon Thomas hadn't heard of Ted's desertion! Then he couldn't know about Dan either. Ben sighed with relief. "Yes, you're right, sir. Jane and her true love were married just before this past Christmas. Ted has left the army and is studying for the ministry."

"I say. That rather arrogant army officer a minister? And our vain, beautiful Jane a minister's wife? Surely you jest."

Nearby church bells bonged out the noon hour.

Morgan swung a conspiratorial glance Ben's way. "Father, Ben has agreed to come home with us and have dinner. I'm sure Mother and the girls would love to hear more of the latest gossip from Rhode Island, as well."

"Splendid, my boy," he said, clapping Ben on the back. "Put the ledger inside, Son, and we'll be off."

Watching his lanky friend's springy strides toward the warehouse, Ben had to smile. He had forgotten how easily Morgan could stretch the truth—and lie outright when the need arose. Morgan's family had no idea he was a patriot to the core, secretly passing Tory information to the Sons of Liberty in Philadelphia. Yet for all his colonial loyalty, he had no problem wallowing luxuriously in the comforts and pleasures of his affluent Loyalist home or his father's social position. Either Morgan had to be the bravest man Ben had ever met, or he was the biggest fool. At the moment, Ben was inclined to believe the latter.

A few minutes later, they strode up the brick walk of the sumptuous Thomas mansion, one of the most impressive on an entire street of stately residences.

As they neared the front steps, three young boys leaped out of the shrubbery. "Lobster lovers! Lobster lovers!" they taunted. Flinging a handful of pebbles at the Thomases, they took off.

Most of the small stones missed and pelted the front porch instead.

"Is everyone all right?" Mr. Thomas asked, looking from Ben to Morgan with deep concern.

Morgan, still glaring after the vanishing hellions, nodded.

Ben rubbed his cheek, where a stone had grazed it. "For two pence, I'd—"

The older man held up a restraining hand. "It would serve no purpose, my boy. Chastising the young urchins would merely escalate matters."

"We've gotten rather used to such abuse," Morgan added, "ever since the Colonies met here this past month and instigated still another boycott against England. We must abide by it, whether or not we approve, otherwise our ships could be torched by the rabble down at the waterfront. Of course, there's more than one way to skin a cat, as the saying goes." A sly smile curved his mouth.

"Don't listen to him, my boy," Mr. Thomas said as he opened the ornate door and waved Ben and Morgan inside. "He wants us to take the ships I've sacrificed dearly to acquire and turn them into smuggling vessels."

Morgan shrugged with mock innocence.

"My warehouses are full," his father continued. "I'm certain we'll be able to slide by until this latest crisis has passed. In fact, with the shortages and elevated prices that are bound to follow on the heels of this boycott, my company should come out of this with quite a tidy profit."

"Ah yes," Morgan chimed in, "Father is so astute at turning profits, he could lecture at colleges regarding the art."

As they walked through the wide entry hall with its marbled floor and exquisite chandeliers, Ben's eyes were drawn to the portraits that lined the walls of the hallway. A succession of somber Thomases stared at him, silent witnesses to generations of prosperity.

"If you would be kind enough to excuse me," Morgan's father said, "I'll go inform the cook to set an extra place at the table." He strode through the massive dining room and went out a large door at the far end.

Morgan moved to the buffet and poured them each a glass of cider.

"Thanks," Ben said, accepting one. "Speaking of colleges, I never did understand why your father allowed you to attend the college of those *radical* anarchist Presbyterians in New Jersey when there's a perfectly adequate school right here in the city."

Morgan tossed his head and laughed. "He *allowed* it for the simple reason it *is* so radical. Of all the school presidents, he knew that the firebrand Witherspoon would never permit a student to bribe his way through. And for once, the old man was right. I even had to spend an entire spring recess at Nassau Hall studying again for orals I'd failed . . . along with Steven Russell and Jonathan Bradford. That's how I came to know Susannah so well, actually."

"Oh?"

He nodded. "Having just arrived from Britain, she knew no one. The three of us were swift to take advantage of that, frequenting the inn where she worked. My friends were my only competition, you might say. Those were the days."

Ben watched a strange expression settle over Morgan's mischievous face.

"What I wouldn't give to see her again." As if he had revealed something unintentionally, Morgan's normally cocky demeanor took over again, and he saluted Ben with his drink. "You know, perhaps I should do something about that. Yes. I do think a trip to Boston is in order about now."

Knowing the young man's reputation with the ladies, Ben leveled his gaze directly at him. "That happens to be my brother's wife we're talking about."

"Yes." Morgan hiked a challenging brow. "Your *imprisoned* brother. Susannah must be getting quite lonely by now. Frightfully lonely . . ." He let the thought trail off.

How satisfying it would be, Ben thought, *to wipe away that overconfident expression.* His hand knotted into a fist.

Morgan shielded his face with his hands. "Just teasing," he said, peering slyly through his fingers.

Ben had to chuckle at the young man's tomfoolery, and Morgan joined in with a hearty laugh as he lowered his hands.

"I was quite serious about going to Boston, however," he elaborated. "From what I've overheard from Crown officers around town, the king and Parliament will never accept these decrees of the Colonies. And now that others are aligning themselves with Massachusetts, it's only a matter of time before there'll be open conflict. I intend to be up there when that happens."

Laughter and feminine voices drifted from the hall, along with light footsteps. Ben picked out Morgan's mother's regal voice and assumed that the others, which were definitely younger, belonged to his sisters.

Morgan stepped close. "Best be on your guard," he whispered. "Mother's in one of her matchmaking moods. Again."

8

The *tap, tap, tap* of dainty shoes walking toward the dining room was yet another reminder of the last time Ben had been in this house. It hardly seemed possible that four years had passed since that fateful Christmas party when Morgan had brought Susannah home for the holidays and tried to pass her off as the daughter of an Anglican church official instead of the lowly bondservant she was. During the festivities the scandalous truth had been exposed, catching Morgan very publicly in a lie.

"I thought I detected a strange voice," Mrs. Thomas said as she swept into the room. Her eyes drifted toward Ben, and a light of recognition registered on her queenly face almost instantly. Even at this hour her fingers were adorned with jewels, and she was dressed fashionably enough to attend court instead of merely having the midday meal. She turned to the young women accompanying her, whose names Ben struggled to recall without success. "Dears, you must remember Benjamin Haynes, Sophia Somerwell's son, of the *Philadelphia Somerwells.*" She strolled to Ben, hand outstretched. "Or should I say—Sophia Somerwell *Haynes.*"

Ben managed to restrain a laugh as he bowed over her hand and kissed it. How typical of her not to mention his father, who was a native of the notoriously rebellious colony of Rhode Island. The family's link to the Somerwells was of far more importance to the woman, for it merited instant acceptance in polite Philadelphia society.

Ben swept a glance over the young ladies before him, feminine versions of Morgan. One had a guileless face and eyes of such a light blue they were almost transparent. The impish gleam in the other one's deep blue eyes was more than a match for Morgan's. "These can't be the two little girls who watched the Christmas ball from the upstairs balcony. Why, they've grown into such lovely young ladies, I hardly recognize them."

"Yes, haven't they." With pride the strikingly handsome woman turned to the younger of the two. "Our sweet Evelyn will be fourteen on her next birthday. We can hardly believe it ourselves."

A faint flush stained Evelyn's cheeks as she rolled her eyes and curtsied.

"And this," Morgan's mother continued as she handed the eldest daughter forward, "is Frances. She is facing quite an exciting year ahead of her. Quite exciting, indeed. The approaching holidays will begin the season of her coming out." Lovingly she smoothed a hand down the girl's rich chestnut curls, which were as glossy as the chocolate silk frock she wore. "And if I know my Frances, gentlemen callers will be at our door in droves."

"Mama!" Frances gasped. Nevertheless, her deep blue eyes sparkled above a most becoming blush. She raised her lashes quite daringly and regarded Ben with a smile.

"Well, darling, they will," her mother continued. "You'll see it soon enough. You're easily as beautiful and accomplished as Melinda was at your age, and she has married quite well." Her attention was distracted by movement at the opposite end of the room. "Oh, here comes the maid with another table setting. And that mindless husband of mine. Waldon, you should have told me we would have a guest."

Mr. Thomas offered her a gracious smile as he approached. "It couldn't be helped, my dear Mildred. We only just arrived." He gestured toward the table. "Cook says we can be seated now."

His wife, glancing toward the maid, fluttered her lace handkerchief. "Lucy! Not there, dear. Mister Haynes will be seated here." She indicated the center of the long, gleaming mahogany table with its eight chairs.

Dutifully the servant gathered Ben's table service from the side which presently had only one setting and circled to the other side, placing the additional plate and utensils between two others.

Ben knew—even without Morgan's significant grin—who would be flanked by the daughters during the meal. Still, he couldn't help but notice that Frances appeared flustered. "May I?" he asked, offering an arm. After seating her and Evelyn, he took his own chair.

"Benjamin, dear," Morgan's mother said as the servants brought in bowls of food. "You must speak to your mother for me. I insist that she—and you, of course—come to Philadelphia for the holiday house parties. It's been far too long. And heaven knows there will be precious little to celebrate in New England this year after Parliament takes punitive action against their dreadful rebellious decrees."

Ben found it exceedingly difficult to contain his less-than-courteous response to her sentiments, so he remained silent until Morgan rescued him.

"I'm famished," Morgan cut in. "Father, would you say the grace now, so we can begin?"

At the head of the table, Mr. Thomas cleared his throat, and even his wife closed her overworked mouth and bowed her head. "Our benevolent heavenly Father, bless this food we are about to receive through thy grace and that of our motherland. I pray for her patience and mercy toward her ungrateful children. Amen."

Ben was grateful that Morgan rather pointedly reached across the table and shoved a platter of cold sliced turkey and ham under his nose. He appreciated the diversion from that ridiculous prayer. He took some and offered it to Frances, then tried a mouthful.

"Benjamin," Mrs. Thomas coaxed as she buttered a warm roll, "you will make an earnest effort to convince your family to come for the holidays, won't you?"

He wiped his mouth on his napkin. "I'm afraid that won't be possible this year. Mother is hoping to arrange a family gathering at home. And," he added, hoping and praying his next words would come to pass, "I am planning to be wed at that time."

Having obviously already speculated on an advantageous match between the Thomases and the Hayneses, her expression fell. "I see." She looked from him to Frances, then shifted her attention to Morgan. "Did you hear that, Son?"

Morgan groaned.

"Morgan is easily two years your senior," his mother elaborated with renewed fervor. "And he is still refusing to choose among our city's young belles. Can you imagine," she asked with a frown, "three and twenty, and not a serious thought toward taking up the responsibilities of wife and family?" Blotting the corners of her mouth, she returned her napkin to her lap.

"You don't say," Ben replied with a conspiratorial smirk at Morgan. He raised his glass to his lips.

A scampish glint in his eye, Morgan swung a slow gaze toward his mother. "But as you well know, dearest Mother, it was Ben's own brother who captured the one true love of my life, leaving me to wither and die a heartbroken, lonely old man."

"I seriously doubt that," she said. "But even if it were true, I'm certain even Ben would agree that his brother's wife is far more suited to being a minister's wife than that of a prominent merchant. It can't be denied that a certain . . . stigma . . . is attached to being a bondservant, no matter how unfortunate the precipitating circumstances."

Ben nearly choked. He had never met a woman with such a propensity for insulting him and his family—and with so little apparent forethought. His own mother was going to owe him dearly for all the stinging retorts he'd had to squelch.

"I say," Morgan cut in, saving him again, "speaking of circumstances, Ben has just made me privy to a rather fortunate one."

If the lout was describing Dan's imprisonment as a "fortunate circumstance," that was the last straw. Ben tossed down his napkin.

"While traveling the countryside," Morgan went on smoothly, "he happened upon a native herb that tastes remarkably like India tea. Isn't that how you described it?"

Ben had no idea what Morgan was talking about, but on the outside chance it had to do with some patriot plan, he decided to go along with it. "Yes. Exactly."

Morgan's mouth twitched as he continued. "Ben has already hired men all across the back country to collect seeds. But now he needs a partner to help him convince farmers to plant the crop, someone he can trust to keep this new venture a secret. He figures that with another tea boycott we could make a fortune marketing this new substitute. And though I know merchants detest the word *monopoly*, we would, for the first year at least, have one."

"Why, this is most incredible," Mr. Thomas said, leaning toward Ben with undisguised interest. "But I find it hard to believe no one came forth with this herb during the last boycott."

Not having the slightest idea how to reply, Ben stabbed a chunk of ham and closed his mouth around it.

Morgan, however, seemed in his glory. "I hear it's a tea the Indians in the Ohio Valley drink. A surveyor brought some of it back with him."

"Ah," his father said with a perplexed nod. "I certainly hope that surveyor was commissioned by Britain. You know as well as I that no colony is supposed to be expanding past the mountains." He turned to Ben. "Under whose authority was he surveying, young man?"

He swallowed. "If you'll forgive me, sir, I never thought to ask." There, he reasoned. No one could accuse *him* of lying.

The elder Thomas snorted his disgust. "Well, what's done is done. Might I ask if you tasted this tea yourself?"

"Not only has he tasted it, Father," Morgan responded instantly, "he went so far as to blindfold two women—not men, mind you—and had them sample the brew along with some India tea. They tasted them both several times before attempting to state which was which. Finally one guessed it was India tea, and the other said Ohio. Now, if that isn't endorsement enough, I don't know what is."

To Ben's utter amazement, he could see that Morgan's father was actually starting to believe the insane fabrication. The man's lips spread into a wide grin. "Well, now, Ben," he said on a much more intimate note, "if this is as good as it sounds, why would you want to share this windfall with us, if you don't mind my asking. Why not with your cousin Landon?"

Again Morgan came to the rescue. "Well, you see, Ben knows what a persuasive person I am, compared to stuffy old Landon. And I informed him that if I were to be a part of this, then so are you. He's agreed to allow us to be the sole agents for all of the middle colonies." He gave a nod for emphasis.

His father's chest puffed out as he harrumphed with pride and beamed at the others around the table.

At the sight of Morgan's artful smile, Ben himself was on the verge of believing the charade. Nevertheless, he was hesitant to actually look the young man in the eye for fear of being drawn even further into it.

"I was thinking, Father, that since importing is bound to be slow for some time to come, you could quite easily do without me right now. I think we're fortunate that this opportunity has arisen at such a perfect time."

"Yes, you are absolutely right," Mr. Thomas said, nodding slowly.

"And the sooner I start canvassing the farmers along the

rivers, the more plants will be sprouting leaves by next spring. Think about it."

"No need for that, Son. I heartily agree. And *while* you're at it, I suggest you go north first, visit some of the merchants in the Boston area. Perhaps you could arrange to have some of their inbound ships rerouted to us, since the blockade will prevent them from brokering their cargos."

"That's an excellent idea."

"Will you be leaving today, Morgan?" Evelyn asked.

"Oh no, dear," her mother said. "There are preparations which must be made when one is to leave on a long journey."

Morgan flashed a pleading look at Ben, who was starting to feel trapped. "Well, I must leave as soon as I've made my deliveries, but I suppose Morgan could come north later—"

Morgan pounded a fist on the table. "Father, there can be only so many Boston ships yet to arrive and be dealt with. This is no time to be dragging our feet. We may never again see an opportunity quite like either of these. And the sooner I fetch the seed and sample leaves to convince the farmers, the more we'll have to sell by spring. Oh yes, and I'll require funds for my expenses."

❧ ❧

"I should be gone no more than an hour or so," Ben said to Morgan as they exited the front door. "I have only one message to deliver."

"Don't worry about me. I'll be saddled and ready upon your return."

"I don't doubt that—if you pack half as quickly as you talk!"

Morgan gave a hearty laugh.

Ben shook his head in wonder at the turn of events. "Just remember, I travel fast and light."

"That does not present a problem," Morgan said. "I'm sure the old man will be more than happy to ship a trunk of extra clothing up to Salem for me. Speaking of fast and light," he added, a devilish twinkle in his eye, "did you tell Mother you were taking a wife merely to throw her off your scent?"

Ben exhaled heavily. "Well, right at the moment, things are a bit unsettled, you might say."

"I knew it!" He whacked Ben on the back. "Why would anyone want to give up the adventure—and danger—of being a courier for the cause?"

"I do plan to continue being a courier as well as marrying." He smiled. "Wait until you meet Abigail. You'll understand why. From the moment I first set eyes on her, I've thought of little else."

"So, why is everything unsettled, then?"

"There's a mother-in-law involved. Her dead husband's mother."

"Ah. Say no more."

"Right. The old battle-ax refuses to let Abby leave the farm with her children."

"Children?" Morgan stopped dead in his tracks. "Poor chap. You must have it rather bad to be willing to take on a wife *and* children."

"I'm not all that noble, actually. As it happens, Abby's children are every bit as adorable as she is." He paused. "Of course, if I were to give up my work for the Committee of Correspondence, stay there and work the farm, Ma Preston would probably be more than willing to agree to our marriage. But with Dan in jail and everything else about to blow, I could never do that. Besides, Abigail needs to get out from under that woman's thumb. She's far too fragile and could so easily be crushed by the likes of Ma Preston and her oaf of a daughter."

They reached Ben's horse, and Ben gathered the reins.

"I'll tell you what I'd do in your place," Morgan offered.

"I'm open to any advice right now."

"Charm the old gal. Tell her whatever she wants to hear. Once you two marry, what can she do? Think it over . . . that is, if you're truly serious about wanting to settle down and set up housekeeping at your tender age."

Ben elevated his chin at Morgan's teasing tone. "I'll have you know I'll be twenty-two on my next birthday."

"And I shall be twenty-four. Yet the very thought of waking up with some whining female every morning for the next fifty or sixty years is enough to send me howling after the moon!"

"You wanted to marry Susannah once."

At the reminder, some of the starch left Morgan's jaunty expression. "Yes. Susannah. Well, that was different," he said. "She was different. Any young woman who would sell herself into servitude merely to be in a place where she could learn and discuss the finer points of theology is a woman with spirit and courage enough to touch any man. Around her I wanted to stretch my own horizons." His gaze wavered, and he glanced away momentarily, then looked back with a shrug. "Having to bury my nose in those dusty old books just so I could keep up with her incessant questions was most likely what got me through college."

This glimpse of the lanky young man's innermost self surprised Ben, and he wanted to lighten Morgan's discomfort. "Well, that's not the only thing Susannah's good at. Her real flair is in the realm of advice. Telling me what's good for me." Turning, he hooked his boot into a stirrup. "Well, I'd better get going. I'll be back in an hour." He swung up into the saddle.

Morgan smiled and nodded. "And I shall be ready in a minute."

"You don't say." Ben nudged Rebel into a walk. "We've got some minutemen of our own up in Massachusetts. Remind me to introduce you to them when we get there."

9

Shivering in the chilly morning air, Abigail wished she had more than her light shawl around her shoulders as she gathered an armful of wood from the shed.

"Psst."

Abby stiffened and looked around.

"Psst."

The signal was more insistent the second time, and it came from behind the woodshed. Had Ben come back for her? "Yes?" she asked tentatively. "Who's there?"

"Wes," he whispered. "Come around back. But make sure nobody sees ya. I want ya alone."

Abigail had more than a few misgivings about being alone with the big dunderhead. She had caught a few very unsettling looks from him of late . . . ever since Ben had asked for her hand, in fact. Had the proposal put some ungentlemanly thoughts into his head? Deciding to ignore him, she went on choosing kindling and wood for the stove. With Ma and Bertha waiting in the kitchen, Wes probably wouldn't try anything so long as she remained in view of the house.

"Abby, gal. What're ya dawdlin' for?" he demanded. "Bertie's likely to come out any minute, wondering why the milking's takin' me so long."

"Well, I have no intention of being alone with you, Wesley, now or ever," Abby whispered back with fervor. "Go away, now, and leave me be."

"But it's you and Ben I need to talk about," he went on impatiently.

"You've heard from Ben?" With a nervous glance toward the house, she slipped out the door and around to the back, where Bertha's husband stood with a milk bucket in one hand and his other hand on his hip. To Abby's relief, he didn't appear amorous in the least. The very thought made her blush. "Sorry it took me so long," she mumbled. "What about Ben? Has he sent a message? A letter?"

"Nope. Nothin' like that. I just wanted you to know I'm on your side. Not that you should take this wrong or nothin', but it would pleasure me to see you and your young'uns gone from here just as it would you."

"I thought you liked my children," she said, offended.

"I do. I do. But the way Ma took on when you said you were taking little Corbin away, she might could go back on her word to me, see? She might deed the whole place to him when he gets older . . . and it ain't fair, not with how I been slaving away here, putting up with her bossin' me around. Besides, she'd be more apt to dote on the young'uns Bertie and me have if her precious Ray's boy ain't underfoot. Hear what I'm saying?"

Abby nodded. "She does set an awful lot of store by Corbin, that's a fact. Too much."

"So, we agree then, right? If you think of any way I might be able to help ya get away from this place, just let me know."

Staring at Wes, Abby couldn't help wondering what he could do. "I'm not even sure Ben's still alive. Are you absolutely sure there's been no word from him?"

"Nope. None a'tall."

Her spirit sank. "Well, if any does come, please don't let them keep it from me. Promise?"

"Word of honor. And if I was you, I'd be thinkin' of sneaking outta here to go to him. Maybe I could arrange some transport for ya. Without Ma knowing, of course."

"You mean, run away?" Abby asked, shocked. "I could never do something so underhanded to Ma. No matter what, she's kept a roof over our heads and food in our bellies since the day Raymond died. I owe her too much." She already felt guilty enough over keeping the clothes money secret. But then she remembered the material she had to buy. "There is something. I need to get to town. There's some business Ben wanted me to take care of, only I'm never allowed to go into Millers Falls by myself."

A conspiratorial smile widened Wes's face, reinforcing her feelings of guilt. "After Bertie goes to sleep tonight I could spirit you out. How's that?"

She shook her head. "That won't do. I need to go during the daytime. But thanks anyway."

"Abby, girl!" Ma hollered from the house.

"Coming." She turned to leave.

"Don't you worry none," Wes whispered behind her. "I'll think of some way to get you where you need to go."

With a slight nod, Abby hurried toward the house, where her mother-in-law glowered at her through the open back door.

"What was ya trying to find in back of the shed?" she said in her grating voice. "The wood's inside, ya know."

"I thought I heard something, that's all. Must've been just a deer."

Ma turned and started back inside, then stopped. "Think I heared something myself."

Abby froze as Ma tromped down the steps. Wes hadn't made a sound. What could the older woman have heard? Abby's pulse picked up. All she needed was for Ma or Bertha to discover she'd had a secret meeting with Wesley. They'd think her wanton, for certain.

But Ma headed around the house toward the road. "Somebody's coming on horseback. And at such a early hour, to boot!"

Abby's relief turned to anticipation. *Ben. Please, Father, let it be Ben.* But as she hastened after her mother-in-law, she saw that it was not. She tried to swallow her disappointment.

The rawboned stranger reined in and removed his hat, but

he did not dismount. "Mistress Preston," he said with a polite nod.

"Mr. Bowman."

"I'm looking for a Mistress Abigail Preston."

Renewed hope sprang to life inside Abby. No one had ever sought her out before except Ben. Perhaps this man had brought a letter from him.

"Well, this is her," Ma said flatly, pushing her forward. "What do you want?"

Mr. Bowman focused his attention on Abigail. "Do you happen to have kin in Millers Falls, young lady?"

"Yes. Yes, I have. A grandaunt, Hattie Fields. But she's quite old now."

"And ailing unto death, I'm afraid. She's been asking for you."

Abigail had to admit she barely knew her distant relative, but nevertheless, she felt sad to hear the woman was dying.

"Maybe she wants to leave ya somethin'," Wes offered, striding up to join them.

"No, that's not possible," Abby said with a shake of her head. "Grandaunt Hattie lives with her deceased husband's nephew."

"So? You never know," he said brightly. "I'll hitch up the wagon right now and drive ya on into town." He turned to Ma. "Tell Bertie to look after the young'uns till we git back, huh? Oh, and tell her I'm hankerin' for some apple pandowdy. If she has some made when I come home, I'll bring a surprise for her. And maybe somethin' for you, too," he added with a wink.

As Abby observed him dangling phantom inheritances and presents at the lot of them, her estimation of his cleverness rose by several degrees. Not only had he kept Ma from having her say, he even had her happy about it! And after seeing Aunt Hattie, Abigail would be able to buy the new material she needed.

"My cloak," she blurted, thinking of the money hidden up in her room. "I'll go fetch it."

"Just don't tarry, missy," Mr. Bowman said. "Your aunt is very poorly."

❦ ❦

Slanted shafts of afternoon light illuminated the smoky interior of Pidge Tavern in Pawtucket as Morgan strolled inside. He waited for his eyes to adjust, then picked out a likely spot at the bar to stand and rest his weary backside while Ben went to seek the minister of the local Baptist church. Ben had set a grueling pace during the past several days of travel. They'd scarcely stopped long enough during the hard ride to catch a bite or to sleep, let alone take time to go visit Ben's parents. All he could talk about was seeing that the banns were posted for his hoped-for marriage, which was far more urgent a matter to him than the return message he carried from Philadelphia to Boston.

Morgan shook his head. Even if Ben were somehow successful in sweet-talking old widow Preston into permitting Abigail to come to Rhode Island for Christmas, did the lad have any idea what he was getting into? No small number of Morgan's own friends back home had succumbed to alluring young maidens—only to discover before the wedding cake grew stale that their expected life of bliss was instead a lifetime of tedium, made up of endless complaints, whining, and nagging. For all Ben knew, even the winsome Abigail could be a shrew. Grimacing at the prospect, Morgan stepped up to the bar.

"Something wrong, lad?" the proprietor inquired with a puzzled frown.

"Why do you ask?"

"It's just that you had a peculiar look on your face. Couldn't help wonderin'."

"Nothing more newsworthy than a nagging woman," Morgan quipped. "I could use a drink, though. Spiced cider, if you have any. Hot."

A customer from a nearby table came to join him. "Did I see you ride in with Ben Haynes? He a friend of yours?"

Morgan met the fellow's more-than-curious gaze. Then, considering Ben's provincial hometown, he decided against making a flip remark. "Our families have been friends for many years. We're just passing through on our way to Boston."

"Running an errand, perchance?" The eyes behind the wire-rimmed spectacles did not waver.

Friend or foe? The man's expression gave no hint as Morgan heard his drink arrive. "Thank you," he said to the proprietor, glad for any diversion.

"You can wipe that scared-rabbit look off your face," the barkeeper said kindly. "We're all family here."

"Sons, you might say," the other added. "How 'bout fetching me one of them ciders, Horace?" He turned again to Morgan. "Passing through, you say? From where?" This time his tone didn't sound so testing.

"Philadelphia, actually." Morgan felt foolish—dangerously foolish—for having displayed his apprehension. Fortunately these men were Sons of Liberty—or so they hinted.

"And you two are heading to Boston, eh? Good," the patron said. "I've some information for Ben to pass along, then."

"He's over at the church. But once he's finished there, we'll be off again. He's in such a hurry, he didn't even stop to see his folks."

"At the church?" The fellow and the barkeeper exchanged smirks. "I'll wait till he comes out. Don't think I need another of them three-hour sermons from our local finger wagger right now. How long do you figure Ben will be?"

"I've not the slightest idea," Morgan said with an affable smile. Speculating about the sort of interesting information the townsman wanted to relate sent Morgan's own curiosity on an upswing. "We shall leave the instant he's through . . . so I'll be more than happy to relay your news to him."

"Aw, go ahead, Fields," the barkeeper said. "Nothin's gonna keep this from the whole seaboard for more than a day or two anyhow."

"Aye, you're right." Turning back to Morgan, he leaned a

fraction nearer. "Some men, who shall remain nameless, sailed out to the island this morning, and—"

"What island?"

"Why, Rhode Island. Where else?"

"But this is Rhode Island." Morgan was thoroughly confused.

The bartender chuckled. "This colony of ours is named after the largest island out in the harbor. Newport Town is on it."

"And a fort," his pal piped in. "It has forty cannon—or should I say, *we* now have forty cannon." He grinned.

Morgan couldn't believe what he was hearing . . . if indeed he was hearing correctly.

The bartender leaned across the bar. "It's like this, son. If dumping a little tea into Boston Bay ends up with a closed harbor, England's probably gonna blockade *all* the ports when they hear the decrees all the colonies signed. So, like Fields says, no sense making things easy for them. They try to block our bay, and they'll find forty cannon aimed right at their heads!"

"You've taken over a military outpost?" Surely they jested.

"There wasn't anything to it, boy," Fields replied. "The place was only manned by a skeleton crew."

"But you must realize you've just declared war," Morgan said, his excitement mounting.

"We did that two years ago," Fields sneered, "when we torched that pirate ship *Gaspee,* of His Highness's royal fleet. The Brits are just slow to figure things out."

Laughing aloud, Morgan slapped the counter. "It's begun! By all that's holy, man, it's begun! I got here just in time!"

10

Susannah gazed down at the cherubic face of Julia Rose asleep in her arms. The silken lashes curling against the baby's chubby cheeks were the same shade as her light brown hair. She was growing quickly . . . so quickly. Dan had already missed out on so many of her little firsts, not to mention the joy her presence brought to these troubled days. After having been robbed of most of Miles's second year, the realization seemed doubly sad. When would they ever be a family again? With a sigh, Susannah got up from the rocking chair and laid her daughter down for her afternoon nap.

A knock sounded on the front door. Someone from the congregation stopping by after visiting Dan, she hoped. Though they had been without a church since British soldiers ransacked it on the pretext of searching for Dan and Ted months ago, the dear members never once blamed her and Dan for the loss. Instead they had stood by them in their tribulations. Susannah felt truly blessed having them as friends.

Before she even reached the landing, two-year-old Miles dashed out of the parlor with Felicia in his wake. He tugged the door open with a grunt.

"Good day, young man," came a stranger's voice from the doorway. "I'm lookin' for Mistress Haynes. Would she happen to be your ma?"

Susannah stepped forward and put a hand on her son's shoulder. "I'm Susannah Haynes. How may I help you?"

The sturdily built farmer removed his hat, turning it around and around in his calloused hands. "How do, mistress. I'm Zeb Swan. Just in from the Grants."

"Oh!" Quickly she checked up and down the street, searching for any strangers lurking about. No one must ever know where Ted and Jane were. "So good of you to stop by, Mr. Swan. Please, come in. May I offer you some tea?"

"Thank you kindly, but no."

As she led the man into the front room, she smiled at Felicia. "Would you be a dear and keep Miles occupied so the two of us might talk freely?"

"Of course." Felicia tousled Miles's hair. "Whoever is first to the kitchen gets a big cookie from the jar."

"I'm the fastest!" The two of them raced up the hall.

Susannah turned to her guest and gestured toward the silver damask settee. After taking one more cursory look through the lace panels adorning the windows, she perched on the edge of one of the wing chairs. "What brings you to Boston, Mr. Swan?"

"I brought in a load of food from the folks up in the Green Mountains. And I bring greetings from a relative of yours."

"How is he?" she asked, hoping with all her heart that Ted had arrived home safely.

"Alas, not so good. He's fearsome worried about how you're doing." The farmer's weathered face bore anxious creases. "To be frank, the lad wants me to find out if the British would accept him in your husband's place. He feels Dan wouldn't be there if not for him."

"You can't mean that!"

"'Fraid I do, mistress. But we convinced him to wait till I return."

"Thank goodness!"

The man's shaggy brows drew together as his expression became even more concerned. "Truth is, we sorely need him up there, what with the turn of events . . . if you know what I mean."

"I'm quite pleased to hear you're seeking more men of God in the wilderness."

"Aye. That, too. But that ain't exactly the skill we're most in need of right now."

"I see. You're referring to his military training, then." At the man's nod, Susannah felt her spirits sag. It was common knowledge in the Colonies how handily the Green Mountain Boys had run off New Yorkers eager to claim the same land that families in the Grants had bought from the governor of New Hampshire. Still, challenging a party of surveyors or New York settlers was not quite the same as opposing professional soldiers. The danger was great for Ted, Susannah knew. But it would be even more dangerous for him to return to Boston. Susannah met Mr. Swan's gaze. "Please tell Ted that I said it's out of the question. Better yet—" Plucking her warm shawl from the arm of an adjacent chair, she rose and started toward the door. "Come with me to visit my husband. I was going to the jail anyway to deliver a letter from his mother. I'm sure he'll voice an even stronger message that will dissuade Ted from doing something so foolhardy. He would surely be shot. Felicia," she called over her shoulder, "I'll be back in a little while."

As usual during the middle of the day, foot traffic along Milk Street was heavy as Susannah and Mr. Swan set out toward the South Battery. Bundled up against a brisk salty breeze, she nodded and smiled at several familiar faces during the walk.

An inebriated soldier stumbled out the door of a mughouse as they passed. He bumped into Susannah, almost knocking her off balance. "Er, pardon, mistress," he said, the words wafting out on a vapor of rum. He made a clumsy attempt to steady her, then with a lopsided grin, chuckled and grabbed her closer.

Shocked, she struggled to free herself.

"Unhand her, you drunken lout!" Mr. Swan seized the

man's shoulder and wrenched him from her. His large fist crashed into the soldier's jaw and sent him slumping to the cobbled street.

Three more king's men joined the melee. They grabbed Mr. Swan and slammed him up against the building.

"Let me at the bloke," the one on the ground railed. Rubbing his chin, he staggered to his feet.

"Merciful heaven," Susannah cried as an angry crowd began to gather. "Don't. Please!"

At the sound of her voice, one of the soldiers turned around. Susannah sighed with relief when she recognized Private Williams, one of the young men who had been posted at her gate during her months of detainment. "I beg your pardon, Mistress Haynes," he said as he hauled one of the soldiers off Mr. Swan and kept hold of him.

The number of onlookers grew by the second, their furor swiftly increasing. "That's your answer to everything, isn't it?" a townsman demanded. "Jump on innocent folk or cart 'em off whenever you please!"

Private Williams ignored the jeer. "You should not be exposed to this sort of scene," he said to Susannah. "What happened?"

"Same thing as happens to any woman who finds herself too close to one of you lobsterbacks!" an angry tradesman yelled.

Knowing that riots often started over far less, Susannah turned anxiously to the private. "It's all a misunderstanding," she blurted. "Mr. Swan was only trying to help me after the other soldier became a—a bit too friendly."

Private Williams clenched his jaw, then gave the offending soldier a curt nod. With a last dark scowl, the culprit swaggered off.

The private removed his tall hat and cradled it under one arm. "Again, Mistress Haynes, our most sincere apologies for any discomfort you may have endured. Do give my greetings to Miss Felicia and your son. And tell little Miles I shall come by soon to toss the ball with him."

Relieved to see the crowd also drifting away, Susannah smiled. "I'm sure he'll be quite pleased to hear that."

Mr. Swan angrily adjusted his coat and came back to her side. Without a word he took her elbow and drew her on down the street.

"May God be with you, Private," Susannah called over her shoulder. Then she breathed a hasty prayer that none of the townspeople would jump into the fray once she was safely out of harm.

"We gotta get this nest of vipers outta here," Mr. Swan grumbled, his voice low and ominous. "We will, too. I heard some serious talk when I was at the Neck, about fortifying the hills behind Charlestown. Yessir, a few well-placed cannon there and on the other side of the bay, and we could put them puppets out of business right quick. Me and the other boys up north will be only too glad to come help you folks out anytime you want us."

"Oh, look," Susannah said airily. "The sun has come out again. Perhaps it'll be a lovely day after all." She knew her efforts were futile. She might be able to change the course of the conversation, but she couldn't keep her mind from dwelling on the farmer's disturbing words. She had heard the same from church members. They, too, wanted to fortify the surrounding high ground. It would be such a shame for a proud and beautiful city like Boston, which had been founded and dedicated by God-fearing men, to face certain destruction. This was the first city in which she'd ever lived where the keeping of the Sabbath was strictly observed—at least by the colonists. When she first arrived, the ringing of the church bells on Sunday served only to call worshipers to gather. Now they tolled throughout the week to announce further turbulence in this divided city.

Susannah hoped General Gage would be successful in maintaining the peace. She knew the townspeople had never elected him governor and that they hated why he was here— to be the leader of an occupying army. His own men thought no better of him, for they were forced to endure insults and

threats from the locals without reprisal. They had even nick-
named the general the Old Woman.

As she and Mr. Swan neared the gate to the South Battery,
Susannah glanced up at him. "My husband has quite enough
to contend with already. I'd greatly appreciate it if you
wouldn't mention today's incident to him."

Mr. Swan eyed her curiously but nodded his assent.

Within a few minutes they were admitted to Dan's cell, and
Susannah rushed into her husband's open arms. "I've
brought someone who needs to speak to you, sweetheart."
She eased back and motioned toward the farmer. "This is Mr.
Swan. He's come from up north."

Dan's dark brows rose with immediate recognition. "Yes, I
believe we've met before."

"Good to see you again, Reverend. Though not in the best
of circumstances."

"Well, no," Dan admitted good-naturedly. "But it can't be
helped just yet. What brings you here?"

"It's Ted, sweetheart," Susannah explained in a hushed
voice. "He's on the verge of offering himself in exchange for
you."

"You can't be serious!" Dan looked from her to the farmer
in amazement. "That's the dumbest thing I've ever heard in
my life!"

"But what if they convict you, Reverend?" Mr. Swan asked.

Dan turned away, pacing to the edge of the cell and back,
shaking his head.

Susannah could feel his utter dismay. She went to him and
put her arms around him.

Dan said nothing for a minute or two, but soon he seemed
to find a measure of encouragement in Susannah's embrace.
He looked intently at Mr. Swan. "Sounds as if your pastor
hasn't preached the Sermon on the Mount for some time,"
he finally responded. "Remember what our Lord said about
worrying? 'Take therefore no thought for the morrow: for the
morrow shall take thought for the things of itself. Sufficient
unto the day is the evil thereof.'"

He turned toward Susannah with a love-filled smile. "And today, except for the fact that I very much miss seeing my babies, I have few complaints. I've had several visitors, among them some of the soldiers my dear wife befriended during the time they guarded our house. Nice lads."

"You wouldn't feel that way if you—"

"Yes," Susannah interrupted, "a number of the baser soldiers are being as rude to the townsfolk as ever, just as our own less charitable ones are to them. But that's nothing new, is it?" She forced a cheerful smile she didn't feel. "I did bring some good news with me, sweetheart. A lovely letter arrived from your mother."

Dan accepted the letter gratefully and scanned it quickly. His dark eyes were soft when he at last looked into Susannah's. "Mother certainly has changed during the past year, hasn't she? Who would expect she'd invite the *entire* family to come for Christmas? And that she'd like us to bring Yancy and Felicia along with us *when*—not *if*—we come."

Susannah laughed lightly. "Yes, and her trust in the Lord has grown so much. It's hard to believe she's the same woman who once disapproved so vehemently of our marriage because of my year of servitude. Now I find myself looking forward to each one of her cheerful, loving letters." She paused, perplexed. "This one, however, I shall find difficult to answer. How can I tell her there's virtually no hope of Alex's return before the end of February?"

Dan drew her close. "Let me save you the trouble, my love. Bring me some writing materials when you visit tomorrow, and I'll send her a nice long letter."

"Would you?" Susannah tilted her head back and gazed lovingly up at him. "I'll also bring the children along to see you. As kind as the guards here have been to me, I'm certain they'll make an exception and permit the little ones. They've yet to refuse my plum tarts."

"I'd like to be included in the party," a voice said from outside the cell.

Susannah whirled around in surprise to see their neighbor, Elder Simms, standing there with . . . could it be?

She rushed forward, arms spread wide, as the guard accompanying the newcomers opened the door. "Morgan! Morgan Thomas! I don't believe it!"

❦ ❦

The joy Morgan felt upon seeing Susannah's radiant smile surprised him. And though he was more than thrilled to be the recipient of her welcoming hug, he allowed himself only the briefest heartbeat to revel in it.

"Marvelous to see you again," he said as he held her at arm's length. He allowed his eyes to wander over her lithe frame so fetchingly attired in indigo and ruffled lace. How could it be that she, the mother of two babes already, had managed to maintain not only her graceful figure but her gentle English beauty as well? He now fully understood why all other young maidens held so little appeal for him.

Just as he began to draw her close again, his gaze met the stare of her unsmiling husband. Morgan swallowed and released Susannah before extending his hand to him. "Dan."

Dan clasped it in a hearty handshake, his expression relaxing into a friendly grin. "Morgan. This certainly is a surprise. What brings you to Boston?"

"You know me. I'm always in search of a good party." He chuckled, including them both in his glance. "Seems I can't turn around without hearing word of another one of your tea parties or ship-burning parties. Why, even yesterday some of your neighbors in Rhode Island threw a party at their fort. How could I stay away?"

Everyone laughed.

"I was quite eager," he added, "to ride up from Philadelphia with Ben. We arrived in Cambridge last eve. I might have gotten here sooner but for that party the British are holding at the Neck. People are lined up for miles just to attend that one."

An even louder round of laughter followed.

"You're what we've been missing around here," Dan admitted, shaking his head with a smile. "We've had nothing but gloom and doom for quite some time."

Morgan grinned. "I daresay, speaking of doom, I couldn't help but notice the redcoats have quite an impressive display of cannon lined up at the Neck, pointed right at folks coming into Boston. Not very friendly, to say the least."

"That's just what me and some of the boys was talkin' about the other day," Mr. Simms piped in. "When Morgan asked me for directions, I was happy to come along and show him us townsfolk ain't paying them Crown puppets much mind."

The other man, who had moved out of the way during Morgan and Susannah's greeting, stepped nearer, his curiosity quite obvious. "I'd like to hear more about what happened at that fort you mentioned. The one in Rhode Island."

"Mr. Swan just arrived from the New Hampshire Grants," Dan explained, and Morgan nodded politely in greeting. "But I'm just as interested. What have my neighbors done this time?"

Morgan felt the attentiveness of the whole group, but he centered his attention on Dan. He couldn't help but note that despite the disreputable interior of this infamous structure, the chap appeared relatively clean and in remarkably good spirits. "It seems they prefer to choose which way their cannons are pointing, so they actually ousted the British from the fort."

Dan's mouth gaped, and Susannah's shock was mirrored on the others' faces as well—all except Mr. Swan's. A man, Morgan decided, with the proper spirit.

"How did you hear this?" Dan asked.

Morgan shrugged. "A friend of Ben's in Pawtucket related it. According to him, the locals there have no intention of putting up with a harbor blockade similar to the one imposed on Boston."

A snort erupted from Mr. Simms. "Mighty big talk from folks who don't have four thousand troops in their streets nor a harbor full of warships staring down their throats."

"Well," Susannah said, her tone indicating her displeasure over the menacing nature of the conversation, "we're so pleased you've come, Morgan. I do hope you weren't inconvenienced awfully by the guards at the Neck."

He tossed his head in triumph and patted the pocket of his chestnut wool frock coat. "Far be it from them to harass someone bearing a letter of introduction to an extremely loyal member of the Clarke family."

No one spoke for a few seconds.

"The Clarkes." Elder Simms eyed him with suspicion. "You referrin' to that bunch of Tory merchants who thought they were gonna get rich off India tea?"

Morgan stretched his neck to make sure no one was lurking beyond the door to the cell block, then he grinned. "The very same, my good man. In fact, the thought came to me that it might be rather entertaining and *enlightening* to wangle an invitation to stay with them through the round of holiday parties. Quite enlightening, indeed."

"You could do that?" Simms asked, fingering his beard in thought. "Stay right there with them in their home?"

He nodded. "My father and the Clarkes are old friends. They've a lot in common, actually. Both greedy merchants, both so loyal to the Crown they might easily have been born at the royal palace—"

"Morgan!" Susannah cut in. "One shouldn't speak so disrespectfully of one's father."

"But, dear Susannah," he returned, winking at Simms, "would you have me bear false witness?"

Dan scratched his head. "If I didn't know better, I'd think we were all back in Princeton at the Lyons' Den, in the midst of one of our famous theological discussions."

"You were with Dan at the Presbyterian college?" Mr. Simms asked.

Morgan nodded and smiled warmly at Susannah. "We had some wonderful times there, did we not?"

A slight rosy flush colored her cheeks. "Yes. And it's ever so good to have you here."

"Perhaps the two of you," Simms said, looking from Morgan to Susannah, "shouldn't be seen together for a while."

The suggestion caught Morgan off guard.

Mr. Simms held up a hand to forestall any protests. "Might be the Committee of Safety here in Boston would appreciate Thomas's services, spying for them. I'd be glad to arrange a discreet meeting. And with that in mind, I don't have to tell you it would be best he not be seen visiting known patriots like yourselves."

"The Committee of Safety," Morgan echoed. "Who are they?"

"The patriot leaders of Boston," Dan explained. "But what you two are talking about could get you hanged."

"With this honest face?" Morgan shot back with his most earnest expression. Then he laughed.

11

Abigail blinked hard, trying to chase away the spots from her eyes as she put a few more stitches in Cassandra's new pink dress. Sewing in secret by candlelight after everyone else had gone to bed was beginning to take its toll. Was this God's judgment on her for keeping her newly purchased yard goods hidden from Ma and Bertha? Just thinking about how gladly she'd received the news of her grandaunt's failing health made Abby's cheeks burn with shame. But it had afforded her the chance she so desperately needed to go into Millers Falls on her own.

Wes, bless his heart, had managed to make sufficient inquiries to find out that Ben had been sent to Philadelphia. He was alive. And if by some miracle Ben really did find a way for them to marry, she intended to be ready.

With a sigh, she set her sewing aside and rose to stretch her aching back—one more indication of the Lord's displeasure, she was sure, for desiring Ben so deeply that nothing else seemed to matter. She had even begun to contemplate the unthinkable, running away with him, which Wes would be more than glad to help her do. But in her heart she knew that was not an option.

Winter's chill was already upon the land, and the unceasing draft that had begun to seep around the window frame and along the bare floor would continue until winter's end. Crossing to the window, Abby drew her woolen shawl tighter over her flannel night shift. She curled her toes inside the knitted house slippers and pushed aside the plain muslin curtains.

Gnarled, leafless trees shone stark in the silvery blue glow of the moonlight. They looked cold, she thought—cold and lonely. Achingly lonely.

The scene before her blurred behind a veil of tears, and Abby's throat closed. She had never known such loneliness in her life—not when her mother died of fever, not when her father's rifle exploded in his face, not even when Ray drowned last year. Perhaps above all else she should feel guilty for that, at least.

Her thoughts drifted to last Sunday's sermon in the Millers Falls church. The minister had preached from the Old Testament, out of one of the only two books, he told the congregation, that the Lord had seen fit to name after a woman. The preacher spoke of the young woman Ruth, who cared so much for her mother-in-law that she gave up any chance of remarrying just to accompany the old woman back to her homeland. It was hard to believe that a whole book in the Bible had been written about not forsaking a mother-in-law for a husband.

Was almighty God so unfeeling that he intended Ruth's story to be an example for other widows to follow? Abby tossed off that dire thought almost at once. After all, the preacher might have said those things simply to pacify Ma. She was a stubborn woman when it came to getting her way. Abby wished she could read so she could get out the family Bible and discover that whole story for herself.

A sudden gust of wind rattled the shutters, sending its icy breath over Abby's slight frame. She rubbed the gooseflesh from her upper arms. Winter wasn't the only thing that got bitter, she realized, for in her heart she could feel what the preacher called a "root of bitterness" beginning to take hold. She must not let herself think uncharitable thoughts about people who cared about her and the children. After all, Pastor Davidson was a kind, godly man. Surely he wouldn't do or say something dishonorable.

Abby took a deep breath and tried to calm herself. Perhaps some warm milk and an oatmeal cookie might quiet her wild thoughts. She glanced lovingly at her two children slumbering peacefully beneath the blankets and left the room.

Halfway down the stairs she noticed a lamp still burning in the hallway below. Someone else was up. Instinctively, Abby turned and started tiptoeing back to her room, then caught herself. Everyone here, after all, was her family. Taking a breath for courage, she continued on, padding along the cold floor of the hall in her knitted slippers.

"I can't understand you, Ma," came Bertha's voice from the kitchen. "I thought you'd be plumb pleased to get rid of that worthless Abigail."

Abby froze in place.

"And what's so all-fired important about losin' one puny grandson?" she went on. "Why, shucks, me and Wes will give ya a whole passel of boys. Big strong ones. People like us, we can't have nothin' but good healthy young'uns. Who needs a runt like that skinny little Corbin anyways?"

Her words cut Abigail to the quick. She clenched her teeth and began inching back toward the stairs.

"You always was jealous of your brother." Ma's voice was harsh. "If it was up to you, we'd forget Raymond ever lived. Well, I ain't about to forget my flesh and blood, nor his neither. Corbin stays right here."

Ma's statement extinguished the last flicker of Abigail's hope. Her whole future passed before her eyes . . . bleak and empty.

"I had every reason in the world to be jealous of Ray," Bertha scoffed. "I knowed he was your favorite. Didn't matter that I worked circles around him scything grain, picking apples, tending the stock—while he was out roaming the countryside, sniffin' around. Pshaw! How else would he have come across that little piece of dandelion fluff he married! It was a good ten miles through the woods to that rundown farm she come from."

"It weren't like that a'tall, me favoring one kid over the

other," Ma returned. "Till you have sons of your own, ya can't understand a mama's feelings. Besides, there's more to it than that."

"Like what?"

"Never you mind. There just is. Now quit that sassing and run up to bed before that husband of yours comes charging down here after ya, shaking the rafters and like to wake the dead."

A kitchen chair screeched back, jolting Abby. She whirled and sprinted up the stairs to her room, where she closed the door and leaned back against it to catch her breath. She heard Bertha's slow, heavy footfalls, followed by Ma's, as the women went to their bedchambers.

Abby remained where she was until her breathing returned to normal. But one painful thought would not settle down in her mind as her gaze came to rest on her sleeping little ones. Not only did Ma and Bertha not care a whit about her, but neither one had mentioned Cassandra either. Ray's family had never made much of a pretense of doing anything but tolerating Abigail's presence in this house since the day he wed her. But they had no reason to look down on Cassie, who was dear and sweet and just as precious as Corbin.

Her gaze drifted to her son's tiny form, and an even darker reality dawned on her. If she were to leave Corbin behind, she and Cassie would more than likely be free to leave whenever they chose. They could go with Ben, far away from this hateful place.

The wrenching thought made Abigail shudder, and she breathed deeply to recover her control. Cassie's pink dress lay on the bedside table where she'd left it—more than proof that Ben was coming back to get her. Maybe he hadn't sent word, but he wouldn't have paid out all that money for new clothes unless he was coming.

But to leave Corbin? Never to see him or hold him again? No. She could never do that. Never.

Drawn to the window once more, Abby fingered the curtain and stared into the night sky. "Oh, Father in heaven, they say you are a loving God. If that is true, why must I stay where I am hated, when such a glorious chance to leave this place lies within my very grasp? It was different for your servant, Ruth. Her mother-in-law, Naomi, cared about her and her well–being. It was Naomi who offered Ruth her freedom. . . ."

Yes, Abby's mind allowed. *Naomi may very well have cared for Ruth. But what if there had been a son to consider? Would she have been so generous then?*

❧ ❧

A fresh layer of December snow blanketed the contours of the Preston farm and crunched under Rebel's hooves in the thin afternoon sunlight. The Committee of Safety had needed Ben to take broadsides to New York regarding the various standoffs between the colonists and the troops. Thanks to those orders, Ben was getting back to western Massachusetts much later than originally planned, especially considering he had intended to strengthen his suit with Abigail.

His pulse began to race with anticipation and worry. There hadn't been an opportunity to obtain any actual legal advice regarding Abigail's position, but he had made sure the banns had been posted. Now all that remained was, as Morgan phrased it, "sweet-talking the old battle-ax" into letting Abby celebrate Christmas in Rhode Island. Once he and Abigail were there, they could wed. Then Ben would become the legal guardian of both Abigail and her children. That much he knew.

For the first time in his life, Ben regretted the strong moral conscience passed down to him by his parents. He could just imagine the tall tale Morgan Thomas might spin—one that would make Ma Preston believe he'd take up residence on her place and become her willing slave until his dying day. Ben knew his own efforts would never measure up to some-thing Morgan might concoct, but hopefully he had rehearsed his little speech sufficiently on the ride here.

Reaching the hitching post at the edge of the yard, Ben gathered his courage and swung down from the saddle. "For

Abby," he murmured. Then he strode up the shoveled pathway to Ma Bear's den and rapped at the door.

He heard at once the familiar clomping of Bertha's feet. The door opened. "Ma!" she hollered over her shoulder at the sight of Ben. "That postrider fella's come again." She turned back to him and raised her chin. "I suppose you're wanting in."

With a polite nod, he stepped past her, aware that he was not nearly so welcome today as on previous occasions. He stood stiffly just inside until she waved him into the parlor.

As Wesley lumbered up from the couch, rubbing sleep from his heavy-lidded eyes, Ben became aware of the unnatural quiet in the normally chaotic home. "I came to call on Abigail," he finally said.

"Hmph." Bertha grimaced. "I'll go hunt her and Ma up." With a last scathing look at Ben, she marched off.

"Have a seat, Haynes," Wes said, reaching to shake hands. "I 'spect you're here to have another run at Bertie's ma. Tough old bird, she is." As if suddenly realizing what he had just said, the lout sneaked to the doorway and peered into the hall, then retreated to his former spot.

In spite of his nervousness, Ben smiled. It hadn't taken Ma Preston long to make sure the pecking order was firmly established here.

"Anything new happened lately?" Wesley asked. "Down to the coast, I mean."

"Yes, as a matter of fact." Ben became aware of footsteps on the second floor above and wondered if they were Abby's. The thought filled him with hope—and dread. "You probably know about the daily brawls in Boston these days, name-calling and the like. Redcoats even threw stones at John Hancock's house and broke his windows. But the broadsides I'm carrying today concern actions General Gage took yesterday."

"What'd he do?" Wes asked, fully alert.

"He confiscated the supply of extra powder and bullets the Massachusetts militia were storing on Castle Island. When they went to move it to a new location, they were informed it was no longer their property."

Wesley's face took on an astounded look.

"I'll admit it wasn't too bright to expect the enemy to safeguard our gunpowder," Ben admitted defensively, "but it had been there since long before the British took over the city."

"And Castle Island along with it."

"Right. And now the island is the main headquarters of the British high command."

Wesley leaned forward, his big freckled hands clamped on his knees. "Ya know, I don't think folks really believed we'd end up going to war with them lobsterbacks. At least not till lately. But now that Parliament gave everything west of our mountains to them Frenchies up in Canada, word up and down the Connecticut River has it that settlers out there are fightin' mad. If the English think they can send reinforcements down here from Quebec, they're in for a big surprise, I can tell ya that."

"They won't be sneaking down Lake Champlain either," Ben said with a grin. "The Green Mountain Boys have sworn—"

Footsteps descending the stairs brought Ben to his feet. He moved to the doorway, where he could see Ma and Bertha coming. Abigail was following behind them, her face as colorless as the faded work dress she wore. Ben noted Ma's granite expression—and Abby's desperate one. He didn't want to do this, but he had no other choice. He had to do it Morgan's way and hope for the best.

"Good day, Ma," he began, manufacturing a look he hoped would appear most sincere.

She flicked him a glance but walked right on by and plopped herself into the rocker. Bertha took up residence on the couch beside her husband, and Abby perched stiffly on the opposite end of it.

Undaunted, Ben smiled at the old woman. "You know, Ma, I don't blame you one bit for being upset with me. I want you to know that. After I left last time, I started seeing things through your eyes, and I understood why you were so upset."

Ma frowned and looked fully at him, her surprise not entirely masked by her austere countenance. "Well, now, I'm right glad to hear that." She relaxed a little and gestured to a nearby chair.

Bertha gawked at him, and Abigail looked totally confused.

Ben wished he could take Abby's hand and squeeze it to reassure her, but the seat Ma had indicated was off by itself. He took a deep breath, then sat down as bidden. "Yes," he went on, directing his attention toward the lady of the house. "My own mother, in fact, would feel exactly the same as you."

"Is that right?" she asked, wariness narrowing her eyes in the shadow of her mobcap.

Tell the old bat you'll live there forever, Morgan's voice urged in his mind. But Ben couldn't even choke the words out. He inhaled to fortify himself. "The only problem is, I still have a commitment to the Committee of Correspondence, and my duties won't be fulfilled until Parliament takes action on the Colonies' latest stand. And that, of course, may not be for another two or three months. I figure that should give you time to get used to the idea of Abigail and me, right?" He forced a smile. "After all, Ma, I like you a lot, and I've been thinking very seriously about your offer of maybe staying on here."

"Well, pshaw," she said, her gravelly voice cracking. "I like you, too, boy. Always did, right from the first." She nodded to Abigail. "Take your young man's coat, then get him something warm to drink."

Abigail rose slowly without even the hint of a smile.

Ben felt like a traitor. He had told her he would be taking her with him when he returned. "No need, really," he blurted. "I can't stay. Duty calls, you know—but maybe Abby could see me out to my horse?" He looked hopefully at Ma.

"Why, sure," the old woman beamed. "Can't do no harm. Run along, girl."

Waiting for Abigail to precede him, Ben turned back at the

door. *Please don't let the old gal see through my next words,* he found himself praying. Then he gave an offhanded gesture. "Oh, I almost forgot. My own ma has ordered me home for Christmas—a lot of my family members are coming this year, for the first time in ages. When I told her about Abby, she said I was to bring her along. She sort of wants to—" he cringed inwardly at his own lie—"look her over, you know?"

Abigail gasped in wide-eyed shock. Ma laughed under her breath.

Ben chuckled with nonchalance while his elbow administered a discreet jab in Abby's ribs. "Oh, don't let her get to you, sweetheart. I'm sure that once she gets to know you, she'll look beyond your shy ways. And the fact that you've had two children should prove you aren't all that frail."

Hating himself completely now, Ben glanced back at Ma. "When I come back through here in a few days, my sister and her husband will be with me. They'll make very proper chaperons, I assure you. Abigail's reputation would not be compromised whatsoever on this trip. I want you to know that right off."

Ma Preston exchanged a sly smile with Bertha, then nodded her head slowly before meeting Ben's gaze. "So your ma wants a good look at the girl, does she? Well, that don't surprise me a'tall. I think she should do just that. It's a right fine idea. A right fine idea, indeed."

"Splendid. I hoped you'd be agreeable to it, Ma. I do thank you for your kind hospitality and generosity. Good day."

With the most charming and unassuming smile he could work up, Ben snatched a cloak from the hall tree and put it around Abigail's shoulders. She was rooted in place, so he had to pull her forcefully out the door before she had time to balk. And before Ma had time to change her mind. Most important, he had a lot of apologizing to do right now.

Outside, Abigail walked woodenly beside him only because he kept a tight hold on her hand. Her eyes were downcast, but Ben could see the teardrops that had fallen on her cloak.

His heart constricted as he pulled Abby into his arms and

rocked her gently. "I hope you can forgive me for all that idiotic balderdash I mouthed to Ma. I was desperate to wangle permission to get you out of here."

She sniffed. "Y-you didn't mean it?"

"Not a word. I promise. How could I?"

"It was all lies?" she asked, tipping her head to look up at him through pain-filled eyes.

He kissed each one. "My friend told me to tell Ma what she wanted to hear, so that's what I did. I trusted that you'd understand when I had a chance to explain. But . . . do you?"

Ben felt as if her intense gaze could see into his very soul. He had hurt her terribly. Morgan's way may have been the easiest for him, but it certainly wasn't for Abby.

When he saw her expression soften to its usual warmth, he reluctantly stepped back and mounted his horse. "I love you, Abigail. I'll be back in a week, then I'll spend the rest of my life making you believe that."

12

Six inches of new-fallen snow lay over the New Hampshire Grants around Bennington. Gusts of wind buffeted the leafless trees on the north rim of the valley and then dipped into the clear expanse of gently rolling land. The sun brought out the full glory of the Green Mountains and the Walloomac River.

As Ben rode toward the village sprawled on a rise along the river flats, he urged his mount into a canter. He was nearing the Catamount Tavern, headquarters of the Green Mountain Boys. He could already smell the wood smoke from the establishment's great chimneys, and no one could miss its famous trademark atop a twenty-five-foot pole. There, symbolizing the fierce defiance of the settlers to keep their lands, perched a stuffed cat-a-mountain with its snarl aimed at New York.

In winter's lush stillness, it was hard to believe there was such unrest in the Colonies. But Ben had to face the reality that the present strife was due to last for some time. Even now, from the grounds around the building, he could hear his brother-in-law's voice, carried on the misty air. Ted was shouting out the steps for the precision loading of muskets to a gathering of the Vermont militia, as they now liked to be called.

Ben halted for several moments and watched the men raise their weapons and take aim, but the insignificant sound of the volley they fired indicated the spare use of the Colonies' short supply of powder.

Off to one side and standing in the bed of a wagon, Colonel Ethan Allen towered above the others, one hand wrapped casually around the long barrel of a flintlock. A strikingly powerful man in fringed garb, the leader of the Green Mountain Boys bellowed at the various groups that were practicing marching in unison. "Let's put some knee into it. Look sharp! Want to be outshone by the militia from New York?"

Ben would have chuckled at the colonel's sarcasm had not the cadence and uniformity of the men's movements instantly improved. He clucked his tongue, and Rebel started up again.

Colonel Allen swung his head, catching sight of Ben. "Ho! Ted!" he called out as he hopped out of the wagon. Ted waved back and quickly joined Allen as Ben rode in. "What news have you brought us this time, lad?" the colonel asked, never one to beat around the bush. His massive hand swallowed Ben's in a hearty handshake.

"Something not so encouraging, actually." Ben withdrew some broadsides from his inside coat pocket and handed them to Allen. "Seems the redcoats have confiscated the Boston militia's supply of gunpowder that was in storage on Castle Island."

"The militia was still keeping their ammunition at *British* headquarters?" Ted asked incredulously.

Ben gave him a sheepish nod.

"Surely no one expected General Gage would release it to them!"

"No," Ben admitted. "But it's further proof of the stranglehold Britain has planned for us. We're now storing our arms and powder in secret and out-of-the-way places. We have stockpiles in Salem and Concord . . . what little we've got."

Ted released a whoosh of air. "I take it Yancy has not yet returned with the shipment."

Ben shook his head. "So if you boys are gonna do any more loading drills, you'd better just go through the motions and do it without powder. From the talk that's circulating, war could break out *before* the British decide on the Colonies' next punishment." He allowed a moment for the statement to sink in.

"What say we go inside out of this cold for a while?" Allen suggested. "I've got some news especially for you, Ben." The three of them headed for the warmth of the tavern.

Jane, seated with some other women in a sewing circle across the common room, let out a gasp when she saw Ben enter. She dropped her quilt block and rushed into his open arms. "Ben! When did you get here?"

"Just arrived, Sis. How've you been?"

Her brown eyes sparkled, adding to a curious glow she seemed to emit. "Fine. Perfectly wonderful, in fact!"

"Second honeymoon?" he asked teasingly.

"*Eternal* honeymoon," she returned just as quickly.

He had to admit, marriage seemed to agree with his spirited older sister. Though she retained a good portion of spunk, she appeared to be making an effort to socialize with the other wives of the area—and even blend in. Her normally lush curls were now tamed into a demure chignon.

"Care to join us for some hot cider? Er, you two don't mind, I assume," Ben added quickly, checking with Ted and Ethan Allen. He knew Jane wasn't very fond of Colonel Allen.

"Not at all," the colonel said. "We'd be delighted for the young lady's company."

"Why, how very gallant of you," she returned, a touch of insincerity in her cool smile.

"I'll get the drinks," Ted offered. He detoured to the bar, where the landlord's wife was already filling mugs with the steaming liquid. After taking the remaining seat at the table, he raised his mug aloft with a tender smile. "To my beloved wife . . . the mother of my firstborn."

Jane went crimson.

"Well, congratulations!" Ethan Allen roared, delivering a stout clap to Ted's back.

Caught off guard, Ben just stared at Jane for several seconds before remembering to lift his drink in a toast. "Congratulations, brat. Oh, and you, too, Ted. May she be a more docile mother than she's been a sister."

Administering a swift punch to his arm, Jane changed the subject. "I received a letter from Mother in the post the other day," she began cheerily. "Even though Dan isn't expected to go to trial until February or even later, she absolutely insists that he, Susannah, and as many of the rest of us as possible come home for Christmas. And, of course, she hopes you'll bring your young lady along so the family can meet her, too."

Ben brightened a little. "Yes. Well, that's why I'm here. I need you and Ted to accompany me to Millers Falls and act as chaperons for us."

"Why, of course," Ted said. "We're going that direction anyway."

"But—" Ben turned to his copper-haired sister—"with you in the family way and all, are you sure such a trip wouldn't be too dangerous?"

She giggled. "I told you, I feel wonderful. Being with child does not turn one into an invalid, little brother. I'm perfectly healthy. As long as we travel at a leisurely pace, I'm sure I'll be fine."

He relaxed, and a wave of relief washed over him. "Speaking of Abigail . . . Colonel Allen?" Ben regarded the man earnestly. "Didn't I hear that you've studied the law some?"

"Had to, boy, to keep ahead of those land-grabbing Yorkers who were trying to claim our New Hampshire Grants . . . our Vermont," he corrected with flair. He then eased back against the chair and unfolded his long legs.

"Well, maybe you wouldn't mind if I asked you a question. I ran into someone the other day who needs to find out a few particulars."

"And?" Allen prompted.

Ben glanced furtively at Jane and Ted. "It's, er, a question regarding guardianship. For instance, when a young wife's husband dies, does she become the legal ward of her mother-in-law? Bound to obey her wishes?"

"Why the mother-in-law?" the colonel asked with a puzzled frown. "Isn't there a father-in-law to consider?"

"No. He died several years ago."

"What business was the husband in?"

"Farming. The widow lives on the family farm with her mother-in-law."

"Did the husband have brothers?"

"No. None."

"Really? Does your young widow have children? Sons, in particular?"

"One, sir. A small boy."

A smile began to spread across Allen's face. "How old?"

"Two."

The smile broadened. "And you say both her husband and her husband's father have passed on."

"Yes."

"And she has no idea the farm belongs to her?"

Ben sat taller in his chair. "To whom?"

"The widow, of course. That is, until her son turns ten years of age . . . at which time he then becomes the legal owner."

The unexpected announcement stunned Ben. He, too, broke into a grin. "Are you telling me Abigail could throw her mother-in-law off the land if she wanted to?"

"Well, yes," Colonel Allen answered. "She could indeed—not that I myself would consider such action a very Christian thing to do to some frail old widow woman."

"Frail!" Ben whacked his knee. "That old battle-ax could wipe out an entire company with one swing of her arm!"

"Hmm." Allen gave him a half smile. "Think we can get her to sign up for the militia?"

13

Morgan left his upstairs guest chamber and strode out into the candlelit hall, where the spicy scent of evergreen mingled with tantalizing aromas from the kitchen. Quite a ploy, he assured himself, managing to acquire such sumptuous and comfortable accommodations in Boston for his spying. Adjusting the lacy cuffs of the silk shirt he wore beneath his violet-brocade frock coat, he strode toward the stairs. He reached the top landing a few seconds before his host, who approached from the opposite end of the hallway. "Sir," Morgan said with a polite nod.

Richard Clarke, a pompous-looking man of medium build with a prominent nose and thick dark brows, inclined his head. "Ah, Morgan, my good lad. An opportune time for us to join the party, don't you agree?"

Morgan grinned and fell into step with the man as they started down the curved staircase.

"I say, are you quite certain you wish to make your friends privy to our little scheme?" Morgan asked, taking care to add to his words the measure of proper British inflection used by so many of his parents' influential friends.

"Indeed." Clarke flashed a conspiratorial smile. "But only a few—whom you'll allow me to select, of course." He brushed imaginary lint off his immaculate embroidered silk sleeve.

The very thought that Clarke had fallen for his fable—that his father had purchased a number of warehouses in Bermuda, where shipments from faraway England could be stored at a more accessible five-hundred-mile distance until the end of the boycott—almost had Morgan laughing aloud. But he met the man's gaze evenly. "By all means. I shall trust you implicitly. I'm sure there will be adequate room for at least three or four of your friends' cargoes—and perhaps an extra measure of profit for the two of us, as well."

Just listening to his tale, Morgan became acutely aware of the real potential of diverting goods. "You know, sir," he began, "we might give some thought to adding a bit of New England ingenuity to our plan."

A curious light gleamed in Mr. Clarke's eye as he paused on the steps. "What do you mean?"

Morgan stopped also. "Perhaps while our British goods are languishing in the Bermuda sun, they could conceivably find their way into a few Dutch and French crates and be sent on to colonial ports, don't you think? I'm sure any necessary changes in shipping manifests could be made without too much effort."

The older man's generous mouth spread into a slow smile. "Why, even the British could not fault such a plan—privately, of course—since our trade with them could then resume, at least to a small degree. Yes. Your scheme has merit, my boy." He draped an arm around Morgan's shoulder, and they continued their descent. "I must endeavor to write your father at once and thank him for sending us such an enterprising young man."

"Splendid," he replied automatically as he searched for a solution. Clarke saying too much to Morgan's father would simply not do. "However, I trust you will keep the exact details of our arrangement just between the two of us." At the older gent's puzzled frown, he rushed on. "It's a bit of a surprise for my father, you see. A bigger return on his investment than he expected."

Clarke smiled knowingly. "Your father will be very proud, my boy. Very proud indeed."

They stepped onto the polished hardwood floor of the foyer, where the butler was admitting guests, adding to the number already milling about. "In the meantime," Morgan said, "I should not mind in the least if you would introduce me to a few of your lovely Boston belles."

"Aha! I'll see that you make their acquaintance, but I wouldn't count on having their undivided attention. The town is fairly bursting with army and naval officers. You'll easily find half a dozen bachelors for every available female at these gatherings." Then, nodding to some arriving guests making their way toward the grand ballroom, Clarke grinned suddenly and took several strides forward. "Andrew," he said, clasping a young man's outstretched hand and drawing him in Morgan's direction, "I'd like you to meet someone. This is Morgan Thomas, from Philadelphia. Morgan, this is Andrew Sewell, son of a close friend. Do be a good lad, Andy, and introduce my young guest around, would you?" With a nod he hurried toward some other arrivals.

"Philadelphia, eh?" Andrew Sewell said, shaking Morgan's hand. A jovial smirk crinkled the youthful features beneath his rusty hair. "Good to meet you anyway."

"Ah yes. We make it a point to trek to various backwoods towns now and then," Morgan shot back. "I'm rather enjoying my stay here in your fair city."

Andy grinned. "You'll enjoy it even more when you've seen the fairest aspects of it. They await us even now in the ballroom. Shall we?"

"After you, my good man." Morgan swept a hand graciously in indication for the young fellow to precede him down the hall. He couldn't help but notice the speculative glances from several merchants he had already met. Aware that the poor chaps were in rather desperate straits because of the harbor closure, Morgan knew they were easy pickings . . . for later. He voiced his next thought. "Young ladies are my first order of business."

"My sentiments exactly," Andy said with a grin. They entered the open double doors of the grand room, where strains of soft music blended in with the light laughter and conversation.

Morgan glanced around at the festive setting, taking in the dark wainscoting and the velvet-flocked wallpaper, accented by huge evergreen wreaths with bows of gold satin. The flickering glow of a thousand candles in the ornate chandeliers sparkled back from the women's sequined gowns and jewels.

Andrew turned with a grimace and motioned toward the wall lined with sideboards bearing an immense array of mouthwatering holiday delicacies. "I'm afraid the more delectable creatures have yet to arrive. What say we sample some of the bounty on the tables? Afterward we can take up a post just inside the doors and pick the best peaches before they fall into the hands of the military."

With a nod of agreement, Morgan accompanied him, and they wasted no time helping themselves to the tasty fare. Morgan had already noticed that most of the young women present were rather plain and attired in far less lavish party frocks than might have graced Philadelphia belles—perhaps due to their Puritan heritage.

A serving girl came their way, and Morgan took two drinks from her tray. Then the girl raised her head, and a pair of wide silver eyes lit up her heart-shaped face and locked gazes with him.

Easily the most fetching one present, Morgan decided. He watched as she moved on, assessing her crisp gray dress and white mobcap and the long shining black hair beneath it. If she were an example of Boston womanhood, prospects were looking much better.

He handed one of the drinks to Andy. "I say, old chap. Perhaps we shouldn't dawdle. Let's select those advantageous positions near the door." But even as they did so, Morgan found himself searching out the tray-bearing lass who moved among the guests.

"Now, here comes a tantalizing damsel at last," Andy said with a nudge toward the foyer.

Turning, Morgan found his view interrupted by a middle-aged man entering the room. "I don't care in the least," the older gentleman was saying to his wife. "In fact, I hope they do. It's appalling that any officer would show his face here this eve. They should be out doing what they've been paid to do. If Gage continues to dillydally after this, mark my words, every Loyalist in Boston will eventually be sacked, too."

Morgan smothered a chuckle as a British officer directly behind the couple turned red in the face and glared at another officer by his side. But amazingly, the second one tapped the woman's shoulder. "Your husband, my lady, is quite right."

She and her husband stopped and turned, and the redcoat continued, "We soldiers would appreciate whatever influence the local citizens might have over our commander. We are all imminently aware that he needs to act. Now."

The red-faced one gave a nod of agreement. "How many more insults must we be forced to endure? As if seizing Newport's battery wasn't sufficient, the traitors have gone even further and taken the one guarding Portsmouth harbor as well."

Morgan grinned, then caught himself and pretended to wave to someone across the room.

"I say," one of the king's men said, eyeing him with suspicion. "Let us discuss more pleasant topics elsewhere, shall we?"

Disappointed at missing further details as the group moved out of earshot, Morgan realized he had tightened his lips. Deliberately he relaxed his expression and turned back to Andrew Sewell.

Andy was bowing to a young woman in sage green taffeta coming toward the ballroom. "I've never seen you look lovelier," he gushed, then glanced sheepishly at Morgan. "I'd like to introduce my new friend, Morgan Thomas, from Philadelphia."

Still straining to catch a phrase or two from the redcoats, Morgan didn't even hear the lass's name. Still, he flashed his most charming smile and bowed over her hand. "Please allow me to fetch you both some punch. I shan't be but a moment."

Extracting himself from the twosome, he hastened to the refreshment table—and the cluster of soldiers standing there. Surely one of them might let a word slip regarding this latest attack by the patriots.

Approaching them, he saw the dark-haired servant girl nearby. He made his way over to her and put his and Andy's empty goblets on her tray, giving his gaze free rein as he took two fresh drinks. Her full lips had an enchanting upward curve at the corners, even though she was not smiling. But she seemed somewhat distracted—almost, he thought, as though she were hesitant to move on to other guests. Too soon, she did.

Reluctant to depart, since he could easily hear the redcoats chatting, Morgan paused and took a sip from one of the drinks.

"There was not the least subterfuge," one of the men snorted. "The culprits had the audacity to march right through town in broad daylight—drummer boy and all—calling the Portsmouth citizens to take the fort."

"That's out-and-out treason!" another snapped. "Where were the authorities, I ask?"

"Quite right. They should have been shot. Traitors, every last one."

The opening notes of a minuet drifted from the string quartet at the far end of the ballroom. Morgan feigned an intent interest in observing the dancers take their positions in the middle of the floor as the conversation continued.

"From what I understand," came the first voice again, "Captain Cochran did just that."

"I've heard nothing regarding a battle."

"The poor bloke tried, but he managed only to get off one cannonball before he and his five men were overrun. Four or five hundred scoundrels swarmed over the walls, took the powder, and dismantled the cannons."

"What? Is there no law left outside Boston?"

"New Hampshire's Governor Wentworth sent his chief justice out to try to reason with the rabble, but to no avail."

"I daresay," a voice scoffed, "most likely the man was afraid to go himself."

"Quite right. General Gage is furious, to say the least. He—"

A crash of glass a few feet away interrupted the account. Morgan swung toward the sound.

A lock of long black hair fell forward over one shoulder of the slender maid, who knelt gathering the broken shards and placing them on her tray.

The sight of her so nearby surprised Morgan. He could have sworn she had gone off toward the opposite end of the room.

After an awkward pause, the soldiers resumed talking, but at a somewhat lower volume.

"General Gage called in his second-in-command—"

Morgan's glance fell upon the ebony-haired lass, who had all but stopped retrieving fragments of glass while the officer spoke.

"And from what his adjutant claimed . . ." The lobsterback halted his story again.

The girl flushed and quickly returned to her chore.

Her barely disguised interest in the soldiers' conversation irked Morgan. Because of her clumsy eavesdropping, he, too, might be noticed. He forced himself to head back to Andy and his belle before the most important part was related— what General Gage intended to do.

Nearing the pair, Morgan saw two additional scarlet-clad officers entering. Red, by far, was becoming the dominant color in the ballroom, he groused inwardly. Then he noticed that one of the newcomers was staring at him with a confused expression. Recognizing the officer who had been on duty when he had visited Dan at the South Battery, Morgan raised the drinks in his hands high to shield his face until he had passed them. Then after excusing himself from Andy, he did his best to blend in with a group of stodgy old merchants chatting in the opposite corner of the room. Better to remain out of sight with them for a while—even if that did entail enduring some dull shipping talk.

For the greater portion of the next hour, Morgan contented himself with tuning out the drone of the men and their business dealings and observing how the British redcoats monopolized every available female at the gathering. Now and again he would catch sight of the fetching maid gracefully weaving around the various clusters of guests, her tray filled alternately with drinks or hors d'oeuvres. But most unsettling was the fact that he saw her lingering far too often in very advantageous listening spots.

The little vixen must actually fancy herself a spy! Morgan rubbed his temples. Surely if her actions were so obvious to him, it would be only a matter of time before others would discover them also.

"Excuse me," he said to the group of men when he saw her begin working toward the kitchen. He would go there and wait to have a private word with her.

He had gone not two yards when he spied the battery officer. Ducking quickly, Morgan skirted him and took a roundabout route.

Some of the regular household servants looked up and exchanged furtive glances when Morgan entered the room, then continued working as if the sight of a guest in their bustling domain was commonplace. He approached one of them. "I beg your pardon. I'm curious to know the name of a black-haired serving girl who's been carrying drinks to the guests this eve. Rather comely. About so tall . . ." He gestured with a hand and a devilish lifting of a brow.

"Oh, aye," the heavyset cook said with a knowing smile. "That'd be Prudence Endecott. She and some of the others were just hired for the night."

If she lasts that long without being discovered, Morgan almost blurted. As it was, the lass should have made it back here by now. He'd better go and find—

The door swung open, and Prudence Endecott came in carrying empty goblets. Her lips parted as she caught sight of Morgan, but she quickly composed her expression and continued to the sideboard, where she began emptying her tray.

Morgan crossed the room in three strides. "I must speak with you."

Prudence did not hide her disapproval as she looked askance at him.

"It's about your spying."

She stopped midmotion.

"Giggle as if I'm flirting with you," Morgan went on, "then come with me to the pantry."

To his surprise, she cast a glance toward the others, then tittered coyly, picked up an oil lamp, and went along with him.

He closed the door behind them. But instead of going into the discourse he'd planned on the finer points of spying, uncontrollable anger surfaced instead. "Do you have the slightest idea what you're doing?"

Charcoal flecks in her light gray eyes glinted as she hiked her chin. "I don't know what you're talking about."

"Oh yes, you do." Morgan shook his head. "Do you think no one but me has observed your rather clumsy attempts at gathering information? I can't believe you would put yourself in such danger. If you've even a fraction of sanity, I suggest you plead illness and leave the party at once—before you endanger those of us who are far more polished in the art."

Prudence's mouth gaped in shock. "Is that right?" she huffed. "As a matter of fact, I *do* believe you were the only one observing my every step this eve—and for reasons most *unprofessional*, to say the least!"

The lass was not far off the mark, but Morgan was not about to admit it. "Think what you will, *on your way home*, Miss Endecott," he said, staring her down.

"And on *your* way home," she replied icily, "think about this. I have no intention of walking out on a commitment to my employer merely because some total stranger—whom, I might add, is such a dolt he'd admit to being a spy—ordered me to. I have been hired to serve at this festivity, and that is what I shall do. And if, from time to time, I happen upon an interesting conversation, there is no crime in listening." She fluttered her hand in a gesture of dismissal. "Now, go about your own business and leave me to mine."

"*Go about my own business?* If you're so forthright and innocent, why aren't you running out of here this instant, shouting to all those soldiers that I'm a spy?"

For several seconds she could only offer a blank stare. "Well, I . . . that is . . . it would be a shame, that's all," she muttered lamely.

He had her cold, and he knew it. "What would? Turning in a fellow patriot?"

She sniffed. "Don't imagine you're going to trap me that easily into admitting anything. I don't happen to be the simpleton you are." With a last glare, she spun to leave.

Morgan caught her elbow and swung her back. "And don't you imagine I'll let you go until you tell me why it would be a shame to expose me."

She plucked his hand from her arm, then dropped her gaze with a self-conscious shrug. "I wouldn't want to be the cause of having that . . . noble face of yours smashed in."

"Noble?" he echoed with a smirk.

"Handsome, then. Is that better?" she asked, her color heightening as she peered at him through her long lashes.

"Much, much better," he admitted. He rather liked this unexpected turn in the conversation. Perhaps he'd test it with a little kiss. He reached out and pulled her close.

The spitfire administered a swift kick to his shin and then backed to the door, her chin in the air, her fine eyebrows arched high. "Handsome is as handsome does," she said coolly. "And your particular appeal is fading by the second. Now, if you will excuse me, I have work to do." She turned and grasped the latch.

With one hand, Morgan held the door closed. "That's what you think," he informed her. "Go home, will you? I can't do *my* job with half my mind occupied with worrying about you." He tipped his head and peered suggestively at her. "Now, will you leave willingly . . . or would you prefer to be carried bodily from the premises? It's your call."

Lips pursed, she scowled at him in fury for several seconds. "Very well," she ground out. "But I'll not forget *you.*" Then, in a swirl of gray skirts, she trounced from the pantry.

"Nor I, you," Morgan murmured as he watched her stomp off. Her kind of ineptness was the cause of Boston's sad state, he affirmed inwardly. Lucky for them he'd come to town.

But one thing was for certain, he conceded, breaking into a smile. Prudence Endecott had the most incredibly lovely— and lively—eyes he had ever seen.

14

A chill wind cut like a knife beneath the sluggish morning sky. Ben shivered and hunkered down into the warmth of his scarf as he guided Rebel along the uneven, frozen hills near Millers Falls. He took a firmer grip on the lead of the gentle gelding he had rented in town for Abigail, then checked over his shoulder at Jane and Ted, who were riding double a few paces behind. Having their company on the trip made it far less lonely than usual but had done nothing toward easing Ben's apprehension. Abigail had been very disappointed in him.

The nearer they got to the Preston farm, the more time he spent rationalizing the situation in his mind. The fact that he had misled Ma, and quite deliberately at that, caused him less and less guilt. The old woman hadn't been altogether honest with him either. Or Abigail. Ma had misused her terribly. That realization made him draw sharply on the reins. "Hold up, you two."

Ted moved his pacer alongside and stopped. "What's the matter?"

"I should have mentioned this before, but when we get to the farm, let me handle things with Abby's mother-in-law—even if what I say isn't exactly what you'd consider *correct.*"

For a second Ted didn't answer. "You're going to lie to the woman?" he asked in disbelief. "You're aware, are you not, that lying only gets a person into more trouble."

Ben grimaced. "Not in this case. You'll have to trust me on this."

Jane, whose eyes remained fixed on his face, appeared less than pleased at this exchange. "Do you mean to say you've brought us along merely to be party to your duplicity?"

She was a fine one to talk, Ben told himself. Until recently, when she had suddenly become pure as the driven snow, her antics far exceeded anything he could have come up with. "This is for a good cause," he said in his own defense. "Abigail is much too timid to stand up to Ma—and I have no right to. Not yet, anyway."

"Hmph." His sister's shiny curls lurched with the toss of her head. "Never let it be said that you'd trust anyone except yourself to set things right . . . not even the Lord."

"We'll try not to interfere, Ben," Ted said evenly. "But we won't lie for you. So do take care what you say."

Ben knew the conditional promise would have to suffice. "I'll do my best." He nudged his mount onward, even as his pulse began gaining speed at the thought of seeing Abigail face-to-face.

When they reached the farm and dismounted, they walked up the steps, and Ben rapped at the door. *Please, oh, please, let it be Abby who answers. I need the calmness in those beautiful turquoise eyes. And please, let there be calmness.*

But the footfalls approaching from inside were heavy. The door opened to reveal Ma Preston, coarse brown attire adding even more austerity to her pursed lips and stern face.

"Good day, Ma," Ben said with as much enthusiasm as he could gather. "I've brought the chaperons with me that I mentioned last time I was here. This is my sister, Jane, and her husband, Ted Harrington. Ted, Jane, this is Mistress Preston."

Jane smiled and bobbed into a slight curtsy. "So pleased to meet you, Mistress Preston. Ben's spoken with great affection about you and your family."

The older woman nodded without expression, then eyed Ted. "Ain't you that feller who came ridin' by a few weeks ago? In too big a hurry to give us the time of day, as I recall."

"Quite right." Ted extended his hand and clasped hers. "Terribly rude of me—I'm afraid I was dealing with a bit of a family emergency. You have my sincerest apologies."

As if sizing them up, Ma continued staring for several seconds. Then her countenance began to relax. "Oh, well, I suppose the lot of you should come in out of the cold." Straggly gray hairs stirred beneath her limp house cap as she turned in the open doorway.

Ben released a pent-up breath and gestured for Jane and Ted to go ahead, then he followed and closed the door. Single file, they paraded after Ma into the kitchen.

A quick glance around the efficient workroom revealed that only Bertha and Wesley were present, and the pair broke into delighted grins. "Well, look who's here!" Bertie said. "We was just talkin' about ya."

Ben had the impression their enthusiasm had a lot to do with the intended departure of Abigail and her children. And from Ma's black expression, he knew she felt just the opposite. "Go on outside," she ordered, "and see to Ben's horses."

"Yes, Ma." Dutifully the couple got up, and while Bertha began tugging on her boots near the back door, Wes leaned his head out into the hallway. "Abigail!" he bellowed. "Get down here. You got company."

    ❦ ❦

Upstairs, Abby paused from patching Corbin's breeches. Company? It could only be Ben! But even as her heart gave a joyous lurch, it was squelched by the memory of her painful decision not to go with him. All that was left now was for her to inform him. With a sigh, she laid aside her mending, glancing at the closet, where the beautiful clothes she'd sewn were folded and neatly tucked inside two old flour sacks. It would not be easy, disappointing him. She and Ben had both done wrong, deceiving Ma. Ma might not deserve better, but the children did. And a solid marriage could not be built on quicksand.

It would be hard saying no to this man who had been so

good to her, so loving. But drawing strength from the sight of the children napping on their cots, she picked up the sacks and walked to the door. Of all the goods she had purchased with Ben's funds, she particularly regretted having to return the pink dress she had made for Cassie. It was by far more beautiful than anything her daughter ever owned, and Abby had not even been able to see it on her. Yet another cost associated with deception.

Corbin coughed in his sleep. He had a bad case of the sniffles, only one of many reasons not to take a trip in the cold of winter. Her resolve thus fortified, she closed the door behind her and headed downstairs.

She set the bags on the front porch, then walked the long mile through the parlor to the back of the house.

The first person she saw was Ben, his love for her written clearly on his face. The very sight of him made Abby's throat close up.

"This here's Jane. Ben's sister," Ma grated, cutting into Abby's inner turmoil and indicating the couple. "Her and her husband have come with Ben to fetch ya."

Abigail's attention was drawn to the attractive young woman smiling at her. Eyes and hair much darker than Ben's, she noticed, but still a definite family resemblance—and ever so elegantly dressed in a hooded, fur-lined cloak. Abby glanced down briefly at her own shabby work dress, and a flash of shame overwhelmed her.

Ted Harrington she recognized from his previous visit. "It-it's nice of you to come," she stammered, then concentrated on Ben. Steeling herself against the desire to run into his arms, she forced her little speech past her frozen mouth. "Forgive me . . . I . . . cannot go with you to your family's home."

The color fled his face, and a muscle flinched in his jaw. He swung to Ma. "But you agreed." His tone left no room for discussion.

The older woman scowled. "The gal's decision, not mine."

Abby watched Ben's fist clench and flex beneath the sleeve

of his wool greatcoat. His other hand crushed his three-cornered hat in a death grip. When he turned back to her, she almost relented at the anguish so evident on his face. Her fingers ached to go smooth away the hurt, but instead, she held on to her reserve all the more. "There are many reasons. And besides, it's Christmas. I can't be away from my little son on such a special day. I—I'm sorry."

Devouring her with his eyes, Ben shook his head. "The invitation was for all of you, Abby. You and the children. I told you that."

"Yes. But with this bad weather, the bitter cold and all, I don't think I should take Corbin on such a long trip. He's been croupy for the last few days. It's not a good time."

"I would never let anything happen to him—or you," Ben pleaded. "I would die first."

Abby swallowed and cut a glance to Ma. "Ma's already lost her only son. I can't ask her to let me put her only grandson at risk as well."

"Everybody set down," the older woman's coarse voice announced. "You need somethin' hot inside before ya go back out."

Grateful for the distraction, Abby flew to the stove and started dipping chicken soup into bowls. She took extra care not to look at Ben. She needed more time to work up enough courage to tell him the rest. She had cried her heart out over it for several nights already . . . surely by now she'd be able to say the words.

"Abigail," Ben's sister said, breaking into the awkward silence. "I don't mean to interfere, put perhaps you haven't thought this through."

Abby met Jane's gaze for a second, then filled the next bowl.

"My brother told me your little boy is only two," Jane continued. "At that age, he's far too young to understand the significance of Christmas. And as for Mistress Preston, she might consider having her grandson all to herself for a few days a marvelous gift."

Ma's expression eased considerably. "Yep, I would. That's a fact."

"See?" Jane sounded even more hopeful. "Meanwhile, Abigail, you and your daughter could make this a special time for just the two of you . . . especially while you help her search for the most perfect present to bring back to her little brother."

It sounded ever so plausible, put that way, Abby reasoned. But nothing could justify the lies.

Ma whacked the tabletop. "Why, I could even bake Corbin some of them gingerbread men he favors so much. And all my other gals is comin' for the holidays. With the houseful of kids here to play with, he'll have himself a great time."

"If he's well enough." Abby leaned the handle of the ladle against the big pot.

"Don't want him turnin' into a mama's boy, do ya?" Ma returned.

Abby looked to Ben. "Could we talk? Alone? Please?" Without waiting for his answer, she walked through the doorway into the parlor. She didn't stop until she reached the front door, where her gaze fell to the slumping totes of beautiful clothes.

Ben followed swiftly after her, the sounds of his footsteps keeping time with the rhythm of her heart. He caught up and turned her to face him. "What is it, Abby? I thought you cared for me. That you'd agreed to be my wife."

She could barely speak for the sorrow. "I did. But . . . I can't. I . . ."

He drew her close, rocking her in his arms. "Don't be afraid, sweet Abby. Talk to me. Whatever it is, I know we can make it right."

A sob burst forth from deep inside her. She'd been so sure she had cried all her tears, but a new flood was cresting behind her eyes, struggling to spill out. It was all she could do to hold them back. She swallowed hard. "I don't see how. We've both . . . sinned. Awfully."

He eased her to arm's length, a disturbed expression darkening his light brown eyes as they silently searched hers.

"We've both deceived Ma." She tilted her head toward the flour sacks. "And there are the fruits of my deception—the lovely clothes I made from the money you gave me. It's only proper that I return them along with my . . . my promise of marriage. A union that starts out with such falsehoods is surely doomed to fail."

Ben still did not speak. The strength of his grip on her arms gradually lessened.

"Did ya talk her into it yet, boy?" Ma Preston hollered from the kitchen.

Abby could tell from the eagerness in Ma's tone she was all for Ben's taking her away.

"We'd appreciate a few more minutes," Ben answered. Then he took Abby's elbow and stepped outside.

The crisp chilly air somehow reinforced her inner strength. She breathed deeply of it, waiting for him to speak. Dreading it. Wanting him to make everything right, but knowing there was no possible way he could.

Gently he brushed some stray hairs from her temple with his fingers and studied her. "I have no defense, Abigail. I did just what you said. I was so afraid of losing you. . . . I'm still afraid. My very first thought was to tell you whatever you wanted to hear, whatever it would take to make you leave with me. But I love you so much more than that. I can only tell you I will never again cheapen the love I have for you with lies. I promise you this with all my heart. It's all I have to say . . . all I can offer you."

"All?" she breathed. Her eyes misting, she touched his cheek. "That's the most wonderful gift you could give to me, to my children."

"Our children." Laying his hand over hers, he drew her palm to his lips and kissed it. "If you will do me the honor of marrying me."

Too choked to answer, she could only nod, smiling through tears.

"Then, will you come with me to my family's farm?"

"Yes," she whispered. In a burst of joy, she threw her arms around his neck.

Ben swept her up into his arms and swung her in joyous circles. After a breathless moment, he set her down again and offered his arm. "Come along, my sweet Abigail. Ma's waiting to hear some good news."

❦ ❦

When Abby went to pack the rest of her things, Ben became acutely aware of the room's emptiness without her. Longingly he watched her graceful form as she left for the stairs.

As if from faraway he heard Ma speaking to Ted and Jane. "I expect the two of you to keep that boy in line, if ya catch my meaning. I don't want—"

The back door opened, admitting Bertha and Wes on a blast of cold air.

"Bertie," Ma ordered. "Go up and help Abby. Cassie will need to get dressed."

"They're goin'?" Bertha shrieked in delight.

"Just her and the girl."

Bertha's broad smile faded. With a cursory glance at Ben, she went to do as she was told.

Wesley hung his coat on a hook and shed his boots at the bootjack, then dropped his hulking mass down on a chair near Ben. "Seein' as how you all just came back from mountain country, I don't expect you heared the latest."

"What's that?" Ben asked. Hopefully it would be something to help the patriot cause this time.

From the sideboard, Ma guffawed as she carried spoons and bowls of soup to the table. "Wish I'd been there to see them lobsterbacks tuck tail."

"What happened?" Ted asked in alarm.

"Just taking back what's ours," Wes replied.

Ma snickered. "You said a mouthful, boy! That uppity general mighta got away with cleaning our gunpowder out of Cambridge, but the boys in Rhode Island decided it was time we took some back."

"Oh, *that,*" Ben said. "It's old news."

"You didn't let me finish," Ma piped in. "The men up in Portsmouth took *another* of His Majesty's harbor forts. That oughta get the general's dander up, for sure." She chuckled to herself. "We'll get our powder back one way or t'other."

Ted, however, did not appear so cheerful about it. "General Gage abhors the idea of open conflict. Being wed to a colonial, he's always been privately sympathetic. I'm sure he'll do whatever he can to keep peace."

"He needs a lot more troops, anyway," Ben said, "before he can lift a finger to do anything." Providing Ben ample time for things like marrying Abby and getting her settled—*if* his luck held.

Wes laughed aloud. "The general's making a big mistake if he thinks he'll be safe till *he* decides it's time to attack. He's a bottled-up man who even plugged his own cork when he barricaded Boston Neck. I, for one, think it's time we started throwin' some rocks at that bottle."

"Attack Boston?" Jane gasped. "Think of the townspeople! My brother and sister-in-law!"

"Time they got out," Ma said flatly.

"Ayc." Wesley gave a confident nod. "I been teaching Bertie to shoot. She's getting purty good, too. Way I figure, Bertie and me won't have us no trouble taking on ten, maybe twenty of them mealymouthed redcoats, single-handed."

At that moment, Bertha tromped in with Cassandra, and Ben couldn't help but agree that the farm gal and her husband made quite a formidable pair. Wes was probably right.

Cassie caught sight of Ben and squealed. She shrugged out of her aunt's hold and raced into his arms.

He hugged her tightly, chasing away some of his emptiness. How he loved the little angel and her golden-haired mommy. And he would have them. Corbin, too. Despite Ma Preston.

15

Abigail watched Ben secure her bags to the horse he had rented. Another expense this good-hearted man had taken upon himself because of her.

"Steady there," he said gently as the animal shifted.

"Steady there," Cassandra echoed happily from her perch on the horse's back. She clapped her mittened hands with glee, her face glowing with excitement beneath her navy bonnet.

Ben finished with the last bag, then turned to Abby. He placed his hands on either side of her waist.

He expected her to ride that huge animal with Cassie? Alone? The two of them? "Wait. I—I can't do this."

"What?" He spun her to face him, and the hem of her heavy wool cloak belled outward.

One look at Ben's frustrated face, and Abby knew she had upset him yet again. "You'd best go on without me. I'll only hold you back."

"We won't be traveling fast." A weariness colored his tone.

Abigail looked reluctantly up at Jane. Ben's sister had mounted behind her husband with ease, appearing so confident, so competent, even fearless. Abby leaned nearer to Ben. "I told you, I've never been anywhere before," she whispered.

He frowned. "So?"

"I . . . don't know how to handle a horse," she whispered even more softly.

Approaching footsteps broke the awkward silence. "Now what's the matter, girl?" Ma rasped. "No call for you to be keeping these good folks waiting."

An uncomfortable warmth flooded Abby's cheeks. "I— um—"

"She's a little nervous about the horse," Ben explained.

Ma snorted. "Don't reckon she's ever ridden before, being nothin' but a penniless orphan child." She shot a scathing glance at Abby. "Pretty near useless she's been around here, too. Never did know what my Raymond saw in her. Even her own aunt said she wasn't good for much besides watching after young'uns."

Abigail had never seen such a malicious gleam in her mother-in-law's eyes. How could Ma say such things? How could she lay Abby's unfortunate past out like a boot mat, fit only for wiping feet on? And in front of the man she loved, no less. Crushed, Abby began backing away. She could never go with Ben. Not now.

"You've no cause to hurt her, Ma." The tightness in Ben's voice was obvious as he snagged Abby's arm, halting her flight. She could not bear to meet his face.

Jane slid down from the horse and came to her, placing a hand on her shoulder. "I'll ride with you, Abby," she said kindly. "I don't know why we didn't plan it that way from the first. It's far better for the horses if the weight is distributed more evenly. They don't tire quite so quickly."

"Yes, that's a fact," Ted added, his smile doing much to ease Abby's humiliation. "We'd undoubtedly make far better time."

Having felt so low a mere moment ago, Abigail was deeply touched by their kindness. Ben raised her chin with a fingertip. "And by the time we reach Pawtucket, sweetheart, you'll be an expert horsewoman. I promise."

This fine young man should have been mortified to have his family find out he'd made such an unworthy choice . . . but instead, he could only speak of teaching her to ride a horse! Abigail was nearly overcome by his thoughtfulness.

After giving Abby a hug, Ben turned to Cassandra. "What do you think about riding with me, angel? You and your dolly."

"Uh-huh!" Without hesitation, Cassie held out her arms to him, and he transferred her to Rebel's back.

Jane effortlessly mounted the rented gelding, then turned a supportive smile to Abby as Ben returned and lifted her up behind his sister in a demure sidesaddle position. "I'll always love you," he whispered. "No matter what."

As Ben swung up into Rebel's saddle, Corbin came crashing out the door, feet bare, his nose running. "I go, too," he cried, his arms outstretched. "Go, too."

Abby's heart wrenched within her breast, and a constriction in her throat almost strangled her.

"Remember the ball I got you, buddy?" Ben blurted out. "And the stage wagon? Well, we're off to find you something else just as good."

The child brightened. "You are?" His gaze drifted to his sister, and he frowned. "Cassie go. I go, too!"

How can I leave my little son behind? Abby cried inside. *He's so little, so precious.*

"And I got a present for ya right now," Ma said. She scooped him up, shielding him with her long apron. "Yessir, I surely do. Out in the shed, hid. Let's go find it."

Before Abigail could protest, her mother-in-law was leaving with her son. Abby blinked back stinging tears. Her baby was being tricked. She could not allow it. She opened her mouth to call after Ma.

Ben whacked the rump of her horse.

The animal jerked forward, almost unseating her as she grabbed onto Jane and held on for dear life.

When she looked back, Ma and Corbin were already out of sight behind the house, and she was bouncing along on a fast-moving beast. She was getting away from that miserable farmhouse at last. But without her Corbin.

Determined not to cry, she bit her lip hard, drawing blood.

❦ ❦

The house was strangely quiet when Morgan drifted downstairs well after noon. The holly and evergreen remained in place to herald the season, but the servants had cleared the clutter from last night.

Seeing no one stirring about in the downstairs rooms, Morgan figured that the Clarkes, after hosting the gala, must still be asleep. No doubt they had remained up until the last guest departed, whereas he had turned in quite soon after learning General Gage's response to the Portsmouth incident. The mix of Puritan propriety and ill-tempered officers did not make for a gay party.

The one bright spot of the whole affair had been dark-haired Prudence—so pretty, yet so reckless, fancying herself a spy. She had lingered in the misty nether lands of Morgan's mind before sleep claimed him. Surely someone among the kitchen staff would know where the fetching lass lived.

He reached the kitchen and strode right in. The servants didn't appear to notice him as they huddled together across the room at the back door, speaking in excited whispers to someone on the stoop just outside.

Morgan strained to hear but caught only disjointed words. "Portsmouth . . . harbor . . . fort."

He took a few steps backward, removing himself from view while he continued to eavesdrop.

"Ye say 'twas Paul Revere, now?" someone remarked.

"Aye. He carried the news to Portsmouth about the Boston powder being seized and got the folks up there all riled. That's all I know."

Muttered expressions circulated the group.

In the ensuing break in the conversation, Morgan stepped forth. "I say, what's for breakfast?"

The servants started in obvious surprise and closed the door even as the outsider bid a hasty farewell.

Paying them no mind, Morgan took a seat at the table near

a batch of biscuits partway along the process of being cut out and placed on baking sheets.

The butler, small in stature but obviously relishing his exalted position among the servitude, jutted out a firm chin and eyed him with wariness. He reminded Morgan of a calculating cat. "The family, sir, takes meals in the dining room."

"I'm sure they do," Morgan said evenly. "But they have yet to come downstairs. I shouldn't want to put you to trouble for my sake alone."

"It's no trouble, I assure you." Striding purposely toward the aforementioned room, the hawk-nosed butler paused and stared back at him, a less than subtle hint for Morgan to follow.

"Pity." Morgan grinned. "At my home, the choicest gossip can be heard in the kitchen."

The cook drew a quick intake of breath.

It was so tempting to stay and egg them on, but Morgan thought better of it. He rose and started toward the door that separated the dining room from the kitchen, then paused and looked back. "By the by, I wonder if you might help me. The serving girl who was here last eve—Prudence Endecott. Some friends of mine are in need of good help at the moment. Would any of you happen to know where she resides?"

The cook appeared on the verge of answering, but a glance from the butler kept her silent.

Having caught the woman's fleeting expression, Morgan was not about to let her off. "Yes?" he asked.

The butler interceded. "She came to our door after hearing about the party, requesting to be hired—a common practice nowadays with so many folk out of work." He slid an accusatory glance up and down Morgan.

Morgan flinched at the insinuation that he was to blame for the harbor blockade. Still, he could understand the animosity in the room. After all, to them, he was a Loyalist stranger— and it was just as well not too many people knew he was a patriot. There were other means of finding Prudence Endecott. He would pursue the matter later on, at the Green

Dragon Tavern, when he reported the information he had gleaned last evening. "On second thought," he said to the butler, "I would appreciate having someone saddle my horse. I must attend to some business."

Within a quarter of an hour, Morgan rode away from the grand homes of the North End. The hooves of his horse clattered over the crooked cobbled streets as he headed for the more modest central part of Boston and the Green Dragon Tavern, the unofficial headquarters of the rebels. The stately elms along the way seemed stark and barren skeletons in the cold dampness. But even in the icy mist of December, townspeople stood outside, watching, waiting, their tension obvious in their anxious expressions.

By now everyone knew about the people in New Hampshire taking the fort, and there was much speculation concerning what General Gage would do about it. Morgan smiled smugly. He was probably the one patriot in town who had the answer. And after he delivered the news, he would ask the whereabouts of the beautiful spy, then chance a visit to Susannah, since both the citizens and the military alike were so preoccupied.

The tavern came into view, a brick structure two and a half stories tall, gray smoke from its chimneys dissipating in the mist. Morgan rode discreetly by the main entrance, continuing on to the next corner. He dismounted on a side street, then headed up an alley for the back door.

Quite a crowd had gathered in the smoky confines of the Green Dragon, the laughter and chatter unusually boisterous for the middle of the day. Lingering off to one side, Morgan scanned the room, searching for his contact. He spied the man on the far side, seated with a gentleman who seemed extremely well dressed for conservative Boston.

The contact, a man of medium stature with salt-and-pepper hair and known only as Garrick, looked up from his drink just then and waved Morgan toward an interior door as he and the gentleman with him stood.

The small dining room Morgan entered offered far more

privacy and seclusion than the crowded common room. Within seconds, Garrick and the other man joined him there.

"Just as soon not have the general population see you talking to us," Garrick explained, closing the door, "no matter how loyal they profess to be." He winked a shrewd eye.

"Rather." Morgan grinned. "One never knows who's spying on whom."

"I like your style," the other gentleman said. Fashionably attired himself, he peered over a long, straight nose, dark brows flaring upward on his high forehead.

"I suppose that should not surprise me," Morgan retorted, straightening the ruffle on his own expensive shirt.

The man extended the fine-boned fingers of his right hand. "I hardly meant that kind of style," he said lightly. "I'm Hancock. John Hancock."

"Ah," Morgan said, nodding as he clasped the fellow's hand. "And from what I've heard, one of the richest merchants in all of New England."

Hancock chuckled. "That, too, young man. That, too." He sobered. "Garrick tells me you're the son of Waldon Thomas, from the fair city of Philadelphia. I was under the impression that your father is staunchly loyal to Britain. Has he had a recent change of heart?"

"No, sir, he has not."

"But his son has?"

Morgan cocked a smile. "No, sir."

Hancock and Garrick appeared taken aback, which amused Morgan all the more. "No change of heart here, gentlemen," he said lightly. "I've been a patriot for a number of years. And not only do I have pertinent military information for you but I have what I believe will be a rather advantageous business proposition as well."

Both men relaxed noticeably. "Splendid," Garrick said.

"However," Morgan added, turning to John Hancock, *"first* I'd like to make inquiry regarding someone I feel must be one of Boston's loveliest flowers of womanhood."

16

Susannah removed a tray of raisin-walnut cookies from the oven and slid in another. Somehow, having little things to do for Dan made their separation easier to bear . . . far easier than when he had been off in the Grants and letters were their only link. Both he and the guards looked forward to the special treats she brought along on visits to the South Battery, and she was taking extra pains with this particular batch to ensure they were absolutely perfect.

Light footsteps carried from outside, and Felicia came in the back door. She set down a bucket of milk from the dairy up the street and dispensed with her boots and cloak. Then, her cheeks still glowing from winter's cold breath, she brought the milk to the table. "You should see all the activity going on out there!"

"Oh?"

The sparkle in her friend's dark brown eyes was mirrored in her expression. "The very air seems charged with excitement. Townspeople are everywhere—and in high spirits, too." Felicia continued talking as she went about her work. "People are laughing, baiting the soldiers—what few soldiers are brave enough to show their faces around the city these days."

Susannah didn't know whether the news was good or bad, considering the volatile state of affairs in the Colonies. "What was the word on the street?"

"Apparently, the fort at Portsmouth has been taken by the locals, right from the hands of the British. Can you imagine?"

Susannah stopped spooning dough onto the half-filled baking sheet and met Felicia's gaze. "Oh, my. I hope it doesn't lead to open warfare. I pray every night that Alex will arrive here from England before Boston explodes like a tinderbox. Dan could become a prisoner of war and be forced to remain in prison indefinitely." The grim possibility was too much to think about. Susannah had to keep busy, had to keep her mind off what might happen. She had to trust God. With a deep sigh she turned back to her cookies.

A knock rattled the back door.

Felicia glanced at Susannah's floury hands. "I'll get it." She had scarcely opened it before Morgan Thomas pushed past her.

"Why have *you* come?" Susannah gasped as he removed his hat. "In broad daylight, no less, when you were warned not a week ago against doing something so foolhardy!"

Oblivious to anything as inconsequential as a flour-covered apron or sticky hands, Morgan laughed and grabbed her in a hug, swinging her twice in a circle before setting her down.

Susannah stifled the giggle that burst forth, and as she regained her feet again, she could see poor Felicia was completely bewildered. She gathered her dignity and composed herself. "Felicia, I'd like to introduce Morgan Thomas, an old friend of ours from Princeton. Morgan, this is Yancy's wife, Felicia Curtis."

His cobalt eyes swept a glance of appraisal over Felicia, head to toe, then he flashed a smile. "So you're the lass who did the impossible, eh? Never thought I'd meet someone with wiles enough to worm a proposal of marriage from that barnacled sea rat."

Felicia's delicate brows flared, but she joined right in, her tone far from serious. "Worm? *Worm*, you say? I'll have you know that sailor counted himself most fortunate when I allowed him to court me. Make no mistake about that." She gave a toss of her dark hair.

"Ah yes. So any woman would have a man believe," Morgan teased.

"Hmph! If that's how you feel about the gentle sex," she said, planting her fists on her hips, "I can only pity the poor woman you deign to set your cap for." With a searing glare, she swirled around, grabbed the cheesecloth, and immersed it in the water bucket.

Morgan laughed heartily, but Susannah managed to keep her own smile in check as she pushed the last pan of cookies into the oven. The scamp was in his glory brandishing his charms and wit in the presence of the fairer gender.

"Speaking of women," he said on a more serious note, "would either of you happen to know a Prudence Endecott? Or where she lives?"

"Don't tell him if you do," Felicia flung over her shoulder.

Susannah had no way of knowing whether her friend was joking or not, but it made no difference anyway. "Sorry, I've not had the pleasure. Do have a seat, Morgan, and I'll pour you some coffee. Who is she?"

Pulling out a chair, Morgan caught Felicia's eye and winked. "Oh, just a passing fancy."

"Apparently," Felicia huffed, "your passing fancy had the good sense her name implies and has passed you by with all due haste, or you wouldn't have to ask."

He chuckled as Susannah brought him a steaming mug. "Yancy must have to keep on his toes with that one."

Spots of color rose high on Felicia's cheeks, tinting them almost the same shade as her raspberry frock. She started toward him, empty bucket in hand.

He raised his arms to fend her off. "Only jesting, I swear. No doubt our seafaring friend would be the first to tell us how lucky he is."

Somewhat placated, Felicia relaxed and went back to the sideboard.

Morgan's smile died. He turned to Susannah. "Truly, I'd be forever grateful if you could check around for me. See if anyone in your congregation might know Miss Endecott."

"How did you meet the young woman?" Susannah asked, her interest piqued.

He gave a casual shrug. "She was spying last evening at the Clarkes' . . . and doing a rather poor job of it, I must say. It would be a miracle if no one other than myself noticed. Someone needs to tell her to stay at home, where she belongs, and let those of us who are better skilled at such things take over."

"And I suppose," Felicia said with a contrary smile, "you consider yourself one of them."

Morgan grinned. "Quite right, actually."

She glanced sideways at him. "Then why don't you prove it?"

"What do you mean?"

"If you're so skilled at spying, pray tell us . . . what's General Gage going to do to the settlers at Portsmouth? Burn them out? Sack the place? What? Everyone is desperate to know."

He regarded her evenly, no longer playing the tease. He raked his fingers through his hair, leaving furrows among the glossy brown strands. "There's nothing to know," he admitted. "The coward will not do one single thing about it."

"Well, that is good news," Susannah breathed. "I was telling Felicia just before you came that the military could consider Dan a prisoner of war were open rebellion to break out."

"It takes two sides to make a war, my dear Susannah. Gage is being cautious, far too cautious. In fact," he went on optimistically, "I'll wager I can even spring Dan out of prison—at least for the holidays. Under house arrest, perhaps, but out, nonetheless. I'm quite the popular fellow with our gentlemen in red, you know."

A wave of hope washed over Susannah. "You could do that? Truly?" She hardly dared to let herself think of the possibility.

He shrugged. "Seriously, I made several influential acquaintances last eve—acquaintances who believe I'm about to aid them in increasing their present fortunes substantially. I wouldn't be the least surprised to find them rather eager to help such an industrious chap with the army." He chuckled under his breath.

"Don't you think you're quite the clever fellow," Felicia said on a caustic note.

"No more clever than your illustrious John Hancock thinks I am." He glanced from her to Susannah and back, and when he spoke again, his voice was much softer. "What I'm about to say must not for any reason leave this room."

Susannah exchanged a puzzled glance with Felicia, but before either of them could voice a question, Morgan elaborated.

"I've convinced a number of Loyalist merchants to continue to load their ships with English goods and then sail them to Bermuda, where, supposedly, my father owns some empty warehouses. Once the cargoes arrive in Bermuda, I've graciously volunteered to repack them into French or Dutch crates and send them on to my father in Philadelphia, thereby outwitting those who advocate the boycott."

"But wouldn't you be aiding your adversaries?" Susannah asked.

He grinned. "That's the best part! In truth, I've arranged with Mr. Hancock to have the cargoes diverted from my father to the patriot warehouses. Quite ingenious, I daresay."

"Suddenly I understand why you and my husband are friends," Felicia said, moving nearer. "Both of you have a burning desire to get yourselves hanged!"

"I'm afraid I must agree with Felicia," Susannah said with a nod. "That sounds quite underhanded, at best. I'm far more interested in what you suggested regarding Dan. I'm afraid to hope, though, that you're crafty enough to secure his release, however temporarily, from that horrid jail."

Morgan feigned intense pain. "For Dan, you would have me risk all. About me and my neck you care not a whit."

"I care whit enough to implore you to take yet a second risk."

"For you?" He cocked his head, his easy manner returning. "Name it."

"Spend Christmas day with us."

His slow smile almost made Susannah regret suggesting such a thing. "You have my word, unless actual conflict breaks out in the streets—in which case, I'd prefer to be right in the thick of it."

Susannah stared at him for a few seconds. "Oh, Morgan. Whatever became of that enthusiastic student of theology I once knew?"

His grin slowly evaporated. "I can't say, to be truthful. Time passes. Things change. People change. And speaking of change," he said more cheerfully, "where are those children I was led to believe you have? And for that matter, have you heard that Jonathan and Mary Clare now have two? They've left his father's farm and moved farther west. And my other classmate, Steven Russell, has taken a church in Germantown."

Only marginally aware of Morgan's ramblings, Susannah knew her last question had pricked his soul. A few years ago his main quest had been for God's light. And now, Morgan, along with so many other young patriots, had turned his zeal toward gaining political freedom instead. How could they not see that no freedom could be complete without the freedom one found when following Christ?

Dear Father in heaven, please let Dan come home—if even for a short time. The patriots need him almost as much as I do.

✤ ✤

Morgan guided his mount toward Clarke's Wharf. He was hoping to find Andy there, at the Sewell family warehouse. If Morgan had the congenial young man pegged correctly, Andy was the most likely candidate to lend a hand with the military—and be the least suspicious when he did so. And he might have some knowledge of Miss Endecott, though Morgan wasn't all that sure he wanted Andy to know anything about her.

He pushed the lovely Prudence to the back of his mind and turned his thoughts to the conversation he'd had with Susannah. How could he have made such a rash promise to her, of all people? The glorious light that had shone in her blue-gray eyes at the mere mention of Dan's freedom had pierced his soul. But what would the Tory community think of Morgan Thomas helping a known patriot? Surely being in Susannah's presence had caused him to take leave of his senses!

Expelling a ragged breath, Morgan shook his head. Perhaps he could come up with some plausible story about Dan's being a black sheep. After all, even the best of families these days seemed to have one or two.

But try as he might to convince himself that his anxiety had to do with Dan, Morgan knew the truth. Susannah's remark about his theological studies had cut him to the quick. He had gotten far afield from his dedication as a Christian. When he had been surrounded by so many friends at Princeton who were as immersed in the search for God's truth as he, his spiritual walk had been much easier. But college was far away now, and so were the shining ideals taught there. His present-day existence centered around spying and lying, whether justified by the cause or not.

As he turned onto Ana Street, the sea smells of fish and brine assaulted him. He grimaced and forced himself to concentrate on the maze of streets he navigated.

A few blocks ahead, he caught sight of a young woman with long dark hair. Her height seemed about right, and her form and walk seemed familiar, but with her back to him, Morgan could not be sure. His pulse raced as he urged his horse to a faster gait.

Just as he was about to draw abreast of her, she turned and knocked on the door of a house, then went inside.

Morgan clenched his teeth in disappointment. There was every chance the girl was a complete stranger, but with that unusual black hair of hers, she might also be Miss Endecott. There was only one way to find out.

He reined in his horse, wondering what he'd say when he rapped on the door. He hesitated, staring at the home.

"Morgan Thomas!" Andy Sewell, just the man he was looking for, approached on horseback from the opposite direction. He drew up alongside. "On your way to Mr. Clarke's place of business?"

"Quite right. But actually I was hoping to see you first. I've a small favor to ask."

"What a fortuitous happenstance! I was just about to go to my favorite tavern for dinner—or should I say the tavern with my favorite serving girl." He gave a sly smile. "Join me?"

For a fleeting moment, Morgan was reluctant to relinquish the chance of seeing his own favorite serving girl. He glanced at the house again and sighed. It was highly likely that the girl he'd seen had not been Prudence. Perhaps his own wishful thinking had conjured up someone who merely resembled her. Anyway, he could come back later. He *would* come back later.

He forced a grin at Andy. "Delighted. After you."

17

Abigail stroked Cassandra's forehead until the child's breathing slowed in sleep. The sight of the coaching inn had been most welcome after their first day of travel, and though Cassie had been amazingly patient and cheerful on the tiring ride, she started nodding off before she had even finished supper. Ben had carried her up to the room Abigail was sharing with Jane, and Jane helped Abby change the exhausted child into her nightclothes.

Now studying the little angel's sleeping face, Abby pressed the blankets snugly around her. Had Corbin fallen asleep so easily tonight without his mama to tuck him in? An aching void in the pit of Abby's stomach had tormented her since the moment she had ridden away from her little son. How she prayed the days would pass swiftly until she could return to him.

With a last look at Cassie, she turned to Jane. "Are you sure you won't mind staying with her for a little while?"

"Not at all. I know Ben is eager for your company." Jane smiled. "Run along. Cassie and I will be just fine. And to be truthful, I could use a little extra rest myself." She patted her rounding tummy.

Returning the smile, Abigail crossed to the door. "I'll try not to be long." As she made her way downstairs, she chuckled over Ben's sister's dedication to the duties of chaperon. Jane had instructed Ted to keep either Ben or Abigail—or ideally, both—in sight at all times. Ben had not been amused.

The bright golden glow from the hearth of the common room chased away the chill of the enclosed staircase. Abigail loosened her crocheted shawl and walked over to Ben and Ted, seated near the fire.

Ben's face brightened, and he stood to welcome her.

Ted got up as well. "Excuse me, will you? I made a solemn vow to my wife, but I shall allow you both a measure of privacy. You'll find me over yonder." Indicating with his mug a table not too far from theirs, he inclined his head slightly and left.

"We must keep our dear Jane satisfied, mustn't we?" Ben teased while Ted was still within earshot. He pulled out a chair for Abby and seated her. "I'll go get you some hot cider."

Watching him walk to the bar, Abby acknowledged how solicitous Ben had been on today's journey not only to her but to Cassandra also. He seemed to know an amazing number of nonsense songs and stories, which he employed to keep the child entertained during the endless hours on horseback.

How Corbin would have laughed at them! The thought cinched itself around Abby's heart in another painful reminder that the distance between her and her little son was growing wider with each mile. But then, with his cold, Corbin's coming had been out of the question, particularly since the sky hinted that a blizzard could let loose at any time. Still, her two-year-old would have loved this adventure. Most of all, she hated that Ma had tricked him into going into the barn with her while his own mother deserted him.

Ben returned with two drinks and set them down, then moved his chair very close to hers. Abby cut a nervous glance at Ted. It wouldn't do to have Ben's family think ill of her when she so coveted their approval. But Ted didn't appear to be paying them any mind as he perused a broadside.

Ben's hand covered hers and curled around it. "I've wanted to talk to you alone all day."

"I . . . longed to be with you, too." With great effort she met his piercing gaze.

His expression softened as he raised her hand slightly and slid his other one under it. "Even when we're apart I carry you with me in my thoughts, do you know that?" Without waiting for an answer, he went on, "But before I get lost feasting my eyes on that beautiful face of yours, I have some information you need to know."

Lost in watching the hearth flames flickering and dancing in Ben's eyes, Abigail had to struggle to concentrate.

"I spoke with a learned man a few days ago, a man of law. What he told me should lighten your heart considerably. At least, I pray it will. I only wish I'd known this before I succumbed to the temptation of lying to Ma Preston."

"You spoke to a man of law about me?" The thought was unsettling, at the very least.

"Right. And you'll be pleased to know that your mother-in-law has no hold on you whatsoever."

"She hasn't?" The moment of joy died almost as quickly as it had come. "Not a legal hold, perhaps. But she's provided us with a home, food, and clothing. I owe her a great deal."

Ben tipped his head, and a wayward lock of light brown hair fell onto his forehead. "That's where you're wrong. You owe her nothing."

"How can you say such a thing?" Abby asked with a frown.

"Easily, my love. Your mother-in-law happens to be the person who is in debt here. *She* owes *you* for each and every bite she has taken since her son died, even for the roof over her head."

"I don't understand."

He squeezed her hand and chuckled. "The fact is, as your husband's widow, the farm belongs to *you* . . . and will until your son reaches the age of ten, at which time it will pass to him."

"I'm afraid you're wrong about that. It wasn't Ray's to give."

Ben merely grinned. "Apparently Ma had him hood-winked, too. When his father died, ownership automatically went to him as the oldest male child. Not to Ma. That's the law."

Abby searched his face as she tried to assimilate this startling revelation. "The farm is . . . mine?" As the knowledge began to sink in, her anger flared. "All this time, Ma and Bertha have made me feel like an intruder—a charity case—someone who didn't belong there. Oh yes, they allowed me to stay—out of their *Christian duty,* they said."

"That's right. They've said the same to me."

"And I'll tell you something else," Abby said, fury raging through her from head to toe as she recalled the conversation she had recently overheard. "Ma has lied to Bertha, too. Telling her if she stays there and works hard, half the farm will one day belong to her. And it won't!" Abby sighed and shook her head. "Poor Bertie. She's toiled so tirelessly on that acreage for all these years. My husband wasn't all that interested in the place, really. He cared more about fishing and watching the clouds roll by. Oh, dear, and Wes. He's believed Ma's promises, too. Yet you say it all will go to Corbin one day?"

"Absolutely. The law will ensure his rightful inheritance."

The disclosure played in Abby's mind, bringing a smile. Now Ma and Bertha could no longer make her feel worthless, penniless. Now she could hold her head up, consider herself as good as anyone else. But before she had time enough to relish that thought, one less appealing surfaced. "But I don't *want* to stay there with Ma and Bertha! Even if the farm belongs to me, Ma would still run it. And me and my children besides. That's how she is."

"I know, sweetheart." Ben smiled gently. "But you don't have to stay on the farm. I'm sure Ma would be more than agreeable to run the place until Corbin comes of age, keep a roof over her head and all that. The only difference is, she won't have you or your little ones there to bully. You'll be with me. After Corbin grows up, it will be for him to decide if he even wants the farm."

It all sounded so feasible, so sensible. But Ben didn't know her formidable mother-in-law. Not really. "Ma will think of some way to stop me, Ben, I just know she will. She'll never give up Corbin."

With a comforting pat on her hand, Ben grinned. "She can't stop us. It's too late. The banns have already been posted in Pawtucket. We can be wed at my folks' house, just as we originally planned." Suddenly he reddened. "Of course, that is, if you still want to be married then."

Married? In the next few days? Abby could only imagine the rage Ma would fly into when she went back there.

"Abigail? Please . . . will you be my Christmas bride?"

Abby had to close her eyes to the pleading in his. There was something else to consider. She raised her gaze and sought the refuge of his face. "When Ma finds out about this, she'll stop me from taking Corbin. I know her. She will never give him to me."

"She will give him to me!" Ben's voice was rife with conviction and purpose. "As your husband, I'll have the right to claim your child as my own. I know what I'm talking about, Abby. Please trust me to take care of you."

"I will. I do. But—" the fact remained, he hadn't been truthful with Ma—"she'll fight you more because you lied to her."

He stiffened. "You're right. As always, I was in too much of a hurry to wait for the right answers. I had to take matters into my own hands."

"You mean, you forgot to pray and wait on the Lord. Trust God to intervene."

Ben released a lungful of air and clutched her hand all the tighter. "Oh, Abigail, I love you so very much. And I'm so unworthy of you. I'm afraid that waiting on the Lord was about the last thing on my mind. What I meant was that I should have waited until I'd spoken to a lawyer." He hesitated. "Now that you know you're an independent woman and you don't really need me to save you, I release you from your promise to marry me. You were right about me. You deserve better. Someone you can respect and look up to. Someone who isn't always in too big a hurry."

His words shocked her. Had he been in too big a hurry when he proposed marriage? His face blurred beyond a sheen of tears. Withdrawing her hand, Abby slowly rose. "I . . . thought you loved me."

Ben sprang up and crushed her to himself. "I do love you, Abby. I love you so much it hurts. If you'll still have me, I promise that from this day forth, I'll try very, very hard to make you proud of me."

For a moment, Abigail revelled in his words, in the feel of his arms around her. Then, pulling back slightly, she gave him a watery smile. "I'm proud of you already, Benjamin Haynes. And maybe if we start learning to wait on the Lord together, we can always be proud of each other. Don't you think?"

"I think," he said, wiping her tears, "I need to kiss you."

Suddenly Ted's shadow loomed darkly over them. "And *I* think it's time I escorted the young lady to her room."

18

"Don't worry," Andy Sewell said confidently.

Morgan looked askance at the new friend accompanying him to the South Battery. *Don't worry?* Perhaps the Sewells and their influential friends had indeed done much to aid in the comfort of many newly arrived army officers, but that knowledge did not help calm Morgan's nerves. He had hoped to be going to the island headquarters at Castle William right now, not making another appearance at the jail where he had visited Dan. All Morgan could do was pray that the same redcoat who had escorted him to Dan's cell and then spotted him at the Clarkes' party a mere two nights ago would not be present today. Now that Morgan was engaged in clandestine spying ventures, the fewer British who might connect him with the notorious Haynes family the better.

The walls of the fortification closed in on Morgan as he and Andy rode past the sentries at the gate and into the brick yard. But oddly enough, the initial feeling swiftly diminished under the thrill of the challenge. Should the officer in question suspect him, Morgan would simply outwit the bloke. After all, the man was only a lobsterback, and the lot of them were little more than dull-witted louts.

Once inside the anteroom, Andy's friendly grin flashed as he strode right to the desk. "Good day, Corporal. I wonder if I might have a word with Captain Long, if this is a convenient time for him."

The young redcoat laid aside an official-looking document and stood almost instantly. "I'll get him for you at once, Mr. Sewell. Please, have a seat." With a polite nod indicating the seats along one wall, he exited a side door.

Morgan was both surprised and encouraged by the fellow's quick and cordial response. Andy and his parents certainly must have spread their generosity around to more than just the officers. Still a little amazed, he crossed to the chairs and sat down.

Lowering himself to an adjacent seat, Andy flashed a smug grin. "You'd best let me do the talking. Captain Long owes me."

"By all means. I can't tell you how much I appreciate your help, my friend. If you ever find yourself in Philadelphia, don't hesitate to expect me to reciprocate."

The side door opened, and Morgan's worst fear was realized. The familiar ruddy face of the officer he had seen on the two previous occasions came into view as the man entered the room. A few steps behind him, the corporal resumed his position at the cluttered desk. Captain Long straightened his cuffs as he strode toward Andy, but his steps slowed when his hooded eyes sought out Morgan's face.

Morgan opted for the offensive, extending his right hand. "So glad to finally meet you formally, Captain. Morgan Thomas, of Philadelphia."

"He's the son of a loyal merchant there," Andy piped in. "Acting as liaison for his father. He's helping to coordinate some business endeavors that will help all of us."

"Now I remember you," the officer remarked and ceased shaking Morgan's hand. He squinted in speculation. "You were here some days ago visiting one of our prisoners. A man accused of aiding a deserter, in fact. One of those rebellious Presbyterian ministers."

"Ah yes," Morgan admitted, instantly formulating a plausible tale. "But then, one can never account for a young belle's choice of a husband, eh? You can only imagine her parents' opposition to Susannah's union with a Presbyterian. Nonetheless, the family in Philadelphia wants her home to ring in the New Year with them."

"Hmm." Long's expression became pensive. "No more than mine would like to see me in London."

"Clayton hasn't been here long enough to appreciate our mild winters," Andy explained, then chuckled at his own joke. He turned to the captain. "Are the rooms we secured for you adequate, sir?"

"Quite. I'm in your debt, young man—and the envy of the other officers who accompanied me here from England."

"We try to do our best for our friends." He glanced casually at Morgan. "Speaking of friends, Morgan has been dispatched by his family on a rather difficult mission, as I'm sure you can appreciate. But he's managed to extract an agreement from the stubborn lady. If he can arrange for her husband to spend a few days at home with her—under house arrest, of course—she's agreed to leave for Philadelphia to visit her family."

Captain Long smirked. "I hear that city is far more welcoming to officers of the Crown than this Puritan pesthole."

"Quite right. As its name implies, it truly is a 'City of Brotherly Love.' And forgive me, Andy," Morgan said with a look of innocence at his friend, "but I might as well inform you that our parties are also considerably more lively than those here."

His chum did not appear offended.

The captain nodded purposefully. "I should like very much to be transferred there." It was a thinly veiled cue.

Sewell regarded the man with sympathy. "Considering that General Gage is doing his best to reinforce his position here, sir, I don't see much likelihood of accomplishing that at the moment. The situation in Boston is bound to remain extremely tense for at least another month or so. However, when things settle down, I'm sure a few discreet hints on your behalf could be made. Yes, I do believe it could be accomplished."

"But not for months to come." Long's countenance hardened. "Pity. But then you seem to be having the same sort of problems I am. In such tense times, I couldn't possibly arrange for the furlough of a known traitor."

One look at Andy told Morgan that the chap's resolve had turned to defeat. But Morgan knew this was not the time to give up so easily. "Might I suggest the possibility of vast . . . improvements, shall we say . . . in your day-to-day living conditions while you await your transfer, then, sir." Regarding him shrewdly, Morgan reached into his waistcoat pocket and withdrew a wad of bills, unfolding them slowly, elaborately.

The greed in the officer's face was barely disguised. After a slight hesitation, he reached for the money.

In the background, something clattered on the desk, a grim reminder that the young corporal was present . . . and staring.

Captain Long cleared his throat. Puffing out his chest, he glared at Morgan. "I'll have you know, young man, that I happen to be a man of honor. It appalls me that you would even stoop to something so low as an attempt to bribe a British officer. Particularly when the charges concern abetting a deserting army officer who not only brought shame to his regiment, but the entire British force in the Colonies."

"Ah well," Morgan said with a shrug of nonchalance, "I thought that in the light of present circumstances, you might just see your way clear to mollify Mrs. Haynes. But if not, there's nothing I can do about it. I do hope this little misunderstanding won't impinge on our further acquaintance. Perhaps we'll rub shoulders this eve at the round of parties."

Long didn't appear satisfied with the explanation, feeble as it was. He scowled and muttered something under his breath.

Morgan was all too aware of his blunder in not taking the presence of the corporal into consideration. Not only were the captain's fingers almost trembling in their eagerness to latch onto the money that had been under his nose, but he was also more than itching for a transfer out of Boston. Losing face in front of an enlisted man would be a bitter pill for an officer as proud as Long to swallow.

Morgan had just acquired his first enemy.

❧ ❧

The sturdy workhorse clopped steadily through the maze of Boston streets as Prudence guided the wagon toward the dock of the Charlestown ferry. Pa would be more than pleased that she had been able to purchase the rope, sailcloth, baskets, and new kegs needed to replenish their store across the Charles River. But her satisfaction was short lived when she thought of her humiliation—or rather, defeat—at the hands of that Tory brute. To think she had lied to Pa just so he would allow her to spend the night in Boston . . . and for naught.

Well, it wasn't exactly a lie, she assured herself. She had, in fact, spent the night with her friend, Judith . . . just not the entire evening. But oh, what a grand plan it had been. *Or could have been, if not for that man.* Still, it was gratifying to discover that she had been right—there had been many high-ranking officers at the party and so many loose tongues wagging.

Boisterous hoots ahead drew her attention to a group of soldiers who were squatting between two buildings, wagering on a game of dice. She glared at them in scorn as she passed by. Boston had certainly gone to the dogs. Redcoated dogs.

It was a pity her efforts had been cut short when she had merely been doing her part to help return the beloved city to its original state. In all likelihood she could have discovered any number of things that might have been of benefit to the patriots. After all, she hadn't been wasting *her* time ogling members of the opposite gender—however dashing they might be. She had been occupied with the business at hand.

At the memory of that compelling face, Prudence pressed her lips more tightly together. Mr. Thomas was nothing but a bounder in fancy clothes. She had half a mind to seek him out and ask if he had stopped eyeing the young women at the party long enough to learn anything of actual value.

If he was a spy at all. He might have been merely toying with her, scheming to get her in his debt for his own carnal purposes later on. Her cheeks warmed. Papa had warned her often enough about that sort of fellow.

"Hey, there, me bonny lass," a lout in uniform called from the doorway of a mughouse. "You need a hand?"

Another redcoat swaggered out beside him with a lopsided grin. "Aye, sweets, Gordy's real good with his hands."

Prudence, appalled by their brashness in broad daylight, ignored them and slapped the traces slightly on the horse's back, coaxing it a little more quickly despite the abundance of other traffic.

"Hey, wait up," they yelled.

Glancing over her shoulder, Prudence saw them staggering unevenly after her. Her fingers closed around the handle of the whip.

Just ahead, a kindly townsman set down a barrel he and another man had been loading onto a wagon. "Don't worry none, missy," he said as she neared. "You just go on home. The two of us'll handle things here."

"Thank you," she breathed. With a smile and a wave, she drove away from the inevitable brawl about to take place. As the voices behind her grew louder, a part of her wished she could stay to watch the two lobsterbacks receive their come-uppance. Next time she came into town for supplies, she decided, she'd have Pa's musket with her. Then she would see who ran away and who stayed.

As she drove by the Green Dragon Tavern, Prudence eyed the notorious patriot enclave with disappointment. Had she been successful at the party, she might have been able to walk calmly and confidently in there today and announce some key bit of information to the patriot leaders who frequented it. She pictured herself imparting the monumental details of General Gage's next takeover—New York. Or Philadelphia. Just envisioning her part in such a coup brought a smile. Gage's efforts would be doomed to failure, and freedom for the Colonies would be within sight. All thanks to her.

But as she basked in imaginary glory, her conscience reminded her that glory belongs to the Lord. God's glory and the furtherance of his holy and righteous cause was what she should be seeking.

A bit deflated, she stole a quick backward glance at the tavern. Was that upstart spy inside even now, passing on information she might easily have garnered herself? If she ever set eyes on him again, she'd give him a piece of her mind about interfering in other people's lives and callings.

She longed to rein in and peek through a window, but she managed to resist the temptation—barely. There really wasn't time for such nonsense, she assured herself. And anyway, he probably wasn't even a real spy.

19

Another in an endless series of giggles erupted from across the Clarkes' sitting room, drawing Morgan's glance to the two outrageously flirtatious young ladies Andy Sewell had brought with him for a visit. The damsels, seated demurely upon the settee, alternately sipped from bone-china cups and tittered at the various comments Andy tossed about. Morgan found their voices irritating, their personalities sadly lacking, and the whole scene aggravating.

Occupying a chair some distance away, he ceased studying the wallpaper and contemplated instead the high-ceilinged room with its heavy moldings. A clock similar to one at his parents' home ticked away the seconds, the reflected light from its pendulum glittering against a crystal vase on the nearby desk.

It wasn't that the belles weren't attractive, he decided, as he raked them with a critical glance. The one with auburn hair, in fact, had a captivating face, albeit a little long and thin in keeping with her waiflike form. The other, a brunette elaborately coiffed and dressed, leaned toward plumpness. She appeared uncomfortably constrained by the whalebone corset that squeezed her into the contours of her stylish morning gown. Morgan couldn't remember either of their names, but it was of no consequence, for he knew he would be leaving shortly.

Andy's voice cut across his musings. "Of course, I must

admit, I was far off the mark in handling the captain at the South Battery. I'm only hoping Morgan, here, will not hold it against me."

"Don't be ridiculous," Morgan answered, entering the conversation. "You're not in the least to blame."

"That may be," his friend returned. "But a person would have to be blind not to notice the animosity the officer has shown toward you these past two nights. The man has been quite adept at putting a damper on the festivities. From the way he's been watching you, one would think you were one of those traitorous ruffians from down on the ropewalks."

The auburn-haired girl frowned. "Why, how positively shocking that an honored guest from Philadelphia would be treated in such an offensive manner. Who is the officer in question?"

"It doesn't matter." Morgan saw through her ploy at once. After having danced with any number of the high-handed king's puppets on the previous evening, she now felt the need to butter him up. He flicked a stray thread from his breeches. "The ill temper of some transient soldier is not worth discussing."

"Tsk, tsk. I know just what you mean," the plump one said. "The officers do seem quite moody of late."

The two girls exchanged mirthful glances and erupted into another giggle, as if sharing some silly secret.

"What, pray tell, is so funny?" Andy asked.

Approaching footsteps precluded their response as Richard Clarke strode into the room. "A letter has just arrived from Philadelphia for you, Morgan. Hand delivered." The distinguished man held it out, obviously curious but not crass enough to ask questions.

Fully aware of the contents of the missive, since he had penned it himself early that morning and then arranged for its delivery, Morgan feigned considerable interest as he ripped open the envelope and scanned the contents. He glanced up at everyone present. "I'm afraid my father has taken ill. I must pack and leave at once to look after the business. Especially," he added for Mr. Clarke's benefit, "now that we've so much new business to attend to."

"Oh. Sorry the news wasn't of something more pleasant." Mr. Clarke pursed his thick lips in thought. "I only wish I could disassemble some of our empty warehouses and send them along with you, my boy. But alas, even if I could do such a thing, they're scheduled for use by the troops for housing facilities. The army sent a man by yesterday informing me of their need, what with extra troops due to arrive at any time."

Andy turned to Morgan with a crestfallen expression. "Well, I admit I shall be truly sorry to see you leave. As soon as I escort these delightful young ladies home, I'll be glad to accompany you as far as the Neck. You should be finished packing by the time I return."

His friend's generosity touched Morgan, but he had important stops to make before he left the city. He tried not to think about the possibility that one day soon he and Andy might be facing one another across battle lines. "No need for you to bother, old man. I'll just throw a few necessities together now. My trunk can be picked up later."

"Please allow us to have it transported at least as far as the port at Salem for you," Mr. Clarke offered. "It would be no trouble at all."

"Thank you, but no," Morgan said quickly. He had no intention of going any farther than Rhode Island. "You've done far too much on my behalf as it is. You've been a gracious host, making me feel most welcome during my stay. I'll just arrange for shipment on my way out of town."

His host gave a nod of acceptance.

Morgan turned to Andy. "If you and your lovely ladies will wait a few minutes for me to gather my things, I'd be happy to ride along with you a bit."

"Splendid." Sewell's happy grin included the two belles.

A flicker of guilt pricked him at Andy's sincerity, for Morgan had done nothing but use the fellow since arriving in town. But he quickly hardened himself against it. A conscience was a dangerous luxury no spy could afford.

❦ ❧

Leftover wisps of fog rolled gradually out to sea, leaving the misty freshness of late morning in its place. Morgan inhaled the salty air and waved as Andy and his young maidens turned off Middle Street. He continued a block farther in the direction of the Neck, then detoured toward the harbor and Ana Street instead. No sense leaving Boston without one last attempt to locate the enchanting Miss Endecott. After all, it was a mission of mercy. Someone must convince the beautiful creature that spying would put her at peril.

Unbidden memories of her graceful movements drifted across his mind. He could still see the candlelight sparkling against the long, dark strands of her hair, see her slender fingers offering him a drink from the ornate tray. But it was the daring gleam in her silver-gray eyes that worried him.

Coming upon the modest house where he thought he had seen her a few days ago, he reasoned that she couldn't live there, or she wouldn't have knocked. But neither could she be a stranger, or she wouldn't have walked right in. He dismounted, went to the door, and rapped lightly.

"Come in," a voice called from inside.

So much for that last brilliant theory, Morgan thought wryly as he entered the structure.

The room was small and dim, cluttered with bundles of reeds and straw. Stacks of baskets in assorted sizes and shapes lined one whole wall. Opposite them, a large woman sat in the light of the window, weaving a basket.

"Forgive me manners, laddie," she said pleasantly, "but I've got me hands full, as ye can see. Pick out whatever kind ye need." With a nod of her head she indicated her inventory. "I'll give ye a good price."

Considering her appraisal of the fine quality clothes he wore, Morgan had his doubts about her last remark. He smiled thinly. "Actually, mistress, I've come hoping to find someone. Prudence Endecott, by name."

The woman's flabby cheeks plumped as she pressed her lips together momentarily. "Don't sound familiar."

"Are you quite certain? I saw her come here just two days ago . . . long black hair, gray eyes, hires out as a maid."

"Fancy the skinny ones, eh?" She laughed, causing the basket to bounce on the broad expanse of her belly. From another straw container lying at her feet, an overfed cat emerged with an elaborate stretch. It gave Morgan an imperious glance. "What would a rich lad like yourself want with a poor workin' gal?"

"You do know her, then," Morgan said with relief, ignoring both the question and the cat, who had begun winding itself around his legs.

"Now, I didn't say that." She narrowed her sly eyes.

Apparently this was going to take some persuasion. Already toying with coins in his pocket, he pulled some out and looked them over with casual disinterest. "I'd be most grateful for whatever information you might be able to give me." Her gaze was riveted on the money, and he dropped several coins into her hand, hoping *this* attempt at bribery might meet with a little more success than the last.

While he gingerly tried to nudge aside the pesky animal, the old lady slipped the coins into her apron, then wagged a finger at him. "I better not hear you've been anything but a gentleman, hear?"

"What? You would doubt my honor?" Morgan asked with a devilish grin.

Her gaze did not waver. "A laddie as good lookin' as you gets used to things coming to him pretty easy. But I s'pose if I don't tell ye where the gal is, you'll likely find out from somebody else." She hesitated, as if about to reconsider.

Morgan held his breath.

"The gal you're talking about came here to buy some baskets. A dozen of the big ones and a dozen of the next smaller size. She came back later with a horse and wagon and took 'em away with her."

Surely that wasn't the whole story. There had to be more. "Where?"

"How should I know? Back home, I 'spect." She resumed her weaving.

The impulse to shake the rest out of her was quite tempting. But grousing inwardly, Morgan withdrew a few more coins instead. These he let clink idly from one hand to the other, while she eyed them with a hungry desperation. "And where might that be, I wonder?"

She focused on him for a second, then went back to staring at the money. "To her pa's store in one of them little villages north of here. Lexington, Bedford . . . you know, one of them little farm towns." She reached to intercept a coin.

Morgan inched it back, just beyond her grasp. It hadn't even dawned on him that the maid could live somewhere other than Boston. How had she come to be spying at the Clarkes'? He glared at the weaver. "If you're lying, I'll be back."

Stiffening righteously, she shook her head. "Me word's as good as me workmanship."

Morgan switched his attention to the nearest baskets—tidy weaving, perfect symmetry. It told a lot about the old gal. He dropped two coins into her palm with a tiny wink. "And if it's not, *mine* is."

❦ ❦

"I do hope this is everything," Susannah said as she picked up Felicia's overstuffed carpetbag and started down the stairs with Julia Rose balanced on her other hip.

"It feels like almost everything I possess!" Felicia admitted, a flush rising to her cheeks as she struggled with two other heavy bags.

A ball bounced past them and down the steps. Brushing their skirts aside, Miles scampered after it.

"I'm going to miss that noisy tyke," Felicia said wistfully.

Susannah laughed. "If it's noise you crave, I'm quite sure you'll find plenty of it at Dan's parents'. From what I understand, the house will be filled to overflowing with children of every shape and size. Between Dan's sisters, there are ten grandchildren—and if Ben brings his Abigail, there'll be two more."

"Wonderful. It'll do Yancy good, give him some practice for the day the Lord blesses our household with little ones." She stopped abruptly. "You do think he'll be there, don't you?"

Susannah paused and turned to her. "Yancy said he'd meet you in Rhode Island for Christmas, and if I know the man, he'll keep his word even if it means breaking out the oars and rowing the ship by himself."

"Yes, you're right." With a far more cheerful smile, Felicia continued down the steps. "I pray Dan will be home here with you, too."

Susannah had her doubts, since Morgan had never returned with the good news. Still, she wasn't ready to give in to hopelessness just yet. It had only been a few days. "When did Mr. Keith say he'd be by with his wagon?"

"Around noon. He says it will likely take most of the day to get past the Neck, but that's wiser than waiting to leave tomorrow before dawn. I don't want to chance missing the morning stage to Providence."

Such a wonderful gathering it would be, so much of Dan's family all in one place at the same time. Wishing for all the world that she and Dan were going, too, Susannah blinked back her tears. She was determined not to put a damper on her friend's excitement. "Give my best regards to Mr. and Mrs. Burns in Cambridge, will you, dear? They've been such a godsend to us all, taking in so many of our strays without a thought of their own well-being."

The sound of hoofbeats filtered in from behind the house.

"Did you hear that?" Susannah whispered. "Only someone who doesn't wish to be seen comes 'round the back way."

She and Felicia set the valises down on the landing, then hurried to the kitchen as someone rapped on the door.

Susannah gathered herself and calmly answered the summons. "Morgan!" Tucking the baby under one arm, she cast a quick look around and stepped aside so he could enter. Then, closing the door, she took closer note of his expression. She held her breath.

Beneath worried brows, his dark blue eyes held none of their usual roguish glint. He shook his head sadly. "I can't tell you how sorry I am, Susannah. I was careless, and the man balked."

Her heart sank at the dire finality of his words, but Susannah knew there would be plenty of opportunity to brood and weep later, when she was alone. She composed a cheerful face and forced a smile. "I'm sure you did your very best. After all, there really wasn't much hope for Dan's release from the start. I'm deeply grateful for your effort." She motioned toward the table. "Won't you have a seat? I'll put on the kettle."

He merely stared at her, his remorse—and possible guilt— making him appear vulnerable. Then his gaze dropped to the baby, and he brushed a hand over her silky head. "So this is the one you named after Julia Chandler."

At the reminder of the childhood friend she'd come to the Colonies to live with, Susannah recalled with sadness that Morgan and his classmates were among the last ones to hear dear Julia's lilting laughter. "Have you heard from her husband recently?" she finally managed.

"Not for more than a year now. Last I heard, Robert was still down in North Carolina, running his father's plantation. To my knowledge, he's never remarried. He took his wife's death rather hard."

"Yes, so I've been told," Susannah sighed. Lonely though these solitary days might be, at least her Dan was still alive and near enough to visit almost at will.

"And this," Felicia cut in brightly, "is Miles Edmond." Stepping forward, she tugged the child along. "He's named for his grandfathers. Aren't you, dear?" Bending down to his level, she nodded in Morgan's direction. "This is an old friend of your mama's. His name is Mr. Thomas."

The child shot a quizzical gaze upward. "You don't look old.

Not like Mr. Simms." He proudly thrust out his hand. "See my ball?"

Morgan chuckled and stooped down. "Best ball I've ever seen, young man."

"Corp'l Williams gave it to me."

Elevating a brow, Morgan glanced up at Susannah.

"You needn't look so haughty," Felicia piped in. "He and several other soldiers were ever so kind to us when they were guarding the house. In fact, they still are, despite our differences."

"I know what you mean," Morgan said, standing again. "I've recently become acquainted with a singularly pleasant young fellow while I've been staying with the Clarkes. Under other circumstances I would have enjoyed . . ." He gave a resigned shrug, then turned to Susannah. "But that's not why I've come. I know Ben was very adamant, Susannah, about your going home for Christmas, whether or not Dan could accompany you. And we're running out of time. It's already the twentieth. So, as soon as you run down to the Battery and bid farewell, we shall take our leave."

"Why, that's very kind of you, Morgan. But I'm afraid I can't."

His mouth tightened. "I promised Ben I'd bring you. He says his mother is really counting on having you there. Surely you wouldn't want to disappoint the family."

Susannah placed a hand on his sleeve and smiled. "Dan and I were separated last year at Christmas, and it's exceptionally special to us, you know. It was on Christmas Eve four years ago that he asked me to be his wife."

"I see." Morgan's expression was impossible to read as he shifted his gaze away from her.

"However," she went on, "since you did offer to be our escort, dear Morgan, I should very much appreciate having you accompany Felicia and—" she mustered all the strength she had to say her son's name—"Miles. His grandparents have never seen him, and perhaps his presence will help make up for Dan's absence." With a questioning glance toward Felicia, she attempted her most cheerful tone. "You wouldn't mind taking him, would you, dear?"

"If you're really sure you want me to."

"I do, truly. And if Morgan goes with you, you can rent a horse and start today, be there by tomorrow eve." With a look down at her son's bright face, Susannah took hold of his hand and led him to the nearest chair. She sat and hugged him against herself and the baby. His little-boy smell and the scent of his hair caught at her heart, making her miss him already. She had to close her eyes for a second against the pain, but then she quickly opened them and dredged up one more smile from the depths of her being. "How would you like to go on a horsey ride, sweetheart? All the way to Grandpa's!"

20

"So kind of you to accompany me to see Dan this afternoon," Susannah told Elder Simms on their way to the South Battery. "I know it takes time away from your cabinetmaking." She adjusted her cloak against the chilly dampness and stepped carefully around a patch of ice in the walkway.

The man's bearded face scrunched into a smile. "Well, missy, truth is, it's getting more difficult all the time to bring in the hardwoods I need to keep me busy. Besides, the reverend needs your visits, him bein' stuck like he is in that rat hole of a prison. He needs to see his baby daughter, too." He tucked a corner of the carriage shawl more securely about Julia Rose in his arms. "Nothin' like a wee little gal to bring hope to a papa."

Susannah answered the man's smile with a wistful one of her own. "I hope so. She's growing so quickly. I don't want him to miss out on seeing her as often as possible."

"No doubt he'll be glad for the news you said you had for him, too," the elder added pleasantly. He nodded to an acquaintance who waved at them from a bakery window.

"Yes." Averting her gaze to the passersby on Milk Street, Susannah didn't know if she should feel contrite for leading the man to believe the information she had for Dan was urgent. It was far from that. She did have something to pass on to her husband, but the only real urgency in this visit was hers. From the moment Miles and Felicia left for Pawtucket, the house had seemed empty beyond endurance, lifeless as a tomb. Susannah needed to be with Dan. She craved the boost to her own hope that their precious time together provided. At least during their visits she was able to block out his surroundings and bleak predicament for a little while and imagine they were together in their home, living a normal family life.

"Don't seem nearly as cheery in the city as it should," Elder Simms commented as he looked about. "Especially seein' as how Christmas is only four days away."

Susannah followed his gaze. Noticeably few people were frequenting the shops, and the cobbled streets were amazingly clear of horse-drawn wagons. "Yes, so many have left the city. But still, I also expected far more hustle and bustle." Susannah took note of the subdued chatter and somber faces on the few townspeople in view. A far cry from so many merry Christmases she had known before coming to Boston. Now each holiday season became more depressing than the one before.

Just ahead at last stood the Battery, the stark official complex jutting against the backdrop of the partly clouded sky. As they approached, Susannah saw a young soldier break off from other army personnel and start toward her with a friendly grin.

Elder Simms muttered something unintelligible, and Susannah was glad not to have heard it clearly. The harsh phrase was best left a mystery.

The private tucked his military hat under his arm as he came near. He bowed politely. "Mistress Haynes."

"Private Blake," she answered, tipping her head.

"Begging your pardon," the young man said, "but some of the fellows would like to know if you'll be home tomorrow eve. We'd like to come by with our Christmas tidings. However—" his cautious gaze flicked toward Elder Simms— "should you be entertaining other friends, we shan't intrude, of course."

His offer touched Susannah deeply. There was a decided

lack of cheer at the moment in that big, empty parsonage. She hoped the exuberance of the young men might do much toward dispelling some of its gloom. "Why, how very sweet. I shall look forward to your visit very much." Noting an impish sparkle in the lad's eye, another thought came to her. "And I suppose the lot of you would particularly appreciate my extending an invitation to the lovely Miss Brown and some of her young lady friends, as well."

"Well, er . . ." The private turned the shade of his uniform and gave a sheepish nod. "But you needn't go out of your way. I assure you, I'd be most honored to save you the trouble and deliver it for you."

"Oh, would you, Private Blake?" Susannah managed somehow not to laugh at the love-struck youth. After all, he'd have been embarrassed in front of stern Elder Simms. "That would be truly helpful."

"Marvelous!" Replacing his military hat with a pat, he turned to leave, then whirled back. "Oh! Forgive my manners! Thank you so much." Straightening with a click of his heels, he then dashed to where his friends waited.

"Young love," Susannah declared with a giggle, recalling her own fragile first feelings of attraction to a certain dashing postrider a scant few years past.

The bearded elder scowled. "You know, don't you, that by encouraging Liza Brown to associate with that lobsterback, you're setting her up for severe criticism. Fraternizin' with the enemy, and all."

"Oh, but they're both so young and innocent . . . and so in love. People can understand that, surely."

"Personally, I don't see how any lass in her right mind could fancy a redcoat," the man said with a snort. "Even a young rattlesnake can be deadly."

"Why, Elder Simms, that hardly sounds charitable. The Good Book instructs us to love our enemies."

He gave a huff. "I don't think Jesus was referrin' to an occupyin' force, missy."

"I wouldn't be too sure," she said gently. "During the time

our Lord walked the earth, Jerusalem was occupied by Rome. And one of the people he healed was the servant of a soldier, remember?"

"Nevertheless," came his adamant response, "that didn't prevent the Romans from destroying Jerusalem, if you recall. Tearing it down stone by stone . . . and here we are in the same boat again."

Susannah found his words disturbing and sent aloft a quick prayer that history would not repeat itself, that Boston would not be reduced to rubble.

The morbid thought nagged her as she and the elder entered the battery's gates. Among the uniformed men scattered about the grounds, Susannah spied Captain Long directly ahead.

Catching sight of her at that same moment, he stiffened and jutted out his already prominent chin as he stepped into their path. "I understand, madam," he said crisply, "you've requested a holiday furlough for your husband."

The niggle of apprehension she felt upon seeing the officer lessened. "Yes," she murmured. "I would be most grateful, Captain."

"Most grateful." In the insinuating way he mimicked her phrase, his beady eyes became slits in his ruddy face. "And how grateful, might I ask, would you be toward that philanderer, Morgan Thomas?"

Susannah cringed at the blatant insult. She reached out a hand to restrain the bristling Mr. Simms while she spoke as calmly as possible. "I agreed to then leave with him to spend the remainder of the holidays with my family."

"Hmm." The officer rubbed his chin in thought. "Then what he told me is true." His cool expression wavered, and he removed his hat. "I humbly beg your pardon, Mistress Haynes, for any wayward thoughts I might have had regarding your honor."

With renewed hope, Susannah accepted the apology and nodded.

"However," he continued, "I'm afraid releasing a suspected traitor is quite out of the question."

Her hope evaporated as quickly as it had come, leaving an empty cavern inside her.

"I suppose that means," Elder Simms piped in, "that your superiors won't be releasing Boston from your heinous barricade either."

Cold hard eyes flared his way. "I'll have your name, sir."

"Simms," he said evenly. "Ian Simms of Milk Street. Journeyman cabinetmaker."

"I'll not be forgetting." The captain's stare remained for another few seconds, then he turned to Susannah. "Good day, mistress." Pivoting on his heel, he marched toward the gate.

Susannah watched his stiff strides momentarily. "I do wish you hadn't provoked him," she said quietly. "He could cause you untold trouble."

"Not for much longer, missy," the elder scoffed. "Not for much longer."

His comment, though spoken casually enough, made Susannah uneasy as they continued to headquarters and entered the door. Inside, she paused. "Would you mind keeping Julia just a little longer while I spend a few private moments with my husband?" This was one time she truly needed to be close to Dan, to feel the strength of his arms.

The elder flashed an understanding smile. "Not at all. We'll wait in the anteroom, the little missy and me. You take your time. Come and get us when you want us."

As the guard accompanied her to the cell block, Susannah's gaze locked with Dan's. How would she tell him the news? She was certain he had been harboring hope of furlough even though he had told her there was very little chance of it.

Somehow she endured the endless seconds' wait until the guard left the cell, then wordlessly gravitated to her husband's open arms. "I'm sorry," she whispered, "so very sorry. Morgan was unable to secure your leave."

Dan cupped the back of her head and pressed her against

his chest. She felt him inhale a ragged breath. "I already knew that, sweetheart." He tightened his embrace. "And I'm the one who should be saying I'm sorry. If only I hadn't—"

"Shh." She leaned back and touched his mouth lightly with her fingertips. "I shall come and spend the entire day with you on Christmas. They'll let me, I know they will. We'll pretend we're at home, and we'll sing carols, reminisce about the gifts we've given each other in the past—"

He silenced her with a tender kiss, then rocked her in his arms. "And above all, we'll remember the promise of marriage you gave this poor excuse for a husband our very first Christmas."

"Dan!" Susannah jerked back enough to look into his face. "Please, don't *ever* say such a thing. Not even in jest. You are the most—"

Susannah stopped midsentence as the outer door squeaked open, admitting the guard and her lawyer, Samuel Quincy. After Dan's cell was unlocked and the door swung ajar, the solicitor merely stood in the opening. His expression gave no indication as to the purpose of this visit. "Would you mind following me, Daniel? There's been a new development in your case, which must be discussed upstairs."

Susannah's mouth went dry. She latched onto Dan's hand, but the encouraging squeeze he gave did little to slow the rapid pace of her heartbeat as she felt herself being tugged along behind him. A wordless prayer, fraught with all her anxiety, winged upward from the deepest inner longings of her soul.

Walking past the confused Elder Simms with baby Julia, Susannah put her hands together in a silent plea for his added prayers. Then she and Dan were ushered into Captain Long's rather drab office. Long stood rigid—and obviously fuming—beside a second officer of the British army, who was seated at the worktable. The stranger, clothed in the uniform of a regiment with which Susannah was unfamiliar, looked up at them. At his elbow, Captain Long clenched an official document in his fist. His eyes blazed in repressed fury, and he kept them trained on some object in the distance.

Quincy, motioning for Dan and Susannah to follow, approached the table.

The visiting officer put down the quill he was holding, picked up a paper, and blotted it. Then he handed the document to the solicitor. "I believe you will find this to be in order." Rising, he turned to Captain Long. "Seems I've developed a considerable thirst. Care to join me?"

Without so much as a by-your-leave, the two king's men walked past Quincy, Susannah, and Dan and strode out the door.

In the curious silence that settled in the officers' wake, Susannah saw the lawyer study the paper. "Yes," he finally said, the word ricocheting back from the stark surfaces in the still room, "it does seem quite satisfactory. Shall we go?"

Susannah felt suddenly light-headed and swayed against Dan.

"Go?" he echoed. "Go where?"

"Why, home, of course," Quincy announced, his mouth spreading into an enormous smile. "You've been exonerated, Daniel. You're free to go."

21

Sunlight glazed the snowy contours of Pawtucket, making everything glisten like the facets of a diamond. To Abigail, the spectacle was breathtaking. She surveyed the gently rolling landscape all around her, and when at last she set eyes upon the Narragansett Pacer farm belonging to Ben's parents, that sight crowned it all.

Abby gazed in awe at the neatly fenced sections of open land ringed by woods, the reddish brown horses sporting their thick winter coats, the sprawling two-story home that crested the far rise. She found herself caught up in visions of a reckless, wavy-haired youth, daring and adventuresome as he romped through the vast fields and forests in search of dragons to slay and peasants to avenge. It made her smile in spite of the introduction to his family that loomed just ahead.

Ben reached over and gave her gloved hand a squeeze as they rode side by side. Cassandra's eyes, too, were filled with wonder as she viewed the scene snuggled safely in front of her soon-to-be father.

Observing her daughter's contentment, Abigail found her own feelings of inadequacy had subsided considerably. And having listened to Ben and Jane recount family memories throughout the trip, Abby couldn't help but feel that being part of a happy and loving family, however large it might be, must be one of the grandest treasures of life.

She retained a few misgivings regarding keeping all the

names straight, however. She would thank Ben to her dying day for coaching her during the ride. Think of them in sets, he'd said. Caroline and Philip, Nancy and Lawrence, Emily and Robby, Susannah and Dan. Such a help. But adding all the children, plus the extra friends who might come, she began to feel doubtful again. How would she ever remember everyone? For a fleeting second, she entertained thoughts of turning her horse around and galloping all the way home. At least she had learned to ride her horse on the way here, and she wouldn't embarrass Ben on that account.

"Don't be nervous," Ben said, obviously catching her unguarded moment. "My parents are quite harmless, and they'll love you as much as I do."

Ted and Jane, riding double, came alongside. "And everyone is going to just love you, Abby," Jane assured her. "And you, too, Cassie. You're going to have such fun here."

"Will we, Mama?"

"Yes, angel." Abigail hoped her growing anxiety wasn't too apparent. The Preston farm had been a big step up from her humble beginnings. It had never entered her mind that Ben's family could be so prosperous. She had noticed, of course, that Jane's traveling clothes were of a much finer quality than hers or Cassie's. Would Mr. and Mrs. Haynes think her dowdy? She dreaded watching their reaction when Ben announced he intended to marry someone so insignificant as she. And the new gowns she had sewn for the festivities—were they truly the latest fashion? Had she done a good enough job on them?

As she thought of all the things that could possibly go wrong in the coming days, Abigail's discomfort increased to sheer terror.

Ted picked up the pace, and Jane tightened her hold around his waist. "Halloo the house!" he called, grinning from ear to ear.

Abigail's heart leaped into her throat. At any moment, Ben's parents would emerge and come to inspect her.

"Relax. You're going to love my folks," Ben said. "My father is a lot like Dan, whom you met a while back, only older and wiser. And Mother is always a gracious hostess, but she'll absolutely dote on you and Cassandra."

Ben's remark lingered in Abby's mind, and her pulse pounded like a runaway horse as they, too, drew up to the house. *A gracious hostess?* Mrs. Haynes sounded so grand, so frightening.

"Be assured," Jane went on lightly, "anyone who can put up with my brother will be welcomed here with open arms."

"If that's the case, sister of mine," he quipped back, "Ted should find himself a recipient of far grander treatment than Abby. I'm surprised he hasn't already run off to the wild frontier to escape your clutches."

At that moment, a horde of nameless faces poured out the front door and down the porch steps in a flurry of shouted greetings and laughter. Abigail picked out a handsome older woman who had to be Ben's mother. She was dressed in rich butternut with dark brown trim, and her regal bearing and countenance froze Abby in place.

Ben dismounted, helped her down, then drew her securely against his side. "I'm going to hold you tight until you feel ready to be on your own," he murmured for her ears alone.

Ben's mother, her arms wide, came straight for them. Her light auburn pompadour seemed to Abby like a queenly crown. It took great effort not to cower.

"Ben, my darling." Enveloping the two of them in a welcoming hug, she then pulled back and looked at Abby. "And this must be your sweet Abigail, the subject of so many letters of late. The first ones," she added with a playful jab of a finger, "you've bothered to write to your poor lonely mother."

"I didn't have anything worth writing about before," he said above the other noisy greetings.

Mrs. Haynes placed a consoling hand on Abigail's shoulder. "I do hope, my dear, that you won't let this horde frighten you. I'm sure you'll find us pretty harmless, once you get to know us." The warmth in her light green eyes and her kind smile did much to lessen the tension of the moment.

Abby suddenly realized that Ben's mother appeared to

have been worried that Abby wouldn't like *them,* rather than the other way around. Taking in all the hugging and the happy faces, she felt the sting of tears behind her eyes. She dipped in a slight curtsy.

Cassandra yanked at her skirts and held up her arms.

"Mistress Haynes," Abby said, picking up Cassie, "I'd like you to meet my daughter, Cassandra."

The older woman's face melted into a grandmotherly smile, and with a fingertip she brushed a golden curl out of Cassie's rounded eyes. "Why, you're just as pretty as your mommy. I do hope you'll call me Grandma, sweetheart. That is," she added, arching a brow at Ben, "if what the pastor says is true, about the banns being posted."

Abby was afraid to breathe. Perhaps Ben's mother did disapprove after all.

Ben had grace enough to look a little guilty despite his offhanded shrug. "I know I should have stopped by that day, Mother, but I simply did not have the time." He drew Abby again to his side. "But, yes, we do hope to be wed while all the family is here for the holidays."

The huge smile Mrs. Haynes bestowed on them more than bespoke her blessing as she stepped near once more and embraced the three of them. "Your father and I thought it might be nice if you took your vows on Christmas Day. What a very special gift that would be for us all." She looked from Ben to Abigail. "If it would please you, of course."

Such incredible things Ben must have penned to his mother to result in such a lavish and wonderful welcome! "Oh yes," Abby breathed. She raised her lashes to him and let her love speak for itself.

Ben's heart returned the message in a tender smile, and he hugged her. "I only wish Dan could be here to perform the ceremony."

"I haven't quite relinquished all hope," his mother said confidently, taking Abby's hand. "And now, sweet daughter, please allow me to introduce you to the rest of our rowdy bunch."

❧ ❧

Morgan had never known such a jubilant reunion as that which had taken place at the Haynes farm. By now the excitement had dwindled to quiet conversations, but the air retained a sweet, joyful spirit. He could not imagine his own mother ever willingly accommodating this many guests, related or not. Curious. In their visits to Philadelphia, he had thought Dan's mother was as rigid as his own when it came to propriety. But the night before, when he had arrived with Felicia and Miles, he didn't even recognize the once-haughty woman. Obviously she must have undergone considerable mellowing over the past few years.

He smiled and looked about the sitting room as the men prepared for bed. All the furnishings were butted up against the walls, and sleeping pallets covered the center of the floor. In the bedroom directly above, women and children still stirred around, their muffled footsteps barely heard over the buzz of low male voices in the sitting room.

In the center of it all, lying on his back with his eyes wide open, lay Ben—who, in Morgan's opinion, had mellowed quite a lot himself from the rash youth he used to be. Now the poor fellow was so smitten he couldn't see straight. No doubt he had managed to discover which bed had been assigned to Abigail, for he all but stared a hole through one spot in the ceiling, as if by magic he might catch a glimpse of his lady love.

A thud sounded overhead, followed by a scolding motherly voice.

"It sounds as if the stampede up there is coming to an end," Morgan remarked.

"I do hope so," Mr. Haynes admitted as he selected a place to retire for the night. "It's been quite a hectic day, however enjoyable." The weariness in his voice was also evident in his eyes and tired smile.

"The girls seem amazingly talented at corralling the herd, actually," Philip, an older brother-in-law of Ben's, remarked.

A round of quiet laughter followed.

"Speaking of herds," Caroline's docile husband continued, "since the Colonies met in Philadelphia, several of our most outspoken supporters of the Crown have packed up their families and left Worcester. Moved on."

"When ye say moved on," Yancy began, "ye don't mean to the west, do you? Now that the bigwigs in London have given control of the western territories over to the governor of Canada, our settlers out there won't be real friendly to any bootlicking Tories who show up. Especially since the British fur-trading companies are gettin' the only franchises. They're callin' the rest of us trespassers." Shaking out his blanket, he pulled it over himself and lay down.

Philip cocked his head. "I wouldn't worry overmuch about that. Our Tories were all making a beeline for Boston, back into the bosom of their redcoated cohorts."

"Benjamin," Mr. Haynes broke in, "you've been all over New England lately. Are those who are loyal to the Crown actually abandoning their farms and businesses out of fear of patriot reprisal?"

His son blinked and shifted his attention from the floor above. "I don't know a town that hasn't had at least one tar and feathering. No one is allowed to sit on the fence anymore. Everyone must choose a side. And the patriots greatly outnumber the Loyalists, especially here in Rhode Island. And, of course, in Massachusetts."

Ted, the last one still up, bent and blew out the lamp, leaving only the dim glow from the banked hearth. "There's never been any fence-sitting in the Green Mountains. They're the most freedom-loving bunch I've ever encountered."

"I pray they're as strong in their desire for the freedom and power in Christ," Emily's husband, Robby MacKinnon, said quietly, his Scottish accent rolling the r's. He gave his pillow a few punches before lying down.

Impressed by the Scot's strong religious convictions, Morgan remembered that Emily and Robby had only recently returned from living in Princeton, New Jersey, where they had probably rubbed shoulders with Dr. Witherspoon and come under the influence of the high ideals he passed on to his students at the theological college. A tiny twinge of jealousy flickered through him. He dearly missed his own years at Princeton.

"I rather wish that were true myself, Robby," Ted answered. "But most of the men in the Grants are hotheads who don't want to be controlled by anyone or anything. I don't believe the Lord could have placed Jane and me in a more challenging spot." He hesitated, then went on, "I haven't found the proper time to tell Jane yet, but I've agreed to be chaplain of the Bennington militia."

Ben snickered. "You won't, either."

"Won't what?" Robby asked.

"He won't ever find a right time to tell Jane." Ben cupped one ear. "Listen . . . I think I hear her upstairs even now, sharpening her skinning knife."

As the ensuing laughter died down, Yancy sat forward. "I'm facing a similar situation myself. We battled a fierce storm sailin' up from the Caribbean. Had to off-load the gunpowder in a remote cove at the north end of Long Island, then make port at New London. I dread tellin' me wife I'll be leaving right after the holiday to retrieve it."

Morgan, more than aware of Felicia's sharp tongue, chuckled. "Do warn me when you plan to let her in on it. My ears are sensitive to great explosions!"

The redheaded sailor laughed. "Ah, mate, but the makin' up, now, it does take away the sting."

"Right," Ben said, his dreamy focus again on the ceiling.

The room settled into a brooding silence. The men seemed to have lapsed into quiet reflections that Morgan assumed had to do with being deprived of their sleeping mates. It only served to reinforce his own conviction that marriage actually stole the freedom they talked about so much . . . not that any of the blokes seemed to realize it, much less care. That was the strangest thing of all.

Releasing a sigh, he settled down onto his pillow. But all too soon, his own thoughts wandered to the alluring charms of a certain winsome spy whose heart-shaped face and incredible gray eyes refused to remain forgotten for long. Still, Morgan smiled with the assurance that a person careful with his promises could enjoy feminine company aplenty without becoming trapped for the rest of his life.

"Something's disturbing the horses," Ben's father said, bolting upright and grabbing his boots.

Robby and Ted, both wanted by the British, pulled on their breeches and boots, while Morgan and Ben hurried stocking-footed to the door.

Two riders on horseback came into view, dark silhouettes against the bluish night snow as they came up the lane.

As the horses drew up in front of the house, Ben let out a whoop. "Susannah! And Dan!" Leaping over the porch steps, he ran to meet them.

22

In the wake of Ben's yell, Susannah saw oil lamps light one by one in nearly every room of the big white house. Faces appeared in the windows, then vanished as quickly.

Ben skidded to a stop mere inches from where Dan had dismounted. He grabbed him in a huge hug, then pulled back for a second look. "I can't believe it! I can't believe it!"

Family and friends streamed out the door, their excited voices carrying on the still night air.

Susannah clutched the baby tightly to herself and leaned into her husband's outstretched arms to be lowered to the ground. One niggling doubt had plagued her on the ride from Boston, and it concerned Mrs. Haynes. What if, despite the loving letters Dan's mother had posted begging forgiveness for her initial ill treatment of Susannah, the older woman reverted back to her cool reserve in a face-to-face meeting? Susannah fervently prayed that both his parents would truly accept her now, for Dan's sake as much as her own.

Dan, always able to read her thoughts in a most uncanny fashion, smiled and wrapped an arm around her for an instant before both of them were engulfed by Morgan, Ted, and little Miles.

"Praise the Lord!" Ted remarked with a stout clap on Dan's back. "You're here! You're really here!"

"Daddy! Mama!"

Dan's eyes shone as he scooped up his son in a fierce embrace. Susannah looked on tearfully at the touching reunion, then leaned in to kiss their oldest child tenderly.

"Come on, you two," Jane called from the crowded porch, where the rest of the assembly huddled together in their nightclothes. "It's freezing out here—and Ben's barefoot!"

Ben, hopping from one foot to the other, seized the bags tied behind their saddles as Ted steered Dan and Susannah toward the house. They were lost at once in another flurry of hugs and kisses. And when the most sincere embrace and welcome of all came from Dan's mother, Susannah had to fight back tears of relief.

Baby Julia, however, let out a full-throated wail amid all the ruckus.

"Let Susannah bring my granddaughter inside where it's warm," Mrs. Haynes ordered in her no-room-for-argument tone. "We're all going to catch our death."

How everyone fit into the parlor, Susannah had no idea. Someone had coaxed the fire back to life, and the heat from the dancing flames felt glorious against her frozen cheeks—almost as glorious as the warmth from the wall-to-wall smiles.

Then came a barrage of questions.

"How did you manage to get out, big brother?" Ben shouted above the rest. "Was it an escape? Did somebody arrange it?"

The volume from the infant went up a notch.

"Oh, please keep your voices down!" Mrs. Haynes scolded in exasperation. "Can't you see you're scaring the baby?"

Felicia came and took Julia to a more subdued corner while a dozen hands offered to take Susannah's and Dan's winter cloaks.

"Emily, dear," Mrs. Haynes said, "I think some tea might help to warm us all up. Would you set the kettle to boil?"

With a cheery nod, her youngest daughter whirled around in a swirl of nightclothes and left for the kitchen.

"Now," her mother continued, a surprisingly droll curve to her lips as she looked around the completely dishevelled room, "I'm sure there must be some seats around here some-where."

Susannah accepted Dan's assistance and stepped over the sleeping pallets to the gray-striped settee his father was hastily clearing of discarded clothing. Others claimed whatever chairs happened to be nearby. Most of the children had no qualms about dropping to their knees on the mats, but Miles rubbed his sleepy eyes and went straight to his daddy.

Mrs. Haynes cleared her throat, a pointed cue for quiet. "Tell us, my darlings," she said, including Dan and Susannah in her gaze, "by what wondrous miracle has God brought you to us?"

So much heartfelt tenderness showed in her expression and calm smile that Susannah felt the last vestige of fear vanish.

"Yes, Dan, do tell," Morgan prompted. "My efforts on your behalf fell miserably short."

Just beyond Morgan, Susannah noticed Yancy's dear face among Dan's siblings. Her adopted family was complete.

"Yes, Son. We're all eager to hear." Mr. Haynes took his wife's hand and tugged her down beside him.

The gesture had an almost habitual quality to it, a show of devotion that was second nature to them both. Susannah reached for Dan's hand and waited for him to relate the amazing story once more.

"Well, I guess it was pretty miraculous at that," he admitted. "All I can tell you is that my release came about as the result of a letter written by Alex Fontaine."

"But how can that be?" his father asked. "There's scarcely been time for a ship to sail to England with the news of your arrest, much less return."

"You're absolutely right." Dan gave Susannah a conspiratorial smile, then turned to her brother, who was sitting on the floor with Jane. "I think you will find this of considerable interest, Ted. It seems Alex truly did have the change of heart his note to Susannah suggested when he removed the guards from outside our house and returned to London."

"But what about the party of soldiers who raided Ben's place?" Ted asked.

Dan shrugged. "They must have been given orders by some other officer looking for a way to gain favor with his superior."

"Well." Ted relaxed quite visibly. "I'm most pleased to hear that. For several years, I considered Alex a true and dear friend."

A soft murmur circulated the room as the family tried to absorb the news.

Mrs. Haynes silenced it. "But there must be more to the story, surely."

"Yes." Dan's nod punctuated the word. "There were two copies of this particular letter. One went to military headquarters, one to Faneuil Hall. That dispatch, I'm certain, was meant to prevent the army from conveniently *losing* theirs."

"And?" Ben prompted.

"In the letter, Alex laid out the possibility that my disappearance was due more to his threats of arrest than to any guilt I might have had in abetting Ted's desertion. He had never uncovered the slightest shred of proof that I had, in fact, participated in the matter in any way—save my own disappearance from Boston. Thank the Good Lord, I might add."

"Don't forget the last paragraph, sweetheart," Susannah reminded him.

"Oh, yes. Alex, of course, had not received news of my arrest and thought I was still a fugitive. He wrote that he fervently hoped the letter would reach the proper hands in time for word to get to me. He was returning home for Christmas, and it was his sincere desire that I might be able to do the same."

It took a few seconds for everyone to digest the information. Susannah watched Jane and Ted exchange looks, and an expression of relief flooded Jane's face. All the trouble Jane had brewed before her change of heart had finally been set right.

"Well, thank the Good Lord, here you are," his mother said. "And here you'll stay."

"I only wish I could," Dan confessed quietly. "But I belong with my congregation in Boston. They need me now more than ever."

Emily came back from the kitchen bearing a tray of steaming mugs, which she began passing around.

Susannah observed Dan's graceful younger sister, who was already the mother of two little ones in the years since the hasty wedding Dan had performed in the parsonage. Emily and her fugitive husband appeared quite happy.

Sipping her hot tea, Susannah caught Yancy's eye over the rim of her mug, and he winked. It made her smile to realize that their dashing seafaring friend was now as much a part of this big family as the rest of them. And the Lord had provided him a wife as grateful to have him as he was to have her.

With a deep sigh, Dan's mother gazed, smiling, around the room. "You know, I had faith we'd all be here together for Christmas. Although I had no idea how, I knew our heavenly Father is wise and powerful beyond anything we can possibly imagine."

"See, Ben?" Jane looked askance at him. "Perhaps now you'll stop being such a bothersome doubting Thomas."

For the first time, Susannah noticed that her brother-in-law had his arm around a lovely young woman with golden blonde hair and startling turquoise eyes. No doubt she was the one who had caused so much of Ben's confusion these past months. "Ben, I don't believe you've introduced us to your companion."

He grinned. "I was just waiting for an opening. May I present my betrothed . . . Abigail Preston of Millers Falls."

Abigail's gaze wavered as a flush rose high on her cheeks.

Susannah thought she looked like a fragile fawn being protected by a proud buck. "Dan and I are pleased to meet you, Abigail. Ben has spoken so highly of you."

"Thank you," she all but whispered.

"Oh, but Mistress Preston and I have already met, sweetheart," Dan told Susannah. "I had the pleasure of enjoying her family's hospitality last summer." He beamed at the bashful blonde. "And I hope she will feel equally welcome here."

"It is our prayer," Mrs. Haynes began, "that Abigail will feel far more than just welcome. We want her to feel a part of the family . . . which is why we'll be calling on you, Daniel, to perform a wedding ceremony on Christmas Day."

"What? Why, that's splendid!" Dan grinned at Ben.

Abigail's blush heightened as she nestled more closely against her fiancé.

Then Susannah's view of the girl was blocked as Dan's mother stood and offered her hand to Susannah. "I think just now that one of my other daughters is sorely in need of a little pampering. Come along, my dear. It's time we took you upstairs and tucked you into a nice warm bed."

❧ ❧

Morgan saw Dan's face fall as his father restrained him from following Susannah.

"Sorry, son," the man said kindly. "With the number of people present at the moment, the only way we can house everyone is by putting the ladies on the second floor while we gents remain down here. I'll go search out some more bedding."

"You can have my pallet," Morgan offered as the older man left the room. Knowing Dan had been separated from his wife for most of the past year, he was more than aware of his friend's keen disappointment.

"Thanks," Dan said halfheartedly, his longing glance still roving the staircase as he unbuttoned his shirt. Then he exhaled a slow breath and sought what little comfort the sleeping mat provided.

The others, after a round of grumbling about the hard floor, also reclaimed their earlier positions, and within minutes soft snoring could be heard.

Morgan took up a post in an empty chair to wait for his bedding and, in the solitude, mulled over his own unrequited love for Dan's beautiful wife. The spirited English lass was everything he hoped to find in a woman, and he had been drawn to her from the first. Always vying with the other students to be the person nearest to the kitchen entrance whenever they frequented the coaching inn, Morgan had hoped to gain the upper hand and win their favorite serving maid's favor. But alas, the fair Susannah had already lost her heart to dashing postrider Daniel Haynes, and she treated all the theological students in the same friendly but quite proper manner.

Morgan had been prepared to dislike Haynes when Dan finally rode into Princeton to claim his love. But to his own chagrin, Morgan found the chap to be loyal and steadfast, completely companionable. And a person would have been blind not to see the love he and Susannah shared. At last Morgan could admit that the two were destined to be together . . . after mooning over her for the past several years. It was foolish to think he could have been a proper husband to her himself, with his penchant for living an adventurous and danger-filled life. The fact was, Susannah was completely happy, and that was worth as much to him as anything else.

He shifted his position as a few more snores cut irregular snatches in the cadence of their breathing.

Actually, he told himself, the kind of woman who would suit him was one who was as daring as he, adventurous enough to take risks of her own—and he vowed to scour every village north of Boston until he found her. With that heady realization, the weight of an old lost love slowly slipped from his shoulders, and an amazingly buoyant hope for the future took its place. Who knows, perhaps someday he'd find the same happiness Dan and Susannah shared.

"Are you asleep, Dan?" he asked softly.

"Afraid not." Dan turned and propped his head in his palm.

"Good. I'd very much like to give you and Susannah a gift. Call it an early Christmas present. I want to pay for your supper tomorrow eve at the inn in Providence—and the finest room they have."

"A night alone with the woman I love?" Dan gave an exaggerated sigh. "Heaven," he murmured. "Sheer heaven."

Benjamin let out a disgusted grunt. "You have all the luck, big brother," he muttered. "Between Ted and Jane and the rest of this clan, I'll be fortunate even to *see* Abby between now and the wedding."

"I guess I know what my wedding present to you and Abigail will be," Morgan told the soon-to-be bridegroom. "How about three nights at the inn?"

Ben turned back. "Make it five?"

The three laughed.

Morgan considered the request for a few seconds. "Well, I suppose I do owe you for helping me to extricate myself from my monotonous existence in Philadelphia. Five it is."

Dan suddenly sat up. "That reminds me." He reached for his frock coat on the nearby chair and withdrew a thick packet from the inside breast pocket, then tossed it at Morgan. "John Hancock came by the house within an hour of my release and wanted me to give that to you. Pretty fast work, I'd say . . . in Boston less than a fortnight and already in correspondence with the illustrious Mr. Hancock."

"I've never been one to start at the bottom," Morgan said flippantly. He rose and stoked the fire, then lit a lamp. He wondered if his spying had drawn too much attention, if he had been seen frequenting the Green Dragon. He had tried not to make any mistakes, but one never knew. He broke the seal and removed the documents—the written orders he had collected from the merchants authorizing him to take custody of their various cargos—and a letter:

My dear M. Thomas,

> *The Massachusetts patriots join me in expressing our appreciation for your efforts and ingenuity on our behalf. War with Britain now is imminent and very near, and considering her naval supremacy, our acquisition of direly needed supplies is certain to be hampered. Therefore, as we discussed earlier, increased importation for the patriot cause at this time is vital.*
>
> *To warrant the smooth transfer of cargos in Bermuda, we of*

the Safety Committee would be most grateful if you would sail for the island personally, as soon as possible. The enclosed bank draft should cover the rental of sufficient warehouses and, hopefully, expedite the re-crating.

You will be contacted there with further instructions for shipping as soon as those arrangements have been made. To ensure that my instructions are legitimate, the bearer will relate to you the name of a certain female about whom you made inquiry.

We thank you not only for your invaluable help this far, but for any future assistance on your part as well. If for any reason you find you are unable to comply with our request, please notify me at once.

This correspondence must be destroyed immediately.

Your most humble comrade in the cause,

J. Hancock

Not at all thrilled about this development, Morgan expelled a frustrated breath on his way to the hearth. He tossed the missive on the glowing embers and watched as it burst into flames and curled into ashes. He knew it was imperative for him to comply with Hancock's wishes, but he did not appreciate being relegated to tiresome warehouse work just now—especially since he had only recently escaped a similar fate in Philadelphia.

Not only that, but while he would be stuck in the middle of the ocean, the assigned password for the venture would be a constant reminder of the woman he had vowed to turn the Colonies inside out to find.

He fingered through the authorizations for a quick count, and his spirit deflated. Aside from the danger of being caught by some snoopy Loyalist merchant, it could take months for all these shipments to arrive in Bermuda and be rerouted. Months! He sagged down into the chair.

"Bad news?" Dan asked quietly.

Morgan answered in a tone as flat as his own discarded plans. "Sometimes I'm too clever for my own good."

23

The rosy glow of candles cast a tinge of pink over the lace and seed pearls on Abigail's ivory taffeta gown as she slowly entered the hushed parlor. She had expected to be nervous and fluttery when the moment arrived linking her life to Ben's for all time. But when her satin slippers whispered over the rug and dozens of loving faces turned expectantly toward her, a feeling of wondrous peace washed over her, completely erasing her fears.

Ben had never looked so handsome or dashing, standing resplendent in a burgundy frock coat and ruffled shirt over charcoal satin breeches, his love written on his face for all to see. And when his eyes met hers, Abby's heart tripped over itself, and no one else existed in the world.

When she reached him, his hand gently closed over hers, and they turned to Dan to repeat the age-old vows. Abby was lost in the beauty of the words, the sureness of Ben's responses. She scarcely heard her own voice as she repeated the same promises. Too soon the lovely service ended.

"You may kiss your bride."

Kiss, before his entire family? she thought in panic. But Ben's touch on her shoulders as he drew her near was so gentle, the smile in his eyes so tender. She lifted her lips to his.

From far away she heard clapping and laughter. She swayed against Ben and deepened the kiss.

Someone tugged on her skirt. "Are we married now, Mama?"

Abigail and Ben laughed and scooped Cassandra up into their embrace. "Yes, angel. We're a family now."

"Goody!" Beaming, she hugged them both.

Only one thing marred the perfection of this moment, Abby realized during that sweet embrace—the absence of her little man. Her Corbin.

❦ ❦

Ben and Abigail, still in their bedclothes, stood at the open window of their room on the second floor of the Grey Swan Inn in Providence, searching the harbor. "There they are," Ben said, pointing to a ship preparing to set sail on the morning tide. The woolen blanket enshrouding them both tugged a little off kilter as Ben leaned out. "Yancy! Morgan! Godspeed, you two," he called. "We'll pray for fair winds."

On the deck, Yancy grinned broadly and waved a farewell with his tricorn. "And much happiness to ye both. Take care."

Morgan, somewhat less enthusiastic, appeared to manage a thin smile as he, too, gave a nod and lifted a hand in a parting wave.

"Poor fellow," Ben said, drawing Abby tighter against his side.

"Why do you say that?"

"He's not relishing the idea of setting off on a voyage that's going to keep him from finding a young woman with whom he's recently become enamored."

"How sad. People should be together when they're in love."

"I don't know if I'd call it love, exactly. Not yet, anyway. But she certainly caught his attention. Must be someone really special for a man so cavalier as Morgan Thomas to be interested in her. He asked me to seek information on her in my travels, find out where she lives."

"Mmm," Abby murmured dreamily. She nuzzled against him, resting her head on his shoulder.

Ben filled his lungs with her fragrance, the essence of her

shining hair, which still bore the lingering scent of rose water. Whoever this Prudence Endecott was, she couldn't possibly hold a candle to his own sweet bride.

"What a lovely morning," Abby breathed. "Just watching the sun rise over the water, glowing bright orange through the thicket of ships' masts . . . it's the most glorious sight I've ever seen." She turned in his arms and smiled up at him. "Except for yesterday, when you took Cassie and me to look out over the vast Atlantic. I've always believed in God, but after viewing some of his awesome handiwork, I realize how truly great and marvelous are his ways, as the preacher says."

Ben drank in the vision of her luminous eyes and glowing face, her golden hair tumbled in shining disarray about her shoulders. Capturing a lock of it, he drew it slowly through his fingers. "It was morning when I fell in love with you. Did I ever tell you that?"

She shook her head, seeming more curious than shy.

Ben loved the changes he had observed, the trust that had grown in her during the five days since they had wed. "During a raging blizzard, I sought refuge with the Prestons. I was awakened the next morning by soft laughter. When I went to find the source, I discovered you and your babies playing on your bed. The early sun cast your hair in a halo of light . . . and I knew at once I'd found my angel."

"Angel?" she said teasingly, sliding her arms around his neck as the blanket slipped to the floor and pooled at their feet. "My first thoughts upon finding a handsome stranger in the house were far from what you'd call angelic." Her tempting smile faded. "And speaking of babies, it's time we go and collect them, don't you think? *Both* of them."

Ben sobered also. "Please don't go stubborn on me, Abby. Stay at my parents' farm with Cassie, where you'll be safe and warm. Let me brave the uncertain winter and bring Corbin to you, as I promised when I married you."

"And wait?" she asked, incredulous. "Not knowing? I *must* go back with you to get Corbin, I must. He'll need me if there's trouble. He'll be afraid."

"But you know I'd—"

She stopped his words with her fingertips. "Please, Ben. Don't expect me to stay here, so far away from him. This is something I must do. I'm his mother."

❦ ❦

With each returning mile, Abigail's anticipation increased. And so did her apprehension . . . especially as the landscape of the Preston farm came into sight. She couldn't help wondering if they should have brought Ted and Jane along this time also. Ted might have been able to help Ben, and Jane's faith seemed ever so much stronger than Abby's wavering acceptance of God's power. Fears and doubts had made Abby's attempts at prayer during the three days of riding all but nil.

Ben had done his best to bolster her optimism with smiles, hugs, and encouraging words all along the way. But Abby couldn't forget that Ma was like a wall—her voice, her will, even her bodily strength. *Stop it!* she commanded herself silently. *We have right on our side, and that must count for something.*

At last they broke out of the trees and could see the house nestled in the clearing. It looked so dismal now, much less grand than it used to seem to Abby. Among other things, it needed a new coat of paint. And yet this house, this land—all of it—belonged to her. She must remember that when Ma started in with her bullying.

"Look." Ben tipped his head. "It's Wesley."

Abby glanced nervously toward the house, where a grinning Wes waved his hammer at them from atop the roof. She saw him move to the edge and begin climbing down the ladder. Remembering his earlier offer to her, she felt a little more hopeful. "I think he'll help us."

"That wouldn't surprise me," Ben replied. "He was willing to help you leave in secret."

"He fears Ma won't keep her promise to him if Corbin is around."

"I see his point."

"I've never seen him stand up to Ma, though. He usually goes along with whatever either of them wants."

"All I need is for him to stay out of my way," Ben said flatly. "Not interfere when I confront Ma. And you don't have to be there, either," he added, bringing his mount to a halt. "I'd really rather you waited here at the end of the lane till I bring Corbin out to you."

Abby did not stop, but veered from the post road onto the lane and kept going. "That's ever so kind of you, my dearest husband," she said sweetly over her shoulder. "But it's time I grew up. I'm almost twenty-one, and this would be a perfect time to stop acting like a little girl." She sat up straighter and raised her chin.

Wesley strode to meet them at the hitching post. "Welcome back. Where's Cassie?"

"Still with my folks in Rhode Island," Ben answered, dismounting.

"Oh? That don't make no sense." He rubbed his chin.

Ben nodded and helped Abigail to the ground. "Abby and I are married. We've come back to pack her belongings and fetch Corbin."

Wes let out a low whistle.

At his expression, Abby felt a jolt of uneasiness.

The front door flew open, framing Ma Preston, hands on her hips. *What was that you said?*

Abby's knees threatened to buckle.

Ben steadied her with his hand at her elbow and ushered her forward. "I said, Abby has done me the honor of becoming my wife. We've come to fetch her son—*our* son."

The older woman turned every bit as white as the snow. She crossed the threshold and closed the door behind her. "Over my dead body. You take that useless girl and get off my property before I get my flintlock and blow your heads off."

Bertha's running footsteps pounded out her approach. "What's wrong, Ma? What's goin' on?"

"That fool girl up and married the postrider, is what," she

spat. "Now they think they can come in here and take my Corbin off somewhere. Well, they got another think comin'. I let 'em take that snivelling Cassie, but they ain't laying a hand on my Corbin. He's *mine*, you hear?"

Snivelling? Abby railed inwardly. Cassie was *not* snivelling . . . and Corbin was not *hers*. It was high time she quit knuckling under Ma's abuse—if not for herself, at least for her children. The older woman was no more like Naomi of the Bible than she herself was like Ruth. And Ruth didn't have a child caught in the middle.

Clenching her teeth, Abby started up the porch steps. "You are not going to insult my daughter ever again, Ma." The authority in her voice amazed even her. "And I won't let you use *my* Corbin just to keep a roof over your own head."

Ma Preston's mouth gaped in shock.

Bertha quickly stepped into the breach. "Sounds to me like you marrying up with some no-account message runner's made you forgit who your betters are." She began stalking toward Abigail.

Wesley caught his wife and held her fast, despite her squirming to get free. "What d'ya mean, Abby?"

Abigail nailed her mother-in-law with a knowing glare. "Do you want to tell him, or shall I?"

"I ain't got nothin' to say. To you *or* him." Ma folded her arms in defiance.

"Very well, then. I'll do it." Abby turned to Wesley and the still-struggling Bertha. "I hate to have to tell you this, I really do. But Ma had no right to offer the two of you half of this farm. It isn't hers to give."

Bertie went still. She looked at her mother. "What's she talkin' about, Ma? What's she mean?"

Ma's hazel eyes narrowed and darkened. "Hmph. Don't make no difference to me *what* she says. Now or ever. This place is mine. I'm the one who did the clearing, not that lazy pa of yours. I did all the work. I *earned* this farm, and nothin' nobody says to me makes it any different."

Ben turned to Wesley. "According to the law, property

passes from father to son. This land went from Bertha's pa to her brother, and then to Corbin. When Corbin turns ten, this farm will belong entirely to him. Until that time, as his legal guardian, I am the steward of this property."

Wrenching out of her husband's grip, Bertha started toward her mother. "Is that true? All these years you been keeping me here with lies, Ma? Your own daughter?"

Wes caught up to her and took her hand. "It's a pure shock, it is. But you know, with or without this farm, I love you. We'll make out, the two of us. I'll take you with me back to the river. I'll get my old job back and take care of you. You won't be sorry, I promise."

"Wait," Ben interrupted with an upraised hand. "Neither of us has any intention of throwing you out of your home." He pulled Abby close. "If it's all right with Abigail, I think it would be more than fair to deed half the farm to you right now, for taking care of it until Corbin is old enough to take over his share. In the meantime, half the profits would be yours, and the rest would go toward improving the place." He bent his head and looked to Abby. "Is that agreeable to you?"

"Of course. Bertha has worked very hard here, and so has Wes since he married her. It's a fine idea."

"Yep," Wes said, narrowing his eyes suspiciously. "That's fine, all right. Too fine, if you ask me. What's the catch?"

"No catch," Ben reassured. "I'll even have a lawyer draw up a contract to that effect. What do you say?" He offered his hand.

Wes stared at the proffered hand and then at Ben. At last he grinned and gave Ben a hearty handshake. "You got yourself a deal. And you can count on me. Corbin will have a fine place to come back to. A real fine place."

Abigail wondered if Bertha shared her husband's delight. She had been unusually quiet. Would she accept this offer?

Bertie glanced around, then slid toward the porch. "Ma! Where's Ma?"

The bar inside the door clunked with a thud into its slot.

Abby's breath caught. She flew up the steps and yanked on

the latch, but to no avail. "I hear her running to the kitchen. She's gonna bar the back door, too, and lock us all out!"

"Ma! Ma!" Bertie pounded on the door until it rattled. "Let me in. I'm your daughter. Don't do this to me!"

"Bertie," Abby cried, grabbing her by the shoulders. "Where's Corbin?" But her sister-in-law had only a dazed expression.

"He's in the house with Ma," Wes answered as the sound of the older woman's footfalls echoed in the hallway, coming toward the front again.

"And this is where he stays!" Ma hollered. "Ain't *nobody* gonna take my boy. Anybody who tries'll get their head blowed off!"

"Mama?" came the child's wavery voice. "Mama? Are you there?"

Abigail swayed against the door. "Yes, angel, it's me."

"What did you bring me?"

"She didn't bring ya nuthin'," Ma railed. "Go back upstairs."

"No. I don't want to," he whined. "Mama? Come in." He banged on his side of the door.

A resounding smack split the air, followed by a little boy's wail.

"Ben!" Abby moaned, swinging around, unable to endure her son's whimpering. But Ben was gone! Then she saw him checking the parlor window. She rushed to him. "No! Ma said she'll shoot anybody who tries to break in."

"The gal's right," Wesley said, then motioned for Abby to go back to the door. "Keep on talking to her," he whispered.

Still worried about what Ben might do, Abby reluctantly complied. She saw Wes mutter under his breath to Ben before ducking low and slipping around to the side of the house.

Ben rejoined her, a determined look on his face. "Ma," he called. "Why are you doing this? You had to know that one day Abby would learn the truth about the farm."

"Not if you hadn't come sniffing around here, she wouldn't,"

Ma said. "That ignorant girl don't know nothin'. She can't even read. How was she to find out?"

"And what about me, Ma?" Bertha asked in desperation.

"You shut up. You always got what you needed or wanted. I didn't stop you from marrying up with that lazy river rat, did I? No. I didn't complain when you brought him home to live off us, did I? No—even though the big ox eats more than three men put together. Go on out to the barn, and set yourself down till these thieving buzzards go off and leave us be. And don't come beggin' to get back in again until they're at least a mile down the road."

A big tear rolled down Bertie's cheek. "Aw, Ma, you know Abby can't go without her boy."

The older woman did not respond.

Ben nudged Abby. "Keep talking," he whispered.

"Bertie's right," Abigail said bravely. "I'll never go without Corbin."

"Yeah? Well, you just listen to me, you ungrateful bag of rags. That's my boy's son, he is. Bone of my bone. Flesh of my flesh. Get on outta here and leave us be, so I don't have to hurt you."

Bertha sagged forward, letting her forehead rest on the door. "Did you ever love me, Ma? Ever?" Her voice broke on the last word as her big shoulders heaved with a sob.

"Aw, quit bellyachin'. And get away from the door, unless you want to stop a bullet meant for one of them. I'm a pretty good shot, ya know. Time was I could pick me off a wild turkey easy as . . ."

Ben turned Abigail around as Ma droned on.

Corbin, riding Wesley's arm with his mouth covered by his uncle's big freckled hand, blinked his huge eyes. Nothing could hide his excitement upon seeing his mama.

Wes motioned with his head for Ben and Abby to go to their horses, and they raced on winged feet to follow him.

Ben all but tossed Abby onto her saddle, and Wes handed the bundled Corbin up to her.

He felt so much bigger than he had been since her last hug,

and he clung so much harder. Abby smothered him with kisses.

"I'll have that contract drawn up as soon as we get home," Ben told Wes, shaking his hand with heartfelt gratitude.

"I don't have a problem trusting your word till then. Take care. The Lord be with ya both."

Abby, a little surprised that Bertha hadn't given them away yet, looked back at the porch.

Her sister-in-law was slumped in a heap on the porch floor, bawling her eyes out.

Abby couldn't help feeling sad for her. "I don't know how I'll ever thank you, Wes. We'll be praying for you. But you'd best go to Bertie. She needs you now."

He shrugged and nodded, sliding a glance toward the house. "I expect they both do. More than they know." His whack on the rump of Abby's horse set it into motion, and it clattered to a gallop.

"Faster! Faster!" Corbin cried in childish delight.

Abby allowed herself one backward look at the farm where she had known such despair and hopelessness. "But, Ben, how did you and Wes—"

Then she saw it. The ladder Wes had been using to fix the roof still leaned against the side of the house.

And Abigail smiled with the realization of the way God had arranged things for his own.

24

March 6, 1775

After putting the children to bed for a nap, Susannah cast an uneasy glance toward the parlor. Dan stood at the front window sipping coffee, engrossed in the activity out on the street. From his intent gaze, his restlessness, the drumming of fingers against his thigh, she could see he yearned to join the throng heading toward the Old South Meeting House.

On this the fifth anniversary of the Boston Massacre, Sam Adams and some of the other patriots had scheduled a church service to commemorate the infamous event. But underlying the surface of the memorial lurked a far more disquieting intent—to goad the unwanted military presence. The very use of the term *massacre* incited the army, for Boston's own courts had exonerated the soldiers who had opened fire on that day when they were cornered by a mob of townsmen.

Last night Dan had given Susannah his word that he would not be party to another gathering that could become as volatile as the last he had attended there—when a shipload of tea had been dumped in the bay. Still, she couldn't help but see the regret in his stance. Hoping to emit calm from her presence, she moved near and stroked his arm.

A company of soldiers trotted by in swift cadence, their expressions as murderous as those of the civilians they forced to the side of the street. The sight disturbed Susannah's spirit, and she saw Dan's jaw clench. "If only . . . ," she murmured.

He turned. "If only what?"

"Oh, I don't know," she said with a sigh. "It's just that there's so much hatred—everyone blaming everyone else, wanting justice, revenge."

He patted her hand on his arm. "It's the wait, love. Everybody's impatient with waiting for England's next move, soldiers and civilians alike."

Withdrawing her gaze from his sable eyes, she noticed the postmaster, a member of their congregation, approaching the wrought-iron gate. He came up the walk and within seconds knocked on the door.

Dan tucked her hand into the curve of his elbow and went to answer. "Won't you come in, Mr. Vickers?"

"Nay," the lanky, white-haired man said. "Just on my way to the memorial. Thought I'd drop this letter by. Want to tag along?"

Dan accepted the missive with a resolute shake of his head. "Thank you, not just now. Later, perhaps."

With a polite bow of his head, Mr. Vickers took his leave.

Susannah had wondered if her husband would truly keep his promise, and she hated that he had hedged. Nevertheless, she found some relief when the door closed and shut off the clamor from the street. She watched Dan scan the handwriting. "Who is it from, sweetheart?"

"It was posted from North Carolina and is addressed to both of us."

"How very odd." Susannah knew no one in that entire colony save Julia's widower, who would have no reason to contact them. "Well, open it. Perhaps it's good news."

Dan ripped the envelope open and unfolded two sheets of paper, then checked the signature. "It's from Morgan."

"Morgan? I thought he had gone off to Bermuda."

Dan chuckled. "Well, if you remember, he didn't remain in Boston more than a fortnight. Maybe someone caught on to that scheme of his to divert supplies to the patriots."

"I certainly hope not." Susannah fought back a feeling of anxiety. "Parliament might just come to their senses and allow each of the Colonies to send representatives to London, to have a say in the laws concerning us. If that happens, Morgan could easily be charged with—what? Piracy? That would be dreadful."

"That's a gamble I guess he's willing to take. But enough speculation, let's see what he has to say. It's dated two weeks ago." He held the sheets of paper out so they could read them together.

My dear Dan and Susannah,

I trust this finds you both well and happy as when we were last together at Christmas. What a joyous time that was for the lot of us. I must admit, I do envy you such a grand family. Ben turned out to be the happiest surprise. Never have I seen such a transformation in one who had been so caught up in the adventure of our cause. Without a single nagging word, his timid little bride has turned him into her stalwart champion. How I should have liked to stay around long enough to witness his taking on the dreaded dragon of Millers Falls! But alas, duty called.

My ventures on behalf of the merchants of Boston Town are proving quite successful. However, lest I tarry too long and chance the tides of misfortune, I felt it wise to move on. I secured passage on a ship bound for New Bern, North Carolina. Being in close proximity to former classmate Robert Chandler, I chanced to drop in on him. As I suspected, Chan is still rather morose about Julia's death. I have convinced him to accompany me northward. Perhaps the stimulation Massachusetts provides will bring him out of his doldrums. Most certainly burying himself on this backwater plantation has not been of much benefit.

We shall be leaving within the next few days, as soon as Chan obtains a manager for the place. I shall send word when we arrive. I will bypass the Neck, since my recent activities might render a visit less than prudent.

Speaking of prudent, I was wondering if you might have chanced to uncover any information regarding Prudence Endecott. I am still most concerned for her welfare.

Your devoted friend,
M. Thomas

A chuckle rumbled from deep within Dan. "The lad sounds as blithely reckless as ever."

"Oh, and I suppose you are not," Susannah chided. "After all that has happened to you, you still want to march up to Old South, when nothing but trouble can come of it."

"You know as well as I, love, why we returned to Boston. Thank the Lord, many of our laity have managed to leave the city until the blockade is lifted. But those of our flock who had to remain need to be confident their shepherd won't forsake them as well. And in order to guide them effectively, I must keep abreast of events."

The truth of Dan's statement could not be denied. But still, Susannah was unwilling to relinquish the joy of having him home . . . safe. She clutched the edge of her long apron in one hand as if by holding on to it hard enough, she might forestall his inevitable leaving. "Oh, Dan, I have no doubt whatsoever how this day will turn out. It can't be any different from when the Boston patriots called for a day of prayer and fasting for their lost liberties. General Gage countered with his Proclamation against Hypocrisy and appointed soldiers to pitch marquee tents just outside the church windows, where their fifes and drums drowned out the service. Both sides, remember, came within a hairsbreadth of bloodshed."

"Yes, love. And a riot was avoided because our more level-headed leaders did *not* stay away."

In spite of her desire to keep him as far away from trouble as possible, Susannah understood Dan's feelings. And from the determined set of his chin, she knew the argument was already a lost cause. She might as well accept the inevitable. "You are so good at twisting words to your favor. Very well. Go, if you must. But please, *please* don't get yourself arrested again. Or hurt. Will you promise me at least that much?"

An exhilarated grin widened his mouth as he nodded and plucked his coat from the entry-hall peg. "Thank you, my darling." Lingering only long enough to administer a quick hug and a peck on her cheek, he dashed out the door, pulling his coat on as he went. "Pray for me," he called back.

"When have I ever done less than that?" she said to nothing but the emptiness he left behind. Her charming but adventuresome husband had managed to slide ever so smoothly right out from under a promise. Again.

❦ ❦

Dan gathered his greatcoat around him and exited Widow Frank's front door. She had intercepted him on his way to the Old South Meeting House, and he was eager to get going.

"Let me know if you hear the least little word," the frazzled woman pleaded from the threshold. "Two nights is a long time for someone not to show up when he's supposed to. What if there's been foul play?" She wrung her bony hands. "Oh, I pray nothing has happened to him."

"Yes, ma'am. I'll do my best to discover your son's whereabouts. Try not to worry." Into his pocket Dan jammed the paper on which she'd taken an exasperating amount of time to list the names and addresses of the lad's friends. His instincts told him the kid had most likely run off to join a militia on the other side of the Neck, as had so many other rash youths who expressed a vocal hatred of the military presence in Boston. But in any event, he would learn what he could about the young man.

Meanwhile, his conscience nagged him about his promise to Susannah. Of course, he wouldn't seek any action that might bring harm to himself. Along with the lovely, wonderful wife the Lord had given him, there were two very sweet babies to consider now. Susannah had been forced to bear the responsibility of caring for their welfare far too long already. All he really wanted was to observe the meeting. Certainly there was little peril in that.

"Shame!" someone shouted from inside the big church as he neared the structure, and Dan surmised that Dr. Joseph Warren was in the process of delivering yet another rousing speech to those who had gathered for the memorial. Articulate and persuasive, the man was an expert at ruthless public attacks.

A fairly large group of redcoats milled about on the corner near the entrance while the citizens crowding the doorway of the church repeatedly flung nervous glances toward them.

Dan wedged inside the crowded building, disregarding the mumbling and grumbling of some of the spectators as he looked toward the pulpit.

There stood Dr. Warren, his generally pleasing countenance now stern, his long face troubled. Beside him stood the frail Sam Adams.

"Fie! Shame!" Several British officers brazenly took positions on the steps leading up to the pulpit, thereby trapping Warren and Adams with glares of utter disgust.

The cry of outrage echoed from another area of the huge sanctuary, drawing Dan's attention to even more army scarlet. There were dozens, and all of them came to their feet. "Fie! Shame!"

In an instant, the entire room turned to a chaos of angry shouts.

The soldiers drew their swords.

Panicked townsmen rushed toward the doors or threw open the windows.

To keep from being trampled underfoot, Dan beat a hasty retreat to a doorway across the street while hundreds fled the meetinghouse through whatever doors or windows provided the nearest means of escape.

The lobsterbacks followed them out, laughing in derision as they swaggered down the steps, still brandishing their weapons. "Fie! Shame!" they chanted. "Fie! Shame!"

The entire scene appalled Dan. How dare the British defy the sanctity of a church building and threaten those gathered in the house of God? His mind flashed to the sacking of his own church by soldiers on the pretext of searching for Ted. They had completely desecrated the sacred house of God.

For the first time he realized with complete certainty that there would be no turning back for the Colonies. And along with that thought, a strange calmness washed over him, and the words of Ecclesiastes filled his mind: *To every thing there is a season, and a time to every purpose under the heaven: A time to be born, and a time to die . . . A time to love, and a time to hate; a time of war, and a time of peace.*

Deep in his spirit, Dan knew that very soon a time of war would come to the Colonies.

And with all his heart he wished he had left Susannah and their precious children in the safe haven of Rhode Island when he had had the chance.

25

Ben left the Brass Horn Coaching Inn and walked outside, shading his eyes under his hat brim as the midday sunshine glared off the choppy waters of Salem's bay. Along the busy wharf, merchants and shipowners were overseeing the loading and unloading of cargos, both destined for and received from distant points of call. The waterfront hubbub carried easily on the salt-laden breeze.

A sharp whistle sliced the air.

Ben caught a jaunty wave as Yancy Curtis came down the steps of the Baptist church. Splendid surprise! The sailor's long, sweeping strides ate up the distance between them in a flash.

"Whoo-ee! Look at you," Ben teased, beholding his friend's stylish attire. Even his hair appeared relatively tame, all slicked back in a queue.

The tips of the seaman's ears reddened slightly beneath his tricorn as he clasped Ben's outstretched hand warmly. "Me wife's idea," he said with chagrin. "Says seafaring clothes are better worn aboard ship than to church. What brings you to this bustling harbor?"

"I just got in from Newburyport a little while ago. Thought I'd have something to eat before crowds of folks emptied out of the service."

"Ye should've joined us, mate," Yancy said with a grin. "The minister gave a rousin' sermon about not gettin' so caught up in the cause that we neglect to seek the Lord's will. The core of it was that as long as we stand by God, he'll stand by us."

Ben gave a hint of a nod. "How's the smuggling business treating you?"

The sailor cast a look of caution over his shoulder at churchgoers passing by, then leaned nearer and lowered his voice. "Ye might be happy to hear we managed to off-load a dozen more barrels of powder a few days ago before coming on in to the docks. But thanks to British paperwork," he added with a grimace, "I now have to twiddle me thumbs waitin' for our ship to get a sailing permit."

"Well, at least you're getting some rest," Ben said jokingly. "There's so much happening right now, it seems the only sitting down I get to do is in the saddle, riding hither and yon to spread the news!"

Yancy gave a knowing chuckle.

"I expect you've heard the latest, since our outlawed Massachusetts assembly met here only a few days ago."

"Aye. Ye must mean their vote to call for a second Continental Congress. In May, I think they said."

"Right. And it shouldn't be dull, seeing as how both Sam and John Adams intend to go again. Are they still here, do you know?" He glanced at the Congregational church farther down the street.

"Ye must be joking. Old Sam had to move on—or be thrown in jail for treason by General Gage. Word has it he had another meeting to go to in Concord anyway. Oh, enough talk about the revolt. I worked up a powerful hunger singin' all them psalms at church. Come keep me company while I grab a bite. You could tell me how things are faring with that wee bride of yours." Reaching for the door of the inn, he opened it, and they went in to claim the nearest table.

Ben's lungs deflated on a wistful sigh. "I've only made it home twice this whole month, and even then it was for only one day each time. Oh, by the way," he added a little more cheerfully, "your Felicia asked me to give you her love if we happened to cross paths."

A longing smile spread across Yancy's freckled face. "I take it Abigail decided to stay in Pawtucket with your parents, then, along with Felicia."

"Right. There wasn't much point in leaving her in a crowded room in Cambridge with the children to look after. Besides, any day now, trouble could spill out of Boston to the surrounding towns. I must admit, Mother took to Abby right off, as if she were just one more daughter. There's no way I could have convinced her Abby'd be better off alone—nor would I have tried."

A buxom serving girl brought over two glasses of ale and lingered expectantly.

"I'll try some of that good venison stew ye served last eve," Yancy said. Ben ordered the same, and the girl strolled back to the kitchen. Yancy returned his gaze to Ben. "Did your efforts to get your wife's son back meet with success?"

Ben nodded. "Old Ma Preston's a hard one, I must admit, but her new son-in-law, Wes, helped us considerably. She may hold that against him—for a while, anyway. It wouldn't surprise me if she even tried to ax his marriage to her daughter."

"Well, what happened?" As a steaming bowl was set before him, Yancy broke off a chunk of bread and dipped it into the broth.

With a shrug of nonchalance, Ben condensed the experience to a reasonably short version while he and Yancy devoured the meal. "So," he said in conclusion, "I'm afraid we had no alternative but to leave poor Wes to deal with the aftermath."

"He sounds like a decent sort. No doubt he'll do what's right."

Ben nodded in agreement. "Oh, and one thing you'll be glad to know. This crisis taught Abby and me to start praying together. It's brought us even closer than we were."

Grinning, Yancy shoved the empty bowl away and took a gulp of ale. "So things are fine with you and your little family, sounds like."

"Fine as they can be with me gone so much. I sure miss them."

"Glad to hear that." The seaman drained his glass. "Oh, by the by, somebody needs to find that Endecott wench Morgan's so taken with, before the lad chucks it all and comes to do it himself. Last I saw him, he must've asked me a hundred times to find her. He was pretty nigh desperate, being so far away."

"I've been asking around, too, with no success. But for someone who had himself such a good laugh at my expense a few months ago, he sure is addlepated over a gal he's scarcely met." Suddenly Ben recalled his first glimpse of Abigail frolicking with her babies. He sighed. "Then again, I suppose it can happen like that from time to time."

"Aye." Yancy chuckled, then rose, slapping a coin onto the tabletop.

Outside once more, Ben noticed the sound of singing floating to them from the other church down the road. He cocked a grin. "Guess those folks have more sins to pray about this morning than you Baptists."

"Thought ye were one of—"

Approaching hoofbeats interrupted Yancy midsentence, and they both peered toward the source.

A galloping horse veered toward the Congregational church. Its rider swung off before his mount came to a stop, and he dashed up the steps and into the building. "The regulars are coming!" he shouted, the announcement easily heard by anyone in close proximity. "Marching fast toward Northfields Bridge!"

Ben and Yancy sprinted over to the church even as the congregation inside began to stream out the doors.

"I need some help hiding the fieldpieces," someone yelled.

"We'll hold 'em at the bridge!" another hollered. "Get the gunpowder!"

The locals scattered in all directions. They wouldn't willingly give up their arsenal as Cambridge had.

Ben wished he, too, had a home nearby and could grab an

assortment of weapons. But he had to settle for the pistol he carried in his saddlebags. He bolted for his mount. "Meet you at the bridge, Yance."

Seconds later, as he emerged from the stable behind the coaching inn with his pistol and cartridge box, distant notes from the farcical tune "Yankee Doodle" carried on the wind from a Crown marching band. The song, written to make sport of the homespun colonials, irked Ben.

The number of men converging on both sides of the deep inlet separating Salem from Northfields was increasing steadily. As Ben joined the armed townsmen of Salem, a splash of red uniforms came into view across the river—several squads of them, in full dress, marching right behind the band.

But the next sight almost made him laugh aloud. A drawbridge . . . in the process of being raised! And dangling from its ascending leaf was Yancy, Sunday coat and all.

Sobering, however, at the mutinous expressions all around him, Ben could make out equally rebellious ones on the faces of other colonials gathering on the Northfields side—their position a far more vulnerable one. On the Salem bank, an ominous silence settled over the group, as if collectively holding their breath to see what would happen next.

A Northfields man strode bravely up to the British commander at the head of the column. Ben had no idea what the fellow said, but the commander's response reverberated over the surface of the swiftly flowing water. "In the name of His Majesty, King George, I command this bridge be lowered!"

The colonial did not back off. With a musket cradled in the crook of his arm and a sword hanging at his side, he stepped right in front of the officer's face. A garbled exchange followed, interspersed with elaborate gestures and heated tones.

Around Ben, murmurs of disgust made the rounds, and the voices across the water could not be clearly heard over the din. The colonial raised a fist. "If any British soldier discharges his weapon, they'll all be dead men!" he railed.

"Give it to the bloke, Captain Felt!" someone near Ben shouted in encouragement, hoisting his flintlock aloft.

"Yancy!" Ben bellowed. "Quit being a target! Climb down!"

The redhead caught his eye and started to comply, then suddenly pointed across the water.

Ben followed the seaman's line of vision and noticed several locals racing to some beached boats the military clearly intended to use to cross the river. Leaping into the small vessels, they attacked them with hatchets and knives.

A detachment of regulars charged after them, bayonets extending the forty-two-inch barrels of their Brown Besses. "Desist, or we'll run you through!"

One Northfields fellow sprang from a splintered boat. Head high, he ripped open his shirtfront, baring his chest. "Do your worst," he challenged.

Red uniforms crashed into one another as the soldiers came to an abrupt stop, gaping in momentary shock and confusion. Then one of them stepped ahead and poked the outspoken soul with the tip of his bayonet.

It drew a fine trickle of blood.

An audible gasp burst from the spectators around Ben, and he was almost knocked off balance when they surged forward to the river's edge. He could only speculate what would happen next, but the offending king's man was ordered back into formation.

"Red jackets, lobster coats, cowards!" came a jeer from the top of the drawbridge. "A pox on your government!"

"Shut up!" someone hissed from below. "Want to get us all shot?"

On the other side of the watery barrier, uniformed personnel began to line the bank, their intent unmistakable.

Ben's heart clogged his throat. Visions of a volley of musket fire, of the blood and destruction that would follow, came to the fore. If he died, what would happen to Abigail?

Just then, a minister, still attired in clerical robes, quickly made his way past the soldiers to their commanding officer.

With his own pistol raised, Ben heard himself beseeching almighty God in a most fervent whisper for a peaceful end to the confrontation. He didn't even breathe as he observed the unheard conversation across the way. It did appear that the cleric's presence resulted in a calming effect on the leader. Another hush fell on the Salem side.

In the quietness, the officer's response was audible. "I shall break into those buildings," he ranted, "and make barracks of them. I shall not leave here until I can get across the river. By all that's holy, I *will not be defeated!*"

"Sir," the militia's captain answered, "you have already been. Now you must acknowledge it."

The commander puffed up like a turkey and stepped to the water's brink, tossing a scathing look at Salem. "'Tis the king's highway which crosses that bridge, and I will not be prevented from crossing it!"

"It's not the king's highway," someone yelled. "It's a road built by the owners of the lots on the other side. No king, country, or town has anything to do with it!"

The officer's chest deflated beneath the impeccable uniform, and his resolve wavered. "There may be two words of truth to that," he said quite lamely.

After a few seconds of silence, the commander motioned to the militia's Captain Felt, and the two walked a good four rods away from the troops and civilians.

All eyes trained on the leaders. No one so much as whispered.

Ben peeled off his gloves and checked his pistol's load, deciding that at any second, the commander could wheel around and bark out the order to fire. And from the look on the faces of his troops, they would be only too happy to comply.

An icy breeze from off the bay to the east had been gaining strength, and Ben noticed that his fingers were numb around the handle of his firearm.

At last the two men returned. Felt cupped his hands around his mouth. "Listen up, men!" he shouted. "Colonel Powell has been issued orders to enter Salem. He cannot leave until he does. However, he has given his word that he will not trouble or disturb anything. He simply wishes to march over and march back. That is all."

Yancy shot a look of incredulity to Ben and sneered. "The blighter's tryin' to save face, if not the day."

"He's trying to do more than that," another voice replied. "The bloke must think we're a bunch of country simpletons. Nothin' but a bunch of Yankee Doodle dandies."

"Perhaps," someone else added. "But if what he says is true, we've won!"

"Aye—and without using up any of our arsenal, at that!" a fourth man pointed out.

"Be good lads, and lower the leaf," the minister called from across the river. "The colonel has given his word as an officer and a gentleman."

Several of the locals scoffed in disbelief, but after a slight pause, relented. A bridge guardian gestured to Yancy and the others up on the perch. "Come on down, men."

Within seconds of their compliance, the section creaked downward to settle against the other half.

The marching order rang out.

The Salem townsmen backed out of the roadway but kept their eyes riveted on the scarlet column now stepping in unison over the bridge.

Yancy came to join Ben. "I'd sure feel better if I had a Pennsylvania rifle in me hand right about now," he muttered.

"And I'd feel a lot better if we had the entire Massachusetts militia here."

Hard leather boots striking the surface of the drawbridge made a sound more harsh than the drums keeping cadence with them. And the demeanors of the redcoats were no less haughty as they passed by.

What utter fools we were to allow them to cross, Ben thought, tightening his grip on his pistol.

Yancy laid a calming hand on Ben's tensed arm. "Not just yet, mate. Let's give the Lord a chance."

The sudden softening of the sailor's tone caught Ben by surprise. Before the seaman had come to know the Savior, he had always been one to act first, think later. Ben relaxed his grip, and Abigail's words rose full force in his mind. *If we learn to wait on the Lord together, maybe we can both be proud of each other.* Exhaling, he closed his eyes and lowered his weapon. "I'm trusting, Lord," he murmured. "I'm trusting."

"Company, halt!"

Ben opened his eyes. The moment of truth had come. The army would either form battle lines or retreat.

"About face!"

Pivoting as one, heels clicked into place.

"Forward march!"

Ben's mouth fell open as soldiers with faces as red as their uniforms marched back over the bridge. It was nothing short of a miracle.

The British band struck up another tune, and this time "The World Turned Upside Down" blared forth from the instruments—as if they could not resist informing the Salem colonists what fools they were for not bending to the authority and *superiority* of His Majesty's own.

The upstairs window of a roadside house flew open, and a woman leaned out of it. "Go home and tell your master he has sent *you* on a fool's errand! And broken the peace of our Lord's Day, as well!" Her shrill voice carried over the noise of the instruments. "What did you think? We were born in the woods to be frightened by owls?"

From near the end of the column, a private broke rank and turned. He leveled his musket at her.

Ben raised his pistol and cocked it, taking aim at the soldier even as the woman flung one last insult.

"Fire, *if* you have the courage," she challenged.

26

Prudence expelled an anxious sigh and weighed the same sack of nails for the third time. Inventory was taking far too long, especially with most of her concern focused on Papa and how poor he looked. She glanced across the cluttered mercantile at him, where he sat having coffee with four of his cronies near the potbellied stove. Though he was making an effort to enter into the good-natured chiding and chatter, he appeared extremely pale and somewhat distracted. He blamed his lack of color on a restless night with his and Miriam's little ones. But Prudence hadn't heard anything unusual through the dark hours, and she suspected that Pa's appearance had to do with something far more serious than mere weariness. He had been losing weight, his walk had become halting, his posture noticeably more stooped. And when had his hair shown more white than gray?

She withdrew her worried gaze and concentrated on the scale once more, then wrote the poundage on the tally sheet before reaching for the next sack. Pa cared very deeply for his second family and would have been the last to admit he'd been too old to start over with a new wife after Ma died. But now, eight years later, the ruckus from four young, energetic children tearing through the house was the impetus that sent him to work in the store even on a day when he would be better off resting in bed. Why, he was even insisting he could drive the wagon all the way to Salem to pick up merchandise, since nearby Boston was blockaded by the dastardly British.

Prudence was sure she should be the one to make that Salem trip. What had been the use of Pa's teaching her to shoot the musket if he didn't expect her to take care of herself? It wasn't as if she'd be running into any of those foulmouthed soldiers . . . they would be foolhardy to venture beyond the Boston Neck these days.

There had to be some way to get through to her father, make him realize it would be best for him to remain here. She set the nails aside and moved from behind the counter, navigating through barrels of goods as she went to join the men.

"Well, let's face facts," one of them was saying. "We ain't never gonna be free unless we rid our shores of that pack of heathen redcoats. What we need is to—"

"Excuse me, gentlemen," Prudence cut in.

Their attention swung impatiently to her, obviously disturbed at the interruption.

She met her father's eyes and noticed dark circles starting to form beneath them. "Pa, I'd be most grateful if you'd reconsider and let me go to Salem. It's been ever so long since I've had a chance to visit Penelope Chester, and just the other day she sent me a card requesting I come to see her."

"Isn't that the young gal you used to call a featherhead?" he asked pointedly, not about to fall for her ploy. "As I recall, you didn't care all that much for her when she lived a few doors down from here."

One of the other elderly men snorted. "Featherhead or not, she did manage to catch herself a husband, didn't she?" He gave a playful wink.

Accustomed to their teasing, Prudence didn't let the remark get to her. If and when she ever chose to marry—and it would be *her* choice—she wouldn't settle for anything less than a man with grit and honor. Someone she could look up to. Someone who respected *all* her qualities, including her quick mind. It most certainly would not be the type who thought that a woman who could think intelligently was an upstart. "Pa," she coaxed, "I want to go. Truly I do. I'll take the musket. You wouldn't have to worry about me at all."

"Seems to me," one of the other men interjected with a smirk, "it's high time this old pappy of yours did have somethin' to worry about concerning you, Miss Pru . . . like maybe a beau or two that preachy mouth of yours ain't run off."

The group laughed, and despite her best intentions, anger began to boil inside her. She'd love to give the lot of them an example of how her "preachy mouth" could put them in their place. But this was not the time. Choking back a caustic reply, she stooped before her father and took his bony hands in hers. "I could hire one of Heber's lads to go with me."

He dropped his gaze and appeared to be giving the matter some thought. She could tell he was wavering.

Outside, a loud clatter of footsteps bounded up the steps, and a neighbor burst through the doorway, still holding the latch. "They run 'em off at Salem!" he all but yelled, gasping for breath. "Run them slimy lobsterbacks clean off!"

"What?" The men shot to their feet and brushed past Prudence in their haste to get to the newcomer. "Tell us what happened, Fred. We want all the details."

Prudence followed and pushed herself into the circle.

He nodded. "Sure ya do. Just let a feller catch his breath."

"No need to be standing in the cold, Fred," Pa said from the outer fringe. "Come in by the stove. My girl will bring you some coffee."

"Aye," one of the others agreed. "Miss Prudence, you heard your pa. Coffee for Mr. Dale." They moved as one to the ring of straightback chairs.

With enormous effort, Prudence pushed down her irritation at being ordered around by someone other than her father. But as she picked up the coffeepot, she discovered with dismay that it was nearly empty. "I'll run next door to the house. Miriam always keeps coffee on. Don't start without me, I'll be just a moment."

By the time she returned, however, steaming mug in hand, there was nothing to hear but knee slapping and hooting. She gave Mr. Dale his coffee, then moved to stand behind her pa. Certainly she hadn't missed everything. *Please, let there be something left to hear.*

The hawk-nosed newcomer took a grateful sip of the hot liquid, then raised a hand. "But that wasn't the end of it, I tell ya. The best part's yet to come. Just as them soldiers was high-stepping it outta town with their tails tucked between their jackboots, a woman by the name of Nurse Tarrant leaned out an upstairs window and started taunting them. Called them king's fools and heathens for breaking the Lord's Day. Them arrogant braggarts weren't about to take that off a woman. One of 'em broke rank and leveled his Brown Bess on her." He paused dramatically, obviously enjoying his own tale.

Prudence didn't take the bait, but one of the others did. "And? Out with it!"

He merely smiled and eased back in his chair. "She made herself an even bigger target, she did, leaned clear out the window, daring him to fire." He took another sip.

"Aw, come on, Fred," another said in exasperation. "Cough up the rest, or the bunch of us'll throttle you."

Mr. Dale laughed aloud. "Well, the cur *woulda* shot her, except he happened to glance around. Turns out he was wearing the only red jacket in sight . . . and a whole bunch of muskets was trained dead on him. Took off like a scared rabbit, he did, all the way back over the bridge! Ah, 'twas a grand day. A grand day."

It took several minutes for the story to sink in. "You mean to say," Pa began, "that the British were thwarted from capturing Salem's arsenal, forced to return to their ships, and our boys did it without firing a single shot?"

"That's about the size of it," he answered. "You shoulda been there!"

"Wisht I was," one of the men said, wagging his head. "That would have been a tale to tell the grandkids one day."

Prudence was overcome with elation. "And all the grander for the bravery of a woman," she said in wonder. Not all the courage in this world was limited to men. Women had just as much a place in this struggle for freedom as the men had. In fact, if that dandified bounder Morgan Thomas hadn't stuck his nose into her business, those soldiers might never have disembarked from their boat in Salem. She might have been able to discover their plot and warn the port town in advance. Obviously that *far superior* spy had failed miserably in unearthing that bit of information.

She folded her arms and regarded the men in the mercantile with disdain. Taken up with all their big talk and brave plans, there wasn't one of them who'd give her any more credence than Morgan Thomas had. Even now they sat rehashing the details of the incident from the beginning so they could all ooh and ahh over the event. And not once, *not once,* would it enter their minds that freedom's holy cause was every bit as dear and precious to her, a woman, as it was to them. After all, having been raised with strict Christian principles, the need to honor them and defend them was just as deeply rooted within her, woman or not.

"Well, gents," Mr. Dale said, breaking into her thoughts. "I'd like to sit around and keep jawin' with ya, but I'd best be getting back to work." He stood and plucked his greatcoat from the back of his chair.

"Same with Smitty and me," one of the others said. With much scuffling, the pair followed Mr. Dale out the door.

Work! As Prudence watched them leave, the sudden realization that she had yet to finish making out her purchasing list struck her full force. And she still hadn't gotten Pa to agree to let her go to Salem in his place either. She glanced toward him, and her breath caught. He was slumped forward in the chair, gripping his left shoulder.

"Pa! Pa!" She rushed around to the front of his chair and knelt there while the remaining two men came to help. Prudence lifted her father's chin. "Speak to me, Pa. Please, please speak to me."

His eyelids fluttered open, revealing faded blue eyes racked with pain. His face contorted in agony. "My . . . chest," he grunted.

27

Dan made a quick maneuver with the hand wagon around an imaginary obstruction, and Miles, riding along with the foodstuffs and supplies, squealed in glee.

"Be careful," Susannah said lightly, enjoying the carefree April sunshine as they strolled home from the market stalls. How many times she had envisioned this very scene, the four of them together, taking care of everyday needs as a normal family. The few months since her husband's release had seemed more like a few weeks, the time had flown by so quickly. And on such a day as this she could almost convince herself everything was right with their world. She shifted Julia's weight in her arms to a more comfortable position.

"Why don't you hop in, too?" Dan challenged, an impish spark in his eyes. "I'll give you a wagon ride you won't soon forget."

"I'll just bet you would." She drew a breath fragrant with the scent of spring flowers as they passed under a tree in full bloom. "Doesn't it smell like the very gates of Eden? I just love spring."

"I know. Me, too." With his free hand, he smoothed some stray hairs from her eyes and gazed at her tenderly. "It's the best time of the year, all fresh and crisp, new life bursting forth. It's a blessed thing."

Dan navigated the turn at the intersection with Milk Street, and the stick Miles dragged along scratched a crooked arc in the soft earth beside the walkway. "And look," Dan said, peering up the road. "Another blessing."

Unable to see anything particular in her husband's line of view, Susannah glanced to the right and left and then back to him. "What?"

He gestured with relish. "Not a redcoat in sight. Anywhere!"

"Oh, you! You're impossible." Despite her cheery smile, the reminder of the unwelcome military presence in Boston cast a momentary shadow on her happy mood. For a brief moment she had been able to pretend that everyone was at peace with his neighbor.

"Good day, Reverend. Missus," called a woman's voice.

Susannah and Dan both glanced toward the next house, where a church member on the second floor was draping a feather tick out an open window to air. They waved and nodded. "Lovely day, Mrs. Howard," Dan said.

"Yes, isn't it though."

"And doesn't it smell divine," Susannah said lightly. Nature's exquisite perfume awakened a longing to work in her flower garden. The instant she put her slumbering baby in the crib, she would do just that.

Arriving at their newly painted clapboard home, Dan turned along the side of their fenced yard, heading to the back door.

"Reverend Haynes, I believe?" a man said, rising from the front stoop as they drew opposite him. Tall and quite thin, he removed his hat as he walked toward them, revealing slightly wavy dark brown hair. His somber eyes, though a rich blue, seemed to harbor immeasurable sadness.

"Yes." Dan stopped. "Can I help you?"

"I've brought y'all a message from Morgan Thomas."

His voice was unusually deep and husky, and Susannah couldn't quite place his accent. It seemed slower, softer than the typical New England one she had grown so accustomed to hearing. And though he looked vaguely familiar, she had no idea why he should.

Dan gave a polite nod. "Splendid. Susannah, why don't you let our guest in the front while Miles and I take the food in through the back?"

The newcomer strode to the gate and held it open for her.

With a tentative smile of thanks, Susannah stepped inside. "Would that be your baby girl?" he drawled as she passed him. "Julia, I believe?"

"Why, yes. Morgan mentioned our daughter to you?"

He tipped his head slightly and looked at the child with a gentle smile. "She's even sweeter than he described."

"Thank you. Won't you come and have a seat in the parlor while I put the baby down? I'll bring you a nice cool glass of cider."

"I'd be very grateful," he said, opening the door and then following her inside.

Susannah indicated the parlor with a nod of her head. "Please, make yourself comfortable, will you? I shan't be more than a few moments. And Dan will be right with you."

"I thank you."

A curious feeling coursed through her as she hastened upstairs to the nursery and then came down as quickly. By the time she started toward the front room with a tray of drinks, Dan and the newcomer were already chatting. She heard the port of Salem mentioned and concluded they were discussing the recent disturbing incident there.

Both men stood as she entered the room.

"Please sit," she said, passing out the refreshment. "And you, young man," she warned Miles, handing him a half-filled cup, "be careful not to spill yours on the rug." Then she set the tray on one of the lamp tables and took a seat.

Dan was smiling. Quite an odd smile, she thought fleetingly.

He cleared his throat. "Our guest has come from North Carolina, sweetheart."

Switching her attention to the tall stranger, she noticed that he seemed in similarly good spirit.

"You don't remember me, do you, Susannah?"

"Actually, I've not been to North Carolina, but—"

"I'm Robert Chandler."

Susannah's palm flew to the open neck of her muslin afternoon gown. "Julia's husband?" she gasped in surprise. Scarcely aware that she'd gotten up, she crossed the room and held out her hands, unable not to stare at him.

He rose and took one of her hands, then bent and kissed it. When he straightened, his bittersweet smile did not quite touch his eyes. "It's been a long time since Ashford, England."

"Yes, it has. No wonder you looked familiar when I first saw you! It's so good to see you again, Robert. You're somewhat thinner than when we first met, but—if I may say it—just as handsome." She turned to Dan. "Now do you see how my best friend could be swept off her feet and whisked ever so willingly to the other side of the ocean? Oh, Robert," she gushed, smiling at him once more, "you made Julia deliriously happy. Her letters were filled with you and her new life here. I shall forever thank you for . . . making her last days such joyous ones."

"Mama," Miles interrupted, tugging at her skirt. "Are you talking about sissy?"

"No, dear. My very best friend in the whole world was named Julia."

"But you said you liked Felicia."

"I do," she said, tousling his tawny hair. "I have many, many dear friends." Glancing back to their guest, Susannah knew the reason for the sadness lurking in his eyes. Morgan had been right; Robert was still mourning his wife's death—and his baby's—even after all this time. Perhaps a change of subject was in order. "Do sit down, Robert," she said, returning to her own chair. "You said you brought a message from Morgan? A letter we received from him said you would be traveling together."

"For the most part." A look of mild merriment softened his features. "But he wasn't sure he'd find much of a welcome in Boston at the moment."

Dan chuckled. "Well, so far I haven't heard of anyone

threatening to tar and feather him, but then, I'm not exactly privy to Tory gossip."

"Morgan posted a letter here to Mr. Clarke," Robert said, "concocting some wild tale of thieves and pirates, in hopes of shifting blame away from himself before the merchants discover their missing shipments. He felt that if he cried foul first, he might just slide through without their realizing he had duped them completely from the start. He does hope to be able to go home again someday."

"He is one of a kind," Dan admitted.

"Yes, he's that. Anyway," Robert went on in his soft drawl, "he's asked me to check with a few individuals here before I return to Concord. That's where we're quartered. He and I have joined the minutemen there—which brings me to the most pressing reason he asked me to come. Please tell me you have learned the whereabouts of Miss Prudence Endecott."

Grinning, Dan shook his head. "Sorry. But tell Morgan it's not that I haven't tried. I've inquired after his mysterious female spy at the Green Dragon and the Bunch of Grapes Tavern, but to no avail. I even went, as a last resort, to the basket weaver's house where he said he had inquired. But the woman is no longer there. According to her neighbor, the weaver's son came and moved her out of Boston until things settle down."

"That's what Morgan was afraid of." Robert's shoulders sagged. "The basket maker led him to believe the girl came from a village north of Boston. That's why we went on up to Concord instead of securing rooms in Cambridge."

"Oh, yes," Susannah said, unable to stifle her amusement. "I can understand his reasoning."

"And since we set foot in Concord," Robert said, "every minute we aren't drilling, pouring lead for balls, or assembling cartridges, Morgan is out scouring the countryside in search of the girl." He shook his head good-naturedly. "I can't help hoping he finds her soon, so the rest of us can have some peace at last."

Susannah burst out laughing, and Dan joined her, but then quickly sobered. "Morgan may find the girl, but I'm afraid peace may be quite another matter entirely. Particularly where you've gone."

"We've noticed the folks up that way do seem a mite nervous," Robert said.

Dan nodded. "General Gage has spies everywhere. They've been pretty adept at finding out where our firearms and powder are being stored . . . and one of our largest caches is at Concord. Don't be surprised if the general pays you a spur-of-the-moment visit like he did the folks at Salem."

"I doubt the man can sneak up there with the same ease," Robert said. "Concord isn't a seaport."

"True." Dan shot a guilty glance at Susannah. "Perhaps we can save this discussion for another time."

"Oh, don't feel you must stop on my account," she answered pointedly. "Be assured, I'd far rather know what's happening and be prepared for it than be kept in the dark and be caught unaware. After all, rumors are rampant, as you both know. Why, every man in Dan's congregation can hardly wait for the *bloodletting* to start—despite what open conflict would do to our families and our town. We are virtually surrounded by warships with huge cannons."

"Then wouldn't it be wise to leave, as the basket maker did?" Robert asked.

"That's just what I've been trying to tell her, isn't it, my love?" Dan asked evenly.

Susannah was every bit as stubborn as her husband, and she set her chin resolutely. "I shan't go without you."

"But you know I can't go just now."

Suddenly Susannah realized they were arguing in front of company, and she turned a slightly awkward smile at Robert. "So, you see," she added in an overly bright tone, "we shall all be staying. And in that case, I insist you join us for supper. You can tell us all about North Carolina. I've heard almost nothing about that colony, except that winters are much milder there. That alone sounds quite appealing."

"Thank you, I'd very much like to stay," Robert said. "Julia spoke so frequently of you and the grand times you had growing up together. She was so looking forward to your coming to stay with us in Princeton. I'd purely enjoy an opportunity to get to know my Julia's Susannah. Perhaps we can compare accounts of some of your girlhood adventures."

Susannah laughed airily. "I'm rather afraid my dear friend's storytelling made far better entertainment. Julia had such a way of . . . elaborating, shall we say? Adding ever so much more excitement."

"Yes," he said on a ragged breath. "That she did." He turned to gaze out the window.

But Susannah caught the gleam of a tear in his eye. Poor Robert. It was taking such a long time for his heart to mend.

28

April 18, 1775

Dan felt Susannah stir beside him and sit up in the bed. "Something's amiss." Her voice remained throaty from sleep.

Becoming aware of the commotion outside, he groaned and flung the blankets aside, then padded to the window.

The night was cold and overcast, but in the dim glow of street lamps he could see a sizable throng of townsmen already gathered and more of his neighbors coming out of their homes to join them. He had a fairly good idea what the stir was about, but he remained casual. "Just some men talking down below, sweetheart. I'll go ask them to be more quiet. Go back to sleep."

Rumors of an expected large movement of British troops had been circulating for days. Dan and the other men of his dwindling congregation had made every effort to keep them quiet and shield their wives from undue concern, particularly since last Sunday was Easter, a holy day. But no one could deny any longer the implication of the substantial tally of landing boats General Gage had been amassing at the bottom of the Common or the conspicuous disruption of normal camp routine.

Dan pulled on his breeches, then quickly slipped into his boots and headed downstairs. The patriots' speculation regarding the general's plan must have become a reality—Gage must have dispatched his troops to Concord to seize the colony's stockpile of munitions. Word also had it that Sam Adams and John Hancock, the very men the general intended to arrest and ship to England for trial, were at this very time visiting friends in Lexington before traveling south for a second colonial congress.

Grabbing his greatcoat, Dan hastened outside and crossed the street to the yard of Ian Simms.

The church elder spied him coming and gave a concerned grimace as Dan approached. "It's just like 'em, Reverend," he muttered, "sneaking outta town in the dead of night."

Someone guffawed. "As if no one would notice hundreds of lobsterbacks marching down to the water!"

"Hundreds?" Dan asked.

"More than seven hundred is the latest count," another neighbor replied. "The light infantry and grenadiers, at that. Must be planning to move fast."

"I suppose someone's sent warning to Concord," Dan said.

"And Lexington," Simms said with a nod. "What a hard blow it would be to Massachusetts if Adams and Hancock were taken."

"I'm surprised old Gage has allowed most of our leaders free rein this long," another man remarked.

Someone near him snickered. "He's just keeping a lid on this simmering Boston pot until *he* decides it's time to blow it off."

From far away, the hollow sound of church bells bonged on the night air.

Dan exchanged glances with the others. "Charlestown. The redcoats must be landing across the back bay in Charlestown."

"If they march straight through," Mr. Simms said, "they could be in Lexington before morning. I certainly hope our express riders get through. There'll be plenty of British patrols scouting ahead. Baker said close to a hundred horses were transported to Charlestown yesterday."

Dan couldn't help wondering about Morgan Thomas and

Robert Chandler, now quartered in Concord. And heaven only knew where Ben was right now. "Yes, let us pray for all those in harm's way. Kneel with me, gentlemen. I fear it's begun."

❧ ❧

From a small window in the unlit attic of her house, Prudence stared out in disquietude at the waterway separating Charlestown from Boston. It appeared that every house around the bay had at least one lamp burning. No doubt everyone else had been observing the succession of longboats that had been bringing soldiers over from the other side for the past hour. One by one, the bells from here to Cambridge had stopped tolling the news.

Word of the British plan to march in force to Concord had circulated yesterday, and Prudence had to wonder if Morgan Thomas had been the one who managed to uncover that information. Whoever had discovered the plot should have dug a little deeper and found out the time and route the Crown puppets would be taking.

There were no more boats rowing across the Charles now in the deadly quiet, but hundreds of redcoats could be seen milling about the ferry dock.

"Prudence?" her stepmother's voice called up the steep staircase.

"Yes?" Prudence moved to the hatch opening, but she could not make out Miriam in the deep darkness below.

"Your father is asking why the bells stopped. Can you see anything from up there?"

"A great horde of soldiers has landed on this side, but it doesn't appear that anyone's issued an order to march as yet." *Poor Pa,* she thought, taking her position at the window again. Like most of the people of Charlestown, he had belonged to the local militia for years and was equally anxious to send those meddling English packing. To be stricken with a failing heart and left to lie in bed at such a time had to be very hard on him.

Is it any less hard on me—tied to the mercantile and the house now, not able to venture elsewhere? Even the store's merchandise must be brought in by others.

"Your father wants to know how many soldiers you can see," Miriam called again.

"Tell him hundreds, maybe a thousand. Wait! I hear something." Having gone to the hatch to answer, she flew quickly to the window.

A troop of mounted dragoons clattered past, their horses galloping over the cobbles. An advance party, Prudence realized, to scout ahead and terrorize every village, every soul, who got in their path.

The yearning to have a fast horse of her own rushed through her. She could envision herself saddling up and riding with the wind to warn Concord. There were all kinds of shortcuts through the countryside she could take and be there long before the British.

"Prudence. Prudence!"

Brought back to reality, she grimaced. *"If* I had a fast horse, of course," she muttered under her breath. *"If* Pa hadn't gotten sick and left me with the mercantile and an entire household to care for. *If . . ."*

❦ ❦

"Morgan! Wake up!"

In the thick fuzziness of sleep, Morgan felt someone shaking his shoulder, and none too gently. He managed to connect the voice to Robert Chandler. Opening one eye, he saw nothing but predawn darkness through the window.

Bells were ringing, he realized groggily. Loud bells, from the meetinghouse on the edge of town. He swung his legs to the floor and rubbed his eyes.

"Get up," Chandler said, standing at the window now. "Lamps are being lit all around. Men are running out of their homes with their muskets."

"What time is it?" Morgan stretched, then staggered from bed to grab his clothes while his friend lit a lamp and hastily dressed. "Sure hope my horse is rested after getting stabled so late."

"I have no idea what hour it is. There's no sign of dawn."

Stomping into his boots, Morgan collected his powder, cartridge box, and flints. "Is my musket primed? I can't even remember."

"Come to, Morgan, will you? We've kept our weapons loaded and ready for a week now in case the British came to break up the Massachusetts Assembly."

"Right. Yes. We're minutemen."

Chandler gave him an exasperated nod.

"But the assembly has already disbanded. Why would there be trouble now?"

Throwing on his coat and hat, Robert snatched his firearm and gear. "Maybe the redcoats don't know that."

From out in the hall, hurried footsteps and excited voices thundered past the room. Someone banged on the door. "Get a move on!"

Chandler flung it open. "Hurry up." He tossed the words over his shoulder.

Still combatting drowsiness after arriving from Sudbury around midnight, Morgan shoved his belongings into his haversack. He had searched every town and village within a twenty-mile radius but had yet to find Prudence Endecott. Perhaps he was the fool everyone made him out to be. He poured icy water from the bedside pitcher into the bowl, splashed some on his face, then slammed out after his friend.

As he exited the building, he saw men hastening toward the meetinghouse from all directions, talking to one another and asking questions.

Someone nudged his arm. "What's happened?"

"Is this a drill?" another asked.

Morgan had no answers and responded with a shrug. The incessant bells were making his head throb, and the cold was making his teeth chatter. If only there had been time to gulp some hot coffee before reporting to the assigned location on the edge of town. Men were coming from every direction, some swinging lanterns, some as bleary eyed as he felt, and all similarly confused.

When at last he reached the church, the company commander, Captain Brown, still buttoning his uniform coat, waited on the top step. His face was unreadable in the faint lamp glow, his stance impatient.

Morgan moved beside Robert Chandler. "What is it?" he mouthed over the din of the bells and other melee.

"The British are coming."

As the expected answer sank in, Morgan's pulse gathered intensity, and he came fully awake.

The commander held up a hand. "Quiet! I need everyone's attention." He motioned with his head to the nearest man. "Go in and tell that zealous bell ringer he can stop."

"Yes, sir."

Within seconds came the relief of blessed silence.

Brown swept a glance over the gathering. "Sam Prescott just rode in from Lexington. He barely escaped a detachment of mounted officers near there—a scouting party for a large column of soldiers heading our way. He also crossed paths with Paul Revere from Boston. Revere told him hundreds, maybe even a thousand, are coming."

Anxious muttering circulated among the pathetic number of men in sight. Even with more riding in by the moment, what were so few against so many?

The captain pointed to a minuteman sitting atop a long-legged mount. "You. Reubens. Ride down the road. Find out if the regulars have reached Lexington yet."

"Yes, sir!" The young man smacked the reins against his horse, and it lurched into a gallop.

"Will." Brown nodded to another. "Form details and start moving the munitions. And don't stash it all in the same place."

Put off by the mere idea of having to start the morning with heavy lifting and hauling without so much as a bite of breakfast, Morgan started melting back into the crowd.

At that moment a militia lieutenant in the near proximity

stepped up. "All you men, follow me," he said, his gesture including Morgan and Robert.

Chandler whacked Morgan's back. "I find it's best to keep busy, myself. Keeps one's mind otherwise occupied."

Morgan moaned and cast him a sidelong look. "I don't think so. At least not this time."

❧ ❧

It was close to ten o'clock before Morgan and Robert trudged back to the township. The munitions and stores had finally all been moved to more remote locations, and leave had been given for the men to eat breakfast.

Morgan took measure of his once fine clothes, now soiled with mud and grease. "Look at me. I'm filthy. Let's breakfast at the tavern, then go to our room and clean up."

Chandler grinned. "We were told there'd be coffee outside the meetinghouse, along with our rations."

"Surely you'd prefer a more substantial hot breakfast, would you not?"

"Under normal circumstances," came Robert's slow reply. "But right now, I reckon we better do just as we're told. Soon we're going to face the mightiest army on earth."

Morgan gazed longingly at the tavern as they passed by. "For such a notorious prankster, Chan, you've turned out to be quite the serious old man."

The meetinghouse, a squat building tucked within a grove of birch and elm trees, had upward of three hundred men milling around when they arrived. Morgan concluded that militias from the neighboring towns had joined Concord's. Everywhere he looked, men were busy checking their weapons or organizing the equipment in their haversacks. Off to one side, musicians were practicing on fifes and drums.

Distant hoofbeats echoed and grew louder as their scout, Jack Reubens, rode into the encampment.

The waiting men sprang to their feet, shouting a dozen questions at once, but their queries remained unanswered as

Reubens headed directly for the steps and joined Captain Brown.

From the dire look on the captain's face as the scout swiftly delivered his report, it wasn't good news. Morgan and Robert exchanged significant glances, and the rest of the group gradually quieted down.

Captain Brown turned to the men, his face rigid and red with fury. "The king's troops have fired on the people of Lexington."

A gasp escaped, then was silenced as quickly.

"A deadly volley," he continued. "Ordered by an officer. Men are lying dead on Lexington Green."

A great cry of anguish, punctuated by curses and threats, burst forth as the militia men waved muskets and clenched fists in the air.

Suddenly a shot fired into the air.

"Silence!" Colonel Bartlett, Brown's superior, lowered the still-smoking pistol. "Remember your training." He seemed to meet the eye of every man in the gathering when he spoke again. "The British have now left Lexington. As of an hour ago, they had already set out to march the six miles between Lexington and Concord. Before you report to your companies to await orders, Pastor Emerson will lead us in prayer, to ask that we be guided this day by Divine Providence."

Morgan bowed his head along with the rest. Faced with the reality of his own mortality, he regretted as never before having drifted so far from the Almighty. Silently he vowed to rectify that position, if he survived.

At the reverend's amen, Morgan opened his eyes and found his hand latched onto Chandler's sleeve. Suddenly he was extremely glad his old school chum was with him. Morgan had invited Chan along in the hopes of lifting the widower's spirits, but now it seemed that their roles were reversed. Morgan didn't want to die alone in a strange town among people he scarcely knew, and having his friend by his side helped. He gave Robert's arm a comradely squeeze, then let go.

The crowd began assembling into their separate companies, and the Concord militia, some hundred and fifty strong, lined up on the road east of the church.

"I think we should go give them lobsterbacks a proper greeting!" someone shouted near the front.

The group instantly agreed.

Captain Brown, appearing interested in the idea, excused himself and walked over to his superiors. During the few minutes the leaders conversed, it seemed as if everyone was afraid to breathe.

"Men," he said upon returning, "we've been given permission to march down the road and make visual contact. Determine their strength. Let them know they won't be dealing with a mere handful of men, as in Lexington."

Another roar of approval went up.

"Fall in!" the captain ordered.

Morgan felt escalating excitement and grinned at Robert.

They were about to face the enemy. At last.

29

Morgan and Robert Chandler, along with a ragtag group of approximately 150 men from sixteen to sixty years of age, marched two abreast along the road to Lexington. Around the newly budding trees, leftover fog still clung in the low areas of the rolling, hilly landscape.

The British were coming.

Near the front of the column, Morgan felt his excitement increasing with each step. He slid a glance toward Robert. His friend's purposeful steps and squared shoulders revealed exhilaration equal to Morgan's, though he refrained from smiling or idle talk. A serious atmosphere enveloped the entire group.

At any time now the militia would come within sight of the British forces. Morgan sent a wordless plea heavenward, a prayer that God's will would be done this day—a belated petition at best. He hoped fervently that he would be brave, that all of them would be.

Up ahead, cresting the wooded knoll of the hill, Captain Brown raised a hand and brought them to a halt. He took out a spyglass and peered through it.

Morgan, desperate to know what the leader found so engrossing, held his breath and listened. Only the rustle of the breeze and the chirping of an occasional bird broke the silence.

Then from far away, almost like a heartbeat, came a faint

thud. Then another, and a third. Slight at first, the beats became stronger, echoing through the woods.

Several at the front of the Concord column broke ranks and ran forward. Morgan and Robert sprang to join them as all the rest poured toward the crown of the hill and spread across the woody rise.

Below, the first redcoats emerged from the mist and dark woods, the sun glittering off their weapons. Lined up four abreast, they came along the road through a stretch of almost treeless fields. And more—hundreds more—streamed behind them.

Morgan's pulse beat an erratic pattern. He checked to his right and left for advantageous and protected positions on both sides of the road where the militia might be able to ambush some of the British regulars as soon as they reached the treed knoll.

About 160 rods away, the first Crown unit halted quite suddenly, and the following troops did likewise.

"They've seen us," Brown said, lowering his spyglass.

Morgan felt a rush of disappointment. There would be no ambush today. Beside him, he saw Robert's knuckles go white as he gripped his firearm.

"Fall in!" the sergeants ordered.

The colonists, more concerned now than excited, ran back to form their own columns. Tension wound tight as a spring. As the ensuing commotion of regrouping settled, distant strains of a tune floated toward them.

"'Yankee Doodle Dandy'!" someone muttered. "The blackguards are playin' 'Yankee Doodle Dandy'!"

Morgan ground his teeth and lurched forward with the others.

"Fall in!" a sergeant ordered a second time. He glared adamantly at them while Captain Brown rode to the rear of the column. "About face!"

"We're retreating!" Morgan groused in disbelief as he and Robert pivoted in place.

"Forward march!" came the yell from the front. The drummer boy struck up the marching beat, but it did not quite drown out the obnoxious British song.

Morgan shook his head bitterly. "Why on earth did we come all the way out here?"

"I thought the captain was as tired as the rest of us of waiting around," someone behind him grated.

As the fife players struck up their own practiced tune, "The White Cockade," the pep of it seemed to perk up the militia. Some even smiled as the company set out in lively step.

The man in back of Morgan and Chandler harrumphed. "Well, blokes, we may not be engaging the enemy right now, but we can deliver 'em to Concord in a sprightly fashion."

Morgan shifted the heavy weight of his field gear slightly and took heart. Even after having only gotten three hours of sleep, he knew his pack felt amazingly light compared to the hundred-plus pounds the lobsterbacks carried—and they had been marching all night.

The Liberty Pole on the hill directly across from the meeting hall was a most welcome sight when the militia passed it on their way into town. Their hearts swelled with pride at the assortment of colorful flags strung along the tall, graceful length of it, dancing on the breeze.

The fifers added a measure of enthusiasm as the company passed the church. Men from additional militias lined the road on either side, the butts of their muskets resting on the ground, hats waving from their other hands. There were many, many more of them now, Morgan noticed. Companies from several other villages had arrived while they were gone.

"Get ready, boys," someone up front hollered. "We're bringin' the bloody backs to you! They're not half a mile behind us."

At once the various companies of men dispersed into their own groups and marched to allotted locations.

Captain Brown turned. "Men, form a firing line at the top of the hill, off to the right."

"First line of defense," Morgan said to Robert. "And what a

grand place to take a stand. Beneath the flying standards of the Liberty Pole."

"Think so?" Chandler asked, his tone mocking. "Let's just hope it doesn't end up as our grave marker."

The long line of crimson was only fifty or sixty rods away now. A flanker spotted Morgan's company, and the leaders grouped together briefly, then broke up and rode back to their positions. An unintelligible command followed, and the regulars fixed bayonets onto the ends of their Brown Besses.

The commanding officer raised his sword aloft and held it for several seconds, then brought it down.

To the rapid beat of drums, the first column of redcoats ran into new positions, at least fifty abreast. Three lines. The cadence changed, and they charged forward and up the hill with a blood-lusting shout, their tall hats giving them ominous height.

Morgan felt his heart freeze. He fixed his own bayonet. Cocked his musket. The clicks of others scarcely penetrated his thoughts in the horrific threat.

"Wait for my order to fire!" a nearby sergeant commanded.

Captain Brown took several steps forward, making himself a target, and raised his sword.

Morgan found it almost impossible to keep his eye fixed on his superior with the British horde clambering up the hillside like a pack of wild dogs. They were halfway now, no more than four rods off. Too close! *Too close!*

"Fire!" the captain bellowed, slicing downward with his saber.

A great roar spewed from dozens of flintlocks at once.

Screams pierced the air.

Morgan peered through the smoke billowing from the blast of his musket and saw at least half the red line fall. Dropping to one knee, he retrieved and bit open a ball and powder cartridge, trying desperately to shorten the costly fifteen seconds it took to reload.

"Fire!" a Crown officer midway up the hill cried.

The earth around Morgan shook. He flattened to the

ground even as rifle balls hissed by him and struck his comrades. His mouth went dry. His hands took on a trembling he could not control as he sat up to pour a measure of gunpowder into the priming pan of the musket. All around him he was aware of others frantically doing the same. He dared not look up to see how close the enemy had advanced. Making quick work of pouring powder down the barrel and adding the ball and cartridge paper, he snatched his ramrod and tamped the load. "Are you all right, Chan?" he asked, the unnatural pitch of his voice sounding foreign to his own ears.

"So far."

Flash. Explosion. Whizzing bullets dug up earth as the second line of redcoats fired.

Ignoring the dirt that sprayed into his face and eyes, Morgan continued packing the load with his ramrod.

"Retreat!" his sergeant yelled. "Retreat to the North Bridge! Assist the wounded!"

Morgan hunched low. Scrambling backward, he almost stumbled over a man lying in the way. He gingerly turned the body over, stunned to see most of the fellow's face was missing.

"Come on!" Robert pleaded, snatching him up by his coat as another British battle cry issued.

Redcoats who had reached the top of the hill began jabbing bayonets unmercifully into the wounded sprawled on the ground, heedless of their agonizing cries.

The savage barbarity stunned Morgan. It infuriated him that there was nothing he could do but dash after Robert down the back side of the hill. He kept his friend in sight the whole way. Together they had survived this battle. Together they would make it to the bridge. God willing.

Chancing a look over his shoulder, Morgan saw only a handful of redcoats giving chase, but having spent so much effort charging up the hill, their pace was slower and lumbering.

He heard a cheer from the Crown force.

Turning, he saw that a soldier had shimmied up the Liberty

Pole. The scoundrel had a rope dangling from his waist—one they would use to pull down this symbol of what the patriots were fighting for.

Morgan stopped to take a bead on the blackguard.

Robert snagged his arm. "Leave them to it. It'll give us time to regroup on the other side of the bridge. They'll be heading this way, thinking our arsenal is still at Colonel Barret's."

Their footfalls made the only sound in the unnatural quiet as they raced through the town. Not a person was in sight. Even most of the stables were empty of animals. The whole place had been abandoned. Finally leaving the houses behind, they moved into the fields beyond the town and joined their comrades.

"Look," came a call from up ahead.

Following the minuteman's pointing finger, Morgan saw a large gathering of patriots on a hill beyond the far side of the bridge—easily twice the number of their just thinned ranks. A wave of relief washed over him.

"Halt! Form up!" Captain Brown called out as he rode past them. "Attention, drummers." He continued on to the front.

Woefully short of breath, Morgan and the others fell into line.

"To the bridge! Forward, march!"

"Commence cadence," someone told the drummers.

Morgan fell into step with the rest. Slowly an incredible realization made its way into his brain. They were an organized fighting unit once more—one that had withstood a confrontation with the mighty British and given as good as they'd gotten. A small smile tugged at his mouth, and he straightened his spine, stepping smartly toward the North Bridge.

He flashed a grin at Robert, but it vanished at the same instant. A fine stream of blood coursed down his friend's arm. "Chan! You've been shot!"

"Me? Where?" Robert took stock without so much as losing step. He slid his coat down for a better look and tossed his head. "Just a crease."

Morgan handed over his kerchief. "Well, hold this over it until we stop. When did it happen?"

"I haven't the slightest idea."

"Surely you must've felt it."

Robert shook his head. "Later, after this is over—I'm sure I'll feel it then."

Morgan shifted his concerned gaze from his friend to the country folk who had gathered on the other side of the bridge. Lining a hill to the east, another company of farmers and craftsmen stood at the ready. Attired in shirts all the same hue and all wearing tricorn hats, they looked amazingly like an actual army with one purpose.

A new confidence and feeling of pride surged through Morgan. He pulled a paper cartridge from his box and grinned at Robert. "Aye, you'll probably feel the wound later. *After* we've routed those red devils. After we've sent them running back to Boston. No—back to England where they belong!"

30

Just outside Cambridge, Ben knew he had to hurry. He had remained much too long with his enchanting new bride and was a whole day late in his return to Boston. But he cared not in the least.

The clear blue sky promised more perfect weather to come. Soon spring would chase away all trace of winter, and the temperature would begin to climb. But for the moment, he reveled in the mild coolness that made his afternoon ride so pleasant . . . that and the sweet memories of his time with Abigail.

Abby was more than he ever dreamed of, all a man could want. He adored her sweet, soft-spoken ways, her breathless voice, the shimmering eyes that told him everything he ever wanted to hear, to feel. Thinking of the way she fit against him, her softness and warmth, her murmured words of love, he smiled.

The road led past a farmhouse, and when he noticed the somber people outside the dwelling, Ben did his best to subdue his silly grin. No sense giving folks the idea that a simpleton was riding by.

But he was so happy. He had never been this happy in his life, and when he got beyond the farmhouse, he didn't bother trying to restrain himself from smiling. Everything was so perfect when he and Abby were together. At least, almost perfect. With her and the children residing at the Pawtucket farm, quite a lot of their precious time had to be shared with his parents. What he and Abigail needed was a place of their own.

As he mulled the idea over in his mind, Ben sat up straighter. He could easily picture Abby the mistress of her own home. No doubt it would help her to overcome some of her timidity, too. Of course, it would be wise to get a place near his folks' house so she would have help when he was on the road.

Perhaps, Ben mused, a house could be built on the rise above the north pasture, overlooking the Blackstone River. It was a nice sunny spot and offered an easy walk down to the shade of the riverbank. The children would probably love romping in the shallows on hot summer days. He and Corbin could go fishing, and sometimes all four of them could go out in Pa's rowboat. Yes, the next warm day, he'd take Abby and the kids there.

Suddenly aware that Rebel had slowed almost to a stop, Ben discovered he was nearing the Charles River. There seemed a noticeable lack of wagon traffic for this time of day, yet he could see women and children everywhere, in their yards along the roadside. Most of them seemed quite serious, and without exception, they all had their gazes fixed in the direction of Cambridge.

Ben shifted his attention off into the distance. Beyond the town, quite a bit to the north, a dark cloud of smoke stained the sky. He guided Rebel up a rise in the road, and from that vantage point, he could tell that the smoke was not all coming from a single source. A pair of columns rose skyward and joined together in a clump of gray. Odd.

A heavy foreboding pressed upon his chest. He drew in on the reins and stopped beside two women along the edge of the road. "Excuse me," he said. "What's burning?"

"Don't know," the older one answered. "Appears to be closer to Menotomy. I'm just prayin' to God my boy don't get himself killed. He's not but fifteen."

"Now, Leah," the other said as she slid an arm around her.

"You've got to stop going on so. Your man's with him, and so's mine."

"But what—" A faraway boom interrupted Ben's question.

"Oh, Lord, help us," the older woman moaned, then pressed her fingertips to her mouth and stared ahead.

"Cannons?" Ben asked.

She nodded. "Them redcoats are shooting cannons at my boy. It's not enough, all the sacking and killing they already done, looting and burning clear to Concord. Now they're coming back here."

Her companion stroked her arm. "But the planks have been taken off the bridge, Leah, remember? The soldiers won't be so quick to cross back."

Ben didn't need to hear more. He spurred his mount into a gallop. While he had been basking in Abby's love with scarcely a care in the world, the British had gone on the rampage! Flying down to the river, he saw all the proof he needed. Only the skeleton of a bridge remained over the Charles.

"What's happened?" Ben called to a group of men as he swung down from the saddle.

"Wish I knew for sure, Ben," one of his own Cambridge neighbors answered. "Old Gage dispatched two regiments to Concord last night by way of Charlestown, and three more came from the Neck and marched over the bridge this morning. We figured if we tore the thing down, we could slow their retreat considerable."

"That is," someone else added, "if they even make it back this far. They mighta lit outta Boston hoping to seize our powder stores at Concord—"

"Plan was to capture Adams and Hancock while they was at it," Ben's neighbor inserted. "But from what we hear, they didn't have much success in either venture."

The news shocked Ben, until he recalled how close they had come to bloodshed in Salem before the Crown forces backed down. "The women up the road told me there's been some shooting."

"Aye. The red-jacket cowards gunned down some good Lexington folk. By the time they tried the same thing in Concord, though, our boys up there were better prepared. Got themselves off a couple real good volleys before the mighty British tucked tail and came running back this way. Not even their reinforcements have been able to stop our Sons of Liberty, I'll tell ya. Men all along the way have rallied to the call and are doggin' the road. There's plenty of trees and stone walls to hide behind while they keep them blasted puppets under fire all the way back."

One of the others grinned proudly. "Me and the boys here rigged ourselves a ferry, upriver aways. Been ferrying militias across all afternoon."

"But the fires," Ben cut in. "What about the fires?"

"Well, them lobsterbacks ain't exactly toothless, lad. Their flanking parties go after snipers, whether in houses or trees. The greedy louts are looting and burning as they go."

"Then how can you be so sure *we* have *them* on the run?" Ben asked, seriously doubting the supposed success of the patriots.

"Because that's what an express rider told us an hour ago on his way through."

"Aye," the second added. "And if it wasn't for all them war tubs in the harbor, we'd go in and retake Boston while most of the soldiers are away. Can't be more than a thousand or so left on the other side of the Neck."

The very thought gave Ben a sickening feeling. All those big guns could so easily turn on Boston. Susannah! Her babies! Dan should have insisted she remain in Rhode Island. "It'll be dark soon. Think maybe I'll sneak over to Boston. See what's brewing there."

His neighbor eyed him thoughtfully. "Better slide in real smooth and quiet. Them lobsters'll be crawlin' up and down the shoreline, watching to see if we make the next move."

❦ ❦

Among the great assemblage of Boston townsmen gathered in front of the lighthouse on Beacon Hill, hardly a man spoke.

They gazed as one across the back bay at the panoramic view from Charlestown to Roxbury. The deepening dusk made the smoke rising above Menotomy less visible . . . and the flames ominously more so. Faraway trees were silhouetted against the red-orange glow flaring high into the sky.

Dan wondered how many of the colonists he had met during his own postriding days had been caught in the middle of that melee and come to harm. The grave possibility had him praying unceasingly.

"Look, Reverend," Elder Simms said softly in the grim silence. He lifted a gloved hand from his coat pocket and pointed northeast of Cambridge. "As the sky darkens, the fires grow brighter. That one must be a house or a barn."

Dan, hesitant to break the solemnity of the moment, kept his voice low also. "How many houses have the British burned, I wonder? How many families find themselves homeless, without so much as a bed on this night? How many have lost fathers, husbands, sons—" His throat constricted in sorrow.

A sudden flash ripped the darkness, followed scant few seconds later by a muffled boom.

"Cannon," Simms grated. "Do you suppose we could calculate the distance they are away from us, as with lightning and thunder?"

"Most likely."

Smaller flashes flickered without a sound from opposing points, like summer fireflies. A ripple of muted exclamations swept across the hill. Soon the muskets would be close enough to hear.

Gradually, before their eyes, the scattered bursts crept nearer and became more frequent.

Turning away from the sight for an instant, Dan barely detected a familiar form a few yards off. "Ben!" In three quick strides, he crossed to his younger brother and grabbed him in a hug. "Thank the Lord you're not in the thick of it!" He then held Ben at arm's length. "Hey, you're all wet!"

"You don't say." With a wry smirk, Ben brushed at his coat. "The skiff I *borrowed* had a bit of a leak."

"You've just come over from the mainland?" Deacon Simms asked, joining them. "Tell us, lad. What's happening? Are the redcoats truly bein' attacked all the way back from Concord? Why, that's near twenty miles!"

"So I've heard. Oh! Look at that!"

Dan and the elder swung back toward the conflict, where the musket flashes appeared now to be more on the outer fringe than in the center, where the troops were.

"Man," Ben murmured. "What a thrill it must be to be out there taking those bullies to task."

Dan shot him a concerned glance. "You need to think beyond that, little brother. Men are dying along the Concord road this eve. Women are becoming widows—children, orphans."

Ben's expression sobered considerably.

Dan knew his brother's thoughts must have gone to his own bride and her little ones. "Morgan Thomas has returned from Bermuda. He and his friend Robert Chandler were in Concord. They had joined Concord's militia when the assembly was meeting there. Morgan thought there might be trouble. Hoped for it, actually."

"Seems he got his wish, then," Ben said, his tone flat.

"Susannah and I have been praying for him all day. By the way, did you stop by the house? Is that how you knew where to find me?"

Ben nodded. "She's wondering when you'll be home. Says you've been up here for hours."

Dan grimaced. "I hated to leave her and the children by themselves, but—"

Another distant boom sounded.

"I was surprised," Ben began, "that the city is so quiet. Thought maybe the patriots here would be taking advantage of the absence of half the garrison. And I couldn't help worrying about Susannah and the babies."

Dan gazed toward Milk Street. If, indeed, trouble broke out all of a sudden, he might have difficulty getting to her.

Mr. Simms fingered his beard. "When the rider brought

news that the folks in the country were giving those lobsterbacks what for, there was some talk of taking action here. But how much hope would we have, surrounded like we are with that blasted navy?" He tipped his head toward the harbor. "The *Empress of Russia* has moved into position just below. And see there? And there—" He pointed to the spots. "No doubt they'd all be more than happy to open fire on us."

"Quiet!" someone said from nearby.

Dan heard the low command echoed throughout the gathering, and a hush fell over them all.

There it was, faint but distinct. Musket shots that accompanied the almost constant flashes from just north of Cambridge resembled Chinese fireworks.

"I pray the regiments will split up at Cambridge," Elder Simms muttered, "each group returning the way they came. 'Divide and conquer,' so they say."

Dan's gaze shifted toward the university town. Bonfires blazed all along the main road heading into it—which would more than enable the people to see the bright red uniforms. But how would Harvard fare, considering the army's field-pieces? Could the navy's big guns shoot that far? Severe damage was most probable. Loss of the college would be devastating.

"Looks to me the British are taking quite a beating," Ben said. "I'm not so sure they can afford to split up right now. Notice how all the flashes are shifting to the right? It looks as if the entire force is headed toward Charlestown Neck. If the people can't stop them, they'll soon be within the protection of British cannons."

"Wait!" Simms cried. "I can see torch fires coming down Medford Road. More militia! If folks can just hold the blackguards until our reinforcements hit them from the other side, the redcoats'll be stopped but good. Cut 'em right to pieces."

At the thought of such slaughter, Dan found himself hoping the British forces would somehow be spared. Most of them had been on the march for over twenty-four hours and must be nearing utter exhaustion. No telling how many wounded they were transporting back with them.

For several minutes everyone was absorbed in watching the flashes from the conflict. Surely General Gage and the other Crown officials were watching, too, and beginning to realize the futility of trying to repress the Colonies' right to govern themselves.

Embattled British troops moved slowly closer and closer to Charlestown Neck. But the Medford militia was making swifter gains. Soon they would cut the enemy off, block the entrance to the Neck.

Abruptly, firing ceased from the center area. It went dark.

"Have we won?" Ben asked. "Did they surrender?"

An instant streak of light flickered, then vanished. Within seconds, another one flashed, then a third.

"Volleys," Dan said almost to himself. "The rear guard is firing volleys so the rest can dash to safety." Moments later, another line of light came closer to the Charlestown Neck, followed by two more. Judging from each new position, the British were much closer now to the Neck. They would reach it before the Medford militia.

The sound of gunfire gradually ceased. For several minutes the ensuing quiet was as deafening in its own way as the roar of battle had been.

A disappointed grumble circulated among the Bostonians. Dan was fairly certain most everyone would have preferred for the patriots to give the soldiers their just deserts.

He glanced down on the Common, at the huge lamplit military encampment. Gage had recently ordered barracks built—very imposing permanent buildings. What would the general do now? On the one hand, the man was commander of all Crown forces, not to mention being Britain's appointed governor of the Massachusetts Bay Colony. On the other hand, Gage married a colonist some years ago and had proved rather sympathetic to the cause. Would he load up his troops now and depart? Or would he retaliate? His career in the military might very well be at stake.

As Dan mused over the possibilities, he began to notice an incredible sight. All the way around the bay circling the Boston peninsula, bonfires burst into flame, one after another. They sprang from the darkness across the hills behind Charlestown all the way to Dorchester.

"Well," Simms said. "It don't appear our boys are going back home tonight. Looks like they're all staying put, letting old Gage know we're not sitting still for any more of their bullying."

The men on Beacon Hill cheered.

In the first few days after the patriot forces had routed the British on the Concord road, Prudence Endecott watched the flurry of activity all over Charlestown. The Committee of Safety was urging people to vacate the village while England's army regrouped, and many of the local men had already packed up their wives and children and sent them off to safer locations. All able-bodied men were joining the ever increasing number of volunteers coming from the surrounding farms and villages. The local militias were gathering, rallying to cast out the evildoers . . . the Philistines.

If only I were a man! Prudence thought wistfully. *Then I could take part in this righteous purging.* But alas, it was her lot to be one of the legion of women left behind, out of harm's way, to wait. Perhaps she should be grateful she had no husband to fear for as so many others did. But she felt so useless. Such a great cause, and she could have no part in it. She could only pack up and leave.

Outside the family home, Prudence picked up her tiny half brother James and hugged him. She tucked him into the back of their loaded wagon next to Nathan, the oldest. "Remember not to jostle around back here and disturb Pa," she said in her firm big-sister voice. "And keep Caleb and Hester from getting into mischief, you hear?" She checked to see that each one was seated securely among the bags and crates.

"Yes, Pru," the boy said, casting a look of superiority at his younger siblings.

Prudence shifted her attention to their father, lying pale and weak on a makeshift pallet in the center of the wagon bed. She reached out and stroked his cheek. He appeared even more wan in the sunlight. "Don't fret, Papa. There's sure to be a building we can rent in one of the neighboring towns."

"You're a good daughter," he said earnestly.

The compliment caught Prudence off guard. Though she knew her father loved her, tender sentiments had been few and far between, particularly since his remarriage to Miriam, barely eight years Prudence's senior. She tried not to let it bother her, especially since it had never been Papa's way to shower a person with useless flattery. Besides, Prudence did get along well with Papa's plump little wife, even though Miriam seemed more an older sister to her than a stepmother.

Prudence let her gaze linger on her father's frail features. His condition had worsened in the last two days. He had lost even more weight, and all the uproar of the other night, the yelling and musket fire, had taken a toll on his already weak heart. She slid a glance toward fair-haired Miriam, who returned it with a bewildered shrug.

"Prudence," her father said. "Just pack up the store. Leave Charlestown as soon as you can."

"I will, Pa. I have most of the goods already crated. It shouldn't take too long to find another location for the mercantile."

"Why did I have to be struck down at this crucial time?" he rasped, breathing hard. "Heber's two boys can help. Hire them. Today."

She attempted an obedient smile.

"And my musket—"

"It's behind the storeroom door."

"You remember how to load? Shoot?"

"Yes, you were a good teacher."

"You must be out of here by tomorrow afternoon. No later." He tried to raise up a little but fell back.

She cupped his shoulder with her hand. "Don't exert yourself, Pa. We're quite safe. The redcoats will probably be licking their wounds for days to come—and heaven knows, they can't think for themselves. They'll wait for orders from Lord North and Parliament before they make another move."

"When are we going?" four-year-old Hester whined, toying with one of her short brown braids as she got up.

Nathan gently pushed her back down beside James with a big-brother glare.

"This minute, honey," Prudence said brightly and nodded to Miriam.

"Wait, Daughter," Pa said. "Parliament has already spoken, and their first words were loud and clear. They'll make their next move—soon." He turned his head toward the driver's seat and met his wife's concerned expression. "We must have this wagon unloaded tonight, Miriam, and back here tomorrow . . . no matter what the cost."

No matter what the cost? Scervant Endecott had never spent a frivolous shilling in his life! He truly was worried!

"As you wish, dear." Miriam's pleasant features softened in a smile. "With three strong men on my father's place, I'm sure it can be easily accomplished." But despite her feigned cheerfulness, the lines of worry creasing her forehead did not disappear, and her light blue eyes, ever prone to tears, now seemed on the verge of pooling and spilling over.

Prudence heard footsteps coming in their direction, and she looked up just as the town barber, Mr. Upton, entered the mercantile. "You just relax, Papa. Miriam and I are more than able to handle things for the time being, and I must tend to business now. Godspeed. I'll see you all in Medford tomorrow eve."

"Bye, Pru," the children chorused, all of them waving.

She returned their wave with as much optimism as she could muster. Then, as the wagon pulled away with her family aboard, Prudence straightened her shoulders and raised her chin purposefully. They were at war now, and she would do her part, no matter how trivial. And she wasn't alone. All up and down the street, other households were being loaded up in carts and wagons and packed off just the same as hers.

She took a breath of the fragrant April air, and it struck her how paradoxical this somber scene was. The world she knew was being torn apart by strife, and yet the forsythia, lilacs, and hollyhocks continued to bloom as if nothing at all were amiss.

Starting up the two steps into the store, Prudence paused and gazed toward the docks at the ominous British warships on the Charles River. Troops were encamped on Boston Common, just across the water. So close. So threatening. It was no wonder so many neighbors had already left town. Yet no matter that England had the mightiest army and navy in the world. They would be driven away. The people of Massachusetts had far greater determination *and* the power of almighty God.

Stout Mr. Upton, his long mustache elaborately waxed, stood at the rope spool measuring a length of hemp. "Afternoon, Miss Prudence," he said matter-of-factly as she came in. "I need about ten yards of sailcloth." Absently he pushed his wire-rimmed spectacles higher up the bridge of his nose.

"I'm sorry, sir, but I doubt we have that much left, with everyone wanting to cover their wagonloads."

"Aye." He shook his head. "'Tis a sad day for our town."

"It's only thanks to you and the other selectmen we still have a town," she returned sincerely. "If you hadn't taken your lives in your hands Wednesday night and gone into the fray to speak with Brigadier General Percy, I'm certain his returning soldiers would have sacked and burned us all out. They were in such a vile temper. Such cursing and foul language as they passed through. I've never heard the like of it."

He nodded. "They're a scurrilous lot. I'd liked to have gone to the Charlestown Neck, held them there until the boys from Salem and Marblehead arrived. But with the warships a stone's throw away, too many women and children were at risk."

"Well, our fellows showed them we mean business. And with hundreds more pouring in from the back country every day, it'll be a while before the British take any more strolls, I'm sure." Prudence began crating the items he had already put on the counter.

"Personally, I won't be happy until they board those ships of theirs and sail back where they came from, every last one of them. And I wouldn't mind in the least helping them get going. In fact, I'm quite looking forward to rejoining my company as soon as I get my family resettled. Speaking of that," he said, tilting his head to indicate the remnant of canvas, "I'll take however much you've got left."

Prudence again was reminded of the fact that she, too, would be resettled, while the men set out on a great and noble adventure. With a deep sense of disappointment she started measuring the heavy cloth.

When the barber finished selecting the remaining goods he required, Prudence helped load him up, then held the door open for him. "Godspeed, Mr. Upton. I hope we'll be seeing one another back here very soon."

"Aye, and so do I, Miss Endecott. Godspeed to you." Outside, he turned and peered around the stack of provisions he carried. "Give your father my best. Tell him we're all praying for him."

"I will, thank you. That will comfort him. It's very hard on someone like Pa not to be able to take his place beside you and the rest of the men." She smiled sadly.

"How well I know, dear girl. We'll miss him, too."

With a grimace, Prudence crossed her arms. "If only I were a man, I could take Pa's place."

Mr. Upton chuckled. "You'll do well to finish up here and get your little self to safety. Your father has enough to worry about without having you entertain such foolish thoughts. Take care, my dear."

Prudence stifled the anger and resentment rising within her and schooled her lips into a polite smile as he walked away. If she had entertained more of those *foolish* thoughts, Pa could very well have been moved to the quiet and safety of his wife's family long *before* the battle . . . only she had been intimidated out of spying by that bully at the Clarkes' Christmas ball.

When Mr. Upton was gone, Prudence set out in the opposite direction to find Heber's two boys to build more packing crates. As she walked, she mulled over that night. Ironically, she had fallen into the scheme of becoming a spy quite by accident. She had taken a ferry across to the city to pick up merchandise in late November, as she had a hundred times before. Down in the warehouse district, she happened to run into Molly, an acquaintance from Charlestown who had secured a place in the home of a Tory shipowner. A silly young woman with simply no principles when it came to the dire straits of Massachusetts, Molly had asked if Prudence knew of any honest young women interested in serving at the round of holiday parties. At first, Prudence discarded the idea without consideration, but when Molly gushed on and on about the illustrious military guests certain to attend, it became apparent that a true daughter of liberty could not let such a golden opportunity pass.

Prudence pursed her lips in indignation. She should never have allowed that browbeater at the party to deter her from trying to ferret out crucial information. After she had given the humiliating matter some thought, she realized he had most likely noticed her only because he chose to engage in the very same activity himself. But the fact was—and such an incredibly satisfying one at that—recent events proved that the pompous peacock was the failure, or Charlestown wouldn't have been caught off guard.

Perhaps one of these days she would run into that sorry young egotist again. For all his dashing appearance and excessive confidence, it would be her purest pleasure to remind him of his debacle, to rub his snooty nose in the mess of his failure.

At the thought of such sublime vengeance, Prudence found herself smiling. But then she reminded herself that she had more important matters to take care of than daydreaming. She brushed some stray fibers of hemp from her dark calico skirt and continued in search of those boys.

32

"It must really be happening. Finally," Morgan said as he and Robert Chandler, along with about twelve hundred other militiamen, left their camp on the outskirts of Cambridge and marched toward Charlestown. "It's been almost two months since we came here from Concord. I thought the British would retaliate long before this."

Robert nodded. "That's for sure. Particularly after your friend Ted assisted the Green Mountain Boys in the takeover of Fort Ticonderoga. It's been over a month, and General Gage still hasn't made a move. All we hear are rumors."

"And those are thicker than mosquitoes in a swamp." Morgan swatted at a particularly pesky one without missing a step in the muggy darkness. "But this latest rumor might be true, about the British plan to take the heights on both sides of the bay."

"Beats me that old Gage waited this long," a narrow-faced man on the other side of Robert commented. "He received reinforcements weeks ago, not to mention three more uppity generals."

"Well," Morgan said, "it looks like our own generals are tired of waiting, after the taste we got on the islands."

"Were you with us when we were sent after some farmer's

pigs on Hog Island a couple weeks back?" Robert asked the other man.

He wagged his head. "Nay. I came from up north just the other day. Name's Jones."

"Too bad you missed it," Robert drawled. "Seems the British soldiers had been makin' forays to the harbor islands to steal livestock and grain, so when they saw us loading up those pigs, they sent a company of marines to stop us."

Morgan leaned around Robert with a grin. "We showed those puppets what for. Gage had to send over more troops. Before the day was over, I thought he'd dispatch the rest of his army against us. But he backed off one more time. We won. Again."

"Well, I don't mind admitting I was a little surprised," Robert said. "With all those musket balls whistling around us, I doubted we'd make it."

"Quite." Morgan grimaced. "But the general did the prudent thing, easing off. As it was, far too much ammunition was wasted over a herd of smelly hogs."

"Still a bit upset that you ended up in a mud bath, are you?" Chandler said on a teasing note. "We had been ordered to drive the porkers down to the barges," he explained to Mr. Jones, "and Morgan slipped into some very fragrant slime."

Morgan edged forward enough to talk around his friend. "I came up here from Philadelphia to fight, not herd swine—nor, as Chandler can attest, to be a beast of burden myself. Seems all we do is move, stack, and then restack supplies."

"Sounds to me," a stout mustached man on Morgan's other side piped in, "you joined the wrong army, if you can't stand a little *honest* work."

The remark, though made in a jesting tone, irritated Morgan. He didn't answer for a few minutes as they marched in steady cadence. Then he perked up. "Think I need to get myself elected an officer. Then I'll ride my horse while others tromp through the muck and mire."

Chandler gave him a playful nudge. "Best you get used to this lowly rank. Unless our colonies send militias from our own neighborhoods, we're just two more strangers in the band. Not much hope of being elected to lead."

"Let's just hope that from now on we do what we came here to do—fight," Morgan grated. "How much farther to Charlestown Neck, anyway? My blisters are starting to get blisters."

"We're almost there, lad," the mustached man said. "But then it's one more mile to the center of town." His chuckle sounded as if he took particular delight in passing on that information.

"You're from around here?" Robert asked.

"Aye. Vernon Upton's the name. Barber and surgeon of Charlestown—or what *was* Charlestown before we were all forced to abandon it. I hate to think it'll end up being sacrificed."

Morgan considered the statement, but he had no comfort to offer the man. "I fear there's not much hope of saving the place if the British attempt what we've heard they're planning."

"By tomorrow morning we should have a little surprise of our own waiting for them," Jones said. "In fact, here comes Colonel Putnam now." He pointed to a caravan emerging from the dark.

"What's he bringing?" Morgan noted a large number of teams and wagons. "Fieldpieces, I hope? Wait! I see barrels. May they be full of gunpowder! For once I'd like to have plenty of that!"

Upton tilted his head with another grin. "Afraid not, lad. The wagons are full of shovels and picks for digging trenches. And the barrels—we'll be filling those with some of the dirt."

Morgan stopped dead, and the man behind him bumped him back into step. "They expect us to dig trenches and then carry the dirt away?!"

Seeming to enjoy himself at Morgan's expense, the barber laughed. "Nay. We'll not be carrying the barrels off. They're to reinforce our earthworks . . . against all the cannonballs."

Morgan realized the man must consider him a green kid

shaking in his boots. "Never fear, Mr. Upton. Stick close to Chandler and me. We'll see you through."

Robert nodded. "Yes, sir. My friend and I dodged our share of bullets and balls in Concord—fired in volleys, no less. Then again, all along the road to here."

"You two were in Concord?"

Morgan found the new tone of respect, however belated, greatly satisfying. "Chandler was shot—he's got the scar to prove it."

"Oh, well, it only grazed me," Robert admitted.

"Graze or not, young man," Mr. Jones said, "it's an honor to march alongside you. I came from the Newburyport area, and we didn't learn of the fighting soon enough to be much help."

"Newburyport?" Morgan echoed. "Isn't that north of Salem?"

"Aye, the next port beyond."

"Hmm. I need to locate a particular person. Perhaps she lives in that direction."

Robert chuckled. "Please, sir, if you actually know of this young woman, do tell my friend. This is one quest I long to see completed."

Searing Chandler with a scowl, Morgan edged forward again to see around him. "Her name is Miss Prudence Endecott. Do you know her?"

"Actually, *I* am acquainted with someone by that name."

Morgan whirled around to see Upton grinning at him. "You are?" Barely able to contain his excitement, Morgan grabbed the barber's sleeve. "The woman you know, is she a lovely dark-haired miss with wide gray eyes? A heart-shaped face?"

"I'd say that's a pretty fair description."

"It is? Well, then, can you tell me where she lives?"

Upton's smirk flashed once more. "She did live right here in Charlestown." He pointed toward the dark outline of the village ahead. "But as you can see, everyone's moved on."

Morgan's elation crashed. "Where did she go? Surely you must know."

"Do tell him," Chandler pleaded. "My sanity's at stake."

The barber gave a nonchalant shrug. "Most likely 'twas to her stepmother's family they went. But I'm afraid I can't recall the name of the village."

"Still, you could find out, right?" Morgan asked, not to be put off.

"I suppose so." He pushed his spectacles higher and looked Morgan up and down. "But from those fancy clothes of yours, young man, and your aversion to honest labor, I doubt you'd be the least acceptable to our Prudence. She's an old-fashioned lass, a plain and simple Puritan girl through and through."

That news mattered not a whit to Morgan. All he cared about was the possibility of finding the gorgeous spy after his long and fruitless search. He turned to the barber. "If you can find out where she's staying, my good man, I'll make it worth your while. Surely in your situation you could use some extra money."

Upton studied Morgan a moment, then nodded. "Aye, that I could. Tell you what. If we survive, I'll do what I can."

"Stay by my side. I'll see that you do."

❦ ❦

Ignoring the dull ache in his back, Morgan brushed the dirt off his blistered hands as the sun peaked over the top of the redoubt. The militiamen had spent the entire night digging and building the earthwork fortification atop a high grassy knoll known as Breed's Hill. All in all, he decided as he peered out of the trench, the odd-shaped structure wasn't half bad. Barrels and woven twigs reinforced the packed earth, and there were sally ports on either side and at the rear for a quick escape if need be. For extra coverage, two apple trees shaded the front. It would not be easily taken by the enemy.

"Colonel Gridley has done well by us, eh?" Upton commented from beside Morgan as he wiped his spectacles on a grubby kerchief.

"Gridley?" Morgan asked, too thirsty to care overmuch about particulars.

"Aye. Fine engineer. Earned his reputation during the French and Indian War, from what I hear."

Morgan glanced absently at the subject of the conversation. The man appeared to be at least sixty-five years of age—and looked almost as dirty and far more weary than Morgan felt himself. Obviously the man had done at least as much physical labor as the workers he had directed. "Quite. He's done a remarkable job. And now that we've finished, I hope he'll see to it that something besides that cheap rum gets passed around. I don't know whether I'm more tired, thirsty, or starved."

Robert Chandler, tamping down the pile of dirt above the trench, leaned on his shovel and turned his soil-streaked face to Morgan. "It's sleep for me. I'd forego even a drink of spring water for a few hours of blessed sleep."

With a half smile of acknowledgment, Morgan climbed over the top for a look at their handiwork. Odd that with all the warships at anchor in the Charles River estuary, no one on deck watching through the long night had so much as spotted the activity on this hill. Even with the growing morning light there was not a soul in sight nor any movement aboard the vessels. Despite the other miracles he'd witnessed thus far, it amazed Morgan that the navy could ring their ships' bells every half hour and greet one another with "All's well," yet be unaware of mass labor being conducted such a short distance away.

Just then, he spotted a sailor running along the deck of the *Lively*. Then others. Booms were swung and the vessel turned broadside.

"Look out!" someone shouted from the wall of the redoubt.

A loud blast shattered the quiet, followed closely by a second.

Morgan slid down just as a cannonball slammed into the hillside below them. The next hit farther afield.

As more cannon shots exploded across the hill, Colonel

Prescott came running along the ledge above their trench. "Men! Bring your tools! Your weapons! Gear! Follow me!"

At that moment, the *Somerset,* just below them, fired its first cannon burst, joined by blasts from several of the big guns lining Copps Hill on the Boston peninsula. The balls exploded all over the eastern end of Charlestown's own peninsula.

Amid the thunder and explosions from every direction, Morgan and the others in their section vaulted out to follow the colonel. Surely the earthworks must have been breached. So much for Gridley's engineering genius—and after that night of backbreaking labor, no less.

Prescott led them out the sally port on the side, away from the shelling ships. But instead of heading for the front of the redoubt, he ran down the hillside toward the Mystic River, which bordered the north side of the peninsula. He stopped. "Here. Dig here—" he sprinted several rods farther—"to here. We need a breastworks to protect our flank."

Morgan could not believe his ears. *He wanted them to dig new trenches out here? In the open? Now? With cannonballs raining down?*

The force of one cannon blast knocked Morgan to his knees. Smoke and dust obscured his view as he got up and furiously jammed his spade into the hard earth. Even though the British military lacked accuracy in their firing, the roar and turbulence from the cannons quaked earth and air alike. He paused and looked fleetingly back at the shelter of the redoubt, wishing he were still within its protection. Had it been only a few hours since he had finally received the first hopeful news regarding Prudence Endecott? He couldn't help wondering now if he would live to find her.

Chandler seized his arm. "Dig, man!" he shouted over the noise. "It's our only chance!"

33

Prudence revelled in the balmy June morning. Her father had sent her to retrieve the remainder of her family's furniture from Charlestown. Seated on the wagon between her two young stepuncles, sent along to help her, she could feel their excitement mounting the nearer they drew to Boston Bay. They talked of little except the siege.

"I didn't want to say anything in front of Miriam," Prudence said, voicing her thoughts aloud to Nicholas and Franklin Randolph. "She has enough to worry about with Papa's failing health. But now that Charlestown is deserted, I wouldn't put it past those good-for-nothing redcoats to sneak across the river in the dead of night and loot the empty houses. I hate to think of them rifling through our things."

Nicholas, a little over a year Prudence's senior, tossed his head, and a sneer contorted his long face. "Don't worry, our boys are watching all around the bay. They wouldn't let 'em."

Whether his words were true or not, Prudence felt somewhat encouraged by his confidence. "I do hope you're right. It would break Miriam's heart if she were to lose her fretwork looking glass."

"Them lobsterbacks don't make a move we don't know about," dark-haired Frank scoffed. Easily the more handsome of the pair, in an obnoxious sort of way, his cockiness had always been the most notable trait of Miriam's youngest brother. Now the lad snatched up Nick's musket from the footboard and pointed it at a tree, the powder horn dangling from it by a thong. "Pow, pow!" he mimicked. "That's what I'd do if I found any of them pointy hats stealing Sis's property." He leered at Prudence. "Never fear, fair niece, I'm here to protect our property *and your person!*" A suggestive smile flared in his hazel eyes.

Nearly two years younger than Prudence, Frank was not one to allow something so insignificant as an age difference dampen his forward manner. He had flirted persistently with her since the day she and the family came to stay with the Randolphs, and she had quickly wearied of it—and of him. "As you well know," she said, "I've brought my own weapon and can take care of myself."

"Thank Providence your pa didn't think so," Nick replied, guiding the horse around a large hole in the road, "or ours wouldn't have let us come."

"Yep," Frank railed. "Ain't fair, neither. Everybody I know's been given leave to join the militia in Cambridge. Everybody except us."

"Pa treats us like slaves." Nick grimaced. "All he ever cares about is getting that miserable dairy herd milked."

"If it was milk being taxed instead of tea," Frank added, "I'll wager he'd be glad to let us go, huh, Nick?"

"No doubt he would. I wish Pa would understand the shame he's bringing on us. My Patsy hinted last eve that pretty soon folks are going to start thinkin' I'm a coward." His face darkened as he clucked the horse to a faster pace. The wagon lurched.

"Perhaps if your father attended church more often—," Prudence started to say.

"Ha!" Frank cut in. "Pa says that's a waste of time *and* money. Says a body can read the Bible and pray at home for free."

Prudence shrugged. "But when a person is left to himself, there's often precious little of either done. Had your father attended church meeting this Sunday past, the good minister would have informed him of the righteousness of our cause.

This isn't merely about taxes, you know. It's about protecting all the freedoms we've enjoyed for so long. Freedom to govern ourselves as well as our tax money, freedom to worship God in our own manner, freedom to buy from whomever we please and sell whatever we want, wherever our ships take us."

Nick turned his head, his mouth curled up in scorn. "You and your speeches. Small wonder you have no suitors. You should be more like Pat. All she knows and wants is for me to shoot those foulmouthed redjackets for the insults they've heaped on our young women."

Unable to think of an appropriate response to such inane nonsense, Prudence could do nothing but stare at him.

Frank snickered. "That's right—we're out to save all our sweet flowers of womanhood." He directed the musket at another tree. "Pow!"

Enraged at the ignorant farm boys, Prudence found her tongue. "Sweet flowers of—"

"Look!" Frank shouted. "Smoke!"

Prudence swung her gaze forward. Black smoke churned upward in the sunny sky—more smoke than she'd ever seen in her entire life. "Charlestown! The red devils must be burning the town!" She snatched the traces from Nick's hands and slapped them across the horse's back to speed him to the top of the hill.

"Hey!" Nick hollered, grabbing the reins again.

"Well, hurry!" she snapped. "I need to make sure it's not my house!"

A distant cannon boom echoed across the stillness.

Frank sprung to his feet as they continued the climb. "The whole place must be on fire!"

Nick halted the horse on the crest of the rise, and Prudence watched in horror the destruction of her village. Flames shot high into the sky from the church spires . . . surely a beacon to God of the evil being done. And the cannons were not only aimed at the town but were also exploding across Breed's Hill behind it.

"Is your house among those burning?" Nick asked.

She nodded, too angry to cry. "It must be. And so is the store. How will I tell Papa? His heart will never stand such a shock."

"Well, I want a closer look," Frank announced. "Get the nag moving."

"Wait, you idiot!" Nick glanced at Prudence. "We can't take a girl down there." He handed over the reins. "Here, Prudence. Take the wagon back home. I'm getting out here."

"Not without me, you're not," Frank said, their father's flintlock and bullet pouch in hand as he leaped down right behind his older brother.

"But what will I tell your father?" Prudence asked.

Nick turned. "Tell him . . . tell him . . ." He eyed the musket at her feet, then reached for it.

She stamped a foot on it. "No. This flower of womanhood will not be left defenseless."

"Aw, I guess you're right," he grated, obviously still coveting her weapon.

"Report to the first militia captain you find," she told him. "He'll issue you one of your own."

Nick nodded, backing away. "Tell Patsy where I've gone, will you? Tell her I love her." Wheeling around, he took off at a dead run after Frank.

Watching the two young men growing smaller against the flame and smoke of the city, Prudence felt disgust—and envy—growing within her. Disgust because men were so thrilled to be going off to fight without the slightest idea of what the conflict was about. And envy because she, a daughter of liberty, who knew the noble and righteous cause for what it truly was, could not go. If only . . .

Suddenly from out of nowhere, a wagon barreled up behind hers. She hadn't even heard it coming. "Out of my way!" the driver shouted frantically.

She snatched the traces and guided her horse from the middle of the road just in time.

As it rumbled past, her attention was drawn to a cluster of women and children standing on a grassy knoll, looking down at the Charlestown spectacle. Behind them was a small farmhouse. And behind that, clothes fluttered on a line.

Surely no one was doing the wash while the bombardment of Charlestown was taking place. It must have been left overnight in all the excitement.

A pair of men's trousers flapped on the breeze, almost beckoning her. And a man's shirt. Dare she take them? The women and children were still engrossed in the fire and taking no notice of her. It was a sign. It simply had to be. God knew how deeply she cared about the cause. Surely he wanted her to join the fight.

As she took hold of the top of the wagon wheel and hopped down, a rush of exuberance completely filled her, the likes of which she had never before experienced in her whole sensible, practical life.

❦ ❦

When the earth-shattering barrage of cannon fire finally ceased, the afternoon silence seemed eerily quiet. Morgan could hear nothing but the ringing in his ears and his exhausted, overworked body screaming at him. He looked at Robert, also slumped against the dirt wall of the breastwork they had dug. Chandler was covered head to toe with sweaty dirt, and Morgan knew he hadn't fared much better himself.

"Do you think it's over?" Chan asked, the rounds of his eyes the only recognizable part of him as he raked Morgan with an appraising glance.

Morgan climbed up the earthen parapet to take a peek.

Smoke billowed up from beyond the redoubt where Charlestown still smoldered and burned. It darkened most of the sky. He wondered fleetingly if Prudence Endecott's home had been lost or spared. If only she were safe, dwellings and possessions could be replaced.

On either side of him, from their positions in the long trench they had dug to widen their defense line, other patriots poked up like so many moles to peer through the smoke.

Farther down the hill behind them, three V-shaped earthworks had just been finished to defend the road below.

"Would ye look at that!" someone yelled, pointing toward Morton's Point at the far end of Charlestown Neck.

A string of boats and barges loaded with redcoated soldiers came through the murky cloud. More had already debarked and were making their way to the shore.

So that's why the bombardment stopped, Morgan thought, sliding down beside Robert again. "The invasion is about to begin. Must be a hundred boatloads. Can you believe that? Now, after we're tired, sore, and beyond being merely famished—now they want to fight."

Chandler, in his unflappable southern manner, pulled his pocket timepiece out and clicked it open. "It's after two." Then he slipped the watch back into its place.

Chan had been a brave and trusted fighting companion during the Concord fight. Still, Morgan often got the impression that he would have no aversion to joining his dear departed wife when it came right down to it.

"Appears the generals must have gotten together and decided we weren't about to be scared off this hill," Robert drawled.

"Scared off?" Morgan asked flippantly. "Not hardly. But I could be bought off, perhaps. Some food, a warm bed. I might be willing to negotiate for a soak in a hot tub."

Chandler and the others nearby chuckled.

"What I want to know," someone said, "is where are all those thousands of men who've been struttin' around for weeks, bragging about what they was gonna do when the lobsters dared to crawl outta Boston? We've been stuck here without food or water for hours. Where's our relief?"

"Well, Morgan, my friend," Robert said lightly, "you're a smooth talker. Go up to the redoubt while there's still time and see if they've forgotten we're down here."

"Aye," another said in agreement. "Tell them what's left of us would sure like a bite to eat about now. From the look of things, we'll not get another chance for who knows how long."

Morgan gazed down the line to a much wider spot that had taken a direct hit an hour ago. Three men had been killed there, among them Mr. Upton, the one man who might have been able to help him find Prudence. And from the startling number of British being unloaded down the hill, many, many more militia would be joining the dead.

"If you don't want to go, I will," Chandler offered.

"Never mind," someone else said. "I see men coming out through the sally port. They haven't forgotten us after all."

Morgan looked to see the additional militia, in clean clothes, dropping down into their trench. They had an officer at their head.

"Where's your captain?" the officer asked.

"We don't have one, sir. Colonel Prescott sent us out here to dig this breastwork early this morning—*after* we'd been digging in the redoubt all night. We could use some food, water. . . ."

The man appeared slightly confused. "The British are lining up, lad. Prepare for battle."

Scarcely had the words left his mouth when the bombardment from the British ships began again with far more intensity than before. *No doubt they had merely wanted their barrels to cool down,* Morgan thought facetiously. But with hardly enough time to console himself that the cannons would have to desist when their infantry neared the fortification, he suddenly realized he had just been ordered to pick up his weapon instead of a shovel and do what he originally came here to do.

The officer continued down the line. "We have very little powder to go around," he announced.

Thousands of troops on the way up this hill, and we're short of powder? Again?

"Colonel Prescott says we need to use our limited supply wisely," the officer continued. "Don't fire till you see the whites of their eyes."

34

"Appears the British are sending their grenadiers and light infantry first," Robert muttered during an unexpected lull in the cannon blasts. "We'll be facing their best, as we did in Concord."

Through suffocating clouds of smoke from the cannon fire, Morgan inched to the top of the trench. Hordes of British troops milled about at the bottom of the hill in various loose-jointed clusters with stragglers on the edges.

Then movement at the far end of the entrenchment drew his attention. Two fieldpieces of their own rolled into position down the slope to be aimed at the redcoats on the beach—the first encouraging sight since the whole business began.

It took only scant seconds for the guns to be loaded and fire put to the fuse. For a change the loud blast was music to Morgan's ears. But, alas, both cannonballs sailed over the enemies' heads and splashed into the bay, sending a mighty spray of water ashore.

Morgan's disappointment abated when he noted the British soldiers scurrying nervously about. They had suddenly become targets—and very hot targets, at that. In their heavy uniforms, lugging weighty field packs, they'd surely be as apprehensive and miserable when they started up the hill as Morgan was tired and hungry.

Cannons from HMS *Lively* and *Falcon* blasted again as the last boat reached the shore. This one included several fieldpieces. "They'll be able to fire at closer range now," he grimly told Chandler. "More accurately."

"Forget about them. We've withstood bombardment all day. It's those troops being deployed that worry me."

At the foot of the hill, soldiers who at one moment were moving around like ants now merged into a long red line, three men deep. The awesome sight stretched from the Mystic River on the north side of the peninsula nearly to Charlestown. The British had no intention of losing this time.

Morgan cast a glance toward the top of the redoubt, where their own militia leader, Colonel Prescott, strode quickly along with the much older General Putnam. The colonel stopped and shouted down to the men within the earthen walls of the fort. "Major Wood! With all speed, take your men down to Charlestown and occupy whatever buildings still remain. We cannot allow the British to flank us on that side." When there was no response, he came farther down. "Major Wood!"

Well, Morgan concluded, at least he and Robert would not be called on to go elsewhere. They were needed exactly where they were. Plenty of redcoats were beginning the ascent. And heading straight for them.

Firing ceased from the ships, and British fifes and drums struck up a military tune. Standard bearers hoisted regimental banners, which fluttered little in the windless afternoon warmth. But the sun glittered off a multitude of bayonet blades as the long, long wave of troops started up the hill.

Morgan heard the men around him opening their pouches, laying out their premade paper cartridges packed with ball and powder and tied with thread. And some of their mumblings were easily recognized as prayers. Knowing it was an opportune moment to send some fervent petitions to the Lord, he flicked a glance at Robert.

Chandler's jaw was rigid. But then he bowed his head— making peace with the Almighty, Morgan assumed, in case he might soon be allowed to join his wife in the hereafter.

Morgan lowered his own eyelids. *Father, I know so many others*

*here are far more worthy of your grace than I, but I have been trying
lately, praying every night. I haven't attempted to lie my way in or out
of anything since Concord, though I've been sorely tempted, considering all this ditch digging. However, I do realize my thoughts have been
excessively occupied with finding Miss Endecott. How one brief encounter with her has managed to consume me so, I do not understand.
But I promise to find a Bible and start reading it every day again,
instead of thinking about her my every waking moment.* "I promise."

"Did you say somethin'?"

Morgan shook his head, too embarrassed to admit to Robert the rash vow he had just made. Chan knew better than
anyone how obsessed with Prudence he'd been.

Well, no more.

Tossing a look out of their haven, he saw the British were
now less than a hundred yards away. A surge of fear assailed
him.

Colonel Prescott, who didn't appear to share Morgan's
trepidation, continued to pace the parapet along the front of
the redoubt, as if oblivious of the excellent target he made if
the British chose to waste a volley.

"The colonel must want to be sure none of us fires before
he orders," Robert said. "The men in the redoubt would have
to shoot through him."

Morgan nodded. "How close do you suppose the redcoats
have to get before we see the whites of their eyes? Closer than
at Concord?"

Chandler didn't answer.

The beating of the drums, from behind the infantry, was
growing louder by the second, and a slight breeze fluttered
the enemy flags.

Watching the oncoming force, Morgan could understand
why the British were known throughout the world for their
military might. Without exception, the soldiers maintained
their steady march, bayonet first, into the face of hundreds of
muskets, as if they were invincible.

The militia officer in the breastwork was slowly working
back up the line. "Don't fire at the same time as the men in

the redoubt," he said, grim reminder of the short supply of powder. "We're farther back. Wait for my order—and make every shot count! Take turns. Remember, only every other person will fire, then reload while the man next to him shoots. Don't give the enemy an opening to rush us."

At last came the order up at the redoubt. "Fire!"

Hundreds of muskets and flintlocks exploded at once, a thunderous roar of flashes and smoke.

Screams pierced the air, and a multitude of regulars crumpled to the ground.

Morgan blinked and looked again. *Almost the entire first line of grenadiers, down? Unbelievable!* The few that remained gazed around in stunned horror, then turned and bolted down the hill—right past the equally shocked next wave. And his own company had yet to receive the order to fire!

In the redoubt, the militiamen with spent weapons slid down to reload, while others stood and took aim.

That volley was equally deadly and came before the stunned British officers had issued an order of their own.

Once again came bloodcurdling shrieks of pain. And once again, only a handful of redcoats remained on their feet. A few managed to get off a wild shot before breaking rank and sprinting down the slope. The panicked third wave wheeled around and ran with them.

"Aw," a man near Morgan groused. "I didn't even get a chance at 'em! Look at 'em showing their heels." With a huff, he leveled his flintlock and shot, order or not.

"Take heart," Morgan said. "They'll be back. They're too stubborn to give up so soon. You'd better reload."

To his utter dismay, Morgan watched his prediction fulfilled time and again as the British regrouped, were reinforced, and kept coming. They came up the middle. They marched around the flanks. They circled along the Mystic River beach and cut in behind the militia. But everywhere there were more militiamen lined up behind walls and fences to thin out the ranks. British blood reddened the grass throughout the afternoon.

No longer panicked by their own fallen comrades, the incredibly disciplined redcoats managed to hit their mark from time to time. But the day belonged to the patriots.

Until they ran out of gunpowder.

And the British kept coming . . . like endless waves of the ocean, a never-ending sea of crimson coats and tall hats, of flashes and smoke from long Brown Besses, of shouted orders and battle cries.

The militia, many now virtually defenseless, began beating a chaotic retreat toward Bunker Hill, seeking a last stronghold. The few who still had a shot or two left covered them.

One after another the enemy claimed each abandoned trench and fencepost, usurping control of Breed's Hill.

Morgan, also out of powder, leaped over a stone wall. A glance over his shoulder revealed the heart-wrenching sight of Crown soldiers entering the side ports of the redoubt even as the last of the militia poured out the back sally port.

If only this brand-new Provincial Army had garnered an adequate supply of gunpowder! But there was no time to spare for such contemplations. The battle was far from over.

Now that they had taken Breed's Hill, scarlet-coated troops began surging up Bunker Hill after the militia.

"Powder!" Morgan yelled at a man defending the stone fence. "Can you spare some?"

"Nay, lad. Only got enough for one more shot meself. Best get on up the hill with the rest."

Bullets and balls came closer, whistling past Morgan and Chandler, slamming into nearby trees and ricocheting from rocks as they scrambled toward the top of the rise. But when they reached it, even that could be held no longer and was being abandoned by its defenders. "Does no one have powder to spare?"

A skinny youth leaned around from behind a rock, musket in hand. "Everybody's run out. Get across the Neck while there's still a chance. I'll hold them off till my powder's gone."

That one's voice hasn't even changed yet! Morgan thought

wildly. "You're just a kid. Give us what you have, and get going before it's too late."

The lad glared angrily up at him, eyes wide . . . wide and unmistakable!

Staring openmouthed, Morgan grabbed Chandler's sleeve. "It's her, do you hear me? Prudence Endecott! Dressed like a man!"

A bullet screeched past his ear.

"Duck down, you fool," she yelled, "before you get your head shot off!"

As he and Robert dropped to the ground beside her, Morgan regained his senses. This was no place for a woman. "Take her powder, Chan. Cover us while I get her out of here."

Prudence's silvery eyes flashed. "You can't do—"

But Robert snatched the powder horn from her as Morgan took hold of her and dragged her, kicking and struggling, down the back side of the hill. In her gyrations, her tricorn flew off, revealing a loose knot of long, black hair.

Morgan slowed long enough to glance back at his friend. *Please, Lord, keep him safe.*

"Let . . . me . . . go!" Prudence rasped, twisting to free herself from his grip.

"Not this time," he said firmly, forcing her along once more. "Why is it, I wonder, that the two of us must always meet under such dangerous circumstances?"

She stopped struggling and swung a puzzled look up at him.

"I confess I'm a touch unkempt at the moment, rather than in a powdered wig or satin frock coat. And there's the sound of gunfire instead of a stringed quartet. But does Richard Clarke's Christmas ball ring a bell?" The corner of Morgan's mouth twitched as he searched her smudged face for a sign of recognition.

It came. Her lips gaped in surprise.

"Seems I'm destined to save your neck this time, too."

35

It was no use fighting this brute, Prudence concluded as his superior strength forced her to keep up with his long, sweeping strides. Morgan Thomas's huge hand gripped her wrist like a vise as they and hundreds of other fleeing militia reached the Charlestown Common on the mainland side of the Neck. He had foiled her attempts again.

The large triangle of grazing land where the Cambridge and Medford roads split was barely recognizable, crowded as it was with such a throng of tired, sweaty, bedraggled men. And even the kind-faced women directing the flow of people onto the Common with promises of food and water were unfamiliar.

Mr. Thomas emitted a weary sigh, and Prudence could see his exhaustion written all over his face. For the flicker of a second his grasp relaxed, but just as quickly tightened again, as if he owned her.

"A water wagon. Thank the Lord," he murmured, veering toward it with her in tow.

With so many others converging there, Prudence was buffeted back and forth as he threaded his way through the mob. She had to admit the poor man was desperate, so, surprising even herself, she stopped dragging her feet and fell into step.

At last they reached the back of the wagon containing spigoted barrels filled to the brim with cool water.

"Would you mind unhooking my cup from my haversack?" he asked. "I'm afraid I haven't got a free hand."

"Well, if you look close enough," Prudence huffed, not allowing her compassion to bridle her tongue, "you'll notice that neither have I."

Without a change in his expression, he reached for her musket and cradled it with his. "Now you do."

"Such a clever fellow," she snapped. Unhooking the metal cup, she saw it was caked with dirt and grime. She untucked her shirttail and began wiping it out.

"Don't bother," he said, pushing both muskets at her and taking the cup from her. "The last thing I care about just now is a little dirt. I haven't had a drink of water in over twenty-four hours." He thrust it forward, vying with other men for the water spigot.

When at last he managed to get some into the cup, his hand shook as he brought it to his mouth. But just shy of his lips, he stopped suddenly and lowered it. "Forgive me. You first."

Prudence was stunned. He could stand there trembling with thirst, his lips cracked and dry, and sacrifice his first sip—for her? She eased it back toward him. "No, thank you. I've had plenty today." It wasn't really a lie, she rationalized. Compared to his need, hers was nothing.

As he gulped down great draughts and refilled the container again and again, she studied him. Still handsome beneath the dirt, he now seemed more manly than before, more . . . well, a far cry from the limp toads who had attempted to court her. A little on the bossy side, but after all, what man could bring himself to admit a woman might actually be of value in battle?

When his thirst had been quenched, she reached for the cup. "I suppose I would like a little," she admitted.

After they were sated, they moved apart from the host of men still seeking respite and found an empty space on the grass.

Prudence peered up at him. "May I have your kerchief?"

He shot her an odd glance, but pulled it from a back pocket

and handed it to her. She poured the remainder of the water on the cloth square.

His mouth curved up as she began scrubbing the grime from his face. Sure enough, as the layers of dirt came off, she realized her earlier assessment hadn't been wrong. Despite the unmistakably bloodshot appearance of his dark blue eyes, they made a nice contrast to his tanned and handsomely masculine face—until she noticed his mocking expression.

Now she truly did recognize that know-it-all who had sent her packing at the party! Just like today. Any pity she might have felt a moment ago vanished.

"Well," she said, putting her hand on her hip, "now that you've intruded in my life again, *saved me from myself,* there's no need to keep me prisoner any longer. As you see, we are well away from danger now." Shoving his cup at him, she whirled to leave.

Mr. Thomas caught her arm, impeding her flight. "We don't know that. The redcoats are aware we've run out of powder. They probably won't stop at the Charlestown Neck. They'll keep right on coming. I must see you safely away from here. First, though, I smell food, and I'm famished. Let's find it."

She planted her feet. "Only if you let me borrow your hat. Please, Mr. Thomas. People are starting to notice me and the way I'm dressed. If I happen upon anyone who knows my family, I'll never be able to live it down."

"Ha!" Morgan swept his tricorn off and held it over her head. "You can have it on two conditions. First, that you call me Morgan, not stuffy old Mr. Thomas. And second, that you'll admit you're not supposed to be here."

"I'll admit no such thing . . . *Morgan.* It's just that it would be awkward. Come along, will you?" She snatched the hat and tucked her hair up under it, then tugged him to his feet. "Let's get something to eat. Perhaps with a full belly you might be more rational. More reasonable."

In line with the others, Prudence suddenly became aware of a whole new problem. She might have clothes similar to the rest of the militia, but she lacked a haversack loaded with gear. The only plate between the two of them was Morgan's. Her gaze fell to it as he held it idly in his hands. He followed her line of vision and gave the merest hint of a wink.

When they reached the huge vat of beans and salt pork, he ladled a great mound of them onto his dish while she filled her hands with as many biscuits as she could hold.

"Let's go over there to eat," he said, indicating with his elbow a spot near the road. "I'd like to keep an eye out for my friend . . . if he makes it back."

She followed him to a grassy mound where they could observe the tail end of the ragtag militias from the various colonial towns. As the men of all ages streamed past with lagging feet, bloody bandages, and defeated spirits, Prudence wondered why the Lord hadn't worked another miracle for his people as he had on the Concord road and at Fort Ticonderoga. The surprise attack at the fort had been so successful not a soul had been killed.

Morgan nudged her and held the plate and a spoon out to her. "After you."

Aware of his great hunger, Prudence quickly took a small sampling, then left the remainder for him. He wolfed it down in seconds, his attention glued all the while to the road from Charlestown Neck.

She had good eyes and should be able to help him find his friend, she decided. But the weary, smoke-streaked men all looked alike as they trudged past in the fading daylight. At last she gave up.

Sporadic gunfire could still be heard, and despite Morgan Thomas's arrogance, Prudence noted how he watched the men intently, uneasiness creasing his tired face. She found herself praying his friend would be all right.

Then he met her gaze. "How much gunpowder would you say remained in your horn when we left?"

"Actually, I had quite a lot. I wasn't able to join the others until later in the day, and the captain ordered me to Bunker Hill—nowhere near the fighting. And just when the British had finally gotten close enough for me to shoot, *you jerked me away.* I only managed to get off two rounds. Two measly shots," she repeated for emphasis. But he was still so absorbed in the stragglers coming up the road that her words had no effect whatsoever.

"Then there's still hope he'll make it. With that much powder, he would naturally be one of the last to retreat. He'd provide cover for the others."

"I assume, then, he's a man of righteous purpose."

Morgan slanted her a disapproving look. "And mercy. Robert would never leave the other men in the hands of the enemy."

"Of course." Breaking eye contact, Prudence gazed into the distance, only slightly mollified. "But our cause . . . almighty God destined us to have this land as surely as he gave Canaan to the children of Israel. The discovery of this land was no accident. Christopher Columbus was brought here—we were all brought here—to bring God's light to the lost, not to have it snuffed out by mighty England." She paused. "Did you know the name Christopher means 'light bearer'? And as children of our Puritan forefathers, surely we have a duty—"

An annoying flicker of amusement crossed his face. "The barber, Mr. Upton, told me you liked to make speeches."

"You know Mr. Upton? You spoke to him about me? When was that?"

"A good portion of last night, while we worked side by side digging trenches. He told me quite a lot about you, actually."

"You don't say." She crossed her arms.

"All good, I might add. He mentioned your ailing father, the great help you were to him in the store—"

Prudence felt herself relax a little.

"That you'd had a few suitors, but usually drove them off because you refuse to accept your place—"

That did it! Pressing her lips into a tight line, she flung him a withering glare.

It didn't dampen his grin in the least as he patted her hand comfortingly. "But you needn't worry. He didn't scare me off.

I've never appreciated anyone trying to keep me in my place either."

Prudence wasn't sure what to make of Morgan Thomas. One minute he acted like her lord and master . . . the next, her confidant. Confused, she pulled her hand out from under his. "Well, I will certainly have a word with Mr. Upton when I see him." She folded her arms again.

Morgan's expression took an abrupt turn, a pained and rather solemn one. "Please, forgive me. It was thoughtless of me to bring up the man's name in such a careless manner. You see . . ." He hesitated, as if debating how to explain. "I'm . . . sorry to say, he was taken from us. A cannonball exploded right next to him."

The news came as a shock. The barber had not exactly been a close family friend, but everyone in town knew and respected him. To learn that he— "May the Lord grant him peace," Prudence said softly. "There was so much cannon fire. So much . . . everything."

Morgan nodded in agreement and switched his attention back up the road. "What I saw mostly were dead redcoats, scattered everywhere, all across the hill. But they kept on coming, as if there was no end to them. Wait!" He brightened. "I think I see Robert!" Staggering to his feet, Morgan bolted toward someone coming toward the Common. "Chan! Chandler! Over here!"

The tall, slender man raised his blackened face and altered his tired steps slightly.

Morgan seized his friend in an impassioned hug as he approached. "You sure took your time! Come on over and sit down. I'll go get you something to eat and drink." He slid Robert's haversack off him and took out his plate and cup.

"No," Prudence offered, getting up. "You're both tired. I'll go."

"That won't be necessary," Morgan said firmly, pressing her none too gently back to her seat. "Chandler, this young woman is in my charge, and I'll personally be seeing to it that she gets home safely. Keep an eye on her for me. I'll only be a minute."

Prudence stared, aghast, as the imperious, insufferable man took his leave. "That—that *tyrant* cannot hold me prisoner, Mr. Chandler," she announced. "Tell him!"

Obviously uncomfortable at being in the middle of this conflict, his friend only gave a worn-out shrug. "Soon as he gets back with my drink, miss. I'm dyin' of thirst."

Morgan took only a few steps away, then turned. "How close are the British, Chan? The shooting seems to have all but stopped."

"They halted at the Neck. But once that's secured I'm sure they'll keep coming. They've got us on the run."

He nodded toward Prudence. "Well, keep her here."

"Odious, arrogant boor," Prudence grumbled as her tormentor strode off.

"Don't be too hard on the poor fellow, miss," Mr. Chandler said quietly. "In the months we've been together, he's had but one thing on his mind. You."

His slow manner of speech had a hypnotic quality. "Me?"

He gave her a knowing smile. "You must have made quite the impression on him the night you met. He's been turning the Massachusetts countryside upside down ever since tryin' to find you."

"Why would he be so interested in me, I ask?"

"Frankly, he's been worried that you'd be caught spying and be hanged." Reaching up for Morgan's tricorn, he removed it from her head. "And now that I'm able to get a good look at you, I can see there's much more to it than that. Whether he's ready to admit it or not, I'm afraid our nonchalant friend is thoroughly smitten."

Prudence felt the warmth of a blush creep over her cheeks as she searched the sea of backs and smudged faces congregated near the water wagon and food line. But her uninvited champion was lost in the crowd. "Smitten?" she echoed, barely aware she had spoken aloud. The thought of that swaggering, overconfident—

Her mind suddenly flew to two other like-minded males, her stepuncles. It had been hours since she had given any thought to their well-being. How shameless. "I really should try to find my stepmother's two younger brothers," she said. "We came together this morning in my father's wagon."

"They ought to be horsewhipped," he said with a frown. "Letting you get involved in this bloody battle."

"I assure you, Mr. Chandler, it was nothing like that. When they saw what was happening, they came down here to volunteer but told *me* to go home." Somehow she suppressed her bitterness over that sort of male reasoning.

She watched him relax. His eyelids were getting heavier by the minute, his blinks lasting longer.

"Wonder how much longer Morgan will be," he finally said on a yawn. "I've never been so tired in my life. And it's not even sunset."

Prudence smiled gently. "Why don't you lie down and rest till he returns."

"I have a promise to keep."

"Yes. Well, I won't go anywhere. On my honor."

"On your honor as a soldier or a spy?" he challenged with a quirk of his lips.

She considered the words before answering. "On my honor as a soldier *and* a spy."

He slumped gratefully down and in less than a minute was asleep.

It was a perfect chance for her to escape. She checked to be sure Morgan Thomas was still not coming, then quietly rose. But her Puritan upbringing caught up with her at once. After all, she had just given her solemn word. And whether *she* was quite ready to admit it to herself or not, a very small part of her harbored a tantalizing new curiosity regarding the dark-haired rescuer she had acquired.

Moments later, he came back, heaping plate and brimming cup in hand. His gaze took in his sleeping friend, then flitted to her with relief. "You're still here."

She had to avert her eyes from the intensity in his. Instead, she gazed at Robert. "I, um, made him a promise." Gently she shook his arm. "Wake up, Mr. Chandler. Your food and water are here."

"Water," he said, groggily coming to. He braced himself up on an elbow.

Morgan dropped to one knee and handed him the drink, placing the plate on the ground by him. "Better eat fast. We've just gotten new orders. We're to go on up the Medford road to Winter Hill. Old Put says more powder's coming, and we're to dig in there while we wait for it."

"Why, that's an excellent spot," Prudence said excitedly, remembering the view from that same hill when she had "borrowed" the men's clothes earlier that day. "We'll be able to see everything from there."

"How far is it?" Chandler asked, biting a biscuit in half. "I don't think I can walk one more step."

"But you don't have to," she said. "I'll fetch my father's wagon. We can take as many men as the horse can pull. Have you any powder at all left?"

"Wait just one minute," Morgan cut in. "You, my pretty, are not staying on Winter Hill, just passing through. I'm escorting you home. Personally."

She glared in defiance. "I'll have you know, *Mr.* Thomas—"

Grabbing her arm, the bully pulled her unceremoniously to her feet. "Come on, we'll get that wagon. On the way to the hill, you can argue to your heart's content, and I'll listen to that charming little voice of yours. I love watching you talk . . . no matter what comes out of your mouth."

36

The night was unbearably hot, the flames from the street lamps only adding to the temperature. And like the oppressive humidity, the weight of uncertainty hung heavy on everyone's hearts.

Susannah lingered outside with most of the other women on Milk Street, all of them anxious for news of the conflict across the Charles River. After enduring the horrendous noise of the battle throughout the day, the quiet now seemed equally ominous. The whole town was crawling with rumors, repeated over and over again as if sheer repetition might make them more true . . . or less so.

Where was Dan? He had promised to come home before dark when he went with Mr. Simms to Beacon Hill to watch the battle. It must have been hard for them to view the slaughter from afar when they were so badly needed. But they would never have been permitted past the barricade.

Liza Brown, the petite and willowy daughter of the midwife, hurried up the street to Susannah's side, her eyes misty and red rimmed from crying. She cast a glance around to make sure no one was too near, then spoke in a whisper. "Do you think it's true what they're saying, Mistress Haynes? About the British casualties bein' too many to count? Mama won't let me go down to where they're unloading the wounded. But I can't bear the thought Gerald may be lying there hurt and bleeding and alone. I keep praying that somehow he isn't maimed or

. . . or . . ." Unable to finish, she pressed her fingertips to her trembling mouth as tears spilled down her cheeks.

A wave of guilt assailed Susannah. She had introduced the graceful sixteen-year-old girl to charming and shy Gerald Blake, a private in the king's army. She shifted little Julia to her other arm and hugged Liza close. "There's no way of knowing anything for certain yet, dear. We can only pray. For both sides." Despite the fact she felt a part of the Colonies now, her heart trembled for her English countrymen bound by duty to carry out the king's orders.

"But what if it's true?" Liza insisted. "I heard they've been ferrying the wounded back here all evening in a steady stream—and still are. If Gerald was alive, he'd get word to me. Somehow or other."

"Perhaps it's a good sign that he hasn't. He may very well still be on duty across the river."

"Do you think so?" Hope flickered in the girl's tortured eyes.

With a comforting squeeze, Susannah braved a smile, then released her. "We must hope for the best." But her words sounded hollow, even to her own ears.

"Mama," Miles said, getting up from playing on the grass and sliding his hand into hers, "where's Daddy?"

"I really don't know, honey. I'm sure he'll come when he can. He . . . might be visiting one of our sick friends."

A frown drew the boy's thin brows close. Then with a shrug, he went back to the carved horses and figures he had lined up in the grass and continued playing in childish oblivion, making shooting noises under his breath.

The odious sounds did little to help Susannah contain her apprehension, and she wished dearly that the interminable waiting would come to an end. Why didn't Dan come home?

Spying Mistress Simms talking animatedly on the opposite side of the street with some other women from the church, she turned to Liza. "Would you mind terribly taking the baby for a few minutes while I see if they've learned something new?"

Still sniffing, Liza nodded and held out her arms. "I'll watch Miles, too," she offered.

"Oh, thank you. I shan't be long." Handing Julia over, she grasped a fold of her skirt and hurried to join them.

Mistress Simms and the women with her nodded a solemn greeting as she approached.

"Has there been any further news?" Susannah asked.

The middle-aged housewife grimaced. "Charity says the plan to march up Copps Hill to take the battery was a flop. But nobody's sure if the men actually tried or how many might be under arrest."

"I just came from my sister's," Charity Calloway, another deacon's wife, began. "She said many of the patriots' houses were viciously vandalized. Some of the redcoats left in Boston to guard the town went on the rampage."

"How dreadful."

"Yes. Awful. Just awful." Mistress Simms toyed with a handkerchief from her skirt pocket. "I wonder what they'll do now that the king's men are being carried off the battlefield in great numbers."

Susannah could only wonder how Massachusetts' own brave fighting men had fared—inexperienced farmers and tradesmen against professional soldiers. Not knowing made the waiting all the harder.

Suddenly one of the women gasped and pointed up the street. "Look!"

They all turned to see a small group of men coming toward them, still a block off. Wiry little Elder McKnight was easily recognizable, the bearded face of Elder Simms, and—Susannah's heart leaped—Dan, on the outer fringe, his steps dogged and weary as the rest. Emitting a cry of relief, Susannah and the others ran to meet them.

She stopped short a few feet from him. "Oh, Dan! You're bleeding! Are you badly hurt?"

He shook his head. "No." But his tired smile barely lifted his mouth. "We've been aiding the wounded as the British bring them back to this side."

"Aye," McKnight grumbled. "Reverend Haynes said it was our Christian duty, part of loving our enemies, and all. Fact is, there's entire regiments of lobsterbacks layin' on the wharf cryin' out for help. The surgeons and doctors can't get to 'em fast enough."

"Lots of the poor souls were beyond help," Elder Simms said gravely, giving his plump wife a peck on the cheek as she wiped a red stain from his ear with her apron.

Susannah looked to Dan and saw a deep and pain-wracked sorrow in his eyes.

"It was . . . there are no words, Susannah. No words."

"Someone said more than half their troops got shot," Mistress Calloway said.

"Could be," Simms agreed.

"But—what about our boys?" his wife asked.

"Can't be sure yet," he answered. "All we know is the British are now in control of Charlestown Neck and are fortifying it, like they did with Boston."

Several seconds of silence lapsed. All Susannah could think was that if the Crown had gained control of Charlestown, thousands of militiamen could have been killed. The British had the battery on Copps Hill, men-of-war in the harbor, and at least two thousand soldiers across the river—all pitted against ill-trained, ill-equipped patriots. How many militia could possibly be left alive, if the British casualties were so unspeakable?

Her gaze was drawn with the rest toward Charlestown. Not a person in the group was without some friend or loved one who in all likelihood had been part of that great battle.

"I heard very little about the fate of our men from the returning redcoats," Dan said, as if reading her thoughts. "However, there's been no mention of a great slaughter of the patriots. Let's pray that God in his mercy spared them."

"That's all we've been doing the livelong day, Reverend," Mistress Simms muttered.

"Then," Dan answered, "there's nothing left but to trust in our heavenly Father's wisdom and mercy."

Everyone seemed to take encouragement in Dan's comment. They began walking again toward their homes.

Susannah slid an arm around him. "Morgan and Robert have been on my mind all day. We've yet to hear if they survived Concord. Surely they must have been in the thick of things, along with so many others from our dispersed congregation. And Ben. Who knows where *he* is?"

Dan tugged her tighter, acknowledging without words her concern. "Miles," he called as they came across the street. "Time for bed, Son." Then he glanced down at Susannah. "I wouldn't worry about my brother. He's been dispatched to Philadelphia to bring back the results of the Second Continental Congress." He let out a weary breath. "I wonder how our leaders will react when they learn what went on here this day."

But at the moment, Susannah's sympathy went out to Liza Brown, who stood openly crying as she held little Julia.

❧ ❧

Ben drank in the sight of the Haynes farm as he rode up his parents' lane. It had been a hard two-day ride from Philadelphia, and in this peaceful setting, the strife taking place in the Colonies seemed even further away.

Surprisingly, lanterns glowed from either end of the porch, and he could see family members gathered there. The warm night must have driven them outside. He put his fingers to his mouth and gave a sharp whistle.

Everyone sprang up, and Abigail ran lightly down the steps and out to meet him.

He swung down and pulled her into his arms, breathing in the fragrance of her hair. "I missed you so. Are the children well?"

She nodded. "They've never been so happy. But I've missed you terribly."

"And I've missed you. I—"

"Hey, you two lovebirds," Pa said, striding up to them. "Come join us. You've brought more news, I trust."

Ben bestowed a promising smile on Abby that made her blush, and he hugged her to him as they climbed the steps. He could tell from everyone's expressions that they were more than just a little interested in news from the congress. Robby and Emily, occupying the porch swing with one of their little ones spread across their laps, leaned slightly forward. Mother's fan lay motionless in her hands, and she was uncharacteristically silent. So was Felicia. And Pa had yet to resume his seat.

"I rode hard to get here quickly," he began. "The Continental Congress has taken our plight a lot more seriously than any of us hoped. They elected a commander in chief—the Virginian George Washington. We'll have a real army now."

"Hmm," Pa said thoughtfully. "I've heard good things about that man ever since the French and Indian War. And he's been chosen to lead us, eh?"

Ben nodded. "He's well respected. Should be a pretty popular choice, I'd say."

"That means they'll not only be sending a commander but men and supplies from all the Colonies as well."

"I only pray our laddies can hold out till they get there," Robby added.

"That's why we're waiting outside," Emily announced. "We were hoping someone would come by with more news of the battle."

"Battle?" Ben looked at his father.

"Once word leaked out that Gage's new generals planned to take Charlestown, Dorchester Heights, *and* Cambridge simultaneously," Pa explained, "the patriots hightailed it to Charlestown and dug in."

"General Putnam sent men out to round up more recruits," Pa said. "Someone came by late this afternoon. That's how we heard."

"It seems," Robby explained, "last night our laddies sneaked onto the Charlestown Neck and entrenched themselves on the hill behind it. 'Twas a big surprise to the British. The Crown started bombarding the hill with their men-of-war and their big guns in Boston, destroyin' the town while they were at it. But that's the last we heard. We hoped ye'd know more."

At such distressing news, Ben was vastly relieved he hadn't housed Abby and the children in his room in Cambridge.

"Well, *I'm* thankful Ben was nowhere near there," Abigail said.

Hearing her speak out so freely after her years at Ma Preston's, Ben was even more convinced it had been the right thing to do to bring her here to live, where she was loved and accepted. At the same time, disappointment at having missed yet another battle irritated him, but he knew better than to worry her by voicing it. He cleared his throat. "Yes, well, I'll be leaving at first light. It's more important than ever for me to deliver my news to Cambridge."

"I'll be goin' with ye, Ben," Robby said as he stood up and propped the sleeping child against the arm of the swing. "'Tis only right I join up, as I should've done long before this."

Ben glanced at his youngest sister. Emily's guileless face and light green eyes harbored eloquent pain, but knowing her as well as he did, he could see she was struggling to be brave despite her fears. She came to Robby's side, encircling his arm with both of hers in a silent show of support.

Abigail, on the other hand, wore an expression that cut Ben to the core as she swayed against him. She had already lost one husband, after all. He released a lungful of air and tightened his embrace. "Well, angel, I've had a really long day." At her wordless nod, he led her toward the door to the house. They had this whole night to be together, for him to assure her that he would take no unnecessary risks. And he planned to spend the entire time holding her, breathing in her sweetness, calming her fears.

It might have to last him for some time to come.

37

It was almost midnight when Prudence finally neared the home of her stepmother's family. As the wagon lurched in and out of a hole, she glanced around at Morgan, still sound asleep on a pile of blankets and quilts in the back. A smile tugged at her lips. Wouldn't he be gratified to discover she'd actually kept her word and driven straight home! She had made him the promise more from pity than anything else. The poor man was so exhausted after working more than forty hours with no sleep, he had been dead on his feet.

But his waking up wasn't her main cause for worry. Coming within sight of the farmstead, she saw lights still burning. Because of the lateness of the hour, she expected everyone in the house would be in bed, thereby saving her the awkward explanations regarding her missing stepuncles as well as her own whereabouts all day—not to mention the strange man now slumbering in the wagon bed. The quilts she had brought along to protect the furniture they'd been sent to fetch now bore the soil and blood of dozens of wounded men that she and Morgan had tended and driven back to Cambridge. She was trying not to think about the untold multitudes of British who lay mangled and dying on the battlefield. It would be difficult enough to erase from her mind the suffering souls she'd seen with her own eyes. Who could imagine the ghastly damage one musket ball could wreak?

Turning onto the lane that led to the Randolph dairy farm,

Prudence dreaded confronting whoever was waiting up. One person or more, it made no difference. Now she would have to explain the happenings of the day.

She looked behind her again at Morgan's sleeping form. To think he had actually been searching for her since Christmas! How strange that he had stumbled across her that day . . . and how unfortunate that under all that grime, someone so unbearably flippant had such a handsome face. In fact, the man was *too* handsome, she concluded. A serious-minded girl like herself would do well to steer clear of his sort.

With a sigh, she turned forward again, absently lowering her eyes. *She still had on men's clothes!* That would never do. Heart pounding, she reined to a halt near a clump of trees, then climbed down. Her dress and petticoat were in a bundle in the corner of the wagon. Retrieving it, she hurried behind a thick tree trunk and peeled off her soiled shirt and trousers.

"Prudence? Miss Endecott?"

He was awake! And here she stood, half naked! If she answered, he'd surely catch her before she finished dressing! And if she didn't, he'd likely holler loud enough to bring everybody out of the house. "Shh!" she finally hissed in a loud whisper. "I'll be right there."

Footsteps crunched toward her in the underbrush. "I thought for a moment you'd run off."

"Keep your voice down," she said, leaning around the tree to wave him aside. " I told you to stay back!" Frantically she shimmied into her petticoat, then fumbled with the ribbons on the front of her chemise.

"Why are you whispering?" Morgan asked, yawning.

"Because there are still lights on over yonder."

"Oh, I see. That's your house."

"Yes. Now, keep your voice down."

He snickered.

"It belongs to my stepmother's father, if that means anything to you." She gave up trying to lace herself evenly. However the dress ended up, it would have to do. Giving it a tug here and there, she scooped up the dirty clothing and came out.

"Oh," he said with a wicked half smile. "You should have called me. I'd have been glad to help."

"Why does that not surprise me?" It was the least of the biting retorts that had come to mind.

He didn't seem put off. "All in all," he said thoughtfully, "I'd say changing was a wise move, considering your activities this day. Perhaps my earlier assumption was wrong. You just might have a mind devious enough to be a spy after all."

Her eyebrows arched high. "Devious? I'll have you know, I am not in the least devious. We happen to be caught in extraordinary times, calling for sometimes unorthodox actions."

A chuckle rumbled from deep inside him. "When the day comes for me to explain myself to my father, I shall be sure to bring you along."

"Really? Well, I'd just as soon *not* explain you to *my* father. In fact, now that I am safely home, your services are no longer required. Run along." Her smile was anything but sweet. "It's no more than a couple of miles back to Winter Hill."

"What? After, lo, these many days and nights of doing nothing but worrying over you? I think not. Why, the very least I can do is place you in your father's loving hands *and* make sure you never try anything so foolish again." His tone was light, but the purposeful set of his jaw was obvious.

Prudence crushed the bundle in her arms. "Please, Mr. Thomas."

"Morgan," he corrected. "We've been through this already."

She sighed. "Please, *Morgan.* My father is gravely ill. It's his heart. We have no idea how much longer he'll . . . be with us. See here, if I promise—and you know by now I'm as good as my word—if I promise never to place myself in deliberate danger again, would you please just go away? Please?"

He tipped his head and studied her. "Well, I suppose I can forgive you this once for—"

"Forgive me?"

"For not knowing how important it is that you stay safely tucked at home at times like these."

"I am not a piece of precious china to be packed in straw," she huffed.

"When a man is out fighting for his wife and family, he needs to know they are where he left them. Safe. Waiting."

"I am not your wife—or your family!"

Morgan merely took her arm. "Come along. There'll be plenty of time for arguing later. I must meet your father, then get more sleep. I'm really quite tired, you know."

After allowing a few steps while she gathered her wits, Prudence again balked. "You have to be the most infuriatingly stubborn man I have ever had the occasion to meet."

His teeth glowed white as he grinned in the darkness.

"Look, *Morgan*. I'll make a promise if you will, too. I will stop arguing right now . . . *if*, after I let you come inside, you will go along with whatever I tell them."

"That would make things hard for me. I'll have to think it over."

Prudence tightened her arms around the bundle. "This is ridiculous. Absolutely ridiculous."

"It's just that I made a solemn vow to God recently to stop lying my way out of things."

"You?" she scoffed, incredulous. "A silver-tongued spy, making promises to the Almighty? I seriously doubt that."

He continued to regard her in silence. "I'd truly prefer to keep this particular oath."

From his tone, Prudence could tell he spoke the truth. He really was a man of honor, worthy of quite a bit more trust than she had given him. Meekly she allowed him to guide her to the wagon and hand her up. "I . . . will do my best not to compromise your vow." She paused. "Or my own conscience," she added under her breath.

❦ ❦

As the wagon rumbled and squeaked up to the barn, Morgan saw a man of medium stature charge out the side door, a lantern swinging crazily from his hand. "Did you figure the cows could milk themselves?" he yelled, coming toward them. "I'll be takin' a strap to your—" He stopped short, confusion adding even more creases to the furious lines in his face. "Where's my boys? And who's he?" Sly weasel eyes stared at Morgan.

Morgan felt Prudence stiffen and inch closer to him on the wagon seat. This man was her father? Though slight of build, the fellow's wiry frame bore muscles formed by steady hard work. He didn't appear a frail invalid at all. And the hardness of his expression was echoed in his overbearing stance.

"Mr. Randolph," she said, her voice unnaturally high, "I'd like you to meet Morgan Thomas. Morgan, this is Lucas Randolph, my stepmother's father."

So this is where Prudence and her family were forced to seek refuge? Morgan wondered as he leaned out to offer his hand.

Randolph ignored it and gave a nod, but the glare in his beady eyes did not soften as Morgan hopped down, then assisted Prudence. "Where's Nick and Frank?" he asked her.

"When we got to the bay, there was a battle raging on the Charlestown Neck. They insisted on going to help."

"I figured," he grated, his thin lips in a grim line. "They been wantin' to run off for weeks now, but I wouldn't let 'em. I worked too long and hard for this place to lose it by taking on somebody else's senseless squabble."

Morgan and Prudence exchanged sidelong glances.

"If that pa of yours and the rest of them city folks did half the work I put in every day," the farmer went on, "they wouldn't be so all-fired anxious to stir up a hornet's nest. Every man alive oughta have twenty dairy cows to look after. Maybe then they wouldn't have idle time to fill up with trouble. How am I to get all my cows milked now is what I'd like to know."

"Yes. Well—"

Randolph motioned his grizzled chin toward Morgan. "That sorry-lookin' feller supposed to be a replacement for my boys?"

The light in the open doorway of the house was blocked abruptly. Morgan looked up to see a silhouette of an older man in nightclothes hobbling out on the arm of a much younger woman, plump and fair haired. "Is that you, my dear?" he asked in a thin, feeble voice.

Sidestepping the farmer, Prudence went to him. "Yes, Papa. I'm sorry it's so late, but it couldn't be helped."

"I'm just thankful you're home," he said, reaching out a shaky hand and gathering her close.

Witnessing the touching scene, Morgan caught the worried looks that passed between Prudence and the other young woman.

"We heard there was trouble not more than an hour after the three of you left," the woman said, a warm glow in her blue eyes. "We expected you would turn right around and come home. It was hard on your pa when you didn't."

"And what about me," Randolph railed. "Me and Miriam had to milk and feed the whole herd this evening. And she couldn't do more'n five."

"Sorry, Papa," Prudence answered, ignoring the dairyman. "But all our furniture was burned with the rest of the town. And, Miriam, I know how much you treasured your mother's looking glass. . . ." She shook her head.

"Now, now, dearest," Mr. Endecott murmured to his wife. "Once we're settled again I'll find you another equally lovely one for our wall." He switched his attention to Prudence. "It's certain now. We'll not be going back there. As soon as things quiet down some, we'll start looking for another location for the store." His inquiring gaze swung to Morgan, then back to her. "Why were you so long coming home, child?"

"Well, with that empty wagon full of quilts, I was asked to help move wounded men to Cambridge."

He shook his gray head slowly. "I should have been fit enough to be there."

"Well, you ain't," Randolph snapped. "Any more than you are to help around here."

The crass remark deeply offended Morgan; he could only

imagine how it cut Prudence and her family. He felt sorry they had to live under the roof of such a mean-spirited man.

Mr. Endecott closed his eyes for a few seconds, then slanted another glance at Morgan. "Daughter, you've yet to introduce your escort."

Moistening her lips, Prudence managed a smile. "Papa, Miriam, this is Morgan Thomas. He was kind enough to see me safely home. Morgan—" she turned to him—"my father, Scervant Endecott, and my stepmother, Miriam."

"I do thank you, young man, for your kindness," her father said as they shook hands. "Is there something we can do to repay you for your time, son?"

"A bed, perhaps? And a few hours' sleep? I've been up since yesterday morning."

"You can use the boys' room, Mr. Thomas," Miriam said with a kind smile. "Prudence, why don't you take him upstairs and see that he gets settled in."

"And perhaps tomorrow," the older man said, "you can tell us all you know about the battle."

"Battle this, battle that," Randolph groused under his breath.

Morgan put a gentle hand on Mr. Endecott's bony shoulder. "I'd be very glad to, sir."

"Well, come along." Prudence's cheery tone was so unlike her earlier attitude that it was the closest thing to a lie so far. She preceded him into the cramped but tidy dwelling and retrieved a lighted candlestick from the kitchen sideboard. Up the stairwell they went, the flickering flame emitting only a small circle of light for them on the climb to the second floor. "I'll get some clean linens for your—"

"Don't bother. I'm far too filthy to even be sleeping inside."

She eyed him. "You're right. I'll put a sheet over the bed. It's quite a warm night. You'll not need blankets."

He gave her a weary smile. "Would you please wake me before dawn? I wouldn't want the captain to think I've deserted."

"You left without permission?"

"In all the confusion on Winter Hill, I saw no reason."

As they reached the landing, Prudence opened the door to

a bedchamber. "Nor was there a reason to accompany me home. All the soldiers were far too busy to notice me."

"Yes, they were," he conceded.

Prudence stepped inside, the glow of her candle revealing a low-ceilinged room furnished with two single beds. She reached to light his lamp with her candle.

"But alas," he finished, "not everyone is as dedicated to the cause. Your stepgrandfather, for example."

"I'll thank you not to refer to the man as any relation whatsoever," she said through gritted teeth. "As far as I am concerned, acknowledging him as the father of my stepmother is all I'll admit to." She ducked out into the hallway and returned with a sheet, which she shook open and let settle over one of the beds.

"You're quite good at improvising, do you know that?" Morgan teased with as much smile as he could work up. "Neither of us had to lie. And I was able to keep my word. And since I'm being so honest, you've no choice but to believe me when I say I've never in my life met a woman who intrigues me as much as you do. Nor one so beautiful."

Her luminous eyes rounded and locked on his momentarily. Then she gave him a gentle push down to the bed and started for the door. When she turned back, the candle in her hand sparkled over a most bewitching smile. "And I have never met a man so out of his head for lack of sleep. Good night, Morgan Thomas. Perhaps by morning you will have regained your senses."

As the latch clicked shut behind her, Morgan inhaled a slow breath. He must be more tired than he thought possible, not to have carried the conversation a little further just as it was on the verge of taking a far more delicious turn.

She was right. In the morning, with dreams of her to replace the nightmare of battle, he would be rested . . . and she wouldn't have the last word then.

What was it she had called him a while back? Silver-tongued? Well, the enchanting and alluring Miss Prudence Endecott was about to discover how right she was.

38

The morning sun was haloing the trees with gold by the time the cows were finally milked. Prudence looked down at her shaky hands as she trudged back to the house alongside Miriam. "I don't know how I'll manage to cook breakfast. I don't think I could pick up that heavy iron skillet, my hands ache so."

"It does take time to get used to that much milking," her stepmother said, rubbing her own tired back. "But I might be able to come up with strength enough to strangle those brothers of mine, should they happen to show their faces around here anytime soon."

Prudence tried unsuccessfully to stifle a soft laugh.

"I can understand Nick and Frank wanting to get away from Pa and his bossing, but just to up and leave out of the blue—" Miriam shook her head, stirring light blonde hairs beneath the ruffle of her house cap. "The least they could've done was given us time to arrange for some help first. Of course, with everyone going off to fight, that isn't going to be easy. Speaking of which, you'd best go wake your young man. I'll see what I can rustle together for breakfast."

At the mention of Morgan, Prudence checked the brightening sky with dismay. She should have roused him an hour ago. But since she hadn't, a few extra minutes shouldn't matter. After all, she wasn't exactly presentable, just coming back from the barn. Not that he would care what she looked like, considering that he had proclaimed her beautiful last night when she'd been a complete mess, but still. . . .

Ignoring the flip-flop of her heart, Prudence tried to convince herself she would have cleaned up after milking anyway, really, even if he weren't here. "Miriam, would you heat some extra water for Mr. Thomas? I'm sure he'll want to wash off a few pounds of dirt before he leaves." She hurried to her room.

Shortly after she had changed into an indigo dress and a clean white apron, then brushed and retied her hair, Prudence slipped into the bedchamber where her fellow spy had spent the night. He was still sound asleep.

She tiptoed near and tilted her head to study him, smiling at the marked contrast between his present dishevelled condition and the dapper figure he had made at the Christmas ball in a ruffled shirt, elegant frock coat, and powdered wig. Now his abundant brown hair was matted and dull, with even his thick eyebrows askew, as if he had rubbed his hands over his face. In the peacefulness of slumber, his mouth was relaxed, the customary mocking expression absent, and his closed eyelids hid the hint of devilment so often apparent in his eyes.

Torn between his request to awaken him and his obvious need for several more hours of rest, Prudence hesitated another fraction of a second, then gently shook his shoulder. "Mr. Thomas? Morgan?"

He stirred, then came to with a start. His gaze, when it finally focused on her, transformed into one of sleepy pleasure. "Good morning." He yawned and stretched his obviously stiff muscles.

Prudence tried unsuccessfully to subdue the pounding of her heart. It was all she could do to refrain from asking if he'd like her to rub his knotted shoulders and back. Instead, she murmured, "I'll get you something clean to wear." Moving to the wardrobe, she selected a few things of Nick's, then laid them on the bed. "These should fit you fairly well. There's water heating in the kitchen. I'll bring some up directly, and when you've changed, I'll see to washing your clothes."

"I'll be forever in your debt." The mischievous grin returned, and for a moment Prudence was lost in his rich blue eyes, unable to move. At last she gathered her composure and started for the door while she still could.

"I'll return the borrowed clothes when I come back to pick up mine," he offered. "Medford's just a short ride."

Prudence intended merely to nod politely, but to her dismay, she began to blush. With a flustered smile, she rushed out of the room.

When Morgan at last came downstairs to the kitchen, Prudence was more in control of herself. She bustled about with Miriam, seeing to everyone's needs.

The children occupied one side of the long table, their heads in a line like so many steps, with Lucas Randolph at the head and her father at the foot.

"I'm hungry," six-year-old Nathan whined.

"Quiet!" Lucas Randolph slammed his palm down on the table with a loud smack. "We'll have none of that!"

The child immediately burst into tears, joined instantly by little James at the opposite end. Between them, Hester's round blue eyes swam, and Caleb froze in place, hardly daring to look up at the dark scowling face occupying the head chair.

Prudence saw the look of shock on Morgan's face and gave him an apologetic grimace as she gestured to the vacant seat opposite Nathan. "Please, sit down, won't you?" She served scrambled eggs to the children while her stepmother set heaping plates before the two older men, then snatched up the wailing tot without a word and left the room.

Morgan seemed not to notice as he took the spot across from Prudence's dark-haired half brother. He pulled a shiny coin out of his trouser pocket and offered it to the boy. "Here, lad, I found this the other day. Might even be enough for a whole bag of rock candy. What do you think?"

Nathan stopped sniffing and took the treasure with a watery smile.

"Ya shouldn't spoil the brat," Randolph spewed around a mouthful of food.

Prudence saw her father's jaw clench, but he made no reply.

"Well, then," Morgan said blandly, "I daresay, I shall have to think of some means for him to earn it." He winked at Nathan. "Are you willing to work for the money?"

"Yes, sir!"

He smiled, then switched his attention to the farmer. "And I'll, of course, pay you for your kind hospitality."

"You'll do no such thing," Papa said with surprising force. "You did me a great service, bringing my daughter and the wagon safely home. If there's further restitution required, I'll settle it."

Noting her father's strained and colorless face, Prudence wondered—again—about the wisdom of their coming here to stay. She slid a glance in Lucas Randolph's direction. Certainly her father would have been far better off in a quieter, more restful place. And one where the host was not an ungracious lout who kept a tally of every bite they took. She set a plate of scrambled eggs and ham before Morgan.

"Mm," he murmured, meeting her gaze. "Cooking like this is worth a goodly amount. It far surpasses the military fare I've had to choke down of late—when there was any."

"I'm sorry there are no biscuits this morning," Prudence confessed. "But having to milk the cows first thing, we didn't have time to get them rolled out. I do pray Thursday's bread will do."

"It's fine." Then his brow creased. "Didn't someone mention there are twenty head? And *you* had to milk them all?"

She nodded. "Miriam, her father, and I."

"That's right," Randolph announced. "So if you see them boys of mine, tell 'em to get themselves back here where they belong. If I have to come looking for 'em, they'll be sorry."

Morgan regarded him evenly. "I regret, sir, but I've never met your sons. I'll ask around."

Prudence replenished his plate with a nervous smile, then brought her own plate over and took the seat next to him.

"Here, Nathan," she said, offering her napkin across the table. "Wipe your mouth." She was more than aware that Morgan followed her every move, and when her arm accidentally brushed his sleeve, she blushed and concentrated on eating in the uneasy quiet. When he finally pulled his gaze from her, she relaxed.

"The militia camped around Cambridge these past two months," Morgan began, "haven't had much in the way of milk or butter. I'd be more than willing to pay a fair price for any *fresh* milk cows you might be able to spare, Mr. Randolph."

Prudence nearly laughed aloud. Obviously, Morgan Thomas understood the farmer's character. The man wasn't beyond trying to pass off a cow whose milk supply was dwindling from not having calved recently.

Randolph rubbed his gristled chin. "Well, now, I might be able to let ya have one or two. I'll think on it. I been pondering hauling milk into Cambridge myself."

"That would be quite enterprising of you. In the meantime, if you could let me have a couple, it would make less work for the fair ladies."

Prudence was touched by his concern. But Miriam's father was gloating as he shoved more food into his mouth. "While I'm at it," he sneered, "I could hunt up them no-account boys of mine."

Her father set down his coffee mug. "You don't speak like a New Englander, Mr. Thomas. From whence do you hail?"

"Philadelphia, sir. My father's a merchant there, but he operates chiefly out of warehouses, selling to stores like the one your daughter told me you had. We also have several ships, but naturally business is slow, considering the current situation."

"That why your pa let ya go?" Randolph said, an insinuating smirk on his thin lips. "Or did ya run off like my sons?"

Morgan always had a quick answer for everything, Prudence knew, and his hesitation was obvious. Then she recalled his vow not to lie and wondered briefly what his answer would be. When he said nothing, she finally decided to rescue him. "Your friend Robert Chandler," she said, offering Morgan a change of subject, "said you met at college. What university did you attend?"

"The College of New Jersey, at Princeton." His voice held a note of relief, and he smiled gratefuly at her.

"I've heard of that school," Papa said. "Run by Presbyterians, if I recall correctly. Your parents are of that persuasion?"

"Not exactly. My father enrolled me there because of its academic strictness."

He nodded in thought. "Wise man. A good businessman always wants to get his money's worth. So much else in life is so unpredictable."

"Papa," Prudence said quickly, catching the sadness in his voice, "you'll be well soon, back behind another store counter, making profits. See if you're not."

"I only hope you're right, Daughter. But I do wish your older brothers had stayed around to keep the store going instead of going off to sea. There is, as your gentleman friend reminded us, a shipping situation. They may soon find themselves blocked out of all New England harbors for heaven knows how long. It could be years before we see them again."

"Like I'm always saying," Randolph cut in, "ya can't count on nothin' or nobody but yourself."

Morgan drained his coffee cup and stood. "Speaking of counting on someone," he said with a mildly disappointed look at Prudence, "I really must get back and *be* counted myself. I intended to return directly last eve, but I was too tired. Now I'm quite late."

"If you don't mind riding bareback, son, you may take our horse. Return it when you can."

"I thank you, Mr. Endecott."

"I'll go out with you and show you which harness is ours," Papa said as he slowly rose to his feet.

Prudence, concerned about her father's sallow features,

went to his side. "Are you sure you're up to that long walk to the barn?"

"Yes, Daughter. I'm fine." He turned to Morgan, who managed one backward glance as the two started out of the kitchen. "Prudence told me a little about the battle that raged yesterday. I'm mighty interested in hearing further details, if you wouldn't mind."

Watching Pa and Morgan leave, Prudence was amazed over her father's uncharacteristic generosity—or was it that he only seemed generous in comparison to greedy Lucas Randolph? She couldn't decide. But there had been a marked change in Papa since his illness.

"If ya see hide or hair of my young'uns," Randolph hollered after Morgan, "send 'em home on that horse."

Prudence couldn't help but wish she, too, might put some distance between herself and the unpleasant farmer. If she hurried up, she could wish Morgan Godspeed before he left. She turned her attention to the little ones at the table. "Good boy, Nathan, you cleaned your whole plate. Caleb, you need to finish up, too. Here, Hester, let me wash your sticky hands. . . ."

❦ ❦

Purposely withholding many of the gruesome details, Morgan relayed the militia's early victories on the walk to the barn. When the older man's steps faltered, Morgan slid a hand under his frail arm and steadied him. Despite his brave-sounding words to his daughter, Mr. Endecott appeared to Morgan even more shaky than he had the previous night. "The only reason we had to retreat was the lack of gunpowder," Morgan went on. "The lads made a proud showing up until that shameful moment. I daresay the British won't soon forget us, though, considering their enormous casualties."

"Sounds to me like our brave patriots were given more a victory than a loss, regardless of our forced retreat."

The man's kind words put the incident in a far better light

for Morgan, and suddenly he didn't feel quite so dispirited about the outcome.

They reached the big barn and went inside, Mr. Endecott's uneven steps slowing even more as he leaned on Morgan and shuffled beside him. "That's our rope halter hanging on the end spike," he said, raising a hand to point. "Old Jupiter is gentle. He'll go along fine with only that. He's in the second stall over there. I think I'll sit for a spell, if you don't mind."

Morgan led him to a nearby milking stool and settled him down, then went to take the halter off its hook.

"From the glances you and my daughter have been stealing since you've arrived here," the older man announced, "I'd venture to say you two are taken with each other."

Morgan's initial shock at the pronouncement vanished in the realization that he himself hadn't been imagining Prudence's interest, or else her father wouldn't have noticed. "You have a brave and lovely daughter, sir." He opened the stall and walked in next to the horse.

"Yes, that I have. She's got a good head on her shoulders and a good share of her mother's spirit, too." A wistful smile fluttered over his lips. "When my first wife passed on, rest her soul, little Prudence threw herself into helping however she could. And years later, when her brothers went to sea, she took over for them, keeping my records and such. She wasn't one to go all muddlebrained, either, over every strapping young buck who set foot in our store." He sighed. "Yes, she's been a great help to me."

Morgan couldn't help wondering if the man was insinuating that his daughter was now beginning to show early signs of "muddlebrain" since he had come along. He slipped the halter over the bay's ears.

"Takes after me, my Prudence does. More than either of my sons, if the truth be told."

Was his father that disappointed in him? Morgan wondered suddenly. Only worse? Much worse? Had he discovered Morgan's duplicitous diversion of the Boston merchants' ships?

"I've always understood the value of honest work and

thrift," Mr. Endecott rambled on. "It never once entered my mind there'd come a day when I could no longer provide for my family. But now, in spite of my most careful planning, everything seems to have been taken out of my hands. First my heart nearly failed me, then I lost my store and my home. Now, I fear I . . . will not be long on this earth."

Morgan, backing the bay out of the stall, was caught not so much by the actual statement as he was by its unemotional and resigned delivery. "You shouldn't say such things, sir."

"Perhaps." He shrugged. "But as I said, I've always been a practical man. It's my sincere desire to remove my dear family from this place and have another mercantile up and running before I pass on. But I must consider the possibility that I may have no more say in that matter than I had over the other recent happenings." After a slight pause, he continued. "I know Lucas Randolph's greed. If I were to die while we're still here, he would surely bully Miriam into handing over our life's savings as payment for raising our children. And could you imagine the lack of charity he'd have toward my precious Prudence?" He shuddered.

"Sir, you needn't worry about your daughter. I—" Morgan stopped suddenly. *What was he saying?*

But before he had a chance to recant, Mr. Endecott uttered a vast sigh of relief. "I was hoping you'd say that. And, my wife—if I knew she, too, was well situated away from here, I would go to my grave a contented man. I've been praying most fervently about the matter of late, and I can't help but feel you're God's answer. From what you've said regarding your background, you sound like someone who would have few problems reestablishing my store."

Me? God's answer? Morgan swallowed. "Sir, I've signed up with the militia for six months. In fact, I should be there this moment. Have you a horse blanket, perchance?"

"In the trunk over yonder." Grasping hold of the rail of the stall near himself, Mr. Endecott labored to his feet and hobbled over to Morgan while he settled the woven blanket over the animal's back. "I'm quite sure your superiors would consider allowing you an occasional hour or two to tend to personal matters. Perhaps even today you might ask the men camped in Cambridge to suggest some locations for an enterprise."

"Well," Morgan said, "the fact is, a postrider friend of mine might know of some likely spots."

Endecott brightened considerably. "I wouldn't normally point this out, but I don't mind telling you, son. I'm not by any means a pauper—no matter how things may appear presently."

"I never thought you were." Morgan tried not to show his surprise at the unexpected statement.

The older man averted his gaze. "I'm aware that these inquiries on my behalf may take time—time I'm afraid I may not have. To keep my wife's father at bay, I need a son—one who hasn't gone off to sea. One who's here, now, to get my business going once more." He looked Morgan in the eye. "Marry my daughter, and I'll settle a generous dowry on her. We could put it all in writing right now, before you leave."

Morgan, stunned, heard a gasp behind him. He turned to see Prudence standing in the open doorway. How long had she been there? How much had she heard?

But in light of his own inner turmoil, that thought faded into insignificance. He had been desperately trying to find her for what seemed like forever. And now, within a day of crossing her path, she was being offered to him on a silver platter. But—marriage? That had never seriously entered his mind. Not really. Not yet.

Prudence narrowed her incredible eyes as she stalked over to them, hands on her hips. "How dare you! Haggling over me as if I'm of no more importance than one more barrel of pork!"

Feasting his eyes on the fiery little zealot with her pouty lips trembling irresistibly, Morgan fought the desire to stay right here and watch her fume and blow for a while. But the whole thing was insane! He had only met the girl twice in his life—and her father wanted a commitment this very minute. In writing!

"I think it would be best," he finally said, "if we continue this conversation when I return the clothes and the horse."

Morgan started to lead the horse toward the door, but he couldn't resist looking back at Prudence, aglow with a lively flush of anger. An overpowering impulse took hold. He stopped and glanced at Mr. Endecott. "But first, sir, with your permission, perhaps I'd better have a small sampling of that pork barrel." Before Prudence could protest, he dropped the horse's lead, hauled her into his arms, and covered her luscious mouth with his.

She stiffened at first. Then, wonder of wonders, she slowly melted against him, her lips moving, seeking, in sweet, sweet—

"A *small* sampling, I believe you said," came her father's stern reprimand.

With the greatest reluctance, Morgan managed to relax his hold, to draw away from her.

She appeared no less dazed than he . . . for a heartbeat. "You—you despicable toad!"

Morgan, recognizing the opportune time to leave, leaped onto the big horse and nudged it toward the barn door. "Mighty tasty pork you have there, Mr. Endecott," he tossed over his shoulder. His gaze lingered on Prudence's flushed face, and he grinned. "Mighty tasty, indeed."

Once outside, he urged the reluctant horse into a gallop.

As Morgan passed the house, Lucas Randolph came running out. "Hey! What about them cows you were gonna buy?"

"Soon, my good man," he promised, grinning from ear to ear. "I do think I'm in a rare buying mood."

39

Thank goodness the townspeople had gathered whatever seeds they could garner in order to cultivate food of their own, Susannah thought as she paused from hoeing a long row of green beans to blot perspiration from her face.

Once the simmering tension in the Colonies had exploded into actual conflict in April, Boston had found itself more isolated than ever. Farmers from outside were no longer permitted to bring their harvests to town to sell. Food supplies, scarce enough before, now dwindled even further. The city relied solely upon shipments from Britain to sustain itself, but what stale fare finally trickled into the market—after the military and loyal Tories finished picking over the cargo—was meager and exorbitantly priced. And after yesterday's battle, even that would most likely stop.

But praise be, this once-barren field that stretched behind the house had been converted to a huge garden plot. Now it was filled with their neighbors and church friends, who lovingly tended the healthy young vegetables in the hot summer sun. Having everyone working together for the common good provided much to be thankful for.

She switched her gaze to check on her growing children. In the backyard, Miles happily played tag with some of the other children from the congregation. Despite having formed attachments to numerous British soldiers, the little boy displayed no effects from yesterday's troubles and indeed seemed oblivious to them.

In the shade of a nearby elm, Liza Brown was caring for Julia. Susannah couldn't help but notice the girl's downcast eyes and listless demeanor as she halfheartedly kept the tot occupied. When Liza finally received word this morning that her young soldier had been slightly wounded, she'd been unable to hide her distress. Now the entire congregation knew of her involvement with the "enemy," and people were treating her coolly at best—some with barely concealed disdain.

Susannah found herself caught between righteous anger and guilt. She had ignored the warning.

Becoming aware of a heated conversation at the end of the row, Susannah looked toward Dan. He and Elder Simms had forsaken the task at hand for some serious talk, as the men seemed to do so often these days.

"Oh, but it pleasures me," Mistress Simms said a few feet away, "to see the variety this garden of ours is sporting." Her round face glowed pink from the warmth of the sun as she leaned on the handle of a hoe.

Susannah pushed the troubling thoughts aside and smiled. "With our folk pooling every last seed we could possibly get our hands on, it was destined to bring forth this glorious bounty. Sometimes when I look out my kitchen window at the display, I just stand in awe at the wonder of God's provision."

"I've such a hankerin' for corn, I keep walking over to that acre we planted to see how it's coming along. I wouldn't put it past those thievin' redcoats to try and reap the fruit of our labors."

"Let's pray they don't." Resuming her chore, Susannah attacked the weeds with renewed energy. "The Howards, next door, lost some of their chickens to robbers a few nights ago. Since then, Mr. Howard has padlocked the gate and strung bells and tins all around their roost."

"Tsk, tsk." The plump older woman shook her head and

took up her work again. "I suppose our menfolk will have to start takin' turns guarding our plot."

"Quite likely," Susannah agreed. "I heard it said that the milk cows down the street may be slaughtered for meat. Since the army has taken over so much of the Common, there's not nearly enough grazing for the cattle now."

"Well, I hope they keep a few alive, for the sake of the children, at least."

"Yes. With milk, eggs, and this wonderful garden, plus nuts from the trees, we should be able to get by adequately until this terrible time is over." But even to Susannah the words sounded hollow. She could voice such optimism, but she didn't really feel it in her heart.

They continued working steadily down the rows toward their husbands. Susannah could tell from the slump of Dan's shoulders and his dejected posture that Elder Simms must have told him something disconcerting. Wiping her hands on her apron, she went over to him. "What's amiss, sweetheart?"

Elder Simms looked at her, his bearded face tight with rage. "Bobby Jones stopped off to tell us those blasphemous lobsters have beheaded West Church."

"Dismantled the steeple, if you can believe that," Dan grated. "To prevent the patriots from signalling Cambridge."

"Why, how perfectly horrid," Susannah gasped.

"Well," Mistress Simms piped in, "at least that congregation can still hold services there. Look what was done to our church . . . bustin' doors and windows and what all on the pretext of lookin' for Mistress Haynes's brother. Every time I look at the place, all boarded up against further ruin, it nearly brings tears to my eyes."

Susannah glanced across the field toward Long Lane and the lonely shell of their meetinghouse. A sad sigh escaped.

Dan forced a smile. "Well, look at it this way, my love. Perhaps the Lord wanted our worshipers to meet in closer confines at a time when we most needed one another."

His comment gave her some comfort. "It does seem particularly cozy, now that you mention it. Particularly since so many of our church family have left Boston. There are but a few of us Presbyterians left among our Puritan friends."

"Well," Mr. Simms announced, "the people of West Church are about to be blessed with that same coziness, too. The army confiscated their building for a barracks."

"What?" his wife railed. "They already have soldiers fillin' every last empty house *and* the Common. What more will they be wanting, I ask?"

He gave a humorless chuckle. "Mostly they want our provincial army to disband, only they haven't figured out a way to make 'em. Not yet, anyway."

"Reverend Haynes!" a tall white-haired man called from the edge of the cultivated plot.

"I'd better go see what Mr. Jeffries wants. His wife has been ailing for some time; perhaps she's taken a turn for the worse." With a quick peck on Susannah's cheek, Dan started toward him.

The impatient man hopped over several rows and met him halfway. "Didn't know who else to tell, Pastor," he said, raking fingers through his thick thatch of white hair. "Most of our Congregational ministers have escaped from the city rather than be arrested for their inflammatory sermons."

"What's happened?" Dan asked him.

"It's that new general. Burgoyne. He has a swarm of regulars in the Old South Meeting House. They're tearing out all the pews, carting in gravel, turning the place into some fool European horse academy. They'll be riding those infernal animals of theirs in there just like it was some old barn. As if it was never consecrated to almighty God."

Susannah, overhearing the exchange, stared in disbelief. As well as being the natural gathering place of Boston's citizens, the huge meetinghouse was an old and revered landmark. This was more than just a slap in the face.

With a resigned shake of his head, Dan placed an arm around the man. "Our Lord said, 'Heaven and earth shall pass away: but my words shall not pass away.' All we can do right now is draw comfort from the fact that God's Word will go on despite the ravages man can inflict upon earthly structures. The church, dear friend, is not a building. The church is Christ's believers. And while the army may be doing their best to destroy it, as long as we remain together in our faith, they will never be able to destroy us. Almighty God is our strength . . . and our shelter in these troubled times."

Susannah's anger over the news Mr. Jeffries had related began to diminish. True, it was shocking and sad to witness the hatred and desecration conducted upon so many places of worship all around them—but Dan was right. Believers were the real temples of God, not the buildings made by human hands. She took in the purposeful set of her husband's jaw, the sincerity shining from his eyes, realizing as never before why God had called him to stay here and help those who must remain in the city. The Lord often spoke through Dan to people who most needed comfort. Her heart swelled with pride for her splendid husband—and with gratitude to God for allowing her to be his wife.

❦ ❦

The grays and mauves of dusk painted Winter Hill in soft shades, muted tones that seemed starkly out of place on the new breastworks in the sprawling makeshift camp.

Morgan, up to his elbows in a huge vat of dishwater, gritted his teeth over being delegated such a degrading and odious chore as cooking and cleaning up. He had only been a few hours overdue, and considering all he'd done two days ago—digging, fighting, transporting the wounded—the fact that Captain Brown assigned him punishment duty galled. After all, rumor had it that plenty of the men ran back home *during the battle.* Far better for *them* to be dragged back and forced to do this miserable job.

Sloshing a greasy pot furiously in the slimy lukewarm water, he glanced up to see Robert Chandler sauntering toward him, an uncharacteristic lopsided grin on his face. He might have known Chan was the type who'd find humor in this sort of forced labor.

"Better hurry," Robert said, propping a foot on a nearby stump. "It'll soon be dark."

"Shut up," Morgan growled in disgust, then began mumbling under his breath through gritted teeth. "Dark. That's just great. I'll never get that horse back to the Endecotts tonight." He shot a sheepish look at Robert. "I don't imagine you managed to find someone to give my borrowed clothes a wash."

"I'm pleased to inform you I have," Chandler said. "They'll be ready tomorrow, in fact—which should be soon enough, since you were refused leave tonight."

Ignoring the smug remark, Morgan gave him a grudging nod. "Well, thanks. Perhaps it's for the best," he added as Mr. Endecott's proposition came to mind for the hundredth time. The very idea of marriage had been such a sudden one. Maybe the older man had long since had second thoughts about the insane plan. In any case, Morgan wished the idea would stop nagging at him. He eyed his dark-haired friend, who had taken a seat on the stump and now stared absently into the distance. Chan seemed a decent sort, not easily rattled. He might understand. Morgan cleared his throat and scrubbed harder at some stubborn residue. "Mr. Endecott offered me his daughter in marriage when I was there."

Only Robert's eyes moved as he swept Morgan with a quick glance. "I thought by now I'd heard the last of your grandiose tales."

"I assure you, I'm quite serious. The man has suffered a recent setback in health, and he fears he will soon depart this life. He's concerned his daughter will be at the mercy of his wife's unsavory father."

Chandler didn't offer any counsel.

"Personally, I think he's desperate, grasping at straws. He's barely even met me. For all he knows, I could be a less than honorable character myself." He shook his head and plunged the next pot into the suds.

"Well," Robert began in his slow drawl, "I suppose I can understand your doubts. I also understand a father's fears for his lovely daughter. I'd give the matter some very serious thought before acting in haste. You're talking about the rest of your life, you know." He broke a twig from the side of the stump and began peeling bark from it. "Does Miss Endecott happen to be aware of her father's request?"

"Whoo-ee, does she ever!" Morgan chuckled despite himself. "As luck would have it, she managed to overhear the two of us 'haggling over her,' as she put it. I hightailed it out of there before she let loose with a full load."

Just then, Morgan spied approaching riders coming into camp. Recognizing Ben Haynes and Robby MacKinnon, he whistled and waved his scrub brush high, ignoring the trickle of water that ran inside his sleeve.

They guided their mounts toward him. "Well, well," Ben said, taking in Morgan's chore with a droll grin. "Good to know our valiant militia is in such fine, clean hands." He nodded a greeting at Robert. "Glad to see you again, Chandler. I don't believe you have met my brother-in-law, Robby MacKinnon. Robby, the man sitting beside our Morgan of the Soap Vat is Robert Chandler."

A smile widened Robby's black mustache. "'Tis always a pleasure to meet another Robert, noble name that it is."

"How right you are," Chandler answered, standing to administer a warm handshake. "And you're married to one of the Haynes sisters?"

"Aye. 'Tis me great honor to be wed to Ben's bonny wee sister, Emily. By far the prettiest and most delightful lass in the clan."

Ben chuckled, then turned serious. "I've already reported in to Colonel Prescott in Cambridge. From what he said, our militia made a valiant showing in the battle. Congratulations. The congress should be very pleased with that great victory."

Morgan met Chandler's confused expression with one of his own. They both knew the British now controlled the Charlestown Neck.

"Don't tell me you haven't heard," Ben said. "Men with spyglasses have been tallying up the British casualties throughout last night and today. More than a thousand red-coats had to be carted back to Boston, dead or wounded."

"I can believe that," Morgan concurred. "But somehow after being party to it, the term 'victory' has a hollow ring. The thought of the enemy's mangled flesh and bone, a hill-side turned red with blood, only reminds me of our own men."

"That may be," Ben conceded. "But still, their casualties were more than three times ours. That's pretty amazing."

"And would have been even more lopsided," Chandler added, "had we not run out of powder."

Ben dismounted and gathered his horse's reins. "Well, hopefully, the congress will be able to come up with some more sources now. I've just returned with evidence that they're truly committed."

"And in the meantime," Robby piped in as he also swung down, "I've come to add me own musket and powder to the cause."

"Was our pretty little Emily agreeable to that decision?" Morgan asked him.

"Well, now, to be truthful, she dinna want me to leave her. But she believes in the cause with all her heart."

After having seen the horrors of actual combat himself, Morgan wondered if the lad had any real idea of what he'd be up against. Part of him wished someone had warned him and Chandler off before it was too late. But they probably wouldn't have been dissuaded. "Have you signed up yet, Robby?"

"Nay."

"I'll be glad to take you to Captain Brown and have you enlist in our company." With any luck, Morgan figured he'd be able to keep an eye on the young Scot. Emily was always such a cheery little thing, as bright as her shining blonde hair. She deserved to have someone looking out for the man she loved.

"You're busy scrubbing pots," Chandler reminded him. "I'll take Robby to the captain. You finish up."

"Wait a second," Ben said. "You might be interested in the latest news before you go. The congress has sent us a commander in chief—George Washington from Virginia."

Chan perked up. "Say, that is good news. He's from our own neck of the woods, one of the heroes of the French and Indian War. Would you believe the man was commissioned a major by the time he was twenty-one?"

"Twenty-one," Morgan muttered with a scathing glare at the remaining stack of grubby pans. "Poor fellow must've missed out on joys like this."

"Not necessarily," Chandler drawled. "Washington spent a great deal of time in Virginia's back country surveying it before he accepted his commission. I doubt he took along a maidservant to take care of the mundane tasks. Because of his knowledge of the frontier, he led several wilderness campaigns—with heroic courage and integrity, I might add."

"And what's more important, he's a man who prays," Robby added fervently. Morgan noted again, just as he had when they were together last Christmas, that MacKinnon had a very simple yet pure faith—a faith he envied.

Chandler inclined his head. "On the other hand, it's not unheard of for Washington to resort to using a whippin' post. He's a strict disciplinarian, but his men respect him. If he and the Virginia militia had not taken part in the Battle of Monongahela, the entire British force would've been lost along with their general. The lobsterbacks persisted in marchin' out in the open in a straight line—as always—while the Indians hid behind rocks and trees. All in all," he said with a vigorous nod, "he's undoubtedly the best choice for the position."

"In the Continental army," Ben added on a proud note. "That's the name they've given us."

"Let's just hope it's not merely a high-sounding one," Chan said with conviction. "And that the militias and supplies from all the colonies follow Washington's lead. Speaking of which," he added, looking at Robby, "follow me. Let's get you signed up and settled for the night."

As the two departed, Ben turned to Morgan. "Any word of Susannah and Dan?"

"I sent Chandler to check with Sean Burns. But as yet there's no word out of Boston."

"I fear things can only get worse there," Ben admitted, his forehead etched with lines. Then he brightened. "At least Jane is safe for the moment in the Grants, now that Fort Ticonderoga is ours. She's due to give birth soon—and she doesn't need any more worries. Sure hope I manage to get up there beforehand."

Morgan smiled. "From what I recall of your sister, she's quite a strong girl. And Ted will be there for her." That thought brought another to mind. "By the way, I have a lady friend with a small problem you might be able to help us with."

"Lady friend." A sly smile softened Ben's boyish countenance. "Don't tell me you actually found your Prudence!"

Morgan felt himself redden. He had teased Ben unmercifully about Abigail not too long ago. Shrugging, he smiled with chagrin.

"And did your *lady friend* turn out to be everything you'd hoped for?"

"Does anything ever turn out exactly the way one expects?" Morgan returned. "But she does have a problem I need to discuss, if you don't mind."

Ben's humorous smirk faded.

"Her family's home and store were burned down along with the rest of Charlestown—"

"Charlestown?" Ben cut in. "Are you saying she was just across the bay all along? Where's she now? I'd like to meet this damsel who's turned you into a yowling hound dog!"

Morgan wasn't in the mood for this kind of banter. "While you were out on the road, did you chance upon a place in dire need of a store? One with a solid vacant building?"

"Anyone wanting to open a new business should go west, to the new territories."

"No, I need a spot close to Boston. Her father is quite ill and unable to travel a long distance."

"And you wouldn't be able to, either. Not with the war here at Boston Bay."

Morgan glared at him.

"They could consider Salem. As long as the Boston port is blockaded, folks will have to go there for supplies. The town is sure to grow. It should be safe enough. From the hundreds of encampments I passed, Gage has as much as he can handle right here."

"Salem? Nothing closer? I volunteered to help them get set up again whenever I have free time."

Ben rubbed the bridge of his nose in thought. "Well, scout the road to Salem. But stick closer to Cambridge."

The suggestion at least sounded hopeful. "Thanks. I'll do that." Mulling the idea over in his mind, Morgan felt renewed optimism. If he were able to help the Endecotts get established again fairly quickly, there would be no need for Prudence's father to be pushing her off on him. Things would settle down to near normalcy. And he'd be able to come calling at his leisure, when he wanted to.

If he wanted to.

40

Morgan rode away from the bay and headed for Medford with the Endecotts' horse trailing on a lead. His sleep had been far from restful the past several nights; he had tossed and turned, assaulted by a myriad of thoughts until the wee hours of the morning. For months, one purpose had propelled him onward—finding his enchanting, silver-eyed spy. And now, practically the moment their paths crossed again, her father wanted to drop her into Morgan's lap. Permanently.

He rubbed his thumbs over his scratchy eyelids and blinked to clear his vision. Marriage. That was one institution he had managed to avoid. In fact, he had often congratulated himself on perfecting the art of skirting it, even as one after another of his peers succumbed to the temptations of feminine wiles and fell by the wayside.

Even before he had gone off to college, his mother had tried manipulating him toward an endless succession of tittering females—daughters of other society matrons, nieces of Philadelphia clergy, siblings of his sisters' friends. Her clever schemes knew no limit. But always Morgan outwitted them—and derived immense pleasure in doing so. It was so much more gratifying merely to dabble in Mother's games without any commitment, play along for a while until he grew tired, and then move on to the next pretty face. The last thing he planned to do was get tied down with one of those spoiled females. Having to face day after tedious day of nagging and whining would sour him on life altogether.

As he shifted to a more comfortable position in the leather saddle, Morgan wondered whether he knew of even one happy marriage. His own mother and the other fine ladies in her snobbish circles schooled their daughters in coquettish ways of twisting a man into doing their bidding. The only women he had met who seemed the least bit forthright were Susannah Haynes, her young sister-in-law, Emily, and more recently, Jane and her mother. Their husbands, he had to admit, seemed truly content with their wives. But from what he had heard, poor Mr. Haynes had suffered untold years of misery before his wife developed a new godly selflessness.

Maybe that was what he should strive for instead of the adventurous life, Morgan decided. Simple contentment. A wife who would remain selfless throughout the years—if that were even possible.

Then a sudden and disconcerting thought struck Morgan. If such a woman did exist, why would she want *him?* He certainly wasn't selfless, as Susannah had pointed out. He had, indeed, strayed from the ideals of his college days—ideals that once were uppermost in his zeal. Well, almost.

But now, seeing the gruesome handiwork of the Grim Reaper around him at every turn, Morgan again found himself desiring to spend time studying the Scriptures and praying . . . even though present circumstances often made that impossible.

Morgan released a ragged breath and shook his head. Surely his nightly exhaustion wasn't all his fault. If there was so much as a bump on the ground, Captain Brown had them dig a redoubt there. The captain worked the men until they were too tired to care about anything else. And trenches! If someone took all those trenches and strung them in a straight line, they'd reach halfway to Providence!

But as yet the British had made no effort to regroup for another attack, or Morgan wouldn't have found even a brief respite from the constant digging, much less time enough to return the borrowed horse. And despite the threat of marriage, he had to admit he was looking forward to feasting his eyes on feisty Prudence, with her long midnight hair and incredible heart-shaped face.

On the Concord road out of Cambridge, Morgan neared the crossroad that cut across to Medford. Just ahead sat a building, its lower half made of fieldstone, the upper of wood. The windowpanes had all been broken out, and there was a gaping hole in one side—possibly from a cannonball. *A souvenir of the Concord Road Battle,* he mused. But the structure was in a great location.

He urged his mount over to the abandoned place and dismounted, then went inside. A second hole on the opposite side indicated the shot had passed right on through it. Long shelves lined the walls, and a couple of knocked-over wooden benches littered the plank floor. Obviously, the building had been someone's workshop.

Lying behind Winter Hill, it was beyond the range of the British ships. And most traffic coming from the north would end up at this juncture of crossroads, along with all the freight coming from Salem and the ports beyond. Men pouring down to the bay to fight would surely have coins jingling in their pockets—and it was near enough to camp that he could drop by himself every day or so.

If he could only find out who owned the place!

As Morgan strode outside, he spotted a woman herding some geese toward a small pond not too far away. He hastened over to her and tipped his hat. "Good day, madam. I wonder if you can tell me the name of the owner of that building."

"'Twas my brother-in-law's gun shop until the conflict along the road," she said, looking Morgan up and down with small, close-set eyes. "He packed up and moved to Sudbury so he wouldn't be a target so quick next time."

"Do you suppose he'd be interested in selling?"

A quirk of interest twitched in her long face. "What for?"

Astute enough to conclude she might take advantage of someone who might expect to profit from the location, Morgan decided to give only the most necessary information. "Friends of mine were burned out in Charlestown and need a place right now."

Her look of pity brought him a twinge of guilt, but he assured himself he hadn't exactly lied. "Is there any land that goes with it?"

She peered at him shrewdly. "How much would they need?"

"An acre, no more."

"Come back later this afternoon or tomorrow. My husband will be home then."

"Splendid. I bid you good day." Morgan bowed his head with his most charming grin and returned to the horses.

As he rode toward Medford, Morgan congratulated himself for his brilliant solution to the Endecotts' most pressing problems. Then he began having second thoughts. The location, which at first seemed so perfect, was still fairly close to the bay if trouble should erupt again soon. The store, and perhaps even Prudence, could be overrun by the redcoats. But, he reasoned, that might very well not happen. The colonists were a tough, stubborn breed. And in the meantime her family could do quite well reestablished in a prime spot, their income secured even if Mr. Endecott passed on. He'd discuss the idea with the older man and let him decide.

As he turned onto the dairy farm, another weight lifted from his shoulders. With such a promising location, the frail storekeeper might be less anxious to marry off his daughter to the first likely prospect!

❦ ❦

Outside beating a rug on the clothesline, Prudence heard horses coming in the distance. Her heart skipped a beat when she recognized the lanky rider, but she quickly quelled her ridiculous reaction. The man had promised to return their horse a full week ago. Not that Jupiter was worth all that much, if the truth were told, but still, she and Pa didn't really know that cocky Morgan Thomas. He could easily have kept the old bay for good.

But worse, much worse, Pa had tried to foist her off on him! As if she wasn't capable of attracting a suitor on her own!

Her cheeks flamed.

Well, perhaps she had no suitor at the moment. But if she *wanted* one—which she certainly did not—she could find any number of them soon enough. She simply had more important things to think about. After all, there was a war going on, and she intended to be a part of it. Somehow.

Prudence slammed the beater into the rug, sending a cloud of dust into the air. In a fit of coughing, she stepped back. Then she realized what a dust-covered sight she must be. She couldn't let Morgan see her like this!

"Are you all right, Daughter?" Pa asked from the rocking chair on the porch as she flew by.

"Yes. Fine." She stopped just short of the entrance. "You might as well know, Morgan Thomas has finally decided to bring Jupiter home." Ignoring the manner in which her father perked up, she gave a disgusted sigh. "And I'd better not hear you two bandying about that ridiculous matrimony scheme again, either!" Too flustered to care overmuch about the tone of voice she had used to her ailing father, she flung open the door and darted inside.

"Hmm," she heard him mutter as she stepped out of her dirty work shoes in the entry hall. "Thought my gal had a better head on her shoulders. It appears she's just another silly female after all, with nothing more to think about than a man."

It had to be Pa's illness speaking, she told herself angrily. He hadn't really been right since his heart started giving out. The last thing he needed was time alone with that arrogant Morgan Thomas—who had kissed her full on the mouth! Right in front of Pa!

Racing upstairs, she fairly tore off her dress and pulled on a fresh one, then yanked the brush through her tangled hair, retying it with her best ribbon. "Well, I have to look presentable," she hissed at her reflection. Then she crossed the room to retrieve a clean starched apron.

Through the bedroom window she caught sight of Miriam out back in the garden. The children were cavorting nearby, and Lucas had gone to muck out the barn. She hoped they'd all just stay where they were. She would absolutely die if they, too, happened on Pa and Morgan discussing her as if she were a slab of meat on a hook.

She was hastily tying her apron when the sound of Morgan's voice floated up to her. "Oh, no! He's already with Papa." She peered into the mirror and saw her flushed face staring back at her. With a single motion she blotted it with a damp cloth, straightened her shawl collar and, with a deep breath, bolted for the stairs.

Near the bottom, she slowed to a ladylike walk. It wouldn't do for that rascal to think his appearance here was any concern of hers.

His profile was visible through the open front door, and she couldn't help but notice what a fine masculine figure he made. He really was quite handsome. . . .

With a huff at herself for such wayward thoughts, Prudence hiked her chin. The ribbon holding her hair had worked loose, so she fumbled with it as best she could, then drew a calming breath and walked gracefully out the door as if she hadn't a care in the world.

Her father, standing with Morgan, turned to her.

Morgan's cobalt eyes locked onto hers, their intensity disabling her ability to look away. "Miss Endecott," he said softly, taking her hand.

She swallowed, still imprisoned by his gaze. "Mr. Thomas." She needed to think of something to say. Something light and witty. Something—

"It's been decided, Daughter." Pa's voice drifted to her, drawing her back. "You're to go with Mr. Thomas."

❧ ❧

If Morgan lived to be a hundred, he would never forget Prudence's breathless gasp or the sight of her face going absolutely white with shock when she thought her father was callously handing her over to him. But then, equally priceless had been her flush upon learning the real meaning of her father's words. After that humiliation, she now sat stiff as a broomstick on old Jupiter, looking neither to the right nor left as she rode in silence beside Morgan to see the location he had found for the store.

After some time had passed, he became sorry for her dismay. Nevertheless, he could not resist teasing her just a little. "You must find me quite a loathsome chap."

She cut him a furtive glance, then quickly looked forward again. "Don't be ridiculous. I told you once before how dashing—and handsome—you are."

He was taken aback by her directness. He had never met a girl as straightforward as she. Nonetheless, if that's how she felt about him, why had she been so outraged earlier at the Randolph farm?

"It's just—" she met his gaze with a tiny shrug—"a woman likes to have a say in whom she marries."

"Yet you do consider me handsome and dashing."

The tiny smile she could not quite smother seemed especially captivating against the fragile pink of her rising blush.

"How, er, *handsome* would you say I am? Personally."

"Surely not as handsome as you are vain." With a toss of her head, she turned her attention to the opposite side.

"Ouch. You've cut me to the quick. And just when I was contemplating the striking couple the two of us would make."

Her light gray eyes swiftly returned to him. "I do wish you would not refer to us as a couple. We are far from that, I assure you. By the way, exactly what *did* you and Papa agree upon, if I might ask? I know he hasn't told me the whole of it. How much has he offered you to take me?"

He fought to remain serious. "What would you consider a fair price for a woman who refuses to stay home where she belongs?"

"Far more than *you*, sir, are worth," she said with disdain.

He shook his head and chuckled. "Go on, try to deny it if

you must, my sweet spy. But the attraction between us is just as evident to you as it is to me. I'd stake my life on it."

Pursing her tantalizing lips, Prudence jerked her gaze from his. "I refuse to be party to this ludicrous conversation."

"And probably for the best. After all, I know how mindful you are of the folly of lying."

Her mouth gaped as she swung back again. "You—"

"There's the store," he said, interrupting what he knew would have been a scathing retort. He pointed directly ahead.

The diversion effectively silenced her, and a pleasantly astonished expression settled over her fine features as they reined in for passing traffic and then crossed the Concord road.

Morgan halted outside the abandoned building, dismounted, then strode to help Prudence.

Her eyes met his as she leaned into his upraised arms.

It took a few seconds more than necessary to lower her slowly to the ground. Eventually he managed to release his hold on her slender waist. It might have been his imagination, he assured himself, but she hadn't seemed all that eager to let go of him either.

She was the first to break eye contact. "I expected much worse," she said breathlessly, turning and assessing the outside walls. "A little wood, some glass, and most of the damage would be repaired. We could board up the side windows rather than doing them all at once. Come, let's look inside." She grabbed his hand and started tugging him along . . . then dropped it like a hot poker.

Morgan smiled to himself as he kept up with her quick steps.

"The size seems more than adequate," she said, turning a slow circle. "A good supply of hardware, nails, cutlery, utensils, some basic dry goods, and we should manage quite admirably here. Don't you think? Of course, once the shelves have been put up and the repairs are finished, I'll be able to run it by myself. The hard part will be keeping it stocked."

Morgan pulled his gaze from her shining eyes and shook

his head. *Of course.* Why hadn't he thought about how difficult it would be for Prudence to get merchandise? Probably because he had become too—*muddlebrained*—to think clearly.

Ah, but not too far gone, he corrected himself, for he immediately thought of certain cargos that had recently been diverted. After all his hard work this past winter, he should be able to get his hands on some of that merchandise. With the British ships preoccupied in protecting their Boston forces, perhaps now would be a good time to arrange their transfers into other Massachusetts ports. Even John Hancock would agree that a small percentage of the goods was due him for his efforts. Of course, almost everything sold here in the store would be going to the patriots.

"You let me worry about the stock," he finally told her. "That's been my family's business for generations."

"We can count on you? Truly?"

At that one last heartfelt word—or maybe it was the gratefulness of her tone—his heart melted. He turned before she could read the depth of the strange new feelings surging through him. "Out back are some storage sheds and a fair-sized clearing. Come, I'll show you." Without thinking, he offered his hand.

To his delight, she placed her much smaller one in his and smiled.

Morgan's heart pounded as he held her hand and they walked outside. He felt the protection of the worldly man falling away, and the bumbling youth coming to the fore again.

But the intimacy of the moment was shattered when the woman he had spoken to earlier approached with a man Morgan presumed to be her husband. Reluctantly he turned to Prudence. "Those are the people with whom I made arrangements for the place. I omitted that you wanted it for a store. I figured they'd raise the price."

He watched Prudence look up and down the road and then toward Winter Hill. Several militiamen were walking from the fort, most likely heading for Cambridge. A wagon was coming from the north, and another mounted pair were slowing at the cutoff from the south.

"Oh, Morgan!" she cried, her face radiant with hope. "We must pay whatever price they ask. You're absolutely right. There's a great deal of money to be made here. Of course, we must stock more of the soldiers' needs. Tobacco, jerky, writing paper, soap, boots . . ."

As Morgan took a closer look at the passing men and saw how they ogled Prudence, his own enthusiasm evaporated. These were merely the first—of heaven only knew how many—to come. To see.

And to want.

41

The steady drizzle that began early the next morning continued to fall throughout the afternoon, making soggy rivulets in the zigzagged trench the men had just dug to protect Cambridge from another British attack. Morgan eyed Chandler and Robby, still in their muddy clothes, sitting beside him on a long bench under a tarp. They looked no better than he.

"I dinna think," Robby began, tongue in cheek, "that as the fightin' comrade ye were so eager to have by your side, I'd be sharpenin' me soldiering skills with a shovel."

Morgan chuckled.

"Ah, but becoming proficient in that particular art may very well save your life," Chandler said. "And we did promise Ben we'd return you to your wife in one piece."

"Quite," Morgan agreed. "If we don't, she'll likely take a pitchfork to us. Personally, I'd prefer to be a dragoon on horseback. Chan and I had great sport when we chased the redcoats back to Boston on the Concord road." The mention of that specific site brought Prudence to his mind . . . as did everything since yesterday evening. He exhaled a troubled breath. "I think I've made a grave error."

Confusion reigned on both his friends' faces as they turned to him.

"I went yesterday, as you know, to return the Endecotts' horse."

"Yes?" Chandler prompted, not quite containing a smirk. "And how is our lovely belle? Still angry, I suppose?"

Morgan almost regretted bringing the subject up after having successfully sidestepped their curiosity until now. But perhaps it would do him good to get it out in the open. "No. Actually, she's quite the opposite."

"Are you saying you've asked her to marry you, after all? I thought you were going to take things slowly."

"No, no, nothing like that. I knew her father had proposed the marriage idea only out of concern for her security, so I did the only sensible thing—I found a profitable place for their store. And since every able-bodied man has joined the militia and there's no help to be had, I pledged my efforts in helping them get reestablished."

"Then why, pray tell, do ye look as if ye just buried your own dear mother?" Robby asked.

Morgan grimaced. "You know me and my clever ideas. I picked what I considered to be the perfect spot for them. More than perfect, really—a veritable gold mine. When I showed it to Prudence yesterday, she was quite excited about opening a store there. Afterward nothing I said would dissuade her."

"But why would ye want to do that, laddie?"

"My sentiments exactly," Chandler affirmed with a frown.

"The building is situated on the Concord road—at the Medford cutoff. I'm sure you know it."

Chandler nodded. "Just past the Winter Hill redoubt?"

"Yes. The vacant building right there."

"I remember the place. Ideal spot. Everyone coming from the north and west will pass by."

"Precisely," Morgan said on a regretful sigh. "Every jack here on his first adventure away from his mother's watchful eye, feeling his wild oats. Not to mention the dozens of men left with nothing but dull guard duty at the redoubt. And that's where she'll be. Alone. A father too ill to help out, nothing save a farmhouse in sight—and that not even within shouting distance. Village idiot that I am, I showed it to her."

"Ah," Chandler said knowingly.

"I'm sure I'd not be wanting me wife in that circumstance either," Robby added. "Bonny as she is, she'd be the devil's own temptation."

"That's what I tried to explain to Prudence. But the willful lass is cocksure she's capable of taking care of herself. And I don't have to tell *you*, Chan, how foolhardy she is. But she's not my wife. I can't order her not to open a store there. As if she'd listen to me even if she *were* my wife! Plus, I'm obligated to lend a hand. I gave my word. To make matters worse," he added, casting a nervous glance at them, "she's actually accused me of being jealous! Can you believe it?" He whacked his knee. "It's ridiculous. She has to know I'm only concerned about the danger to her. Pure and simple."

A maddening grin passed between his two friends, but they wisely said nothing.

After a few minutes of silence, Morgan decided to change the subject. "Wonder when the cook's going to ring the bell for supper."

As they looked toward the cook fire, they saw a tall officer approaching on a long-legged horse. Even in the drizzle his blue uniform appeared perfectly tailored, with cream-colored facings and trousers, and fancy epaulets. Squarely atop his head sat a plumed tricorn. He halted his mount and took out a spyglass, peering through it at Boston Bay.

"George Washington," Chandler said.

Morgan looked from the striking figure to his friend. "He can't be here already. They've planned a big welcome for his arrival."

"Then I reckon the surprise is his."

"And he seems none too happy," Robby piped in.

"Well, look at us, will you?" Morgan said, taking a gander at their shambles of a military camp. "The lot of us are covered with mud from head to toe, tents and huts scattered about without rhyme or reason. He must find us an unholy mess. No doubt he already regrets leaving Virginia."

"He might today, laddie," Robby said. "But these men have

earned the respect of the British, and that's what counts. If he's the sort of man Chandler says he is, 'twill not be long before he sees that, too."

❦ ❧

After Morgan bathed and changed into conservatively fashionable clothing in the privacy of Ben's rented room, he crossed the shaded expanse of Harvard Common with the confidence that finely tailored clothing instilled. He couldn't help but compare the university buildings here with the College of New Jersey, comprised only of Nassau Hall. His alma mater seemed small by comparison, even though its single building was reported to be the largest of any in the Colonies.

Morgan strode over the Common, imagining the grounds filled with black-robed students. Classes had ceased the day of the Lexington and Concord conflicts, the dormitory and classrooms having been converted to barracks to house the Continental army. It grated him to think that certain companies of militia stayed in such a tight structure while his own company had to be quartered under canvas. Pity that Colonel Brown hadn't acted quickly to secure better facilities for his men, who had actually fought in Concord.

He continued on to the president's house, where General Washington was residing temporarily. The entrances were guarded, and a number of officers and civilians were waiting outside. He suddenly realized that, as a lowly private, he could face serious difficulty procuring an audience with the commander, let alone convincing the general to go along with his plan. But he simply couldn't go back on his word to Prudence and her father to keep their store stocked . . . and the army truly needed a mess of supplies as well.

There was no recourse but to resort to one more fabrication. Surely God would understand how desperately he needed this audience with the general. Surely God would excuse this one little exaggeration.

Morgan strode purposefully up to the main entrance,

flanked on each side by guards, their muskets resting butt down on the floor. He attempted to pass.

"Halt!" Their rifles crossed in front of him.

"I must speak to General Washington as soon as he's finished with his present business."

"You and the rest of Cambridge, sir," one of the sentries snapped.

"But you don't understand," Morgan insisted, using what he hoped was his most intimidating stare. "I've come on behalf of John Hancock, president of the Continental Congress. I believe the general will want to see me. Right away."

The officer blanched. "I'll inform the commander's aide that you're here. Whom shall I say is calling?"

"Thomas. Mr. Thomas." Morgan made it a point to keep from being noticed by the other officers milling about. The last thing he needed was to be recognized by one of them as a mere private about to usurp their places in line.

"Come this way," the sentry said upon his return. He ushered Morgan inside and motioned toward a chair beneath the stairs. "The general will see you as soon as he's free."

"Thank you." With a polite nod, Morgan sat down.

Undistinguishable voices drifted from behind the double doors straight across the hall. Morgan began to have cold feet. What if the man wasn't exactly enthusiastic about the brilliant proposal he was about to put before him? He didn't want to think about the peck of trouble he could find himself in for bypassing the chain of command.

After a few moments, the doors opened. "I'll do my best, sir," a man said, clad in a uniform of the Rhode Island militia. "But it may take several days."

"Several days?" The responding voice spoke with quiet authority. "You can't give me an accurate roster for several days?"

"Sir, at least half the men have gone home to arrange their affairs. You must understand, we literally dropped everything to run to the aid of our Massachusetts brothers. It's entirely possible that not all will be able to return."

"Not return? I thought you men up here were committed to this cause."

"We are, sir, I assure you. But some are simply unable to return until their families have been provided for."

There was a slight pause. "One week. I must have an accurate number in one week."

"Yes, sir. Good day, sir." Visibly relieved, the Rhode Islander left.

An aide followed the officer into the hall, then approached Morgan. "You may come in."

Morgan felt his knees shake as he steeled himself to follow. He could be thrown into the guardhouse for this. After he was deposited before a massive desk in the book-lined study, he watched the aide take a seat at a corner table.

Commander Washington, without his coat and wig on this warm afternoon, raised his pockmarked face, and his clear blue eyes met Morgan's. "I understand you're from the Continental Congress. I wasn't expecting anyone so soon."

Impressed momentarily by the tall general's courtly manners and noble presence, Morgan almost forgot to remove his hat. He quickly whipped it off. "No, sir. The guard must have misunderstood. I said I came on behalf of John Hancock, not from the congress in Philadelphia."

A slight intensifying of the man's stare indicated that not a moment of his time was to be wasted.

Morgan swallowed. "Sir, during the winter, Mr. Hancock and I executed a plan to divert several of Boston's Tory merchant ships to warehouses in the middle and southern colonies. We scattered the merchandise to make it harder to trace. I feel that with the British preoccupied with Boston Bay, this would be an excellent time to retrieve the various shipments. They could be off-loaded in Providence to the south or in Salem. Or smuggled into any of our numerous coves, if need be."

Washington motioned to a nearby chair. "Sit down, Mr. . . . Thomas, isn't it? I don't detect a northern accent."

"No, sir." Morgan, vastly relieved that his legs hadn't buckled, sank to the proffered seat and drew some manifests from an inside pocket of his frock coat, handing them to the general. "I hail from Philadelphia. My father is a prominent merchant there. But, alas, a Tory."

"You have my sympathy." Washington looked over the cargo lists, then smiled. "This is the best news I've had all day. Tell me, how did you manage such an endeavor?"

Morgan didn't try to hide his own grin. "Actually, my Tory connections from home only enhanced my efforts to ingratiate myself with the Boston Tories. They're an amazingly greedy lot, I must say. It was quite easy to dupe them into believing that with their authorization I could intercept and store their cargos in warehouses my family owns in Bermuda. Then, after repacking the shipments into French and Dutch crates and forging appropriate manifests, they'd become much more acceptable to the Colonies. That was the part which pleased them most. They'd be defying the boycott against British goods while increasing their profits—or so they thought. But, unbeknownst to them, we diverted the merchandise to the patriot cause."

The dignified commander was completely expressionless. "How on earth did anyone come up with such an elaborate—and devious—plan? Did you think of it yourself?"

From his bland tone, Morgan sensed his disapproval. The Virginian was known for his high standards of integrity. "Sir, I have considered myself at war with the British since they blockaded Boston Harbor—a war they declared by that very act. Therefore, I regard my efforts on the Colonies' behalf nothing less than honorable. And I'm sure Dr. Witherspoon, president of my alma mater, would agree," he added for good measure, since Witherspoon was a respected patriot and member of the congress.

Washington sat back and steepled his fingers, seeming to assimilate the information as he studied Morgan. "I presume you have shipping connections you can trust."

"With my life, sir."

"And Hancock—have you discussed with him recently the possibility of shipping the merchandise up here?"

"No, sir. We've both been rather busy—he, with his election to presidency of the congress, and I with shooting redcoats and digging trenches." He took a steadying breath. "You see, sir, I cast my lot with the Concord militia and am but a lowly private. You may think I should have gone through proper channels to see you. But in matters of espionage, I've always felt the fewer who know, the better."

"I'm surprised someone with your education and ability hasn't been given a commission."

The statement was gratifying. "Sir, things are done differently here in New England. Very democratically. Officers are elected by their men—and naturally, the men of Concord would prefer one of their own to lead them."

"Yes, I've recently been apprised of this system. Many of the officers I've spoken with have no qualifications, no military experience or knowledge whatsoever. Some can neither read nor write."

"But don't discount their hearts, sir, or their courage. I've fought alongside them from Concord to Cambridge and on Breed's Hill. For the most part, they're made of sturdy stuff . . . even if they don't march so smartly." He smiled. "Yet."

The general smiled, too, then turned serious again. "Who actually went to Bermuda to implement the diversion of the ships?"

"I did, sir."

"Excellent. Excellent."

Not one to waste opportunity, now that the commander was in such a light mood, Morgan went for broke. "Sir, I would deem it an honor to take charge of the inventory as it comes in and administer its dispersement. I've had years of experience, working for my father."

"And what is his name?"

"Waldon Thomas, sir."

"Yes, I believe we met in the late sixties. He has a fine

reputation. 'Tis sad he's unable to divorce himself from the old ties."

"Yes. Quite. But concerning the merchandise that will be coming—" he took out another list—"I would like to purchase these goods from the shipments. A store owner in Charlestown was burned out by British artillery, and I'd appreciate the opportunity to help him reestablish. The store would be set up just outside Cambridge, so the soldiers would not be deprived in any way."

Washington averted his gaze, definitely suspicious again. "And this is for friends, you say."

"Sir, truly, I am not trying to skim cream off for myself. I'll give you whatever information you deem necessary. These people are very respected patriots, above reproach."

"Yes," he said thoughtfully, "I would expect a full report along with your written request. But first, let's deal with getting the goods here, shall we? Along with any gunpowder you can garner along the way."

"Me, sir?"

"Of course. You are the logical one to retrieve the shipments."

"But, sir—it's strung out from Maryland to South Carolina."

"Precisely. So we've no time to waste." The general turned to his aide. "See if General Putnam is around." He swung back to Morgan. "We need to commission you an officer and send you on your way on the first tide. There's not a day to spare. From what I can tell, except for food, we're short of everything." Leaving Morgan sitting there dumbfounded, General Washington rose and strode after the aide to the door.

This was not the way it was supposed to happen, Morgan railed inwardly. He was supposed to stay here, be given the much easier job of preparing *for* the shipments. He had promised to help Prudence set up the store. He had given his word. And he had vowed to see to it personally that no interlopers harassed her. Were all these promises to be broken? Why was everything going wrong again?

But as his thoughts tumbled about in his brain, there was a stirring in his conscience. Before he broke another promise to God, maybe he had better take time to pray about it first. Perhaps even wait upon the Lord for an answer. It was pretty obvious he wasn't faring too well on his own.

But blast it all, he had just outsmarted himself again.

And Prudence would now be left to the mercy of thousands of soldiers!

42

Inside her father's newly purchased mercantile, Prudence placed a stool carefully atop the bench to give her the added height she needed. Then, a hammer in one hand and a board under her other arm, she climbed up, positioned the new wood over the gaping cannonball hole, and removed one of the nails clenched between her teeth.

How gratifying, this first step toward the resettlement of her family! Once she managed to get the store operational she would be able to concentrate all her efforts on finding a home for them nearby. After that, they would *finally* get away from that despicable Lucas Randolph. Even today—when she'd be working all day in the mercantile—the surly farmer had made her promise to be home in time to milk the cows. She barely refrained from picturing his swarthy face as she pounded in the nail and reached for another.

It wasn't as if Pa wasn't shelling out plenty of money for the family's room and board. Randolph never had it so good, she was certain. Once Pa and Miriam moved out on their own again, that miser would have himself a setback. With the war going on, workers were hard to come by, especially for a tight-pursed man who rebelled at having to pay an honest wage. With renewed energy, she slammed a few more strokes, driving in another nail.

"What do you think you're doing?" a voice behind her demanded gruffly.

Morgan!

His hands reached from behind and snatched her from her precarious perch. The stool tumbled after her.

Prudence swung around the instant her feet touched the ground.

"So, you've already bought the place," he said, his fury so near the surface it was almost palpable. "You paid no heed whatsoever to my warnings, and now, to cause me more grief, you're set on breaking your neck before your first customer has the chance to ravage you."

Prudence spit the remaining nails into her palm. "Really, Morgan. Must you speak of such things? They're most unseemly."

"I do with you," he returned. "You refuse to listen to my more gentle attempts at persuasion."

"Well, your fears are quite unfounded," she announced with assurance. "It's a rare Massachusetts man who is not a gentleman around a woman. Perhaps you've only been around Pennsylvania men who've not been so properly reared."

He ignored the insult. "And let us not forget those uncouth frontiersmen. A company of those wild men arrived just today."

Prudence, still heady from obtaining the mercantile just yesterday, didn't let his insinuations rile her. She picked a splinter from her apron with feigned indifference. "If a problem should happen to arise, I'll handle it. You'll note, I do have my musket propped right alongside the lumber." She tilted her head toward the wall she had been patching. "And before you say another word, understand this. I cannot—I repeat, *cannot*—be dissuaded. My family is counting on me in this time of crisis."

Morgan growled, then snatched the hammer from her, seized nails from the open sack, and hopped onto the bench. He pounded viciously until the board was secured, then he spun around to peer down at her. "And suppose you just happen to miss your shot. What then? Will you ask the marauder to please wait until you reload?"

Prudence rolled her eyes at his arrogance. "No. I'll bash his head in with the barrel, *then* ask him to wait."

Without speaking, he grabbed another board and began hammering it into place over the remainder of the hole.

Prudence sighed as she watched Morgan work. He was, to be certain, an infuriating man—especially when he insinuated that she was incapable of taking care of herself. But, still, he was rather sweet to be so worried about her and all. She moved closer, wishing that he'd allow her to defuse some of his anger. "Morgan, my dear friend, please don't be mad at me. This is something I must do for my family . . . and in my small way, perhaps for the cause."

He paused briefly, then banged the nails even faster.

"It's more comfort than you can possibly know," she added, "having you drop by every day or so to see how I'm getting along."

Morgan stepped down and set the tools on the floor. A muscle flexed in his jaw as he turned to her and met her gaze. "But that's my greatest distress," he said quietly, taking hold of her shoulders. "I won't *be* here. General Washington is dispatching me on a mission this very afternoon which will keep me away for several months. I'm heading to Salem now to board a ship."

The news was most unsettling. Prudence had let herself count on his coming often . . . and not merely to help with the store. She clutched his arms. "You're going away? But why?"

"It has something to do with my activities for the cause before the outbreak of the war. It's best I don't give you any particulars beyond that."

"Oh, I—I see. I . . . understand." She didn't, actually, unless he was to become a spy again.

"Well, *I* don't. I need to be here, looking after you. That's what I've been counting on." His grip on her shoulders tightened. "Promise me something."

"Yes?"

"Promise me that before this week is over you'll find some man or boy—even another woman, if that's the best you can do—to help you here, so you're not by yourself. Will you do that?"

His plea touched her deeply. "Morgan, any man or lad I might trust has joined a militia. We women are having to take their places and look after their duties. As it is, Miriam and I are seeing to two jobs, milking her father's cows. And countless other women are doing the same thing."

At her words, the furrows deepened in his brow, making him look even more despondent. "But I'll do my very best to find someone to help," she added. "Truly, I will."

"I was afraid this is how it would turn out," he said on an exasperated breath. "So I arranged with the captain for either Robert Chandler, whom you met the day of the Bunker Hill battle, or another friend, Robby MacKinnon, to come by every day. They'll see to all the repair work and the building of any shelves you need."

"You, Morgan Thomas, are quite the thoughtful man. With countless preparations to deal with before you go, you took time to—" She smiled as another thought came to her. "Arranged with the captain, you say? The one who made you scrub pots for a week?"

He grinned—the first smile he had offered since his arrival—and the customary twinkle in his eyes returned.

For the flicker of a second, Prudence thought he had been on the verge of drawing her close. She wondered what it would be like being pressed to his heart by those strong arms, being held there, close to him. But she dismissed the wild notion instantly and made a greater effort to concentrate on what he was saying.

"The very same," he went on. "But General Washington thought it best I be commissioned an officer, which made it possible for me to reason with the captain on more level ground. And with a small, shall we say, inducement, he was more than happy to agree."

She had to laugh. "Shall we say, stipend? I insist upon repaying you."

He waved it off. "Take it out of the profits later. And

speaking of business," he said, his expression becoming less animated, "in my absence, I'll actually be able to see that this store is better stocked. My travels will take me to ports with a much greater selection of available goods."

"Why, that's . . . wonderful. Providence has truly arranged for you to help us in this time of need." Then a sudden thought struck her. *Ports*, he said. More than one. The word itself sounded distant, unreachable. She looked deep into his eyes. "Please, Morgan. Whatever you do, wherever you go . . . be careful, will you? Don't you get yourself killed."

This time he did tug her closer, wrapping her in his arms. "It's not going to be easy," he said huskily, "leaving you here on your own. It's not what I'd planned. At all."

"I know." Prudence slid her arms about him and tightened the embrace, cherishing the way his heart thundered against hers. She tried desperately not to think beyond the moment, beyond this embrace. She was determined not to give in to the inevitable anguish to come.

Morgan tipped her face up to his searching gaze. Then his lips descended to hers.

The deep reverence, the tenderness, the desperation of this kiss was completely unlike that first mocking kiss in Lucas Randolph's barn. She melted against him, returning the kiss with a passion she had never realized she possessed.

Too soon, the kiss ended, replaced by a longing she knew would only intensify.

He brushed the backs of his fingers over the curve of her cheekbone with a worshipful smile. "I must leave. I've miles to ride to make high tide." With a last long look, he turned and strode to his horse, leaving as abruptly as he'd come.

Prudence, not daring to breathe for the intensity of the pain inside, felt as if her heart had been torn out and now raced away with him on that steed.

"God be with you," she whispered. "Until he brings you back to me."

43

"Here you are, sir." Prudence assumed a smile and handed a penny's worth of candy to the leering soldier, then exhaled with relief as he left the store. *One down, two to go,* she thought, trying not to be obvious as she watched another pair of unsavory characters in militia shirts. They had been browsing most suspiciously for an extraordinary amount of time, all the while casting vulgar glances at her, confirming with sickening dread Morgan's predictions regarding her vulnerability here in the store alone. She glanced up and caught the heavier of the two staring in a most disgusting fashion.

She tried to still her nerves by adding hard candy to her list of needed goods. *If* they were to be had. The warehouses in both Salem and Newburyport were not able to keep up with the added demands. Hopefully, Morgan would have better luck in whatever ports he had sailed to.

At last one of the soldiers beckoned to the other and they departed.

Prudence drew a calming breath, then shook off her uneasiness. She had merely been overworking her imagination. Tossing back her long hair, she focused all her attention on adding items to the steadily growing list.

The mercantile was an overwhelming success. Many of the young men eager to join the militia left home ill prepared. Robert Chandler and Robby MacKinnon had constructed numerous shelves and counters with used lumber from other damaged buildings; they had all been put to good use. And if only there was room, she'd ask for more.

Even if she had bungled her spying effort to serve the cause, God had substituted this endeavor to help fill the supply gap until the army was better established.

The British had not launched another assault, and it had been almost two months. For that reason, Prudence was more sure than ever that the Lord was with her and the patriots. The militia was in dire need of gunpowder, and the Almighty knew it. Just this morning she had overheard soldiers commenting that at most there was only enough powder for each man to fire a pitiful total of nine rounds!

But while they waited for gunpowder, the poorly supplied patriot soldiers had other needs as well—needs she was determined to fill. Somehow she had to find a source for shirts, blankets, metal plates and utensils, boots, haversacks—all things Morgan Thomas had promised to obtain before he was called away last month.

Morgan. How she missed him! But he had sent her the two Roberts: Chandler, with a sadness that saw but fleeting moments of cheerfulness, and the younger Robby, homesick for his sweet wife and children back home. They were loyal helpers. They spent all of their limited time off here in the store, despite Robby's guilt about laboring for a woman other than his Emily.

Most of the hard work, however, fell to Prudence. Daily she felt the effects of rising before dawn to help Miriam with the milking, then laboring at the store until dusk. The roads no longer seemed as safe as they'd been before the fighting started, and the weight and feel of a musket was as familiar to her now as it was to any militia soldier.

She returned her attention to the list at hand and scanned it with resignation. Between the colonists' boycott and the British navy hindering manufactured goods from reaching New England shores . . . Prudence slowly shook her head. If only the Colonies had textile mills, not to mention gunpowder manufacturers. No doubt Commander Washington would agree with the latter.

The brass bell above the door tinkled, and Prudence looked up.

One of the two repugnant fellows she'd so recently been thankful to see leave now grinned at her, his thick, grubby finger jingling the bell. The sight of him and his cohort returning was not a welcome one.

This time, instead of staying together, they split up and moved in opposite directions to browse. She had the uneasy feeling she was being flanked as they drifted along, handling an unnatural number of items.

Many of the soldiers who came in foraged through as they might in a forest, trying to find things that might be of some use at a later time. And far too many of them seemed to be foraging for her as well. She was beginning to rue her hasty words to Morgan. Once a man was far from home and away from people who knew him, he was more likely to act rash. And these two, closing in on either side, were making her jittery. Could she handle them?

Casually she let her hand slide down to the loaded musket on the special shelf Chandler had built for her just below the counter. "Are you men with the Continental army?" she asked, hoping to distract them, praying they'd give up on the mischief they had on their minds.

"Why?" one asked with an insinuating smirk. "Like soldier boys, do you?" He slid a glance to his crony and back to her, undressing her with his bulgy eyes.

In an attempt to wither their carnal hopes and inspire them to higher ideals, Prudence schooled her features into the most pious expression she could muster. "I believe in the noble and righteous cause of our soldiers. Almighty God will honor our humble efforts to his glory; therefore, any who serve the Lord in this army will be rewarded—if not in this life, then surely in the next."

The two oafs went slack-jawed and looked askance at each other as Prudence babbled on. "We must not falter but persevere in humble obedience to God toward the victory he will give us. And I am not alone in this persuasion, of course. It is said our very own commander, General Washington, spends much time in closeted prayer. What a blessing that our leader understands the importance of habitually seeking heavenly wisdom and blessing. All of us may derive comfort from the fact that among his first orders to the army was one that required all officers and enlisted men to attend church meeting every Sabbath."

"Now, don't that beat all, Clem," the shorter of the two drawled. "All them words, spewin' outta that one purty, little mouth, and ain't a pulpit to be seen anywheres about."

"Purty, *sweet* little mouth," his cohort mocked. They made their way past crates and barrels, closing in on her.

Prudence gripped the musket in both hands, wondering how quickly she could clear the woefully long weapon from beneath the counter . . . and which one to aim at first. She opted for the more disgusting of the pair as she began drawing it from its place.

He stopped abruptly.

"There's a wagon rollin' into the yard!" he sputtered, and they both turned to stare at the doorway.

"Thank you, heavenly Father," Prudence whispered as she glanced out the open window and saw Chandler and the young Scot arriving on the seat of a huge freight wagon. She shoved the musket back.

With one last predatory glance at her, the ruffians muttered under their breaths and lumbered outside.

And thank you, Morgan, she thought, *for making the two Roberts promise to check up on me!* She had to admit, the sight of *his* face would have delighted her even more than theirs, but she'd make do. After all, her champion truly must be important to be singled out by General Washington himself. For all she knew, Morgan had always been more than an ordinary run-of-the-mill private. Perhaps he had been on some secret mission for the cause all along.

By the time she reached the wagon, Chandler and Robby

had hopped down and were gazing after the departing louts, who were walking down the road toward Cambridge. *Good riddance,* Prudence railed inwardly, then flashed a bright smile. "Good day."

"Have those gents yonder been botherin' ye, lass?" Robby began uncertainly. "'Tis sure they dinna look up to much good."

"Not at all," she answered lightly. These two gallants could be as worrisome as Morgan about such things, were she to give them reason. And the scoundrels hadn't actually *done* anything except set her heart to racing.

"Perhaps not this time," Chandler said evenly. "But it's not wise for you to be here alone. Is your father any better yet?"

"Yes, but not quite enough to endure the ride from Medford every day." When Prudence saw Robert's expression, she thought it best to put his mind at ease as quickly as possible. "Today, however, I heard of a place for us to live just down the road from here. The Loyalist who owns it barely escaped with his family to Boston the day after the first battle. Folks say it would be only right for us to use it until the war is over, since our home was destroyed by the man's British friends."

"Sounds fair enough," Robby said. "When might ye be movin'?"

"Well, actually, I haven't been to see it yet," Prudence admitted. "But if it has even three walls standing, I'm sure Papa will be more than glad to take it. He's been having an awful time keeping peace with Mr. Randolph."

"Emily and I have been truly blessed in the homes the Lord has provided for us," Robby went on. "Good Christian homes, they've been. What I'd give to be in one of them right now with me sweet wife and wee bairns. But 'twas six months I signed up for. And all this time has been a waste, with the British not about to make a move."

She smiled. "Perhaps the Almighty will show them the error of their ways, and they'll simply set sail for England."

The idea brought the nearest thing to a smile that she had seen yet on Chandler's normally grim face. "That would take a miracle akin to when the Lord walked on water! I've been to Britain. You can't even imagine the wealth of that country, the power, their utterly unquenchable pride—"

"One might think you were describing Egypt in the day of Moses," she returned. "We must never forget, God's power is vastly more immense."

"Don't always count on bein' saved just because ye want it, lassie," Robby said. "We Scots thought our own Moses had arrived a time or two—but the Union Jack still waves over the heather."

Prudence met his clear blue eyes. "That may well be. But neither the Lord's timing nor his ways are ours. The Israelites were in Egypt four hundred years before they were delivered." Even as she spoke, the story the Scotsman had related about his own abduction by a British naval captain came to her mind. "And didn't you tell me once that you'd been in this country only a short time before you realized you'd been delivered from something far more deadly than the British? Your unbelief."

"Aye." His dark mustache spread with a slow grin. "But don't be forgettin' your own words, lass. We never know God's timing. And wouldn't it be grand to be delivered for once, soul *and* body, from the blasted British dogs?"

"Aye, that it would," she mimicked good-naturedly, affecting a brogue like his. "'Twould be Moses and Joshua and Jesus' resurrection, all rolled into one."

"I do wish the two of you could talk about something else now and again," Chandler cajoled. "After listening to you for a while, attending a service on the Lord's Day is merely an afterthought."

Robby's ears reddened. "I suppose I do get carried away at times. We'd best get the wagon unloaded if we're to take it back to Salem in the morning."

"Well, it's wonderful of you both to stop by on your way to Cambridge," Prudence said.

"We're not heading anywhere," Chandler said. "This load is all yours."

"Mine?"

"The port authority in Salem sent us a note informing us of the cargo's arrival. Apparently Morgan shipped these goods from New York before he left to go south. The manifest stated it was to be delivered here."

"How sweet. How dear of him!" Realizing she'd spoken aloud, Prudence felt warmth flood her face. "To keep a promise when he's so busy," she added lamely.

One of several riders passing by reined into the yard. "There you are, Robby! I've been all over looking for you." He dismounted and shook hands with the Scot and Chandler.

"Have you met Miss Endecott?" Chandler asked. "Prudence, this is our good friend, Ben Haynes."

"Mr. Haynes," she said politely. Many of the young men serving the militia so faithfully were incredibly handsome, and this one was no exception.

"I'm happy to have the pleasure at last," he said, turning light brown eyes upon her. He whisked off his tricorn, revealing a neat queue of golden brown hair. A curious smile tweaked his lips.

Prudence had the impression he was mildly surprised about something but had no idea what.

"Have ye been home lately?" Robby asked him.

"I'm just back from the Grants. My sister, Jane, has just become a new mama. She had a baby girl."

Robby cleared his throat. "What has she named the bairn?"

"Joy Sophia. The Sophia part after our mother."

"And Jane? How's she doing?" he asked.

"Better than Ted, that's for sure," Ben said with a chuckle.

"Ye may laugh now," Robby said, "but when your turn comes, ye'll see things in a different light. Not knowin' whether they'll live or—" With an uncomfortable glance at Chandler, he changed the subject. "Any new word about Fort Ticonderoga? Have the Brits in Canada made a move down Lake Champlain to take it back?"

Ben propped a foot on a rung of the wagon wheel and grinned.

Feeling a long story coming on, Prudence moved to the rear of the oversized conveyance and took out the shipping manifest stuffed under the strap of one of the crates. She was interested in the war talk, of course, but at the moment her curiosity over the shipment was greater. She turned one ear toward the conversation while she scanned the manifest.

"To begin with," Ben said, "Ted is pretty fed up with the heroes of Fort Ti. He says Ethan Allen and Benedict Arnold are both glory seekers, squabbling like unruly children to outdo each other. They've now come up with separate plans to take the garrisons at Montreal and Quebec."

"You can't be serious. We've got enough to deal with right here in New England," Chandler piped in, "without stirrin' things up in Canada."

Ben snorted. "Ted would agree. But you know my brother-in-law. His reasons are more of a spiritual nature. Nonetheless, Colonel Arnold has sent a letter to Congress stating that if he's given permission to take Quebec, he can hand them all of Canada."

"All I can say is, there must have been tons of gunpowder stored at Ticonderoga if Arnold is certain he can take that entire territory," Chandler said. "He should share his good fortune and send some to us."

Ben laughed with relish this time. "Don't hold your breath. What's there is needed for the protection of that crucial waterway. Arnold expects Congress to outfit him."

Prudence joined in the laughter at Arnold's misplaced hope. She wagged the bill of lading at them. "Colonel Arnold should ask Morgan to outfit him instead! I can't believe all the goods we've just received. Morgan surely bought out an entire warehouse. How on earth did he have enough money?"

A burst of laughter issued from Ben. "I take it he hasn't told you. Our Morgan is a very inventive young man. He told his father a hilarious tale about a native tea that supposedly tasted exactly like India tea. With sufficient funding, he alleged, the profits would be unimaginable. Thus, by duping his father, he managed to leave Philadelphia to come north with enough money to last even a spendthrift like him for some time to come."

Morgan? Deceived his own father? Why, how perfectly horrid! How sinful! Glancing from Ben to Robby, she noticed that the Scot didn't see much humor in his brother-in-law's tale either.

"And that's not the half of it," Ben went on. "You should hear how he hoodwinked a dozen rich Boston Tories with a scheme they believed would protect their cargos from England and multiply their profits, but instead wrested their shipments right out of their very hands!" His last words spilled out on an unconscionable guffaw.

Chandler stepped forward. "Don't let these stories disturb you, Prudence," he said in a placating tone. "Morgan acted out of loyalty to the patriots. He knew we'd run short of supplies. Everything he's done has been for the cause. General Washington, a man with high principals of his own, knew of his scheme yet had no qualms about commissioning Morgan an officer and dispatching him on a highly confidential mission."

In Prudence's present state of mind, Chandler's words seemed little more than a cover-up for a friend. "To swindle his own father? How utterly contemptible! Now I understand what he meant when he told me he'd like to have me along when he had to explain things to his father." Angrily she took stock of the big wagon, piled high with merchandise he had secured with ill-gotten funds. She must send it back, that was all there was to it.

Then reason prevailed. The goods were already here. Morgan's father was already out the money—and the fact was, all the items in the wagon were sorely needed here and now. And they would help to assure her own ailing father that the store was, indeed, flourishing.

She suddenly realized that while she was standing around thinking, the men had begun unloading. She caught a sheepish glance that passed between them as they worked. She figured they simply wanted to escape from here as quickly as they could.

Turning her back on her three helpers, she walked into the store to give herself time to regain some composure. What an idiot she had been to believe in Morgan Thomas! That lying blasphemer had used her own faith in God against her when he said he had made a vow to God never to lie. Everything that came out of his mouth must have been a lie. Everything!

Well, not quite. He *had* sent the supplies.

Utterly distraught and confused, she grabbed a broom and attacked a vacant corner with vengeance.

Perhaps he made the vow after *he did those other despicable things,* she thought, slowing in her work. Perhaps he did care about her . . . did consider her pretty.

Foolish mooning, that's all it was. She resumed her task with a fury.

And frogs turn into princes!

44

January 1776

Susannah's melancholy mood matched the bleak January morning. She finished the plain but filling breakfast of biscuits and milk gravy she had served her little family, then relaxed against the chair.

"One good thing," Dan said at the head of the table, his expression as grim as hers. "I'll be able to tear down the stable for firewood."

Susannah nodded, then glanced across to Miles, who appeared too occupied with making silly faces at Julia to be listening. "Yes. The wood will be welcome. Hopefully it will be enough for a while, since we've been warming only the kitchen."

Dan lifted his coffee cup and took a drink, then set it down. "If you think we're bad off, the British have resorted to stripping wood from North Church this whole last week to warm their backsides. It won't be long until there's nothing left."

"North Church, too? Will there be no house of worship left unscathed?"

A loud boom precluded his response. Three more explosions followed closely.

Susannah felt grateful that the children hadn't paid the racket much mind. But how ironic it was that they had become so accustomed to the sound of cannon fire!

"I figured the artillery would be at it again this morning," Dan said. "Last eve, when I was down at Bull's Wharf hoping to catch a fish, I heard that another of the grenadiers had been—" he cast a covert glance at their son, who was now feeding the baby part of his biscuit—"you know . . . while guarding the Charlestown Neck." He put the last of a biscuit into his mouth and chewed slowly. "Remember when Yancy was telling us about his Pennsylvania rifle, its superior range, and how accurate he had gotten when he needed to put food on the table? Well, rumor has it, a couple of militias of frontiersmen have shown up. They've been positioning themselves well out of range of the regulars' Brown Besses, then picking off any soldier at the barricades who doesn't keep his head down."

Another boom sounded in the distance.

Susannah held her breath, knowing return fire would be forthcoming.

From somewhere near the Boston Neck, the report from the single exploding cannonball sounded. It was common knowledge that the patriots had a limited number of artillery pieces and could ill afford powder for multiple firing. But even though the Royal Navy managed to keep mostly out of range, the militia fired often enough to remind the British of the colonists' capabilities.

"I suppose we should be thankful the militia doesn't have bigger guns or a plentiful supply of powder," Susannah mused, "or the noise would never end. At least the Mystic and the Charles haven't frozen over as yet." Glancing at Miles once more, she tried to choose bigger words he might not understand. "I want the siege to cease, of course, but not badly enough to risk having hordes of young heroes rampaging across the ice to clash with the old order."

The child, clearly paying the grown-ups no mind, mopped up the rest of his gravy as much with his sticky fingers as his biscuit, then licked his lips.

"It's hard to know exactly what to pray for these days," Dan agreed. "Perhaps it's best for now to lean only on God's wisdom." After a slight hesitation, he rose and met Susannah's troubled gaze. "Well, there's not much sense putting it off. Do you want to come outside and say g-o-o-d-b-y-e?"

She cringed. "No. You just go on. Take him."

Resignation tightened his lips. "I, uh, won't be long."

Susannah carried her dirty plate to the sideboard. Unable to keep herself from peering through the window, she watched Dan lead their faithful sorrel, Flame, out of the stable. Since the first day she'd met Dan, the gentle pacer had been his constant companion. Now she watched her husband dejectedly leading him away. No matter how hungry she became, she would never be able to choke down any part of that horse. She saw Dan reach up and pat Flame's mane, then brush a gloved hand over his own face. The sight wavered as her eyes brimmed, and she felt tears spill over her lashes and roll down her face.

"Ma-ma. All done," the baby said, slapping her palms onto some crumbs in front of herself.

Susannah sniffed and picked up a wet cloth, then went to wipe Julia's hands and face. Anything was better than having to watch the dear pacer plodding out of view on his way to the butcher. "Miles," she said, setting the baby on a blanket in the corner, "would you play with Julia while Mama does the dishes?"

"Mm-hmm." Sliding off the high stool, her son wiped his hands on his breeches and galloped over on his broomstick horse.

Susannah drew a fortifying breath, then poured hot water into the washpan and added soap flakes. Only a week ago the elders had asked everyone for an accounting of their foodstuffs. The bountiful harvest from the garden was now depleting at an alarming rate, the meat supply completely exhausted. Once the McClures' last three ganders had been roasted for the church's Christmas dinner, the lot had fallen to the three men who still had horses. They drew straws to see which beast would be sacrificed first. With more than forty mouths to feed, the meat from even a large animal wouldn't last more than a month—and if the siege continued for another three more months, no one knew how they'd survive. The men had little success casting lines off the pier, since the bombardment had all but emptied the harbor of fish. And a Brown Bess would threaten anyone attempting to use a boat to go farther out.

In the corner, Miles and Julia shared a giggle, and Susannah turned to enjoy the light moment. Present circumstances were extremely serious, but just as the Lord fed the children of Israel those forty years in the wilderness, his flock in Boston had not gone hungry so far. She must not allow her trust to falter. The Lord would be faithful in his provisions. Even the outbreak of smallpox had bypassed the congregation thus far.

If only letters from the rest of the family could get through, things would not seem so bad.

Susannah tried to concentrate on the quiet but meaningful Christmas that had just passed. She and Dan had shared it with the few remaining people from their church. There had even been a fresh blanket of snow, thick and white, to cover some of the dreariness around them.

As she turned back to her chore, however, the walls of the kitchen seemed to close in on her. How much smaller would the cramped room look and feel before winter finally came to an end?

A sharp pounding shook the back door. It banged open.

"There you are!" Mistress Brown, the midwife, railed, barging in without an invitation.

"What is it, mistress?" Susannah asked, a noticeable chill coursing through her that had nothing to do with the outside temperature.

"Playin' the innocent, are we now? The good pastor's wife?" The woman's plump fists balled as if ready to do battle.

"I beg your pardon?" Puzzled, Susannah motioned toward an empty chair. "Please, sit down, won't you? I'll fetch you a cup of coffee."

Mistress Brown remained in her fighting stance, face rigid, eyes cold and challenging. "I'll not be partakin' of any more of you *or* your *genteel* English poison. You'd have done better to take a knife to my girl. At least that would've been kinder."

"Are you speaking about Liza? What's happened to her?"

"Is Liza sick?" Miles sprang up and ran to Susannah's side, throwing his arms around her legs, and she pressed a comforting hand against his back.

Mistress Brown, her gaze fixed on Susannah, moved a step closer. "At least if she was in the grave, I could mourn her proper . . . without shame."

Her tone gnawed Susannah to her very core. It had been a long, long time since anyone had spewed such open hatred at her. "Please, Mistress Brown. What has happened? Tell me."

"You. That's what happened. You and your la-ti-dah, high-falutin English ways, turning my girl's head, making her want to be just like you. Be nice to the soldiers, just like you."

The woman had to be referring to Private Blake, the young soldier Liza had been smitten with. The girl had feared for him desperately after the Charlestown battle. She had been so upset then she had forgotten to be careful about who knew she loved him. Her mother had forbidden her to see him since the first conflict in April, yet many from the congregation shunned her, considered her a traitor.

"Wasn't causing our church to be sacked because of you enough? Bringin' the wrath of your heathen countrymen down on innocent church folk because of that lobsterback brother of yours?"

"I beg you, tell me what's happened to Liza," Susannah pleaded once again.

"You think I don't know you've been encouragin' her all along?" the older woman huffed, her face red and contorted with rage. "Well, I caught the little hussy myself, this time— sneaking in the back door just before dawn. Beat her, I did, till she confessed what she's been up to. Thanks to you, my girl's ruined for marriage now. No decent man'll have her. And if my neighbors find out what Liza's been up to, they're sure to tar and feather the girl. Stone her, maybe, who knows? All thanks to you."

Aware that Miles was now shaking as he clung to her, Susannah stroked the top of his silky head, trying to remain composed. "Surely no one would resort to such violence against a young girl."

"Where on earth have you been this past year, I ask? Does bein' a *lady* make you deaf and blind?"

"If you'll just permit me to see Liza, perhaps I can—"

"You must be out of your mind." Each word came out deliberately and slowly as her eyes became slits in her plump face. "I came here for one reason, *Mistress Haynes*. To give you fair warning. If I ever, *ever* see you within ten rods of my Liza again, I'll wring that fine lady neck of yours with my bare hands. Remember that." She wheeled toward the still open door and stomped down the steps.

Susannah felt she should make amends, somehow. She took a step forward. "I—I have wronged you and your daughter greatly, Mistress Brown. I shall pray to God for—"

The woman whirled around. "I'll do my own praying, thank you. Save yours for yourself. Me and the others have had all the holier-than-thou, love-thine-enemy speeches we can stomach from you and your kind." With one final loathsome glare, she turned and stalked away.

Tears welled up in Susannah's eyes as she felt her son shiver and cling to her all the harder. She lifted her chin and then bent to comfort him. "There, there, sweetheart. She's gone. Everything will be fine."

She only wished it were true.

45

Morgan kept a tight rein on his skittish new horse as a jubilant, jostling throng clogged the bridge into Cambridge. He had the misfortune of arriving on the day when General Washington's chief engineer, Colonel Knox, was returning cross country from the wilds of the western mountains with the cannons of Fort Ticonderoga. The feat would have been a major triumph even in summer. In winter it was a near miracle, and the people had turned out to give Knox and his men a hero's welcome.

Morgan managed to contain his irritation at the snail's pace of the horde. It was yet another delay after the insufferable five and a half months it had taken him to locate friendly ship captains in the southern ports who were willing to take cargos north. With pockets of open rebellion becoming increasingly widespread throughout the Colonies, all non-British vessels now faced danger of seizure.

He longed to know how Prudence had fared in his absence. He hoped the small percentage of each shipment General Washington had allowed him in payment for his own expenses had been diverted to her mercantile. He had received no reply to the letters he'd sent from various ports informing her of his whereabouts. With the less-than-adequate postal service in the south, he couldn't help but wonder if they ever reached her. For sanity's sake, he had relied on the hope that the two Roberts had kept their word to maintain a watchful eye and discourage all scoundrels and bounders.

But a far worse possibility kept nagging at him, one he refused to consider. Was he returning only to find her married? Among the many thousands of men camped around the bay, had some attractive and unattached young man caught her eye? His own friend Robert Chandler was far from homely, and his sadness might easily have stirred within her a need to comfort him and cheer him up, to help him at last put aside the loss of his Julia. What if that possibility turned out to be a reality? What then? Would he be able to find within himself enough grace to wish them happiness? Releasing a ragged breath, Morgan ignored all the chatter and shouting as he guided his mount through the crowd.

If he wasn't bound by duty to report to Washington upon his arrival, he would have circled Cambridge and put his mind at rest posthaste. Couldn't the Charles River, at least, have cooperated and frozen over in the center so he might have bypassed the bridge?

Finally gaining the other side, the crowd melded with an even greater throng of people, dampening his hopes of making any faster progress.

"Hey!" someone shouted. "That must be them coming!"

Everyone surged forward, stretching to see over the vast assemblage in front of them.

"I say, madam," Morgan yelled above the roar to a woman waving a flag. "What militia banner is that?" He eyed the Union Jack in one upper corner and the red and white stripes that made up the remainder.

"'Tis not militia colors," she announced proudly. "'Tis our own bonny new flag. Thirteen stripes for thirteen colonies. Grand, is it not?"

"Yes! That it is!" Already spying others like it held aloft, Morgan also felt a rush of pride—despite his own preference that would have eliminated the British insignia.

Morgan finally reached the street where everyone had stopped to witness the parade of cannons, and he heard a cheer starting up at the far end. From his perch astride the horse, he could see the tip of a cannon barrel poke forth around the bend, drawn on a crude sled by a team of eight oxen. The animals strained and puffed in the cold afternoon air as they plodded over the frozen road. More followed. Men on foot alongside the beasts cracked bullwhips sporadically above their heaving backs.

The sight of the huge guns being brought to Cambridge sent a thrill coursing through Morgan. At closer inspection, he knew the first cannons at the head of the long caravan were certain to have tremendous range and would be a boon to the patriots—able to do tremendous damage to the Crown forces *and* their battleships!

"Morgan! Morgan Thomas!"

He craned his neck and scanned the crowd to see who had called out, then discovered Ted Harrington, accompanying the caravan, waving at him. He returned the wave and maneuvered his mount through the bystanders to intercept his whip-snapping friend. "This must have been one impressive undertaking, I daresay," Morgan said above the racket as he reined in alongside Susannah's brother.

Ted grinned up at him. His face was chapped from the cold, his boots badly worn. "Quite. You don't know the half of it, my good man. If not for God and his miracles, there's no way on earth we'd have managed this. We've crossed lakes and mountains knee deep in snow and mud. But we're here at last." He sobered. "Have you, perchance, any news of my sister?"

Morgan glanced in the direction of Boston, then back at Ted with a solemn shake of his head. "Wish I had. But I'm just returning from the southern colonies myself."

"What?" Ted gave a nod of confusion. "It's hard to hear over all this. Meet me at Ben's room later?"

A swarm of noisy youngsters caused Morgan's horse to shy before he could decline the invitation. When he regained control, a wall of people separated him from Ted. *What's one more delay,* he thought with dismay. As much as he would have liked to ride straight to the mercantile and see Prudence, he probably should find Robby and Chandler first anyway. *And,* he thought as his chest tightened, *avoid any unwanted surprises.*

It took the usual tedious couple of hours for Morgan to be admitted into the general's presence and give his report, but after that had been taken care of, he rode through the still crowded streets toward Ben's rooming house. He glanced at the sun, already low in the sky. Its weak winter rays had done little to alleviate the chill, and tonight was sure to be colder still. Perhaps he would stop by Ben's room for just a minute and make an excuse, then ride out to see Prudence. He didn't necessarily have to talk to Chandler and MacKinnon first.

Morgan dismounted at Ben's building and hitched his horse, then dashed inside and up the stairs, taking them two at a time. But before he knocked the door swung open. There stood Robert Chandler, all smiles. "Well, look who's finally here!" He grabbed Morgan in a back-thumping hug, then passed him on to Robby MacKinnon.

"You're here, too. Both of you. Good."

"See, I told you he was in town," Ted said with the hint of a smile, then concentrated on Morgan. "They were just mentioning the possibility that you'd deserted us and gone on to see that Miss Endecott you told us about at Christmas a year ago."

Christmas a year ago! he thought, sliding out of his greatcoat. All that time, and he had spent precious few moments of it with her.

"Here, have some spiced cider," Chan said, offering him a glass. "It's only lukewarm, I'm afraid. Robby fetched it from the tavern a while ago."

Morgan draped the coat over the back of a chair. "Thanks." As the first gulp of the tasty liquid coursed down his throat, he remembered he'd had nothing to eat or drink all day in his haste to reach Cambridge. He had left Providence at dawn and only stopped occasionally to rest the horse. "Where's Ben?" he asked, sinking down onto the comfort of the extra cot. "Anyone seen or heard from him lately?"

"The lad had urgent news to pass on to Philadelphia,"

Robby answered. "Pertained to the invasion in Canada, but he dinna go into details about it with us."

Morgan nodded. "General Washington mentioned it during our meeting. He said the news isn't good. I think he'll keep it under his hat, though, to maintain the men's morale."

"What did he say, exactly?" Ted asked, leaning forward from the edge of the big bed. "A number of my friends and neighbors in the Grants took part in the expedition. I'd appreciate knowing how it went."

"The general didn't say an awful lot. Ethan Allen was captured early on."

"That I've already heard. Anything else?"

"General Benedict Arnold, the one who marched up through the wilds of Maine, was wounded, but not seriously. And, I'm sorry to say, they weren't able to take Quebec. The commander who went north by way of your Lake Champlain, General Montgomery, was killed. What's left of our forces are in retreat."

"And the Green Mountain Boys," Ted said with dismay, "with Seth Warner. What happened to them?"

Morgan reached to administer a comforting pat. "Sorry, old man. That's all I know. On the other hand," he went on, switching his attention to Chandler, "all the news isn't bad. The southern colonies—including your own North Carolina—are no longer sitting on the fence."

"Is that a fact?" He brightened.

Morgan chuckled. "While I was in the warehouse district of Charleston, I heard one of the British tobacco merchants relate something of interest." He assumed a snobbish face. "'The stench of a lowborn insurrection is growing more putrid by the hour.' I think those were his words."

The others laughed along with him.

"In fact," he went on, "when I made my last port stop at Norfolk, Virginia, it seems the governor, Lord Dunsmore, had been having a jolly good time with a company of Tory irregulars he had formed. They had been out pillaging and burning the plantations of the patriots—which, of course, upset the local folks to no end."

"What about my place?" Chandler asked. "Did they cross into North Carolina?"

"No, everything's fine there. Besides, you're not close to the coast. However, I did stop by to see your family on my way through. The overseer you hired is doing an excellent job."

"Well, I can breathe easier, then," Chandler said.

Morgan drank the rest of his cider, then put the glass down on the floor beside him. "Getting back to the Norfolk news, the good citizens thought it was time to throw a party of their own. I don't mind telling you, as much as I enjoyed their efforts, it proved a might inconvenient for me. It made me have to load the merchandise I had stored there onto wagons and go up to Yorktown to ship it."

Chan frowned. "Why?"

"Because," Morgan continued, "our boys ran the governor and all his cohorts quite literally into the sea, along with the detachment of redcoats garrisoned there. They had to take refuge on His Majesty's ships out in the harbor. Needless to say, they were in such ill humor after that, they bombarded any vessel that tried to get past them!"

"Sounds like the Virginians managed to do something we haven't," Robby mused. "Chase their own wigged peacocks right out of town."

"Speaking of peacocks," Morgan said once the round of chuckles quieted, "General Washington wants all his officers to look professional. Legitimate. I'm to have a uniform made immediately."

"No doubt that will affect me as well," Ted cut in. "I've signed with General Knox. I'll not be going home until I'm certain Sue and her family have been safely rescued."

"I'd say Jane will take exception to that," Morgan teased.

"Quite. But she'll understand. I took her to stay with her sister in Worcester."

"I may take leave myself," Robby piped in, "and move me

family back to Princeton. The British navy bombarded Bristol in October, and that's not twenty miles from the farm."

Morgan nodded. "I hear they burned a small port city up north, too."

"That's right," Chandler said, restraining a grin. "They actually insinuated the folks up there were dabbling in a bit of smuggling."

"You don't say." Morgan wondered if their old friend Yancy had a hand in it.

"Morgan," Robby said. "Don't forget to find a proper place to lay your head. Ye won't be permitted to bunk with us."

"Of course I will."

"Afraid not." Chandler stretched out on the cot behind him and crossed his forearms beneath his head. "Officers are no longer allowed to fraternize with the enlisted men. It'll be against regulations for the two of us to sit around chitchattin' with you from now on. Washington spent most of the time you were gone shaping us into a real army. The militias have all been disbanded, and the enlistees have been formed into new companies with appointed officers instead of elected ones. He selected men for their ability rather than their popularity. You have no idea of the grumbling goin' on in the ranks."

Morgan couldn't help recalling some of the men with whom the two of them had served. They were, for the most part, an independent lot, each wanting his own way. "So. They're looking for well-educated, capable men with leadership qualities, eh? Then why aren't you in an officer's uniform, Chan? You've been to college, you've had experience leading men in the field." He grinned. "Tobacco field—battlefield, what's the difference?"

"They asked, but he turned 'em down," Robby answered.

Chandler shrugged. "I told you before we ever left North Carolina. I needed to get away from that kind of burden. I don't want to be responsible for the lives of a single platoon, let alone an entire company of men."

Morgan had to wonder if his chum would ever be ready or willing to pick up his life again. It was time to lighten this conversation. "Well," he began, making sport of himself, "I won't have to worry about *my* men getting shot. I'm to be a quartermaster, doing the very same thing I left Philadelphia to avoid—running a warehouse. My main responsibility will be to guard against pilferage and theft. Now, were I to have a couple of men under me whom I could really trust . . ." He waggled his brows suggestively.

"Ye don't mean give up me life's dream of bein' a journeyman ditch digger," Robby said, pretending alarm.

Morgan grinned. "Life is full of sacrifices."

Chandler swung to a sitting position and raised a mug of cider high. "No sacrifice is too great for the cause."

After their quiet bout of laughter faded, Morgan rose to his feet. "Er, speaking of causes, how is Miss Endecott?"

The two Roberts exchanged glances.

"The young lady you were so interested in finding last year?" Ted asked. "I heard from Ben that she was just on the north side of the bay all the time."

"Until her family was bombed out." Morgan looked to Chandler. "Well, man, how is she? And her father? The store?"

"Prospering just fine," Chan finally answered, his expression unreadable. "We received three shipments from you. Business is steady. Brisk, you might say."

"They found a house not a quarter mile from the mercantile," Robby said with a nod, "and the lass's father is feelin' well enough to sit with her at the store most of the time. Chandler and I nailed a cot in the back for him to rest on. And we drop by almost every day."

Morgan drew his first free breath since his arrival in Cambridge. They hadn't told him what he most wanted to know, but at least there'd been no indication that Chandler had gotten romantically involved with Prudence. He'd best find out for himself where her feelings lay. If she remembered his last words to her . . . the kiss . . . the promise her eyes made. He gave an elaborate stretch. "Well, I guess I'd better ride on over if I expect to get there before they lock up."

"Will you be coming back to Cambridge tonight?" Ted asked.

"Oh, that's right." He looked from one Robert to the other. "I'm no longer welcome in the cozy little abode I helped build with my own two hands."

"You'd better stay here until they assign us quarters," Ted offered. "If there are any left to assign, that is."

Thinking back on last year's shortage of living quarters, Morgan deduced they probably hadn't improved much. "Capital idea. I'm sure Ben wouldn't mind, since he's hardly ever here."

His own words reminded him that Ben wasn't the only one who wasn't often around. But now that he had been designated quartermaster, that would change. There would be regular hours of duty, and he would be able to see Prudence any evening he wanted. Every evening, for that matter—and right now he was wasting one of them.

His heart jolted with anticipation, and he cleared his throat. "Well, I'll be off, gentlemen." He tipped his head and took his leave, expending a great effort to depart at a normal pace. He was about to see Prudence again . . . at long, long last.

46

"Here's your total, sir." Prudence turned the sheet around on which she'd tallied her customer's purchases and passed it across the counter for him to see.

"That all?" A pleased grin spread over the man's mouth as he checked her sums. "Somebody said this mercantile charged fair prices, but I figured we'd be gouged here just the same as everywhere else these days. I'm used to payin' two and three times what things are worth."

"For a store to charge so much is downright sinful." She glanced at her father dozing in a rocking chair near the small stove, a lap robe over his legs. "We don't believe in taking advantage of the brave young men who've sacrificed everything to come here to defend our righteous cause. Besides, when this war is over, we'll still need customers."

"Well, I'm sure to be one of them, missy. And I'll spread the word in my camp, too. You'll have more business from now on, wait and see. You have yourself a good evening, now." With a polite dip of his three-cornered hat, he gathered his purchases into his arms.

Occupied with straightening the top of the counter, Prudence heard the tiny brass bell jingle as he left, then jingle again. She looked up, noting first the fine clothes, which contrasted markedly from the typical garb worn by the soldiers. But as her eyes continued their upward sweep, her heart skipped a beat. Morgan!

A most peculiar half smile tilted his mouth.

She immediately pushed down the fluttering sensation inside with the stern reminder that he had broken three commandments out of the ten. He had deliberately lied to and stolen from his father in a shockingly dishonorable fashion. And she must never forget that fact, never allow herself to succumb to yearnings of a most carnal nature. She must see past the outside, to the man's heart and behavior. Now in keeping with such thoughtless actions, here he was, so inconsiderate as to barge right in without warning. And after her long tiresome day, just when she was about to close.

She saw his smile fade and disappear as he crossed to her.

Prudence moved a step backward, inadvertently bumping into a stack of empty crates as she did.

One crashed to the floor, jolting her father awake. "Oh. Mr. Thomas," he said sleepily, adjusting the coverlet with a yawn. "Nice to see you. It's been ages."

"It's wonderful to be back, Mr. Endecott. You're looking well."

"I've had better days. But I'm gaining strength, if more slowly than I might have liked. My wife and daughter mother me to death, making sure I don't overdo."

"Yes, I can understand their concern." Morgan switched his attention to Prudence once more.

"Mr. Thomas," she said with a businesslike nod. Forcibly she restrained her trembling hand from flying up to check for wayward strands of hair. "It's been a long time."

"Much longer than I'd hoped."

Fortunately, the counter that separated them gave Prudence room to breathe. She quickly plucked the ledger from a shelf below, then opened it to the current page, more than aware that his eyes were riveted on her. "I've kept very detailed records," she said, amazed that her voice didn't waver.

He opened his mouth and started to shape a word.

"I received a bill of sale only with the first shipment," she blurted. "The one from New York. But I used them as a guideline for estimating the prices of the next two." She turned the big book around to enable him to read the figures easily. "We will, of course, pay any extra out-of-pocket expenditures you incurred on our behalf."

Again he tried to break in. "I—"

"As you can see right here," she rushed on, turning to the next page, "I've listed the profits we've made from the first two deliveries. And here at the bottom—" her finger trailed down the columns—"are the store's expenses, giving us a total of the profits thus far. Since Papa and I share the work, I've concluded we're entitled to two-thirds of those monies. This figure, plus the one on the previous page, is approximately what we owe you—excluding your travel expenses. Of course, if you happen to have the bills of lading, I'll gladly give you a more accurate tally."

Morgan's hand covered hers.

Her lashes raised, and she looked up to his face.

"I want you to have it all."

For a lying schemer, his expression was incredibly sincere. All reason fled momentarily under his scrutiny. "I—I wouldn't think of it," she heard herself utter.

"I don't wish to discuss business anyway," he said quietly. "I'm far more interested in hearing how you and your father have been getting on."

Suddenly aware that her hand was still trapped, Prudence slid her fingers out of his grasp. "I'm sure Papa is better suited to answering that. Now, if you'll excuse me, I must batten everything down and lock up. It'll soon be dark, and I must get him home while we can still see." Head high, she willed her shaky legs to carry her to the end of the counter and on to the back.

Morgan stared after her as she left the room, watched her wooden movements, the stiff set of her dark head. There had to be some reason why she had brushed him off like that. His own recollections of their last time together were sweet—sweet and very tender. What had changed her? Or whom?

He perused the well-organized shelves and the burgeoning

stock that bore testimony to the fact that he had remained faithful to his promises.

"Come over here, lad," Mr. Endecott said, "and warm yourself by the fire."

Her father undoubtedly would have the answer. Morgan smiled politely and did as bidden. Upon closer inspection he saw the older man was more than pale. His skin had a translucent quality to it, and his veined hands shook when not clasped together atop the lap robe. "How have you been, sir?" Morgan put a palm lightly on one bony shoulder.

Mr. Endecott shrugged. "Getting stronger all the time. I spend most days here with my Prudence so I can help with paperwork. And I give lots of advice," he added with a thin smile. "Those other two lads you sent us, Chandler and MacKinnon, fixed up a cot in the back room for whenever I need to lie down. They've been a godsend."

"I hear you found a house nearby."

"Yes. A nice tight one. Used to belong to a Tory. My good wife walks over with our noon meal every day."

"Sounds like everything has worked out fine. I'd venture you're all much happier now."

"True, true. My wife, my family, and my affairs are now separated again from Miriam's father." He paused, and his whitening head leaned to one side. "My sons, however, have no plans of returning home in the near future. That's my one regret. I received a letter some weeks ago that they're together on a merchant ship plying the waters of the Indian Ocean. Who knows how long the pleas I posted to Zanzibar and Bombay will gather dust in those faraway posts before the boys ever make port and learn they're needed at home?" He inhaled slowly. "But I'm feeling stronger. Things are better now."

Morgan had his doubts. "I couldn't help but notice your daughter seemed less than pleased I've come back."

"And I can see you're more than a little disappointed about it."

Morgan, meeting Mr. Endecott's shrewd blue eyes, put voice to his fear. "Has she—is there someone else? Is that it?"

He smiled. "No. The poor girl's far too busy keeping this place going to give any thought to something even as urgent as finding a husband. Particularly since those two chaperons you provided have been quite dedicated in discouraging suitors—not that she's noticed."

Morgan felt slightly encouraged by the old gentleman's response, even though it lacked substance. "Well, I'm glad to learn my friends have done well by her. Are you certain there is no one else?"

Neither Mr. Endecott's smile nor the slow shake of his head seemed all that emphatic. Or all that reassuring.

"I had hoped to come back long before this," Morgan continued, "but I was forced to put my own plans aside."

"Prudence and I both understood that, lad. You've been most honorable, honest, and generous in all your dealings with us. We're truly grateful. But—" he grimaced—"what my daughter is struggling with is your dishonest dealings with others. Your father, to be precise."

"Has he been here?" Morgan asked with alarm.

"No, no. A friend of yours came by last fall. A lad by the name of Haynes, I believe. Somehow in conversation he related to Prudence the story of how you duped your father into letting you leave the business and come here. Some nefarious tale regarding native tea, as I recall."

"I see." That more than explained the coolness from one whose loyalty to her family equalled her virtue and her valor. She surely must have found his actions reprehensible and impossible to forget. Though bound as a Christian to forgive, mere forgiveness would never be enough, not for her. She needed—she *deserved*—a man of honor. Morgan sank to a chair beside the old man.

"Take heart, son. Perhaps young Mr. Haynes exaggerated the details. I know my daughter cared deeply for you. You were the first to capture her heart, you know. And, I fear, you may be the last. Of the men passing through here, no other has caught her eye. Why not go to her and explain?"

"It would be pointless. Ben didn't exaggerate, I'm sure."

"Then, I suppose it would be pointless. Prudence has always had very high ideals. The girl has a great zest for them."

"Ah, yes," Morgan said with a defeated sigh. "And the Lord has surely made her his instrument. The Almighty has had trouble getting through to me. I would wager he placed her in my path quite deliberately. Now I'm forced to view my sin through her eyes, and it's not a pretty picture, I avow."

"But acknowledging one's sin is half the battle, son."

Son. Mr. Endecott had used the endearment more than once this evening. Morgan doubted his own father would do the same in the future after he heard the truth of his son's actions. That thought had been eating at him for a while already, but he'd done his best to suppress it. Until now. "Well, I know what I must do to put my life to rights once more. Even if it means I'll never again be welcome in my father's house as long as I live—and rightly so. I must write and confess how I've wronged not only him but many of his influential friends as well. Even if he is a Tory and even if I consider his loyalty to Britain sadly misplaced, he deserved much better from his own son."

Mr. Endecott sat without speaking, a look of quiet understanding among the lines on his aged face.

"Lately I've been remembering the story of Jonathan and David in the Bible," Morgan went on. "Jonathan knew his father, the king, was wrong to try to kill David. But even after doing what he could to protect David from the king, he remained a loyal son . . . even to the end, when his father's follies cost them both their lives."

"I doubt our heavenly Father expects that sort of blind loyalty from any of us. Perhaps fewer would have died back then had Jonathan left his father's side—honorably, of course. Perhaps Israel's turmoil might have ended sooner."

"I appreciate your kind words more than I can say. But they don't really change anything."

"I know. The path ahead of you just now is a hard one. But it's the righteous one. And should the possibility you fear come to pass, of not being accepted back into the fold anytime soon, you might reconsider your decision not to take your share of the store's profits. After all, you've earned them. In these trying days, it's likely you'll need the money eventually."

"Thank you," Morgan said with a wistful smile, "but no. For my part, the gain was ill gotten." Bone weary, he rose. "Well, it's been a rather long day, riding this distance from Rhode Island in haste, only to meet disappointment. Before I leave, though, I'd like to ask just one small favor of you, if I may."

"What is it, son?"

"I'd like Prudence *personally* to have whatever monies were supposed to come to me. It's little enough payment for restoring me to the Lord's fold—a road another dear and loyal friend tried to point me toward some time ago. It's a bitter pill to swallow—knowing that not only have I forfeited any hope of having your daughter in my life, but I'll probably be cast out of my own family." He paused. "Still, I've been told that time will share its healing power with me. Tomorrow's a bright new day, and all that."

The older man smiled gently. "Why not put everything you've just told me into a letter to your father? And write a similar one to my Prudence. Certainly once she's aware of this struggle of yours, she'll be more receptive."

"Sounds simple enough," Morgan said without bitterness. "But a young woman as wonderful as your daughter deserves someone she can look upon with respect as well as love. I would be the last to wish her any less. Someday I'm sure she'll find someone worthy of her. Just see that she gets my share, will you? It's important to me that she never sacrifice her courageous spirit or ideals for security for herself or her family."

Morgan shook Mr. Endecott's hand in parting, then walked numbly outside and back to his horse.

47

March 1776

A head-splitting boom rattled the walls of Ben's rooming house. Morgan, awakened from a dead sleep, bolted to his feet.

In the other cot, Ted raised himself up on an elbow and yawned. "General Washington is bidding us good morning rather early today. One of His Majesty's ships must have drifted within range during the night."

"Not necessarily." Morgan plopped back onto the bed. "Washington's probably celebrating after that shipload of gunpowder made its way right past the British navy. Wagon-loads rolled in all yesterday afternoon despite the muddy roads."

"Would you say the interminable wait is over?"

"I would." Morgan raked his fingers through his hair. "After waiting fruitlessly all winter for the river to ice over, it appears the balls from our big guns will be crossing the Neck without us."

Ted linked his palms beneath his head. "Have you heard when the cannons will be moved to Dorchester Heights?"

"What makes you think they'll be positioned there?"

"It's the logical choice, old boy. The British have Charlestown Heights, so Dorchester's the next best site."

Morgan considered the statement. "It's also the most vulnerable, when you think about it. Even Castle William would have a clear shot."

"Not really. We'd have the high ground. But, I hate to say, Sue and Dan's house would be within range for the first time. I only pray they've had foresight enough to stock their cellar with plenty of food and water."

"If they have any," Morgan muttered. "Considering how frequently the redcoats have been sending out ships with foraging parties over the last month, I'd imagine the food supply in the town is scarce. If there's a cow or pig that hasn't been pirated up and down the coast for a hundred miles in either direction, it's a miracle."

Ted nodded in solemn silence. "I've been in constant prayer that the Lord will meet the needs of his own during this time. Yesterday a peculiar thought came to me during my meditation. After almost a year since Lexington and Concord, the British in Boston are still under siege—a very long time for the most powerful nation in the world. Yet Washington needed every single one of these months to merge all the fraternal militias into one unified army." He exhaled and sat up. "Even if we do manage to dislodge the Crown forces from Boston, they'll not soon give up. They won't back down simply because a few thousand Yankee Doodle dandies try to throw them out of one of their own possessions."

"They may *say* they own this land, but hardly a one of those powdered-wigged *dandies* ever so much as set foot on colonial soil. It belongs to the people who've carved out an existence here. Not to mention their children and their children's children."

Though the rooming house was well out of range, return blasts from British cannons, coming in close succession, rattled the windowpanes. The balls landed in loud explosions somewhere near the breastworks facing the bay.

"It also belongs," Ted mused as he rose and started dressing, "to the people who were here before any of us came."

"The Indians?" Morgan's thoughts turned to stories of entire tribes that had been wiped out after contracting diseases brought by the white man. There were very few natives left on this side of the mountains. The Iroquois Nations in the west, however, had not succumbed so readily to the diseases and had become vastly stronger since acquiring firearms. "Now that settlers are trickling into their territory, I doubt the Indians will show us any loyalty. Most likely the British will hire them to fight for their side."

Ted nodded. "Looking at the situation as a whole, the odds seem stacked quite heavily against a victory for us."

"Rather," Morgan agreed. "The reality is pretty grim, *if* one does not weigh the power of God."

"Well, I'll be," Ted said in amazement. "You've spent so much time with Robby and me you're actually beginning to talk like us!"

"I suppose I could do far worse," Morgan admitted with chagrin. His reckless past had left him with an empty void inside—a hollow place where once he had known the love of his family and a hope of marriage to lively and beautiful Prudence Endecott. After sacrificing himself on the altar of confession by writing his father, there had been more than ample time to try to elevate his thoughts to a higher plane.

"Speaking of Robby," Ted said, "has he returned yet from the leave his *superior officer* so generously granted?"

Morgan grinned. "Yes, he got back last night. He told me that Ben, too, managed to get to the farm three times during the two weeks Robby was there." He chuckled.

A slow smile spread across Ted's mouth. "Ben does love that shy new wife of his."

"Quite." Morgan's thoughts drifted to someone far less shy. Prudence, with that spirit of hers, was a magnificent woman. He couldn't help wondering if her father had given her the extra share of the profits as Morgan had requested. Perhaps one day, after his heart stopped aching—*if* it stopped aching—he'd ride by and see how they were getting along. Right now he could feel himself turning into another Robert Chandler, shrinking away to nothing but an empty, lonely shell of a man.

Fastening the last of his buttons, Ted headed for the door.

"Robby may have word of Jane. Or even Susannah," he added hopefully. "I'm going over to their camp. Sue might have managed to get a letter out."

And surely my father has received the one I wrote more than six weeks ago, Morgan reminded himself. Even if it had stirred up nothing but rage, there had been time enough for sufficient anger to subside, time enough to permit some response. Any response.

Nor had there been a single word from Prudence—not that he had expected any. But nevertheless, that, too, hurt far more than he would have surmised.

Morgan reached for his trousers and pulled them on, then stomped into his boots. He pocketed the remaining funds from his pittance of army pay—a reminder of how little he must get by on these days. After paying for all the Endecotts' store supplies, plus financing his travel expenses, he was down to the last of it. And these were inflationary times to boot. He might as well try his luck at the morning mess rather than eating at the tavern.

A knock sounded at the door, and Morgan opened to a breathless, freckled lad.

"Mr. Thomas? Here's a message. I gotta go. I left in the middle of chores." The boy turned and scampered down the stairs.

The envelope simply bore Morgan's name, nothing more. Curious, he quickly removed the paper inside:

My dear M. Thomas,

> *Father is gravely ill and desires to speak to you. Please come at once.*

P. Endecott

Prudence needed him.

❧ ❧

Morgan had galloped halfway along the Concord road and almost reached the store before he realized he didn't even know where Prudence lived. But there was nothing to be done about that until he found someone to ask.

He expected the mercantile to be closed, but the door was not padlocked, and a horse was tied out front. He skidded his mount to a stop and swung down.

Running inside, he spied Lucas Randolph's swarthy face as the man looked up from behind the counter, where he had the ledgers spread out.

"I was summoned to see Mr. Endecott," Morgan blurted. "But I see I must be too late. He's already passed on?"

"No," Randolph scowled. "He was still kickin' at dawn when I was at the house." He returned his attention to the columns of figures Prudence had painstakingly recorded in the books.

"Where *is* their house?" Morgan asked, barely able to stomach the sight of the vulture already circling, hoping to devour his daughter's future, his grandchildren's legacy.

He didn't so much as look up, but flicked an index finger in the general direction. "Fourth one on the left."

Within moments, Morgan reached the small, run-down dwelling and rapped softly.

Prudence opened the door. At the sight of her eyes, bright with unshed tears, and her bleak face, it took every ounce of strength Morgan possessed not to pull her into his arms and impart whatever comfort and strength he had to offer her.

"Forgive me for bothering you," she said in a near whisper. "He would not rest until I sent you word. I'm not sure it was wise."

"Where is he?"

"The minister is with him now, trying to calm him. The doctor doesn't give Papa much hope."

With the image of Lucas Randolph fresh in his mind, Morgan could easily conclude the cause for the older man's unrest. "I'll do what I can to reassure him."

A nearby door opened, and a bald, spectacled man stuck out his head. "Is that you, Mr. Thomas? Please, come in."

He obeyed at once, conscious that Prudence was only a step behind him as he entered the darkened room. Curtains shut out the glaring light of day, and only a candlestick dispelled the gloom.

Scervant Endecott lay propped up on pillows in the bed. Miriam, puffy eyed and looking far too young and vulnerable, sat in a chair beside him, holding his bony white hand. His labored breathing had an ominous rattle to it, his face as gray as death. His dark-rimmed eyelids raised slowly, then flickered with recognition. Withdrawing his frail hand from Miriam, he beckoned to Morgan.

His wife rose and stepped back to make room.

"No . . . more time." He struggled to say. "Do you . . . still want . . . my daughter?"

"Papa!" Prudence gasped.

"Do you?" he repeated, slightly more fervently.

"I—" How could he lie? Yet this was not the time. There had to be more time for explaining things to Prudence. Hoping against hope she'd come to love the new him.

"Do you want her?"

"Yes. Yes, sir, I do. More than you know."

The minister quietly moved closer. "Considering the dire circumstances, I've agreed to wave the banns and perform the ceremony now."

Miriam flung a pleading look to Morgan. "We've just found out that my father has spoken to a lawyer for the purpose of gaining power of attorney of my husband's estate."

Her words scarcely penetrated his thoughts. All he could think was, *They want me to marry Prudence. Now.* "But I can't."

Prudence gave a tiny cry and whirled away.

Morgan barely caught her hand. He drew her back. "How can I marry someone who has no respect for me?" he asked, searching the stormy depths of her eyes.

Her gaze wavered momentarily, then focused on his. "Papa told me everything. Did . . . did you write to your father and confess your sins against him?"

He inhaled a ragged breath. "Yes. So I'm afraid I'm no longer much of a catch. I've no doubt my father has seen a lawyer of his own and drawn up a new will disinheriting me."

"You did it? Truly?" A tremulous smile softened her lips. She placed her silken palm to his cheek, her touch telling him far more than words. "I'm sure that must have been a difficult letter to write."

Her hand slipped away as he nodded, but the warmth remained. "You gave up everything to do what's right. I'm very, very proud of you, Morgan Thomas."

"You are?" He felt his chest contract. His hands cupped her face. "Do you know what you're saying, after all the things I did . . . all those years?"

She nodded. "Your yesterdays have been washed clean. Today is a new beginning." Tears welled in her eyes, shimmered and slid down her face, framing her sweet smile.

He couldn't see very clearly himself as he drew her into his arms and held her close. Her heart kept pace with his own throbbing pulse.

Someone tapped his shoulder. "We may not have much time, son," the minister said.

Morgan saw that Mr. Endecott's eyes were closed, but he wore a small smile. "Then, will you have me, dearest Prudence?" he asked, easing her gently away. "Will you marry me?"

"Yes. I will," she whispered. "For all our tomorrows. Forever."

"And will you have her, Morgan Thomas?" the minister asked. "For better or worse, for richer or poorer, in sickness and in health, until death do you part?"

Realizing the ceremony was being performed at that very moment, Morgan took Prudence's hands in his. "As God is my witness, I will, and I do."

"Then, by the power vested in me, in the name of the Father, the Son, and the Holy Spirit, I pronounce you man and wife." Reverend Stillwell adjusted his spectacles, then turned to her father. "You can rest easy, friend."

"Thank you."

Mr. Endecott's faint response seemed a bit stronger. A hopeful sign. Morgan would hate for Mr. Endecott's death to mar this day of blessed union to his beloved. Looking at her, he wondered if it were his own hands trembling or hers as he continued to hold them tight.

He had considered her beautiful before, when he had first seen her. And later, when they had sparred and when the two of them worked together to help the wounded soldiers. But now, in a simple dress and apron, with the dazzling splendor of love lighting her wondrous face, there were no words to describe her. He couldn't think of anything but the goodness of God. How was it possible? Prudence loved him!

"I said," Reverend Stillwell announced pointedly, "you may kiss your bride, young man. Then I have a marriage certificate you both need to sign."

Prudence lifted her trusting face, and her lips parted slightly as she wrapped her arms around his neck.

The remembrance of their first kiss made him pause. What had he called it? Sampling the merchandise? Such a rake he'd been . . . back then.

Reverently, softly, he lowered his mouth to the glorious sweetness of hers.

48

A muffled sound awakened Prudence. Fearing it was a distant cannon blast, she rolled over and opened her eyes, and her surroundings came into focus. There was no danger here, she remembered. She and Morgan had taken a room far enough inland on the Worcester post road to enable them to forget about the war for one precious week . . . and it was coming to an end.

But she refused to think about that yet. She quickly brushed the thought aside as the door opened to admit her husband, fully dressed except for shoes and bearing a tray laden with food. Quickly she fluffed the pillows and leaned back against the head of the bedstead while he crossed the room.

The other side of the mattress dipped slightly beneath his weight as he sat down. "Good morning, my beautiful wife."

"Yes. It is lovely, isn't it?" An effortless smile bubbled forth . . . or was it that she hadn't stopped smiling since their simple little wedding ceremony? She wasn't sure as she beheld her wonderfully thoughtful mate raising the tray aloft and slipping back into bed beside her.

He set the burden on the sheet between them, then plucked an apricot half from an assortment of dried fruit on a plate and lifted it to her lips with an adoring smile.

She bit into the apricot, delighting in its tart sweetness.

Then she chose one and held it a hairsbreadth from his mouth.

He nipped the tip of her finger along with the fruit, an impish glint in his eyes.

Prudence allowed her smile to lessen as she widened her eyes. "Why, Morgan Thomas. You weren't completely truthful to me when we married."

"Oh?" He trailed the edge of his index finger over the curve of her cheekbone and, with splayed hand, coaxed her nearer for a tender kiss. "And how is that?"

"You said you'd changed your devilish ways, and not only is that statement in question, but just look at how you've corrupted me in just a matter of days. Breakfast in bed."

Morgan filled his lungs and gazed at her with a gentle smile, then gathered her fingers and kissed them. "Ah, my sweet, sweet Prudence. This is our time. 'Rise up, my love, my fair one, and come away. For, lo, the winter is past, the rain is over and gone; the flowers appear on the earth; the time of the singing of the birds is come, and the voice of the turtle-dove is heard in our land.'"

She arched a chastising brow. "Penned by Shakespeare, no doubt?"

"No." He smiled smugly. "King Solomon."

"Ha! You would, of course, choose to memorize the Song of Solomon." She tried her very best to scowl.

His grin widened. "No self-respecting College of New Jersey man would leave Nassau Hall without committing to memory every single tantalizing word of it."

"Well," Prudence began while she broke a blueberry scone in half and held it for him to bite, "from now on, my love, we'll be reading that particular book together only."

"As you wish, dear heart." He bit the soft biscuit, then offered her a sip of coffee. "But it will have to wait for another time."

She frowned. "But you said *this* is our time."

"Yes, well . . ." His peculiar expression transformed into

one of guilt. He sat up straight. "I'm afraid I must return to duty today."

"You said we were to have a week," she said. "We've had but five days."

"That was all the time I was able to get. Forgive me. With all that's going on lately, five days' reprieve sounded like a month. I had no idea it would be over so swiftly."

"Oh, Morgan, you should have told me last night." Prudence folded her arms in despair.

"And mar a moment of our beautiful time together? We may not have another chance like this for quite a while."

She searched his face. "Why do you say that?"

"Because, for better or worse, General Washington is ready to make his move now. Any day, the war will begin in earnest."

Even as he spoke, Prudence swayed against him, seeking the solace, strength, and comfort of his arms. There, held tight, she listened over the beating of his heart to the deep resonance of his voice.

"But no matter what happens, my love, I'll see that you and your family are never in harm's way. I promise you that."

Her throat constricted, making it almost impossible to speak. "But what about you?" she whispered, clinging to his nearness. "I know I'll lose Papa soon. I've accepted that. But if anything should happen to you—" Her breath caught.

Morgan crushed her to himself. He kissed the top of her head, the tip of her nose, then raised her chin with his finger. Their breath mingled for a heartbeat before his lips lowered to hers and sealed the promise. "Don't you worry about me, my darling. Nothing in this world is going to keep me from coming back to you."

"Please don't forget that." She paused. "Morgan?"

He eased away enough to meet her gaze.

Still new to the ways of love, she let her eyes ask what her lips could not.

He smiled gently and disposed of the tray, then took her in his arms.

❧ ❧

Looking back, Morgan could not have explained where he found the strength to leave Prudence. In his wildest imaginings he never expected to find such happiness, such peace, or such contentment as he'd known since taking her for his wife. The depth of love they had found in even those few magical days and nights together was all the proof he needed that their union was blessed by God.

But mustering every ounce of willpower he possessed— spurred by the stark realization that Washington had installed a whipping post for disciplinary measures—he came up with just enough gumption to take Prudence home and tear himself from her loving arms.

Mr. Endecott had not fared any better in their absence. He clung to life, but by only a thread. Morgan wanted more than anything to be with Prudence when her father's end did come. She would need her husband then as never before.

Releasing a tortured breath as he passed the padlocked mercantile, Morgan wondered if his wife would reopen it again now that she was back, considering her father's precarious condition.

Suddenly Morgan realized that it was *his* store now as much as Prudence's. And her family was now his, too, to care for, plan for, and help. But somehow these new responsibilities did not weigh him down. Nor did the idea that he might indeed turn into a workhorse just like everyone else in these Colonies and be the "fool" he'd vowed never to be. He chuckled.

An inordinate amount of activity ahead of him at the crossroad pulled him out of his reverie, and he noticed a steady stream of wagons coming and going from the Winter Hill fortification. Nearing Cambridge and the din of almost constant artillery reports, there was even more bustle. It seemed that every rider on horseback, every soldier and rig, seemed to be going somewhere with purpose. Seeing the increased movement toward the British-held Charlestown and Boston

Necks, both of which were targets for most of the more recent cannon fire, he knew that something was definitely in the wind. Had his men at the warehouses been keeping up with the demand for supplies during his absence?

Morgan nudged his horse to a gallop, riding for the farmyard on the west side of Cambridge that he had converted to a supply depot. When the big barn and sheds came into sight, along with the additional sail-tarped structures he'd had constructed in the past month, he saw that all but one of the wagons and oxen teams were gone. The remaining outfit was backed up to the drastically reduced stacks of lumber and in the process of being loaded by the two Roberts, along with several other men. An unmistakable shock of red hair also met his gaze. Yancy Curtis.

Guiding the mount over in their direction, Morgan drew up alongside of them.

"'Tis the blushin' bridegroom!" the sailor called as Morgan drew up alongside them. "The honeymoon over already, mate?"

A knowing chuckle circulated among them.

"And how is the wee bride?" Robby asked, not bothering to control his broad grin.

Yancy heaved two boards into the wagon bed. "When I tell Felicia the 'flippant scoundrel' found someone to tame his wild streak, she'll be rendered speechless! And ye know what a wonder *that'll* be!"

With chagrin, Morgan felt a flush rising around his collar. He hoped it wasn't too obvious. "Yes, I was rather unchivalrous in my teasing of the lass, as I recall," he admitted. "But with all that's going on here right now, I need to know what's happened since last week."

"Actually," Chandler drawled, with an only slightly more serious smirk, "the lot of us probably didn't get much more sleep than you." Then he sobered. "Privateers commissioned by the congress have been keeping the Crown ships pretty occupied of late, so more supplies and powder have been getting through to us. Needless to say, we're putting them to good use. I'm sure you can tell from the sound of it, we are giving back as much as we're getting from the British artillery. Finally."

Robby nodded. "There's rumors, of course, of an attack, but nothing official yet. A messenger lad rode by this mornin'. You're to report to General Knox in Dorchester as soon as ye can."

"That's where all this lumber's bound," Yancy piped in. "And since I made port day before yesterday with a whole *cargohold* of gunpowder out of St. Eustatius, I've been haulin' wood for the boys. That engineer Knox is having somethin' called 'chandeliers' built out of it."

"Chandeliers?" Morgan asked. "Of lumber? That doesn't make sense."

The sailor gave a nod. "'Tis some big secret, mind ye. But I'll tell ye this. They'll not be hangin' from a ceiling to grace a dining table. They're a kind of sturdy framework for some purpose known only to the men in charge."

Morgan couldn't fathom such a concept. "But the cannons are pounding the other side of the bay. And I saw wagons full of supplies heading for Charlestown Neck."

"Just a diversion," Chan said offhandedly. "They're nothing but empty crates, movin' back and forth between the two necks. Most of the oxen have been driven down to Dorchester."

"Aye," Yancy added. "Masses of 'em. And all the activity is hidden from Boston behind the hills of Dorchester."

Morgan tightened his hold on the reins. "Guess I'd better ride on down there myself."

Robby tossed back a lock of black hair that had fallen into his eyes. "And ye best hurry, lad. We covered for ye this morn when ye hadn't returned from your leave."

As a gleam of devilment washed over Yancy's freckled face, Morgan spurred his horse and galloped out of there before he had to suffer through another bout of teasing.

It took nearly an hour to reach Dorchester, a small village inland of the hilly peninsula that stretched strategically into the bay south of Boston. When Morgan arrived, the smell of fresh-cut lumber assailed his nostrils, and the sound of sawing almost drowned out the lowing of oxen penned up in every available enclosure. A quick scan of the area revealed tall, brash General Knox at the base of a hill just east of the hamlet, where men hammered wooden frames together. Though only in his midtwenties, the general's military bearing seemed accented by the fancy uniform he wore.

Morgan dismounted, saluting as Knox looked up from inspecting a bundle of sticks. "Quartermaster Thomas reporting as ordered, sir."

He returned the salute, merry blue eyes assessing Morgan. "Glad to have you back, Thomas. Your new bride, is she well?"

"Fine, sir."

The general gave a nod, then withdrew a book from an inside breast pocket and flipped it open to a page of sketches. "Ingenious, wouldn't you say? I've got to hand it to the French."

Morgan perused the various drawings held out for his observation. One showed cannons mounted on wooden frames, and a second depicted bundles of sticks positioned in and around the framework. All written matter was in French.

"They came up with a means of installing a battery when the ground is frozen," the general went on.

"Yes, I see that." Morgan realized with a sickening sense of dread that the possibility of Dan and Susannah's house being within range of a bombardment was now a reality.

"We think they'll make for a nice celebration on the sixth of March, Boston Massacre Day," Knox continued. He pulled out a list from between pages. "And we'll need this on the hill and distributed to all my artillery crews by then."

Morgan ran his eyes down the column, an incredible accounting of balls, mortar shells, powder, and flints. The general actually took it for granted that all the brass and iron would be mounted and ready to fire by then! "That's just two days from now, sir. Surely the British aren't going to sit idly by while we install an entire battery, no matter how much noise is going on over at the other necks."

"Oh, we plan to mount them under cover of darkness on the night of the fifth. And, I might add, with the same success we had building the fortifications on Breed's and Bunker Hills."

"But we were only digging ditches, sir. You propose to set up something strong enough to withstand the tremendous kick of a big gun without so much as the light of a single candle?"

Knox merely smiled. "Have a little faith, doubting Thomas. With God, anything is possible."

49

Even from the relatively safe distance of the mercantile, Prudence found the noise of the constant bombardment unsettling, especially after the peace and solitude she and Morgan experienced during their first wondrous week together. She never would have guessed that her new husband was capable of the gentleness and tenderness he had shown her during those precious days of their honeymoon. Even now she had to remind herself not to smile.

But where was he? He hadn't come home since he left her at her father's house two days ago.

A cloud of tobacco smoke and a burst of raucous laughter drifted toward her from several soldiers holding their hands out to the red-hot stove. She had kept the store open later than usual these last nights, more to provide a warm shelter for them than anything.

"That's fer sure!" one of them spat. "The only thing them Brits are sufferin' from is lack of sleep. You and me, we'll lose our toes and fingers to frostbite yet. Mark my words."

Prudence moved past them to the little potbellied stove and plucked the coffeepot from it to pour each of them a warm-up.

"March, march, march," another grumbled. "It's all we do in this miserable cold. Washington's brain must've froze."

On her way by the window, she searched the length of the

road for the dozenth time. Surely Morgan would come home this eve. But it was getting so late.

They had to be on the brink of some significant happening. Something more than these foot soldiers had any inkling of.

Well, regardless, she reasoned, her husband had a safe duty to perform. Surely running a warehouse didn't put him at serious risk. But it was ever so lonely without him.

Taking her winter cloak from a hook behind the counter, Prudence flung it around her shoulders and stepped out of the smoky room into the brisk cold, where she stood gazing up into the night. The rolling landscape blocked any view of the bay, but intermittent flashes from the cannon explosions lit up the cloudless sky in random patterns, momentarily blotting out the tiny, brittle stars in the broad expanse of the heavens.

It was almost midnight. She really should lock up. She needed to check in on Papa again. He slept most of the time now, Miriam told her, and he rarely had strength enough to eat even a bite. Neither of them retained a shred of hope for his recovery. They knew without saying that he could slip away at any moment.

Now that she understood the indescribable wonder of love shared by a husband and wife, Prudence felt an added sympathy for her stepmother. Despite the vast age difference between Miriam and Papa, their love had been very real from the first. How would Miriam ever go on without him? It was a thought far too sad to dwell upon.

Suddenly, just as Prudence was about to go back inside, the entire sky burst with horrific brilliance. Her heart leaped to her throat at the blinding spectacle. Every British cannon must have fired simultaneously. And if the colonists were even now advancing on Boston Neck, as rumored, she didn't want to think about the devastation that blast must have caused.

She pulled her cloak tighter, trying to fend off her mounting fear. Morgan should have gotten word to her if he wasn't able to come home again tonight. She knew firsthand his love of danger—from choosing the hazards of being a spy to being among the last to leave Bunker Hill. Might he have taken it upon himself to jump into the middle of some fray? Could he have been wounded or killed by that horrendous cannon blast?

She searched the sky with heartfelt urgency as she whispered a prayer. "Please, heavenly Father, you've already taken my mother and both sisters. My father is at death's very door even as I come before you. My brothers—who knows when or if I'll ever see them again in this life. Please, please, I beg of you. Keep Morgan safe from harm. I love him so . . . and I don't know what I'd do if I had to deal with Mr. Randolph alone."

As Prudence continued her pleas to the Almighty, a disturbing realization worked gradually through her confused and jumbled thoughts. She caught her breath and closed her eyes. "It's true, dear Lord, very true. I've always been so sure of myself, so certain I could get through things all on my own. And I have looked down on others for their weaknesses. But now I understand how sinful and unloving that was. My strength comes from you, Lord. All glory belongs to you, not to someone as judgmental as I. Please forgive my unforgiving spirit. Forgive my vain pride. And most of all, thank you for being a God of mercy, love, and forgiveness."

Breathing out slowly, Prudence began to wonder how long all her waking moments and actions had been centered around herself. What on earth had Morgan found to love about her?

Perhaps he'd had second thoughts by now. With a little distance between them, maybe he had progressed beyond being enchanted with whatever outward beauty he thought she possessed and realized how uppity and self-righteous she truly was. Could that be why he hadn't come home?

The tramp of boots from inside the store shook her out of her troubling reflections. She sent up another quick prayer as the infantrymen neared the door. "Dear Father, please help me. Replace my pride with love for others. And give me the faith to really trust you . . . trust you to be in charge, instead of myself. Please."

The soldiers emerged from the warm haven. "Oh, Miss Endecott," one said with an off-center smile.

About to inform him of her new name, she thought better of it, hoping she still *had* a husband.

"I plumb forgot." He tugged off his glove with his buckteeth and reached into a pocket. "The officer at the warehouse gave me a letter for ya yesterday. Hope it weren't nothin' important."

"Why . . . why thank you!" She snatched it from him and dashed joyfully inside to the lamplight. Morgan hadn't abandoned her after all! "Thank you, Father," she breathed as the door slammed shut behind her.

❧ ❧

In the wee hours of morning, Morgan glanced at Yancy beside him on the hard seat of the wagon, steering it up the hill between Brookline and Roxbury. "You say they're almost finished mounting all the cannons on those twigs and glorified sawhorses?"

"Aye." The redhead's toothy grin glowed in the cannon-lit sky. "And they work just fine. The men have carted tons of rocks up there, too, and are filling barrels with 'em to help support the chandeliers. Course, if need be, they could always roll the barrels down the hill and flatten a bunch of lobsterbacks."

"I just have a hard time believing everything will be in place by morning!"

"It'll be ready enough to put one surefire scare into General Howe, ye can count on that."

"And the munitions—are you sure you and the others delivered the proper size balls or shells to each cannon crew?"

"Relax, mate. I know *I* have, at least."

"Well, I'll feel better when I've checked the line for myself."

Another of Yancy's grins flashed in the light of an explosion when they reached the summit of the hill. "I figured once ye made sure the supplies were all there, ye'd have flown to that pretty little bride everybody's been tellin' me about."

"There'll be time for that once I'm positive nothing else is required hereabouts. But have no doubt, Yance, these past two days have been the longest of my life! I miss Pru so much. Why didn't somebody tell me married life was so wonderful? Why is that kept such a secret?"

Yancy laughed aloud. "Ye think young Ben's been close-mouthed about his wee Abigail?" He whacked Morgan on the knee. "But thinkin' it over," he said in a more serious tone, "it's kinda like when a body first comes to the Lord. Who can understand the wonder of it till ye take that step yourself?"

"You know," Morgan remarked, "for a carrottop smuggler, you're turning into quite the wise old sage."

Yancy's dimpled grin took a lopsided twist. "Aye, but I'm no longer a smuggler. We've declared all our ports tariff free. Now if only them hardheaded British bigwigs would accept it."

Morgan gave an understanding nod. Then, as usual, thoughts of Prudence teased his mind. He took out his spy-glass and peered toward the northwest, trying to find the mercantile, but the hills surrounding Cambridge prevented any view of it. He aimed it toward the east and south instead, at the excellent panorama of the back bay waters edging either side of Boston Neck. The Neck was clearly visible in the light of the cannon fire. "Hold up a minute, Yance. I want to take a closer look."

When the wagon rolled to a stop, Morgan pointed the instrument toward the bay on the south side of the Neck. The reflecting water changed abruptly to rugged black at the closest point of the ragged shoreline of the Dorchester Neck. "Hard to believe the British haven't discovered the activity on the Dorchester peninsula. It's such a clear night." He raised the spyglass higher and studied the dark outline. "Shouldn't we be able to see the emplacements from here?" He passed the telescope to Yancy and let him peer through it.

"Not really, mate. We never tried to put any cannons on the

closest hill overlookin' the Neck. General Washington had them set up farther down, on the heights." He didn't speak for a few seconds, then chuckled. "And lest ye ever doubted the Good Lord's on our side, you'll not doubt again. The Almighty's providing us with some fog. Thick, low fog that's hugging the top of the heights, but nowhere else. An' he didn't stop there. Look at the direction of the breeze. It's carryin' the sounds of our workmen away from Boston. I've seen me share of miracles lately, but considering the thousands of men and beasts workin' up there, this ranks high on the list."

Morgan took the spyglass back and gazed toward Dorchester peninsula again. "I don't see any fog. Just a dark silhouette against the sky. Could it have lifted by now?"

"Nay. It just appears that way. It's still there." The sailor snapped the traces over the horses' backs. "God is a wonder, sometimes. Don't ye think?"

❦ ❦

As he took inventory of the last cannon crew's supply of ammunition with Robert Chandler in the light of dawn, Morgan noticed that the misty shroud was beginning to lift. And as it did, he could see the massive amount of work that had been finished overnight. This was much more impressive an undertaking than what they'd accomplished on Breed's and Bunker Hills. Orchards had been chopped down, and securely mounted and fortified cannon lined the flat tops of two steep, frozen hills.

Morgan exchanged an amazed look with Chan, then his friend nodded toward the bay. Across the water, wisps of fog floated past wharves crowded with confiscated merchant vessels, whalers, and fishing boats, their masts sticking up like a barren forest. Long Wharf, jutting out more than a quarter mile into the water, was most noticeable, lined with British warships. Beyond the waterfront a myriad of buildings covered the Boston peninsula. "See the South Battery?" Morgan said with a lift of his chin. "I visited Dan there when he was

❦ 426 ❦

confined. Milk Street, where their house is, runs inland right behind it."

Robert's expression darkened. He tilted his head and indicated the hill just to the left of them, where exhausted workers were assessing their night's handiwork, the row of cannons. "Susannah and Dan will be within easy range of those. And that sweet little Julia . . . she's such a dear, fragile thing." He drew a sad breath.

This was not the time to encourage his friend's morose imaginings. But Morgan was beginning to understand the depth of pain that must be involved in the loss of a beloved mate. He attempted an optimistic tone. "And when she grows up, she's sure to be a joy, if she's anywhere near as wonderful as her namesake." *Or my Prudence,* his heart added.

"I only pray the child has the chance to grow up."

The cannons firing at the Boston Neck fortifications suddenly ceased.

Morgan put a hand on Chandler's coat sleeve. "Listen. It's unbelievably silent all of a sudden." Their diversionary forces must have seen Dorchester Heights clearly and now knew their task was completed.

A volley of cannon fire from the English emplacement ended the short silence. Then a moment later, with Dorchester Heights emerging clearly into view of the British side, the Crown's battery at the Neck stopped as well.

Morgan would have given anything to have brought his spyglass up the hill with him this time. It would have been one sight to behold, he was sure . . . all those redcoats running for cover like an army of ants who had just lost their hole!

50

A thin ray of light beamed through an opening between the heavy window draperies. Susannah opened her eyes and moved the quilts aside enough to raise her head, then peered around the frigid bedchamber.

"What is it, sweetheart?" Dan muttered huskily.

"I don't know." An uncanny sensation she could not quite name sent gooseflesh tingling over her whole body. She sat up, clutching the heavy blankets to her.

Dan joined her and put an arm around her, adding his own warmth to that of the bedcoverings as their breath came out in frosty puffs.

Susannah looked at him in puzzlement. "It's quiet. Much too quiet."

"The bombardment stopped. That must be what woke us." He yawned and flopped back down on his pillow.

"Wouldn't it be marvelous if it's ended for good? But I suppose it will start up again tonight. Oh, I pray it won't. I've had precious little sleep the last four nights."

He pulled her down into the bedding and hugged her. "I know the uproar has been extremely hard on you, love . . . plus trying to maintain some semblance of normalcy while cramped in the kitchen every day with our two rambunctious little ones."

Snuggling against him, she nodded. "I'll tell you one thing. I'll not take firewood for granted ever again. What I wouldn't give to be able to heat the whole house—and be *too* warm for even one day."

He chuckled. "And find food in the market stalls, the way we used to. Or drop by the bakery for some fresh cranberry tarts. Wouldn't that be a treat?"

But Susannah couldn't manage even a tiny smile. Her stomach knotted with far more urgency than it had since she and Dan first began giving most of their share of the meager meals to the children. "Miles and Julia. I can endure almost anything but seeing them go hungry. How ever can we stretch what's in our larder for even a few more days, Dan? I'll tell you, before I watch my babies starve to death, I'll take them down to the shore and set them adrift as Moses' mother did him. I swear I will."

Dan's arms tightened around her, and he kissed her temple. "God has been faithful thus far. Somehow we must find the strength to trust the Lord a little while longer."

Searching her heart, Susannah couldn't help wondering where that last ounce of strength would come from. She was certain she had used up all she had ever possessed long ago. "Oh, Dan, I should have listened to you when you wanted me to stay in Rhode Island. Because of my stubbornness, our two little children are now in dire peril." Her eyes stung with tears, and she closed them until the threat subsided. "And to add to our trials, because of my liberal ways, I've caused Mistress Brown to leave our congregation. She'll never forgive me for Liza's involvement with that young British soldier."

Dan gave her an encouraging peck on the cheek. "If you'll stop beating yourself to death with hindsight, I'll brave the cold and go down to the kitchen to start the fire for you."

"You will?" The loving gesture made her perk up a little. She watched him sit up and reach for his clothes.

Outside, the clatter of a horse's hooves sounded on the cobbled street.

Dan, fastening his trousers, moved to the window and parted the drapes. "A soldier, racing from the wharf. And . . .

wait a minute." He looped the heavy panel out of the way, then unlatched and opened the window. He leaned out.

The air that floated inside was scarcely colder than that already in the room. And it brought with it something even more peculiar—the tinkling of a multitude of bells.

"Where is it coming from?" she asked.

"The wharf area. Sounds like ships' bells."

One even closer and clearer pealed.

Dan whirled around and faced her. "That's from our church on Long Lane." He tugged the window closed, then returned to the bed to finish dressing. Leaning over, he bestowed a quick kiss on her lips, then rose. "I'm going to go see what's happening. I've been expecting something for days. General Howe has dispatched several regiments closer to the Neck and has been ferrying troops over to Charlestown every day. I think he's heard our boys are planning to storm those two necks."

"Would they be so foolhardy?" Susannah asked. "They'd surely be slaughtered, just as the British were at Breed's Hill."

"Yes, I know. I've been praying they won't do anything reckless. I'll try not to be too long."

She grasped his hand. "Promise you won't be. I can't stand it when you're gone for hours and hours, leaving me to wonder and worry."

Dan sat down beside her again and pressed her hand to his heart. "I give you my solemn promise. This time I will not leave you here endlessly." He hurried out of the room and down the steps.

Susannah tightened her lips. "Your promise to hasten home is about as good as your promise to light the fire." With an unhappy sigh of defeat, she tugged the quilts higher in the cold empty bedchamber.

❦ ❦

Dan exited his front door to discover many other curious townsmen rushing out of the homes along Milk Street. Some were still fastening buttons and putting on hats and gloves as they started toward the wharves. And quite a few king's men, still donning the final pieces of their uniforms, emerged from the houses where they had been residing since so many patriots had departed the city. They appeared as confused as the rest of the crowd going to the harbor.

A loud blast from the South Battery almost deafened them, and they all halted abruptly just short of the wharves, waiting for the explosion.

The report boomed in the southeast. The Dorchester peninsula!

While the redcoats continued on in the same direction they had been heading, Dan and the locals veered swiftly to the right. On Mackerel Street, which curved around Fort Hill and ended at the dock on the other side, there would be a much better view of the target.

"Maybe our militias are launching a surprise invasion from Dorchester," someone huffed as he jogged past. Even though the remark drew no response, the men picked up the pace as the battery fired its big guns several more times.

By now an ever increasing crowd was hastening along in what bordered on a stampede. Running pell-mell, Dan reached the graying planks of a deserted wharf cluttered with broken barrels and hogsheads. He stopped at the water's edge and centered his attention on the explosions on the opposite shore. Just as many cannonballs were falling into empty water as reaching the land. But there wasn't a militiaman in sight, nor a single boat attempting to cross.

Someone nudged him. "Look! On top!" He pointed across the bay.

Dan squinted at what appeared to be lethal cannon emplacements positioned atop two steep hills.

The British cannonballs were beginning to gain the Dorchester shore now, and each firing exploded farther up the heights.

Wondering if the big guns at the South Battery could elevate their barrels to a high enough angle to reach that distance, Dan watched in fascination as the breeze began to shift, blowing the thick black smoke back toward the city. He knew that Susannah would smell the stench of burned powder any minute, and he had promised to return soon. But he had to stay for a little while—at least until he was certain of one thing.

After two more unsuccessful cannon blasts, a fellow beside him hollered with glee. "They can't do it! The shots can't go that high!"

Catching the spirit of jubilation already spreading like wildfire, Dan grabbed the man and hugged him.

"Our boys have done it again!" came another exuberant voice. "Done the impossible in one night!"

"Aye, that they did!" someone else yelled. "Would you believe it! Long Wharf, the South Battery—and everything else on this end of Boston—is now at the mercy of the Continental army!"

❦ ❧

"Thank you ever so much for coming over, Mistress Simms," Susannah said, admitting her neighbor into the house later that afternoon. "I do appreciate your offer to stay with the children while they nap."

"Those sweet babes are no trouble." The elder's wife hung her warm coat and scarf on a peg. "I'm just surprised the reverend's taking you down to the wharf with him."

"Yes, I can hardly believe it myself." Her complaint earlier this morning had not fallen on deaf ears. "But Dan thinks the militia will hold off bombarding for a few more hours, at least. Give the people a chance to get out of harm's way. *And* give the British time to rethink their position here."

"Well, you just hurry back before dark. They'll start up for sure by then. You might need to take the children farther inland to keep 'em safe. Me, I'm too old to concern myself with this sort of business. I'll just take myself down to the cellar."

"At the very first hint of danger we'll be back, the two of us. You can be assured of that."

The faint thrumming of marching drums grew steadily louder in the distance.

"Wonder if that's one of the regiments comin' back from the Neck?"

"Dan told me regiments are being moved to the North End, out of range of the Dorchester guns. And he heard that the British are moving many of their landing boats and smaller vessels from the Charlestown side, too. He thinks they may launch an infantry assault on the Dorchester peninsula's flank."

"But Washington's no fool," Dan said, coming downstairs, a spyglass in his gloved hand. "He's sure to have his own regiments waiting for them to land." He snatched Susannah's warm cloak off a hall peg and put it about her shoulders. "It's a long walk to the North End. If we don't hurry, we may miss it all."

❦ ❦

Susannah found it difficult to walk against a steadily rising southeastern wind, and she was exhausted by the time they reached the far side of Clarke's Wharf. There they were somewhat protected by the hordes of other townspeople braving the cold to witness the latest spectacle.

A long line of heavily armed redcoats, four abreast, extended a considerable distance back from the end of the pier as they waited to board landing craft. A few fully manned longboats were trying to make headway in the stiff breeze while an even greater number of empty ones were being buffeted mercilessly against the pilings by the turbulent sea.

Susannah watched apprehensively as the determined soldiers climbed down the ladders and ropes to board the wildly rocking vessels. Suddenly two boats collided, spilling uniformed men into the frigid, choppy sea.

A cheer went up around her.

Upset by such callous disregard for others' lives, British or not, she glanced at her husband, but he was gazing at something else. "Dan!" she said over the noise of the wind.

He lowered his spyglass. "Yes, sweetheart?"

"Soldiers," she said, pointing toward the bay. "In the water."

His expression sobered as he observed the drama below.

"May I see?" She reached for the telescope and watched the drenched soldiers splashing and paddling in frenzied horror, trying to grasp the ropes being tossed to them. She hoped against hope that none of the young redcoats who had befriended her while guarding the house were among the unfortunates. She breathed a prayer that all would be rescued. One of them might even be Gerald Blake, Liza's young private.

When finally the last one had been hauled up onto the pier, Susannah relinquished the spyglass.

Dan quickly directed the telescope toward the open passage, and she followed his lead.

Several longboats, each bearing at least fifty British soldiers, were struggling farther out in the roiling water. Dozens of soldiers leaned hard into their oars, but they were fighting a losing battle against the force of the vicious gusts. Even if they did reach the back side of Dorchester, they'd be too exhausted to battle a patriot force.

At the pier, the commotion and racket grew louder, with empty boats crashing together. All attempts to board them had ceased while His Majesty's own had their hands full trying desperately to haul on lines to separate the beleaguered craft.

The force of the wind intensified even more.

Out in the bay the manned boats teetered precariously on huge white-capped swells, only to be hurled back to Boston, losing more distance than they gained.

"They'll never make it, Dan," Susannah cried, holding the throat of her flapping cloak together as she tugged on the sleeve of his greatcoat. "The whole thing is a disaster."

He pulled her close, blocking her from the worst of the bitter gale, and leaned to speak into her ear. "Or a miracle."

51

March 17, 1776

The great wind, the wind all the colonists said was from God, lasted three days and nights. Added to this miracle, Prudence's father's fragile hold on life continued into the next week—a blessed gift to her. And with the arrival of the Sabbath to free her from her duties, she gratefully relieved Miriam and spent the morning at Papa's side. As she spooned clear chicken broth into his wan lips, it brought fleeting memories of her own childhood when Papa would cut her meat into bite-sized chunks for her. How sad, this reversal of roles. And how quickly in one's lifetime the child was called upon to take up duties of the parent while the parent became the dependent one.

The front door squeaked open and closed, and the sound of her husband's spritely footsteps banished the melancholy turn of Prudence's thoughts.

Morgan, all smiles, peeked around the doorjamb before coming into the dimly lit room. He planted a kiss on her upturned lips, then nodded to Papa. "Father Endecott."

"My goodness." Rising, she let her eyes roam freely over his splendid new blue-and-buff uniform. "Aren't you the handsome one! You look like the cock of the walk. I didn't expect you home so early . . . even if it is the Lord's Day."

"Yes, I know." He eased himself down on the bed in the spot

she'd just vacated and gave her father's frail shoulder a pat. "I've spent the whole morning witnessing one of the most beautiful sights either of you can imagine."

"What was it, Son?" Papa asked, his voice a thin whisper.

Morgan snagged Prudence and pulled her down on his lap, grinning over her attempts to keep from spilling the bowl she still held. "Sailing ships, sir. The bay is billowing white with them. The British have given up. They're leaving!"

"Are you serious?" Prudence asked.

"More than I've ever been in my life, dear heart. I left my duties long enough to fetch you so you could watch the glorious show with me."

"Then it's truly happening at last! Praise the Lord!"

"Indeed. That three-day gale the Almighty sent us kept the redcoats trapped in Boston while our militia set up another battery facing Castle William. Then one went up on Noddles Island. And as of this morning, we've got another brand-new fortification on Nooks Hill, overlooking Boston Neck. There's not one place left that's safe for the Crown. And all the glory certainly belongs to God."

"The redcoats . . . pulling out," Papa sighed, the warmth in his eyes stronger than his wavery voice.

"Quite right, sir. Every last uppity one of them, along with their lackey Loyalists. They've been loading supplies for several days now—and from what our lookouts have reported, loading troops, too. By the hundreds. Thousands."

Papa gave an almost imperceptible nod. "I'm thankful I lived to hear this." He paused, gathering strength, then slowly labored on as both Morgan and Prudence leaned closer to make out his fading words. "Great day for our people. My children, free from tyranny. Splendid legacy."

Then Morgan straightened. "I've more good news. My father has at last written in response to my letter. It arrived yesterday. Chandler gave it to me this morning."

Prudence swiveled to him. "Is it truly good news?"

"See for yourself." Reaching into his breast pocket, he withdrew the missive and handed it to her.

As she caught her bottom lip in her teeth and unwrapped the letter, Morgan slid his arms around her, sending all serious thought skittering. How ever would she read it aloud? And when he blew lightly, teasingly, on the back of her neck, she checked to see if Papa had noticed his scandalous behavior.

If he had, he gave no sign. He gestured for her to begin.

The handwriting was bold and precise, liberally flourished. Obviously, Mr. Thomas took pride in it. She started reading aloud:

Dear Son,

Needless to say, your letter of confession came as a great shock to me. It took considerable time to calm myself sufficiently to pen an answer. But after giving the matter much thought, I realize I must in all truthfulness bear an equal share of the blame for your actions. It was I who insisted upon your attending a college separate from your friends, an institution I heard would afford you no slack. But I was not unaware that the Presbyterian professors there were caught up in the nonsense of the tea rebellion, and young minds are often easily misled.

I have chosen not to make mention of your letter to your mother or any of our associates. Politics and business partnerships change with the wind, but I have only one son. It is, after all, entirely possible that it is I who am misled. Of late, I find myself questioning who is right and wrong regarding this very great conflict in the Colonies. If a highly respected planter and statesman such as George Washington would lend himself so wholly to the cause, I must sit back and take stock of my position and consider making some difficult decisions of my own.

Now I have a request to make which I beseech you to give your utmost deliberation. When your enlistment is completed, I should like very much to have you come directly home. It is most imperative that we talk.

I do thank you most sincerely for the honesty and forthrightness of your letter, however painful it might have been for you to

write or me to receive. May the Lord bless and keep you until we
meet again.

I remain your faithful and loving father,
Waldon Thomas

By the end of the missive, Prudence had to fight tears of joy. She couldn't utter a word of her own but scanned again the carefully written pages in silence.

"Good letter," Papa murmured. "And honest. You did the right thing, Son."

Morgan smiled. "In his own way, my father has always been a rather decent sort."

"And your mother?" Prudence asked.

"Mother's, uh . . ." Abruptly he set Prudence on her feet, then stood up behind her. "It's wonderful you were awake for my news, Father Endecott. But your daughter and I must make haste. I've a long train of wagons readying to enter Boston with badly needed food and firewood. And I want her to be at my side as we make our triumphant entrance."

❧ ❧

Approaching what until today had been a no-man's-land between the colonial and British artilleries at the Boston Neck, Morgan observed that the train of wagons had pressed as near as possible to the barricade. The British had to have left the area! Surely this was the most glorious of all days—forgiveness from his father plus the vacating of the Crown forces, all on the very same morning!

Now with his beautiful Prudence behind him on the horse, her arms securely about his waist, the breeze against his face felt clean. Fresh. Hopeful. Especially with the heady knowledge regarding the armada of British ships poised in the harbor, waiting only for the tide to turn before they set sail for England.

"Oh, my," Prudence murmured, leaning to see around him. "Are all those wagons yours?"

He chuckled and turned his head slightly to speak. "Actually, they belong to the Continental army, but they do happen to be my responsibility."

"How thrilling! Just think, they'll be the very first to roll into Boston bearing such needed gifts. I'm so very proud of my enterprising husband." Tightening her embrace, she rested her cheek against his back.

Morgan cupped a hand over hers, clasped together in front of him. "By the by, I forgot to tell you. Yancy's wife, Felicia, surprised him nigh unto death yesterday when she and Emily, Robby's wife, arrived here out of the blue. Apparently a number of Rhode Islanders got wind of the imminent British departure and had to come see for themselves."

"Oh?"

"Mm-hmm. The women came without their husbands' permissions. But I can't truthfully blame young Emily. Undoubtedly it was Felicia who came up with that harebrained idea. She's quite the independent sort. Rather like you, I might add."

"Is that so? But I've been a most obedient wife since we were wed."

"Ah yes, for an entire two weeks."

To Morgan's relief, Prudence laughed softly. "I'm truly eager to meet them. Particularly Robby's wife. He scarcely came by the mercantile without speaking fondly of her and their two 'wee bairns,' as he called them."

Morgan nodded and began threading a pathway through the throng amassing at the Neck to the line of wagons. "For someone who had quite literally been washed ashore, MacKinnon stumbled across a rare find in his Emily. In her younger tomboy years, I thought of her as just another one of us fellows."

"Just another one of the—"

Morgan straightened his posture and removed his hand from Prudence's to return a salute from one of his wagon drivers. Passing the piled-high conveyance, he mentally checked off some of the items visible in that bed and the next two: flour, molasses, maple syrup, coffee, krauts and pickles, potatoes and other vegetables, apples, cheese, sausages. The sight of the latter, along with its full-bodied aroma, reminded him he hadn't taken time for the midday meal.

A little farther down the line, he spied Ted on the seat of a wagon and beside him, his auburn-haired wife. He spurred his mount forward, skirting the pedestrians, and drew up alongside. "I say, Jane. When did you arrive?"

She turned a friendly smile. "An hour ago. I rode in with Philip, my brother-in-law. And it seems we didn't get here any too soon."

"And she quite surprised me," Ted admitted, hugging her close, "even though I distinctly told her to stay put."

"Well, *I* told *you* not to join up," she said with a false pout, "and I notice you're clad in a new uniform." At his apologetic grimace, she shifted her attention to Prudence.

Morgan followed her gaze. "I believe an introduction is in order. The enchanting lass with me happens to be my lovely bride, Prudence. Dear heart, I'd like you to meet Jane Harrington, Ted's wife."

"*The* Prudence?" A merry gleam sparkled in Jane's brown eyes. "The one you turned the earth upside down to find?"

Prudence leaned to peer up at Morgan. "Honestly, is there no one you didn't mention me to?" But her lips softened into a smile as she turned to Jane. "It's very nice to meet you. I've heard so much about you."

"And I, you."

Before the mischievous Jane could utter any further word, Morgan spotted Robby and Chandler a few wagons ahead and urged his horse toward them. "Excuse us," he said, making his escape. He was positive the honey blonde curls beneath the bonnet of the lass between the two men on the seat could only belong to the more compassionate Emily. "Well, well," he called as he rode near, "'tis the lovely Mistress MacKinnon."

Emily's glance took in both him and Prudence, and a guileless smile of greeting lit her face. "And this must be your new bride my Robby said was so fetching. I'm happy for you,

Morgan. And ever so delighted to make your acquaintance, Mistress Thomas."

"Please, call me Prudence. After hearing your husband declaring his undying love for his wee yellow-haired lassie with the bonny green eyes, I'd recognize you anywhere, Emily MacKinnon."

As Robby gazed adoringly at the pretty wife beside him, Morgan couldn't help but catch the poignant expression on Chandler's face. Surrounded by friends, Chan was still profoundly alone.

"I say, down with it!" a man shouted from a gathering at the barricade.

A narrow section of the barrier was yanked away by several pairs of bare hands.

A loud cheer went up as lads from Boston surged through to freedom, hugging everyone in their path. Morgan's heart caught at the sight of their painfully thin forms, the hungry eyes they turned upon the food-laden wagons.

A church bell from Roxbury started clanging, followed almost immediately by others in the surrounding area.

More people climbed across the rubble, and deafening cheers went up as the two crowds converged.

"Let's give a hand," Robby said to Chandler as he turned the reins over to Emily. The two leaped down and raced into the melee to help make the opening wide enough for the wagons.

Morgan glimpsed a shock of red hair in the thick of things, ripping and tossing boards. He pressed his mount's flanks and started forward through the mob. Just as he was about to yell out the seaman's name, he recognized Felicia on the seat of the lead wagon.

She saw him at almost the same moment. "Morgan Thomas, as I live and breathe!"

Much as he might have preferred to shield his wife from becoming acquainted with someone even more mouthy than Jane, he had to laugh at the irony of it all. He tipped his head politely, then turned to Prudence. "I'd like you to meet Felicia

Curtis, dear heart, the wife of my smuggler friend. Felicia, this is my wife, Prudence."

To his dismay, he saw a definite kindred spark pass between the two dark-haired lasses as they exchanged greetings. He only hoped that time and circumstance would preclude any opportunity for them to find out exactly how much they had in common. But he was blocked from moving forward by the milling throng.

Too late.

A slow, knowing smile spilled across Felicia's lips. She looked from Prudence to him and then back. "I believe you're just the woman who can whip that particular rebel into shape. Yes, quite nicely."

At that very moment, the horde in front pulled away a large section of the barricade, clearing the entire roadway. Felicia slapped the traces across the team's back, and they lurched ahead while Yancy deftly hopped aboard.

Another rousing cheer rose heavenward as the first wagon passed into Boston—the first one in eleven months.

❦ ❦

Susannah could only gaze in amazement at the kissing, hugging, dancing, and laughter that joined in splendid harmony with the ringing of Boston's bells.

Dan, with a grin broader than any he had worn in a very long time, scooped Julia Rose up in one arm, then turned to Susannah. "Let's go, sweetheart. To the Neck. This is one thing we'll not miss." He offered her his free hand.

She took it without hesitation. Then, with Miles securely in tow, they set out after the throng. It was all she could do to hold back the tears of thankfulness and joy. Whenever had she felt so happy, so hopeful?

But without warning, Mistress Brown stepped in front of Dan, her pudgy face contorted with pain.

The delightful sensations evaporated.

The older woman's eyes were swollen and red from weeping. "Please, Reverend," she wailed above the raucous confusion. "It's my Liza. You have to help me!" Her hazel eyes darted back and forth between Dan and Susannah.

"What is it, Mistress?" he asked.

"She left. With the British. She's on one of them ships in the bay. You've got to do somethin'. You've got to get her back for me." She wept uncontrollably in her misery.

Dan pulled his kerchief out and handed it to her. "I'm so sorry. Only the Lord knows how truly sorry I am. But I'm afraid there's nothing I *can* do. Liza chose to go with her young man."

"But . . . but she's my baby. My darlin' girl. She'll end up nothin' but a camp follower, a trollop."

"Try not to think such thoughts," he said reassuringly. "Her young man believes in the Lord. I know the two of them are not acting responsibly at the moment, but I feel the young man will do the honorable thing by her. They love each other very much."

"Honorable!" she sobbed. "Them heathens don't know the meaning of the word!"

He put an arm about her heaving shoulders. "Mistress Brown. Even if you're not able to trust Private Blake just yet, you do know your daughter and all the things you've instilled within her throughout her life. The Lord promised us in the book of Proverbs that a child who has been trained in ways that are right and proper will not depart from them. You must cling to that promise with every ounce of faith you have."

She searched his eyes. "Oh, Reverend . . . if only I could."

Susannah ached to take the older woman's hand to comfort her, but she didn't dare. Mistress Brown blamed her for her daughter's downfall.

Dan, however, hugged her tighter. "We'll pray night and day with you that the Almighty will surround her always with his merciful protection—and perhaps, one day, guide her back home."

"B-but do you think it's really true? What the Bible says?"

He nodded gently. "If I didn't believe in every one of God's precious promises, I could not be a minister of the gospel.

❧ 445 ❧

Liza is in God's hands right now. We must trust him to take care of her. He would never forsake those who belong to him any more than he could forsake this city, which has always been dedicated to him." He gave her a comforting squeeze. "Come with us to the Neck, will you? Come and celebrate the Lord's faithful care of his flock."

Dan was asking something nearly impossible of the still crying midwife—bottomless faith.

Susannah, unable to restrain herself any longer, slipped her free hand into the older woman's cushiony one. "Yes, please, do come with us."

The midwife raised her watery eyes and stared for a frozen moment, as if trying to lay hold of the things Dan had said. Then with a heart-wrenching sob, she grabbed Susannah and hauled her into a hug and clung desperately.

"Mama?" Miles's young voice broke into the emotion of the moment. "Does Mistress Brown like you again?"

After a ragged sigh, the older woman let go and gathered herself together. She smiled at the child, then swept him up into her arms. "Yes, she does, my little man. Now, let's go see what all that shouting's about."

As they neared the corner of Marlborough Street, riders on horseback raced past them from the Neck, one waving a large flag made mostly of red and white stripes. "No king but King Jesus!" they shouted, flying onward.

Everyone in the vicinity cheered.

"Wagons!" someone yelled. "With food!"

"Food," Susannah whispered, and she heard the word echoed up and down the street along with even more cheering.

Everyone moved aside to make room for the outfits to come down the center of the broad street.

Susannah stretched on tiptoe, trying to see past the heads of the taller folk. At last she made out the lead wagon. "Yancy! Oh, Dan, it's Yancy Curtis! And Felicia!"

Dan was already grinning from ear to ear and holding the giggling Julia aloft so she could see, too.

Susannah smiled at Mistress Brown, then grabbed Miles's hand and followed Dan as he wedged a path for them through the townspeople lining the street.

When they broke through, Yancy halted the team of horses, jumped from the wagon, and seized Dan, thumping him on the back. "Good to see ye, mate!" Then he helped Felicia down, and the hugs started up again, with everyone talking, laughing, kissing, and crying at once.

Someone tapped Susannah's shoulder.

She turned to find herself lost in Emily's arms, then Robby's, and even Robert Chandler's. Overwhelmed with joy, Susannah caught sight of her brother and Jane trying to make their way through from a few wagons down the line. She dissolved completely into tears and tugged Miles doggedly after her to meet them halfway. When she reached them, Susannah threw herself into Ted's embrace, not even caring that she was bawling all over his new uniform.

"Hey! What's the holdup?" a masculine voice called out.

"Morgan, too?" Susannah cried as she made out his broad-shouldered frame coming toward them atop a splendid chestnut horse. A rather comely young woman was riding behind him. Susannah waved. "Morgan!"

How he managed to dismount so smoothly and quickly was a mystery, but within seconds, he and his companion were both on the ground. "Susannah! Come here," he said, yanking her into a hard, long hug before holding her at arm's length. "The rest of your family, are they well?"

"Yes, yes," she laughed, wiping helplessly at her joyful tears. With so many others around her involved in their own happy reunions, she had no time to be embarrassed.

Morgan tugged the lovely black-haired girl forward. "I'd like to present Prudence, the young lady I told you about in Rhode Island the Christmas before last. Two weeks ago she did me the honor of becoming my wife."

Susannah, rendered speechless, found the girl's appearance somewhat surprising. A striking and exotic beauty, Prudence nonetheless was far from the fashion plate one might expect someone of Morgan's background to choose. Her Puritan dress was plain to the point of severity. And her shining black hair, parted in the middle and tied back beneath a ruffled cap, hung nearly to her waist. Susannah finally recovered her voice. "I cannot tell you what a joy it is to meet you. I wish you a long and fulfilled life with our dear Morgan."

"Thank you." Prudence dipped into a slight curtsy. "But the honor is mine. I've heard quite a lot about you and your family."

Just then, Robby descended upon them. "Prudence, come with me. Susannah's husband, Dan, is eager to meet ye."

As the two wove their way out of sight, Susannah shook her head. "Oh, Morgan, I couldn't be happier for you. In fact, I couldn't be happier—period! But I must admit, Prudence seems quite a departure from your usual young ladies."

"Rather." He chuckled. "I didn't know what I was looking for before she came along."

"You've found it, then?"

"Completely."

"And your family? Your mother . . . has she met Prudence?"

Morgan laughed aloud. "No. But I always did love high adventure."

"That's good to hear," Ted cut in, stepping up to them. "I just learned our generals have been discussing the possibility that the British will try to attack New York next. We'll be moving out right away."

"Oh, no!" Susannah felt her joy wilting. "So soon?"

"Is that not the fate of all Crusader knights, fair lass?" Morgan asked lightly.

She gave a grudging nod. "I'm just so very pleased the Almighty chose to send you to save this beacon on the hill rather than destroy it."

Dan and Prudence joined them then. "Yes," Dan said. "This will be a day Boston will never forget."

Morgan drew his wife close to his side and smiled worshipfully at her.

Prudence's silvery eyes widened in a combination of innocence and challenge, and she quirked a smile reminiscent of one Morgan might have used himself. "Since, Sir Galahad, you are the good knight chosen to bring succor to the masses, why don't we quit dawdling and get this food to market, where it can do some good?"

Watching the lively exchange, Susannah felt an immediate liking for Morgan's dark-haired beauty. Pretty, practical, Puritan. She was going to be quite a surprise to the Philadelphia Thomases. Quite a surprise, indeed.

Susannah turned to Dan. "Shall we go, my love? I believe we'll be having company this eve."

Dear Reader,

We highly regard your interest in our series, and we would be pleased to receive your comments and to answer any question you might have.

Sally Laity and Dianna Crawford
P.O. Box 80176
Bakersfield, CA 93380-0176

P.S. Your self-addressed, stamped return envelope would be appreciated.

The Embers of Hope

The
Embers of Hope

Sally Laity
&
Dianna Crawford

Tyndale House Publishers, Inc.
Wheaton, Illinois

Scripture quotations are taken from the *Holy Bible,* King James Version.

Library of Congress Cataloging-in-Publication Data

Laity, Sally.
  The embers of hope / Sally Laity and Dianna Crawford.
    p.   cm.—(Freedom's holy light ; v. 5)
  ISBN 0-8423-1362-1 (sc : alk. paper)
    1. United States—History—Revolution, 1775-1783—Fiction.   I. Crawford,
Dianna, date.   II. Title.   III. Series: Laity, Sally.   Freedom's holy light ; v. 5.
PS3553.R27884E47   1996
813'.54—dc20   96-14241

Printed in the United States of America

02 01 00 99 98 97 96
8   7   6   5   4   3   2   1

1

August 1776

Summer reigned in proud glory, hot and seemingly endless in the rolling, wooded countryside of New York.

To Prudence Thomas, who had never been more than twenty miles from Boston in all her eighteen years, the foliage of Manhattan Island seemed particularly lush and verdant as she rode her newly purchased Narragansett mare along the post road. She tried her best to focus on the rich green beauty surrounding her . . . anything to keep her mind off the very real possibility that her husband would be furious when she arrived at his encampment. *Please, don't let Morgan be too angry,* she prayed silently. *He knows the patriot cause is as important to me as it is to him.*

It couldn't be much farther. Almost all the traffic she had passed since crossing on the ferry an hour ago had been military. Now, as one more band of Continental soldiers marched toward her, she fought the impulse to check and see that no telltale lock of black hair had escaped her tricorn. Instead, she guided her gentle mount into a bank of moss and ferns along the edge of the roadway to allow the platoon to pass.

Up ahead she could make out a sprinkling of tents and crude wooden shelters, and her heart began to race.

She tried to convince herself that her husband's handsome

face would light up when she rode into his supply camp out of the blue. Surely he would be so overcome with joy it wouldn't matter that she had come with neither his permission nor an escort. After all, there was no longer any reason for her to remain at home, and her brother's clothes had kept her from undue attention during the journey.

Soldiers seemed to be everywhere. The prevailing air of expectancy reminded her of Boston during those months when the patriots laid siege to the Crown forces that occupied the town. Here, royal warships had been anchored in the outer bay for weeks, with more arriving by the day. Thousands of enemy soldiers gathered on Staten Island, poised to attack the port of New York, a few miles away at Manhattan's southern tip.

Nearing the conglomeration of canvas shelters, Prudence could see that it wasn't a supply camp after all. She released a tense breath and pressed onward, careful not to make eye contact with any of the men lounging idly about. How much farther could it be? Morgan had written that he was stationed a mile or so this side of New York. As quartermaster, he would be positioned a sufficient distance from the English ships.

The road before her looked deserted as it curved into the woods. Without passersby to pay her any mind, she mulled over for the hundredth time the speech she had memorized. A convincing argument and very logical, she had no doubt. But when she emerged from the trees and found herself in a large clearing filled with acres of supplies and equipment, her noble sentiments rang hollow. Trying not to pass her own skittishness on to her mare, Prudence reined in near the center cluster of makeshift buildings.

A handful of soldiers were unloading a wagon, and another pair stacked barrels against the side of a wooden shack. Nary a woman was in sight—another gaping hole in her prepared argument. But Prudence could not give in to her cowardice and leave, not after having ridden so far. At the very least she had to see Morgan. It had been so long.

Gathering her courage, she nudged the horse's sides, and the weary animal moved forward.

Just then, a strikingly tall man exited one of the large tents on the far side of the camp. She recognized Morgan's stride immediately, and her heart skipped a beat as she took in the sight of her husband. An immaculate blue and cream uniform molded itself to his strong contours, the shining boots and crisp three-cornered military hat adding to his height. His face, with its compelling planes and angles, was averted from her, the deep-set eyes hidden in the shadow of his tricorn.

To her dismay, Prudence saw her husband move swiftly to a waiting horse and swing into the saddle. He then wheeled around and trotted the chestnut Thoroughbred down the road toward New York.

There was nothing to do but chase after him, regardless of the attention she might attract crossing the compound. Perhaps it was for the best that their reunion would be out of earshot of his men. If he happened to unleash a tirade, no one would know. She urged her tired mare into a gallop.

"Morgan!" she called as she drew near.

He glanced backward, then hauled his mount to a stop. "What on earth are you doing here?"

The instant she drew abreast of him, he reached over and plucked her right off her horse, settling her across his lap.

Prudence felt her body flood with warmth as she leaned into his kiss. Evidently he, too, had longed for her over the past five lonely months.

But all too soon, the kiss came to an abrupt end. Morgan's cobalt eyes darkened to a deep indigo as he searched hers.

"How did you get here?"

"I-I rode my new mare. Isn't she beautiful?"

His even brows met in a stern line. "From where?"

"Why, Boston, of course."

Morgan's gaze raked her from head to toe. "And look at you. Wearing men's clothes again!"

Prudence felt the heat of a flush and promptly forgot every

word of the logical speech she had spent miles and miles perfecting. Only one recourse remained. "I was expecting a far more affectionate greeting," she said in her sweetest tone.

Her words did not distract him. "Please do not tell me you rode all the way from Boston by yourself."

He had always been a little too clever. Still, a wife was not a slave. Prudence mustered what little dignity she could in her present awkward position. "I did. And without the slightest problem. Certainly you must know by now that I'm perfectly capable of taking care of myself."

He shook his head in frustration. "This entire island is on the brink of blowing up in all-out war, and you pick today to come for a little visit. And what did you do with the store? Leave it in the care of your stepmother and all her babies?"

"I did not," she spewed back, highly insulted that he would even think such a thing. "My brothers have returned. I wrote and told you weeks ago."

"It's been more than a month since I've gotten a letter."

"Oh. Well, I can hardly help that," Prudence said, beginning to soften. "Word of the patriot revolt reached all the way to the Indian Ocean, you see. When Nathaniel and Zachary heard about it, they immediately set sail for home. Of course, no more had they arrived, when Nat signed on with a privateer, leaving Zachary to run *my* store. He, in typical high-handedness, expected me to go on home and help Miriam with the little ones."

Prudence thought she detected the beginnings of a smile, but Morgan quickly squelched it.

She reared back. "Oh, you're as bad as every other man. Not one of you will take a woman seriously, no matter how much you promise to do just that."

He tightened his hold and eyed her. "I take very seriously the fact that you placed yourself in jeopardy *again* by spending days on the road all alone."

"Well," she huffed, "as you can see, I'm perfectly fine. Besides, are you the only one allowed to be concerned? We've received nothing but ominous news in Boston, and you're the only husband I've got. And—" Her voice became breathy. "I missed you far more than I ever dreamed possible."

Morgan exhaled and folded her within his arms again, holding her tight.

"Please, let me stay, won't you? I could keep the supply-camp ledgers. I know how you hate dealing with those. Surely General Washington would not object to your having help."

"Washington?" He shoved her to arm's length. "I'm supposed to be at headquarters this very instant. The general himself summoned me." He maneuvered his horse closer to hers and helped her remount.

"Does he request your presence often?" she asked, impressed that the commander in chief of the Continental army would meet with her very own husband personally.

"No, only rarely. It's quite possible the British are about to commence their invasion. I do wish you hadn't chosen this moment to arrive, Prudence. But then, you do have a knack for jumping into the middle of things."

She tossed him a flippant smile. "I thought that's what you loved most about me."

Morgan stared at her for a moment, his gaze smoldering as he reached to cup her cheek. "Trust me, my dear," he returned with a very familiar smile. "That is not what I love most about you. And as you know, I've vowed never to lie again."

❦ ❦

In a straightback chair at Washington's headquarters, Morgan clicked open the cover of his pocket watch and grimaced at the lengthy wait. It had been more than two hours. But if the commander had expressly requested to see him, he must have discovered details regarding a British attack and wanted Morgan to organize the disbursement of specific supplies.

Back in his own spying days, Morgan realized with chagrin, he might have uncovered such prime information himself. Now he could only sit and wait . . . and worry about Prudence becoming impatient enough to wander from the room at the coaching inn. The streets of New York were crawling with uncouth soldiers and ne'er-do-wells. One close look at the refreshing beauty of her heart-shaped face and luminous silver eyes, and her ridiculous men's attire would be of little protection.

After all it had taken to win her love, he could not bear the thought of his fetching black-haired bride being in peril. Why could he not convince her that part of the reason for this struggle against British tyranny was to make the colonies a safe haven for his own priceless wife and the wives and children of the other colonists? And why couldn't he make her see that he would be a far better soldier if he had the peace of knowing his loved ones were out of danger?

Yet he couldn't forget how her soft words and comforting hands had eased so many in the aftermath of the Bunker Hill battle. He could still see the grateful eyes of those she had tended, men whose bodies had been ripped open by a musket ball or bayonet. Despite her usefulness, however, Morgan was not willing to have Prudence within a hundred miles of any conflict.

Expelling an impatient breath, Morgan observed the other equally anxious men pacing the anteroom as they waited for an audience with the commander in chief.

"Aye," he heard one of them remarking. "The hills of Staten Island are white from top to bottom with British tents. What are those English blackguards waiting for, more reinforcements?"

"It was bad enough to have General Howe's lobsterbacks breathing down our necks," another said. "Now that his brother, Admiral Lord Howe, sailed his fleet into our backyard with his high-priced mercenaries from Germany, I'd call that a few too many already."

Morgan couldn't resist joining in. "Don't forget General Clinton. He and his force are now out in the outer bay as well."

One of the men guffawed. "That shouldn't scare anyone. The bloke's attempt to take the southern colonies was a miserable failure. He came sailing in here still licking his wounds."

"Aye. With his tail tucked between his legs," snorted another.

"Morgan Thomas," a voice announced from an open doorway.

At last! He unfolded himself from the uncomfortable seat and strode into the large book-lined room where General Washington sat behind a desk. Struck, as always, by the commanding presence of the Continental army's leader, Morgan gave a sharp salute. "Reporting as ordered, sir."

Washington rose and returned the salute, then extended his big hand with a weary smile. "Lieutenant Thomas."

"At your service, sir."

The general nodded. "Have a seat, Lieutenant." Indicating a chair facing the large mahogany desk, he sank back down to his own. "I've a mission, a vital one, I'd like you to handle. I won't order it, but I do hope you'll volunteer. I can't think of anyone as suited for the job."

The last statement particularly piqued Morgan's interest, and he was more than flattered. "Of course you can count on me, sir. I'll do whatever you ask."

"It might be prudent to wait until you've heard me out," Washington said, his gaze unflinching. "Your name was put to me by some of your fellow officers. They report that your spying activities in Philadelphia and Boston remain to this day undetected—that you somehow managed to skirt the blame for all those Tory ships which were diverted to the cause."

"I believe that's true. From what I've been able to discern, no Loyalist other than my father has any knowledge of my subversive work, and he has promised to keep silent."

The general's pox-scarred countenance brightened considerably. He leaned forward, resting his forearms on the open maps spread across the desktop. "It's gratifying to hear that one of the staunchest Tory merchants in all of Philadelphia is wavering in his resolve to support the British. You're quite positive you can trust your father, Lieutenant?"

"Completely. He would not betray his son. As he once put it, 'Political differences come and go, but family is forever.'"

"I only hope that is true, lad," he said, eyeing him steadily, "because I need your services again."

Morgan raised his brows. Being dispatched on a secret mission would solve his problem with Prudence. He would be obliged to send her back to Boston, where she'd be much safer.

"I need someone I can trust in Philadelphia," Washington went on, scarcely stopping for breath. "Someone who'll attend all the parties, the theater, be included in all the gala events and gatherings. The British army has been close-mouthed with the New York Loyalists. My spies have gleaned nothing. Perhaps letters to their Philadelphia friends have been somewhat less discreet. I seriously doubt Crown secrets would be so closely guarded that far from the battlefield."

"Philadelphia," Morgan declared flatly, trying to cover his disappointment. Back to living the useless life of a Tory dandy among his family's friends. He sighed. "I'll do as you wish, sir."

"Splendid, Lieutenant! Splendid." The general rose. "Then I shall dispatch you immediately. It's imperative for us to ferret out information regarding when General Howe plans to launch his attack."

❦ ❦

Morgan trudged wearily up the enclosed staircase of the coaching inn where he had deposited Prudence in a rented room. A part of him couldn't help worrying that she'd gotten bored and wandered out on the street. He had been gone a long time, and it was now late afternoon. With some trepidation, he inserted the brass key into the lock and opened the door.

Morgan smiled at the sight that greeted him. His new wife lay asleep on the bed, looking soft and angelic, her fine features outlined by the subdued window light. Awake, her feisty spirit came swiftly to the fore, but now . . . ah, now, he could revel in her fragile beauty. She was so much more than he had ever hoped for, so different from the raft of simpering, manipulative females his mother had constantly prodded in his direction, mirror images of his mother herself. Unable to resist, he bent down and brushed his lips across hers.

She stirred, and her lashes fluttered open. "You're back," she murmured in a sleepy voice, a tender smile on her lips. Then the smile vanished, and she sat up. "You left me for hours in this dreary place."

Not at all perturbed by how quickly she came to herself, Morgan sank down beside her and took her into his arms, bestowing a promising kiss on her upturned lips. "I know, my sweet. But I'm afraid it could not be helped. I had to wait my turn to see General Washington."

She melted against him. "What did he want?"

"That I go at once to Philadelphia to spy for him."

"Philadelphia!" Prudence drew away slightly and looked up at him. "Why, that's wonderful!"

"Won't you miss me even a little?" he asked, deflated by her response.

"How can I, when I'll be right there with you?"

"I think not. I'm going to arrange to have you escorted safely home."

Her loosened topknot shifted off-kilter as she shook her head. "Just listen to yourself, sweetheart. Wouldn't it look more than a little suspicious for you to return to your own family's home without bringing your new wife along with you?"

He breathed out slowly. "I'll simply tell them the truth. That you have a store to look after and aren't able at the moment to shirk those duties."

"I'm sure *that* will please your parents," she said with a frown. "They'll be thrilled to learn that their son has married a common shopkeeper."

Morgan tightened his embrace. "You are not common," he insisted fiercely. "Besides, all I care about is getting you home, where you'll be safe and out of trouble."

In one fluid motion, Prudence withdrew from his arms and sprang to her feet. "I know in my heart I was meant to be of great service to the cause. I've always known it. If God didn't want me to serve, then he wouldn't have instilled within me this compelling need to do so."

Morgan also rose and squared off, his nose a mere fraction from hers. "And if I had a burning desire to go downstairs and get myself roaring drunk, would that, too, be God's will for me right now? or simply my own wish to escape this endless argument?"

With a huff, Prudence crossed her arms and presented her back. "Very well. We shan't argue about it anymore."

"Then you agree not to go?"

"Certainly not."

Though she put up minor resistance, Morgan turned her around and grasped her upper arms. "What you're suggesting could get us both hanged. You know that, don't you?"

A spark of stubbornness flashed in her eyes. "You don't consider me clever enough to prevent that?"

"Cleverness has nothing to do with it," he said gently. "Spying is a very subtle art. One must be able to move about with undue notice, and you are incredibly lovely. Who wouldn't notice you? And you've never socialized in the circles I grew up in. You've no concept of the accepted mode of dress, the particular way city belles have of talking, flirting, conducting themselves. Not that I have any desire to have you putting on those kinds of airs in the first place. I love you the way you are. That's what drew me to you, what made me want you for my wife."

"But as your wife, I *need* to help you. I can learn whatever is required. You can teach me. I'm a very fast learner, you'll see. And, my dear husband, I am not averse to obtaining a fashionable wardrobe. In times like these, old standards must be put aside for the greater good."

He hugged her to his chest. "Prudence, Prudence. What am I going to do with you?"

"You're going to teach me how to become a proper wife. After all, I do happen to be married to a prominent member of the merchant class of Philadelphia. It's high time I acquired the necessary graces required to be an asset to you."

Gazing down into her shimmering eyes, Morgan felt his pulse gathering intensity. "You have no idea what you're asking. If you knew my mother, you'd turn around right now and run for your life. All through my youth she was determined to handpick the belle I wed. Even if your manner and mode of dress were absolutely perfect, she would never forget that you weren't her personal choice. I shudder to think of how abominably she'll treat you."

"And I," she whispered with an impish smile, "will be all sweetness and charm to her. I'm ever so clever, you know."

A muffled boom rattled the windowpane, followed by another.

Morgan grabbed her hand and rushed with her to the window, flinging open the sash. "What's happened?" he shouted down to the street.

"More British ships are sailing in," someone hollered back. "The tubs at anchor are giving them a cannon salute."

Exhaling, Morgan settled back onto his heels and drew Prudence close again—but not before he caught the glint of excitement in her eyes. Suddenly a heavy realization all but pressed the air from his lungs.

Left on her own, his beautiful bride would always get herself dangerously close to the fray. Like it or not, he would never have peace of mind unless he knew her whereabouts at all times.

But how much safer would she be as an accomplice to a spy?

Prudence adjusted to a more comfortable stance atop the stool in the dressmaker's shop. Elated at the thought of actually accompanying Morgan to Philadelphia rather than being sent back to live with her stepmother, she found herself more than enjoying the experience of having a gown expertly fitted to her by two nimble-fingered women.

"It's truly a pity," Mistress Jennings, the proprietor, remarked around the straight pins clenched between her thin lips. "Maddie and I could have sewn some new frocks for you if you could've waited a few days." Small and slight as a broomstick, she removed the remaining three pins and put them in place one by one along the seam she was adjusting. "Of course, these lovely secondhand gowns your husband purchased for you cannot be faulted. He has an excellent eye for fabric and fashion."

Prudence had to restrain a giggle as the plump fingers of the employee called Maddie gathered a fold of excess material at Prudence's waist, tickling her in the process. She tried not to breathe too hard, lest she hinder either woman's work.

"'Tis a wonder 'e managed to find three day gowns in such marvelous condition," Maddie said in her thick London accent.

"We did have to rummage through five used-clothing shops before anything caught his attention," Prudence admitted. "He seemed to know exactly what he was seeking."

"Ah, but this apricot lawn is exquisite," Mistress Jennings said, taking a few steps back, her blue eyes critically assessing her handiwork. "It must have belonged to a very rich merchant's lady."

Maddie wagged her braided head and clucked her tongue. "*Spoiled* merchant's lady'd be more like it, I'd say." She tied off a final stitch, then snipped the thread. "Couldn't 'ave been worn but once or twice."

"I'm really sorry you've both been put to such an unduly quick task," Prudence said. "But my husband and I are in extreme haste and must leave your fine city to go to Philadelphia. He wants to be sure his own merchant family will find no fault with my appearance. We New Englanders, I'm afraid, tend to be quite conservative in our dress."

Two pairs of sharp eyes swung to her plain, gray linen gown, draped over the back of a chair. The women exchanged a wordless glance, but at least they had the grace not to smile.

"I'm glad I set up shop here in New York," the owner said, reaching to check the shoulders and lace-edged sleeves on Prudence's frock. "I would find Boston somewhat . . . tiresome."

The comment, though said without rancor, might have incited Prudence to indignation. But as a spy she was convinced she must learn to adapt to new places and new situations—blend in, rather than draw attention. Still, she couldn't help but take stock of the excessively bright bolts of fabric lining the shelves behind the counter, the jars of colored beads and bouquets of dyed feathers. Several dress forms bore gaudy party gowns in various stages of progress. Obviously the women of this city had no qualms about arraying themselves like strutting peacocks. "From things my husband has told me, I assume the ladies of Philadelphia dress much the same as those here in New York."

"If not even more elegantly," Mistress Jennings said as Maddie fluffed out the sweeping skirt of Prudence's gown and checked to see that it draped evenly. "You'll find you'll need many more afternoon and evening gowns than these three."

Prudence felt a jolt of excitement. That also meant there would be an abundance of spying opportunities . . . beyond her imaginings.

The proprietor stepped away and joined Maddie, eyeing the finished product.

"And all three done before your husband came back for you," Maddie said with a nod. She brushed perspiration from her damp forehead. "Seemed he was in a bit of a lather to get on the road."

Mistress Jennings shrugged. "Perhaps, with General Howe's ship anchored off the Long Island coast, Lieutenant Thomas wants to escort his bride to safety before the British start bombarding us in earnest."

"Or worse," Maddie said, her faded brown eyes wide. "Unruly and uncouth as those former countrymen of mine were in Boston, with us at war now, no woman along the seaboard will be safe from bein' ravaged."

"I wouldn't be borrowing trouble, Maddie," the head seamstress remarked. "Our brave boys drove them out of Boston. They'll do no less here. Certainly are enough of them underfoot," she added, chuckling.

"Aye, they—" Maddie, on the verge of elaborating, caught Prudence staring. She flushed and cleared her throat. "Well, now. We've got you properly dressed—except for the hair. We'll see what Florence, next door, can do about that severe bun of yours." She snatched Prudence's hand, pulling her to a chair. "Sit."

❧ ❧

Robert Chandler watched his two closest friends strap a secondhand trunk to the packhorse Morgan had just obtained.

"What do you say, Robby?" he heard Morgan ask the younger Scotsman, whose wiry frame had acquired strong muscles from his former duties as a wheelwright. "Think it's secure?" He yanked at the straps, testing them.

Narrowing his clear blue eyes to appraise the load, Robby MacKinnon raked fingers through his thatch of black hair, then replaced his tricornered hat. "Aye, 'tis secure."

"Excellent." Morgan brushed off his hands. "Then it should hold all the extras I've had to purchase today. It wasn't my plan to take Prudence home to my family so suddenly, but if I don't, heaven only knows what folly she'll get herself into."

Chan shook his head in disapproval, amazed that his friend had not taken time to consider the daftness of such a hasty decision. "Do you think allowing her to be part of your spying venture is safe?"

"Not entirely." Morgan looked at him in frustration. "What I'm hoping is that by the time we arrive in Philadelphia, I will have convinced her that she'll be my greatest asset by becoming so enchantingly distracting that attention will be diverted from me."

Robby leaned against the horse's rump with a chuckle. "'Enchantingly distracting'? Our Prudence—the Puritan? the Yankee-thrift shopkeeper? That'll take a bit more than convincin'. I doubt she even dances."

Morgan pulled a wry grimace, then brightened. "Imagine how many people she'll be able to enlist to teach her the fine art. In fact, there's a jeweler yonder. Perhaps I'll find her some earbobs to wear with her new gowns. Come on."

"Say, Morgan," Chandler remarked as they headed toward the jewelry shop. "Prudence went out of her way to be kind to Robby and me when we were repairing the store. Would you be opposed to my picking up some little trinket in appreciation?"

"Not at all. And I'm sure she'd be pleased as well."

Chandler, drawn to a heart-shaped locket displayed in the window, lagged behind as the other two entered the shop. Habitually, he pulled the similar one of Julia's from his fob pocket and smoothed his fingers over it. It was the one keepsake of hers that he had kept near his own heart.

He looked again at the one in the window. On a simpler chain and not quite so intricately filigreed as Julia's, it was beautiful in its own quiet way. Perhaps Prudence would admire its simple elegance. With a last long look at Julia's locket, he tucked the treasure back into its haven and went inside.

In a surprisingly short time, Morgan found two pairs of earbobs and a fancy comb for Prudence's hair and gave them to the clerk to wrap.

Meanwhile, Robby decided against a cameo brooch he had been admiring and instead placed a bracelet of inlaid silver on the counter for his wife, Emily.

"Splendid choice." Chandler put the locket that would soon belong to Prudence near Emily's present. The simple locket would suit Prudence, he was certain—just as the more elaborate design had suited his wife.

Moments later, their gifts tucked away, the men arrived at Estelle Jennings's dress shop. The tiny bell above the door announced their entrance.

Three women near the back of the establishment glanced up. The one seated in the center, willowy and dark haired, rose gracefully. The small smile on her lips added astonishing beauty to an already perfect face as she glided toward them. "How wonderful, Morgan. You found them both!"

Chandler stared in wonder at the transformation before his eyes. When last he had seen Prudence, she had worn her typically austere dress beneath a crisp starched apron and house cap, with her waist-length hair tied at the nape of her neck. But now, wearing a lavish apricot gown cut surprisingly low and her glorious black hair piled in a swirl of curls and peach ribbons, she was a vision. An absolute vision. He swallowed.

"Robby!" she gushed, drawing him into a warm hug before turning to Chandler. "And Chan! So lovely to see my two Roberts again. Though you, Chan, appear to have lost weight again—and after those pains I took to fatten you up. What a shame."

Morgan closed his own gaping mouth. "You make him sound like a pig," he said teasingly. "One you were trying to ready for market." He paused momentarily and shook his head, lost in the sight of his bride. "Here, let me take a good look at you."

Blushing, Prudence smiled and tilted her head, her silver eyes dancing as she turned in a slow, fluid circle.

"I daresay," he remarked, letting out a whoosh of breath, "you've never looked more enchanting. I do believe even my mother will be forced to approve."

The shop owner tapped Morgan's arm. "Your wife said that you haven't purchased a powdered wig for evening as yet. I've a friend in Philadelphia who makes the most glamorous wigs in the entire city."

"If that is so," Morgan answered cheerfully, "without a doubt, my mother and sisters have already found her." He returned his gaze to Prudence as he took the package from his breast pocket. "These may complement that enticing gown, love."

"Why, thank you." Nibbling her lip, she untied the ribbon and removed the wrapping. A sparkle lit her eyes when she discovered the diamond earbobs. "Oh, how very lovely. They're just beautiful! I've never owned anything so exquisite." She raised on tiptoe and gave him a kiss, then held one of the bobs to her ear for him to admire.

Chandler couldn't have spoken then if his life had depended on it. He was caught in misty memories of gifts he had bestowed upon Julia during their short time together. Her responses had been much the same as Prudence's, and the recollection stabbed at his heart.

"No one will ever know I'm a fraud, sweetheart," Prudence said gaily, going to a looking glass to try on her new jewelry. "I'll try very hard to make you proud of me."

"You're no fraud, young lady," the seamstress assured her. "You're every inch a lady."

But Chandler caught Prudence's deeper meaning . . . that she, the staunch patriot, hoped to assume the role of a Loyalist in a city of Crown supporters. Yet as honest and forthright as she'd always been, and outspoken to a fault, he had to wonder if she would be able to pull off the deception for long. For her sake and Morgan's, he prayed she would.

Chandler retrieved the little package from his pocket and placed it in her hand. "I, too, saw something I hoped you might like."

"Why, I don't know what to say. How thoughtful." She tugged the ribbon free and spread the paper open, exposing the locket. She raised her eyes to his.

"It reminded me of the shape and beauty of your face. I hope it'll remind you of the pleasant times Robby and I spent with you."

Prudence lifted the fragile chain. "I'll think of you both whenever I wear it. Thank you." After clasping it around her neck, she touched it lightly, then turned to him and Robby. "And while Morgan and I are away, you both must be careful. Really careful. Chandler, I'd better not hear ever again about your being the last to leave a battle scene, as you were at Bunker Hill. I insist that both of you dig the deepest trenches for yourselves and don't take foolish risks. I don't wish to think of you as dead heroes—and Robby, neither does Emily, I'm sure."

Morgan stepped to her side and slid a proprietary arm around her slender waist. "That goes double for me. After all, I won't be around to look after you—"

"You have a job of your own to concentrate on now," Chandler interrupted sternly. "Looking after your wife. Nothing in this life is more important, believe me." He clamped a hand on Morgan's shoulder. "Promise me y'all won't get so caught up in the game that you lose sight of that. Promise."

The stout helper tittered in the background. "Truly, Lieutenant Thomas has nothin' to worry about concernin' his little wife. These gowns are all of the latest fashion. No one will fault them—*or* her."

Chan suddenly realized he had almost betrayed their confidence. He dropped his hand and stepped back, collecting himself. "Of-of course. There could be no fault to find in someone so . . . lovely." Then, before he uttered anything else that might place them under suspicion—or anything that might disclose the morose thoughts threatening to swamp him—he tipped his head. "Farewell, my friends. I'll be thinking about you night and day."

3

Prudence fanned herself with her hand, but the slight breeze did little to assuage the mugginess of the hot day as she and Morgan rode their horses over the cobbled streets of Philadelphia.

Compared to New York, she found the "Red Brick City" much more attractive, with its streets neatly laid out in a grid, its brick buildings symmetrical and elegant. Many of the fashionable homes were lavish, indeed. Even the trees and shrubbery appeared well tended. The townspeople they passed were attired in finely tailored clothing, and those who recognized Morgan seemed especially amiable.

But she did have definite qualms about meeting Morgan's well-to-do family. "How much farther is it to your parents' home?"

Oddly enough, her husband didn't look much more at ease himself. "Before I take you there, I plan to stop at my father's warehouses."

Prudence knew that Morgan was anxious to discover if his Loyalist father had experienced a change of heart since his last letter. The man's response to Morgan's written confession had been a surprise, to be sure. Mr. Thomas, after a considerable span of silence, corresponded by claiming he had forgiven Morgan for swindling him and his fellow businessmen by diverting their cargo to the patriot cause. He had decided to remain silent about the matter.

"I'm sure you realize that should Father have changed his mind about me and betrayed me to his business associates, we will have come here for naught," Morgan continued. "But now that I think about it, perhaps that would be best. I could take you back to Boston and return to my duties with the army."

Prudence arched her brows. "You'll not get rid of me quite so easily, Morgan Thomas."

"It's far more than that, sweetheart. If you'll recall, a few short months ago I made a vow to the Lord to stop lying. Now here I am, all too ready to lie and spy again. The two go hand in hand."

Reaching to give his arm a squeeze, Prudence offered him an encouraging smile. "We've already talked about this, haven't we? Don't forget how Moses sent spies into the land of Canaan. Joshua and others also sent out spies. It's part of the process of war—and I truly believe deep within my heart that we are in a holy war just like those in the Bible. If we remain faithful to the cause and do not become weary or faint of heart, God will be faithful to us."

"I know, I know. And afterward," he went on, parroting earlier statements she had made, "we'll have the freedom to worship almighty God as we see fit, to decide how our taxes are spent, to trade with any country we choose." His exasperation was far from comforting as he exhaled wearily, guiding his mount around a freight wagon directly ahead of them.

A sudden surge of guilt caught her off guard. *But am I right?* she wondered. *Or am I his Eve? his Delilah?* She immediately rejected such inane comparisons. Tapping her quirt, she caught up to Morgan. "Sweetheart, please don't be upset with me."

"You know you're not the problem, Prudence," he answered quietly. "It's the complexity of lying on a grand scale that worries me. Keeping all the stories straight, knowing what I've said to one person and what I've said to someone else. Floating on a sea of lies is very harrowing."

It did sound ominous, put that way. Prudence pondered his

comments for a few silent moments. "But *together* we'll help each other not to forget. We've rehearsed our story often enough. And this time you won't be alone. I'll be here with you. We can do this, Morgan. We can. You'll see. We'll be wonderful, working together, praying together, helping each other. We can do it."

With a thin smile, he tenderly brushed a lock of hair behind her ear. "You have the faith of a child, love. If only I could see with the same clarity."

Another stab of uneasiness made it harder to maintain her own reassuring smile. She *was* beginning to see . . . far more clearly than she was willing to admit.

As they approached the waterfront district, she could hear the noise and bustle, the increased traffic and shouting hawkers, the clatter of goods being loaded aboard ship or hefted down gangplanks. She saw the name *Thomas* emblazoned across several warehouses—huge, looming buildings that testified to the power of Morgan's family. They were more than merely affluent. They were very wealthy, indeed.

Morgan reined in at the largest of the warehouses and dismounted, then turned to her. "I probably should have given you an opportunity to change into one of your new gowns before reaching the city. But I've told my father a bit about your strict New England background. I think he'll rather appreciate your simplicity. Aside from his ruthless business dealings, you'll find he's quite a decent sort."

Prudence blanched and pushed his hands away the instant her feet touched the ground. "You think I'm a simpleton?"

With a laugh, Morgan grabbed her and hugged her. "You, my dearest? a simpleton? By no means. But when you meet the women in my family, you'll discover I've just paid you a sincere compliment." He released her and placed an arm around her waist. "Come along, we'll find Father."

The cool interior of the building provided welcome relief from the sticky heat outside. Prudence blinked as her eyes adjusted to the shade. She was taken aback by the vast amount of open space everywhere.

So, apparently, was Morgan. "I've never seen it so empty," he remarked, looking around with a frown.

Prudence surveyed the cavernous structure. Morgan had more than proven how inventive he was in procuring supplies for her own new mercantile, as well as for the patriots. Perhaps he now experienced guilt over having left his father's service. If the Loyalists of Boston ever discovered the ways in which he had diverted their shipments to the Continental army, his career as a spy—not to mention his life—would be in dire jeopardy.

"I can see how sorely my presence here was needed," Morgan admitted. "By now it has become all but impossible to get a Tory merchant shipment past the British navy—or the patriot privateers, for that matter."

"Do try not to feel bad about it," Prudence said in reassurance. "No matter how many shiploads of men and cannons the British send, with God on our side the patriots will win. I'm sure the war will not outlast the summer."

"I pray you're right."

Scraping and muffled thuds of crates being moved echoed from the opposite end of the warehouse. From above them, a man on a catwalk gave a sharp whistle, then shouted directions.

"Father!" Morgan called out with a wave. Grabbing Prudence's hand, he hastened toward an open staircase.

When they paused on the top landing, Prudence bit back her nervousness as the distinguished gentleman approached them.

Not quite as tall as Morgan, yet somehow almost as handsome, he made no effort to disguise his delight. Dark blue eyes crimped at the corners as a wide smile lifted his well-shaped lips. His neatly combed hair was somewhat less abundant than Morgan's, but it was the same rich shade of brown, with a sprinkling of gray at the temples. "Well, well," he said, spreading his arms open as he neared. "You've finally come." Wasting no time at all on proprieties, he embraced his son exuberantly.

"I was afraid you might have changed your mind," Morgan admitted, "considering my rather thoughtless betrayal of you and your friends."

"Well, be that as it may, Son, it's in the past. And best forgotten. I'm extremely glad to have you back where you belong." He released Morgan and took Prudence's arms. "And you, my dear, would have to be Prudence." His slow gaze took in her plain riding attire but revealed neither approval nor disapproval. It was a relief when he smiled warmly. "What a delightful surprise."

After a moment he turned back to Morgan. "Well, Son, left to your own devices, you've done admirably well. Admirably, indeed. She's quite flawless. With an added frill here and there, not even your mother will be able to find fault."

Instead of easing her tension, his complimentary words increased Prudence's disquiet. She had heard only curious, guarded remarks about the "Lady" Thomas.

"Have you told Mother about my marriage?" Morgan asked.

Embarrassment tilted the older man's awkward grin. "If I'd had word you were coming, I would have had the chance to prepare her. But no, I'm afraid not."

Morgan nodded, his expression obviously worried. He recovered quickly and flicked a casual glance at Prudence, but he was a few seconds too late. "Actually," he said to his father, "this trip was unexpected—and when I disclose the reason behind it, you may be less than happy I've come." He drew Prudence close. "I've been sent back here to spy again—*if* I've not already been exposed, of course. General Washington feels I can be of far more use here than with the army in New York."

Mr. Thomas's countenance, which had sagged noticeably within the last few seconds, darkened even more.

"Have I been found out?" Morgan asked.

The older man shook his head. "No. But—"

"I'm more than aware how difficult this whole thing is for

you, sir. I'll turn around and go back to New York at once if you ask me to."

Mr. Thomas searched his son's face for a moment, obviously mulling over the disturbing news he had just been given. Then he inhaled a deep breath and slowly released it. He placed a hand on Morgan's shoulder. "To be quite honest, I never once thought Pennsylvania would succumb to rebellion's call. We've always been the most reasonable, the most civilized of all the colonies. But since Ben Franklin returned from London, he's been chipping away little by little at the people's resolve. Of course, that dissertation of Thomas Paine's, *Common Sense,* has fueled the fervor. Then last month even William Penn signed that fool Declaration of Independence, so our colony has now aligned itself with all the other radicals intent upon shedding the motherland once and for all."

Prudence looked from one grim face to the other. There was a distinct resemblance, not only in the stance of the two men, but in the way they held their heads, in their stalwart features. When Mr. Thomas glowered, Prudence could see Morgan in his eyes.

"When I told your mother about it," he went on, "she became quite hysterical. She's convinced there'll be no stopping the rebels now, that they'll burn us out—or worse."

"I wouldn't expect that sort of thing here in Philadelphia," Morgan said. "At least, not for the time being. After all, the Congress meets here. They'll want to appear as legitimate as possible. Allowing mobs to run amok in the streets would be most detrimental."

"Yes. I hadn't thought about it in that light. I do pray you're right." The older man pulled a wry grimace. "As a Loyalist, maybe the best insurance I could have against fire is the presence of my rebel son in the house."

"It would be . . . but only if my true affiliation were discovered." Morgan paused significantly to let the words sink in.

"Ah, well . . ." Morgan's father cocked his head. "I'm becoming more and more a man with two faces myself. I once was dead certain exactly who was right and who was wrong in the world of politics. But I have serious doubts now." He exhaled in frustration. "I just don't want to lose all that I've worked for all these years. Most particularly, I don't want to lose you. I'll be no hindrance . . . but neither will I assist you. I hope you can understand that."

Morgan nodded, and Prudence saw him relax slightly. "I thank you for that, Father."

The older man stepped closer and hugged him hard. "I'm so delighted to have you back, Son. It's a comfort that you'll be away from New York when the British do finally decide to attack."

His sincerity touched Prudence deeply. Perhaps in business dealings he might be considered ruthless, as Morgan termed it, but he certainly had the utmost respect and love for his son. It made her feel closer to her distinguished father-in-law.

"Is there some private place where Prudence might change into something more elegant, sir?" Morgan asked with a grin. "I'm about to introduce her as my very wealthy, very loyal, *Tory* bride."

"You're not serious!"

Morgan chuckled and gestured graciously toward Prudence. "Yes, Father. My beautiful, hardheaded Yankee insists upon being my fellow conspirator."

❧ ❧

"He's . . . *married?*" The woman's gasp carried remarkably well from upstairs. So did the ensuing silence.

Prudence stood like a statue, afraid to draw a breath.

Morgan, beside her in the mansion's marble foyer, chuckled as he squeezed her hand and gave an excessively nonchalant shrug.

Running footsteps echoed from the floor above. "What's happened, Mama?" a younger voice asked. Then a door clicked shut, leaving only muted voices . . . but the flustered tones and exclamations were surprisingly distinct.

Prudence chewed the inside corner of her lip. "Perhaps we should come back later. . . ."

"Oh, don't despair," Morgan said. "She'll recover from the shock quite quickly, you'll see. Mother's amazingly . . . *adaptable*, when she has to be. However, if you'd like, we might take a walk in the garden." He led her across the hall and through the magnificent ballroom to a bank of glass doors opening onto a flagstone veranda.

The fresh air, sweet with the perfume of roses and other late summer flowers, wafted over Prudence like a blessing. Despite the immensity of the huge home, she had begun to feel confined, strangled. Now she drew a strengthening breath and tried to shrug off her dread while Morgan strolled with her to an intricate fountain flanked by curved marble benches. For several minutes, she watched the slender arches of crystal water shooting from the mouths of a trio of dolphins.

"I would love to have seen Mother's face when Father broke the news," Morgan said, the rakish gleam in his eye adding to his devilish grin. "High drama is her dearest forte."

Prudence, trying unsuccessfully to lose herself in the grandeur of immaculate hedges and exquisite flowers, dragged her gaze from them and looked disapprovingly at her husband. "That sounds uncommonly callous of you."

"Quite right." He reddened. "I suppose over time I've become insensitive to Mother's theatrics and manipulations. But be alert, my love. She is a formidable adversary. Never let down your guard around her. As they say, forewarned is forearmed."

Unable to truly believe such alarming statements, Prudence turned to face him. "And you, my dear husband, are more than clever yourself. Methinks you're trying to scare me into returning to Massachusetts." Taking his hands in hers, she looked directly into his eyes. "But home for me is wherever you happen to be."

"Then this, dear child," a well-modulated female voice said, "is surely your home. We have no intention of allowing our son out of our sight again for a very, very long time."

Prudence turned with Morgan and saw a stately woman of medium build coming toward them on Mr. Thomas's arm. Her corseted figure matched perfectly the contours of the understated gold taffeta gown she wore. A lace cap hid some of the silvering strands amid the elaborately dressed, dark brown hair, and her eyes, nearly the same cobalt blue as Morgan's, stopped just short of smiling. Prudence was more than relieved to see a distinctly pleasant expression on the woman's oval face, especially when she reached out a tapered and manicured hand in welcome.

A younger girl, dark-haired and appealing, stood a few steps behind and off to one side, but she did not speak.

"Welcome, my dear," Morgan's mother said. "Welcome to the family."

Taking the proffered hand with its jeweled rings, Prudence dipped into a polite curtsy. "Thank you, Mistress Thomas. I've been so looking forward to meeting you." Surely Morgan, for some reason known only to him, must have exaggerated, she told herself. Mrs. Thomas couldn't have been more gracious.

"And, Morgan," she went on, sweeping a glance to him with arched brows, "such a lovely bride you've brought us. I do commend your choice—though you are, nonetheless, a most naughty boy. With all the trouble that brewed up in Boston, you might at least have sent us word regarding your well-being, especially when you were held in that city's siege by those unsavory outlaws. When the situation worsened to such a degree that all those loyal to the Crown had to retreat to Halifax with the British, you must have known we'd be concerned."

"I've no excuse for my thoughtless neglect," he admitted. Smiling sheepishly, he took her shoulders and kissed her on both cheeks.

She gave him no chance to elaborate further. "And now you've finally come home, just as handsome and unscathed as ever, *and* with a new bride. We do have considerable catching up to do, don't we?"

"That's a fact, Mother."

"Well, you must tell us everything. And what of Dan, Sophia Haynes's son, up in Boston? I assume he, too, was trapped in that city during the besiegement, along with that—wife—of his. You remember, don't you, Waldon," she went on, tilting her head toward her husband, "that bondservant he married to spite his poor, dear mother?"

Prudence felt a sudden chill.

4

Though every last word his mother uttered to Prudence had been gracious, *excessively* so, Morgan could not escape the conviction that the woman's actual feelings were anything but accepting. After having endured her scheming and manipulation throughout his entire life—her attempts at arranging an advantageous marriage for him, in particular—he knew she had to be in high dudgeon over his having taken matters into his own hands. He could only wonder how long this farce would last before her true emotions came to the surface.

As the family meandered back up the walkway to the house, his mother gestured toward Morgan's sister. "Our Evelyn, I'm delighted to say, has a young admirer taking supper with us this eve—Clayborne Judson Raleigh. He's in the colonies with his father, a tobacco buyer."

"Is that so?" Morgan asked, catching up to his youngest sibling. He slid an arm around her narrow waist and hugged her.

Evelyn smiled becomingly, adding striking beauty to her fragile feminine features . . . but the guileless smile lost some of its appeal when spoiled by a self-satisfied glimmer in her pale blue eyes. "A very rich tobacco buyer with close royal ties," she announced proudly.

Morgan thought he had detected a change in the winsome fifteen-year-old when he first glimpsed her flying to Mother's room a short while ago, and his suspicions were confirmed by both her carriage and her reply. She had blossomed in the time since he went to Boston. During his absence, not only had she become a captivating young woman, but evidently she had been Mother's apt pupil as well—molded in her image.

His spirits sank. So far he hadn't found it necessary to speak less than truthfully, but how long would that last? On this, his very first night home, there would be some British pup to entertain. "What about Frances?" he asked, returning his attention to his parents.

His mother fluttered her hand. "Why, your sister has made a most fortuitous match *while you were incommunicado,*" she answered pointedly, "to Bradford Hendricks, that young man she had been seeing before you went away. He's from a good British family, you recall, and has now been made an officer of the king's army. Your sister returned with him to England. Southampton, to be precise. Of course we miss her terribly. Your father and I are already planning a trip there next summer—if this awful rebellion business doesn't prevent us from doing so."

"It was the *loveliest* spring wedding," Evelyn murmured dreamily. "Wasn't it, Mother?" She reached the back door ahead of the others, opened it, and went inside ahead of them.

"Absolutely," her mother gushed as they crossed the ballroom again. "Even though the worst troublemakers from all the colonies were stirring up a hornet's nest over at Carpenter's Hall. 'The Continental Congress,' they call themselves." She sighed and shook her head in distaste. "We do our best to ignore them. But sometimes . . ."

Morgan met Prudence's gaze and squeezed her hand as they returned to the foyer. "Speaking of married couples, you might be interested to hear that Dan and Susannah are now living in northeastern Pennsylvania's wilderness." He watched his mother's eyebrows arch. "By the time of the Boston siege, their church had been sacked by the British, and most of the city's Presbyterians had left. Dan has been sent to start a new flock in the Wyoming Valley."

"You don't say," his father remarked. "That's the place we've been disputing with Connecticut regarding ownership, is it not?"

"Quite right. But from what I understand, the settlers there have switched to fighting the British."

"It's enough to make one swoon," his mother said, fanning herself. "Sophia Haynes must be beside herself, knowing her oldest son is forever embroiling himself in one hotbed of revolt or another. Thank heaven you've kept a cool head on your shoulders. If those Continental delegates have their way, everything we've ever worked for will go to rack and ruin." She pursed her lips.

"I agree wholeheartedly," Prudence chimed in.

Morgan held his breath, waiting to hear what she would say next.

"Without the civilizing influence of the mother country," his wife went on smoothly, "these colonies will degenerate into an uncouth rabble, as did my own poor dear Boston."

Flabbergasted at the depth of Prudence's sincerity, Morgan could not believe someone who had always held the truth in highest reverence would now utter lies without a qualm—and after she had once found his own dishonor toward his parents so sinful.

A manservant hired in Morgan's absence walked into the foyer. "You needed me, madam?"

Mother considered the small trunk and valise Morgan and Prudence had left sitting in the marbled entry, and she frowned slightly. "Yes. See that their luggage is taken upstairs, Charles."

"It pains me to admit it," Prudence said as the uniformed man complied, "but I'm afraid your son married an impoverished woman. During the siege, my family's home and business were wantonly burned to the ground by the most despicable criminals."

At least that much was true, Morgan conceded. The Crown

forces did cannonade her family's house and store—and she did consider them despicable. Yet she seemed to possess amazing skill at twisting the truth, and that made him very uncomfortable.

"I've scarcely more than the clothes on my back, now," Prudence went on coyly. She shrugged a shoulder in helpless embarrassment.

"Why, my dear." Mother stepped near and took her hand. "How absolutely dreadful. What you must have suffered." She turned to her husband. "I'm telling you, Waldon, if something is not done soon, the same fate could be ours."

Prudence rushed to Morgan's side, her eyes enormous and frightened. "You told me we'd be safe here. You promised."

Even to him her charade appeared convincing. He put an arm about her as he caught the twinkle in his father's eye.

"Never you worry, dear," Mother cooed, patting Prudence's shoulder. "That won't actually happen in this city. Will it, Waldon?"

"Of course not," he answered. "This is, after all, the City of Brotherly Love."

Prudence pulled a kerchief from Morgan's pocket and dabbed elaborately at nonexistent tears, then swung back to his mother. "And merry, isn't it?" She sniffed. "I've always heard Philadelphia is very lively. Even with this bothersome trouble, there are still parties and plays and balls. Morgan has promised to take me to all of them—and in an entirely new wardrobe, too. Fashioned from the latest Paris fabrics and designs." She whirled around to him. "He's quite the dearest thing, isn't he?" Her back to the others, she winked as she raised on tiptoe to kiss his cheek.

Morgan realized, to his dismay, that she was having the time of her life!

His mother, coming near once more, placed an arm about her and turned her around, leading her toward the curved staircase. "Why, of course you shall. The wife of my only son does have a certain *standard* to maintain when we introduce her to our friends. But first, come upstairs, and I'll show you to your room. You must be exhausted from your long journey. You can rest awhile before supper. Afterward we can discuss which fabrics and colors will set you off to your best advantage. Your eyes, of course, are your greatest asset."

Evelyn wasted no time chasing after them. She grabbed Prudence's hand. "It'll be just like having a sister at home again. What grand times we shall have! Mother, may I have some new gowns made, also? All the girls have already seen everything I own."

Morgan was almost hesitant to look at his father. In his earlier spying ventures, he'd had no one but himself to worry about. Despite the success of these initial moments, heaven only knew what still lay ahead.

❦ ❦

Robert Chandler and Robby MacKinnon, crossing from Manhattan to Nassau Island with a wagonload of supplies, reached the top of the Guan Heights, west of Brooklyn village. The wooded hill overlooked the outer bay, where the afternoon sunshine glistened over the choppy water—and the vast array of British ships at anchor off Sandy Hook.

Robby halted the two-horse team. "Would ye look at that."

"An awesome sight, that's for sure."

"Every time we come up here, there's more of them. No wonder our ranks are beginning to thin. I overheard some captains just this morning talkin' about daily desertions in their camps. One of them sounded frightened himself. He said General Washington should've swallowed his pride and gone over to Staten Island when the British were wantin' to talk. I canna' help but agree."

Mildly amused, Chandler smiled. "Ah, my friend, you would have to be a southern gentleman to understand his reasoning. To have a letter addressed to *Mister* Washington, rather than *General,* was a low-down insult—one the good general would find impossible to swallow."

"But with so many inlets and beaches down there, we'll not be able to defend them all. Every night I pray for a miracle, yet I canna' shake me feelin' of doom. And with naught but a small portion of those men and their mighty armada, they could overrun Rhode Island in a day. I should've taken leave. Emily and the bairns are in grave danger so close to Narragansett Bay. I've no doubt General Howe will detach a force to take Providence. They won't ignore the rebellious Rhode Islanders much longer. Me family would be far safer in Princeton."

Chandler, having visited with Emily MacKinnon and their children on the march south from Boston, remembered her winsome beauty. She had a fragile quality about her, yet she seemed to possess the same steady strength Robby normally displayed. He knew the couple shared not only a deep love for one another but a strong and abiding faith in God as well. But if they ever were truly tested, as he himself had been, were ever to suffer a loss beyond belief, how would they fare then?

He shook off his morbid thoughts. "Better get the team moving again if we want to get unloaded and back to New York before dark."

Robby cast a last long look at the ships, then snapped the reins over the animals' backs.

Chandler promised himself that if he had anything to say in the matter, the Scot would never know a loss similar to his own crushing experience. "Tell you what," he suggested. "Nothing's stirring down there yet, no sign of the redcoats getting ready for an assault. Let's report sick tomorrow and get some men to cover for us. In less than three days we could be at the Hayneses' farm."

His friend's dark mustache quirked beneath doubtful blue eyes.

"I'm sure that in no more than nine or ten days at the most," Chan insisted, "we could have your family safely tucked away at Princeton and be back here. I'd stake my life that the English will still be sitting down there, with no more than an occasional growl coming from their cannons. Their mere presence is scaring so many into deserting. Soon all they'll have to do is just sail into New York and plant their flag."

"Ye know better than that. Going after me Emily is mighty tempting. But we canna' be sure they won't attack before we get back. I deserted once. No matter that I'd been unjustly impressed into service aboard an English ship, I don't want that dishonorable word attached to me name again. Ever." He paused. "But perhaps we could ask permission. . . ."

Chandler gave a dubious shake of the head. "We could try, but that new quartermaster doesn't know us from Adam. I wish Morgan hadn't been fool enough to traipse off to Philadelphia and drag our little Puritan along. Speaking of Prudence, can you even imagine her trying to spy? or even more unbelievable, lie? The two of us should have stopped them somehow."

Robby chuckled and nodded. "Aye, perhaps. But the lass is as stubborn as she is persuasive. Puts me in mind of me bonny Emily when we first met. But for her stubborn logic, I'd have been hanged as a deserter. She saved me life . . . her and the Lord, of course."

Chandler rubbed his thumb over the lump Julia's locket made in his pocket. He and Robby should have tried harder to stop Prudence from going into the lions' den . . . but by hook or crook, he'd see to it that Emily was taken to the safe haven of Princeton.

Princeton. The thought of setting foot in the place where he and Julia had known their brief time of happiness—and where he had experienced immeasurable sorrow—was almost unspeakable. But hard as it was, somehow he'd do it.

Hoofbeats sounded from behind them as a rider approached. Out of habit, Chan reached for his musket and checked its load.

"'Tis me brother-in-law!" Robby remarked. "Ye remember Ben, don't ye?"

"The courier? Of course."

"Could be he's got a letter from Emily."

Chandler felt deader than ever inside. There would never be such a letter for him, ever again.

5

"Will that be all, mum?" Lucy, a thin, pleasant maid of the Thomas household, asked Prudence.

"Yes, thank you so much."

"Very good." The servant quietly exited the guest chamber.

Prudence stared in awe at her own elegant reflection in the winged looking glass of the dressing table. Lucy had styled her hair into a braided coronet with a cluster of ringlets dangling behind one ear.

Her gaze lowered to the sprigged muslin gown. The color, a soft ivory trimmed with violet-edged lace, made her olive skin glow. But was it fashionable enough to fit in here? The word of a mere New York seamstress didn't seem sufficient for someone hoping to give the impression of being a spoiled belle—and soon she would be expected to select an entire wardrobe! Merciful heavens!

Thinking back on when she'd sought employment as a serving girl in order to spy on the Boston Tories and their British allies, she recalled how the women in attendance had spoken of little other than the frocks other attendees had worn. How would she ever carry off this charade?

The bedroom door opened, and Morgan strode in. His eyes met hers in the mirror.

Springing to her feet, she turned to face him. "Do you think I'm presentable?"

His admiring gaze meandered slowly downward from her

hair to her toes and back; then he shook his head in wonder as he came to her. "More than presentable, actually. You look ravishing. Far more beautiful than any one woman has the right to be." He drew her into his arms and kissed her.

"But am I wearing the latest style?" she asked, drawing away slightly when he attempted a second and more passionate kiss. Flattery might be fine for some, but her husband's biased view would not help her to learn the proper ways to act or dress. She twirled around, then sought his opinion once again.

"All I can say is that any man—wealthy or otherwise—would be proud to have you on his arm. Other than that, I'm afraid I've not paid that much attention to what is all the rage this season."

Prudence's enthusiasm withered.

"If you *should* happen to be lagging behind the others in some small way," Morgan went on, "I'm sure no one will hold it against you. Boston port has been blockaded for over two years, remember."

"Yes," she said with renewed hope. "I hadn't thought of that. So your mother shouldn't find it strange that I'll be putting myself wholly at her disposal, relying upon her good taste and guidance in choosing my wardrobe. I'll be so pliable and appreciative she won't be able to help liking me."

"Quite." Stripping off his shirt, Morgan crossed to the commode. He poured water from the pitcher into the basin and began to wash.

Prudence went to the ornately carved mahogany wardrobe and removed a fresh shirt for him. "I asked Lucy to have this pressed for you. I hope I made a good choice."

He gave it a perfunctory glance.

"Won't it do, Morgan?"

"Hm?" Grabbing a towel, he rubbed his face and arms briskly. "Oh. Of course. It's fine."

"Then what is it? Something's troubling you."

He draped the damp towel over the bar on the edge of the washstand. "It's this whole business."

"What business?"

Morgan turned. "We happen to have come here for the express purpose of deceiving my family. That's what is troubling me. Now, correct me if I'm wrong, but when I told my father a rather elaborate lie in the not too distant past, you were so upset with me that you were ready to shut me out of your life completely. Yet here we are, eager to tell my own mother all the things she wants to hear, simply so we can use her and her social connections to further our own *righteous* cause."

Aware of the warm flush flooding her cheeks, Prudence inhaled deeply. "But that was different."

"I fail to perceive how." Morgan turned away and began pulling on the clean shirt.

"The . . . lie . . . you told your father was done to trick him out of a large sum of money that would ensure your own pleasure and comfort, which was an outright sin. But this isn't the same thing, Morgan. Please know that I will never do anything to deliberately bring hurt to your family."

"Lying or tricking one's mother—no matter *what* the reason—is far from honoring a parent."

Someone rapped on the door.

Prudence caught her breath. Had this conversation carried beyond the room?

Fastening the last of his buttons, Morgan went to answer.

"Dinner will be served in five minutes," a voice said.

"Thank you." He closed the door and turned to Prudence. "One more reason I shouldn't have an accomplice in these circumstances. Sooner or later, we're bound to be overheard."

She fluttered one hand and sat down to put on her shoes. "That is simply rectified. We'll never speak of the matter again unless we're positive it is safe to do so."

Morgan drew on a dove gray dinner coat, and Prudence, having finished with her shoes, rose to adjust the ruffles on his cuffs and shirt front. It was the first time she had seen him dressed like a dandy since their first meeting. "Now I recognize you for certain," she said teasingly. "That flirty, bossy upstart from the Clarkes' Christmas ball."

"Ah, yes," he said wryly. "Back in those sweet carefree days before you became the worry of my life."

Raising up on tiptoe, Prudence caressed the lines from his brow and brushed his lips with hers. "I do hope I've become more to you than that."

The tension left his expression, and a spark of desire darkened his eyes. He pulled her near and kissed her neck.

Prudence laughed lightly and pushed him gently away. "Forgive me, sweetheart, but you mustn't muss my hair just now." She took his arm and looped hers through it. "Afterward," she whispered, "you may tangle it to your heart's content."

With neither the answering grin she'd anticipated nor a glint of mischievous fun, Morgan filled his lungs and gestured toward the hall.

Prudence drew a strengthening breath, also. How would she ever convince him they were doing the right thing? Surely her reasoning was sound, logical. Their motives were pure, the cause righteous.

Nevertheless . . .

           ❧ ❧

As Morgan escorted Prudence downstairs, he could hear his father conversing in the library.

"But to have that happen in New York!" the guest was saying as they drew near. "From what I understand, that city had no fewer Loyalists than your fair city. I fear it does not bode well for Philadelphia."

Father gave a noncommittal shrug, then brightened as he caught sight of Morgan and Prudence entering the book-lined study. "It's my son and his bride." He set down his glass of sherry and came to meet them, kissing Prudence on both cheeks. "You look lovely, my dear."

"Thank you," she said softly.

"Morgan," he went on, "I'd like you to meet Clayborne

Raleigh. He's become so fond of our gracious town, he chose not to accompany his father to the tobacco warehouses of the South. Clay, this is my son, Morgan."

"Your servant," the visitor said, extending his hand.

So this is my baby sister's admirer? Morgan took immediate stock of the well-dressed man. Light brown hair, hooded hazel eyes sloping downward at the corners, snobbish lips, impudent chin. Of medium height, he had to be nearly thirty if he were a day. *Surely of sufficient age to be buying tobacco in his father's stead, not languishing here while his elderly sire labors. Nor dallying with the affections of impressionable young girls. With Evelyn.* But Morgan shook hands and forced out a polite greeting. "How do you do?"

"So you're the brother who found himself trapped in Boston during the bombardment," Raleigh said, the nasal tone of his British accent indicating his distaste. "How utterly tiresome it must have been. I hear that society is devoid of all grace and culture." His interested gaze fastened on Prudence. "And dare I say, even our own soldiers can be quite common, indeed. Circumstances must have been very trying in Boston for one of such beauty." He bent elaborately and kissed her hand.

Morgan's mind was still coming up with labels for the useless bounder. "It's unwise to prejudge a city," he said, pulling Prudence close with a proprietary arm. "After all, I plucked this rare flower from those very gardens."

The newcomer appeared flustered.

Prudence tapped Morgan's chest with the tip of her closed lace fan and smiled. "I fear my husband is jesting at your expense. 'Tis true I'm a daughter of Boston. But its reputation as a city with no sense of humor, no imagination, is more than deserved. And alas, now that it is teeming with rebellious upstarts, it is suffering an even worse fate. Soon, I fear, it will be nothing but rubble."

Clayborne Raleigh sniffed. "Speaking of rubble, I was just relating to Mr. Thomas what I heard at the Barkleys' last night. It seems there is—or perhaps I should say *was*—a marvelous statue of King George astride a steed in New York. The very moment the outlaw army squatting there found out about their *Declaration of Independence,* they dared to pull the figure off its very foundation. Then, from what Barkley said, they melted it down for bullets to shoot at the king's own men."

"Yes," Father remarked. "Appalling conduct, to say the least."

Morgan fought to subdue a smile. His own efforts had been lent to accomplish the deed. He could still feel the tug of the rope in his hand.

"'Tis shocking, I know, Mr. Raleigh," Prudence mused. "But I have faith that this disgusting violence will soon come to an end. Too late, perhaps, for the loyal citizens in Boston, but not for the rest of our beleaguered colonies."

"I say," Morgan cut in. "You seem privy to the latest gossip, sir. Perhaps you've heard something definite regarding the attack General Howe is planning. I'd hoped this dreary business would be over before the first leaves of autumn fell."

His father cleared his throat. "I do believe I hear the ladies coming down." At the hint of discomfort in his tone, Morgan concluded it would be best to refrain from gleaning information while in his father's presence. The man was compromising himself enough as it was.

"And for my own lovely wife's comfort," Morgan announced, his fingertips pressing on her waist, "let us refrain from war talk for the remainder of the evening. It was a long and tiresome ride down from Halifax, and we've heard little conversation along the way save that."

"You poor dear." Raleigh sidled alongside Prudence as they started toward the foyer. "Obliged to evacuate Boston with the army, then forced to endure the ramblings of backwoods Yankee-Doodles all the way here. Well, don't despair. We'll see that you are thoroughly entertained this eve—and each and every one for the next fortnight, as well." Reaching the staircase, he switched his gaze to Evelyn. "Won't we, my pet?"

Morgan was struck by how grown up his sister appeared,

with her shining hair in a cascade of ringlets and her lips sporting a faint touch of lip rouge. Then he caught the way Clay Raleigh's eyes lingered on her budding bosom as she smilingly took the rake's arm. The effort to throw the lecher out on his ear was almost too strong to resist. Morgan was amazed his father didn't appear to have noticed the cur's disgusting conduct . . . and was more than thankful that Evelyn still sparkled with innocence as she tipped her head at her older brother and Prudence.

"I see you two have already met our charming guest," Mother announced, gifting the man with a warm look. "He's the son of one of England's most prominent merchant families. As well as his father's expertise in tobacco, he has an uncle who imports great quantities of spices and another who's deeply involved with the Chinese silk. Isn't that so, Mr. Raleigh?"

"We do try our utmost to keep abreast of the needs of England," he returned.

We? Morgan thought with a smirk. The man appeared worse than useless—unless there was more to him than met the eye, which he seriously doubted. But one never knew. Clayborne Raleigh might bear watching for reasons other than the safeguarding of Evelyn's virtue. Under no circumstances would Morgan leave the cad unchaperoned with his sister. Suddenly he was very glad to be home. It would appear he and Prudence had arrived just in time.

❦ ❦

Prudence crimped her lips in disgust. Morgan had dismissed her to their bedchamber almost immediately after supper on the pretense that she was exhausted from their trip! Why, she had hardly risen from her chair before he began questioning Clay Raleigh regarding the Crown's commitment to loyal merchants. Obviously Morgan intended to exclude her from his activities at every opportunity. Well, he would hear about it when he returned. She had been waiting more than three hours in the unlit room for him to join her!

Emitting an angry breath, she pushed the partially open windows out as far as they would go, then leaned to catch the slight breeze. Her night dress was much too heavy for these sultry climes.

Had it not been for Mistress Thomas, who unwittingly aided Morgan in his ploy by deciding that the men needed to become better acquainted, Prudence might have objected to leaving the supper table. But the older woman had announced that dreary business talk was too dull and uninspiring to endure. She had taken Evelyn upstairs and retired.

The thought of young, dark-haired Evie brought a smile. The girl did possess an abundance of youthful charm. It was not hard to understand why she was already being courted at such a tender age. But not yet sixteen, she was much too naive to be left unattended with a man of the world.

Clay Raleigh epitomized everything Prudence disliked and distrusted . . . and everything the colonies now rebelled against. He didn't bother trying to conceal his own lustful arrogance, his vain intent to devour youthful purity. Advantageous match aside, how could anyone's own mother willingly cast her trusting daughter to such a wolf? Hopefully Morgan would find a way to utilize Raleigh's excessive ego—and perhaps even cajole out of him some detail of major importance.

The grounds below were bathed in silvery glow as the moon emerged from behind a lone cloud and painted the hedges and fountain spray with magical splendor. The lavish gardens attested to the Thomas wealth, as did the elegance of the interior of the mansion. Truly, she and Morgan came from very different worlds. Would she find the same acceptance from Mrs. Thomas as Morgan had found from Pa? But Papa had been in dire need of Morgan's talent and experience. Would Morgan's mother ever have need of her?

Well, no matter. She and Morgan were, in fact, married. His mother would *need* her to be an asset to her son. Prudence smiled. The poor woman had her work cut out for her. Mistress Thomas had been stunned to discover that Prudence had no musical accomplishments whatsoever, and had adamantly declared that the matter would be rectified. Prudence had been unable to resist playing that up for all it was worth, divulging that her father had considered dallying in the arts to be frivolous and had insisted upon instructing her in how to keep ledgers instead. *My father,* she had added without batting an eye, *wanted me to fully understand that money does not simply fall from the sky, as so many young women of my station believe.*

What priceless indignation had flooded Mistress Thomas's patrician features. Prudence savored the memory of it and could still hear the woman's remarks echoing in her mind. *Women,* she had said, *have enough of their own concerns to contend with without being burdened with those of men. Which, my dear,* she had added with an almost sincere smile, *you will soon learn, when you are blessed with children of your own.*

A bittersweet twinge caught at Prudence's heart. She and Morgan had been married for more than five months now, and her time still arrived as surely as the new moon. Of course, he'd been away from her a good portion of those months. Now, at least, they'd be together for a while. But with the uncertainties of war, perhaps it was best they not be blessed just yet.

Returning to the big empty bed, Prudence flopped impatiently across it. What was taking Morgan so long?

Within moments, footsteps and murmured good-nights drifted from outside the chamber door.

Prudence jumped up as Morgan came in, and she rushed to him. "Well?" she whispered, propping her hands on his chest as he wrapped his arms about her.

He pulled her some distance away from the door. "Nothing definite, I'm afraid. With my father present, I was hesitant to pry."

"Oh, you," she groused in disappointment. "Then why did you banish me to my room as if I were no more than a mere child?"

He rubbed her nose in the darkness. "Actually, love, I was far more interested in seeing that Evelyn was taken upstairs.

And it worked, didn't it? There is no way on earth I will allow that philanderer to have his way with my little sister."

Prudence nodded in agreement.

"One thing, though," Morgan continued softly. "The bloke does have a loose tongue. He said the British will initiate an attack before the month is out. That, of course, would be no surprise to anyone." Drawing away, he crossed to a chair and sat down to remove his shoes. "A pity he did not know the exact date. He did confirm what our generals suspect, however. The attack will be massive and—they hope—decisive. They are counting on total victory before winter."

· "Oh, my."

He raised a palm. "The windows are open, and Mother's sitting room is next to this one."

"We haven't spoken above a whisper." Nonetheless, she went to close the windows.

Movement below caught her attention. Stepping back slightly, she motioned for Morgan to join her.

A figure stepped from the shadow of a tree. The blue-white light of the moon illuminated a billowy night shift. Evelyn!

Then from the hedges near the back, a man came forth.

Morgan went rigid. "That sneaky—," he hissed under his breath. He thrust the upper half of his body out the window.

Grabbing his shirttail, Prudence yanked him back inside.

"What in blazes has been going on here while I've been away?" He wheeled around and charged out of the room in his bare feet.

"Oh, dear," Prudence whispered, heading for the window again. She had never seen Morgan in such a rage. If only there were some way to warn her new sister-in-law . . . but that much noise would surely also be heard by the girl's parents.

Then she saw Evelyn melt into the man's embrace.

Prudence tucked her chin. And she and Morgan had actually believed the girl was an innocent!

6

His hand on the latch of the back door, Morgan paused just long enough to gain control of his rage. He was more than merely angry with his sister. He was deeply disappointed in her. Evelyn, always his pet, had claimed to have hated the vapid way their mother and older sisters acted. How could she have changed so much in such a short time? Apparently the two years he had been away had been very crucial ones for her, and all that time he had been such a careless dolt he'd scarcely given her a thought.

Well, that was about to change. He was home now . . . and perhaps this reason for returning was far more important than taking up his role as a spy again. After all, the answer to that dilemma had eluded him thus far.

Inhaling a calming breath, Morgan slipped quietly outside. It would be best to catch the slimy snake in the act. Even as he pictured the despicable spoiler, Morgan's fingers balled into fists. He wouldn't mind giving that aquiline nose a new shape.

He moved toward the steps to the garden and from there could already hear whispering. The trunk of a massive oak provided an effective shield as he eased on silent feet toward the pair.

Peering ever so gradually around the base of the tree, Morgan saw the bounder boldly kissing Evelyn full on the mouth. Livid, he tapped the cad's shoulder.

The man started in surprise and turned. A sharp jab to the chin sent him sprawling onto the grass.

Evie gasped in shock.

Jamie Dodd! Morgan recognized the gangly, copper-haired younger brother of Micah Dodd, one of Philadelphia's Sons of Liberty. The lad sat up, dazed, rubbing his jaw, his eyes narrowed in pain.

Evelyn, too horrified even to look guilty, sent Morgan a withering glare as she reached down to help Jamie up. Then she stared at her brother, hands on her hips.

Morgan looked from one to the other in total confusion as he rubbed absently at his sore knuckles. He cleared his throat. "What were you and my sister doing?" he demanded quietly with as much authority as he could muster.

"Certainly not what you imagined," Evelyn hissed. She glanced at the flustered Jamie with a frown and brushed some grass from his shoulder. "I've never been more humiliated in my entire life."

"I only came to tell Evie good-bye," Jamie said, his voice cracking on the last word. "I'm off to New York tomorrow to join the Continental army."

Morgan was not ready to let go of his doubts yet. "And I suppose you just happened by at the very time my sister decided to take a moonlight stroll in her nightclothes. Surely you don't think I'm such a dunce I'd fall prey to that!"

"Will you be quiet?" Evelyn pleaded under her breath. "You'll wake the entire household." She grabbed Morgan's arm and tugged him into the shaded seclusion while the young man followed. She stopped and turned. "If you must know, dear brother, I've been meeting with Jamie these past two years since you so blithely shirked your duties here without so much as informing the Dodds or any other of your fellow Sons of Liberty that you were leaving Philadelphia. The very night after you left, poor Jamie waited half the night for you. When he didn't give up and go away, I came out to explain."

"You?"

"Yes, me. And since I happened to have heard an interesting tidbit of my own, I passed that along. Otherwise, poor Jamie would have stayed out here all night for nothing."

"You were aware of my affiliation with the Sons of Liberty?" Morgan asked in alarm.

"Of course. Though you didn't have enough confidence in your own favorite sister to tell her yourself."

"Who else knew about me? Frances?"

"That ninny?" Evie scoffed. "She can't see anything beyond her looking glass—unless it's red as a lobster coat."

"Then earlier tonight, with Clay Raleigh . . . You really aren't—"

Evelyn rolled her eyes and shook her head. "I simply allow the useless fop to think anything is possible. It makes him most willing to attend me at parties where talk is as loose and free as he'd like to be with me."

In a surge of brotherly pride, Morgan seized her and hugged her hard. "Oh, bless you. I needn't tell you what I'd been thinking up till now." But then another realization dawned on him. He eased her away. "Wait a minute. You're far too young to be playing such dangerous games. All manner of evil could befall you." He swung to Jamie, seizing him by both arms. "How dare you enlist the aid of my little sister to spy?"

The lad straightened to his full height, which was several inches shorter than Morgan. "I did no such thing. I tried my best to talk her out of it. But she said she would use your signal, then wait until I came—even if it meant days or the risk of being caught. She gave me no choice. So whenever I saw just the one curtain fastened back, I came as soon as it was safe."

"Some excuse that is." Morgan had to fight a strong impulse to throttle them both as he digested the discomforting news.

Evie stepped forward, her eyes aglow in the subdued light of a half-moon. "Well, it's the truth. He tried to get me to quit every time he saw me."

"That's right," the lad said, nodding. "And I did get her to promise not to deliberately spy. Only to pass on information she heard naturally."

"So you might as well let go of him, Morgan. This has all been my idea. Jamie never once used the signal asking me to meet him. Not once."

At the quiet fervor in her voice, Morgan eased his grip and released him.

"So today," Evelyn went on, "when I saw his string tied to the lamp post, I knew he must have something terribly important to tell me. It was the longest, most unbearable evening of my life, with you men downstairs droning on about how the patriots can't possibly hold off the British. I thought you'd never bid Clay good night and go upstairs to bed. And now, to learn Jamie is going away . . . to take part in a hopeless battle . . ." She threw her arms around the lad. "Oh, please don't do it, Jamie. Please, don't go."

He held her tight, his own expression strained. "I must, kitten. Our boys need all the help they can get, or it *will* all be for nothing. We've worked too hard and too long to give up now. You've always wanted to do your part, Evie. Well, your part is to stay here and wait for me. Will you?" As she nodded, he looked over her head to Morgan. "I'll inform my brother you're back—that is, if you are."

Morgan winced at the accusation conveyed in the young man's tone. "I am. But this time I'm here on Washington's orders. Tell Micah that anything of importance must be taken directly to him. Can that be arranged?"

"Of course." A slow grin widened Jamie's cheeks. "So you haven't deserted the cause after all. My brother and the others will be glad to hear that—*and* glad to have you back. You were the best man we had. Now, if you don't mind, I'd like to have a few moments alone with Evie before I depart."

Hesitating, Morgan eyed the two of them.

Evelyn stretched up on her toes to whisper in his ear. "Yes, do go away. Please. He was just confessing his love for me. *Finally.*"

"But—"

She gave him a gentle push. "Go. Now."

With a last stern look at the young couple, Morgan relented and returned to the house. He was getting old. His own baby sister was blossoming into womanhood, and she had been spying for the patriots for two whole years already! Wait till Prudence heard about it!

This was certainly going to muddy things up, though. Now, not only would he spend untold hours worrying over what his wife might be doing, but he'd have to keep track of his sister's actions as well. To say nothing of the new risk posed by the possibility that someone might inadvertently overhear yet a third member of the household discussing matters of extreme importance. Returning inside, Morgan started up the stairs.

And Robby thought he had worries merely because his wife and children were in Rhode Island! At least they were with her parents and a good hundred miles from the nearest enemy . . . *not supping with them!*

🏵 🏵

"The children are finally down for their naps," Emily MacKinnon announced cheerily. "Peace and quiet. Even their doting grandma should appreciate it today." Removing the pins from her bedraggled hair, she twirled the length of it and deftly swirled it into a bun again as she sank down beside her brother Ben's wife.

Abigail smiled and set the big bowl of fresh beans between them on the porch step. "It's nothing like it was when all the other grandchildren were here. Then, a quiet moment was completely unheard of." She snapped the ends off the beans in her hand and took another bunch.

Emily took a handful and began helping with the chore. Having heard quite a bit about timid little Abigail before she met her, Emily had taken to her right away, glad to have another sister around again. Abby still tended to be quiet in large family gatherings, but no remnants of apprehension remained in her turquoise eyes now. Her children and Emily's seemed to get along surprisingly well, too.

"I truly love this wonderful farm," Abby said in her airy voice. "There's always so much happening here. Cassandra and Corbin are fascinated by the horses, especially the foals and colts. And if someone mentions that some of the other cousins are coming for a visit, they can hardly sleep for the excitement."

Emily nodded, gazing off toward the pastures. The animals were mostly clustered in the shade beneath the trees, motionless in the lazy afternoon except for the swishing of their long tails as they kept pesky flies at bay.

"I've even started looking forward to the family visits, if you can believe that. I wondered, at first, if I'd ever truly fit in . . . but everyone has been so kind and caring. They've all gone out of their way to make us feel at home. Now I really enjoy being around the other women . . . especially since we've all been left behind to wait for our husbands."

"You know, of course," Emily teased, "that the lot of us are all quite jealous of you."

"Of me?" Abby said, amazed.

Emily nodded. "Unlike the rest of us, your husband manages to come home every week or so."

"Oh." A flush pinkened Abigail's fair cheeks beneath her wheat gold hair. "Well, I suppose being a courier does have its advantages," she said gently. "But Ben complains that his saddle sores are turning into calluses. Speaking of traveling, I do hope your sister Jane and her husband made it back safely to Vermont."

"I'm sure they did. There's been no word of the British moving down from Canada." She paused, looking off into the distance again. Some of the deep green leaves of summer were just beginning to fade. "From what Papa heard this morning in Providence, every last redcoat in the Americas is camped on an island just offshore from New York. Along with some regiments of mercenaries."

"Mercenaries?" Abby echoed.

"Soldiers King George hired from Europe. Germany, I believe. They're called Hessians."

"How awful." Abigail reached over to squeeze Emily's hand. "That must be very upsetting for you, what with your Robby encamped right there in New York."

"I try not to think about it," Emily confessed. "I pray for him a lot, and I rest in the fact that our heavenly Father loves Robby and all our other men very much, even more than we do. No matter how grim things might seem at the moment, that thought does help a little.

Abby didn't answer for several seconds. "I hope one day I will think that way as naturally as you do. It still takes someone to remind me."

"Don't feel bad about it," Emily said with a chuckle. "I'm still learning, along with many other things, to look to God first and trust that he knows best."

"I'm sure your brother Dan always does. He seems so wise."

Emily laughed aloud. "Considering he's a minister, he was rather a mess when he was separated from Susannah those many months. But, yes, most of the time they're both God's faithful servants. And they know the importance of being examples to their congregation."

Finished with the beans she had been snapping into her apron, Emily spilled them into the bowl, then took more. "I suppose I've always admired their love for God and their devotion to one another despite severe trials.

"But it does amaze me that he and his wife would choose to go to some faraway settlement. With Susannah being an English lady and all, I do pray they fare well in the wilds of Pennsylvania."

"Jonathan Bradford, a good friend from Dan and Susannah's Princeton days, said the troubled Wyoming Valley was in much need of an impartial man of God. His plea was quite convincing. And Felicia will be with them, too. After spending time of her own in the Virginia mountains, she should be a big help."

"I don't understand why Felicia went, really. With her husband being a sailor, she'll never get to see him."

"Yancy needed to know she was safe. Since he's off at sea so much, he didn't want to be worrying about her welfare."

Abby shrugged. "I guess it's not too different with you and Robby. He wanted you to go back to Princeton. But you're still here."

"You mean you don't enjoy my company?" Emily asked with a droll smile.

"Oh, I do. Truly. It's just . . ."

Emily gave a comforting squeeze to her sister-in-law's shoulder, then snapped the last bean. "With all the men away, and old Elijah barely able to work anymore, I don't want to leave Papa with the entire farm to run by himself. When he finds help, then I'll go." Tipping the slender vegetables into the bowl with the rest, she stood. "In fact, it's nigh unto feeding time. I'd best go to the well and start drawing water. If Katie and Rusty wake up before I'm through in the barn, would you mind keeping an eye on them?"

Returning from the water trough a short time later, Emily heard Abigail squeal. She gazed toward the porch of the sprawling two-story house and saw her sister-in-law spring to her feet and run down the lane.

Ben came into view. Emily heard her brother's delighted laugh, then watched him leap down from his mount and gather his wife into his arms, his tricorn tumbling from his tawny head. Abby's feet didn't touch the ground as he swung her in exuberant circles. They smothered each other with kisses.

Emily's heart constricted with loneliness. No wonder all Abby's sisters-in-law envied her. Watching the passionate reunions of the recently married pair intensified their own solitary existences.

Oh, Robby, where are you? How are you? Do you feel as empty as I do?

Emily recalled her own former days with a sad smile. She had been slightly younger than Abigail when Yancy Curtis came to hide Robby MacKinnon in one of the outbuildings of the farm. Ruthlessly impressed into service as a cabin boy aboard the ill-fated *Gaspee*, Robby had jumped ship mere moments before Rhode Islanders torched the vessel, which had run aground on a sandbar. When two British officers came to supper later that afternoon—one of whom was Susannah's own brother, Ted—Emily had whisked the charming Scot to safety right from under their noses. What an adventure! Even yet she smiled at the memory of how Dan had insisted Robby marry her to salvage her name. Her older brother's solicitation hadn't been necessary. Their love had grown so quickly they never wanted to be apart again.

Closing her eyes against the pain of her longing, Emily swallowed hard. Four long months, and only once in all that time had she seen her husband's handsome face. It seemed a year.

Before she started to cry, Emily turned away from the sight of the lovebirds and concentrated on her task.

"Emmy!" Ben called, coming toward her with Abby. "I saw Robby last week. He sent a letter for you. And a little present."

"How is he?" she asked breathlessly. "Does he still look fit? Has he lost weight?"

"You've nothing to fear concerning him. He's in the rear of the army, sitting on all the food and supplies. Trust me, he'll be the last to go hungry. That is, unless he gets transferred to a different company."

"Why?" she asked, suddenly concerned. "What do you mean?"

"Morgan is gone." Ben glanced around. "This information must not leave this farm. Morgan has been relieved of his duties as quartermaster and sent to Philadelphia again to spy."

"I see."

"That's only the half of it," he continued. "The day he received his order to go, who showed up out of the blue but Prudence, and she convinced him to take her along."

"I don't blame her." Emily folded her arms. "If it weren't for the children, I'd have been in New York ages ago!"

A frown connected Ben's straight brows. "As you well know, that is not where Robby wants you. While I was with him and Chandler, he tried to get leave to fetch you back to Princeton. But since the British are poised to attack any day, it was denied."

Denied! Emily had to fight tears. Only once in all this time had Robby been given leave. It wasn't fair.

"He asked me to try to find someone going to New Jersey who would be willing to escort you."

"And what about the horse farm, Ben? Papa's all but alone here, you know. I can't leave him with all the work."

"Where is Pa?" Ben asked, scanning the grounds.

"He left a while ago for Boston with a string of horses. He's had a number of orders since folks up there lost so many during the siege."

"Right." Ben rubbed the bridge of his nose. "Mostly eaten." Stepping away from Abigail, he withdrew a letter and a small package from his inside vest pocket and handed them to Emily. "From your dearly beloved. He told me to kiss you for him, but I declined." He grabbed Abby close. "I'd rather kiss this pretty lass. But you can imagine this is Robby kissing you, if you like." With a teasing smile in his light brown eyes, he claimed Abby's lips.

It was more than Emily could bear to watch. She snatched the water bucket and walked away, Robby's letter and gift clutched tightly in her other hand.

Once she was out of sight, she stopped alongside the barn and set down the pail. She lowered herself to the ground and removed the ribbon and wrapping paper from the present. Her eyes misted at the sight of the lovely silver bracelet Robby had sent her. She could envision him standing at the jeweler's, eyeing every item in stock as he selected just the perfect extravagance. Having come to America with limited funds, he had never been one to waste money on frivolities, but he would sometimes surprise her with a little bauble for no particular reason. She cherished each one. Now he had spent money he could ill afford, just to send his love.

She pressed his unopened letter to her heart. She would save it until she'd finished with the horses and had some time alone without fear of interruption. And for those few precious minutes, she would pretend Robby was there with her, saying all the sweet words he had written . . . and more. So much more.

7

Chandler gradually opened his eyes and stretched his sore muscles. The bed of the tarp-covered wagon hadn't seemed quite so hard when he and Robby first sought shelter there last night. Now, with the arrival of morning, his whole body protested in discomfort.

Beside him, Robby stirred.

"Did you hear the shots?" Chan asked sleepily.

"More thunder, no doubt." The Scot sat up and began untying one of the ropes securing the canvas covering. As he raised the edge of a flap, the brilliant glare of the rising sun reflecting over the bay struck their weary eyes. "On second thought, it couldna' be that. The sky is crystal clear."

Chandler squinted and tugged at another knot pulled tight by the force of last night's wind. Oftentimes throughout the gale he wondered if the meager covering would hold. The storm had prevented their prompt return to New York after delivering supplies to Colonel Hand's outpost.

Three more measured shots ripped the air. Almost instantly movement could be heard outside.

Eyeing one another, they put on their boots and crawled out of the opening Robby had managed to make.

The grass around them was slick and wet. Members of the First Pennsylvania Rifle Battalion were emerging from the various canvas shelters, some still yanking on boots and buckling belts.

Something was amiss. Chandler ran into the open and gazed beyond the planted fields. The Narrows between Staten Island and the shoreline, less than a mile away, glistened white with sails. Landing craft of every shape and size were reaching shore, discharging Crown regiments. Already there were hundreds of redcoats on the beach, while many more longboats ran aground to debark additional soldiers. It had been rumored that the enemy numbered more than twenty-five thousand, and it appeared that at least half that number were on their way. Chan felt a twinge of fear even as adrenaline coursed through him.

"May the Almighty have mercy on us," Robby said beside him. "We should've gone back to New York last night, storm or no."

The rat-a-tat of a drum called the men to arms. Colonel Hand, a levelheaded Irishman who had served most effectively as an officer in the British army before settling in Pennsylvania, raised the flap of a large tent and came out. He pulled on his gloves, then took a spyglass from a young soldier at his side.

To a man, everyone stopped what he was doing and waited while their leader surveyed the distant scene. A few untried men whimpered among themselves. After today, they would be less likely to bawl like babies, Chandler assured himself. If they survived this day, they would be hardened veterans.

"We should get going," Robby whispered. "The ferries crossin' to New York will be clogged soon, and it's a good ten miles from here."

Feeling guilty at the thought of leaving this lonely battalion of sharpshooters here at the forefront, Chan hesitated, but he and Robby did have their own duties to consider. Besides, the Scot had never yet faced a British volley, and Chan would just as soon keep it that way. He joined his friend on the wagon they'd left hitched through the night.

"Atten-tion!" one of the sergeants hollered, mustering the men.

Robby snapped the reins over the team's backs, and the wagon lurched into motion.

"Halt that thing at once!" the colonel yelled.

A sergeant strode quickly toward them. "Where in blazes do you two think you're going?"

"Back to the main storehouses," Robby replied. "We're assigned to a quartermaster on Manhattan Island."

"Not today, you're not," the colonel said, joining them. "Today you will help us move our own stores and be available for any other detail."

Robby's chest puffed out as he saluted. "Yes, sir!"

"Report to the supply sergeant."

"Yes, sir!"

As they obeyed the new order, Chandler couldn't help feeling more than a little apprehensive about this development. He noted the small force of perhaps five hundred around them. Last night he had considered that a substantial number . . . but now, compared with the opposing army, it seemed pitifully small. Certainly no match for what would be coming at them across the open farmlands. On this neck of Nassau Island, barns and other outbuildings were few and far between.

The colonel raised his hand to silence the mumblings in the ranks. "Men, nothing usable is to fall into the hands of the enemy. No field crop, no grain in the barns, no hayricks. Burn the lot of them. Sergeants! Collect torches and disperse half the men. I want to see a wall of fire from the Narrows to the creek."

Wise plan, Chan decided as Robby guided the wagon toward the supply tents. Colonel Hand was covering their backsides, while never actually telling the men they were retreating. They would be kept far too busy to panic . . . and at the same time, a fire of that magnitude would signal the rest of Washington's army.

"We'll be loadin' up again," Robby muttered, "everything we unloaded last eve."

Chandler chuckled grimly. "Or burning it. Just keep your

musket close at hand, and do exactly what I tell you. Emily would never forgive me if I don't get you out of this in one piece."

           ❧ ❧

A knock sounded on the bedchamber door. Prudence, busy composing a letter to her stepmother in Massachusetts, quickly slipped the missive into a desk drawer. The unfamiliar weight of her lavender silk gown and petticoats felt cumbersome as she started to rise.

Evelyn stuck her head into the room before Prudence managed to untangle her feet. "The music instructor is downstairs waiting for you."

"Your mother certainly isn't one to waste time, is she?" With a light laugh, Prudence crossed the room to her new friend. "First you helped me select patterns and fabrics, then went shopping all day yesterday for accessories with me. You've been such a blessing, Evie. I had no idea there could be such a thing as an unfashionable style of wig. You've guided me wondrously through what seems a maze of social dos and don'ts."

Evelyn grinned and tossed her unbound brunette hair. "I've never had so much fun outwitting everyone. All this la-di-da folderol is just so much nonsense anyway."

"Nevertheless, you've been a godsend to me. Most of all, though, I'm so pleased Morgan and I don't have to fear being honest with you. I've already begun to think of you as my little sister . . . which reminds me." Turning to gaze at her reflection, Prudence repositioned a loose hairpin, then turned back. "Morgan asked me to speak to you regarding your—spying." She mouthed the last word. "He told me to convince you to leave that business to him, now that he's come home. He wants you and me to do nothing but continue to be the *lovely distractions* he considers us."

"Lovely distractions!" Evie's expression became sulky. "Surely you don't agree with my stuffy brother, do you? Just last night you told me how much you resented the intrusion of your two brothers into the affairs of your own store after you'd worked so hard to get it running smoothly. Well, Morgan merely walked away from all his responsibilities here. I *had* to take over. And I know for a fact that I've been so good at it no one—not anyone at all—has even begun to suspect this *child* of anything." She batted her lashes most innocently.

Prudence stifled a giggle as she snatched Evie's hand and squeezed it. "That must have been so exciting for you."

"Oh, yes," Evie said with a huge smile. "Ever so."

"Well, you and I, we'll do as Morgan asks. We won't *deliberately* eavesdrop. We'll simply go on as you have in the past, being gracious minglers. *And very attentive listeners.* But we must agree to stay together. Morgan is beside himself with worry as it is, and I've promised to look after you."

"As *I* will look after *you.*" She tugged Prudence toward the door. "As a matter of fact, I've already solved your musical accomplishment dilemma."

Prudence slanted her a curious glance. "I can't imagine how. I've never so much as held a musical instrument in my entire life."

Evelyn fluttered her hand. "Before I came upstairs, I told the music teacher you have the sweetest, however untrained, voice!"

Prudence's mouth fell open. *"You didn't.* Surely I would be expected to get up before company and sing. I'd die of embarrassment."

Evie just grinned. "With the talent you have for playacting, all you need to do is pretend you can sing, and trust me, you'll have no problem whatsoever outdoing Millicent Sears. The silly music teacher once told her she had perfect pitch, and now we can't silence her. Why, I've heard cats yowling on the back wall at night that sound better than she does!"

"I'm sure you're exaggerating to make me feel better."

"I wish I were." Evelyn opened the door and swept out, the ruffled hem of her red polka-dot dimity brushing the jamb. She curled her index finger in a gesture to follow. "Come along, let me introduce you to the insipid Master Stanton.

He's such a namby-pamby; you're sure to hate him as much as I do. Always scraping and bowing to any influential Tory in sight. Just watch . . . no matter what Mother says, he'll agree. Remember, I've already praised you, so he'll rave about your singing and soon have Mother believing you're an enchanting songbird."

Prudence pulled the younger girl back into the bedchamber and closed the door. "Evelyn, please don't lose sight of the fact that mothers are to be treated with respect, even when we don't always agree with them. And as for your Master Stanton—surely you don't really hate the gentleman. You may hate what he stands for, but—"

Evie tipped her head and laughed. "What my brother said about you *is* true. When you're not playacting, you truly are a very proper New England Puritan!"

"Please don't consider that a bad thing. Even though we must perpetrate a charade to aid the cause, I would never want you to lose your sweet spirit. Morgan and I want you to always be as lovely inside as you are on the outside."

The younger girl's confident expression faded noticeably. "Do you think Jamie Dodd would still love me if he knew I was only fifteen and three-quarters? He thinks I'm eighteen, you see. He would never have allowed me to take over when Morgan left two Decembers ago if he'd known I had just turned fourteen that month."

"I see." Prudence knew better than to make light of it. Morgan had already informed her that the Son of Liberty was barely old enough to shave himself. His only expertise as Morgan's contact had been his ability to scale the back wall— though his boyish appearance didn't hurt, either. No one would suspect someone so young. "Well, if he truly does love you, your age won't matter."

"*If* I ever get another chance to see him alive again!" She became even more woeful. "In the last two whole months, I haven't heard a single person express belief that Washington's army has a chance against King George's forces. Our men will all be slaughtered—everyone is saying so. Even Jamie."

Prudence wrapped an arm around her and opened the door, and they stepped into the hall. "Don't you believe it for a minute. God is on our side. Now, come along. Let's go down and make your Master Stanton work for his money. I do believe a duet is in order, don't you? Yes, you and I shall become accomplished harmonizers."

"The . . . two of us?" Evelyn stopped.

Prudence nudged her gently onward. "Yes. You and I."

"But—"

It was almost impossible for Prudence to contain her growing merriment. "And won't we create the very distraction our Morgan desires? The oh-so-talented singing Thomas sisters."

❦ ❦

Distant booms from the British cannons had rarely ceased since the Crown force started their landing some hours ago. Chandler, at the front of the team, hauled on the lead gelding's halter, trying to urge the horses forward. On the seat of the wagon, Robby cracked a whip above their backs. With the trees around them and billowing smoke from the fires to cover their retreat, any view of the scene below was completely obscured.

"Up, you two! Giddap!" he urged.

The animals strained in their traces, hauling the loaded wagon through a dip so it could continue up the steep incline. With a great lunging leap, they finally managed to roll out of the hole and gain the top.

Chan released his hold on the halter and patted both geldings' necks. "Good boys. Good boys." He glanced at Robby. "Let's give them a few minutes' rest."

"Aye. They've earned it." He hopped off the high freight wagon. "'Tis a pity to have to resort to misusing the poor beasts like this."

"I know." Chan blotted his forehead on his sleeve. "But we

couldn't take a chance going up the road." He drew some water from the barrel in back and gave the horses a drink.

"Got any to spare?" someone called from a group of riflemen jogging up the hill.

"Sure do." He filled his and Robby's cups again and again and passed them to the thirsty soldiers.

"Happen to know the way to Green's entrenchments?" an unshaven regular inquired. "We're to regroup there."

"To the north," Robby answered, pointing. "See over yon? The banked dirt on the top of that hill. 'Tis his redoubt."

The fellow nodded and gulped down the cool liquid.

"Have you engaged the enemy yet?" Chan asked.

Wiping his mouth on the back of his hand, the man shook his head. "Hasn't been time. Been burning up and down the neck. Can't believe these local farmers refused to move their grain and livestock when Washington asked 'em to."

"The stupid New Yorkers never would believe there was gonna be an attack," another said. "By the time I had to shoot several fat cows and leave 'em to rot, I'd have gladly done the same to their owners."

A rawboned man came from behind the wagon. "Got me off a clear shot once, thanks to the breeze. Fired at a column of redcoats moving up the road toward Gravesend. Dropped one, too." He grinned, revealing a gap between his front teeth. "Did a little jig while the devils took potshots at me. Always did love that look they get when they discover I'm outta range of their puny Brown Besses. I reloaded to get another shot, but the wind shifted, and I couldn't see them no more through the smoke."

"'Twas one of God's creatures ye killed, me good man," Robby said quietly. "May the Lord rest his soul."

"Lobsterbacks ain't got souls," a low voice grated.

"We don't need to hear any more of your talk, Scotty," a gruff sergeant said. "We got enough on our plate without you trying to heap guilt on it besides. We're at war."

Chandler had to wonder if Robby would be able to hold his own if they found themselves in a heated battle. At Bunker

Hill, there had been no time for philosophizing, only time to load and fire at the redcoats. Load and fire until they ran out of powder. And the British kept right on coming. Climbing over their own dead comrades didn't even slow them down. Nothing stopped them.

"Look!" someone shouted.

Chan turned. For the first time since early morning, a wide panorama slowly became visible. A line of red stretched along the shoreline for five or six miles. Another red line moved inland on the road leading to the redoubt on the hill, exactly as the rifleman had reported . . . the very road Chandler and Robby would have preferred rather than taking the wagon up this rugged terrain. And worse, there wasn't a single soldier down there trying to stop them!

The colonial army had only two defensive positions between Brooklyn Heights and New York—a pair of redoubts, two mud-banked square holes. One was at the top of a ridge on the Heights of Guan, flanked by a few trenches, and the other on the plain between the two heights. They were in dire need of more. Many more.

Chandler wasn't the only one stunned. No one around him uttered a word.

"Stop lollygagging," the sergeant finally ordered. "Get moving again—and step lively."

Robby, ashen-faced, climbed aboard the wagon and snapped the whip.

Chan hopped on as it sprang into motion. He tried to distinguish the redoubt, about half a mile to the north along the ridge, but its size was so insignificant and the trees so many, there was rarely a clear view of it. How could General Washington put all his efforts into protecting only the port city and the Hudson? Surely in the past four months this area could have been fortified much better than this!

But as he mulled over the thought, he knew the answer. Washington wasn't to blame. The general's efforts to build a cohesive army had been blocked at every turn. Congress rarely sent supplies, and they neglected to pay in a timely fashion as well. Most of the volunteers, who hadn't seen the action Massachusetts men had, were not taking the war any more seriously than Congress. By the hundreds they invented ailments to relieve them of duty. Some just plain deserted. It had been reported that last week an entire New Jersey company got tired of digging ditches and went home, saying they'd be back if anything ever happened.

Some army, this Continental force. Well, now they would have to become one . . . or be crushed.

8

Morgan saw his mother glance at the mantel clock and sigh. Evelyn, studying her nails while their father paced the study, met Morgan's glance and raised her eyebrows. Out in the parlor, the grandfather clock bonged seven times.

He cleared his throat. "I'll see what's keeping Prudence. We'll be down directly." Taking the steps two at a time, he made short work of the staircase, then went straight to their bedchamber.

He entered, only to find a glorious profusion of saffron ruffles and white lace sticking up from beside the four-poster. His wife was on her hands and knees, feeling around beneath the bed. "Where *is* it?" she muttered to herself in exasperation.

Unable to resist such an inviting sight, Morgan smiled and crept noiselessly behind her. In one fluid motion he dropped down beside Prudence and rolled her atop himself, her wig sliding askew in the process.

"Morgan!" she gasped, making a futile attempt to right the elaborate powdered creation.

He grinned and pulled her back down, sprinkling her with kisses.

"So, you want to play games, do you?" With a smile, she flung her arm in a wild arc and sent his wig toppling to the floor.

"Ah, now see what you've done," he said, manufacturing a

scowl. "I shall, of course, have to retaliate." He reached to yank one of her white curls.

She dodged, and her skirts billowed about them as she grabbed his wrists. "Do be serious," she pleaded. "You'll spoil my entry into Philadelphia society."

"Now there's a thought," he returned, drawing her face to within inches of his. He took the briefest second to drink in beauty not at all diminished by such trifles as a lopsided wig or a somewhat inglorious pose. "If your attire were to meet with some mishap or other, I shouldn't have to worry about your giving us away this eve."

"Me?" she asked. "You're the one who ran out into the night chasing after your sister, who, incidentally, happened to be spying herself. You might have given her away."

"Is that right?"

"Yes." She brushed her nose playfully across his.

He knew he had but one recourse. Breaking her grip, he grabbed her on either side of her slender waist and squeezed.

"Oh, please, stop!" she giggled. "You know I'm ticklish."

"You are?" he asked in mock innocence as he intensified the assault.

Prudence could only shriek and writhe in helpless laughter.

"Whatever are you doing?" Evelyn cried, looming suddenly over them, the cornflower blue of her gown intensifying the color of her eyes.

"He-he's trying to muss me so I have to stay home," Prudence confessed between giggles. "He knows I'll show him up if I go."

"You don't say. We must see about that." She leaned down and tried to pry his fingers loose. "Let her go, you brute!"

Prudence took a deep breath and seized his other hand.

With a mighty roar, he tossed the girls off but grabbed both of their waists, pulling them close to sit beside him. "Now hear me. I am the lord and master here. Therefore, you must both obey what I say without question."

Prudence rolled her eyes, while Evelyn stuck out her tongue.

"Besides," he went on, relaxing his grip a little, "*I* happen to have orders from the commanding general, and I'm the one who's been ordered forth. You two shall be decoys, and that is all. Delightful, frilly, silly distractions. Evie—" he kissed her nose— "you are to stay close to us. Particularly to Prudence. Help her with the subtle details of etiquette—and nothing else."

"But what about Mr. Raleigh?" she asked. "He does so yearn to take me out into the night air to whisper sweet Tory nothings in my ear."

Morgan turned to Prudence, kissing her upturned nose also. "If I'm occupied, don't you let this *child* out of your sight, even for an instant. It's bad enough I caught her trying to—"

"Caught whom?" Mother demanded from the doorway. "Doing what?" She planted her knuckles on either side of her swagged brocade skirts, her face drawn.

Morgan felt a jolt of panic, wondering how long she had been standing there and exactly what she had overheard.

"And for heaven's sake," she went on in her customary tone, "get off the floor, the lot of you. Here it is, past the time we should have left for the Somerwells', and you're down there crushing everything it took the servants hours to iron."

"It's his fault," Evie said, pointing to Morgan. "He's being a bully. As usual."

"Then, child," Mother retaliated, "since you are so ready to accuse, you won't mind telling the rest of the misdeeds in question. Whom did Morgan catch doing what?"

Evelyn clambered to her feet. "The bully thinks I flirt with Mr. Raleigh." She smiled at Morgan in triumph as she straightened her skirts, fluffing out the ruffles. "He feels that because I occasionally smile at an admirer, I'm acting unladylike."

Mother tightened her lips and shifted her glare to Morgan still on the floor. "Your sister has become quite the accomplished young miss while you were away. It is most acceptable for her to flirt a bit with her young man. And, might I add, most advantageous. The mere thought that he might take more than a passing interest in our dear Evie makes my head light. Do you have any idea what an exceptional catch he would be for her? Not to mention the marvelous business connection for us all." She swung back to her daughter. "Go over to the mirror and center your wig, dear. It's crooked."

While their mother was preoccupied, Morgan stood up, then reached down to assist Prudence.

"Not just yet," she whispered. She lifted the hem of the bedcoverings and resumed her search.

"What are you looking for?"

She turned her eyes up at him. "You'll think I'm careless. I dropped one of those enchanting earbobs you bought me, and it bounced under here."

He knelt to help her.

"Mercy, Prudence," Mother chided. "Get off that floor. Let your husband find it for you. And from now on, if he's not available, ring for a servant. That's what they've been hired for." She whirled around. "And if all of you are not downstairs within the next two minutes, we'll leave without you. I'll not be conspicuously late for you or anyone else." She stomped away.

"Yes, Prudence," Evie said with a giggle. "Don't ever forget. Husbands and servants. Servants and husbands. They're all at your beck and call. So don't let that brute make you think otherwise."

"Oh, I won't, I assure you."

"Ha! I found it." Morgan scooted out from under the bed, the sparkling diamond bauble in his hand. He switched his attention to his sister. "And now, I'm coming to set *you* to rights, brat. 'Tis high time you had a good tanning."

Evelyn squealed and ran from the room as he lunged to his feet.

As Prudence reached for the ornament he held in the palm of his hand, Morgan clamped his fingers tightly over it. "Not so fast, my love. Even a bully deserves some reward."

"Oh. How utterly thoughtless of me." With a beguiling smile, Prudence wrapped her arms about his neck. "Will this do, my handsome and ever so chivalrous brute?" The light kiss turned swiftly to one quite passionate.

Morgan pulled her close, inhaling the enticing perfume she wore as he responded to her with fervor of his own.

"Morgan! Prudence!" came the screech from below.

Releasing a ragged breath, he reluctantly loosened his embrace. "Don't forget where we left off," he breathed against her temple. "When we return, we'll pick up from this point."

Her silver-gray eyes shimmered with unconcealed anticipation as she took the earbob from his hand.

❧ ❧

Chandler lost count of the thousands of British campfires glowing far below the earthen wall of the redoubt. He and Robby wolfed down their biscuits and beans after a long and tiring day, their legs dangling over the enclosed defensive fortification. Occasional rifle shots, undoubtedly from their sniping Pennsylvania riflemen, split the quiet.

With a low chuckle, Chan stretched his sore muscles. "Colonel Hand isn't planning to let them sleep in peace tonight."

"Aye," Robby said, "just like at the Boston and Charlestown barricades. Those awesome long-range rifles will shoot at anything that moves throughout the night."

"Well, we sure don't want those puppets getting it into their heads to take a stroll up here just yet." He took another mouthful. "Hey, there's something odd. I'm surprised I didn't notice it before."

"Notice what?"

"Except for the colonel's riflemen, there aren't any of our regulars in this assembly. Just a couple local militias with virtually no training."

Robby nodded slowly. "When I was fetching our food, I heard somethin' else just as disturbing. General Green, the officer in charge of the defense of this whole island, is down with a fever."

"Someone better send reinforcements soon, or there's no

sense in staying here on Nassau. Funny, isn't it? If the redcoats knew that, they'd be having supper with us right now."

"Ye see humor in that?" Robby asked with a scowl.

Chan averted his eyes and straightened. "Don't look up, but here comes that sergeant we talked to earlier. Landers, I believe someone said his name was."

When the man was too close to ignore, the two put down their plates, then stood and saluted him.

He returned the salute. "One of my men told me you two saw action on the Concord road and at Bunker Hill."

"Only me friend, here, sir," Robby admitted. "He was one of the last to leave Bunker Hill."

Chandler glanced disparagingly at his loose-tongued buddy. What was he trying to do to him? "Nothing to brag about, sir. It just so happened I came upon a full horn of powder as I was in retreat, so I used it up before I left."

"Aye, that he did," Robby added, nodding. "Covered the retreat of scores of others. His friend, Lieutenant Thomas, told me all about his heroism."

Already Chan was composing in his mind the little speech he would soon cram down the Scotsman's throat—just before he throttled him.

"Here. Take this." Ruddy-faced Sergeant Landers thrust his Pennsylvania rifle to Chandler, then followed it with a haver-sack containing the required fixings for it.

Chan suppressed an inward groan. So much for being assigned to safe duty with a quartermaster.

"I don't have enough seasoned men," Landers continued. "I want you to go down there for a couple hours and keep the lobstercoats entertained. Just remember to stay out of range, and keep moving."

"Yes, sir."

"I volunteer to go, too," Robby announced, his expression as wary as it was determined.

"Sure. I'm not fool enough to turn down a volunteer."

"But—sir," Chan cut in. "I'll not be responsible for him out there."

"I'm not askin' ye to be responsible for me," Robby said, hiking his chin. "I can take care of myself."

Chandler shook his head and offered the firearm back to the sergeant. "I'll not go if you send him, sir. He's got a wife and two babies back home."

"So have half the men here, lad."

"But he's never faced a volley of fire. We don't know yet how he'll react under that pressure. He could get the two of us killed." Hating himself for intimating that Robby might be cowardly, Chandler reaffirmed his decision that the young Scot would remain out of harm's way.

"What's your name, Corporal?" the sergeant asked, his tone menacing.

"Chandler, sir. Robert Chandler."

"Well, Corporal, get yourself off this hill—and don't come back until you're out of powder."

"Yes, sir!" Slinging the haversack over his shoulder, Chan picked up his mug and drained the last of his coffee as the older man strode off.

Robby, obviously fuming, reclaimed his plate and stabbed at the food remaining on it.

"Sorry about what I said," Chandler began. "I know you're no coward. That's precisely the problem."

The wiry Scot leveled his gaze at him, his blue eyes unwavering. "You're not responsible for me . . . no matter what Morgan told ye."

"Well, we are responsible for that team and wagon," Chan said pointedly. "One of us should stay alive long enough to return it to our supply camp, right?" With a grim nod, he turned toward the nearest sally port.

"I'll pray for your safety all the while you're down there," Robby said quietly, no lingering trace of anger in his voice.

Chan saluted with his rifle. "Find a deep hole to sleep in. If I know General Howe, he'll have the big guns brought up before morning."

9

As Morgan helped her down from the family carriage, Prudence assessed the brick mansion owned by the wealthy friends of the Thomas family. The setting sun cast a rosy hue over the generous dormers and large Palladian window above the columned portico, lending a lovely contrast to the candle glow pouring from every window of the two-story home. But even in a grand city like Philadelphia, it seemed excessive. With her hands on Morgan's arm, she started up the walk, smiling with as much confidence as she could summon.

The ornate white front door opened, and a uniformed butler admitted them up the hall to an open doorway beyond, where a stately middle-aged couple waited. Both had amazingly similar squarish faces and high foreheads, though the woman's features were noticeably more defined and elegant, and her coloring was fair in contrast to his. "Waldon," the man said with a welcoming smile. "And Mildred. Splendid of you to come."

"Good evening, Landon, Rose." Morgan's father and their host exchanged warm handshakes, while the others entered amid a flurry of greetings.

"And how wonderful to see Morgan," the host went on. "I'm sure the young ladies in attendance will be quite thrilled."

"Landon, dear," his wife said with well-modulated politeness. "I must have forgotten to mention that Morgan has wed.

I was quite taken aback when Mildred told me a few days ago." Switching her attention to Prudence, she offered her hand. "Am I to assume, my dear, that you are the one who somehow managed the impossible?"

Morgan stepped forward. "She is, I am most delighted to confess. I should like to introduce my wife, Prudence." He turned to her. "These are old friends of our family, sweetheart. Mr. and Mrs. Somerwell. We've known them for as far back as I can remember." Smiling graciously, he nodded to them. "This happens to be my darling wife's introduction to Philadelphia society."

Prudence, touched by the love and manly pride in his voice, felt a blush rise on her cheeks as the couple appraised her. "I'm very pleased to meet you both."

"We are most happy all of you were able to come this eve," Rose Somerwell said pleasantly. "Some friends of ours have written a new play, which they will enact for the first time just for us. Later, there will be games, music, and, of course, dancing. It is my fond hope, Prudence, that afterward you'll think kindly of our fair city . . . the true Philadelphia, as it once was before all the uproar. May it soon regain that glory." She closed her blue eyes for a brief second and shook her head.

"And in the meanwhile," her husband announced, "we shall take our seats. Alas, there's not time to offer you refreshments just now. The production is about to begin."

"We must offer you our most sincere apologies," Mother Thomas said, "for being so tardy."

Knowing that it was due in large part to herself, Prudence vowed silently not to repeat this blunder. She certainly didn't intend to earn a bad mark in the eyes of her mother-in-law or any of the family's influential friends.

"Now, Mother," Morgan said smoothly, "you mustn't accept blame that is mine. Cad that I am, 'twas I who made us late. I was holding my beautiful wife captive in our chamber."

At Landon Somerwell's chuckle, Prudence felt her flush

return in force. She didn't have to wonder what he was thinking.

"And but for your age, Son," Mother chided, "I would reprimand you for teasing the poor girl. She lost one of the earbobs Morgan gave her, you see," she explained to the Somerwells, "and wouldn't leave until it was found."

"That was when the bully took her captive," Evelyn blurted in delight.

Her mother branded her with a stern look, then stepped closer to the sequined-gowned hostess. "I simply don't know where I erred with these two. Our other children were so wonderfully pliable." The two women glided toward the rows of chairs in the room as the lighting was subdued in preparation for the performance.

"Evie," Mr. Thomas said, sidling up to her, "knowing the sort of memory your mother has, I would suggest you find a way to make amends before the evening is over."

"You're right, Papa." She gave him a dutiful peck on the cheek, then hooked her arm through his.

Morgan's attempt to follow was interrupted by their host.

"I heard something to the effect that you had left our fine city with Ben Haynes. Have you, perchance, seen Cousin Sophia and the rest of Ben's family while in your travels?"

"Actually, I spent a most delightful time at the Hayneses' farm with the entire family two Christmases past. Due to the blockade and the siege of Boston, however, I've seen them but once since then. They were all in good health—and remarkably good spirits, considering."

Watching the man assimilate this information, Prudence thought of Robby MacKinnon, Sophia Haynes's son-in-law. Not knowing what kind of peril he and Robert Chandler might be in at the moment, she sent a swift prayer heavenward for the safety of both young men.

"A plight which now is affecting all of us," Mr. Somerwell replied sadly. "Well, come along. We wouldn't want to miss the play. It's a farce featuring Saint George and the Dragon." But before they had taken a few steps, the door knocker tapped.

"Excuse me," he said. "We were expecting one more couple. I must go and greet them."

"What a pity the play isn't about King George meeting up with a few fire-breathing, monarch-eating dragons," Prudence whispered to Morgan after the host strode away.

He patted her hand where it rested in the crook of his elbow. "Let's hope, my darling, that Parliament has some of those very animals just waiting for the opportunity to devour him. The force he's assembled in New York harbor is costing a king's ransom, if you'll pardon my pun."

Prudence was amazed to see at least a hundred people gathered to watch the production. When the stage curtains parted to the applause of the audience, she didn't have to feign interest. She looked expectantly toward the set.

The scenes bordered on hilarious, with the man inside the silly dragon costume clumsily and haphazardly trying to manipulate the various parts of the ungainly beast. When he managed to blow red silk streamers from its mouth to simulate fire, it was comical enough to set everyone to laughing. And the hero, "George of the Willow Sword," was equally amusing. The entertainment ended with roaring applause.

Watching the small cast taking their bows, Prudence was convinced that Philadelphia truly was the liveliest city in all the colonies. Such free and easy laughter would have been unheard of in staid Boston.

Of course, there was no denying that in her former days she would have condemned such frivolity herself. Up until quite recently, she would easily have scorned anything or anyone who wasn't as starched and proper as she. But thankfully, the Good Lord had softened those judgmental feelings considerably, and now her only condemnation this eve lay in the fact that the charming, happy people around her were Tories.

As the clapping died down, the servants relit the candle sconces along the walls, illuminating the grand room with its satiny, pale green and ivory wallpaper and the garlands of fresh flowers that draped the tall windows. Musicians mounted the stage.

Mrs. Somerwell rang a small crystal handbell. "Your attention, please," she called above the noise and buzz of voices. "We must ask everyone to help clear the floor for games and dancing. If you would all please carry your chairs to the outer walls, it would help greatly. Thank you."

Evelyn, who had been sitting with friends a few rows ahead, lifted her chair and joined Morgan. "Honestly. That Clay Raleigh is such a dullard," she whispered. "All through the play he kept trying to attract my attention, but I pretended I couldn't hear or see him. You'd think he would take the hint. But," she added, with a mischievous smile reminiscent of her dashing brother's, "innocent-child-with-a-huge-dowry that I am, I'm incapable of deliberately toying with him, aren't I?"

Even as she spoke, the single-minded Englishman threaded his way toward her through the milling crowd. A split second before his arrival she set her chair down and coyly began fanning herself, then whirled around and collided with him—a move which appeared accidental. Her shell fan clattered to the floor.

"Oh, I must beg your pardon," he blustered, bowing to retrieve the fan. "Do forgive my clumsiness."

Prudence looked askance at Morgan, hoping her expression conveyed her amazement that the two of them had been worried about their poor little Evie, so innocent regarding the ways of the world.

"I believe you promised me the first dance," Raleigh said, offering her his arm.

Evelyn batted her lashes. "Why, how gallant of you to remember. But first, I have a dreadful thirst. We arrived too late for refreshments, I'm afraid."

"I noticed," he said, his voice rife with meaning.

"Then, if you'd be so kind." She gifted him with a charming smile, then turned to Prudence. "Oh, I am being rude. Pru, you and Morgan must be equally thirsty. Would you, Mr. Raleigh?"

His eager smile faded a shade. "But of course."

Once the man was out of earshot on his way to the crowded

beverage table, Evelyn rolled her eyes. "Now, isn't he just the handiest sort to have around?"

Morgan frowned. "Just remember, even pets have been known to turn on their masters. Your obedient bear could just as easily do the same to you. Don't let him get you alone, or you might find out exactly how handy he really is."

"I shan't worry about that overmuch," she said brightly. "You've vowed to shadow me this entire evening." Quickly she swung to Prudence. "Of course, I welcome *your* company, so I suppose I shall have to endure the bully's as well."

"Morgan!" a voice called from across the room. "Morgan Thomas!"

Looking toward the source, Prudence observed a young man waving. Within seconds, others converged on Morgan, all smiles, everyone talking at once.

Prudence knew her handsome husband had been rediscovered.

"Don't fret," he whispered with a quick hug. With his other arm he caught hold of Evie and tugged her close, too. "Ah, what a pity," he said with chagrin. "After having been so carefree all my life, now to suddenly be burdened with not one, but two damsels to look after."

❦ ❦

Clumps of recently scythed grass felt prickly and rough through his shirt as Chandler crawled on his belly across an open field. The moon, rising higher, lent a pale blue glow to the world around him. What he would have given for some of the fog that now shrouded the ships anchored in the Narrows. He wasn't completely certain he was beyond the range of the British Brown Besses.

The silhouette of a redcoated sentry passed before a distant campfire. In his tall military hat he presented an excellent target, if only Chan had taken aim quickly enough. He'd wait for another chance.

From far away, a rifle report sounded. At once the guard and three other shadowy figures bolted from the vast encampment and into the field, heading toward the telltale flash from the rifle's pan. Professional soldiers all, each knew precisely what action to take without so much as a whispered order.

Chan could only hope the sniper had possessed sense enough to remove himself immediately from the spot, since the main fault with the long-range Pennsylvania rifle was the extra time needed to reload after firing. The redcoats could easily be upon the man before he managed that feat.

Another flash and crack shattered the air. One of the charging soldiers fell to the ground.

His cohorts halted and fired their muskets at the new flash, one of the balls digging up the ground dangerously close to Chandler. He froze and held his breath, knowing that they, too, would require time to reload.

Within seconds, crunching footsteps revealed the fact that the two king's men had managed to reload and were now running across the field toward the second sniper. A third stopped and brought up his musket but didn't fire.

Chan raised his head enough to scan the dim area.

When another crunch came from a new location, the sentry took aim and fired toward it.

A brief silence followed.

Knowing that the redcoat's musket was now empty, Chandler eyed him. The man was a good fifty yards from the others. A perfect time to take a bead on the fellow.

The sentry became aware of his vulnerability when moonlight glinted off the steel blade of his bayonet. He began backing toward the camp.

With the enemy framed in his sight, Chandler couldn't bring himself to pull the trigger. There seemed something cowardly about lying in wait for an unsuspecting man. Besides, his orders had been to keep the British awake and nervous, nothing more. He relaxed his hold and watched the soldier hesitate cautiously, then return to his post. His two comrades also returned to camp carrying the fallen man. Snatches of angry oaths carried easily to Chan's ears.

More flashes and shots rang out—this time from the British

side. Musket balls fell several yards short of the positions occupied earlier by the snipers. Chandler couldn't help wishing he could trade the cover of darkness for a few sturdy trees to hide behind.

He lay motionless for several minutes. Would they order a column out to send volleys into the night? He waited, tense with the uncertainty of it all. But the camp gradually settled down again. Wood was added to the fire, and several soldiers milled about, pouring coffee and talking.

Still, he couldn't simply lie there all night without doing something. Chan tried to choose a man to fire at . . . pick the one to send a shot ripping through. But the most tempting target hung a few inches above the fire. Steadying his rifle against his shoulder, he took deliberate aim, then squeezed the first trigger. He held his breath and moved his finger to the second, a hair trigger, and tapped it.

The flash blinded him momentarily, but with the explosion he heard a loud ring. Men yelped. The spots before his eyes cleared, and he saw soldiers leaping clear of the scalding coffee sputtering from the flames. He had hit his target.

"Get the blasted coward!" one of them yelled. They scrambled and ran for their weapons.

Chandler sprang to a crouch and beat a swift retreat.

A shot rang out somewhere nearby.

Within seconds another explosion roared, this one much louder, closer. The concussion all but knocked Chan off his feet as he sprinted through the night.

The British had brought up some artillery. The game was about to get rougher.

10

Morgan managed to smile at the merchant sea captains from England who were attending the gala. It was difficult to focus on trying to gain their trust, what with Evelyn flitting about from one man to another on the dance floor and Prudence, too, surrounded by eager swains. Though dancing was an entirely new venture for his wife, she had spent hours under his and Evie's tutelage and managed to learn fairly quickly the intricacies of the various minuets and reels. Now as he watched her glide gracefully over the floor on the arm of their host, he felt a strong surge of pride and struggled against cutting in.

Granted, when a horde of old friends converged on him and Prudence, he figured he was in for a merciless round of teasing—or worse, would have to endure their tattling to Prudence about his wilder days. But to a man, from the moment they gazed upon that incredible heart-shaped face of hers with its wide-set gray eyes, eyes just now perfecting the art of flirting, his so-called friends had stumbled over one another's feet vying for a turn on the dance floor with her. Loathe to be termed a jealous husband, he now had to stand by and watch, however hard that was to do.

"I, too, am becoming most impatient these days," one of the captains remarked to the others, his glance settling on each of them to ensure that they were in complete agreement. Nodding, they lifted their drinks. "Hear! Hear!"

Aren't we all, Morgan mused silently. He expended great effort to turn his attention away from his wife and make some headway toward what he was sent here to do.

"I'll tell you one thing," another ship's master said. "Unless something substantial is done posthaste to resolve this frightful mess, I shall set sail for Canada. I understand our friends in Boston suffered severe privation during the lawless siege, then had to leave most of their belongings behind when they fled to Halifax. That is true, is it not, Mr. Thomas?"

Morgan met the stout captain's concerned gaze. "Quite. Personally, I believe Parliament should see to it that they are reimbursed for all their losses."

A lantern-jawed sea master on the edge of the group scowled. "I hardly see how Britain should be expected to recompense colonists for what other colonists do to them, do you, gentlemen?" He circulated a scathing grimace.

"I daresay," Morgan interjected, "they were dwelling on one tiny peninsula supposedly under the protection of thousands of your military—who, I might add, promised to do just that. Protect them. But alas, the army quite shamefully neglected to fulfill its obligation. Not only did these poor loyal folk have their harbor blockaded by their very own protectors, depriving them of their livelihood, they were then starved, then forced to leave all their worldly goods behind. Do you not consider that appalling?"

One man gestured with his glass. "You know very well, lad, that Parliament's punitive action was directed at the outlaws."

"Ah, yes," Morgan responded. "But whom did it hurt? Not your outlaws, certainly. For the most part they had already left the city and reestablished themselves. But, on the other hand, my own wife's family home and business were burned to the ground. And now my dear mother is in terrible fear for her life as well, and for everything we've worked generations to build. All of this in a city where these Continental Congress rebels are meeting openly, recruiting armies and raising money to finance them. All to wage war against their own motherland."

"Armies?" one man asked in alarm. "Did you say *armies?*"

"I did." Morgan gave a decisive nod. Despite the fact that it was only wishful thinking at the moment, there was something quite appealing about the sound of it. "Why ever else would my mother be so fearful? And speaking of protection, I do believe it is time that I rescue my lovely wife from the wilds of Pennsylvania." Chuckling for effect, he gave them an opportunity to do the same. "If you'll excuse me, gentlemen." He bowed his head graciously and took his leave.

In mere seconds he spotted Prudence on the opposite side of the room, dancing with Dirk Martingale, a chum from his bachelor days. Morgan paused, admiring the beautiful vision she made in her saffron silk and fashionable wig as she dipped and swayed to the patterned steps. While he watched, his thoughts shifted back to the captains. He relished the impression he was certain he had made on them. It had been jolly fun putting the stuffy merchant seamen on the defensive about their government's inability to maintain order. Henceforth, they could only think of him as one more pompous, demanding Loyalist. Or so he hoped.

With the most beautiful wife here, he added, smiling to himself. He observed the way the candlelight sparkled over her necklace and earbobs and radiated from her luminous eyes. She made such an enchanting picture, it was hard to wait for the final strands of the minuet so he could reclaim her.

When the piece at last ended, he strode purposefully to the couple. "Sorry, old man," he told his friend as he snagged Prudence around the waist. "My wife has promised this next dance to me."

"Then I shall, with some reluctance, relinquish the enchanting damsel to you," Dirk said. Always a bit of a rake, he bowed over her hand as she curtsied, the gleam in his eyes more wolfish than anything else. Then he walked away.

Prudence lifted her gaze and smiled at Morgan with relief. "I am utterly parched. Do take me to the nearest cup of punch, or I shall swoon."

"As you wish." But as they started for the refreshment table,

Morgan suddenly remembered Evelyn and made a quick search among the guests. He spied her standing nearby with Clay Raleigh in the midst of a cluster of young people. The Englishman appeared even more feral than Dirk Martingale had, if that were possible. "I rather think we should cool our little Evie down, too," he told Prudence, steering her in that direction.

"That might be wise."

Morgan tapped his sister on the shoulder. "We're stepping across the hall for something cool. Care to join us?"

Evelyn looked from him to Prudence. "Why, that sounds lovely."

"I heartily agree," Raleigh added, without releasing her arm. He fell into step with them. "Afterward, perhaps a nice stroll in the garden might be appropriate." His intent gaze centered on Evie.

More than certain that the cad had some very inappropriate things on his mind, Morgan had to force a grin. "I say, that is an excellent idea. Don't you think, love?"

"Oh, yes," Prudence murmured. "A stroll in the garden would be divine. The late roses smell so wonderful."

The Englishman's own smile stiffened around the edges, while Evie's curved upward in wicked delight.

As they exited the grand ballroom and started across the entry hall to the dining room, a man burst through the front door. Panting and out of breath, he rushed to the wide entrance of the room, which was teeming with guests. "Hear, hear, everyone! Listen! The British landed a force on Nassau Island this morning. And they promise to deliver New York by the end of the week!"

A great commotion broke out. A man raised his arms for silence. "Who told you this?" he asked.

"An express rider by the name of Joseph Galloway just rode in from Staten Island. Said General Howe landed over fifteen thousand infantry and marines. His brother, Black Dick, moved his fleet into the Narrows. The rebels haven't a chance! They'll be nothing but bloody corpses when we're through with them."

With a broad smile, Landon Somerwell stepped onto the stage and raised his glass high. "This calls for a toast!"

"No! A cheer!" someone else yelled, leaping beside the host. "Hip hip hooray!"

"Hip hip hooray!" came the excited echo from all present. "Hip hip hooray!"

Morgan nudged Prudence, and together they made a valiant show of enthusiasm. But he could feel the tense grip of her hand on his arm.

Just as suddenly, she released her hand and took Evelyn by the shoulders, leaning close so Evelyn could hear above the uproar. Then she said something into the younger girl's ear. Morgan noted that Evelyn looked pale as death.

Prudence was up to something, of that he was certain. But what?

"Sweetheart," she said, swinging back to him. "I'm afraid your sister's upset stomach has returned. All this excitement, I'm sure. She needs to leave at once."

Evelyn hadn't been ill earlier. Nonetheless, Morgan picked up his cue. "You mean, she's about to . . ." He clutched at his throat.

Evelyn cupped her hand over her mouth with a frantic nod.

Clay Raleigh, having overheard the exchange, slanted a glance at her. "I must sadly bid you Godspeed, Miss Thomas. I pray you feel better soon." He distanced himself from her with such haste, Morgan might have laughed . . . if only his heart weren't so heavy.

He and Prudence each took one of the younger girl's elbows and led her outside. And none too soon. She all but crumpled the second they closed the door after themselves, her face already awash with tears. Trembling, she flung herself at her older brother. "Oh, Morgan," she sobbed. "Jamie's there. And all that awfulness is about to happen—or has happened. He could be shot. Bayoneted. He might even be

. . . dead." Burrowing her face into the front of his satin frock coat, she cried uncontrollably.

"I know, little one," he crooned, wrapping a comforting arm about her and the other around Prudence. His own fearful thoughts were of the other two patriots he knew personally . . . the two Roberts.

Prudence, understanding his pain, reached up and placed a palm against his cheek, her eyes searching his. "They'll be fine. After all, they're safely tucked away behind the port of New York, aren't they? That's miles from Nassau Island. Miles."

But Morgan knew her assurances were as much for herself as for him. He sent a fervent prayer to heaven for his two good friends and for Jamie. But an unexplainable feeling of dread made it hard to breathe. He tugged the girls close and escorted them to the waiting carriage.

11

Trudging through the incessant drizzle, Robert Chandler made a futile attempt to brush some of the grime and splattered blood from his clothes as he marched along the muddy Gowanus Road paralleling the shoreline of the Narrows. It had been a very long four days since the British landed on Nassau Island. After nights of scant sleep, two of which had been in the pouring rain, the other men in his squad scouting the British advance moved as wearily as Robert.

They stayed at the redoubt on the Heights of Guan only one night after they had been chased back up the hill by the enemy's artillery. The riflemen, with their long-range firearms and excellent marksmanship, had been ordered by Colonel Hand to rout approaching Hessians from advantageous positions on the Bedford Road. But the Germans' muskets could be reloaded twice as quickly and were fitted with bayonets. Despite their losses, the relentless mercenaries had closed the gap, and Chandler's battalion had been forced into a bloody retreat. Now the enemy held possession of all the orchards and fields on the east side of the hills.

Thankfully, Robby MacKinnon had been spared having to face the enemy. He had been given the detail of driving casualties back to the village of Brooklyn. Not having the Scot near the line of fire was a relief to Chandler. One less worry.

Chan hoped that since General Washington had ferried six regiments to the island and had come personally to direct the battles, he would turn their failures into triumph. But rumor had it that all the American positions were under heavy artillery fire. General Stirling, Colonel Hand's superior, now led a force no more than half a mile from the First Pennsylvania's own encampment.

Approaching their makeshift camp on high ground, Chan wondered if Robby had managed to keep their blankets dry. Three or four hours of undisturbed sleep would be pure heaven.

When he saw the wagon parked beneath a tree, its canvas cover dripping from the rain, Chandler's spirits lifted. Perched at the rear of the bed, unharmed, was the gentle-hearted Scot. He veered toward his friend. "Robby!"

"Thank the Good Lord ye survived another day," the younger man said, his dark mustache spreading with his welcoming smile. He patted the space beside him in invitation.

Chan hopped aboard and leaned his tired bones against the side for support as he watched Robby gnawing on a rock-hard biscuit. "Didn't run into anything but one of their scouting parties. We sent them packing. These backwoods Pennsylvanians sure do know how to shoot." He grabbed the biscuit his friend tossed to him and bit into it. "Too bad we don't have more of those sharpshooters."

"I could hear a battle ragin' down near the water," Robby said.

"The redcoats have been trying all afternoon to find a weak spot in General Stirling's line."

"Isn't he guardin' everything from the other side of the road down to the marsh?"

Chan nodded. "So I wouldn't recommend getting too cozy."

"Aye." Robby chewed thoughtfully. "Washington should've sent more than six regiments. We're still outnumbered two to one, and our losses are mountin' all the time. It's been reported that the Brits are movin' into position against General Sullivan and General Woodhull. And the First Pennsylvania has suffered many more casualties than it appears. Our own reinforcements just make it less noticeable."

"You're not telling me anything I don't already know. I've seen it myself."

"Aye, but I'm tellin' ye we've been cut down by half."

"Half?" Chan sat up straighter at the dire news.

Robby gave a grave nod. "The First is down to about two hundred men."

Chan mulled over the numbing fact in his mind. "Well, we were the first line of defense. I suppose seeing action every day since the British landed, we have to expect a large number of casualties."

"Ye wouldna' be thinking of 'em as mere numbers if ye'd been transporting 'em as I've done these last days. Me heart has been nigh onto burstin' at the endless suffering. And, Robert, 'tis even sadder how many of the lads had yet to make peace with the Lord. I'm thankful I was here to help, to answer their questioning spirits." He paused. "Odd, is it not, how often one must sink to the lowest point before he thinks of lookin' to the Lord, before a man will reach up and take the hand that's been waitin' all along to lift him up."

As his friend talked, Chandler found himself even more grateful Robby MacKinnon had been ordered to stay with the wagon. The wounded must have appreciated having someone as sympathetic as this sensitive young man to comfort them. Still, it was a struggle for Chandler to justify the fact that a God whom some called loving would allow the death of youth dedicated to fighting for liberty. Or, for that matter, that God could have taken someone so unselfish and giving as his own Julia for no reason at all.

"I do have a bit of good news, though," Robby said with a grin.

Chan stared incredulously. "Short of the Crown forces magically disappearing from Nassau Island, what news could be good?"

"We're to be sent back to the village near Brooklyn Heights

to rest up, soon as Major Burd's battalion is ferried over to relieve us."

"You mean," Chan said, brightening, "a whole night's sleep?"

"From what I hear. But according to the sergeant, it'll be a few hours before they arrive."

"Is this Landers you're talking about? our favorite sergeant?"

"Aye."

"Did you think to remind the man that we don't even belong here? We should've been permitted to go back to New York days ago."

Robby's mouth curved upward in a smile. "Landers said that Colonel Hand has been so pleased with our efforts, he's requestin' we be transferred to his unit. Busy as he is, he actually noticed us. He's even talkin' about a commendation for ye."

Chan groaned. "Just me, or the whole battalion? I'm not the only one shooting at the enemy."

"Maybe. But you're the one who carried that wounded lad across open ground the first night and back up to the redoubt. Carryin' him under cannon fire all the way up the hill, at that."

"He was just a skinny kid," Chandler protested. "Anyone would've done the same. How's he doing, by the way?"

"That *skinny* kid," Robby chuckled, "owes his very life to ye. He's on the mend."

"Well, that's good to know. But I sure didn't do anything out of the ordinary." Embarrassed that someone was making a big to-do out of nothing, Chan pulled out his blanket roll and curled up in it. "Wake me when the relief column gets here."

❦ ❧

"Chandler?"

The whisper came from far away. Chan huddled deeper into his blanket.

Someone shook his shoulder. "Chan? Wake up. The sergeant wants ye."

"What?" he asked, still groggy. "Are we leaving? Has our relief arrived?"

"Nay, lad," Robby said.

Chandler sat upright and rubbed his gritty eyes. The dim glow from the dying embers of the campfires did little to dispel the darkness under the layer of clouds. "What does our beloved sergeant want this time?" he asked with more than a little sarcasm.

"Didna' say. But he wants ye to go to Colonel Hand's tent."

Sliding down off the wagon, Chan couldn't decide which ached the most, his feet or the rest of his body. He did his best to stretch out a few kinks while taking note that most of the other soldiers within the circles of light remained close to the warmth of their fires. It was not a general order to fall in. "I'd say the sarge has taken a definite liking to me, Robby. Could it be he wants to adopt me?" He laughed at the ridiculous notion.

"For a lad as scruffy looking as yourself at the moment," the Scot chuckled, "ye'd best not get your hopes up too high about that."

"What do you mean? I'm in fine fettle." Running his fingers through his tangled hair to restore some semblance of order, he plunked on his tricorn, then grabbed his rifle and haversack. "See you later."

"Aye. Just be sure ye stay alive. And Godspeed."

All but Colonel Hand's tent had been taken down in anticipation of their imminent departure, so Chandler had to step over a number of slumbering forms to reach the one canvas shelter. Outside it, enough men to form a company were gathering.

The Irish colonel faced the group, looking no more rested than any of the rest of them. "I know you lads expected we'd be behind the lines by now, getting a good night's sleep. But one of the sentries has spotted what he thinks are a couple

British platoons sneaking into the apple orchard to the south."

Groaned rumblings spread through the group as the colonel continued.

"The lobsterbacks are most likely probing, hoping to find a vulnerable spot to breach between us and General Stirling. Divide and conquer, so to speak. Well, we're going to do some sneaking of our own. You men have been handpicked by your sergeants because of your proven ability under fire. You are to crawl down through the watermelon field below us and wait till the redcoats emerge from the trees. I need not tell you to wait until they're in the open," he added with emphasis. "Sergeants, move out your men. And God be with you."

"All right, men," Sergeant Landers added quietly. "Listen up. We're to take the far flank. Spread out. Keep a good rod between each of you. Chandler," he motioned, "take the far outside edge of the patch. Take Trudell, Carter, and Reynolds with you. The rest of you men come with me."

Chan didn't need the knotting of his insides to remind him how he loathed being responsible for the lives of others. Hadn't he left his North Carolina plantation for that very reason? He rued the day he had allowed Morgan to make him a corporal. He started to protest, but Landers had already crouched low and taken off.

Chandler felt three pairs of wary eyes trained on him. He lifted a shoulder in an uneasy shrug. "Never should've given the man my name," he mumbled to the others. He turned and crouched to follow the sergeant, letting his men be responsible for their own fates.

A wide field yawned before them in the gloomy night. Beneath a tangle of watermelon vines, the mud was ankle deep. Chan's rifle, slung high, bounced against his back as he led the way. Knowing that the assigned men were following him added to his tension as he kept an eye out for movement in the deeper darkness of the orchard.

Already they were passing others from the company who had taken up positions on their bellies out of range of the enemy muskets. Nearing the end of the vines, Chandler stopped and motioned for one of his men to drop down. The redcoats would most likely come from the center, so he cut at an angle toward the outer edge, placing his other two men as he went. "Remember to wait for fifteen seconds after the first volley before firing," he told the one in the middle, "so the others will have cover while they reload. We don't want to give the British time to rush into range." The lesson learned on Bedford Road had been invaluable.

At the farthest, most vulnerable, position, Chan sank down to the cold ground, more willing to expose himself to the flank than to place someone else in peril.

Several minutes passed. No sign of lobster red. Another wild-goose chase? Had the sentries been seeing things? Surely if redcoats were coming they would have reached this side of the orchard by now. It was no more than ten acres across. On the other hand, he would rather lie in the mud than fight in it.

He eased up enough to check as far as he could see through the darkness. Barely able to make out his own motionless men to the side, he strained harder to peer into the orchard.

A flash of white—no, two—moved forward. White-clad legs. Another pair followed. Then more. They stopped at the edge of the field. Waited.

Chan held his breath, his pulse racing. At least the melon patch provided cover for his men. It would be hard to make out their heads among the rounded shapes on the vines.

More white legs emerged from the trees. Again they were all down near his end. Chandler caught the faint glint of a large steel barrel. Artillery was being rolled out into the open. *They're planning to set up a battery to fire on our encampment!*

Despite the cold, sweat beaded on his forehead.

A minute passed. Then he saw more cannons being rolled into position, yet no one down his line had ordered a volley. Obviously no one else was aware of what was being planned. It was up to him.

He cocked his rifle and sighted on the nearest pair of legs.

He mopped sweat from his face, pulled the first trigger. Eyes closed against the blinding flash, he tripped the second.

An instant after his shot, his comrades fired a volley. Cries of pain split the night as several British crumpled to the ground.

Patriots at the other end of the line lunged madly across the vines until they sighted the British and got off more shots. No one wanted the redcoats to take cover behind their cannons and discharge them.

Reloading in frenzied haste, Chandler heard an order from down the line. "Fire!"

A second volley downed more redcoats.

"Retreat!" a Crown officer yelled, and those left standing ran back into the trees.

A man to Chan's left leaped up to give chase. Others followed, firing wildly into the deep darkness.

After reloading again, Chandler ran toward the grove. The enemy would soon regroup in the inky blackness of the orchard and get off a volley of their own at the charging Americans.

At the brink of the trees, he stopped and crouched behind the wheel of an abandoned cannon. Not a single telltale click of a hammer could be heard. Only the thudding of feet and the groans of the casualties lying in their own blood mere yards away.

"Disarm the wounded," Chandler shouted to the men who ran up to join him. "Carter, you and Reynolds scout down the west side. Make sure the lobsters don't double back on us."

As the pair took off, Chan recalled Robby's wagon. "Trudell, go back to camp and have MacKinnon come to transport the wounded." Then he swung his attention to the line of fieldpieces. Had the sentry not spotted these redcoats, he and the rest of Hand's men would have had a very lively wake-up call. But now the cannons were theirs, and he had no doubt the Irish colonel would make quite good use of the windfall.

Colonel Hand appeared out of the darkness while Chan

searched for the best route to roll the cannons out of the field and up to the encampment. The leader's face was grim, and so was Sergeant Landers's. "Over here," the sergeant ordered.

Aware that he had been usurping their authority, Chandler traipsed out into the vines to them. He saluted. "Begging your pardon, sir. I don't know what came over me."

Landers shook his head. "You've been so levelheaded up till now. I can't believe you didn't wait to fire until they were farther out in the open where we could all get them in our sights."

"From my vantage point, sir, I could see that the enemy wasn't planning to come any closer. They were lining up their fieldpieces."

"Fieldpieces?" Colonel Hand pushed past Chandler, leaving him and Landers to follow.

The colonel took stock of the cannons and the crates of balls beside each. He turned around. "It would appear we owe you an apology, Corporal—Chandler, isn't it?"

"Yes, sir. Another minute or two and they could've answered our volleys." As Chan spoke, he became aware of a new look of respect from his superiors. He felt all the more awkward. "If you have no other need of me, sir, I'll go help with the prisoners. Oh, I sent Carter and Reynolds down the side of the orchard to make sure the redcoats don't double back."

"Very good, Chandler," Hand said, his expression all the more approving. "I won't forget the initiative you showed here this night. You're dismissed to aid the prisoners."

As he strode away, he heard the colonel speak to Landers. "Yes, sir," the sergeant answered. "That's the same Carolina man who distinguished himself at Bunker Hill."

Chan wasted no time blending in with the other men, trying his best to become anonymous as the wounded were moved away from the dead. Administering whatever help he could while awaiting Robby and the wagon, he hoped against hope that his friend would come bearing news that the relief column had arrived.

None too soon, the slosh of the wagon wheels carried to his

ears. The Scotsman pulled up alongside. "Grand to see ye've not been wounded," he called down.

"We were lucky this time."

Robby wrapped the reins around the brake and climbed over the seat. "Luck, or God?"

Chan shook his head. The Scot never gave up!

Then he turned to a man at his elbow. "Give me a hand, will you?" Together they lifted a grimacing redcoat into the bed, with Robby helping from above. "The relief show up yet?"

Robby grinned down at him. "Aye. Came while you lads were down here shootin' up the place. A green bunch, they are. Ye should've seen their eyes when they heard all the ruckus."

"Sleep." The other soldier thumped Chan's back. "Now we'll get some blessed sleep."

"In a dry place," Chan returned.

"Well, move aside, then, so we can get the rest loaded," Robby said.

Chandler turned to see a line of others waiting with bleeding, gasping men.

From somewhere in the orchard a shot rang out.

Reminded of the two men he had sent to track the enemy, Chan swung toward the trees.

Nearby, someone grunted and fell.

Chandler whirled back to the wagon.

Robby lay crumpled beside the wounded soldier, Scottish blood mingling with English.

12

"No! Robby!" Chandler hurled himself onto the wagon and grabbed his friend, hugging him to his chest. "Please, please," he begged, his eyes seeking the heavens, "don't do this. Not to Robby. Not to Emily." Everything blurred before his face as he looked down again at the limp Scot. As if from a great distance he heard the order given to turn the cannons, and the men nearby began shooting their rifles into the orchard. Chan's only concern was the lad's labored and raspy breathing. A crushing heaviness compressed his lungs. "Oh, Robby, Robby."

He felt his friend stir.

Snatching at even the slimmest hope, Chan held him still. "Robby?"

He moaned.

"Where are you hit?"

"Chest." The word came out on a gasp.

Chandler touched the mushy, bleeding crater in the younger man's torso. *No! It can't be, it can't be.* Desperately he tried to stem the flow, but blood surged through his fingers.

"'Tis . . . bad," the lad whispered.

Chan gathered the remnants of his shredded hope. "Oh, not so bad." But even as he spoke, he knew the truth.

Robby grasped the front of Chandler's shirt. "Take . . . Emmy . . . bairns . . . to . . . Princeton." He coughed.

"Y-you don't know what you're saying," Chan said.

"Please," Robby grunted. "No one . . . else." His grip on Chandler's shirt tightened.

Chan rocked him in his arms. "We'll both take them. You and me. Together."

Robby shuddered, and another coughing spasm racked his wiry frame. In the faint light, Chandler saw his eyes open wide and fill with a wondrous glow. "Mother?" he murmured, a tiny smile lifting the corners of his mouth. "Father? Ye've . . . come."

"*No,*" Chan pleaded softly. "No." But in his heart he knew it was for naught.

And then a peace transformed Robby's face as he looked up at him. "Take care . . . of me . . . sweet . . ." He emitted a long, slow breath. His hand slid down Chan's chest.

Chandler bent over his friend's bloody form and wept.

❦ ❦

"*Robby!*" Waking from a deep sleep, Emily sat up with a start. Her heart pounded with panic, beating almost audibly in the silence. Instinctively, she reached to touch him in the darkened room. Of course. He wasn't there. He was in New York, helping Morgan.

But with the oppressive emptiness, she knew the truth.

Clutching his cold pillow to her breast, Emily buried her face into its softness, trying to capture some tangible remembrance of him there. A very slight, almost imagined trace of him lingered. It stabbed at her heart.

Oh, Lord God in heaven. Why? I need him so. She slid off the bed and onto her knees. Tears coursed down her cheeks and neck and into her nightdress as she crumpled against the wall and looked heavenward. "Please, heavenly Father. Please, let it not be so. Not my Robby."

But the only answer in the depths of her soul was her husband's own whispered words the night he left. *'Twould never be my own choice to have somethin' keep me from coming back to ye. But if it should come to pass, ye must be brave for me, for our wee bairns. 'Tis what drew me to ye those few short years past, sweet*

Emmy. You've been so bonny and brave. If it should happen, be brave again. I'll wait for ye over yonder. Me love will guide ye Home.

Be brave? A cold draft washed over her, raising gooseflesh. "Oh, Robby," she murmured, "I was only brave for you. I don't know if I could be that way again, without you. I love you." Her breath caught on a sob, and she sank to the floor.

❦ ❦

Someone tugged at the leg of Chandler's trousers. "Move aside, man."

Chan looked up to see a pair of soldiers carrying a wounded redcoat.

"Reach down and give us a hand," one of them said. "Help us get him into the wagon."

He just stared. "My friend . . ."

"Sorry, I didn't know the lad." The touch of sympathy in the voice made Chan feel worse as the pain of his loss settled around him like a fog.

"Dreadful shame," the other said. "A lone sniper, from the way it looked. Just when he was about to be relieved, too."

"He-he wasn't even in the fighting," Chan said, his gaze drawn once more to the lad lying so peacefully in death. "All he ever did was try to help people. Took care of our wounded boys—*and* theirs." He shot a scathing glare at the wounded British soldiers whose cohorts were responsible for the senseless waste. "Gave them comforting words. There wasn't a violent bone in his body. He was purely a good man, a godly man."

"The two of us are both plumb sorry, Corporal, but our arms are about to give out. You wouldn't want us to drop this here man, would you now?"

Chandler didn't care one way or the other about the redcoat suspended between them, but he realized he wouldn't be able to take Robby out of here until all casualties were loaded. Before stepping down to lend a hand, he carefully laid the young Scotsman out, closing his eyes, folding his hands, straightening his legs. His dear friend deserved respect.

There was no time for grieving when Chan drove the wagon back to camp. He was ordered to take the prisoners on to the village up on Brooklyn Heights, where a makeshift hospital had been set up. But the drive provided time to think. To decide.

Chan wouldn't bother asking for permission this time. He would simply leave. He would let no one stop him from taking Robby back to Emily and his dear children—not even General Washington himself.

Once the wounded were unloaded, Chan climbed back onto the wagon seat for Robby's journey home and threaded his way through the arriving soldiers clogging his path. Often he was forced to wait while a column of marching men commandeered the roadway. Despite his churning emotions, he forced himself to relax, fearful of attracting attention as he traveled the last mile to the ferry.

Nearing the landing, he gazed out over the half-mile expanse of water. Small boats of every description, heavy with men and supplies, came out of the night, heading toward the dock to be unloaded. With the arrival of so many more troops adding confusion and bustle, he doubted he would be missed.

Torches burned brightly across the wharf. As Chandler unfolded a tarp and gently covered Robby's body, he paused. It had been much too dark before to really see, but now the gaping wound in his chest was shockingly visible, and he looked so young. How would Chan ever find words to explain this to Robby's Emily . . . his widow. The ache in Chan's throat brought back full force his own tragedy. He knew all too well the devastation of Emily's loss.

With a shuddering sigh, he covered the purest friend he'd ever known, then gathered the reins again, flicking them over the horses' backs.

"Halt!" a beefy boatman shouted. "By whose authority are you boarding?

Chan straightened. "We need more powder. I've been dispatched by General Stirling."

"Then you must have a written order."

"No."

"Then you ain't leavin' this dock."

"What's your name?" Chandler challenged.

The muscular man took on a stubborn expression. "What's it to you?"

"If I have to go back for a paper," Chan said evenly, "I want to be sure to tell the general what idiot is responsible for this holdup. I'm fairly certain he'll not forget you. What did you say your name was?"

He moistened his lips. "I got my orders, same as you."

"Then you have no reason not to give your name."

The man rubbed his mouth, then grinned at the other boatmen. "Arnold Pell," he announced defiantly.

"Arnold Pell," Chandler repeated, as if committing it to memory. But he was more than aware his bluff hadn't worked. In despair he pulled on the reins. "Back! Back!" More than likely, every available craft was already in use, leaving none for the ferry dock even as far up as Kip's Bay. Well, if he had to, he'd find some narrow spot and swim across with Robby's body and the horses.

"Wait!"

"Whoa." Chandler pulled up on the reins and stared wordlessly at the boatman.

"Just where's the general sendin' you?"

"The arsenal near the port battery," he lied wearily.

"Oh, all right. Come aboard, then. But next time you make sure you get your orders in writing, hear?"

"Next time. Sure, I'll do that." It was going to be a long night.

With longer days to come.

13

A rhythmic duel between crickets and tree toads kept tempo with the creaking of Emily's rocking chair as she stared pensively into the fading twilight. How could there still be such quietness, such peace in the world, when the dearest dreams of her life had turned to ashes? How could the sky beyond the western rim of trees cast that breathtaking rose and lavender glow over the pastures of her girlhood home, when deep within her all was colorless and bleak?

Moths fluttered against the globes of the lanterns on the porch railing. Their futile struggle to touch the flickering candle flames reminded her how desperately she wished she would wake up and find that the past two days had been nothing but a nightmare, a horrid dream. She had prayed so hard that it was untrue. But the dull ache refused to diminish, a constant testimony that nothing would ever be the same again as long as she lived.

On her lap, two-year-old Rusty stirred in his sleep, and Emily looked down as a tiny smile touched his lips and then vanished as quickly. An angel kiss, Mama had always called sleep-smiles. Could it have been something even more dear . . . a kiss from the daddy who'd been taken from him? The bittersweet thought brought the sting of tears, and she blinked them away.

She should have put her little son up to bed an hour ago with his big sister, but he had been fussing over a new tooth.

And, in truth, Emily needed to hold him. Except for the auburn hair he had inherited from his grandma, he was the very image of Robby. The same smiling blue eyes, the way he walked and carried his head, made him a duplicate in miniature. Somehow it made her feel as though Robby was not so far away. She inhaled the delicate scent of her son's silky reddish hair, loving the smell and feel of him.

Her gaze gravitated to her mother and father, keeping her company on the porch. Her parents' marriage had always been so solid, particularly over the last few years since Mama's spiritual commitment. Emily had planned to follow their splendid example in her own marriage . . . back when she envisioned it lasting forever. Almost from the moment she had told them that she knew Robby was gone, they had been hovering over her in their quiet way, not wanting to intrude, but unable to accept her certainty of his death. "Papa, how long has it been since Ben came through?"

Her father looked up from the leather rope he'd been braiding, his deep brown eyes revealing his love and concern. His calloused hand stilled.

In the chair beside him, Mama paused in her knitting, uncharacteristic worry lines marring her regal features. "It was when your father took that string of horses up to Boston. When was that, dear?"

"I've been back almost two weeks now."

Emily nodded. "Then surely he'll come again soon. He rarely stays away from Abby more than a fortnight."

Mama smiled, but the deep sadness in the depths of her green eyes did not abate. "I never expected Ben would turn out to be such a considerate husband after his reckless and thoughtless boyhood. He was downright rude to your sister Jane."

"And she to him," Papa said with a low chuckle. "But then, of all our children they were the closest in age." He switched his attention to Emily. "Why are you concerned about your brother?"

With a small shrug, she tipped her head. "I . . . need to hear it from him. To have him say the words. So you'll believe me. And . . . it might help me to—" Her voice cracked, and threatening tears made it impossible to finish the thought. She took a firmer hold of Rusty and stood. "I guess it's time to put him to bed."

"I'll do it," Papa said, rising. Gently he took the sleeping tot and went inside, his faint footfalls quickly receding as he carried the child up the stairs.

Arms empty now of her one small comfort, Emily lowered herself once more to the rocker. In a way, she was relieved not to have to go into the bedchamber herself, at least for a while. During the daylight hours, she could keep busy and avoid it. But the endless empty dark of night was another matter. It was then that she would relinquish her brave front and the last shred of hope and surrender to the agony of her loss. Weeping into her pillow at night made putting on her cheerful front a little easier when the morning finally dawned. She had not informed the children of their father's passing.

She shook off her morose thoughts and turned to her mother. "Mama?"

"What is it?"

Emily struggled to formulate the nagging question, then decided just to let the words tumble out in whatever fashion they might. "I've been trying to work something out in my mind. About . . . about God. If he's so very interested in us and in our lives, then why would . . . how could he—" Her words drifted off helplessly.

Mama didn't answer right away. "You must remember, darling, none of us is completely certain Robby . . . is gone."

"But I am, Mama. I can tell you the exact moment he was taken. We were so close. Soul mates. If he were still on this earth, I wouldn't have such an emptiness in my heart. Or such an ache. What I need to know is—*why?* What possible purpose could the Lord have for taking such a good husband, such a wonderful father?"

Her mother glanced down at her hands in wordless silence. Then her eyes met Emily's. "I'm very sure God loves you now as much as he ever did," she answered with quiet conviction. "Having to part from someone dear is truly the hardest thing any of us must face. It's been the curse of humanity since the fall of Adam and Eve. When we lost two of our own dear babes in infancy, I wondered how I could go on. But the Lord's promises are true, and I was never more aware of God's presence than I was then."

She paused, as if caught in the poignant memory, then went on, her voice steady, comforting. "Should the day ever come when your father must depart and leave me behind, I don't know how I'll get through the rest of my life without him. But I know someday God will call one of us to be with him. And should I be the one left here, I know God will be there with me at that moment, providing all that I need."

Emily, in her sorrow, had already experienced moments of indescribable peace. She had not spoken of it as yet, but in the solitary hours, after the tears, the certainty that the Lord was holding her up wrapped itself around her like a comforting blanket. But it was still too new to express in words, and it did little to lessen the deep ache inside.

"And do not forget," Mama continued. "God's very own precious Son was not spared from pain—or from death. So the Father knows and understands how deeply we grieve."

Yes, but we had so many dreams, Emily thought sadly. *Such grand plans. Now they'll never come to pass.*

"Remember how bitter I was when Dan defied me by marrying a lowly bondservant?" Mama asked with a little smile. "My, what a fool I was, and what a hard lesson the Lord had to teach me. But now I thank God every single night for Susannah and *for the things I suffered, as well.* Once I let go of my selfish pride, God enriched my life beyond measure. You tried to tell me this once, as I recall."

Emily almost smiled at the memory. "Me and just about everybody else in the family!" She rose, crossed to her mother's side, and kissed her cheek. "I'll try to trust God for tomorrow. I'll really try."

Her mother caught her hand and squeezed it. "Ask him to

give you his peace, sweetheart." She sadly shook her head. "This awful war has been very hard on all my girls. The waiting, the uncertainty. But please, don't bury your dear Robby prematurely in your mind. For all you know, tomorrow he could quite possibly walk through that door."

"I wish he could," Emily whispered. "You'll never know how deeply I pray that I'm wrong. But think back, Mama, to Christmas two years ago. You knew with utmost certainty that all of us would be here, remember? Even Dan, who was imprisoned in Boston without hope of release. Yet you never wavered in your belief. Well, that's the kind of knowing I have inside *me* now. My Robby will never come back to me alive. He's . . . gone to the Lord."

Mama stood, tears shimmering in her eyes, and wrapped her arms about Emily. "If that were to be so, my darling daughter, I can only tell you how very, very sad I would be. He's been so special to us all."

Emily could not keep her own tears back. She swayed against her mother, desperately needing the reassurance and serenity that were such a part of her. "But I feel so lost, Mama," she said, weeping softly now. "So very lost."

"I know, sweetheart. But I'm here for you now. We all are."

❧ ❧

"Faster, Mommy! Faster!" Katie bounced along on a sedate mare the next day as Emily guided the horse around the field. Behind Katie, Rusty giggled so hard he could barely keep hold of his sister's waist.

Cassandra and Corbin, Abby's children, squealed in delight on a second quiet-tempered mare led by Ben's wife. "Us, too! We wanna go faster, too!"

Emily exchanged a sidelong glance with Abigail and smiled. The children's laughter was like a tonic. She wondered if Robby were looking down on the sweet scene and grinning. It was a nice thought, one to cling to—for a little while.

"Hold on real tight," Abby told her two offspring, then

jogged ahead, trailing the trotting pacer behind her as she navigated a huge circle. Her long wheat-gold tresses ruffled with her movements, shining in the sun.

Emily, more hesitant since her children were a bit younger than Abby's, kept her animal at a more tranquil walk as she turned and headed past her mother, who watched from the fence.

The sun was high in the azure sky and so far had not been obscured by any of the small fluffy clouds blowing in from the coast. Emily found the beauty of the day consoling. It fit with the solace she had derived from her morning Scripture reading in Philippians. She, like Paul, was *in a strait betwixt two, having a desire to depart, and to be with Christ* . . . and her Robby, but knowing all the while that *to abide in the flesh is more needful* for the sake of the children. The unexplainable sense of peace that surrounded her since her husband's passing was even more evident in the perfection of this afternoon, as if the Lord were assuring her that he would always be there, holding her up.

"Faster, Mommy. Please!" Katie begged.

"Well," Emily hedged, "if you promise to hold tight. You, too, Rusty." At their eager nods, she began a near jog in a slightly smaller circle than the one Abby had run. She needed the children to be as lighthearted as possible. Once she told them about their father, they wouldn't have the Psalms to turn to for comfort, or the hymns that had helped keep her own spirits up. She would be all they had. *Oh, precious Lord, help me to find the right words to make them understand. Don't let me fail them or break down. I must be brave for their sakes. For Robby.*

Mother's throaty laugh joined in with the children's, her first cheerful display that day.

Turning the far bend, Emily met up with Abigail on her way back, and the two girls slowed to a walk again, panting side by side. "Somehow I don't feel as young as I used to be," Emily admitted. "All this running has worn me out."

"More! More!" Cassie pleaded, bouncing up and down excitedly on the horse's back.

"Not just now, angel," Abby groaned.

"Your poor beasts of burden are tuckered," Emily told the little girl.

"At least the two-legged ones," Abby added with a giggle.

"Let's do something else," Emily suggested. "Let's sing." Veering the pacer in the direction of her mother, she started the hymn she had been humming most of the morning, one of Robby's very favorites. "Rejoice, the Lord is King! . . ."

"Your Lord and King adore!" Abby chimed in exuberantly.

A baritone voice joined them from the direction of the barn. "Rejoice, give thanks, and sing, and triumph evermore."

Emily smiled at her father, and he doffed his work hat with a flourish as he approached her mother and draped an arm around her shoulders.

The sight of their easy companionship almost made Emily's throat close up. It took all her effort to go on to the chorus with the seemingly personal words. "Lift up your heart, lift up your voice! Rejoice, again I say, rejoice!" She couldn't finish.

Her father, holding her gaze steadily as if to impart his own strength to her, took over. "Jesus, the Saviour, reigns, the God of truth and love; when he had purged our stains, he took his seat above."

Emily let the rest sing the last two verses. The familiar refrains soothed her heart with the sweet assurance that with the Lord and her loving family supporting her faith, she would make it through this hard, sad time. If not for herself, for Katie and Rusty, who needed her so very much. And—she gazed upward into the sky—for Robby.

"Mama! Mama!" Katie exclaimed. "Somebody's coming!"

Down the lane, a wagon rumbled into view . . . and following behind it, a Narragansett pacer tied by a rope.

Emily's heart stopped, then throbbed in ominous thuds. Moving mechanically, she swung the children from the mare and handed them to her parents. "Mama, why don't you give them some of those gingerbread cookies you and Tillie baked this morning?" Then she crawled through the fence boards and smiled at Katie. "You and Rusty go up to the house with Grandma now, and help her fix a treat for our company, will you? We'll make it a nice surprise."

"That sounds splendid," her mother said, her sad gaze offering her understanding. "Come along, Abby. Bring Cassie and Corbin, too." Together they moved quietly off.

Her father stayed behind and gave her an encouraging hug. "It may not be what you think."

Recognizing Robert Chandler now, Emily looked her father squarely in the eye. "Yes, it is, Papa. Pray for me. Help me to be brave."

He inhaled a deep breath and gave her a harder hug as he stood by her side.

On the wagon seat, Chan looked thinner than Emily remembered, and his face was drawn, with dark circles beneath his eyes. He couldn't possibly have eaten or slept on the way. For him to have expended himself so was an indication of the deep friendship he and Robby had formed since her husband had first gone to Boston Bay to join the Continental army. He reined to a stop.

Careful not to allow her eyes to drift to the wagon bed just yet . . . or the canvas-covered form at the edge of her vision, Emily focused on him.

Robert's fingers shook as he wrapped the reins around the brake. He climbed down and took both her hands, and his red-rimmed eyes searched hers. "Emily."

"You've come a very long way," she told him. "Please let Papa take you inside for something to eat and a quiet place to lie down."

"B-but you don't understand. I—"

"I know," she whispered, unable to trust her voice. "I know."

His gaze flicked to her father and returned to her as he released a ragged breath. "I'm so very, very sorry. I tried to keep him from . . ."

Emily tried to see through a haze of tears. She nodded and squeezed his hand, placing it to her cheek. "Please, I-I'd like to have a few moments alone with him."

Papa stepped near and took Chandler's arm. "Come on, lad," he said, gently drawing him away.

For the first time, Emily allowed her gaze to drift fully to the back of the wagon, and her knees grew weak. She inhaled deeply, gathered herself together, then, trembling, climbed aboard.

Kneeling down, she slowly pulled the canvas covering away. Her tears ran freely now, and a sob caught in her throat. Robby lay so still, so peaceful. He appeared merely to be asleep, and he looked so very young. "My love," she whispered on a sob, lightly combing her fingertips through his hair. There wasn't even a hint of silver among the ebony strands yet, barely a line on his face. The clean clothes he wore were evidence that Robert wanted to spare her from whatever wound had taken her husband's life. She wasn't sure she really wanted to know anyway, and a surge of appreciation coursed through her at his thoughtfulness. He had been a faithful and true friend.

But as she continued to gaze at her dear, young, dead husband, anger sliced at her heart. It wasn't really Robby lying there, not now. It was just an empty shell. Robby had gone on ahead, to be with Christ for all eternity. He would never come home to her again. "Why, Robby?" she cried softly. "What possible reason could there be for you to leave us? How am I to go on without you? And the children—" No. She mustn't give in to even a hint of anger. She had to be brave. *Brave.* But right now, she had not the slightest idea how she would accomplish that feat.

She memorized each feature for the last time, the broad forehead, the unruly shock of black hair, his square chin. She tried to imagine life without his lilting laugh, the trill of his *r*s as they rolled from his tongue in the Scottish brogue she loved so dearly. The plans and dreams they had shared would be laid to rest now, too. Forever.

Raising her eyes to heaven, she swallowed hard. "I do thank you, dear God, for hearing my plea, for bringing my Robby back to me so quickly . . . but how will I tell our babies? Please,

please give me your strength. How can they understand something like death? You must give me the right words to say, Father. Please, do this for me."

Looking once more at her gentle husband, she tried to smile. "I will always love you, Robby MacKinnon." She leaned down and brushed a last kiss to the lips so still and cold. New tears speckled the tarp as she gently placed it over his face.

It was time to go and thank a dear friend for his kind thoughtfulness . . . and after that, to have a sad talk with her children.

14

Evelyn's melodious laugh, near the other end of the long table of guests at the Neville Heath mansion, sounded unusually false to Morgan. He knew his sister had to find this gathering of merchant friends of his father's very wearisome. Besides himself and Prudence, Evelyn and Clay Raleigh were the only other young people present. As usual, Father, Mr. Heath, and another distinguished merchant, Jude Rossiter, allowed the topic to drift time and again to the subject uppermost in their minds—the countless affairs concerning importing and exporting, and how they were affected by the war.

To Evie's credit, no one had seen through her inane chatter or the engaging smile she had lavished upon the others during the hour since the Thomas coach had brought the family to supper. Especially fetching in cranberry taffeta and powdered ringlets, she was the very epitome of charm. Even Raleigh had to be basking in his exalted opinion of himself as she laughed at his silly jokes. But Morgan knew that Evelyn's determination to do whatever was necessary to help her sweetheart, Jamie Dodd, and the other patriots was paramount in her mind.

Switching his attention to his parents across the table, Morgan marveled that neither of them seemed to note his sibling's playacting but appeared to be bursting with pride as they beamed at her throughout the meal.

Now, as slices of rich butter cake with plum sauce were

brought in by the servants, Evelyn took a dainty sip of punch and set down the silver goblet. "I feel so much safer, Mr. Heath," she gushed to their host, "knowing we're being so well protected. How many man-of-war ships did you say were plying the colonial waters just now?" Her long lashes fluttered in feminine innocence.

Having already probed the uninformed gentleman along that same line himself, Morgan didn't even bother to wait for the reply as the portly man blotted his trim mustache on his napkin and turned to her.

Morgan's greater concern was the false smile fastened to Prudence's mouth since the moment of arrival here. His mother had magnanimously offered his wife's talents for the entertainment following the meal, and he could see that Prudence was suffering from an acute case of stage fright. She appeared nearly as colorless as her ivory gown, and her fingers trembled as she pushed uneaten cake around her plate with a fork.

He barely managed to stifle a grin. His little Puritan wouldn't be more petrified if she were about to become a sacrificial lamb. Her campaign to win Mother over had a greater price than even she had bargained for. Mother had insisted that Evie merely accompany her on the harpsichord. His mouth twitched into a grin as he swallowed the last morsel of dessert.

"Ahem." Mr. Heath rose to his feet and gave a polite bow to his wife at the foot of the table. "I believe the gentlemen and I will retire to the study. Mr. Raleigh has generously provided us with a rare selection of cigars from several of our Caribbean islands. And—" he turned to Clay, "a new experimental leaf from North Carolina, is it not?"

"That is correct." Raleigh gave a smug nod and stood. The other men, except for Morgan, followed suit.

With Prudence's death grip on his knee, Morgan's attention swung to her face, which was white with panic.

Her eyes widened in desperation. "You must take me home," she whispered. "Now."

He peeled her fingers away and kissed her open palm. "Something must be in the air," he murmured softly, "or we would not have been included on the guest list. Be brave." He got up, elevating his voice to a level others could easily hear. "I shan't desert you for long, my sweet."

"Oh, don't hurry on my account," she said with forced acquiescence. "Take all the time you want."

"Absolutely not," his mother intervened, placing a jeweled hand on the sleeve of his indigo frock coat. "Twenty minutes should be quite sufficient. Any more than that, and we women will join you, won't we, ladies?" She smiled at the three older women who were part of her social circle.

"Only if we may smoke as well," an amply bosomed matron in a royal blue gown announced, chuckling at her own jest.

Mrs. Heath made a distasteful grimace. "What? Those smelly things? Only out of extreme generosity do I permit the disgusting weeds to be lighted, even in that one room. We shall adjourn, ladies, to the music room, where we'll await our husbands."

Morgan cast a backward glance at Prudence, who remained stiffly in place as the others rose. Hoping to allay her fears, he winked at her. Still, Prudence resembled a frightened doe on the verge of darting away. How amazing to recall that she was the same woman who had risked her life to join the army at Bunker Hill.

He expelled a breath and entered his host's private domain and was immediately caught by Mr. Heath's collection of rare Greek and Latin books. Scanning some of the titles, he paused to study a display of ancient coins enclosed in a glass case. The man lived well.

"I urge you to choose the cigar you would most enjoy," Mr. Heath said invitingly as he circulated an embellished wooden humidor.

From the corner of his eye Morgan saw each gentleman sniff two or three before selecting. The host clipped the tips of the cigars with a silver cutter.

"And now you, Morgan," Heath said, extending the bounty toward him.

Withdrawing his gaze from an exquisite Roman coin, he raised a hand of refusal even as the heavy aromas blended in a gray-blue haze. "Thank you, but I'm afraid I shall have to decline. My stomach is unsettled this eve." *And it never hurts to lay the foundation for a hasty exit, just in case.*

Mr. Heath frowned. "What a pity. Perhaps next time, then." He took his seat in an upholstered leather chair behind the desk.

Clayborne Raleigh expertly puffed a smoke ring and smiled as he propped a foot on his opposite knee. "Gentlemen, my father would be most glad to take orders for any of these fine cigars, I'm sure."

Morgan slid him a glance. The stuffy Englishman was no less a pretender than he. It would be difficult to picture him dirtying his hands on something so plebeian as merchandising. Yet with so few aristocrats for the snob to keep company with, why had he even deigned to come to the colonies in the first place?

Comments Evelyn had made about Raleigh's being in love with her dowry rather than herself began to take on deeper meaning. Without a title of his own, Raleigh would need a great deal of money to find acceptance among the upper class. Morgan's respect for his sister's intuition took a sudden rise.

"When do you expect your father to return to our fair city, Mr. Raleigh?" Mr. Rossiter asked.

"I'd say within a week or so, sir." One side of his thin mouth curled upward. "He'd not miss the opportunity to be the first to offer the victorious soldiers and the restored New Yorkers a celebratory cigar."

"Can't fault a businessman for his good sense," Heath remarked.

Morgan restrained himself from voicing his own derisive thoughts. No matter how confident the Loyalists were since word came that the Crown now controlled Nassau Island,

Jamie Dodd's brother, Micah, had discovered that most of Washington's army had evacuated safely. Under cover of night, they had sneaked across the East River to New York, right beneath the noses of the redcoats and the guns of their warships. The patriots termed the feat a miracle, and Morgan was all the more convinced that God was with their cause.

"Speaking of New York," Mr. Heath said, "Mr. Rossiter and I have a proposal to set forth." He turned to Morgan. "We should like to offer you the opportunity to represent our interests in New York. If, that is—" He looked at Morgan's father. "If Waldon can spare you for a time. We believe you are the best choice, since you spent more than a year with General Howe's officers in Boston while it was under siege."

Morgan tried not to show his alarm. He left Boston long before it was barricaded and had spent no more than two weeks in the company of Boston Loyalist merchants and the British army. And, to his dismay, he had managed during that short time to acquire a dangerous enemy. He had made the wise decision to leave the city before the vengeful Captain Long started checking into his business dealings . . . in particular, his unlawful diversions of Loyalist shipments to the patriots.

Nevertheless, he rationalized, New York *would* be an ideal spot for someone trying to ferret out information. Captain Long might not have come from Halifax with General Howe. It was a chance worth taking—one which might be wise to check out with General Washington first, however.

He glanced at his father but could not read his expression. "I say," he said, turning to the host. "It does sound rather interesting. Father and I will discuss it and have an answer within the next few days."

"Splendid." Mr. Heath fairly beamed as he puffed on his fat cigar.

"You do realize, Waldon," Rossiter began, "that unlike Philadelphia, New York will now be open to English trade without fear of rebel reprisals. We could even purchase wharf-front property and build warehouses."

"Yes," Heath agreed, stroking his mustache. "We should not sit idly by while the New York merchants keep all the profits for themselves."

As the men's voices escalated, the door opened, and Mrs. Heath leaned in, waving aside the smoke. "Neville, it's time you and the others joined the ladies, don't you think?"

❧ ❧

Only with utmost effort could Prudence make her rubbery legs carry her toward Morgan as the men filed into the music room. It was imperative she get to him. He simply had to take her home. At once! She was becoming more nauseated by the second. In desperation she mopped the cold perspiration beading her brow. Never in her entire life had she so much as hummed a tune in public. Properly raised Boston Bay women did not make a practice of putting themselves on exhibition. It was simply not done.

Finally reaching her husband, she latched onto his arm.

"Evelyn, my pet," Clay Raleigh piped in from beside Morgan. "I've splendid news. Your brother and I shall be departing for New York very soon."

Prudence sought Morgan's eyes.

"Wouldn't it be marvelous," Clay continued, "if you might accompany him and his wife? A victorious army throws magnificent parties, to be sure."

Mother Thomas moved quietly to their side. "Morgan, you only recently arrived home. I do hope you aren't thinking of leaving again so soon. Tell me you're not."

"Oh, Mother," Evelyn cajoled. "It's only two days by carriage. Just think of the advantages!"

As the older woman pondered her daughter's words, Prudence could see that the possibility of a truly splendid marriage for Evie was not lost on her. But she couldn't know her daughter's secret goal—going north to find Jamie Dodd.

As for herself, Prudence was willing to say or do anything at all to avoid becoming a singing fool. Now *or* later. "Why, darling," she said, turning to Morgan. "This is so sudden.

Surely we women should be included in a discussion of matters that pertain to all of us. I'm in complete agreement with Evelyn. I'd simply love to go to New York. I would leave this eve. This very minute, in fact."

An amused grin revealed that Morgan saw through her ploy. But it vanished as quickly. "Father and I have yet to decide if I'm to go. But regardless, you and my sister will be staying here in Philadelphia. My mission would involve stimulating more business opportunities, not being a constant chaperon—which even you would agree would be necessary in a city overrun with hordes of loose-living soldiers."

"Oh, please," Evie cajoled. "Please!" She grabbed onto Morgan.

Clay Raleigh appeared similarly disappointed. He had likely already counted on this chance to have the elusive young heiress more frequently to himself. "I would be only too glad to see to Evelyn's welfare."

"Why, how very kind of you, Mr. Raleigh," Mother said. "Now, there's been quite enough talk of war and business for one evening." She nodded emphatically toward the other ladies, then at Evelyn. "Evie, dear, go to the harpsichord. We've kept our friends waiting long enough. My new daughter-in-law's tutor, Mr. Stanton, says she is a pure find. He's quite elated with her progress."

Prudence felt her knees begin to fold. Why, oh, *why* hadn't she been more insistent when she tried to coerce Evie into singing a duet?

Morgan's steadying grip kept her from dissolving to the floor. But Prudence knew better than anyone that even if she made it to Evie's side, nothing but a pitiful croak could possibly emerge from her paralyzed throat.

"Actually, Mother," Morgan said smoothly, "Prudence and I have a bit of a surprise for you ourselves."

Prudence clung to this startling announcement with all the fervor she possessed as she gazed up at him. *Oh, please, dear Lord, let him have a plan to save me. Let it be that.*

He appeared somewhat flustered momentarily.

She was doomed.

Morgan cleared his throat. "After much pleading on my part, my dear wife has agreed to allow me to harmonize with her. Isn't that so, sweetheart?" His slightly cornered expression met hers. "We do, after all, like to think of our marriage as a duet in every way."

Speechless with shock, Prudence almost forgot to close her eyes as he lowered his lips to hers amid a chorus of *oohs* and *aahs* from the assemblage.

Could he even carry a tune? What on earth would the two of them sing? Raising her lashes again, she pressed closer to the strong beat of his stalwart heart . . . this man who would willingly make a public spectacle of himself just for her.

Who knows, maybe they could pull it off. Together they could do anything, couldn't they? Even sing.

Morgan nodded to Evelyn, and she took a seat at the harpsichord, fingers poised above the keys. She looked expectantly to him.

"We'll do 'Barbara Allen,'" he said bravely, and donned a magnanimous smile as Evie played a few measures of introduction. "Just come in when I squeeze your hand," he whispered to Prudence, then broke out in a strong baritone:

> " 'Twas in the merry month of May
> When all gay flow'rs were blooming,
> Sweet William on his deathbed lay
> For the love of Barbara Allen.'"

Prudence was hard put not to laugh at the lovesick expression he wore, and some of her fears began to evaporate as he continued:

> "He sent a servant to the town
> Where Barbara, she was dwellin',
> 'My master's sick and sends for you
> If your name be Barb'ra Allen.'"

But when she felt pressure from his hand, her terror rose to the fore. If he hadn't winked in devilment, she might not have gathered her wits so quickly. She moistened her lips and began, timidly at first, then buoyed by his delighted smile, in a clear soprano that surprised even her:

> *"So slowly, slowly she got up,*
> *And slowly went unto him.*
> *And all she said when she got there:*
> *'Young man, I think you're dyin.'"*

Morgan took up with the next verse, and Prudence the one after, as they alternated verses of the sad ballad. Incredibly, Prudence even saw one of the matrons dab at her eyes with a lacy kerchief. The last two stanzas seemed upon them all too quickly as they blended their voices in harmony:

> *"Sweet William was buried in the high churchyard,*
> *And Barbara buried by him.*
> *And out of his grave grew a bloodred rose*
> *And out of hers a brier.*

> *"They grew and grew to the steeple top*
> *Till they could grow no higher;*
> *They lapped and tied in a true love knot—*
> *The rose around the brier."*

As the last notes died away, there was a long silent moment, then a burst of exuberant applause.

Prudence felt herself crushed in Morgan's embrace. "To think you've hidden that talent from me all this time!" she murmured.

He chuckled against her ear. "Just hope they don't plead for an encore. It's the only tune I know, except for a rather humorous version I heard recently of 'Yankee-Doodle.'"

15

"Thank you, Mistress Harnell, for coming," Emily said, escorting the older woman to the door. The neighbor was one of the last of the many who had come to extend condolences. "It would have meant so much to my Robby to know so many people cared."

Mrs. Harnell patted Emily's hand with her own slightly rougher one. "If there is anything we can do for you, dear, anything at all, please do let us know. I fear Robert will not be the last brave young man we'll lay to rest before these dark days are past."

"I pray that isn't so," Emily returned softly.

With a gracious nod and a last kind look, the woman adjusted her lace shawl and joined her husband waiting at the edge of the porch.

Emily sighed and stepped out after them to check on her children. Abigail was supervising Katie and Rusty and several other youngsters under the shade of the big maple in the side yard. For a few seconds, listening to their sweet voices, Emily could almost forget the sadness of this day.

"Ashes, ashes, all fall down!" they chorused. Katie's and Rusty's bright smiles and laughter were as carefree as the rest of the children's as they all tumbled to the ground.

In a way, it seemed a blessing to Emily that the children were too young to grasp the finality of their father's passing. When she had tried to explain that he had gone to heaven to be with God and that they wouldn't see him again for a long, long time, Katie had scrunched up her face in confusion. "Is it more days than this, Mama?" she asked, holding up her fingers. Perhaps it was best. They would understand too soon what death was all about.

Mother and Tillie had a lot of cleaning up to do after the company, Emily remembered. She closed the front door and headed toward the kitchen. But as she passed the parlor, she saw Papa and two friends hovering around Robert Chandler. Chan, seated with his back to the doorway, had scarcely spoken last night when he arrived and had slept long into the morning. If she hadn't felt compelled to awaken him for the funeral service, there was little doubt his exhaustion would have kept him sleeping still.

She paused momentarily, wishing the rest of the mourners would depart. Emily desperately wanted to speak to Robert alone, to find out how Robby had died. She needed to know for her own peace of mind. But that would have to wait.

"If the battle for Nassau Island was going so badly," one of the neighbors remarked, "I'm surprised you were given leave to bring young MacKinnon home."

Curious, Emily pressed closer to the doorway.

"The morning the British landed," Robert drawled in his slow way, his voice flat and without emotion, "he and I were out on the long island, delivering supplies to the battalion stationed there."

"We've heard all manner of wild talk," the other man said. "How many redcoats did the British really send against you?"

"Judging from the number of their landing craft, I'd say somewhere between fifteen and twenty thousand. Their artillery created too much smoke to allow an accurate count. The two of us found ourselves having to stay with the First Riflemen, from Pennsylvania. Their sergeant ordered us to move supplies away from the enemy's advance and do whatever we could to cause delays until Washington was able to send reinforcements from New York. In the end, Robby used the wagon to evacuate the wounded. He was . . ."

Emily strained to hear.

"Speak up, lad," the man told him.

"I said," Robert announced, his voice weary but stronger, "Robby had a way of giving hope to the wounded when they needed it most." He exhaled an uneven breath. "On the fifth night, fresh troops relieved the rifle battalion, and we were sent to the rear to rest. That's when I brought him home."

"With him assigned to a quartermaster," Papa mused, "I figured he'd be out of danger."

"So did I." Chan lurched to his feet. "If y'all will excuse me, I need to check on my horses." He charged out of the room, giving not the slightest indication of whether he noticed Emily.

She felt her heart constrict. If it pained him so to speak of it, then surely Robby's death must have been horrible. But something inside her needed to know the details . . . whatever they might be. She would give Chandler a bit longer, then go to him and find out what she could.

For several hours Emily threw herself into a cleaning frenzy. She washed every last pot and then, on her hands and knees, put every ounce of energy she possessed into scrubbing the plank floor. By the time she finished, the neighbors had all gone, and Abby had settled the children down for the night. Now was the opportune time to seek out Robert. She dried her hands on her apron, then untied the strings and draped it over the back of a chair.

He wasn't in any of the downstairs rooms, she discovered, but voices carried from the front porch. Perhaps he was with her parents.

She saw him as soon as she opened the door. Propped on the railing, he stared pensively into space, seemingly oblivious to her or her parents' conversation. Emily moved quietly to one of the empty chairs and sank into it. The soft breeze felt refreshing on her overheated face. She had been working harder than she realized. She gazed at Robert, wondering how to begin.

He turned then, and his sad blue eyes met hers, reflecting

the depth of her own pain. He had always been a melancholy man, but now . . .

Not expecting him to speak just yet, Emily was startled by his voice. "I know this is probably too soon. Nevertheless, it must be said."

Aware that her mother and father had stopped talking, Emily gave him her full attention.

"I . . . made Robby a promise, just before . . ." He swallowed. "It was something very important to him. He asked me to take you and the children to Princeton."

"New Jersey?" Mother gasped, springing to her feet.

"Now?" Emily asked, astounded. "Leave here?" She had not for an instant considered taking such action, especially since she depended so upon the strength and comfort of her family's presence. She still needed Papa's counsel to get her through periods of anger, jealousy, and sometimes even hopelessness. He had a way of putting things into the proper perspective, which did much to undergird her own faith.

"Robert," Papa began, "this is not a matter that must be decided tonight, is it?" His tone seemed to request Mother's patience as he switched his gaze to her.

She retook her seat.

Emily noted that Chandler's attention had not veered to her parents but remained fixed on her so intently she had the impression he hadn't even heard them speak. "Emily, your husband was certain the British would attack Rhode Island very soon."

"I know," she whispered.

"With his last breath he made me promise to take you and your children where it's safe." He paused. "I . . . could not keep him from dying. Please, don't make me fail him in this, too."

"But our daughter needs her father and me around her now," Mother said.

Emily couldn't imagine leaving the people most dear to her just yet . . . not so soon after laying her beloved mate to his final rest. She felt caught between Robby's last wish and her own needs. She pushed aside the suffocating prospect of leaving the farm. "You must give me time. I . . . I can't make that decision just now. I'm sorry." She paused, gathering her frayed emotions. "What I would like, Robert, is for you to walk with me a bit. If you will excuse us, Mama and Papa," she added, turning to them, "I'd like a few moments alone with this very good friend."

Chan's guarded expression was tinged with panic. After a moment's hesitation, he stood and accompanied her down the steps.

As they passed beneath the trellis at the end of the walkway, the heady fragrance of the last summer roses wafted over them. No more would bloom this season, and the realization almost brought tears to Emily's eyes. She would miss their perfume. Many of them now adorned the fresh mound of earth on the rise. Forevermore, the fragrance of roses would carry a measure of sadness. She struggled to dismiss the memory of fading, wilting blooms scattered on the rich dark soil.

A horse stirred in the nearest paddock, and Emily moved to the fence. Chan, in silence, followed as a leggy year-old colt stretched its head across the top of the rail with a companionable whinny.

Emily smoothed a hand across the soft velvety muzzle, aware that Chandler was staring at her. "I'd like you to tell me," she murmured, turning to him. "I must know everything."

He glanced away.

"Please, Robert," she said, forcing herself to keep using the name she loved above all. She placed a hand on his forearm. "I will never quite be able to lay Robby's memory to rest unless I know all there is to know about his final moments."

Chan didn't look at her as he shifted his weight to his other leg. He let out a shuddering breath and slowly shook his head. "It was me. . . . I issued the order that brought him onto the field. I sent for him to come fetch the wounded." He flicked his gaze directly to hers, then, as if he couldn't bear to witness her sorrow, he averted it once more to stare into the darkness. "I should have waited until we were absolutely certain there were no more redcoats in that orchard, but I didn't. I placed Robby in peril . . . and after vowing I'd do my utmost to keep him from it!" Sagging against the wooden fence, he averted his face.

Emily didn't respond at first. She now understood what had compelled him to bring Robby home to her instead of allowing him to be interred in some lonely place with others who lost their lives that night. He had been driven by guilt. Robby had explained about Julia's untimely death, and now another unbearable weight had been added to that loss.

The more she thought about that, however, the less fair it seemed. Robby had been *her* husband. This loss was *hers*.

It took a few moments, but inhaling deeply, Emily managed to control the anger that surged through her. "You said you sent for him. You and the others were already on the battle-field, then?"

He nodded. "A company of us had just sent an enemy artillery detachment hightailing it back into the orchard without their fieldpieces."

"So you chased them away, and then you needed to see to your wounded."

He uttered a groan. "That's the worst of it. We had no casualties! Not a single scratch in the lot. Robby died as he helped a wounded redcoat aboard. I risked his life for a blasted lobsterback! I'll never forgive myself."

Emily considered that information for a moment, then crossed her arms. "If you had not been there, given the order, would those redcoats have been left out there to suffer? I think not. I know my Robby. He wouldn't have left anyone— friend *or* foe—lying on some field bleeding to death. You know that as well as I do."

Chandler stared at her in mute shock.

"Anyway," Emily said, having relinquished a fraction of the rage inside and now able to quell the remainder, "I need to know—did he suffer? I don't care overmuch about the rest of it."

"No. He did not suffer. The end came quickly, I can assure you of that."

"Is that the absolute truth?"

"Yes, I swear." His hand went to his heart as if in solemn oath. "And you were on his mind to the very last."

Not allowing herself to visualize the unbearable, unthinkable scene, Emily latched onto the facts with a measure of relief. "I never would have been able to bear knowing he had endured endless hours of pain."

Robert gave an empathetic nod.

"I . . . never truly allowed myself to dwell on the possibility that when Robby left to join the army, he . . . he wouldn't . . ." Her voice wavered as a quivering began inside. Emily had to turn away to gather herself, and Chan graciously remained silent until she could go on. "The Bible says that all things work together for our good. I confess, I have my doubts in this instance, but I do not doubt that God dearly loves his children. I have to rely on his promise and his love to get me past all this sadness and emptiness. Katie and Rusty need me more than ever now."

Chandler shook his head in amazement. "You sound exactly like Robby. That's the sort of thing I'd expect him to say. To him, the chance to aid the wounded was but one more opportunity to save someone's soul."

"I'm not the least surprised." Emily resumed stroking the horse. "Robby had great faith in God. It was the most important thing in his life. He was forever poring over the Holy Scriptures and passing on to me the various gems he found there. It would have been his dearest wish to assist others in finding the same peace he had."

"Then knowing he had some success in doing just that should comfort you. He spoke of more than one dying man who came to know the Lord before the end."

She paused and looked at him with a small smile. "Thank

you. That means more to me than you'll ever know. And . . . I shall always be grateful that you brought him home to us."

Another silent moment passed. Then Emily's eyes met his once more. "How soon must you report back? I'm surprised you were given leave at all, considering the great battle you must have left behind."

"I wasn't given leave, actually."

"You . . . deserted?"

"Not exactly. I'll return once I have you and the children safely tucked away with Jasper and Esther Lyons in Princeton."

Emily wasn't quite ready to discuss that subject yet, and she started to turn.

Robert caught her arm. "Don't look away, Emily. It was his dying wish. I can't forget it, and neither can you. Try to think of your children, if not yourself."

His relentless stare touched her deeply. She felt as if it burned straight through to her soul. "In my heart, I know you're right. Everyone around here is certain that should New York fall, the British will come here next."

"Or sooner. With that immense force at their disposal, they could easily spare enough ships and troops to take Rhode Island at any moment. Robby said a number of times that as rebellious and arrogant as the Rhode Islanders have been, the Crown must attack—if for no other reason than pride."

Emily could only agree. She nodded slowly. "Part of me would prefer to stay here with my parents and accept along with them whatever happens. But it would not be fair to Robby to risk the legacy he left me . . . our children. *If* I must go, then I want it to be swift. Tomorrow morning, as soon as I've packed our things. I'm not up to dragging out my farewells." Before any second thoughts assailed her, she turned away. "Good night, Robert. I'd appreciate it if you would have your wagon hitched and at the side door first thing tomorrow."

16

A cool, salty breeze off the Atlantic ruffled across the wagon as Chandler skirted the Narragansett Bay before heading south along the Boston Post Road. It was near sundown, and Emily, on the seat beside him, silently blotted the tears that appeared from time to time. She had been amazingly brave bidding good-bye to her parents earlier this morning, but he shouldn't be surprised. From what he knew of her, she would be strong—would do her best to alleviate her parents' anxieties. He admired her staunch acceptance of life's sad turn as well as the peace that seemed to be with her most of the time. He had to admit, her example put him to shame.

He glanced over his shoulder at the children, sitting on their knees on the pallet their grandmother had fixed for them behind the seat. They gripped the side of the rail in speechless wonder at the passing scenery. Katie, her green eyes wide, clung to a worn rag doll, and Rusty's carved wooden colt was right beside him.

The meager stack of belongings piled beyond them had come as a shock. Even with the incredible amount of foodstuffs Emily's mother had insisted be brought along, there was still quite a lot of space remaining. But then, he remembered, Robby and Emily had left their household goods behind in Princeton when they came north.

Ever watchful, Chan searched the ragged edge of the shore to his left. He needed no reminder of the dangers they could face along this route. A fleet of warships hiding in a sheltered cove or behind one of the islands speckling the bay could be unloading a thousand soldiers at any given moment.

At the clatter of rapid hoofbeats behind them, he quickly swung around to see a strapping young man suddenly slow his horse to a walk. The fellow's attention settled on Emily, who made a very comely picture without a bonnet covering her honey blonde hair.

Chandler glanced at his Pennsylvania rifle. Rammed into a scabbard spiked to the side of the bench, it was within easy reach.

The stranger caught Robert's stare and quickly nudged his gelding to a faster gait and went on.

And he is just one ordinary man, Chan thought grimly. If the enemy had reached the bay, the wagon could be swarmed unexpectedly by an entire regiment, and he had but a single shot to keep Emily safe from a horde of woman-hungry soldiers. All too rampant were stories of the scores of women who'd been ravaged on Staten Island.

"Mama, I didn't like that man," Katie whined.

"Hush, sweetheart," Emily crooned. "He's gone now. And you must remember that God is watching over us."

"See what I mean about taking this route?" Chandler groused. "The interior road would've been far safer."

"Yes, I'm sure it would," she returned evenly, her composed expression making her appear even more innocent. "But this one's faster and more direct. You'll be able to return to duty sooner."

She was only echoing the sentiment she had voiced earlier, when they had argued about which way to go. "I have enough on my conscience right now without having your absence last any longer than absolutely necessary," she had stated with finality. He would never have guessed that someone who appeared so feminine, so gentle and soft, could also be an immovable force at times. Robby had never once hinted at it. He had referred to her only as his "sweet Emily." Well, one thing was certain . . . tomorrow before leaving South Kingston, Chan would purchase more firepower. Two pistols, at the very least.

Sometime later, the darkening evening sky revealed a sprinkling of lamplights as South Kingston came into view. Despite the light load, the cumbersome wagon had not made very good time. Chandler knew he probably couldn't count on more than thirty miles each day on this well-traveled road, not with a woman and small children along. Part of him wished Robby had asked someone more worthy of such a responsibility.

He glanced down at Emily, now lying in back with the children. She looked so much more fragile and vulnerable since she'd curled up with them and drifted off an hour ago. Knowing how weary she must be, he was relieved to see signs of a travelers' inn twinkling in the dimness ahead.

Emily sat up as he pulled the horses to a stop in front of the stable. "Where are we?"

"South Kingston. I thought we'd get rooms for the night."

"The sun has gone down already?"

"Yes." The day might have seemed short to her, but for him it had been interminable. Now the possibility of stretching out on a soft mattress was appealing after so many hours on the wooden wagon seat.

"I didn't think I'd actually fall asleep," she mused.

Without anyone but himself to consider for the past several years now, Chandler at once felt remorse for his selfish thoughts. Of course she would be exhausted, having just buried her husband. He would make a greater effort to be considerate of her from now on.

"Day after tomorrow I'll spell you and take over half the driving. You shouldn't have to do it all," Emily offered.

"Take all the rest you need."

She climbed to the seat and settled her skirts about her. "Did you, perchance, see a Presbyterian church as we rode into town? If not, a Baptist will do nicely."

He stared at her. "I know tomorrow is Sunday, but if we

delay our departure until after services, we won't even make fifteen miles before sundown."

"Robert, surely you don't expect—"

"As I recall, you were the one so adamant about time being of the essence. It's dangerous enough taking this road in the first place. I don't intend to waste half the day singing psalms with total strangers."

She set her lips in determination and didn't immediately respond. "Well, fine. You go on, then. I certainly wouldn't think of stopping you. My children and I, however, will not break any part of the Sabbath . . . especially now, when it's paramount to keep faith."

"If you had no intention of traveling tomorrow, then why did we bother to leave this morning? We could easily have waited until Monday."

"No, that's where you're wrong," she said quietly, with a sad shake of her head. "I really couldn't face prolonged farewells just now. I just couldn't. I'm sorry."

"No, I am the one who must apologize. Of course, if it will comfort you to attend church, that's what you shall do."

She reached over and touched his arm. "Thank you. I appreciate that. My husband thought of you as his kindest, most faithful friend, and a very, very good man. I can see why. Forgive me for not expressing my appreciation once to you this whole long day. I'll try to do better tomorrow."

Emily's green eyes shone with guileless sincerity in the glow of the pair of lanterns hung on either side of the stable door. He could see why his best friend had adored this delicate, yet strong young woman.

Immediately dispelling the thought, he jumped down from the wagon. "Wake the youngsters while I go see about rooms."

❧ ❧

The following morning found Chandler more refreshed than he had been since the day he left North Carolina to join the Continental army. Resigned to the fact that Emily did not want to travel on the Lord's Day, he had settled her and the children into a room, then paid to have a hot bath and to have his clothes pressed. As an added, almost forgotten, luxury, he had even slept late. Now as he came downstairs, a leisurely breakfast was all that was required to round out his respite to perfection.

As he stepped onto the landing, he caught sight of his dull boots, and he rubbed them across the backs of his trousers. Maybe after breakfast he would see about finding someone to polish them. A man coveted small pleasures when denied them for so long, he mused, striding through the foyer into the common room.

Emily waved to him from across the sea of tables. She and the children had not yet eaten, as he might have expected. He wove his way toward her, noticing as he neared the children that she had taken extra care in readying them for church.

Neither did it escape him that Emily herself looked particularly lovely. An abundance of white lace on the shawl collar of the austere widow's-black gown made her features all the softer. How perfect a match she'd been for Robby, he told himself, just as Julia had been for him, with her easy laughter, her nonsensical little pranks. It was the laughter he missed most.

"Good morning," he said, reaching Emily's table.

"Good morning to you. Won't you join us?"

She hadn't quite smiled, but then, Chan knew it would take some time before smiling would come easily again . . . if ever. He wondered if, as time went by, she would retain that quality of honest innocence she had shared with Robby. Or would it die the way his laughter had died with Julia?

"Morning, Mr. Chandler," Katie said, and beside her Rusty giggled.

A mobcapped serving girl appeared with a mug of hot coffee. "Will ye be havin' eggs and bacon with your wife and children? or somethin' else?"

He flicked a look to Emily, who quickly shook her head with a pleading expression. "I'll have the same," he said, and the server left.

"Thank you for not correcting her error," Emily breathed. "I didn't want to . . . hear the words. I hope you understand."

He more than understood. It was far easier to allow strangers the impression that these three were truly his family. After all, had fate not decided otherwise, he might have been papa to a couple of little ones by now. He had already fathered one—the child who died with his wife.

He glanced at the two youngsters at hand. Except for a stubborn cowlick, little Rusty's auburn hair was all slicked down. Katie, in a Sunday dress that was all flounces and lace, now appeared younger than her three and a half years.

It suddenly dawned on Chan that both pairs of wide eyes— one pair green like Emily's, the other blue as Robby's—were staring back. He cleared his throat. "My, don't you look pretty, Katie. All the other little girls at church will feel plain beside you this day."

She glowed. "Will they?" Then her happy smile collapsed. "How do you know? We never came here to church before."

Catching Emily's amusement, Chan knew he was on his own. "Oh, but who else would have such soft black hair or sparkling green eyes as you? I can't imagine a prettier princess anywhere."

The little girl frowned. "But my cousin Cassie said Uncle Ben told her *she's* the prettiest girl in the whole world."

"*Cassie* has *curls,*" Rusty announced emphatically.

Giving Emily's daughter a simple compliment was proving very difficult, Chandler realized, and he sought the mother's help. She, however, was looking away, sipping her coffee. And which child at the funeral had Cassie been, anyway? "Well, your cousin might have curly hair, but yours is as shiny as a polished boot."

"My hair looks like a smelly old boot?" Katie asked in horror. Rusty dissolved into giggles.

"I-I mean—" Chan scratched his head. "Like a thousand black satin ribbons."

Her face looked a bit more hopeful. "Is that more than a hundred?"

He sighed in relief. "Yes. Hundreds and hundreds."

"Oh, goody." She settled back in her chair.

"What about me?" Rusty asked.

The panic that seized Chandler abated as the serving girl returned, her tray piled high with food—a distraction sufficient to keep him from putting his foot in his mouth again.

Rusty was all set to pounce as soon as the plate was set before him, until he caught the stern stare from his mother.

"We will remember our manners, won't we?"

"Yes, Mama," both children chorused. They joined hands with each other and with her.

Emily looked with some hesitation at Chan. "Um, they're used to making a circle while we say grace. Would you mind?" Tentatively she offered her hand.

"Oh. Not at all." Closing his fingers around hers, he took Katie's and bowed his head. In the awkward silence that followed, he realized Emily expected him to do the honors. He felt heat rise from his collar, and he racked his mind trying to remember some snatch of a prayer after so many bitter, prayerless years. "Almighty God," he finally mumbled, "we thank you for this bounty. Amen."

"Amen," the others echoed.

Chan was absolutely certain the tips of his ears must glow, but no one seemed to notice as they began to eat.

"I'd be most grateful," Emily said after a few moments, "if you would escort us to service. I . . . don't quite feel up to talking with strangers, answering questions."

After his own deep and longstanding anger at God, church was the last place Chandler wanted to go. Even at military camp he had been successful in not complying with General Washington's order that all enlisted men attend services. Chan opted for guard duty instead. He fervently wanted to refuse now, too—to make some reasonable excuse why he couldn't do as Emily asked. "I'm afraid I haven't any decent Sunday clothes along," he blurted.

"Considering you're a soldier, you're exceptionally presentable," she replied. "No one would expect better."

"Anyway," Katie piped in, "we need to see if I'm the prettiest, remember?"

"Katherine Faith MacKinnon," Emily said scornfully. "We go to church to become pretty on the inside, not on the outside."

"You mean our bones?" the little girl asked in total confusion. "But nobody can see inside my skin."

Emily silenced Rusty's giggle with an arch of a fine brow. "Perhaps we can't, but our heavenly Father can."

Rusty dropped his spoon. "Is Daddy looking down at us, too?"

His mother's color fled.

Chandler saw Emily swallow, noticed the throb of her pulse in the hollow of her throat. "I'm fairly sure the church bell's about to ring, lad," he said. "We'd better eat up."

"Will you sit next to me, Mr. Chandler?" Katie asked.

"No! Me!" Rusty sprang to his knees.

"No need to fight over the poor man," Emily said, her color almost back to normal. "One of you may sit on his right, and the other on his left."

"Oh, goody." Katie slid her tiny hand into his.

How could a man refuse?

17

Chandler couldn't think of a thing to say on the way to church. With Katie skipping happily along and Rusty running circles around them all, he couldn't very well drag his feet. As the simple whitewashed church loomed before them, growing larger with each step, he assured himself that if he could put up with Robby MacKinnon's constant preaching, an actual sermon couldn't be that much harder to endure. Surely it couldn't last more than an hour or two.

Reaching the meetinghouse and going inside, Chan swiftly ushered everyone to an empty pew in the back, acknowledging nods and polite smiles afforded them as newcomers and strangers. He couldn't help but notice again how handsome his borrowed family was, sitting all prim and proper with their expectant expressions. The sight stirred buried longings deep within, and he realized how honored he felt showing them off.

With a smile, Katie slipped her hand into his, and Rusty snuggled close. Did the little pair even have a concept about death, or were they so used to Robby's being gone that to them heaven was merely somewhere on the other side of New York?

Emily glanced over with a slight smile of approval . . . one that tugged at Chan's heart.

The pump organ off to one side began to wheeze as a stout woman in Sunday finery worked the pedals, and the opening strains of music filled the modest sanctuary. Yet it took several bars before Chan recognized the familiar hymn as the congregation rose and began to sing. It had been so long.

"Come, thou Almighty King,
Help us thy name to sing,
Help us to praise:
Father, all glorious,
O'er all victorious,
Come, and reign over us,
Ancient of Days."

Having tried his best to dismiss everything that reminded him of God, it amazed Robert how much of the piece he still remembered. The many times he had sung this hymn during his student days at the College of New Jersey must have taken deeper root than he realized. By the close of the second verse, and anticipating the moving words of the third, he found himself joining in:

"Come, Holy Comforter,
Thy sacred witness bear
In this glad hour:
Thou who almighty art,
Now rule in ev'ry heart,
And ne'er from us depart,
Spirit of pow'r."

When a sheen of tears misted Emily's eyes, Chandler lost track of the last stanza and fell silent. Katie's gentle tug at the end reminded him to sit down.

The minister, a narrow-faced man in a flowing black robe, climbed the steps of the unadorned pulpit and raised his hand for silence.

Chandler felt the children snuggle against him, getting comfortable for the tedious dronings their young minds could not grasp.

"In these trying times," the man began in strong voice, "with so many of our fine men away from us, I'm pleased to see so many faithful coming together each week to bear one another up. Before I proceed, Mistress Barker requested that I pass along her most sincere thanks for the long hours of unselfish labor provided by so many of you dear brothers and sisters in the replacing of her barn roof after the fire. I'm certain her husband, Lawrence, will be equally grateful when he learns we replenished their grain and straw in his absence as he represents South Kingston in the Continental army."

That said, he drew a breath and continued. "At critical times such as these, I consider it my sacred duty, dear children, to pass along information important to our well-being. Therefore, in lieu of the reading of a sermon, I should like to take this opportunity to answer some of the rumors that have spread like wildfire around us. This, I trust, shall enable you to pray more effectively for the cause, and so I must ask that you pay close attention as I relate some information I've only recently been given myself."

He stopped as if to see if anyone objected, then went on. "The British, it is true, have taken the big island just offshore of New York port. With General Washington concerned more with New York and the passageway up the Hudson, very little had been done to fortify Nassau Island. But even in that loss our Lord has shown his mercy. On the twenty-seventh day of August, the British surrounded our troops on three sides, leaving nothing but the bay to our boys' backs. All the while, the Royal Navy attempted to move into position to bombard our army from the rear. Upon that dire day, both Generals Sullivan and Stirling were captured, along with their commands. . . ."

The news astounded Chandler. Stirling had been to the immediate right of the First Pennsylvania Rifle Battalion when the order came for his battalion to retire from the field. Even if Chan had stayed, he knew he would have been spared death or capture—he, who cared so little whether he lived or died. It was men like Robby MacKinnon who died—ones with so much to live for.

Where was justice in all of this? Couldn't these people see that life was little more than the toss of a coin? What true and loving God would have taken Robby and left someone so much less deserving behind?

"The situation could not have been more grim," the minister said, grabbing Chandler's attention once more. "A complete defeat was imminent . . . except for God's intervention. As the Lord did in biblical times and other periods throughout history, he provided a miracle. A great storm sent the British in search of shelter. The heavy rains fell for days, and the wind blew unceasingly. Complete and total victory at hand, General Howe allowed his army to stay under cover. As the elements raged, the Royal Navy could not maneuver its ships past the Narrows to bombard our army from the rear. However, accustomed to such ill weather as we New Englanders are prone to endure," he paused for effect, a broad smile widening his mouth, "we saw no reason to wait for perfect conditions. If we did, would we ever go to sea?"

"Amen," someone volunteered.

A low chuckle made the rounds.

The pastor nodded. "Men from Marblehead and Salem manned whatever flatboats they could find and ferried our boys across that night, with nary a second's thought to the storm our bountiful Father had provided. Whether or not they figured they could get the whole army across, they simply trusted the Lord. And to honor that faith, near midnight, our Lord changed the direction of the wind, making it possible to then press our sloops and other sailing craft into action. Praise be! They ferried *almost every man* across before the light of dawn!"

Several women drew in audible breaths.

"As the dawn brightened into morning, the rain stopped, and a blessed fog rose up from the water and wrapped itself around the last few boatfuls, just as if the Lord himself had cupped them in his mighty hand. And not a single man who had been rescued doubted that it was a miracle."

He spread his billowy sleeves wide. "Brothers and sisters, have no doubt in your hearts and minds. Because of unwavering faith, because of fervent prayers, God is standing with us in this righteous cause of ours."

Chandler couldn't help his own misgivings. Even at this very moment the Pennsylvania riflemen could be under heavy attack. After all, the English forces had not shown any regard for the Sabbath so far. He felt a surge of guilt for not being with the riflemen now, lending whatever support he could. But when he glanced at Emily, her vulnerability convinced him of the opposite. No matter what, he would have taken Robby home to her.

The booming voice of the minister cut across his wandering thoughts. "I urge every one of you to uphold in prayer all of our men who've been taken prisoner and all of the stalwart soldiers who remain steadfast. And," his voice softened as he lowered a glance to someone near the front, "let us remember, too, the families of those who gave their lives for freedom. It is my sad duty to pass along word that one of South Kingston's own brave Sons of Liberty, Sylvester Jones, has gone to his eternal reward."

Muffled sounds of weeping came from women wiping their eyes with kerchiefs.

Chandler heard Emily take in a ragged breath. He caught the wrenching sight of her, sitting rigid, her eyes closed, with tears seeping between her damp lashes. He shifted Rusty to his lap and tentatively reached a hand toward her.

To his surprise, she gripped his fingers and held on tight as silent sobs shook her slender frame.

It came to him with all certainty then. . . . Robby had been right to send him. No one else could have understood her grief as he did.

"Let us pray," the minister continued, "that the British will be given an unequivocal send-off to England, leaving us to bask in the light and glory of our God-given right to freedom in Christ."

❧ ❧

"And in closing," the Anglican priest in Philadelphia pronounced, much to Prudence's relief, "let us pray that this unpleasant rebellion will soon be quashed. That we can all resume enjoying the benefits of our benevolent mother country." He spread his arms in a wide flourish of luxuriant velvet-trimmed black sleeves. "This mighty empire, lest we forget, has ever possessed the most sane voice of reason and civilized conduct in the entire world."

Prudence ground her teeth in disdain as she observed the pompous representative of the Church of England standing in the intricately carved pulpit. He hovered ten feet above the congregation—high above the mere commoners in the physical sense, she assured herself, as well as in the hierarchy of the Holy Anglican Church.

Sacrificing her own Congregational Church service for the very one her Puritan forefathers had come to the New World to escape had been the most difficult adjustment for her since coming to Philadelphia. How she missed worshiping with her own kind. She ventured a glance at Morgan next to her. He wore a bland expression, but then, he had been raised in this stuffy church with its self-serving clergy. And of course, he had been a successful spy long before her path crossed his.

"Let us pray," the priest went on, "that when next we meet on the Sabbath, we shall be rejoicing in the restoration of New York City and the end of this barbaric rebellion."

On Prudence's other side, Evelyn reached over unobtrusively and applied pressure to her hand. The younger girl was undoubtedly galled by the man's sanctimonious tone and victorious words, but she was also distressed about her Jamie. Prudence hoped with all her heart that someone would soon dispel the rumors of the heavy patriot losses.

When the Eucharist was finished, the final hymn sung, and

the benediction pronounced, Prudence breathed a sigh of relief. She and Evie sprang to their feet.

But Morgan's staying hand dampened his wife's enthusiasm. "We must be sure to relay to the good Father what an inspiring message he delivered today." His attention swung to Evie. "Very encouraging, wouldn't you say, Evelyn? Most uplifting."

Her demeanor became markedly solicitous. "Quite right, Brother, dear. Now that you've mentioned its finer points, I realize how truly wonderful it was."

He grinned. "Ah, look who's trying to get our attention. That fine figure of an heiress-seeking Englishman, Clayborne Raleigh." Morgan waved.

As they made their way up the aisle toward the entrance where Raleigh stood, Evelyn looked at Prudence. "Please don't leave me alone with him. He's getting more persistent by the day."

Prudence had to agree. True to form, he had a decidedly predatory gleam in his watery blue eyes as he reached them and took Evie's hand to kiss it.

Reflexively, she snatched it back, then recovered. "Not in the sanctuary, Clay. I say, did you ever see such boldness?" she asked Prudence in a coy tone, adding a sidelong look of pleading at her brother.

Morgan, obviously at his limit with the pompous oaf, no longer deemed it necessary to keep smiling. He began herding them toward the exit. "Fine sermon, was it not, Mr. Raleigh?" he inquired.

The Englishman gave him a look of tolerant impatience. "Quite. However, one can't help but surmise that with all of General Howe's mighty army, the man should have simply finished off the rebellious trash when he had the chance, instead of allowing them to escape back to New York. Oh, well," he said with a sniff. "Perhaps Lord Howe wants to toy with them a bit longer, like a cat with a mouse."

When he reached the priest, Morgan extended a polite hand. "Splendid sermon, Father, and thought provoking."

The rotund clergyman accepted the flattery with a satisfied tip of his wigged head. "I notice your parents are not present this morning. I do hope they've not fallen ill."

"Not at all, I assure you, Your Grace. They've simply gone to visit friends in Baltimore."

"Ah. Well, then I shall expect to see them next week." He dipped his head toward Clay Raleigh and offered a pudgy white hand.

But Prudence had caught the devilish glint in the Englishman's eye when he heard that Evie's parents were away. Now she watched Raleigh tuck Evie's hand within the crook of his elbow and whisk her down the steps of the grand church.

Evidently, Morgan noticed it, too. Drawing Prudence away slightly, he bent close to her ear. "That London wharf rat seems to think he's going to play with our little kitten while Mama and Papa are away."

She chuckled. "Lucky for us, this little kitten is too quick for the rat. And she does have claws."

"Still, a rat that big might just devour a little kitten when she's not looking. We'll need to keep our eyes on him at all times."

"I say, Thomas," a man behind them said. "Are you, perchance, having a rodent problem?"

Morgan and Prudence both turned to see his father's prissy haberdasher. "No, Mr. Beatty, nothing so serious as that."

"One must not let them get the best of us, you know," the gentleman went on, elevating his brows. "I recently came across a marvelous new poison at the feed store. Here, I'll write down the name of it." Pulling out the stub of a writing stick and a scrap of paper, he scribbled a few words.

"Actually, that won't be necessary," Morgan started to say as Prudence squeezed his arm with an amused smile.

"Don't be silly, my boy, of course it is." Beatty pressed the paper into Morgan's hand. "I'm sure this will help."

"Thank you." Prudence watched as he absently shoved it into his pocket.

"Pray, look at it first," the haberdasher insisted. "It's a Latin name, and my penmanship is not what it used to be."

Prudence suppressed a grin as her husband struggled to be patient with the intrusive man. She rose on tiptoe to read the paper as he opened it.

Your bread is done. A message from Micah Dodd! Micah needed to see Morgan now! Suddenly Mr. Beatty didn't seem quite so irritating.

"Why, thank you, sir," Morgan said with a smile. "I shall purchase some of this at once."

The perfectly tailored and powdered man touched his tricorn. "Good to have you home again, lad. Come by soon and sort through my latest fabrics. I've a royal blue satin that would go fabulously with your eyes." With a wink, he strolled off.

"A blue satin as fabulous as your eyes?" Prudence barely concealed her delight as they joined Evelyn and Raleigh. "Such a find is worthy of announcing to all your gentlemen friends, don't you agree?"

"Sweetheart," he said to Prudence. "Forgive me, but I'm afraid I must go down to the warehouse. I just remembered I neglected to hang the invoices, and the workmen won't know what to crate tomorrow."

"Ohh," she groaned in false disappointment. "Can't you do it in the morning before the men arrive?"

Morgan inched nearer to Clay Raleigh. "Can you imagine? My wife would have me rise before the sun!"

"A ghastly prospect, to say the least," Clay answered with a laugh.

"Well, my good man," Morgan told the Englishman, "if you will be so kind as to see my ladies home for me, I'll join you all within the hour."

Prudence shrugged in resignation. They needed an escort, after all, and as much as they all despised Clay Raleigh, he *was* the logical choice.

"And, of course," Morgan continued, "we shall expect you to join us for Sunday dinner."

Prudence glared at Morgan, but he was already beating a hasty retreat.

❧ ❧

The delicious aroma of freshly baked bread and biscuits permeated the whole area when Morgan arrived at the docks, and it grew even stronger as he entered the Dodd Baking Company. His stomach growled as the bell above the door jangled.

"Morgan!" Micah called out from across the workroom. "Good, you're here." He plucked the baking hat from atop his dark head and beckoned. "Had a special order that couldn't be put off," he added by way of explanation for working on the Sabbath.

With a nod of greeting, Morgan strode through the rows of flour-dusted tables to the back, then followed Jamie's older brother into a small office.

Micah's floury fingers left white impressions on the back of the dark wooden chair he grabbed and tugged to the high window. Climbing up, he peered outside, then pulled the window shut. "Glad you could come so quickly," he said, dusting his hands on his work apron before offering one in a warm handshake. "My good wife has the Sabbath dinner waiting at home. Now that you've fallen from bachelorhood yourself, you must know the pickle being late for Sunday dinner can get a body into."

Morgan grinned. "Actually, I've not had that pleasure as yet. Let's get down to business, shall we? But first, have you news of Jamie? My little sister is on tenterhooks."

"Nay. But he's a quick lad. I gave him my best Pennsylvania rifle and told him to report to Colonel Hand. The man was a professional soldier before he settled here, don't ya know. A no-nonsense man, if ever there was one. He'll keep the boy alive and in line, I'm sure of that."

"That will be welcome news to Evelyn. She's quite taken with the lad."

Micah gave a hearty laugh and nodded. "Puppy love. How well I remember."

"I take it you have a message for me?" Morgan asked.

"Aye. And I want to say, gettin' an audience with His Holiness, General Washington, is like goin' through the eye of a needle! But I managed." He hopped on the chair to take another look outside, then climbed down.

Morgan checked outside the office door.

"The general said that if the merchants of Philadelphia want you to represent their interests with the British army in New York, his answer is an enthusiastic *Godspeed.* Said he couldn't imagine a less suspicious entrance into the privy circles of the Royal High Command."

"That's about what I expected him to say," Morgan admitted. He was all the more glad he would be going, for the deceptions with his family were beginning to bother him as never before—especially since he'd had to withhold from his father his knowledge of Evie's spying activities.

"Speaking of Washington," Micah added, "I seen him comin' and goin' last year, along with the rest of the representatives to Congress. A body couldn't miss that giant. Seemed a bit unapproachable, he did . . . yet when we talked privately, I saw another side to the man. He expressed true concern about you. He wanted me to be sure and tell you not to take any undue chances. If you ever suspect you've been exposed, he said to leave immediately. Spies are not treated like other prisoners. They are executed."

Morgan snorted in derision. "That's exactly what I keep trying to tell my wife . . . *and* that reckless little sister of mine!"

18

"Big stick!" Rusty hollered. He gave a few hearty swings to the large twig he'd managed to find in the underbrush, then jabbed at some dead leaves.

"It sure is," Chandler agreed. He added another branch to the bundle of deadfall in his own arms. "I think we have enough now. We'd best get back to camp."

Katie turned to him, her eyes shining. "I see a real good one, there!" As she hopped over a fallen tree to retrieve it, her foot landed on a protruding twig. She went sprawling, and the tiny bunch of kindling she was carrying flew everywhere.

Chandler watched her jump up without a peep and brush off her dress, then gather in earnest the bounty she had been so proud of. This time she didn't drop any. Observing her movements, he couldn't help but recall that his own son would have been six years old by now, more than two years older than Katie, had Julia not suffered a miscarriage from the fall that claimed her life. Their child would have had neither Katie's dark black hair nor Rusty's auburn, of course, but inheriting some of Julia's fun-loving personality, he'd have been every inch as energetic and exuberant as these two, Chan surmised. "Find all your sticks?" he asked as the little girl started toward him.

"Yep. Every single one."

"Me, too," Rusty piped in, coming over with a swagger reminiscent of his father's.

"Then let's get back to your mommy." Chan couldn't believe how quickly he'd grown used to having the children around. He even enjoyed it.

At that thought, Chandler slowly exhaled. He had felt himself coming back to life during this past week and a half of travel. It was an incredible change for him, after so many dreary years with only himself to think about. Now he anticipated each new day in a way he'd almost forgotten, finding delight in so many little things.

He still chuckled over a remark Katie had made when it had been impossible to secure lodging at a roadside inn because of the hordes of people fleeing New York. The child had stood up in the back of the wagon and planted her hands on her hips. "No room at the inn. Just like Joseph and Mary," she had said in dismay, then brightened. "Oh, goody! Maybe we'll stay in the manger, with lots of cows and horses."

Alas, that night, and every night since, they'd had to resort to camping beside the road, along with so many other families. But even that was not without benefits, for Katie and Rusty could play with other children. Already they had traveled as far as the outskirts of Elizabeth, New Jersey. Tomorrow evening they would arrive at Princeton, and he could deliver Emily and her "wee bairns" into the capable hands of Jasper and Esther Lyons.

So far, Chandler hadn't permitted himself to dwell on returning to the town where he'd lost everything worth living for. Only the promise given to Robby MacKinnon could have made him consider going there. He would do no more than bid the MacKinnons farewell and then make a hasty departure. He could not tarry in the heart of his sorrow . . . nor could he ponder how much more solitary his life would become, once he left this little family behind.

He and the children emerged from the woods into a grassy field where they and several other families were setting up camp for the second night in a row in honor of the Sabbath. Were it not for her rigid beliefs, she and the children might be enjoying this very evening the congenial company of the old Lyons couple in Princeton.

Emily was kneeling in the back of the wagon bed, chatting with a gray-haired woman and a young girl as she put some things into a basket. When he was not beside her for comparison, it was easy to forget how tiny she truly was. Her slender form and long fluid strides seemed deceiving. As always, struck by the natural grace of her movements, he had to remind himself that both Robby and Morgan had told him she was a tomboy as a child, out working with her brothers on the horse farm more often than sitting on the porch with her sewing. It was hard to picture her in anything other than ruffles and lace.

His gaze lingered on her expression. Even as innately friendly as Emily was wont to be, it still wasn't any easier for her to speak of her widowhood to strangers.

Reaching the campfire, Chandler and the children dropped the wood beside it. The supper simmering in the iron kettle gave off a delicious aroma. After more than a year of army fare, this pungent smell was ambrosial.

"Rusty," Katie said, "there's Eddie. Let's go play." And the two started happily off.

"Hey! Wait one minute," Chan called out, stopping them in their tracks. "Supper's about ready."

Emily and the women looked up.

"Oh, it's good that you're back, Mr. MacKinnon," the older one said. "We need you to lift the pot off your fire and tote it over to the Hansons' camp. Being Sunday and all, we thought it would be nice to share our bounty this evening."

Mr. MacKinnon? Chandler cut a glance at Emily, who gave a helpless shrug. Knowing her, she would have been far too polite to refuse the eating arrangement. "Sounds like a mighty tasty idea."

Approaching him with two pot holders, Emily gave him a grateful look. "Thank you," she mouthed, then raised her voice to a normal tone. "I'll bring the basket with our plates and utensils."

"Can I carry something, Mama?" Katie asked as Chandler lifted the kettle off the tripod he had rigged above the coals.

"I suppose we could use a blanket to sit on, honey. Bring the one with the berry stains, all right?"

"Me, too," Rusty chimed in.

Noticing Emily's bewildered frown, Chan racked his brain. "A good strong lad like you might lend a hand with that heavy basket your mama's carrying. Can you do that?"

"Aye. See my muscles?" Shoving up his sleeve and bending his spindly arm, Rusty displayed a minuscule bulge.

Chandler widened his eyes in feigned awe. "I see what you mean." Chuckling, he turned to the women. "Well, ladies, which way to the Hansons'?"

When they arrived at their neighbor's camp, a long table made of boards propped on barrels had already been set up. Chan set the heavy pot on one end, then found himself being waved aside by bustling women readying the feast. His stomach growled in anticipation as he walked toward the men lounging against a fieldstone wall. All of them appeared past fifty, except for one who hobbled about with a decided limp.

"Wait and see," he heard one of the men say. "Washington will outfox those king's puppets yet."

Chandler was not surprised by the topic. Everywhere he went, men discussed little else.

A silver-haired gent eyed him with disdain. "How do. The wife tells me you just come down from Rhode Island on your way to Princeton. Some new trouble up that way?"

Chan shook his head. "Not yet, anyway." He could tell from the mild stares of disapproval that all of them must have been speculating about why a fit man such as himself wasn't with the army. But for Emily's sake he chose not to explain.

"My boys have all enlisted," another remarked pointedly. "So have Rayford's."

A nod came from the one named Rayford. "And I've a mind to enlist myself, just as soon as I get my daughter-in-law and her young'uns to her folks' in Trenton."

"I might just join up with you," a third said. "Maybe I'm not as fast as I used to be, but General Howe's movin' so slow against us that it shouldn't matter much."

"Davis," the crippled one said, "they aren't gonna want a couple of old coots like you two around, gettin' in the way."

Seeing how much the older pair wanted to lend a hand, Chandler shrugged. "I wouldn't say that. If you don't mind loading wagons and taking supplies out to regiments, you could report to Major Kendall. He'd probably be glad to have you. It would free up some younger men to be sent to a fighting unit."

"Think so?" one of them asked, perking up along with his crony. "You know this Major Kendall?"

"I've loaded a wagon or two for him."

"Then you were enlisted for a spell? served under this officer?" A slight note of respect colored his tone now.

"I'm still in, actually," Chan responded. "But I've been transferred to the First Pennsylvania Rifle Battalion. I'll be reporting for duty again in a few days."

Now all the men's expressions became markedly friendlier. "A rifleman, you say," one remarked. "Been in any skirmishes? I'd sure grab at a chance to get off a shot or two at them lobsterbacks."

Chandler didn't bother to elaborate. He didn't especially find the matter of killing or being killed appealing. He decided to change the subject. "Well, don't discount Howe's ability because he seems reluctant to take action. The huge losses he suffered at Bunker Hill would sober any general, make him not want to endure a slaughter like that ever again. I'd wager that from now on when he makes a move, he'll do it confident of a victory."

"Slaughter, eh? Were you at Bunker Hill, lad?" the man with the limp asked. "If I didn't have this cussed leg, I'd have been there, like as not. Must've been one glorious day."

"No one thought so at the time," Chandler assured him, disliking the way the battle on Charlestown Neck was being glorified with the passage of time. "It was a terrible day. A day of smoke. Blood. Broken bodies."

The man seemed no less enthusiastic. "Aye. A glorious victory for us."

"Time to eat," a woman called.

Chan felt a wave of relief. They couldn't truly understand the horrors of a massacre unless they had been part of it. And it was no less horrifying merely because the enemy got the worst of it.

Rejoining Emily, he noticed that her face appeared drawn. Already he was able to read every small change in her expression and demeanor, and obviously she was not coping well. Had there been too many probing questions? He moved to her side to fend off any more queries.

❧ ❧

Emily lay awake long after everyone else was in deep slumber. Only the usual night sounds of crickets and tree toads broke the stillness of the camp as the moments crept past. Gazing up from the pallet she and the children occupied in the wagon, she watched the moon crawl across the sky.

She remembered doing this very same thing the night before Robby MacKinnon had come into her life. She had been stargazing and ruing the fact that God had made her a mere girl, thus delegating her to a life of drudgery, while men sailed off to their high adventures. She had bemoaned her unlucky fate to the Almighty. And, oh, how he'd heard her! And answered. The very next night she had been on the run from a redcoat patrol, aiding and abetting a perfect stranger.

She thought back on what a charming and handsome young Scotsman Robby MacKinnon was then. From the very beginning he had bestowed upon her a gallant respect the rest of her family had never deigned to show "their baby." Her untried heart had quickly become captivated. It was with the utmost joy, after having successfully eluded their captors, that she and Robby agreed to have her brother Dan unite them in marriage. They'd known immeasurable happiness during their life together, and Emily hadn't experienced a day's regret since.

Until now.

She swallowed and took a deep breath for strength. Tomorrow evening she would be at the Lyons' Den Coaching Inn. Just imagining the raft of questions, the motherly concern Mrs. Lyons would heap upon her, made Emily's eyes smart. How would she ever get through telling that sweet old woman of this immeasurable loss? Fresh tears blurred the sight of the starry sky, making the pinpoints of light run together.

Next to her, Rusty mumbled in his sleep.

Emily rolled to her side and tenderly adjusted the blanket covering him. So like Robby, he was, her little man. Mrs. Lyons would love him and his little button nose, his boyish strut. She would be amazed to see how much he had grown. He and Katie both. The old couple had doted on their "little princess" during the time Emily and Robby had made their home in Princeton.

Esther Lyons, childless herself, had agonized with her during the births of both children, crying and struggling and grunting right along with Emily. And Esther's gruff old husband, Jasper, had been as relieved as anyone when it was all over. Why couldn't she be happy at the thought of returning to them now? *Why couldn't she go to sleep!*

Easing onto her back once more, she made out the three stars that made up Orion's belt, just above the horizon. It must have been past midnight.

Robby had taught her a lot about the stars. He had picked up most of it during the months when he was cabin boy on the *Gaspee. Oh, Robby . . . why did you have to leave me all alone like this? You were such a good husband and father, so loving and kind. Why did you go away?* When the intense aching inside threatened to unleash a whole new ocean of tears, Emily threw off her cover and climbed out of the wagon. A quiet walk in the moonlight would get her through this lonely night.

She slipped into the moccasins she had left beside the wheel and quietly left the camp. Glancing back only once, she saw Robert Chandler's sleeping form near the smoldering embers of the campfire. Robby had told her that Chan always shied away from responsibility, yet he had been a rock to her. A listening ear when she needed to talk, a silent tongue when she couldn't bear chatter. She would be grateful to him forever.

And how many times on this journey he had endured being called her husband, without a qualm! The thought would have made her smile, except for the constant pain in her heart. Yes, Robby had sent her a treasured friend. Robby . . . and God.

Reaching the far side of the meadow, Emily passed the outer trees of the woods. The earth smelled damp and piney with the scent of evergreens. The air, though cooler, seemed somehow thicker. She continued on into the forest, becoming aware of the soft scurry of woodland creatures, the fluttering wings of a bird she'd disturbed. Familiar sounds.

But then the remembrance of her first nights in the woods with Robby came back with crashing clarity. That time together had been so innocent, yet so intimate. During those nights her heart had awakened to love.

"Whooo, whooo, whoo," an owl hooted.

The swift flapping of its wings startled Emily, and her night shift snagged on something. She struggled to free it, pricking her finger on a sharp thorn in the darkness. Tears, ever near the surface these days, quickly sprang to her eyes.

"Whooo, whoo," came the call again. Questioning.

She faced so many questions now, so many uncertainties. She had no answers anymore. She dropped helplessly onto a bed of pine needles and moss. Beyond her endurance, she relinquished her struggle and buried her head in her arms, giving in to the sorrow she had tried so hard to fight. There, alone and far from camp, she moaned and sobbed and wept out her anguish. When at last the wrenching cries died down to only whimpers, she sat up and drew her knees to her chest, rocking herself for solace. But she found none.

"Emily?"

She felt a hand on her shoulder, and Chandler dropped

down beside her. Without thinking, she leaned against him, needing to feel close to someone . . . it had been so long. When her trembling and sobs began to subside, Emily raised her head, trying to make out his shadowy face. "If God knows . . . how much it hurts," she struggled to say, but was unable to finish.

"Shh." He took her hand and enclosed it in both of his. The warmth of his nearness was oddly comforting.

Neither spoke for several minutes.

"The closer we get to Princeton," he finally said, his low voice resonating in the darkness, "the more the memories of my days there come back. Not just the cursed reminders of Julia's death, but memories of good times I shared with her and my fellow students, of teachers and some of their lessons. I didn't usually pay much attention to the Bible classes, as I think back. But this morning in church, the pastor said something in regard to one of Jesus' great losses. I remember studying it in one of my classes."

"Wasn't the sermon about the feeding of the five thousand?"

"Yes. But that day was very long, and so much more happened than one miraculous meal. The disciples had just informed the Lord of the death of his cousin John, who had so faithfully heralded his coming. Jesus felt deeply burdened over it. His first thought was to get away from the throng, so he went across the lake and up a hill, taking only his closest friends, the disciples, those who might understand the depth of his grief. But finding solitude was not to be."

Emily marveled at hearing Chandler say so much at once— especially when it concerned the Lord. According to Robby, Chan blamed God for taking his wife . . . yet she had no doubt that the Lord was speaking to her through Chan right now.

"Despite the weight of his burdens, Jesus still had to deal with people by the thousands who clamored after him, crowded around him, begging him to ease their suffering. From his Father, Jesus found strength enough to do just that, until the day was far spent. Then he provided the meal for the crowd."

Emily did not respond but waited to see what Chandler was trying to say.

"But still his day was not finished. After witnessing that incredible miracle of the food, the people turned into a riotous mob, wanting to make Jesus their king. He barely managed to send the disciples off in a boat and spirit himself away. And it wasn't until then that he was finally able to find comfort, in the one true source, his Father."

Mulling over the story, Emily began to grasp Chan's point. For all people's good intentions, truest comfort could be found in God alone. "I've never pieced the whole story together before. It's as sad as it is beautiful. Thank you for this gift."

The moment she said the words, an indescribable peace flowed through her, one even more profound than the first wave of peace she had felt soon after Robby was killed. Somehow in the following days she had let it slip away, and now the Lord restored that which had been lost, and even more. "How perfectly wonderful that almighty God absorbed Jesus' pain and lightened his heavy heart."

"I don't recall the gospel saying that, exactly."

"Oh, but it does, if you read between the lines. If Jesus had remained weighted down with a heavy burden, he never could have walked across the water to join the disciples, could he?"

Chandler regarded her steadily for a long moment, then reached and brushed away a damp lock that clung to her cheek. "I'd hesitate to argue that point with Dr. Witherspoon at the college. . . ."

"No matter." Taking a deep cleansing breath, Emily got to her feet. "It's just something I needed this night. I'll be better from now on. The Lord has eased my awful pain and sorrow by placing them on his own shoulders to help me bear. From now on I'll do my best not to take them back."

With an incredulous shake of his head, Chandler looked

straight at her. "You mean, just like that? You can go on now and live as if the one you loved most in this world were not taken from you?"

Emily heard the doubt in that question, and she knew that though Robert Chandler had given this gift of God's Word to her, even now he didn't understand, because he had never accepted the gift for himself. He had spent years shutting himself away from God's peace. But she also knew it was never too late for him to find his own new beginning and then to go on from there. She mustered all the conviction she possessed. "I know Robby will never come back to me, and of course I shall always miss him. But one day I will see him again. And until that day, in spite of the sorrow I'll feel, I know that God will never let me go."

19

As the houses on the outskirts of Princeton became more and more frequent, Chandler found his dread of coming into the town increasing as well. Until now, the children and their incessant questions had provided some distraction from the prospect of the grievous pain that would inevitably assail him here. But observing Emily's patience with them today, he couldn't help but wonder what sort of mother his beloved English wife might have been.

Who could have known how very fragile life was, back then? He and Julia had known such happiness during their months together . . . so sublime, yet so breathtakingly short. Misty fragments of her tinkling laughter still echoed in his mind, as did haunting visions of her red-gold curls, wild and gloriously beautiful.

But those happy memories seemed inconsequential compared with the unspeakable agony of witnessing her futile struggle to live and her tortured descent into the valley of death along with their premature son. The mental pictures slashed ruthlessly across his consciousness again, making him regret his promise to Robby all the more.

The bell tower of Nassau Hall would be visible above the trees any minute now. Chandler's hands began to sweat, and with a constriction in his chest, he labored to breathe.

"Look, Katie," Emily said, pointing out an upcoming home

to her daughter, who sat between her and Chandler. "That's where your friend Cora Beth lives. Remember?"

"I . . . I think so," the child said with some hesitation.

"I 'member," Rusty announced, puffing out his chest.

"Well," Emily went on, "your daddy worked for her daddy when we lived here in Princeton. You and Cora played together almost every day. Oh, and there's the Smiths' place, and the Harrises', and . . ."

Chan tried to concentrate on her chatter. Emily was returning to a happy past, to old friendships. This venture into yesterday was the opposite for him.

Just beyond the college building where he had attended classes would be the turnoff to Holmby House and the simple little room where he and Julia had spent their sweetest moments together. Since students were required to live in the school dormitory, and Chan did not want to risk expulsion by confessing his untimely marriage, the newlyweds thought it a lark to keep their haven a secret.

Everything had been a lark then. Julia, from an aristocratic British family, would have found instant approval from his parents, he was sure of that. But her folks would have been hesitant to accept the union, since it meant leaving her home and country behind and sailing across the wide ocean to the New World.

They met by accident and became completely enamored with one another while Chandler was touring Britain with his friends. The two threw caution to the wind and followed their hearts. Chandler spirited her aboard his returning ship, and once at sea, they implored the captain to marry them.

In their naïveté, they imagined that by keeping their marriage a secret, they could live on Chandler's allowance for years and be free of both sets of parents. A smile curved his mouth at the way some of his classmates, party to their scheme, helped him outwit the professors, just so he and Julia might enjoy some time together. Thinking back on it now, it was hard to believe he had ever been that young and carefree. And that foolish.

Emily's voice once more interrupted his musings. "Yes, Mr. Chandler did go to that big schoolhouse. Didn't you?"

Robert cast a cursory glance toward the immense structure of native stone that housed the College of New Jersey. "Yes," he managed. But seeing the familiar cutoff coming up, he did not elaborate further.

"And so did your uncle Dan," Emily went on, hugging Rusty close. "Now he's the minister of a church. Perhaps someday, when you're a very big boy, you shall go there, too."

"What about me, Mama?" Katie asked.

She smiled. "Girls don't attend that college, I'm afraid."

"Why not?" the little girl demanded indignantly.

Emily smiled. "We learn other sorts of things. But from the look of the place, I hardly think anyone is learning anything there now. It appears vacant."

"Most likely it is," Chan admitted. "Probably in recess until after the war, just as Harvard is, back in Cambridge."

"The war has altered so much more than I would have expected," Emily remarked sadly, then drew both children tighter. "But I'll wager it hasn't changed Grandma and Grandpa Lyons," she added on a much brighter note. "Won't they be surprised at how much you both have grown! We're almost there now. It's just up the road."

"Hurry, horsies," Rusty pleaded as he bounced up and down in excitement.

Approaching the dreaded street Robert had tried so hard to put out of his mind, he snapped the traces over the animals' backs and did his best to keep his eyes fixed straight ahead. Just a few seconds more . . .

It was God's judgment, that's what, came the hateful, railing voice of the landlady in his mind. His gaze swung on its own down the elm-lined street as the wagon passed, taking in the two-story brick house with white sashes. He could not keep from looking up at the second-floor window of the room, where Julia had breathed her last, having their child. *God's judgment on you for trying to make fools out of your family and that good Doctor Witherspoon over at the college. God's judgment.*

God's judgment.

        ❧ ❧

At last they turned onto the gravel drive fronting the Lyons' Den Coaching Inn. Emily let her gaze freely absorb the welcome familiarity of the huge fieldstone building—three stories, with wide chimneys, neat shrubbery, and a carved, wooden lion's-head sign suspended by chains above the entrance.

Suddenly the doors flew open. *"Emily?"* a young man asked in wonder as he came outside.

She had seen him so seldom once he'd enrolled at the college, it took her several seconds to recognize the now-grown youth who, along with his sister Mary Clare, had been a ward of Jasper and Esther Lyons. He had shot up like a weed, his skinny body had filled out, and his once blond hair had darkened to a sandy shade. "Chip!"

He tucked his chin and grinned, leaping aboard to give her a hug. "I don't go by that nickname anymore. I prefer Christopher. Or even Drummer, sometimes. Some of my friends call me that."

"Well, I like Christopher," Emily said, hugging him back.

Rusty squirmed. "Help! I'm squished!"

"Whoa," Christopher said, rearing back. "What have we here? Your mommy left here with two tiny kids, and came back with a little princess and a big boy. I'm sure glad Robby finally talked you into coming back where it's safe. Ma Lyons will be in her glory with two babies to look after again." He hopped to the ground.

"I am *not* a baby!" Katie announced as she and her brother got to their feet.

Rusty gave an emphatic nod. "Me either."

"Oh. Too bad. I suppose you wouldn't want a piggyback ride, then, would you?" Turning, Christopher took a step away.

Emily gasped as her son flung himself at the young man's back, but she let out a breath of relief when Christopher's arms curved around and held the child secure.

Katie giggled and clambered off the wagon to prance happily alongside. "I know you," she singsonged. "You're my Chip."

"*Uncle* Chip to you, peanut," he teased, giving her nose a tap with one finger.

"Uncle Chip, Uncle Chip," they chorused.

Smiling after them, Emily rose and began to climb down from the wagon. Chandler remained fixed to his seat. "Come on in and greet everyone, won't you? We can see to the horses later."

"No, you go on. I'll tend to the animals first."

From his closed expression, Emily sensed that arguing would serve no purpose, and she let out a quiet sigh. She could understand Chan's grief over the loss of his wife, but she had been praying he would at last begin to accept it. No doubt returning to Princeton, where Julia had died, was bringing up many long-buried memories. She looked at his pain-racked expression, and her heart wrenched with compassion. "Well, please don't be long, all right?" With a thin smile, she stepped down and followed after Christopher and the children.

"Pa Lyons! Look who's here," she heard the lad call as he went inside.

Entering the familiar establishment a few steps after the others, Emily saw scraggly old Jasper Lyons look up from the ledgers he had been studying. "It can't be! Esther!" he bellowed. "Come out here right quick!" His booming voice startled the white cockatoo on a perch in the corner. Methuselah ruffled his feathers and blinked translucent blue eyes, then settled down again.

As Mr. Lyons clomped over and smothered Emily in a huge hug, a pair of chairs screeched back on the plank floor of the common room. Two townsmen who were almost fixtures of the place got up and made a beeline for her, too.

The second the innkeeper released her, she found herself grabbed by barrel-chested Asa Appleton. "Welcome home, Missy," he said, all but suffocating her in his exuberance. "We missed havin' you around."

"That goes double for me," Hiram Brown, next in line, said. Light from candles in the wall sconces glinted off his noticeably balder pate as he beamed from ear to ear.

From behind them, Emily heard a soft cry. She turned right into stout little Mrs. Lyons's cushiony embrace. "My sweet Emmy. Oh, but it's pure heaven to set eyes on you again. Now, where are those 'wee bairns' your Robby's so proud of?"

"Right here, Ma." Christopher, a few feet away, urged the youngsters forward.

"Ohh . . . just look at how my precious babies have grown." Overcome at the sight of the children, the older woman pressed her gnarled fingers to her lips.

"Grandma?" Katie whispered, her eyes shining.

Mrs. Lyons bent over and tenderly wrapped her arms around the child, stroking her long black hair. A tear sparkled in her small eyes when Katie clung back.

"What about this little squirrel?" Christopher asked.

Rusty beamed. "I'm big, too, Gramma."

"You surely are, young man," she returned, tousling his hair before hauling him close.

It truly was like coming home again, Emily decided, relishing the way the old childless couple made them all feel like family. It had been like that from the very first day she and Robby had come to Princeton to live.

"Robby's not with you?" Mrs. Lyons asked.

"No. He's . . ."

"Course he couldn't come, old woman," Jasper said in his usual gruff manner. "There's a war goin' on, remember?"

"Well, at least he sent his dear ones back to us, and that's all that matters now." She gazed lovingly at the children again. "You must be tired after that long trip. But first things first. I want all of you to sit yourselves down, and I'll fetch you some hot stew. Won't be but a minute. Then we'll have time for a nice long chat before the stage wagons get here."

"I'll help," Emily offered, trailing after Esther, while Mr. Lyons began herding the children to one of the long tables in the middle of the ordinary. Since it was Monday, stage wagons would arrive from New York and Philadelphia . . . but not for a few hours, at least. Time enough to relate the sad news to her dear friends.

Mrs. Lyons bustled about the big workroom in her efficient way, seizing a tray and putting it on the table, then plunking bowls from the sideboard on it. She turned to gather utensils.

Emily, on the fringe, whispered a hasty prayer for strength, then stepped in front of the older woman and took hold of her hands. "Would you please sit down first? There's something I must tell you."

A slight frown emphasized the maze of lines on her forehead, but she complied. She drew Emily down beside her, all the while searching her face.

"It-it's Robby," Emily said, struggling to make her voice stop wavering. "He's . . . he's been . . ." She had to take a breath to say the word. It emerged in a whisper. "Killed."

Esther drew an audible gasp, and her hand flew to her heart. Tears glistened at once in her hazel eyes, and for several seconds she appeared unable to respond. "Oh, my poor, poor child," she finally said, tugging Emily to her. "How?"

Being crushed in the older woman's fierce embrace made Emily's throat ache. She struggled to speak. "On the battlefield. Robert Chandler was with him when it happened. He told me Robby didn't suffer."

It took another few moments for Mrs. Lyons to digest the details. "This is such a sad, sad time," she said woefully, gently releasing her hold. "There's a few from the college who can never come back to us . . . and now to hear we've lost our little motherless lad from Scotland, yet. Jasper and I loved him like our own."

"I know," Emily whispered. "I know. And he loved you both

so very much." Her throat clogged completely now. She blinked hard at the tears cresting behind her eyes and tried to keep hold of her composure.

The older woman blotted her own face on the hem of her long apron and sniffed, then drew Emily against her ample self once more. "I'm sorry, child. Truly sorry."

Emily nodded, still in the embrace. "But the Lord has been good. He's helping me through it."

"Sometimes it's hard to understand suffering, though. This will be a tough one for all of us . . . especially Jasper. He set such store by the boy." She wagged her head slowly back and forth, concern evident in her demeanor. "Maybe it would be best to save tellin' Jasper until later, after the babies are in bed."

With such a fragile hold on her own ragged emotions, Emily could only nod.

Mrs. Lyons dried her moist eyes on her apron again, then took a deep breath and rose. "Well, in the meantime, let's see about gettin' the food dished up and served."

When they returned to the common room, Emily found the men all fussing over the children. Katie was snuggled on old Jasper's lap, all smiles, and Rusty was in the middle of the table on his knees, giggling as he tried to catch hold of the timepiece Asa Appleton dangled by its chain inches above the boy's reach.

There had always been an abundance of love here. Even now, with Christopher's hearty laugh and animated face, it was hard to remember his humble beginnings, when the Lyonses had taken him and his sister in. Castoffs of the town drunkard, Christopher and Mary Clare had been worse off than strays. Now the stuttering problem brought on by his father's abuse was only a distant memory, and the young man was studying to become an engineer. Or had been, until the college closed for the war.

Emily and Mrs. Lyons set down their trays, then arranged the sufficient number of place settings.

"Where's Mr. Chandler gonna sit?" Katie asked.

A twinge of conscience reminded Emily that in the excitement she had all but forgotten about Robert. He should have finished tending the horses ages ago.

"I'll see what's keeping him," Christopher offered.

She stayed him with a hand. "No. I'd better go." She turned to her hosts. "It was Robert Chandler who brought us. I'm sure you remember him. He attended the college here for a while."

"Aye," Jasper said, recognition dawning. "That spirited little English gal's husband. There's none of us can forget that sad affair, rest her soul. They took supper here most nights while he was at school, until the day of her passin', and then he up and left for good. After that, his other college friends moped around here for weeks."

"It was real hard on the lads," Esther added. "There wasn't anybody didn't love that Julia. Course, she never lifted a finger to so much as clear a table all her pampered years, I'm sure, but so full of life she was. Always laughing. A room lit up whenever she walked into it."

Emily nodded. "I've heard she was very special. Robert has yet to lay her memory to rest, though. I thought I'd better prepare you before he comes in."

Mrs. Lyons moved near enough to give Emily's shoulder a squeeze. "You're a very special girl yourself, love. Always thinkin' about the feelings of others, no matter what."

The brisk air that greeted Emily when she stepped outside hinted of the coming change of seasons. Soon the leaves would begin to turn all the brilliant hues of autumn. Would cooler weather bring an end to the conflict with Great Britain? Emily could not imagine the militia tramping through cold and snow, facing the enemy across icy rivers. Surely things would be settled by then, husbands and fathers would return to their homes and to everyday life again. Most of them, anyway. She did not allow her train of thought to drift further along that line.

The team, she noticed upon entering the stable, remained hitched to the wagon, though Robby's horse was now settled in a stall with fresh hay and water.

Chandler looked up as he unhooked a feedbag from one of the animals. "I need to get back to New York as soon as possible. With this empty wagon, I could be halfway to Elizabeth Town by midnight."

You're leaving us? she wanted to cry out, but she immediately squelched the thought. She was the cause for his leaving his post without permission for nigh unto a fortnight, as it was. She could not ask any more of him. She had simply come to rely on his steady calm, that was all. She stepped to him, her hand outstretched. "I'll miss you, Robert."

He took her fingers and gently squeezed them. "You'll be fine here, you and the children. The Lyonses will take good care of you."

"As you have. I'll be ever grateful." Unbidden tears gathered, and she blinked quickly and took a deep breath. "And don't ever forget, you'll always be welcome at my hearth. But please won't you come inside and eat before you go? I'll pack food enough to see you back to your battalion."

He shook his head. "I'd best not take the time. I'll be on my way now."

"Without even a good-bye to Katie and Rusty?"

She saw a flicker of remorse in his expression, and she realized that he was probably reluctant to face Jasper and Esther Lyons. But the time had come for him to begin dealing with his feelings, so she pressed on. "Please don't disappoint the children. Not so soon after . . ."

Chandler straightened, visibly fortifying himself. "Very well, I'll bid them farewell, but then I must be off."

"Thank you." Emily grasped his hand. "Come along, then. Perhaps you can eat a few bites before you go. Everyone's waiting."

"Everyone?" The tension was apparent even in his touch.

"And me," she said softly. "I'll be there, too."

20

As he accompanied Emily back to the Lyons' Den, Chandler's feet felt weighted with lead. He berated himself for having dawdled with the horses—he could easily have been miles from here by now. This town had already dredged up far too many gloomy reminders of the past, and the last thing he needed was to call up even more of them. Nevertheless, for Emily and the children he gritted his teeth and trudged after her.

Nothing about the inn had changed. The same carved lion's head filled the wall behind the bar, the same crisp white cloths covered the bare wood tables, the same welcoming fire blazed in the huge hearth at the far end. And as always, happy chatter filled the room.

He felt everyone's eyes on him as he and Emily approached the table where the others were already helping themselves to buttered cornbread and digging in to their stew.

"Mr. Chandler," Katie cried, patting the bench beside her. "Sit by me. See my other grandma and grandpa."

He plastered a smile on his face and moved to take the proffered seat, reaching to shake Jasper's beefy hand on his way. "Good to see you again, lad," the old man said, his shaggy brows winging upward in jovial welcome. On the walk from the stable, Emily had told him that only Esther, so far, knew of Robby's death. He managed a polite nod at Mrs. Lyons and the two other gentlemen he vaguely recalled as regulars.

"You all remember Robert Chandler," Emily said, taking the spot next to him. "He attended the college in '69."

Knowing it was more likely he would be remembered for the scandal his and Julia's secret union had caused than for being a student, Robert cringed inwardly. He was beginning to think that Emily was one of the bravest women he had ever met, with her ability to confront things head-on and get them over with.

"Not only do we remember Robert," Esther replied, a smile rounding out her apple-dumpling cheeks, "but I will always be grateful to him. He's largely responsible for bringing our dear Susannah to us, and then, of course, Daniel. And they, in turn, sent us you," she added, bestowing a look of empathy to Emily. "Yes, Robert, I have a big place in my old heart for you, for all the wonderful people who've become a part of our lives because of you. And certainly we'll never forget your lively Julia."

Robert heard Emily's intake of breath. But somehow, the way the innkeeper's wife had mentioned Julia had not caused the customary jab of pain, only a flurry of happy memories. He could envision her breezing in the front door on a lilt of laughter, her unruly curls bouncing, her eyes sparkling with mischief. He almost smiled. "She did enjoy coming here of an evening."

"Well, have some of this good cornbread, lad," Jasper urged, handing the plate to Christopher to pass. "You look like you could use a few decent meals. Isn't anybody gonna get him a bowl of stew?"

"Oh, my, yes," Esther said in a fluster, getting up and hurrying off. "I'll be back directly."

"Things around here are a sight quieter now that the school shut down," Jasper went on. "Time was, we'd see two or three tables of black-robed students every evening, laughing and carrying on. Now we only see travelers on the stages three times a week, tryin' to leave all the trouble with Britain behind."

Robert heard the last of Jasper's remark as if from a distance. His gaze wandered to the table in the far corner, where he, Julia, and some friends had always sat. Those had been the happiest days of his life. Strange, how that memory did not hurt now, the way he had expected. Maybe it was because everyone here had loved her, too, and felt sorrow themselves that she'd been taken. They had all experienced his loss. Unlike his own family, these people had known her, and loved her.

An unexpected sense of comfort and peace began to flow into him. He leaned to Emily. "Thank you for making me come inside."

Esther returned with a steaming bowl of stew, and as Robert dug in, Christopher grinned at him from across the table. "In one of Robby's letters, he wrote that you and he are assigned to Morgan Thomas, and all you do is haul food and ammunition out to the fighting units. That right?"

Chandler wished the lad hadn't changed the subject so soon after the first truly poignant memories of his and Julia's life together had surfaced. He exhaled a slow breath. "Morgan was sent on special assignment by George Washington. He's no longer at New York. And, well, when the British surprised us by landing on Nassau Island instead of Manhattan, Robby and I happened to be delivering to the only battalion of regular army stationed there. They had urgent need of us and the wagon, so we ended up being attached to the First Pennsylvania Rifle Battalion. I must report to them as soon as I can." He resumed eating.

Now impressed, the young man brightened all the more. "I've got a Pennsylvania rifle myself. Got it two years ago, for my sixteenth birthday. Outshot every single student at the school last winter, right, Pa Lyons?"

"Aye, that's a fact." Jasper bit into a chunk of cornbread and talked around it. "Lad's got a real good eye. Taught him the particulars myself, I did."

"With considerable help from me," the larger of the two townsmen harrumphed.

Not to be outdone, the balding one jutted out his chin. "He shot his first buck with me, I'll have you know."

With his easy smile, Christopher leaned forward. "Any idea when you'll be heading back to New York, Mr. Chandler?"

"First thing in the morning."

Emily met Robert's eyes with a gentle smile of approval. He suddenly realized that he was going to miss her far more than he had a right to.

"You're going away?" Katie puckered her childish features in disappointment.

"'Fraid so, little one." He could tell from her expression that she would feel forsaken, especially since she'd been without her daddy for months before he died. "But first chance I get, I'll come back and see how you're doing. Besides, I need you to teach me a few more songs." He winked at Jasper. "I'll wager your grandpa knows some pretty good ones he could teach you."

The old man chuckled. "Aye, me little Katydid. I've a couple tunes that'll perk up those tender ears of yours right quick."

"*Jasper.*" Amusement twinkled in Esther's small eyes as she shook a finger at him.

"You know, Mr. Chandler," Christopher said tentatively, "I'm thinking about going back with you."

"Chip! You'll do no such thing," Mrs. Lyons shot back, her face white.

The lad's Adam's apple quivered when he swallowed. "But, Ma Lyons, with the college closed, business isn't half what it used to be. And now with Emily around, you won't need me so much."

"That's not the point. I'll not risk losing—" She closed her mouth just in time.

Christopher's face darkened. "I'm eighteen years old. I can take care of myself. It's only right I go."

The old woman jumped up, coffeepot in hand. "Would anyone like more coffee?" she asked, as if the last few remarks had never been made.

Determination became all the more evident in the set of the boy's jaw. "I have to go, Ma. I *have to.*"

"The lad's right, Esther," Jasper said, his own resignation taking the edge off the gruffness of his voice. "We can't be keepin' him here when all the boys in the whole country-side—some even younger than him—went off to do their duty months ago."

Esther's bosom rose and fell rapidly with her breathing, and her plump face became flushed. "And how many will be comin' back, can you tell me that?" she asked, near tears. "I—" with a futile glance at her husband and then Emily, she slammed down the pot and rushed to the kitchen.

A strained silence fell for several seconds.

"That's not like her," Jasper mumbled, a frown knitting his scraggly brows. "Not like her a'tall. Excuse me." He threw a leg back over the bench and got up.

Robert knew exactly what was bothering Esther, and knew that Mr. Lyons would soon understand also. He glanced at Emily, whose eyes were wide and fixed on the innkeeper's retreating form.

"I don't care if she does get mad," Christopher announced defiantly. "I'm going. A man's gotta stand by his convictions."

A man? How young he looked, with that smattering of freckles across his nose, how innocent of the horrors that would soon face him. But Robert knew the boy would not be dissuaded. To a youth, the ideals of going forth to fight injustice ranked on the same plane as saving a fair maiden from threat of harm and then romancing her. The thrill was the same, and as old as time. Not even learning of Robby's death would stop the lad—any more than the possibility of dying prevented a young woman from wanting to bear a child.

Nevertheless, Robert felt it only right to tell him about the Scotsman, to try to change his mind. He stood to his feet. "How about coming out and showing me where to put my team for the night, Christopher?"

Emily caught his hand, obviously reading his mind again, as she had a surprising number of times during the journey.

"Thank you for doing this for me. And, Robert, I'm sure Chip will be going with you to New York. It'll be a comfort to Esther to know you'll be looking after him."

Me? He railed silently. *Responsible for Christopher? Delegated to keep him alive?*

But he could not deny the heartfelt trust, however misplaced, that shone from the depths of Emily's green eyes as she looked up at him. "Just as you looked after us."

⚜ ⚜

On the way back to the military camp, Chandler had expected a delay at the Hudson River ferry, since he, Emily, and the children had spent several long hours waiting there a few days ago. It was the only flatboat within thirty miles that had not been commandeered by the Continental army, and with British warships roving the waters near New York, the ferry had to operate many miles upstream from its normal position. But now he and Christopher faced an added delay at the East River, trapped in a long, slow line to cross King's Bridge at the top of Manhattan Island.

"It's been almost two and a half weeks since I left my battalion," Chandler commented. "I'm real glad I made it back before the British invaded New York. Now I'll be here to lend a hand when they do." *Maybe,* his mind added. *Depending on what punishment Colonel Hand will mete out.* He could almost see a line of men, their rifles trained on him, awaiting only the order to fire. No, they'd hang him—powder was too precious.

Christopher didn't respond. The lad was obviously fascinated by the carts and wagons passing by, piled high with household goods, as families left the city to escape the impending battle.

Finally the stone bridge loomed ahead.

"You know, kid," Chandler began, "it might not be to your advantage to stay too close to me right now. More than likely I'll face arrest the moment I set foot in camp. You should give some thought to signing on with the quartermaster instead. He's always in need of a young man with a sharp mind."

Christopher slanted a glance at him. "I'm not a kid. And what the deuce do you mean, you might be arrested?"

"Well, the pure fact is, I didn't bother to wait around for permission to take MacKinnon's body home. I just left."

Christopher's jaw sagged, adding length to his youthful face. "You deserted? You could be hung."

"Maybe. I don't reckon Colonel Hand's quite that ruthless, but that remains to be seen."

"Then why'd you come back here?"

What difference does it make? Robert almost blurted out. But without voicing the futile question, he suddenly knew it made a profound difference. If he died, he wouldn't be able to keep his promise to little Katie . . . or see Emily's winsome beauty ever again. He immediately chastised himself for that traitorous thought, a betrayal of his own dead comrade's memory as much as Julia's. Maybe hanging would be more fitting than dying a martyred hero in the fight for America's freedom.

He inhaled a steadying breath. "I signed on to fight the redcoats, so that's what I'll do until I'm relieved of that duty. Now, surely you can see the wisdom of putting some space between the two of us. When I drop off the wagon at the supply camp, you stay and enlist there."

"No." Christopher shook his head with slow deliberation. "I've wasted enough of my life loading and unloading supplies back at the inn. When all the talk started up about the colonies going to war, I began practicing to become an expert marksman. Not you or anybody else is gonna talk me out of going straight with you to the riflemen's battalion to enlist."

A short while later, after delivering the supply wagon and obtaining directions to Colonel Hand's command, the two of them walked into the clearing about halfway down the island, where the rifle battalion was camped in a pasture. "I sure hope you know what you're doing," Robert muttered.

"I do." Christopher straightened to his full height. "And I'm staying with you. I'll speak on your behalf."

"Don't be stupid, kid. See that big tent over there where the flag is posted? Go in there and ask to enlist. After you've finished and left, I'll report in. But first—" He latched onto Christopher's sleeve, stopping him. "Think about Mrs. Lyons. From what I hear, she's been the next thing to a real Ma to you since you were a tadpole. And one of her other 'adopted sons' has already been snatched from this earth. Are you sure you want to put her through another loss like Robby's?"

"Don't worry about me," Christopher scoffed. "I'm not gonna get myself killed." He wrenched out of Robert's grip and puffed out his chest, walking briskly to the canvas structure.

Robert, following at a slower pace, ducked his head low, leery of premature recognition. He saw Chip approach the sentry, saw the guard raise the tent flaps and admit him. He released a pent-up breath. It wouldn't be much longer.

The guard then began eyeing him. He strode over. "State your business."

"I'm waiting for the young man who just went in to join up."

"Wait somewhere else."

Just then, Colonel Hand parted the tent flaps and walked out into the daylight, tugging on a glove. Recognition registered at once in his shrewd eyes. "Corporal Chandler."

Something about the way his name rolled off the Irishman's tongue made Robert feel that his head would soon be rolling, as well.

21

"Private, disarm this man! Arrest him."

The sentry ripped Chan's rifle from him and leveled his own on him. "Where do you want him, sir?"

Colonel Hand branded Robert with an intimidating stare. "Lock him in the shed with the gunpowder. If it happens to blow, so much the better."

"Yes, sir!" The young soldier jabbed his rifle at Robert's spine. "Move out!"

"Wait!" Christopher bolted from the tent, the haversack on his back catching on the flap. "You can't arrest a man for just doing what's right."

"Stay out of this, Drummond," Robert commanded. He turned back to the colonel. "Sir, the lad doesn't know yet what's expected of a soldier. But once he knows the rules, he should do fine. He's an expert marksman."

"You brought a recruit back with you?" Hand asked incredulously.

"He insisted on coming, sir. He was adamant about it."

"I see." The colonel regarded the lad evenly. "What sort of battalion do you think I would have, son, if it was made up of men who thought nothing of deserting?"

"He didn't desert, sir. He had business that couldn't wait, and he's back now."

Colonel Hand directed a cold glance to Robert. "I hardly think his fellow soldiers would have considered his absence acceptable had the British attacked Manhattan Island while he was off *conducting business elsewhere.*" He spat out the final phrase.

"Drummond," Robert began, "with the colonel's permission, I'd like you to go back inside and finish signing up. *This does not concern you.*"

A glower twisted the fiery youth's face, and he snorted in defeat. "Very well." But he swung back to the colonel instead. "Sir, Chandler had to leave to bury Robby MacKinnon, one of your own brave soldiers, then get his widow and children resettled."

Hand's eyelids closed momentarily in weary frustration. When they reopened, his attention settled once more on the new recruit. "As justifiable as all of that may seem to you right now, lad, no army can succeed if men take it upon themselves to leave at will in order to take care of personal matters. Now, as your friend has told you, this is not your concern. Go inside. Now!"

Christopher's eyes widened. He glanced at Robert.

"Go!" Robert glared until the lad relented and reentered the tent. "Please don't hold this against him, sir. He's a fine young man."

"I'd say loyal to a fault. But since you returned on your own, I've decided not to have you hanged."

Robert felt some of his tension begin to evaporate.

"Tomorrow morning," the colonel went on, "directly after Sabbath services, you shall be brought before the assembly. The charge against you will be announced, and you will be flogged."

Flogged! Robert felt his blood turn to ice in his veins. As the son of a southern plantation owner, he had firsthand knowledge of floggings.

"Fifty lashes."

Dear Lord, no, he pleaded desperately. A sudden lightheadedness almost made his knees buckle. During his childhood he had twice witnessed their overseer administering that number to a runaway field slave. Scarcely a strip of flesh would remain on a man's back after that many lashes. If Chan survived, he'd be laid up for at least a week. And if the wounds became infected, his life would be doubly endangered.

"Until tomorrow," the colonel said quietly. Then he turned to the sentry. "Take him away!"

"Sir," Robert implored. "I know I don't deserve it, but I seek your mercy in one small thing."

With unbending sternness, the officer cocked his head sharply to the side. "What?"

"Don't make the new lad, Christopher Drummond, watch, sir. It would be too hard on the boy."

Colonel Hand's gaze wavered, giving Robert a measure of hope. Then abruptly, the man swung to the guard. "You have your order. Lock him up."

❦ ❦

The following morning, the fifteenth of September, dawned with a definite hint of autumn. The air held a crispness, and the brittle brightness of a clear autumn sky peeked through the roughly hewn boards of the shed where the powder kegs were stored. But the chill Robert felt came from the apprehension and sickening dread he felt inside. Loathing the rising of the sun, he sat with his back against a wall, already feeling the sting of the cat-o'-nine-tails laid across his naked skin. The whip was splayed into nine knotted rawhide strips that could slice the flesh with ease.

He had slept little during the night, weighing life against death, cowardice against valor. For hours he had struggled with the thought of requesting to be hanged rather than flogged. A month ago, that would have been an easy decision. Hanging would easily have won out. But every time he so much as considered it now, two pairs of shimmering green eyes—Emily's and Katie's—cut into his very soul, pleading with him not to give up his life. He had given the little girl his promise that he would return. So soon after her own daddy departed this world, could he intentionally abandon his own life—never to smile again over Rusty's little-boy imitation of his father's swagger or hear his childish delight over something as inconsequential as a twig?

But—fifty lashes! How would he bear them?

He had to do it, somehow . . . for them. For Emily, the children. He had to.

A rattle came from just outside, then a scrape of metal at the door.

So soon? The colonel had said after church services. In a sudden grip of fear, Robert rose to his feet.

The door opened to admit a soldier with a tray of food. Another directed a rifle at Chan. Neither one quite met his eyes, but their expressions, to some extent, mirrored his feelings. They departed quickly without a word, locking the shed behind them.

Robert studied the gruel, the coffee, the chunk of bread. A thin column of steam wafted upward from the mug into the chilly air. Nothing except the coffee held any appeal whatsoever. In fact, his stomach churned at the sight of the mush in the bowl. He picked up the steaming mug, cupping it in his icy hands, wondering how many more cups it would take to warm the chill of fear running through him.

He had taken only a few sips when a knock sounded on the door.

"Chandler? Chan?" Christopher Drummond called softly.

Robert had hoped that the things the lad had witnessed yesterday would have sent him packing. But no such luck.

"*Chandler!*" His voice held more urgency this time. "You in there?"

"Yeah. And I told you to stay away from me. You shouldn't start off here by keeping bad company."

"You're not bad company. I . . . prayed most of the night for you. And I think the Lord heard me."

Just what I need. Another religious zealot. But then, would Emily know any other kind of people? Robert shook his head in resignation.

"When I told some of the men about you and what you'd done, they suggested you throw yourself on Colonel Hand's mercy. They said he's not gonna want any of his men laid up for weeks with the lobsterbacks ready to attack any day. They said that he's had some time to think on it. He'll cut the sentence by half. At the very least." He paused. "Chandler?"

Beg for mercy? The slaves had begged for mercy. Even Robert's own mother had run out in tears, trying to intercede for the field hand. But that never stopped Father or the overseer. They had to make an example of their poor "runner."

Make an example. Could Colonel Hand feel any less strongly, with a far superior enemy force poised to strike?

"Did you hear me, Chan?"

"Yeah. Look, kid, I want you to stop worrying about me. This is all my doing. I just want you to stay away from the flogging, will you do that, at least? You don't need to watch. I don't want you to. Promise."

He heard the lad exhale. "Can't. We've all been ordered to attend. My sergeant says he was given specific orders to stand me right there, up front."

Robert closed his eyes in defeat. So much for mercy *of any kind.*

❦ ❦

Chandler was astounded that such a large crowd could be so quiet, so still. He could feel every last eye trained on him as the men before him moved aside, making a pathway to the center of the parade ground. Two sentries walked behind him and prodded him with their rifle barrels if he slowed even a fraction, and it was hard to march fast when his legs wouldn't hold him.

The whipping post came into view.

Colonel Hand stood next to it, grim faced and stiffly erect, with all his subordinate officers beside him like so many tin soldiers. And on his other side, Sergeant Landers . . . coiled whip in hand. His ruddy face appeared all the more red from fury—or betrayal. Obviously this was not a duty he looked forward to carrying out.

Robert's heart pounded so fiercely it seemed it would burst out of his chest. *Dear God in heaven,* he begged silently, *help me to suffer this punishment in silence. Please don't let me cry out like a coward. No matter what.*

His gaze stumbled upon Christopher Drummond in the very front of the assembly, just as the colonel had ordered. It was almost enough to rob Chan of his last shred of courage. The lad was sure to write Emily about this, tell her of this shame. And she had been through enough already. Too much. From somewhere deep inside himself, Robert dredged up a wink at the stony-faced youth, hoping to lighten the moment a little for him.

"Strip off his shirt," Sergeant Landers ordered.

The guards both snatched at the cloth, ripping it off, buttons flying.

"Tie him to the post."

The rough wood, when they shoved him against it, scratched his bare chest; the rope binding his wrists burned. *Dear Lord,* he found himself praying once more, but no words would come to him.

From off to the side, he heard Colonel Hand issue the order to read the charge and the sentence.

Another voice took up immediately, monotonous and flat.

Unable to hear the words above the rushing of his pulse in his ears, Robert suddenly became aware that after so many years of forsaking God and hating him, now God was his only hope. He had blamed the Lord all along for his terrible loss—and, in fact, still blamed him. So why should God answer any of his frantic prayers, show him any mercy whatsoever, give him the strength he so desperately needed?

In utter despair, Chan tilted his head upward and searched the heavens. *Lord God, there is no hope for me. I don't know how not to blame you.*

A heavy silence followed the end of the reading, ominous in its weight.

Someone's footsteps crunched close to the post. "You were

one of my best men," Landers groused. "I don't like it in the least, what you've caused me to have to do."

Not having even considered what this would do to the man wielding the whip, Chandler blanched. "Sorry. I'll try to make up for it, later."

The man muttered a curse as he wheeled away.

Robert closed his eyes and held his breath, steeling himself against the cruel, knotted rawhide strips at the end of the lash.

Without warning the first stroke tore into him, and he could barely draw breath. The taste of blood filled his mouth.

"One!" the sergeant yelled.

Another slash, and a poker-hot wave of pain seared through his entire body. Chandler clenched his teeth harder, digging his nails into the splintery post. Already, warm blood trickled down his back from the multiple cuts the whip had inflicted. How would he find strength to endure one more lash, let alone forty-eight?

"Two!"

Father, I beg you! He braced himself.

Suddenly, the silence around him ended. Murmurings spread in all directions, from scores of voices. Low at first, becoming louder, talking all at once.

Then above the tumult came a shout. "Attention! Men, form your platoons. Report to your company commanders for further orders."

From the corner of his eye, Robert saw men disperse. It could mean only one thing—the British were crossing over from Nassau Island!

"Cut him free," he heard Colonel Hand order.

Robert turned his head toward his commander and met his gaze.

Hand was the first to break eye contact. "Have the surgeon bind his wounds; then have him report back to your company. *For now.*" Then he walked away.

The distant sound of a cannon boom confirmed what Chandler already knew.

"This must be your lucky day, son," Sergeant Landers said, sawing the ropes that secured Chan to the whipping post.

Saved! He could scarcely believe it. Unbidden moisture stung Robert's eyes. But was it merely luck, as the sergeant said?

Or . . . against all odds . . . had God heard his prayers?

22

Robert sagged momentarily against the pole and gathered what strength he had left, fortifying himself. He straightened and turned gingerly around, forcing himself to ignore the pain that even the slightest movement caused in every muscle and nerve along his spine.

"Are-are you all right?" Christopher had moved to his side, holding out the discarded shirt. "Can you make it on your own?"

"Boy!" Sergeant Landers barked. "You were given an order. Report to your squad leader."

"Wait." Robert inhaled slowly. "Please, sir. It's only his second day in the army. Assign him to me . . . at least for today. I promised to watch out for him."

The sergeant looked askance. "Quite a rash promise, don't you think? Considering what was in store for you here."

"Yes, but you know how persuasive mothers can be."

With a disbelieving shake of his head, the man peered from Chandler to Christopher and then back. "Leave it to you to be giving me a hard time about another one of your charges! Expecting to keep the lad out of the fray just as you did that Scotsman . . . for all the good it did him."

"Robert MacKinnon," Chandler said. "His name was Robert MacKinnon. And, no, that was not my intent. This young man has no wife or children to leave behind, and he's accomplished with the Pennsylvania rifle. But this is still his first day in the army. He needs someone to show him the ropes. I want it to be me."

"Very well," the sergeant finally relented. "Who was to be your superior?" he asked the lad.

"Sergeant O'Hara, sir."

Before the man could respond, Robert cut in. "Any reason why Private Drummond couldn't be assigned to my squad permanently, Sergeant?"

"For a fellow who won't even open his mouth to plead for himself, Corporal, you sure are persistent when it comes to others!" He then turned to Drummond. "Take Chandler to the tent over there—" He indicated a large canvas structure flying a surgeon's banner. "Have his wounds dressed. And be quick about it! From the sounds of the bombardment, the battle's two or three miles away, and we've got fieldpieces to move into position."

The unkempt surgeon's ministrations, however, turned out to be anything but swift. Between applying Tincture of Myrrh and bandaging the open cuts, the slovenly man spent an inordinate amount of time drinking from a flask. At last the doctor nodded toward the exit. "You can join your battalion."

"Finally," Christopher grated as he and Robert stepped outside into the deserted camp. "I put your gear with mine." While cannon reports boomed constantly in the distance, the two of them went to Chip's campsite. "If anyone could use a good flogging, it's that so-called surgeon. I pity anybody who has to go to him for anything as serious as a bullet wound."

Robert nodded. At least the bandages would keep his heavy linen shirt from chafing—or worse, sticking to the blood as it dried in all the cuts. "Well, I don't approve of drinking to excess," he added, "but that's the way some men have of coping with their fears."

Christopher tossed his sandy head with a bitter grimace. "What's *he* got to be scared of? We're the ones who have to confront those lobsterbacks."

Robert didn't respond. The young man would find out soon enough about the gruesome effects a bullet or a load of grapeshot from a cannon blast could have on a man's body. The doctor faced his own type of battle every day.

He decided against aggravating his tender back with the weight of a food-filled haversack. Besides, being hungry would be the least of his problems. He hooked his ammunition pouch and water flask to his belt. "Come on. We need to catch up to the others." Even as he spoke, the bombardment ceased. "Especially now." He reached for his rifle.

"The cannons have stopped. Is the battle over already?" The lad sounded disappointed.

"No. The quiet means the redcoats have landed. And General Howe always comes with great force." Clenching his teeth against the stinging of his wounds, Robert struck out across the open ground, toward the woods that lay between them and the eastern shore.

But even after an hour of tramping through the forest, there were still no further sounds of battle. Chandler frowned, checking the multitude of tracks on the ground. He and Christopher had to be going in the right direction. As soon as they broke out of the woods, he would know for certain if it had been a false alarm.

Then another sound captured his attention. He put a hand on the lad's arm, stopping him.

The tramp of men's feet carried from the other side of a rise directly ahead.

Robert motioned for Christopher to follow him into a stand of high, thick ferns. There, bracing himself with his rifle, he managed to ease himself down into them. He couldn't stifle the groan, but inhaled deeply as the wave of pain subsided. He saw the fear in the kid's wide blue eyes and gestured for him to crouch down as well. "Probably some of our boys," he whispered. "We'd best check our loads, though, just in case." Holding his breath, Chandler maneuvered himself onto his belly, then propped his weapon on a chunk of log. His pulse throbbed with apprehension.

The sound of the steps grew louder.

Between the leaves, they could see the tops of heads emerging over the crest. All of them in tricorns.

"Patriots!" Robert released a pent-up breath. "Wave your rifle above your head so you don't surprise them, then get up," he instructed. Wincing and grunting, he cautiously did the same.

By the time he regained his feet, what appeared to be a full company of riflemen reached them.

"Well, well. Our very own deserter," one of them chided.

Christopher stiffened. "Chan did not desert. He just took his friend's body back to his wife and got her resettled . . . and I'll fight anybody who says any different."

"Whoa, boy," the soldier said with a chuckle. "I was only joshin' ya. If you wanted to see some real turncoats, you should've been with us! By the time we reached the crest of the hill overlookin' Kip's Bay, the Connecticut militia that was supposed to be guarding it looked more like a swarm of ants. They was spillin' out of their trenches, runnin' for all they was worth!"

"Which isn't much, that's for sure," another scoffed.

"They deserted their posts in the earthenworks?" Chandler asked, incredulous.

"Aye. Before the lobsters even landed, yet! General Washington come chargin' down there on his horse, fit to be tied. Tried to turn 'em back, but they kept on going. Never saw a man so mad."

"'Twas shameful to see," the other elaborated. "Them redjackets will be hootin' and hollerin' about that flock of scared chickens for weeks."

Robert eyed them both. "Well, why didn't you go down and take their places?"

"'Cause we couldn't make it down there in time. Them English devils was already beaching their landin' craft. They'd have beat us to the trenches. Besides, they outnumbered us three to one."

His pal nodded. "We been ordered to go to the west side of the island to cover the retreat from the port up to Harlem

Heights. Kip's Bay ain't the only place catchin' it. Men-of-war have been firin' on New York all morning long."

"One good thing come from this, though," the first said. "Colonel Hand got a good look at what a real deserter looks like. I don't think he'll give that little leave-takin' of yours much mind now, not after what we all seen today."

"So you're just gonna let them land, then?" Christopher asked, his voice cracking. "We're not gonna do anything to stop them?"

One of the returning soldiers gave his shoulder a squeeze. "Don't you worry none about that, lad. You'll get your chance at 'em. Probably before this day's out."

An aborted flogging, and Christopher had been spared the horrors of battle—at least for now. Two blessings in one morning! Sweet Emily must have been down on her knees in prayer.

❧ ❧

Clay Raleigh stepped out of the carriage, then offered a hand to Prudence. She accepted it with a polite nod. "Thank you, Mr. Raleigh. It was ever so kind of you to escort Evelyn and me to her sister's for tea. Such a delightful afternoon. Melinda does make even a New Englander feel welcome—despite my colony's reputation, of late."

"*Of late?*" he countered good-naturedly. "When during the past century hasn't that Bay Colony been up to something decidedly rebellious, I ask?"

"When, indeed," Evie quipped with the air of an empty-headed twit. She allowed him to lift her down in a swirl of ruffles and lace. He was slow in letting her go.

"Evie, dear," Prudence said, coming to her aid. "We'll be late to supper if we don't hurry inside and change. You know how your mother detests tardiness."

"Doesn't she, though?" Artfully, Evelyn extracted herself from Raleigh's arms and started up the walk. "It's best not to get on her bad side if one expects to have one's desires granted later." Reaching the stoop, she turned. "And, dearest

Clayborne, I'm sure you don't need to be told how disadvantageous it would be to upset the apple cart over the trivial things." She made it sound as if the "apple cart" might yet get dumped, but over something much more scintillating. "We'll see you, of course, tomorrow eve at the theater."

He could do little more than give a reluctant nod of agreement before his little sparrow flew inside.

Prudence was careful to hide her amusement. "Yes, good day, Mr. Raleigh. And thank you again." She raised her hand in a wave as he got back into the carriage and drove off.

Pausing just outside the door, she contemplated Evie's remark about her domineering mother. The truth of the comment cut across the grain. Only out of patriotic necessity had she allowed Morgan's mother to *manage* her from the moment she'd walked into the Thomas household.

It was becoming more difficult by the day to display only good humor when the woman prattled on endlessly about "those dreadful rebels" while trying to remold Prudence into her own image. There was never any middle ground with the woman. . . . It was either prepare for battle, or submit. Steeling herself against the next encounter, Prudence stepped inside.

"But you can't!" she heard Evelyn wail. "Not without me."

Glancing toward the staircase, Prudence saw her sister-in-law halfway up. She expected to see Mother Thomas, but instead Evie faced Morgan a few steps above her.

"Tell him, Prudence," Evie said. "Tell him he can't go without us."

"Go?" she echoed. "Go where, pray tell?" She directed her gaze to her husband, noticing now that he carried a valise in each hand . . . and wore a markedly guilty expression besides.

"New York!" Evie cried.

The door to Mr. Thomas's study opened, and he emerged. "Evelyn, I'll not have you making a spectacle of yourself. Go to your room this instant."

"But, Papa—"

"This instant! And Morgan, you and Prudence come into

the study. Business—particularly of a marital nature—should never be conducted in open hallways."

How like a merchant, she thought bitterly, to think of marriage as just one more business deal. Well, she was one item of business that would not be handled so easily. *Not this time.* She crossed her arms and strode into the room. When Morgan came in a few steps after her, she fought a strong urge to pummel him with her fists.

"It's not how it looks, sweetheart," Morgan offered, his expression appearing as lame as the excuse. "While you were at tea, word came that the British have taken control of New York City."

She blanched at the dire news. "And you were going to run off without me?"

"They occupy New York, but not yet the north end of the island. Washington will quite likely regroup and field a counterattack."

"I think not, Son," his father said. "From what I heard at the merchants' club, rebels have been deserting in droves since the Crown took Nassau Island. And when the army landed on Manhattan, they abandoned the beach, running for their lives. I'd say the rebellion is all but over. I'm sorry, Prudence."

Sorry? All her hopes for her country, for freedom, their noble dreams, were being dashed—and all he could say was, I'm sorry?

Morgan's arm slid around her waist, and he pulled her close. "Don't be so quick to give up. This is just one battle, and you know how each side always exaggerates. All I'm certain of is that I must go there at once. If ever General Washington needed accurate information, it's now."

"I agree," she finally answered. "I'll pack only the barest of necessities and arrange for the rest to be shipped."

He shook his head. "No, you won't. You heard Father. Both armies are still on that one little island. It's far too dangerous."

Wrenching free, Prudence opened her mouth to protest, but Morgan placed a finger to her lips.

"Please, love. Leaving you is difficult enough already. Don't make it any worse. I can't deliberately take you into a battle-field. . . . You know that."

"But—"

"No. We've discussed this matter many times." His intractable expression gradually softened. "Please, don't make me leave like this. Send me off with your blessing, wish me Godspeed, . . . and give me a kiss I'll not soon forget. Will you do that for me?"

Prudence had no other alternative but to do as he asked. At least for now.

23

"No! I will not hush!" Evelyn stood at the foot of Prudence's bed, only her white night shift and flashing eyes visible in the faint light from the windows. "I held my tongue all evening, but no more. No more." She shook her head violently in declaration.

Prudence, propped on her pillows in the lonely bed, stared up at the ceiling and folded her arms. She was really not up to this confrontation. The entire evening had been simply dreadful as it was. Missing Morgan was bad enough without having to endure Mother Thomas's endless gossip about one nonsensical tidbit after another all through supper. And Evelyn, clearly in the foulest of tempers the whole time, had sat sullen and pouting until Prudence finally finished the meal and sought refuge in her bedchamber. But even that melancholy quiet was short-lived when her sister-in-law burst into her room, ranting like a madwoman.

Prudence swung her feet off the high bed and went to Evelyn. "You really don't want to wake your mother, now, do you?"

Evie glared and averted her face. "I don't care if I wake the whole blessed household. Morgan knew how urgently I wanted to go to New York. *And I will go. Do you hear me?*" Her tirade all but shook the windowpanes.

Prudence sighed. "Well, we can't even discuss the matter

unless you calm yourself. In the morning we'll take a drive out in the country, where no one will overhear us."

"Fine." Arms crossed over her chest, the younger girl tapped a foot in defiant impatience. "But I have no intention of *discussing* anything." She whirled and tramped to the door, flinging it wide. Halfway across the threshold, however, she swung back, lowering her voice a notch. "Jamie hasn't written me even once. He has to be either hurt or dead. I'm going to find Jamie . . . with or without you."

From the middle of the hallway, the rustle of satin night-clothes could easily be heard as Mother Thomas appeared just behind Evie, her salt-and-pepper hair in a long braid over her shoulder. "What on earth is going on here? And exactly *who*, Evelyn, is this Jamie?"

Her daughter's mouth gaped. She glanced at Prudence with an expression of helplessness.

Someone needed to say something. Prudence crossed the room to stand at Evie's side. "Jamie is her . . . new kitten," she blurted out, immediately regretting the silly lie.

Mother elevated one eyebrow and peered over her patrician nose. "Evelyn has never been able to abide cats. They set her eyes and nose to running."

"Oh, yes, I know," Prudence said, trying for the most off-handed tone she could. "It's just dreadful, is it not? That's why we've been keeping the dear little thing out in the carriage house." She pinned Evie with a conspiratorial glare.

"Yes. And now he's gone, Mother," Evie finally contributed. "Our little stray has disappeared. I'm afraid if we don't find him soon he'll die. But Prudence simply refuses to go out with me and look for him."

The older woman eyed them each in turn, then settled her attention on Prudence. "Well, I'm quite pleased to hear that, at least. Perhaps there's a sensible side to you after all." With a curt nod, she turned and swept back to her room.

Mother Thomas at her best, Prudence concluded. No compliment was complete without an insult tacked on for good measure. "I bid you both good night, then," she called politely after Mother Thomas, while giving Evelyn a firm nudge out the door. "Tomorrow morning, Evie. We'll go looking in the morning."

❧ ❧

Prudence settled back against the plush leather seat, relieved that Evie had taken it upon herself to drive the summer carriage rather than have a groom to worry about. The day was mild, with a gentle breeze stirring the leaves. Letting her gaze rest on the heavily wooded hillsides beyond the city, Prudence knew that soon autumn's palette would stain the countryside, turning all the trees to breathtaking shades of yellow, red, and burgundy. It was always a sight to behold, one that made it possible to forget the strife in the colonies . . . at least for a little while.

Absorbed in her thoughts, Prudence suddenly noticed that Evelyn had turned toward the river instead of heading away from town. "I thought what we had to talk about would best be discussed out in the open countryside."

Evie gave a nonchalant shrug. "There are a few things I must find out first." No amiable smile accompanied the statement, only tight-lipped determination as the horse's hooves clopped over the cobbles.

Her answer made Prudence uneasy. "What kind of things? Where are we going?"

"To see Jamie's older brother. Micah Dodd runs a ship's bakery down near the docks. Morgan told me Jamie left to enlist with a Colonel Hand. Surely by now his brother has had word of some sort. Mr. Dodd must at least know where he is, if he's been wounded or . . ."

"Very well, then. We'll go talk to him, if that will make you feel any better. Nevertheless, if we do end up going to New York, it will be to join Morgan. *Not* to scour the picket lines in search of your young man. You might as well accept that."

Evelyn, obviously in no better humor than she had been the previous evening, cast Prudence an indignant glare. "A fine one you are to talk. Seems I recall a merry tale of you riding all the way from Boston to New York *alone* to be with *your* young man."

"Yes, I must admit it's true. But that was different, I assure you. Your brother was stationed behind the army lines at a supply camp."

With a purposeful sniff, Evie pressed onward. "Who is to say Jamie isn't safely at the rear of things himself?"

Prudence inhaled a steadying breath. It was useless to reason with the willful girl until they'd had a chance to speak to Micah Dodd. Why had she never realized what a handful Morgan's younger sister could be?

Seeking a more pleasant diversion, Prudence switched her attention to the lovely brick homes lining the street. Tall, stately trees with thick crowns of green and yellow contrasted strikingly against the red brick. Once the leaves turned color and fell in droves to the ground, this verdant early autumn hue would be just a memory.

The nearer the carriage got to the warehouses and docks, the more of a curiosity she and Evie became, or so it seemed to Prudence. Workers, tradesmen, and shipbuilders alike paused in their work and gawked at them. One even whistled. Another had the audacity to give a bawdy wink.

Evelyn neither slowed nor indicated her awareness as she guided the horse to the bakery and reined to a stop.

Prudence was struck by the absence of the normal tantalizing smell of baking bread. In fact, the place seemed deserted. Had she and her sister-in-law chanced being accosted by uncouth men for naught?

Evie, nonplussed, stepped down and walked to the front door. It opened to her touch, and she went right in without a moment's pause. "Mr. Dodd," she called. "Are you here?"

By the time Prudence reached the entrance, a stocky man of medium height was coming toward them, weaving between rows of long tables. "Aye? May I help you, miss?"

"Mr. Dodd?" she asked, and at his nod, continued. "My name is Evelyn Thomas. I'm sure you're acquainted with my older brother, Morgan." She extended a gloved hand to him.

"Aye." He wiped his on his apron, then took hers. "I see the resemblance," he said astutely, then looked at Prudence. "And you must be his new bride. I sure hope the message you two young ladies have brought me is worth the risk you took gettin' here." Thick triangular eyebrows dipped into a frown in his round face, darkening his amiable blue eyes.

"Message?" Evie shook her head. "We have no message. I've come to question you."

"Did you now?" Concerned creases furrowed his brow.

"Perhaps while we're here, you might appreciate knowing that Morgan left for New York yesterday," Prudence remarked.

"I would indeed. Thank you, mistress. Thank you very much." He turned back to Evie. "What is it you need to know, missy? And be quick about it. There's no sensible reason I can think of that you two would visit a ship's bakery—one that's not even firing its ovens at the moment. Not a ship has been given permission to sail for days."

His brusqueness had no effect on Evelyn. She took a step closer. "It's about Jamie. Have you heard from him since he left? Is he well?"

The man nodded with a knowing grin. "Ah. I should've guessed. But I'm sorry. Me brother's not much of a hand at writin' home. His colonel, though, would have notified me if he'd been—if there'd been a problem of one sort or another."

"Perhaps we could write to him," Prudence suggested hopefully. "Express our concern at the lack of news."

"Sure thing," Micah Dodd replied, still grinning. "There are pouches leaving here for Washington's army near every day, what with the Congress wantin' to keep in close touch. I'll see the letter gets there, *if* you promise not to bring it here yourselves."

"That's very kind of you," Evelyn said. Then her tone switched to a syrupy coo. "But to which militia should I address it?"

"Not any militia at all. To the First Pennsylvania Rifle Battalion. Can you remember that?"

"I'll try ever so hard to. Good day, Mr. Dodd." With a grateful smile, Evelyn swept gracefully toward the door.

Prudence, observing the younger girl's departure, exchanged a dubious glance with Jamie's brother. It was apparent that Evie was up to something, and Prudence wouldn't rest until she found out precisely what it was.

Leaving the wharves behind, she took charge of the reins this time, planning to do the same with her sister-in-law as well. With a harsh glare at Evie, she clucked the horse into a faster trot.

Evelyn, however, didn't seem disconcerted.

The moment they were on a relatively empty stretch of the street, Prudence let loose. "I know that mind of yours is working like a waterwheel in a spring thaw, Evie, but you might as well tie it down. We are not doing anything or going anywhere until we hear from Morgan. Do you understand?"

The girl huffed and looked away.

"I said, do you understand?"

The lift of one shoulder was the nearest thing to an answer she offered.

"And agree."

Evie narrowed her eyes. "That could take weeks!"

"No, it won't. Morgan gave me his word he'd write as soon as he is settled."

"And what does that mean, exactly—*settled?*"

"We'll receive a letter from him within a week, I'm sure. A fortnight at most. Please, agree to bide your time until then."

Evelyn stared hard for several seconds. Finally her shoulders sagged. "Oh, very well. But not a day longer. You can't count on a man to write. The last time my brother left home, there wasn't a single word from him for more than a year."

❧ ❧

Heavy smoke billowed over the bay from New York. Morgan's horse, Prince, began to whinny and prance nervously.

Standing beside the Thoroughbred, Morgan tightened his grip on the bridle. The flat deck of a ferry was no place to try to calm a frightened stallion. He could kick himself for attempting the trip from Staten Island in the first place. From what the British dragoons at the landing had said, General Howe had given the order that his men *not* fight the fire.

"*Serves them Yankee-Doodles right,*" the dragoon sergeant had sneered. "*Let their saboteurs burn the whole blasted town, for all we care.*" It had taken all of Morgan's restraint not to ram a fist down the bloke's throat.

Stroking the horse's muzzle, he talked softly to the animal. But every few minutes, the wide nostrils would flare, and the stallion would try to jerk free.

As the ferry neared the New York side, the wind shifted, carrying the smoke away from the flames so that they were clearly visible. The Thoroughbred became all the more agitated. Morgan hoped he'd reach land with his arm still attached to his shoulder.

A large crowd of civilians, luggage in hand, waited ashore to be evacuated. Morgan considered remaining aboard the craft and returning, particularly with ash drifting down like snow over the area.

The ferry bumped the dock, and the front man jumped down. "How close is the fire?" he asked the waiting passengers. "Think it'll reach the wharf?"

"Hmph!" railed a hefty woman. She planted a fist on one wide hip. "Now that my house—along with the rest of the whole block—has burned down, our champion, the good General Howe, has deigned to order his men to put out the fire!"

"Aye," another man yelled as he tied off the stern. "It suddenly came to the fool that *he* might not have a place to sleep tonight!"

Well, Morgan decided, that sounded somewhat promising—despite the fact that it looked as if the entire town was ablaze. He could at least go ashore to investigate. He pulled a shirt from his valise, wrapped it over Prince's eyes, and walked him onto the landing.

"A pity about your home, madam," he said, passing the

large-boned woman as she boarded. "I only hope the place where I planned to stay is still standing."

A deafening explosion ripped the air just then, and a blinding light illuminated the sky.

The Thoroughbred wrenched free and bolted, still blinded by Morgan's shirt as it clattered crazily away.

"Must've been a powder magazine," Morgan heard someone holler.

The stallion crashed through the waiting crowd and headlong into a stack of barrels, where it stumbled to its knees with large kegs bouncing and rolling around him.

Morgan finally caught up. He snagged Prince's bridle before the animal regained its feet and sent up a swift prayer of thanks that no one had been trampled. Then, coughing as a drift of smoke wafted by, he did his best to calm the Thoroughbred with soothing words.

"You'd best keep that nag under control," a soldier warned, lifting his musket, "or I'll put a bullet between his eyes." From the man's expression, the deed would clearly have given him pleasure.

Morgan placed himself between the soldier and the horse as he guided the stallion away from the landing, through the dense smoke and fallen ash. Why had he ever volunteered to come here? He was beginning to think the ferry had caught the wrong current and docked in Hades.

And unless things improved drastically, one thing was certain. He would definitely not allow Prudence to come to this place.

Exhaling in resignation, he strode into the hysteria and chaos of a town on fire.

24

"Eighteen . . . nineteen . . ." Robert counted off as Christopher jabbed a ramrod up the long barrel of his rifle. "Twenty . . . twenty-one . . ."

"Done!" The young man said in triumph. "Beat my last time by two seconds!" With his short load, he shot a small branch off a tree a few yards away.

Chandler gave him a noncommittal smile. "Let's see if you can do as well lying on the ground."

"On the ground?"

"Down."

The lad obeyed, and with concentrated fervor, set to the awkward task of reloading.

Chan was more than pleased with Christopher's marksmanship. But that skill needed to be paired with quick, adept loading if there was any hope at all of keeping the kid alive. He might have been unsuccessful with Robby MacKinnon, but he wasn't going to lose this one.

As the lad poured a trickle of powder in the flash pan, Chan moved up behind him and bent down. *"Boom!"*

Christopher started, spilling powder. "Now look what you made me do," he cried indignantly.

"Get used to it." Chan straightened, wincing as his movements pulled at the wounds on his back. "The battlefield is full of surprises. Keep loading. You're wasting time. The enemy could be on you by now."

Hearing approaching footsteps, Robert looked up to see Sergeant Landers coming with a couple of other new privates. "Thought you might as well drill a few more while you're at it," his superior said with an amused quirk of his mouth. "How's the back?"

"Coming along, sir."

"The bandages been changed yet today?"

Preferring not to be reminded of the flogging—or that the sergeant had administered the lashes—Robert shrugged.

"It's been three days, sir," Christopher answered.

The older man grimaced. "Can't afford to have one of our best men laid up, now, can we? The surgeons have set up shop about half a mile down the road. Look for a white farmhouse trimmed with blue. And," he added with an unmistakable grin, "march these boys smartly up there with you. They need the practice." His levity faded. "Wouldn't hurt them to see where they'll end up if they're not quick enough to follow orders."

As Landers left, one of the new recruits turned. "The sarge is just tryin' to scare us into obeying everything he says."

"Because he prefers his men alive," Robert added pointedly. "You heard him. Line up."

Hastily the men fell into step. They kept the cadence as they marched past fields with the remains of buckwheat and corn. Low wooded hills spotted with jumbles of rocks and outcroppings lay on the outer edges.

The farmhouse the sergeant had indicated was situated in a ragged field of moldering wheat that should have been harvested a month ago. Robert couldn't help thinking of his North Carolina home and wondering how the plantation was faring in the war. It had been weeks since he had written to his mother. . . . This evening he would set that to rights.

As they approached the building, Robert saw soldiers with a variety of injuries occupying the narrow porch, seated on chairs and steps, lounging listlessly on the railings.

"You three stay outside," Robert told his men, "and keep these fellows company while I see the doctor." He knew they were apprehensive, but it would do them no harm to observe firsthand some of the consequences of battle. He went on inside the somewhat cramped dwelling.

"What can I do for you?" a soldier asked, peering up from a desk near the door.

"I'm supposed to have some bandages changed," Chan responded.

The soldier flicked a cursory glance over him, then gestured down the hall. "First room on the right."

In what was probably the dining room before the war, three long tables occupied most of the center area. Chandler noted with relief that they appeared clean—and empty, at the moment, which was also comforting. He spotted two men drinking coffee at a small square table in one corner, and he went to them. "Corporal Chandler, First Pennsylvania Rifle Battalion, reporting, sir."

The two eyed him. "What's the problem?" one of them asked, stroking a thick growth of whiskers.

"I need some new dressings on my back."

"Guess you can look after this one," the other surgeon told his companion, "while I go check on our new patients." He nodded in dismissal, and light from the window gleamed over his bald pate as he strode away.

The whiskered man indicated one of the long tables with a wave of his hand. "Take off your shirt, lad."

Robert complied, then eased himself onto the table, turning so that the man could observe his wounds.

"You must be that deserter who didn't know when he was well enough off," the physician said wryly, slowly peeling away the old strips of cloth.

"I didn't desert," Robert grated through his teeth. "I had urgent business that couldn't wait."

"I see. Well, they must've believed you. Never saw a man with so few lash marks after a flogging. And I see you weren't busted to a private, either."

"No, that's a fact. They've been making a sport of threatening to make me a sergeant."

The surgeon laughed. "Hard to say which is worse, considering the precarious state of our army." He applied some ointment and fresh bandages. "I think I heard you mention Colonel Hand's battalion, that right?"

"Yes, sir."

"Well, there's a patient here that you can take back with you. I was fairly sure he was malingering, since his wound isn't severe. Then this morning, when the father of a young gal from the next farm came in threatening to put a bullet in him, I decided the lad's plenty fit to return to his company. There," he said, finishing. "You can put your shirt back on. The cuts are healing quite well. In fact, three more days and you can take the bandages off for good."

"Thanks." Robert slipped into the shirt and tucked it into his trousers.

Christopher and the other two recruits glanced at Robert as he and the doctor stepped onto the porch.

"I'll go round up our faker," the surgeon remarked. "We've taken to calling him the Manhattan Lover."

Robert stopped by his men. "We'll be taking another fellow back to camp with us," he explained as the surgeon strode to a lad lounging beneath a maple tree.

Christopher sidled up to Robert. "What did the doc mean by that?" he whispered.

"No doubt we'll find out soon enough."

"Well, here he is," the older man said, returning with the skinny, copper-haired soldier. "I'll trust you to see that Private Dodd is returned to his superiors."

"Will do. Fall in, Private."

As the surgeon strode back inside, Robert and his small group began the trek back to camp.

"My friends call me Jamie," the lad said with an infectious grin as he marched along with the others.

"What's this we overheard the sawbones sayin', about you bein' called the 'Manhattan Lover'?"

Jamie colored slightly. "Not what it sounds like. I was just keeping company with a kind lass who brings cookies to the wounded soldiers here."

"And," Christopher injected, "who just happens to be as pretty as she is kind, I'll wager."

"Or as pretty as he is brave," another chortled, and the rest hooted with laughter.

Anger set Jamie's jaw in a hard line. "Not that she's any concern of yours." His voice cracked.

"Aw, I was just kinda hankerin' after some cookies," the lad next to him said. "Thought maybe I'd take me a stroll over there of an evening."

"Won't do you any good," Jamie returned. "She's spoken for."

Robert cast him a dubious look. More than likely the young man was merely staking out his territory. "Let's pick up the pace," he ordered, hoping the increased tempo might put an end to the conversation.

When they came within sight of the camp, Robert raised a hand and slowed the lads down to a normal march. "Who's your sergeant, Dodd? I'm supposed to deliver you personally."

"Sergeant Little."

Robert nodded. Sergeant Landers's tent was directly ahead, and the noncommissioned officer sat just outside on a stump, cleaning his rifle as he talked to another officer. "Excuse me, Sergeant," Chan cut in at a break in the conversation. "I'm returning a Private Dodd to Sergeant Little. Can you point out his tent?"

Landers and the other sergeant exchanged glances. "Little and his men were manning the picket line last night. He got shot in the head."

"Sorry to hear that. Who replaced him, sir?"

"That's just what Sergeant Fields and me were talking about. The lieutenant asked us to recommend somebody."

Robert sensed what was coming. He regretted having hurried back from the surgeon.

"All of Fields's men," Landers went on, "are too green. Till we come up with somebody else, Chandler, move your gear over to their camp and keep an eye on them."

"What about me, sir?" Christopher asked. "May I go with Corporal Chandler, too?"

"Yeah, sure, kid. If that's what it takes."

What it takes, Robert thought dolefully. "Sir, I'd rather not—"

"You have no say in the matter, Corporal. Little's platoon is camped on the other side of those boulders." He pointed toward a jumble of rocks on a rise several yards away.

Clenching his teeth, Robert left the other recruits he'd brought back and went to his own tent, where he and Christopher retrieved their belongings. Then they started for the other camp with Jamie Dodd tagging along.

"Meaning no disrespect," Christopher said, turning to Jamie, "but is she pretty? Your girl, I mean."

The fact that this very topic seemed uppermost in most of the lads' minds was singularly irritating to Robert.

"Aye, she sure is. Hair like corn silk, eyes same color as the moss growing down at the creek. . . ."

Like Emily's. A lonely ache gripped Chan's heart. What pure pleasure it would be to find her beyond the boulders ahead, instead of dirty smelly soldiers. For the flicker of a moment, he allowed himself to picture her sitting near a campfire, the flames making a halo of her golden hair as she favored him with a beckoning smile.

A distant gunshot was no less a jolt than the forbidden thoughts. He must have taken leave of his senses. Frowning, he cut a sidelong glance at Christopher and Jamie. "Step lively, you two. We're not out on a Sunday stroll."

25

The tick of the mantle clock echoed in the quiet sitting room, the only sound besides the stab of the embroidery needle in the taut fabric as Prudence labored over her design. Why did this tiresome chore seem to be the only gentle endeavor acceptable for society's elite to pass an afternoon performing?

Across the room on the settee, Mother Thomas held her own project at arm's length while she assessed her handiwork, then resumed stitching. Prudence sighed and glanced at Evelyn, a few yards away in another silk damask chair. The younger girl's oval hoop lay idle on her lap, and she appeared lost in thought.

The front door opened and closed.

"Father!" Evie sprang to her feet, her embroidery falling unnoticed as she rushed to the foyer.

"I often wonder," Mother Thomas commented, eyebrows elevated, "if that child ever recalls a single lesson on the rudiments of proper etiquette."

Not certain exactly how to respond, Prudence smiled.

The older woman returned the smile. "It does please me, however, that my daughter has been inordinately eager to receive word from our Mr. Raleigh since the very day he left for New York. I suppose I should be thankful for that."

"Well, give it to me!" Evie cried, her whine carrying easily from the hall.

Prudence doubted that a letter from Clay Raleigh would even begin to appease her sister-in-law's unrest. The girl wanted to hear from Jamie Dodd . . . almost as desperately as Prudence sought word from Morgan.

"Don't be so hasty," Father reprimanded, coming toward the sitting room. "This happens to be addressed to Prudence."

Praise be! Prudence's heart swelled. Laying aside her stitchery, she rose to meet Morgan's father as he approached with the letter outstretched. From his taciturn expression, she wondered if the missive was from her stepmother in Boston, rather than from Morgan. She quickly checked the handwriting.

"Well?" Mother said in her imperious voice. "Is it from Morgan?"

"Yes."

"Then *read* it!" Evie demanded.

Father Thomas gave her a sharp glare. "It's addressed to Prudence. It is for her to decide if she wishes to share it."

Prudence, hoping Morgan had foresight enough to know that any word he sent her might not be exactly private, barely had time to exchange a thankful glance with her father-in-law before his wife cut in.

"Nonsense. If it's from our son, of course he would want all of us to hear what he has to say."

"So hurry," Evelyn pleaded, coming to Prudence's side.

Prudence pried open the wax seal, then unfolded the two pages, wishing she had time to peruse them alone first.

"Do sit down, dear, while you read," Mother said impatiently.

There was nothing left for Prudence to do but breathe a silent prayer as she returned to her chair and began reading aloud:

"My dearest wife,
I am thankful to report that my journey to New York was without mishap. However, as I am sure you must have heard by now, the city was ablaze when I arrived. The entire town has

been in chaos ever since. Hundreds of families have lost their homes and are now camped on the Common. Fortunately for me, the home of Father's friend, Horace Dillard, was untouched; thus, I have a roof over my head. But alas, I must share it with three junior officers of the king's army.

Please inform Father that Dillard will be of no assistance whatsoever in dealing with the British. He and his family departed for England two days after the fire, leaving me to look after their home."

"Oh," Mother declared, "our poor Hortense. How utterly dreadful this must have been. First having her city overrun by rebellious rabble rousers, then the horror of a great fire. And to make matters absolutely intolerable, she had to suffer having her home occupied by total strangers. A season in London was certainly called for."

"Please, Mother, let her finish," Evelyn begged. "Go on, Pru."

The slight interruption, however, provided Prudence a chance to scan the next paragraph, which concerned the conflict. If Morgan inadvertently revealed his true position regarding the matter, Prudence knew she would have to think fast when she came upon anything compromising. She began reading once more:

"As to the war news, there is not much to tell. Once General Howe secured the city, he made no further effort to take the remainder of Manhattan. He merely set up a picket line about midway up the island, and the rebels have done the same."

Prudence felt herself relax at Morgan's reference to the *rebels*. If the letter had been strictly for her benefit alone, he would never have called the Continental forces by that name. She inhaled with confidence and continued:

"General Howe's primary concern seems to be to establish a comfortable command center for the winter. Most military effort

has been expended on moving supplies from Staten Island and off their huge fleet of ships.

I am sad to report, dear, that Micah's friend was killed while fighting the fire. You might send him our condolences."

Morgan's contact . . . killed? Quickly, Prudence read on, hoping that no one noticed her surprise:

"My darling wife, I know you are waiting impatiently for permission to join me in New York. But until order has been completely restored in the aftermath of this horrendous fire, and until the rebels have been driven from the island, coming here would be most unwise. As much as I desire your presence, I cannot allow it just now."

Evelyn gave a huff of rage. "He cannot allow it? *He cannot allow it?* Who does he think he is? King George?"

Her mother turned a reproachful glare on the girl. *"Evelyn.* That will do. Your brother is only looking out for everyone's best interests."

Evie clenched her fists and appeared ready to explode. She flung a withering glare at all of them and bolted out of the room and up the stairs.

"Our daughter has become completely unmanageable, Waldon," Mother remarked with a wag of her head. "You must do something about it." She paused, then continued. "I don't know what the child expected. She merely toyed with Mr. Raleigh for months on end, never giving him an affirmative response to his proposals. But now that he's gone to New York, she can't wait to follow him. I'll never understand her. Never."

Father shifted uncomfortably. "Is there more to the letter, Prudence?"

"Not much. He misses all of us and asked me to relate his love to the family. Other than that . . ." She felt herself coloring. "There are some private words to me." Which she would read again and again once she was alone. *Oh, pray, let it be soon.*

Mother gave an emphatic nod. "Then, Husband, I expect you to go see to that daughter of yours."

"Oh, let me," Prudence blurted. No telling what Evie might divulge in her present state of mind. "She was so counting on some word from Clay Raleigh, you know. She's terribly disappointed—especially since she's talked of nothing but going there to be a part of the victory celebration."

"Silly girl," her mother scoffed. "Surely even she must know there must first *be* a victory."

Gathering her letter and her stitchery together, Prudence avoided meeting her father-in-law's eyes as she left the room. The man had not the slightest idea of his daughter's secret life, and having to lie outright to him was quite disconcerting. But if her father knew his youngest child had involved herself in a deadly game, he could quite easily side with the Loyalists . . . particularly since his son had also been less than honest in keeping Evie's duplicity from him.

Upstairs, Prudence rapped softly on her sister-in-law's closed door. When she received no reply, she walked in, startling the girl. But Evie was no less shocked than Prudence herself was when she saw the girl throwing things into a large valise on the bed. "What are you doing?" she asked.

With a toss of her dark curls, Evie resumed her task. "Exactly what it looks like."

"I think not," Prudence challenged. "Even if I must resort to tying you to the bedpost, you'll not escape into the dark of night, young lady."

She turned with a huff. "I doubt someone as small as you can stop me."

"You're right," Prudence answered, undaunted. "Your father, however, would find it measurably easier."

"Is that right?" Evie hurled back, eyes flashing. "And I suppose you intend to tell him about me. Well, do what you must. But let's not overlook Mother. I'm sure she would be interested in hearing a few things, too. Shall I call her now?"

Prudence needed no one to tell her that in Evie's present state of hysteria, she would not hesitate to do that very thing.

She inhaled a strengthening breath and forced herself to speak calmly. "Evie, dear. Please, sit down. You know I'm on your side." When the girl refused to move, Prudence took her hand and tugged her down on the bed beside her. "I want to go to New York every bit as badly as you do. Truly I do."

Evelyn pursed her lips, her gaze downcast, but gradually she began to crumble. "It-it's been two months since Jamie left. Two long months! He *promised* me he'd write. I just know he has to be dead, or lying somewhere mortally wounded. It's all I can think about. I have to go. I just have to. Now!"

"But Morgan said—"

"A pox on Morgan!" Jumping to her feet, Evelyn seized her valise and dashed for the door.

Prudence picked up her skirts and gave chase, lunging for her just before Evie gained the back stairs. They landed unceremoniously in a sprawl, and Prudence was more than aware of the racket they were making. She heard herself capitulate. "Very well. We'll go. But there are a few things we must do first."

Evie stopped struggling. She turned, brushing a wayward curl from her eyes. "You'd better not be trying to trick me."

"I—"

"What in the world is going on up there?" Mother Thomas railed, her footsteps echoing from the front stairwell. "It sounds like a herd of wild horses!"

Prudence and Evie scrambled to their feet, smoothing their skirts. Evie deftly positioned hers over the bag at her feet. "Nothing, Mother," she called. "We were just chasing a . . . a mouse."

"A mouse!" her mother gasped. The footsteps stopped.

"Yes." A mischievous smile spread across her lips. "But everything's all right now. We stomped it to death."

A sound of smothered horror came from the older woman.

"Never fear, I'll dispose of it out back."

"Yes . . . well . . . I'd better get back to your father." Her hasty retreat faded from the stairwell.

"She abhors mice," Evie giggled.

Prudence, torn between guilt and relief, was very glad that, if nothing else, at least Evelyn's mood was lighter. "Let's go back to your room. You have a letter to compose."

The younger girl frowned but complied.

Once inside the chamber, Prudence closed the door. "You must pen a convincing letter to your parents, or they'll send agents after us."

"What should I write?"

Prudence thought for a minute. "Tell them that just before Clay left Philadelphia you said some horrid things to him. Say that you won't have any peace until you go to him and make things right. Hopefully, that will take care of your mother."

Evie nodded. Turning to her desk, she sat down and took out a sheet of paper, then dipped a quill into the inkwell.

"Now for your father," Prudence went on. "Write that when you threatened to sneak away at the very first opportunity, I agreed with great reluctance to accompany you as chaperon. And don't forget to say *with great reluctance*. Tell him I will take every precaution, that sort of thing."

As Evelyn nodded and began to write, Prudence stepped to the door. "I'll go and pack a few necessities. For safety's sake we should wear men's clothes. I'll bring some of Morgan's back for you. Oh, and Evie . . . be sure to request that your mother have our clothes shipped to us as soon as possible."

"My, you do think of everything," the younger girl said in amazement.

"That's not all. Before we leave town, we must find Micah Dodd and relay Morgan's message."

"And find out if he's heard from Jamie," Evie added with renewed emotion.

"Yes, dear, that, too. Now, do you know where your father keeps the key to his weapons cabinet?"

"Weapons?" Evie whispered.

"I'm hoping he has a pair of pistols."

Her light blue eyes flared. "But I don't know the first thing about guns."

"Then it's time you learned, don't you think?"

26

A knock rattled the door of Morgan's bedchamber. Assuming that it was either one of the king's men in need of some service or a servant with yet another complaint regarding the same, he reluctantly set down the volume on the history of the Roman Empire that he had obtained from the library downstairs. He did not appreciate being left in charge of the Dillard household. Were it not for Prudence's tendency to snoop herself right into a noose, she could be here now to run the place—not to mention warming his heart and his bed, since winter was not far off. But Morgan knew he could not trust his beautiful wife to remain out of danger. Irritated by the tangle of thoughts, he answered the summons.

Captain Gorton, the highest ranking of the three officers lodging at the house, stood stiffly at the door in full dress, military hat cocked under one arm. "Good evening, Mr. Thomas. I hope I'm not disturbing you. I was unable to return home in time for the supper hour, having accepted a rather last-minute invitation. You mentioned wanting to meet some of the quartermaster officers, did you not?"

"Why, yes. Absolutely." The offer piqued Morgan's interest. "As you know, I've come representing a number of Philadelphia merchants."

"Then throw on your coat, and let's be off. General Howe is hosting an impromptu gathering this eve. I've a feeling he intends to make an announcement of some import. Even the governor himself is expected."

"Splendid. One would not want to miss such a fortuitous occasion. I appreciate this immensely, Captain. I shall have to think up a worthy reward for you."

The man's eyes sparkled with anticipation. "My pleasure, to be sure."

A pity the remainder of the world's problems couldn't be handled as simply, Morgan mused. "Give me five minutes, will you? I must change into something more appropriate."

"As you wish. I shall wait for you downstairs."

A short time later, in his best satin and lace finery, Morgan accompanied Captain Gorton to one of the grandest homes in all of the city. Made of pink brick with white columns, it occupied a broad expanse along one side of a tree-shaded street. But no amount of wealth could dispel the lingering odor of burnt ash that still permeated the air.

Morgan noted a number of fine carriages of the New York elite already lining the horseshoe drive. Apparently, not everyone had been fortunate enough to escape the chaos of the city as the Dillards had. But then, not all had wished to take leave. Wise Loyalist businessmen knew that the opportunities for profit were prime at this time, with lucrative contracts—if not outright monopolies—to be gained.

As Morgan walked up the drive to the entrance, an unexplained feeling of disquiet went through him. Although he had heard nothing to substantiate his strongest fear, it was entirely possible that some of Boston's exiled Tory merchants might have come with the army from Halifax—merchants who might now suspect that he was responsible for the loss of a number of their cargoes last year.

The captain tapped the brass knocker, and a butler ushered them inside to a huge and already crowded room. On the far end of the elegant expanse, a string quartet was making a feeble attempt at being heard above the drone of conversation.

Morgan scanned the face of every man he could see who

was not in uniform, and then he relaxed. Not a familiar Bostonian among them. The evening could be spent quite fruitfully, putting together deals for his father and associates while keeping his ears perked for any valuable military information.

Beside him, the captain groaned. "Not a female here under fifty . . . and precious few even of them."

"Shipped off to the safety of London, no doubt," Morgan said, chuckling, "as were the Dillard daughters."

The officer gave a sly smile. "I don't understand. I volunteered personally to see to the safety of the oldest girl."

"Quite. But don't despair. If ever you happen to be in Philadelphia, I'll introduce you to some of our loveliest." As he casually spoke the words, Morgan realized another reason he could not allow Prudence—and more important, Evie—to come here. With three British officers having the run of the house, he would be forced to keep a constant eye on his wife and young sister.

"I shall hold you to that," Gorton remarked. "I've no doubt we'll be dropping in on that city the moment we tire of New York hospitality . . . which, from the look of things, won't be long."

"The look of things?" Morgan returned. He hadn't thought the man was privy to command decisions, much less that he would have knowledge of a possible movement to Philadelphia.

The officer smirked. "One cannot deny a substantial loss of charm in a town that's been half burned down. And it's said that the farther south one goes, the prettier the belles."

Morgan dismissed the comment as no more than wishful thinking on the captain's part. He gazed around the room again and spotted the commander, William Howe, and his admiral brother, Richard, at one side of the room. A number of high-ranking officers surrounded the pair. "An incentive like that should inspire your soldiers to finish business here quickly so they can move on," Morgan said to Gorton. He began gravitating toward the commander, a large, slow, sleepy-looking man with a dark complexion.

"Morgan Thomas!" The voice came from behind.

Morgan cringed. He only hoped it belonged to friend, rather than foe.

"Morgan," Clay Raleigh said, making his way over to him. "I'm glad I found you here tonight."

"I didn't realize you had already come to New York."

The Englishman drew up his snobbish mouth. "My father, I'm afraid, insisted that I accompany him. Alas, I was obliged to tear myself away from your sister's charm and beauty. And as you can see, those particular qualities are sorely missed here." He took a sip from his goblet. "Have you, perchance, sent for her yet? She said that she would anxiously count the days until her arrival."

"Actually, I thought it might be wiser to wait until things are more settled here."

Clay's expression fell. "When do you think that might be?"

"I've no idea. Perhaps the good captain might be able to tell us. Oh, forgive my rudeness. Captain Gorton, may I present Mr. Clayborne Raleigh."

"Of the tobacco-buying Raleighs?" the officer asked, his eyes widening in undisguised interest.

"Yes. One and the same," Clay said with pride. "And we would be most grateful if you would hurry and make the city a safe place into which our gentle ladies might be brought."

The man looked from him to Morgan and back. "This lovely damsel you spoke of . . . would she be residing with her brother?"

Clay nodded. "Of course."

"Hmm. A lovely young flower at the Dillards' once again. You've come to the right person. I'm captain of the city guard. I should be happy to assume full responsibility for her comfort and safety, once she arrives."

No doubt, Morgan thought wryly. Time to extract himself from yet another womanizer who would care not a whit that the girl was barely sixteen. "Your father," he said, turning to Raleigh. "Is he here this eve?"

"Yes. Busy conducting business, as usual. He's over yonder, talking with the quartermaster of a regiment of light infantry." He motioned with his glass.

"Splendid. I'd like to meet him."

Excusing themselves from Gorton, Morgan and Clay joined the elder Raleigh. Somewhat taller than his impeccably groomed son, the man was far more reserved in demeanor— and more attractive as well, with thick brown hair and clear hazel eyes. Morgan knew him to be a true trader, with his attention squarely on the margin of profit—and he respected the man for not assuming airs as his son did.

Morgan immediately set upon immersing himself into the intricacies of price haggling with the quartermaster, and within moments managed to secure a good price for his proffered cargo of beans and molasses.

"If you don't mind," Clay muttered, obviously bored, "I think I'll mingle a bit."

"I'll join you," Morgan offered. Having concluded a piece of business for his father, it was high time to take care of a few matters for General Washington.

They turned to move on toward the Howes.

Morgan, struck by a sickeningly familiar face directly in his path, stopped dead. "Captain Long," he said with forced enthusiasm. "How delightful." He offered a hand, hoping his initial shock had not been noticed. "I've been in town for nearly a month. How is it we just now meet?"

The man's shrewd, hooded eyes narrowed as he took Morgan's hand. "Mr. Thomas. I've been kept quite busy, preparing for the mass of prisoners we'll soon be incarcerating, questioning those already in my confines . . . executing spies. I trust you heard about the young fellow we sent to the gallows a few weeks back. Nathan Hale, as I recall. A spy posing as a tutor." Though his tone was cordial enough, Morgan knew the comment was little more than a veiled threat.

"Ah, yes. Well, I'm glad I bumped into you," Morgan lied,

hoping to ease the officer's distrust, if not his dislike. "I'm afraid when I left Boston to return to Philadelphia, I lost track of Andy Sewell. Do you know, perchance, if he stayed in Halifax or went all the way to England?" Morgan instantly regretted having this conversation in Clay Raleigh's presence. The young man might mention that Morgan arrived in Philadelphia but a short time ago, rather than the two years he wanted Long to believe.

The captain's expression remained unreadable. "While you were enjoying yourself in the 'City of Brotherly Love,'—and I was enduring endless dull months in Boston, then Halifax—the Sewells sailed to England."

Morgan realized that the man would never forgive him for not wrangling a transfer for him to the detachment in Philadelphia, as he had once offered to do as an attempted bribe . . . only to have one of the man's subordinates inadvertently witness the exchange. "Well, Captain, you have the good fortune to be precisely where all the excitement happens to be. Compared to New York at the moment, Philadelphia is rather tiresome, indeed. In fact, I intend to find the highest vantage point from which to sit and view the unfolding of the great drama when your commander decides to field his attack. I'm sure he'll deploy the most brilliant of strategies."

"Yes," Raleigh added. "And when *is* the big day?"

Only now did Long's gaze withdraw from studying Morgan to fasten instead on Clay.

"Oh, forgive me, Captain Long," Morgan said. "I'd like to introduce Clayborne Raleigh, a tobacco buyer from London."

As the two shook hands, Morgan seized the chance to depart. "If you'll excuse us, sir, there are some other officers I'd like my friend Clay to meet." Then, with no little relief at having wrested himself from Long's presence, he led the way across the room toward the other two lieutenants who were lodging at the Dillard home.

A drumroll interrupted their passage.

General Howe stepped onto the stage, and the instruments lapsed into silence. Quiet immediately descended upon the rest of the room. "Ladies and gentlemen," he began, "I do hope you are enjoying our hospitality. But that's only one of the reasons I invited you here this evening. I am pleased to inform you that within the next few days, the rebel army will be no more."

A great roar of cheers followed the words.

Howe raised his hand. "On a very near day and hour—which, unfortunately, I am not at liberty to divulge—our brave men shall go forth and march down on the enemy like the Roman soldiers of old . . . *and crush them beneath our heels!*" Another cheer exploded.

"Then," he went on, "all you merchants and tradesmen will be pleased to hear that we shall settle here for the winter. We will await Parliament's further orders concerning the punitive action to be taken against any remaining pockets of rebellion in every colony—and particularly, their leaders holding that Yankee-Doodle Congress in Philadelphia."

I must get this news to Washington at once, Morgan thought as the commander stepped down and derisive laughter and happy chatter broke out. But without a contact, he would have to take it himself.

Clay Raleigh, at his shoulder, grabbed him in an exuberant hug. Morgan could only pray he would make it past the pickets alive, for Prudence's sake . . . and his own. The thought of never seeing her or holding her again was almost too much to bear.

Feeling the fine hairs on the back of his neck begin to prickle, Morgan glanced up to find Captain Long's intense gaze on him, as if daring him to pass on the information just related. But then logic took over. If the man even remotely suspected him of spying, he would be only too glad to make the arrest personally. It was merely the thwarting of Long's desired transfer and the accompanying hefty bribe that caused the ill feelings between them. *Merely that.*

Nevertheless, Morgan knew he had to leave. Now. Perhaps if he invited Clay Raleigh to go with him, it would appear less suspicious. As he turned to do just that, he bumped into a middle-aged woman servant.

Wine sloshed over the lip of a decanter she was carrying and spilled down his front. "Oh, I beg your pardon!" she gasped, obviously flustered as she took the corner of her apron and began mopping at Morgan's waistcoat. After a few futile seconds, she grabbed onto his sleeve. "I can do a much better job of this in the kitchen. Come with me, before the stain sets."

There was nothing for him to do but comply. While she labored feverishly over the satin waistcoat, he stood in the flurried workroom in his shirtsleeves, hoping there wouldn't be a water stain. He had brought very few clothes on the journey.

Finally the maid returned and held the garment up for him to slip into. The evidence of the spill was next to invisible, and she had blotted the spot almost dry. "Oh, yes," she said quite cheerfully. "I almost forgot. The baker said your order is ready. You're to pick it up at the Dog's Head Tavern, down at the docks."

Much relieved at not having to sneak through the pickets himself now that there was a new contact, Morgan spun around and planted a kiss on her forehead. "I do thank you for the fine job you did on my waistcoat." With a spritely wink, he exited the kitchen.

His good spirits were swiftly doused, however, upon seeing Clay Raleigh and his father conversing with Captain Long. Hoping fervently that no damage had yet been done, he hurried over to them.

"Yes," the older Raleigh was saying as he approached, "we've had excellent success marketing that particular variety of tobacco. Excellent success, indeed."

Morgan really preferred to meet his contact without the complication of Captain Long's presence in town, but since that was not possible now, he pulled Clay aside. "Some party, is it not, with such a dreadful lack of fetching damsels to liven it up. You must be as weary of it as I. What say we visit a few of the local taprooms?"

Clay perked up at once. "I say, that's a capital idea. If what General Howe says is true, you'll be able to send for your lovely bride and my darling Evie very soon. There might not be many opportunities for an evening free of their genteel restraints then."

"Thomas," Captain Long said, stepping closer. "You didn't mention you'd wed."

"Oh, yes," Clay answered. "To one of Boston's loveliest belles."

"Is that a fact." The more than interested gleam in Long's eyes intensified. "Which one would that be?"

Morgan knew he had to change the subject. Prudence may have been from Boston Bay, but she was far from being one of the Loyalist belles. And with such a limited number, the man would surely have been acquainted with them all. Worse, if he ever saw Prudence, he just might recall a remarkably fetching, remarkably nosy serving girl. "Clayborne, I'm afraid, is much too taken with my youngest sister to give my wife a second glance." He snagged Clay's arm and pulled him away before his loose mouth could get them in any deeper. "Time is of the utmost, old chap."

27

Clay Raleigh peered nervously over his shoulder through the gathering fog. "I should have insisted that we take the carriage."

"The place came highly recommended," Morgan said lamely, feeling no less anxious as the two of them walked to the Dog's Head Tavern. The drunken laughter and occasional woman's cry echoing through the night was enough to set anyone's teeth on edge. "It shouldn't be much farther."

"I should hope not. Next time, I'll do the choosing *and* provide transport."

In the misty dark recesses behind them, a door slammed shut, and Morgan heard someone running. He listened intently, wishing he carried a weapon, but the footfalls receded in the opposite direction.

Morgan shook his head in disgust. Here he was, searching through the dark, deserted streets to find an unknown contact—while accompanied by a British boor whose company he had to pretend to enjoy. How had he gotten himself into this mess?

But even as the question arose, he knew the answer. He had lied. Less than a year ago he'd made a solemn vow to God not to lie again, and he had not been faithful to his promise. No amount of rationalizing that his deceptions were for a higher purpose made his feelings of self-reproach lessen . . . especially with Clay believing that the two of them were even now going to the tavern to get drunk and carouse with fallen women!

Past the corner of one warehouse, they reached the boardwalk fronting the piers. Morgan could make out a lantern glowing through the mist, and as they neared, he recognized the sign with a large carving of a dog's head hanging directly beneath it. Having only casually noticed the tavern a few days before when he'd been in the area discussing sailing permits, Morgan was glad they had found it so swiftly. He breathed easier.

"At last!" Clay said, lengthening his strides.

"Before we go in," Morgan said, matching his pace to Raleigh's, "I feel it only right to confess that I only overheard a few men talking about the place. It might behoove us not to mention where our sympathies lie, until we're sure it's not a rebel den."

"Quite right."

They entered and found themselves in a rather large dim room. Low ceilings confined the tobacco smoke and stench of liquor in a suffocating haze. Raleigh, seeing more redcoats and Royal Navy men than dockworkers and merchant seamen, immediately appeared at ease.

Morgan, however, remained guarded. With the city overflowing with Crown forces, he should have expected them to frequent every mug house in existence. He even spied a group of green-uniformed Hessians in one corner involved in a loud discourse in their native German. And, as was typical for this manner of establishment, a few women in gaudy, revealing dress sat among the patrons, as well.

Raleigh nudged him in the ribs. "Ah, there's a comely wench, old boy." He nodded his head toward a serving girl fetching drinks from the bar.

Morgan, gladder than ever that Evie was merely pretending interest in the rake, barely concealed his disgust. "Get us a table, would you? I'll fetch some drinks."

"Simply order them," Clay said. "Let the girl bring them to us."

"It would appear she's busy enough." Morgan motioned toward a vacant table, and Raleigh strutted over to it. Glad to be rid of the bloke for even a few minutes, he approached the bar. "Two tankards of flip, please, sir. And," he added, with no change in tone or manner, "I was told my bakery order is ready."

The burly barkeeper gave him a blank stare.

Morgan wondered how he would explain away such a nonsensical statement if this was not his contact. He envisioned himself walking about the room uttering the inane inquiry to every civilian present.

"This is a taproom, not a bakery," the man said gruffly, filling the tankards from a spigoted keg. Then he turned with a lazy smile. "You'll find your bread out back."

Morgan breathed a quiet sigh of relief, then suddenly remembered Clay Raleigh. "I'd appreciate it if your serving girl would bring our drinks over. I wouldn't want my companion to become bored and come looking for me while I pick up my order."

"Glad to." The barkeeper pulled a hot poker from a brazier and plunged it, sizzling, into the first tankard while Morgan rejoined the Englishman.

"I can see why this place was so highly recommended," Clay remarked. "Take a gander at the lass entertaining the dragoons."

Morgan slid a glance toward the table of soldiers and noted a comely woman flirting with them.

The flaxen-haired serving girl delivered the flip just then, along with a very inviting smile for Clay Raleigh.

He paid for the drinks with a flourish of coin, adding a hefty tip.

Her smile became much more accommodating.

Raleigh caught her hand when she turned to leave, and he rose to his feet, tugging her close as he held his tankard aloft. "Gentlemen, ladies, I wish to propose a toast. To our gallant fighting men."

A raft of cheers rang out as almost everyone got up to join in the tribute.

Morgan, among those who stood, counted only one table of men who remained seated. Observing their stony faces, he figured they were patriot sympathizers who refused to relinquish their hangout to the enemy.

"And another toast," Clay announced, raising his drink again. "To our commander, General Howe, whom I heard announce this very evening that you brave soldiers will soon be marching forth to mete out swift, decisive, and final punishment to the rebellious colonial rabble."

"Hear! Hear!" The banging of dozens of tankards on the wooden tables accompanied the resounding cheer.

"Refills, lass," someone shouted, and the server slipped away from Clay to tend them.

He took his seat, lounging back with a smug smile. "I rather like this place."

Knowing that Clay had managed to convey in an instant that he was a free-spending Englishman with very influential friends, Morgan felt that it would be only a matter of time before the patrons reciprocated in a most friendly and generous manner. He was not far off the mark.

Before they'd had time to warm their chairs, a handful of lobsterbacks appeared at the table. "Mind if we join you?"

"Certainly, certainly." Clay beamed. "The more the merrier, I always say."

A small crowd quickly congregated, complete with garishly dressed women. A spontaneous celebration began.

"You say you were with the general this eve," one of the soldiers commented.

"Ah, yes." Clay puffed out his chest. "'Twas a grand party, to be sure."

Morgan watched the young man take center stage and grin as he looped one arm over a pair of creamy shoulders. "Pity he's been so lax. I'd have had these colonies whipped into proper submission long ago."

With everyone at the table absorbed in the conversation,

Morgan bowed politely. "If you'll excuse me a moment, I'm afraid I must answer nature's call."

Clay, wallowing in newfound popularity, waved him off.

Outside, a lone lantern burned to dispel the misty darkness. Morgan inhaled deeply, finding the salty tang especially refreshing after the heavy atmosphere in the tavern.

A redcoat emerged from the outhouse and returned to the taproom.

Morgan waited until the soldier was inside again before checking the area. The rear yard was closed in on one side by a long warehouse, and on the other by a ship's outfitter. He wondered when and where he'd meet his contact. Deciding to try behind the store, he started toward the inky darkness beyond the circle of lantern light.

The tavern door opened and closed.

Morgan peered back to the lighted area, recognizing the three men who hadn't cheered with the soldiers. One must surely be his contact, he decided. "Good evening," he called pleasantly, retracing his steps. "I always forget how delicious baking bread smells down on the quay by night. I—"

Without warning, the threesome hurled themselves at him and dragged him to the ground. Before he could land a single blow, his arms and legs were pinned. One slapped a hand over his mouth. "Quick! Look inside his coat."

Morgan struggled to breathe, to wrench free as his frock coat was yanked open.

"Check for a money belt."

He bucked harder, but to no avail. And all his money was on him.

"Aye. There's a coin pouch, and a heavy one it is, too." The bloke lying across his chest sat up and hefted his purse.

"What in blue blazes is going on here?"

Recognizing the bartender's stern voice, Morgan strained to turn his head. The burly man loomed over the lot of them. "Get off him, you idiots. He's one of us!" He yanked the nearest one away.

Morgan managed to shove the other pair aside and regain his feet.

"You sure?" the one with the money pouch asked.

The tavern keeper snatched the bag and handed it back to Morgan, still glowering at the attackers. "Sorry, lad. In times like these, things aren't always as they seem."

One of the threesome shifted his weight and sniffed. "Guess we made a mistake, mister. But you're askin' for trouble, ya know, hobnobbin' with the king's generals and all." He made a futile attempt to brush off the back and shoulders of Morgan's coat. "Tell ya what. To make up for roughin' ya up tonight, if ya find yourself in trouble and in need of something—anything—I'm workin' down here at the docks every day. Just ask anybody for Percy Maxwell. They'll tell ya where I am."

"Thank you, Mr. Maxwell. I appreciate that." Morgan stretched out his hand. "There *is* something. Have any of you heard of a sailor friend of mine? a redheaded joker by the name of Yancy Curtis?"

"No! You're a pal of Yancy's?" another asked, thumping him on the back. "Well, any friend of that barnacled sea rat is a friend of ours."

"Aye," the third piped in. "Only we've been blockaded since the British tubs sailed in . . . 'cept for the odd ship His Highness has allowed to pass."

"I know." Morgan released a long breath. "But knowing Yancy, he's probably hanging from the topsail of some privateer, looking for a man-of-war to blow out of the water."

"We're wasting time," the barkeeper said. "You fellows run on home to your good wives. My friend and me need a couple minutes alone."

❦ ❦

When Morgan returned inside, he had the names of contacts residing in three different sections of New York. And it wasn't hard to see that Clay Raleigh hadn't missed him in the slightest. The rake now had a wench draped across his lap as if she belonged there.

"Sorry to break up the party, Clay," he said, rejoining the group at the table. "But I'm afraid I must have eaten something that didn't agree with me." He rubbed his midsection with a wince.

"So that's why you were gone so long," one of the other women remarked.

"Hmph," another snorted. "Looks to me like he's been down groveling in the dirt."

Morgan realized a bit late that he hadn't bothered to check his clothing before coming back inside. "I was a bit dizzy outside," he returned, rubbing his temples for good measure. "Perhaps we'd better leave."

Clay Raleigh eyed him with a hint of disdain. "Actually, old man, I'm rather enjoying myself at the moment. And the corporal, here, has promised to show me a few souvenirs he acquired in India. Isn't that right, Tupman?"

"Huh?" The soldier frowned. "Oh. Of course. Whatever you say, your lordship."

Morgan fought the urge to laugh aloud at Clay's sudden elevation in station . . . a lord, no less. And all in the time Morgan was occupied out back. "Well then, I'll be off." He took a step away, then turned back. "Do drop by in a day or so, and we'll go to dinner or something."

But Raleigh was otherwise occupied.

Outside once again, Morgan strode along the wharf boardwalk. Did Clayborne Raleigh have a single redeeming quality? Even as he pondered that, an old saying crossed his mind— one his mother had mouthed whenever he'd run into the house covered with dirt, much the same as he was this very night. *Cleanliness is next to godliness.* Morgan chuckled. Well, if nothing else, Clay Raleigh's appearance was always immaculate.

Morgan turned up the street between the warehouses. He conjured up a comical picture of an indignant Raleigh standing before the judgment seat of God, appalled at the audacity of having his sins read off to him when everyone knew he'd always been so very tidy.

A shuffling sound echoed softly behind Morgan.

He had already been set upon once this night. Without slowing, Morgan glanced over his shoulder. He could see nothing. Must be rats, he told himself. But the four-legged kind weren't the only ones that might be lurking in the dark.

28

Prudence roused in her sleep and turned over, her hand brushing the other side of the empty bed. Where was Morgan? It took a moment to remember she was not at home but at a travelers' inn outside Elizabeth Town, New Jersey. And her husband was not with her; his sister was. And she should have been occupying the rest of the bed! Quietly sitting up, Prudence scanned the darkened room.

Prudence exhaled in frustration. Evelyn was nowhere to be seen. The younger girl had been nothing but trouble since the two of them had left Princeton that morning. Looking back, Prudence could see that stopping there had not been one of her more brilliant ideas. Morgan and Chandler and Robby—poor, departed Robby—had spoken so highly of the place. But once Evie had discovered that Robert Chandler and the Lyonses' ward, Christopher Drummond, had been transferred to the very battalion that Jamie Dodd had joined, there was no putting her off. She had questioned Emily and the Lyonses relentlessly regarding rumors of heated battles, and they fed Evie's fear that Jamie was one of the casualties.

The instant Mr. Lyons relayed that Christopher's battalion was camped four miles west of King's Bridge on the Worcester causeway, the girl's stubborn streak took over.

Prudence rose silently from the bed, plucked her wrapper from the foot of the bed, and slipped into it as she padded to the door. Her sister-in-law might have gotten hungry and felt in need of a late-night snack. But a sixth sense told Prudence that that was just wishful thinking. The inn lay at a crossroads. One lane led to British-held Perth Amboy with its ferry to New York, and the other led westward up the Hudson River to a ferry that could transport the girls to within twenty miles of the colonial force. Prudence and Evie had gone to bed in bitter disagreement over which fork they would take in the morning.

Stepping out into the hallway, Prudence glanced in both directions.

The clatter of erratic hoofbeats out back broke into a gallop. Prudence sprang to the end window and peered out. In the moonless night it was impossible to discern anything more than a vague slender outline, but she had little doubt of who it was. The rider was heading west.

Prudence rushed back to the room and lit a candle. Quickly she pulled her breeches and Morgan's shirt on over her night shift, then shoved her stockingless feet into her riding boots. Throwing the rest of her belongings into her satchel, she refrained from thinking about the explanations she would have to give Morgan if she were to actually lose his sister. She would catch that willful brat even if she had to ride all the way to Canada to do it!

Much later that day, Prudence's bottom felt as if she might have covered at least half that distance. The sun's rays had been slanting at her through the trees for nearly an hour now, and still she'd seen neither hide nor hair of the wretched girl. But at least traveling at such a swift pace had prevented anyone from taking notice of her. She hoped it was the same for Evie.

Coming up on a settlement she recognized from when she'd traveled from New York with Morgan, Prudence knew she would soon reach the ferry crossing. Relief filled her as she started down the grade leading to the quay and noted the long line of people waiting to cross—for once, a blessed sight, because Evelyn would have had no choice but to wait her turn. When the young girl was caught, Prudence would give her a talking to she would not soon forget . . . right after she finished strangling her.

She peered along the line as she rode slowly past the waiting carriages, carts, wagons, riders, and quite a number of young men on foot—who, Prudence fervently hoped, were reinforcements for an army whose soldiers were fleeing in droves, according to the letter Mr. Lyons had read them.

No sign of Evie. None at all. Prudence wondered if the girl had seen her coming and hidden. It would be just like her to do such a featherbrained thing. Working her way past the people and down the steep hill, she considered going back up to the top of the palisade and checking some of the buildings.

Absently she glanced out over the water at the crossing flatboat of passengers and animals.

Evie! On the ferry, out in the middle of the water!

In a line as long as this one, how had she managed to get so far ahead? And despite Prudence's lectures about maintaining her disguise and staying inconspicuous, Evie's hat was off. Shining brunette curls were in glorious display for all the world to see.

Prudence bypassed everyone and rode to the front, stopping at a broad-shouldered, whiskered man who was threading the ferry rope, which mules on the far shore were reeling in on a giant wheel. "I beg your pardon, sir."

The scruffy face turned to her, and the stubby cigar he'd been chewing on shifted to the other side of his mouth. "Aye?" His loose glance wandered up and down her.

Prudence ignored it. "I've been trying to catch up with my sister—" Removing her tricorn, she pointed out to the water. "She's wearing men's clothes, too. I can't imagine how she caught such a quick ride. She was only a little way ahead of me."

The man gawked at her like a dumb ox, saying nothing.

Was he deaf? Prudence started to repeat herself more slowly, but a woman with her husband on the seat of the first wagon gave a derisive sniff. "You'll not get a straight answer from the likes of him, dearie. The lass sweet-talked him into lettin' her get in front of all of us who've been sittin' here this whole livelong day."

The fellow spat the cigar stump into the water. "Now that's not exactly how it was. Told me she'd got word her husband had been wounded and was near to dyin'. She needed to get to him before he passed on. Seemed only right, for someone layin' his very life down for his country."

Prudence shook her head. "She has always been good at spinning tales. The truth of the matter is, she's running off to be with her young man. And there's been no word of anything befalling him at all."

"Didn't I tell ya, Phineas?" the woman groused. "Just like an old man to turn to mush when a pretty young miss favors him with a smile."

Prudence looked from her to the ferry tender. "Oh, please, sir. I must catch my sister. She's sure to get into trouble without me to look after her. Please, I beg of you, let me on the next boat."

"What's one more, old man?" the woman challenged. "It's obvious the silly goose needs her big sister with her, before she's ruined for good. That one will be in need of a good dressin' down, too," she added to Prudence.

The boatman peered indecisively up the long line snaking up the hill behind him, and creases deepened in his sun-burned forehead. "Just hope I don't end up with a riot on me hands."

"Oh, thank you. Thank you!" Prudence sank gratefully into her saddle. It had been a long, long day. But the end was finally in sight.

❧ ❧

It was near dusk by the time the flatboat delivered Prudence to the other side of the river. Lamps glowed in the windows of the farmsteads sprinkled along the Hudson. And by that time, her ears were fairly ringing with advice from the woman in the wagon, who had also boarded on the same load. Truly glad to be leaving the talkative Mrs. Downy behind, Prudence turned her horse east and started downriver toward the colonial army.

Her fears for Evelyn had grown steadily with the passing of time. With a heartfelt prayer that she'd catch up to her reckless sister-in-law before it was too late, she tried to calm her disquiet. Deep inside, she had to admit that the younger girl was no less willful than she. It had been her own secret desire to have Evie persuade her into going to Morgan.

The arrival of darkness swiftly brought nippy fall air. Slowing her pace, Prudence took care that she didn't stray from the rutted trace alongside the river. About every half mile she spotted the lights from another farmhouse, and it came to her that Evie might have turned in for the night at one of them. But rather than lose time by checking each out, Prudence continued on. Far better to reach the Pennsylvania Riflemen ahead of Evelyn than after her. Her one consolation was that she had passed no one on the road since it had grown dark. The more deserted the road was, the less Evie's safety would be threatened.

The air along the river grew steadily colder and more damp. Without stopping, Prudence reached behind her saddle for the rolled up blanket and wrapped it around her shoulders. It might very well be another extremely long night.

✼ ✼

Morgan finished the last of his meal alone. None of the other officers had come to join him in the Dillards' formal dining room this eve . . . an ominous sign. Three nights had passed since General Howe proclaimed his announcement of an imminent attack. It could conceivably happen this night—or tomorrow morning at the latest. He rose and went to the foyer to retrieve his greatcoat.

Tossing it about his shoulders, he headed out the door to see what he could ascertain. But before he reached the street, he saw Clay Raleigh stepping out of a carriage. *Not tonight,* Morgan groaned inwardly.

"Ah. Morgan. What a fortuitous coincidence to catch you on your way out. You must come celebrate with me."

Leave it to the useless fop to keep abreast of all the latest happenings, Morgan conceded. He feigned enthusiasm. "Do tell. What's the good news?"

Raleigh looped an arm around him and turned with him toward the carriage. "Let's adjourn to the Dog's Head, and I'll tell you as we go."

Morgan could think of no way out. But once they were aboard the conveyance, he could keep silent no longer. "I insist you tell me what's happened."

In the low lamplight inside the carriage, Raleigh arched his brows. "My, my. I had no idea you were such an impatient sort. When Captain Long inquired after you last eve, I told him you were quite the relaxed fellow."

Morgan's marrow froze. "You spoke with the captain regarding me?"

"Oh, just in passing," Clay said with a flutter of his hand. "He was pretending a rather intense interest in Philadelphia society . . . but I could tell his attention lay more in my father's selection of fine cigars. The man invited himself over to our table at the Provincial House and managed to smoke two while we chatted."

"Two, you say." Plenty of time for Long to find out everything he wanted to know about Morgan. He quickly assessed the situation. As long as the captain didn't meet Prudence, Morgan was confident he could handle the rest. He could come up with a plausible reason why he hadn't gone to Halifax with his wife as Raleigh thought, and why he had just returned to Philadelphia—a good solid alibi. It certainly wouldn't do for the redcoat to discover that he had actually been exchanging musket fire along the Concord road and at Bunker Hill.

Morgan relaxed into the plush cushion. Yes, it was best to face this Captain Long problem head-on, get it behind him, rather than put it off and end up looking over his shoulder as he had while walking home the other night. "Well, Clay, I'm waiting. What's the big news?"

Raleigh smiled smugly. "All soldiers have been ordered to report to their regiments. They'll move out first thing in the morning."

"You don't say. Why, that *is* splendid news. We've been waiting a long time for this." And even more splendid, good fellow that Raleigh was, he was delivering Morgan right to the very doorstep of one of his contacts. He returned a broad smile.

But soon the dire reality of the news struck him. He had heard rumors that so many in Washington's army had deserted, it was down to half-strength. They were bound to be cut to pieces.

Thankfully, Prudence wasn't here to witness it.

❦ ❦

Prudence had been riding for the better part of twenty-four hours. She was cold and miserable, her teeth had taken to chattering, and now as a thick fog began rolling off the river, she had to dismount and continue on foot to be sure she didn't stray from the road. But there was one consolation . . . if Evelyn was still traveling, too, the fog would provide some safety from any evildoer who might be lurking in the night. Anyone with any sense would stay home and keep warm.

Lady's breathing had grown labored and more intense. The poor animal had been cruelly overworked. Prudence stopped walking and ran a hand over the soft muzzle. "You've been such a good girl for me on this trip," she murmured for the dozenth time.

The good-natured mare gave a low rumbly whinny.

Another horse answered out of the darkness.

Prudence felt gooseflesh rise. But then, realizing that it could be Evie's horse, she gave Lady her head, allowing the animal to lead her into the trees and brush. After all, the two had been stabled together for some months now and were quite companionable to one another.

After stumbling through the undergrowth for several minutes, she and Lady came upon a horse that had been picketed for the night. In the heavy mist, Prudence had to come within inches of the animal to confirm from the blaze on its face that it was, indeed, Evie's. But the girl was nowhere in sight.

There was no light from a farmhouse anywhere, either. Prudence knew Evelyn couldn't have gotten far without her horse. She had to be hiding. "Evie," she called out.

No answer.

Prudence cupped her mouth with her hands. "Evie!" she demanded.

Still no answer. Not even a nightingale broke the silence of the fog-enshrouded darkness.

The girl was being unacceptably stubborn. Hands on her hips, Prudence figured Evie would wait for her to fall asleep, then steal away again, as she had last night. But that simply would not do. Prudence knew she needed to deliver Morgan's sister safely to him and in the same unsullied condition she'd been in when the two of them had left home.

"Evelyn. I promise to go with you to the army camp." Prudence strained her ears but heard only silence. "I *promise,* Evie. We'll search for your Jamie until we find him—even if it takes all year."

No response.

Prudence huffed. "Have I ever once broken a solemn promise to you?"

Nothing.

The dreadful thought struck her that perhaps Evie's horse had gone lame, and she'd gone on without it. Prudence peered fleetingly back toward the road.

"No, you haven't." The voice came, small but clear. A slight figure stepped out from behind a tree. "First light. We'll go find Jamie at first light."

"Yes." Prudence nodded, overcome with relief. "Absolutely."

Then, like a whirlwind, the younger girl threw off her

blanket and rushed into Prudence's arms. "I'm so glad to see you! It's scary out here."

Prudence hugged her hard, then held her at arm's length. "Yes. It's very dangerous for lone women in the dark. That's why as soon as we find your friend, we're going on to Morgan. Is that understood?"

"Yes! Yes!" Evie hugged her again. "Whatever you say. But won't Jamie be surprised to see me!"

29

Fields of unharvested corn and buckwheat had been trampled almost flat by hordes of Continental soldiers camped along the road. The misty morning lent a ghostlike appearance to the scene as Prudence and Evie rode their horses toward the encampment of the First Pennsylvania Rifle Battalion.

"Slouch, Evie," Prudence muttered in exasperation as soldiers glanced up at them. "Try to look more like a lad."

The atmosphere here was quite warlike, much different from that of the soldiers they had passed farther inland. Those men had been occupied with varied mundane chores or aimlessly milling about. A few had even been helpful, providing the two of them with directions to the rifle battalion. But here, near the fog-obliterated shoreline facing both Nassau and Manhattan Islands, the soldiers were unusually still, their muskets positioned in readiness. They glanced at Prudence and Evie, then quickly returned their attention to the faint marshy coastline below them.

Robert Chandler and Jamie Dodd were obviously at the forefront of an expected invasion, Prudence concluded. But aside from that danger, what would Morgan say and do when he found out she and his sister had come here?

The queasiness she had been experiencing for the past few mornings added another niggling fear. She tried to dismiss the thought, but it returned. There was every possibility that she might be with child—and perhaps even endangering their firstborn.

Evie guided her mount closer to Lady. "Can't you just feel the excitement? the danger?" Her eyes sparkled as she placed her hand over the big pistol jammed inside her belt. "I just wish you would've had time to teach me more than how to load and aim. I only got to fire two shots."

Prudence swung her a withering glance. "And when, pray tell, was I supposed to teach you? Yesterday, when you were trying your hardest to lose me?"

"Well, if I hadn't, I'll wager we wouldn't be here now."

"Don't remind me. Now hush. An officer is walking out into the road."

The uniformed man faced them and raised a hand. "Halt. This road is closed to all civilians."

"But we're not civilians," Evie said, effecting the lowest voice possible. "We're on our way to join up with the First Pennsylvania."

"A couple of baby faces like you two?" His tone was rife with disdain. "Colonel Hand won't take you on."

"I heard it said he welcomes a lad who can shoot the eye out of a squirrel at a hundred paces," Evie bragged convincingly.

The officer remained skeptical, but relented. "All right, you can pass. You'll find his headquarters a few rods down the road, just before you come to the mill pond. But if I know the colonel, you'll be back this way in short order. See if you aren't."

"Much obliged," Prudence said in her best imitation of a male voice, and they rode on.

"Just a few more rods," Evie whispered.

The younger girl could barely contain her excitement, but when they were safely out of range, Prudence exhaled a sigh of relief. She was anxious to leave the area as quickly as possible. "When we get to headquarters, let me do the talking. I don't want to hear one more outlandish remark from that mouth of yours."

Flattening her lips indignantly, Evie lapsed into silence.

As they rode into a sprawling military encampment, Prudence sought the banner that marked the largest tent. She veered her mount in that direction and noted that a number of men were converging on the very same place. It appeared that she and Evie were riding in just as some kind of gathering of officers and sergeants was taking place.

One of the sergeants noticed them. "Come forward, lads."

There was nothing to do but comply. She and Evie wove their mounts through them toward the tent.

"I'm Colonel Hand," a tall, granite-faced man said, his voice carrying the hint of an Irish brogue. "Have you brought me a message?"

"Sorry, sir, no." Prudence fought the heat rising in her face. "We've come to inquire after a young man we haven't heard from since August."

He stared blankly, incredulously, for a full five seconds. Then his gaze narrowed in barely suppressed anger. "If the lad had been slain, I'd have notified his family. Now, get yourselves out of here and back up the road." He turned away.

"No! Wait!" Evie yanked off her hat, letting her mass of dark tresses tumble around her shoulders and back. "I've come too far to give up now."

Prudence, in irritated defeat, removed her own tricorn as well. No sense trying to pretend any longer.

"Prudence?" a voice called out in shock. "Is that you?"

She swung around in the saddle and saw Robert Chandler striding toward her.

"You know these women, Sergeant Chandler?" Hand inquired.

He came to attention. "Just one, sir. The wife of Lieutenant Thomas, one of Washington's special aides."

The colonel eyed Prudence with scorn. "Then she should surely know better than to come here. Take them aside and deal with this *missing person* problem with the utmost dispatch. I don't have time for such foolishness—the British are landing out on Throg's Neck this very minute."

Prudence wasn't the only one shocked. From the murmurings running through the crowd, she concluded that the soldiers were just now hearing the news.

"Yes, sir!" Robert saluted, then grabbed Lady's bridle and began leading them away from the others and toward a tree on the outskirts of the grounds. Evelyn prepared to dismount when Robert came to a stop.

"Stay put," he ordered. But his expression appeared a bit softer when he all but smiled at Prudence. "I'd like to say how good it is to see you, Prudence, but what in the world are you doing here?" He wagged his head. "I swear, when it comes to danger, you're like a fly to honey."

Evie gave her no chance to answer. "She's not the adventurer. I've had to practically drag her every step of the way."

Robert switched his attention to the younger girl and looked at her quizzically. "And you, I assume, must be some relation of Morgan's."

"His sister," she said.

"His *baby* sister," Prudence amended.

"I'm plenty old enough," Evie huffed.

Robert swung a fleeting glance toward the dispersement taking place behind him. "There's hardly time for pleasantries. Why have you come?"

"It's my friend," Evie answered. "Jamie Dodd. He promised he'd write, but it's been two months. I just know something dreadful has happened to him."

"Dodd? James Dodd?" Chan's brows rose. "I'm sorry, but he's no longer with us."

Evelyn went white. "Oh, no."

"It's not what you think," he added hastily. "He's missing. For three days now."

"Missing?" Prudence echoed. "Have the British captured him?"

"No, I wouldn't say that." Robert appeared hesitant to give more details.

"Then what?" Evie demanded. "We've ridden all the way from Philadelphia. Please tell us."

Robert exhaled heavily. "I'm sorry. You're not going to like this. Private Dodd . . . ran away. With the daughter of a farmer from Manhattan Island."

Evelyn stiffened. "I don't believe it! He would never—he's too patriotic to desert. You must be speaking of someone else."

"Afraid not, Miss Thomas. You have to remember, the lad is young, inexperienced. And the girl's father had declared his own personal war on Dodd."

Evie's eyes shimmered with unshed tears as she sat rigidly in place.

Prudence reached over and touched her shoulder. "I'm so sorry, Evie. Truly I am."

"So am I," Robert said quietly. "I wish you hadn't come so far only to be given such unhappy news. But now our immediate concern is to get the two of you safely out of here."

He looked back at headquarters even as a young sandy-haired soldier started running toward him. "Chan. I just heard. What do you want us to do?" He stopped short upon seeing Prudence and Evelyn. "What are *girls* doing here?"

"Christopher," Robert said, "tell Corporal Meeks to take charge of the men. Have them stay put until they receive further orders. Then you hightail it right back here."

"Yes, sir." Backing up with an uncertain expression, he turned and ran.

"I'd best go speak to the colonel myself," Robert muttered, his lips determined.

Prudence followed on horseback as he struck out for the big tent but held back when he approached the commander and saluted.

"Sir," she heard him say, "Special Aide Thomas's wife and sister are ready to leave now. With your permission, I'd like to take along another man and escort them to safety a mile or so inland."

"The last time you went to help a lady, Chandler, you were gone two weeks."

"One hour, sir," he said evenly. "I give you my word. No more than one hour."

The leader cocked a brow and smirked. "I made you a sergeant last time you were tardy. Any longer and I'll commission you an officer."

※ ※

Robert could not believe this was happening. Riding double behind Prudence, and Christopher riding with Morgan's young sister, they trotted out of camp—with a battle about to break out at any instant. "I hardly know whether to hug you or throttle you," he finally confessed.

"I'd prefer the hug," Prudence said. "No doubt Morgan will personally see to the other."

"And where is he?"

"New York. He's been dispatched there to spy now. Evie and I were on our way to join him . . . but the willful baggage took it upon herself to take this little detour. She's amazingly stubborn."

"And Morgan actually agreed to allow the two of you to go to New York?" Robert asked in disbelief. "Spying in Philadelphia was bad enough. New York will be quite virtually the lions' den."

Prudence nodded. "Speaking of that, Evie and I spent a night with the Lyonses in Princeton on our way here. I was very surprised to find Emily there. Oh, Chan. What a heartbreak to hear about her dear, kind Robby. Such a loss. Morgan will take the news especially hard, I know it."

"Yes. As we all have." Robert did not trust himself to say more.

"But it seems Emily is faring amazingly well," Prudence went on. "Always a smile for her little ones. She seemed rather cheerful, actually . . . or nearly so. I know from what Morgan has told me that she and Robby shared an exceptionally strong faith. That must be what has helped her through this sad time."

"I'm sure."

"That reminds me. She said that if by some happenstance

our paths should cross—little did she know Evelyn would take off for here without me, giving me a merry chase—"

"What did she say?" Chan interrupted. He was astounded at how very deeply he wanted to know what Emily had said.

Prudence swiveled and turned a look of mild surprise on him. "Emily said to give you her warmest regards, and she renewed her thanks for your services. She told me how you took time off to take her and the little ones to safety. I must say, I would most certainly want a friend like you if I ever were called upon to suffer such a loss."

"Don't even think such a thing." Suddenly Robert thought of the British invasion that was happening even now—and very close by. "Let's not take the road, Christopher," he called over his shoulder. "It's too open. Head for the woods."

As the lad complied, Robert couldn't help but notice the tears streaming down Morgan's sister's face. Christopher gave him a helpless shrug.

"I take it your sister-in-law was quite smitten with Private Dodd," Robert commented.

"Yes," Prudence sighed. "They had been friends for a few years. But I think she was as infatuated with the idea of his going off to fight the good fight as anything else. His desertion was probably as much a disappointment to her as knowing he left with another girl."

Robert mulled over Evelyn's sad plight only briefly. His thoughts insisted on drifting back to Princeton, to Emily. Prudence had seen her mere days ago. "You say Emily seems to be settling in at the Lyons' Den all right? And the children . . . how are they?"

Prudence smiled at him, then turned forward again. "Oh, those little ones are really a pair, aren't they? Already they've got everyone wrapped around their little fingers, doting on them, chasing after them. How it brought back memories of my own little half brothers and half sister. And Emily, well, she has scarcely a thought for herself. She's worried about her parents and the horse farm. Oh, and did I mention? She told me to remind you that the children miss you terribly and that you'll always be welcome at their hearth."

Robert was immensely glad that Prudence had turned to the front and couldn't see the smile that had broken out on his face. After all, there was no sense in having someone read anything untoward in it.

They rode in silence for a few minutes. Then Prudence squeezed his arm. "I'm dreadfully sorry for always being such a bother."

"Well," he said good-naturedly, "at least you're a very dear bother. Now, when Christopher and I leave to turn back, stay off the roads for a few miles. Take advantage of whatever cover you can find. Then head straight for the ferry. If you're wise, you'll go back to Philadelphia, where they're throwing parties rather than cannonballs."

She nodded rather unconvincingly.

"You know," he added, "I don't believe Morgan has the slightest idea you're on your way to him. He would never have permitted you and his sister to travel the roads alone, especially with things in such a volatile state."

"Well, we did leave a little earlier than he expected," she admitted. She slumped against him with a sigh of resignation. "Please understand, Robert. I just can't turn back. Especially not now. I need to be with my husband. I . . . I'm beginning to suspect I'm . . . with child."

"What?"

"Shh. I haven't mentioned it to Evie just yet."

"And you've been out riding across the country for days on end?" he whispered angrily. "Not to mention being exposed to all sorts of danger lurking about. . . ."

"Chan!" Christopher called intensely, bringing his mount alongside. "Redcoats! Riding this way! Fast!"

30

"Quick! Dismount!" Robert commanded. "All of you!"

The urgency in his voice chilled Prudence, and before she had time to act, he snatched her from the saddle and dropped her to the ground.

"Down, into the bracken."

She threw herself headlong beneath a canopy of broadleaf ferns and clawed as fast as she could through the under-growth as the others did the same. Their mounts had tramped a telltale path through the greenery, one which could all too easily be followed by mounted redcoats. They needed to get as far from the trail as possible.

When the horses lurched into a rapid gallop, she knew even without looking that their only transportation was gone. But inching up between the fronds, she saw that they weren't running away on their own. Robert had remained in Lady's saddle and was stringing Evie's horse behind as he charged away from the hiding place and out into a small clearing.

"Halt!"

A musket discharged.

Her heart in her throat, Prudence saw Robert speeding onward, apparently unhit. He gained the other side of the clearing and crashed into the dense woods beyond.

The mounted patrol of eight king's men clattered past the stand of ferns in chase.

Prudence's mouth went dry. Cautiously she rose to her

knees to watch, her pulse throbbing in her ears, her breathing hard and shallow.

One of the British soldiers raised his musket as the scouting party crossed the small meadow. Another shot exploded. Then he and the rest of the redcoats vanished from sight into the woods.

"Oh, please, dear Father in heaven," she pleaded with all that was in her. "Please, don't let them catch Robert."

"Amen to that."

Prudence saw Christopher Drummond rise in the midst of the bracken. Evie clung to him, her expression frantic in comparison to his grim but more composed one.

The lanky young man clutched her to him with one hand and pointed his long-barreled rifle with the other. "Let's move into that thicket over there. And try not to disturb these ferns any more than necessary."

Following his lead, Prudence and Evie moved carefully and quickly until they were ensconced within a growth of young trees too close for a horse to pass through without difficulty.

"Might as well get comfortable," Christopher muttered. "We'll have to stay here till Chan comes back for us."

"What if he doesn't?" Evie's voice sounded unnaturally high. She took a firmer grip on the lad's neck.

"Oh, don't worry about him," he said confidently, giving her a reassuring grin. "He can take care of himself."

But Prudence noticed the way the youth's blue eyes remained riveted to the forest in the distance. He didn't appear nearly as strong as Chandler, yet he didn't seem to have a problem calming Evie as he took control of the situation. She suddenly realized that Evelyn no longer had her tricorn covering her hair. "Evie, where's your hat?"

The younger girl's eyes widened. Relinquishing her death grip on poor Christopher, she reached up to feel her head. "I-I don't know."

The lad released a *whoosh* of breath. "You two stay here. I'll go find it."

"Keep low," Evie whispered, her words conveying her fright.

Prudence hoped Evelyn had at last acquired some under-standing of the danger of their present situation. When Rob-ert returned—*if he returned*—she and the younger girl would ride out of here as fast and as hard as their horses could go. She felt her sister-in-law reach over and latch onto her hand as the two of them watched Christopher searching through the bracken.

Eternal minutes later, he poked his rifle into the greenery and retrieved the three-cornered hat from where it had fallen. He waved it at them with a triumphant grin.

Evie, her face still devoid of color, answered with a mute but urgent wave of her hand.

Finally she realizes we are not on a child's backyard adventure, Prudence told herself, *however belated her newfound under-standing may be.*

Once Christopher got back and the three of them settled into a bed of dry pine needles for the wait, Evelyn's terror began to subside. "I thought the British were supposed to be landing on Throg's peninsula. Someone said they'd have a real fight to get from it to the mainland."

"That's right," Christopher conceded. "They're still there, or we'd have heard sounds of battle."

The words were barely out of his mouth before a series of cannon booms thundered one after another from the direc-tion of the mill dam . . . not much more than a mile away.

Evie's eyes flared in horror. "But—but how can that be? They just rode by us."

Christopher, with an earnest smile, wrapped an arm around her. "Pretty scary day, huh? Riding all this way just to learn your trust had been sadly misplaced in someone less than honorable, then being beset by lobsterbacks. But have no fear. On my honor as a gentleman, I'll die before I let any harm come to you."

Evelyn relaxed noticeably, leaned her head against his shoulder, and raised her eyes to his face. Though not the dark cobalt of Morgan's, her eyes were equally deadly in their soft, feminine way. "But where did the soldiers come from?"

"Most likely the scouting party landed many miles to the north and rode through the night to check us out from behind. But don't worry about them," Christopher added valiantly. "They're behind our lines. They'll have to ride fast and keep going if they don't want to be caught."

"If that's true," Prudence mused, "perhaps they've already broken off the chase after Robert."

"If they haven't already shot him," Evie said morbidly.

They fell silent. Evelyn huddled against Christopher, and Prudence positioned herself where she could get a fairly clear view of the bracken and the meadow beyond. For some time there was no movement other than a few squirrels scurrying about, busily gathering nuts and acorns for winter.

After what seemed the longest half hour in history, Prudence spied a lone rider coming toward them. Lady's white forelegs were unmistakable. *Oh, thank you, Lord,* she breathed. "Robert's alive!" She jumped up and ran to him.

Chandler grinned one of the fullest grins she had ever seen displayed on his normally serious face, and he reined toward her.

"Where's my horse?" Evie asked in dismay as she and Christopher joined them.

He shook his head. "Sorry, miss. I had to sacrifice him."

"Dead?" she cried in a high voice. "My horse is dead?"

"No, no. I had to send him off on his own to divert the scouts. I hid until they passed, then I took off in the opposite direction. I'm just glad I was able to find my own way back to this spot."

"But this is terrible," Evelyn moaned. "All my things. My brush, my soap, my clothes. They're all on that horse."

"Never mind, dear," Prudence said, moving near to comfort her. "We'll buy new things when we reach New York City. Until then, we'll share mine. And, of course, we'll ride double on Lady until we can find you another mount."

"In the meantime," Robert added, "Christopher and I will walk awhile longer with you to make sure you don't run into any more redcoats. Then you're to hightail it for the ferry."

He looked straight at Evie. "And there'd better not be any more of your tricks, young miss. You listen to your sister-in-law and ride straight to Perth Amboy and across the bay to Morgan. If I hear one thing to the contrary, you'll get the tanning of your life, I promise. Even if you're not *my* little sister."

His stern look softened when he turned to Prudence and handed her the reins. He put a hand on each of her shoulders and leaned close. "And you take care. You hear? Take very good care of yourself."

For a little while, Prudence had forgotten about the new life she suspected was growing within her, one she'd yearned for since her marriage to Morgan last spring. But Robert hadn't. And, she vowed, neither would she again.

❦ ❦

Robert could see and hear the battle taking place by the time he and Christopher jogged to the top of a rise on their way to rejoin the First Pennsylvania Rifle Battalion. They stopped to catch their breath after the long run and assessed the situation.

High tide had made the peninsula an island, filling in the marshy crossing, which existed only during low tide. Colonel Hand had positioned his men where they could best answer the British field artillery, and the flashes and reports from their rifles carried easily to Robert. But he could see that General Howe was trying to outflank the patriots on all sides. Scores of landing craft were still debarking enemy and equipment onto the neck from New York, and he knew their men-of-war also patrolled the Hudson on the other side of Manhattan.

"Looks like a pretty fierce battle over that way," Christopher remarked, pointing toward the near side of the neck. Causeways and a connecting bridge had been constructed between the peninsula and the mainland to create a milldam—a passage the British appeared determined to take. But twenty or thirty riflemen, high on the back side of a huge pile of cordwood from the sawmill, were doing an admirable job of standing them off. Not even the British cannonballs were making much of a dent in the woodpile.

"Of all the places Howe could've landed his men," Robert mused aloud. "Our battalion has managed to be positioned precisely where the British decide to land . . . two times out of the first three assaults."

"Then it must be more than luck," Christopher remarked. "From what everyone said, the First Pennsylvania did a masterful job of slowing down the British on Nassau . . . unlike those Connecticut boys who took off running at the first sight of redcoats when they landed on Manhattan. Washington must've had a fairly good idea that the lobsterbacks would pick this spot. And this time he wanted men he knew he could count on to stay and fight. That's us, Sarge." He started running again. "Come on," he tossed back. "I don't want to miss a thing."

Robert set off after him. He knew the lad couldn't miss much, considering the size of the landing force. He only hoped General Prescott didn't forget to send up the reinforcements he had promised.

With their line of troops strung out for more than a mile, Robert had no idea where the lieutenant might be. But he spotted Colonel Hand on horseback, riding along his line of defense. Though Robert knew he and Christopher had been gone for more than an hour, he headed toward the commander.

Hand caught sight of them and cut his horse in their direction. He came to an abrupt stop. "Looks like you're bucking for that commission real hard, Sergeant."

Robert gave a sharp salute. "Begging your pardon, sir. We had to outwit a British scouting party."

"*Where?*"

"About a mile into those woods, sir." He indicated the direction.

"I'd better let General Prescott know," Hand said, eyeing the west. "I trust the ladies are a good distance away from here by now." At Chandler's nod, he continued. "I've placed your platoon with Sergeant Morrison. Go out to the woodpile and help those men hold that bridge. Take fixings for at least two hundred rounds."

"Yes, sir!" *Two hundred rounds?* Robert thought incredulously. The colonel certainly was optimistic that they'd be able to hold the British at bay for quite some time.

"Oh, and Private," Hand said to Christopher. "Didn't you say you were a sharpshooter?"

"Yes, sir!" the lad cried, snapping to attention in youthful eagerness.

"Go with your sergeant," he said, jutting his chin in Robert's direction.

"But, sir . . . ," Robert argued. "He's never been under heavy fire before."

The colonel studied Christopher, then wheeled his horse. "Do me proud, son."

31

"Oh, I *do* hope this is the Dillard house," Prudence told Evie wearily as she slid off Lady's rump. "Being turned away at a wrong door once would have been bad enough. But three times? That exceeds mere humiliation!" Shaking her head ruefully, she held the horse's bridle while Evelyn dismounted, then looped the reins around a hitching ring in front of a large stone house.

Evie shoved a loose shirttail beneath the cinched belt of her oversized breeches and started up the wide steps. "Well, the directions the butcher's delivery boy gave me were so vague. Anyone might have misinterpreted them." Lifting the brass knocker, she rapped on the door, then rubbed at horsehair on her trouser leg in disgust. "I declare, I've never smelled so terrible in my whole life. The minute I get these filthy rags off, I'm having them burned."

"Yes, well, we'd best ask Morgan first." Eight days of travel had done little to dull Prudence's apprehension of facing her husband with an explanation for her uninvited presence. *Again.* And destroying his clothing would not earn points in her favor, either.

The door opened, and an impeccable manservant stared for an instant, then stepped back and withdrew a kerchief. He covered his long nose in distaste. "Those seeking work should go around back," he said, starting to close the door in their faces.

❦ 269 ❦

Evelyn propped her foot on the threshold. "Wait! We haven't stated our business."

He maintained his insolent glare. "Very well, then. State it and be gone."

"Is this the Dillard residence?" she asked, a defiant spark in her eyes.

"Yes, it is, young man."

"Oh, good!" Whisking her hat from her head, she shook out her thick curls. "Then you may run inside and inform Mr. Morgan Thomas that his sister and his wife have arrived." Elevating her chin, she pushed audaciously past the pompous servant. "But first, show us to the sitting room."

Regaining his dignity, the butler admitted Prudence also, then closed the door. "This way, if you please."

Prudence and Evelyn followed him across the wide entry to the first door on the left, which opened into a rather somber but quietly elegant open-beamed room.

"I believe you'll be comfortable in here," he said, turning to leave.

"Before you go," Evie said, "inform the housekeeper that I'll be wanting a bath. I'll perish if I don't get one soon. Tell her to heat plenty of water. For both of us."

Graying eyebrows rose high on his narrow forehead. "As you wish."

"How could you order the man about like that?" Prudence asked softly after he had exited the room.

"Like what?" the younger girl asked in mock innocence. "He is a servant, is he not?" She turned and casually began taking stock of the well-turned mahogany furnishings.

Despite Prudence's own anxious state, she couldn't help seeing humor and irony in Evie's conduct. The girl might consider herself in rebellion against everything her parents stood for, but what she didn't realize was how much she took the comfort of their position for granted. Not wanting to soil the lovely upholstery by sitting down, Prudence moved to stand by the cold fireplace.

Evelyn, however, plopped down on a wing chair. She

straightened almost immediately. "Wouldn't it be marvelous if our clothing has arrived already?"

"Ahead of us? I certainly hope not. Morgan would be sick with worry. We're four days overdue." Her hands turned clammy at the very thought.

"Oh, I wouldn't fret overmuch about my brother," Evie said with a sigh. "From the butler's surprise at our arrival, no one could have known we were coming." She caught her breath. "You don't suppose Mother is in such a temper she's refused to send our trunks! Whatever would we do?"

Prudence smiled to herself. The girl had certainly rallied from her disappointment over Jamie Dodd. A bit too quickly, perhaps. "We'd manage. In an emergency there are always the sellers of used clothing."

"*Used!*" Evelyn's big eyes widened in horror, and she gave a shudder. "They could be crawling with lice."

"When you fly out from under your mother's generous wing, dear, you can't always have—"

Running feet pounded down the stairs. Prudence felt her chest tightening with each footfall, and she gripped the mantel for support. Out of the corner of her eye, she saw Evie kick her tricorn under her chair. The younger girl was nervous, too, whether or not she would admit it.

The harried steps echoed across the parquet floor of the entry. Morgan burst into the room, his eyes latching instantly on Prudence's. "It's true! I can't leave you alone for one minute!"

"Two weeks," his sister corrected pointedly. She planted her hands on the arms of her chair. "You didn't write for more than two whole weeks. Then when you finally did, you had the audacity to tell us not to come. Well, *I* refuse to be ordered about by my brother."

After her tirade, Morgan refocused on Prudence, his face completely unreadable.

Prudence's mind went utterly blank. She knew she must look a terrible sight, her hair unkempt, clothing rumpled—she even smelled bad.

"You needn't blame Pru," Evie said in her defense. "She had the choice of either coming with me or explaining to Mother why I'd gone off alone. And, of course, with her being such a devoted 'big sister,' and all, what else could she do?"

"I see. And since you're masquerading about in men's clothing, I can also deduce that my permission was not the only one you lacked. Mother and Father must be quite livid. Traveling alone, no escort . . ." He narrowed his eyes. "And that waistcoat looks very familiar."

"That's not the half of it," Evie almost bragged, baiting him. "I left Prudence behind along the way and rode off by myself to find Jamie Dodd. I am a thoroughly willful and disobedient girl." Abruptly, she stood. "And now that we're all in agreement on the matter, I would really appreciate a hot bath and a soft, bug-free bed. Which room will be mine?"

Morgan's guarded expression turned to astonishment. He opened his mouth to speak.

"Oh, it sounds like that uppity butler is in the hall," she interrupted, starting for the doorway. "When can I expect my bath?" she called to him.

Prudence remained rooted to the same spot as Morgan followed his sister out of the room; then she bolted after them.

"Mr. Chester," Morgan said. "Please put my sister in the Dillard girls' room for now, since the other guest rooms are all occupied."

The servant's face registered the same disapproval it had earlier, but he escorted Evelyn upstairs.

Obviously the man thought it inappropriate to house a stranger in the Dillard family's private chambers, Prudence realized. Everything about her and Evie's arrival had been dreadfully wrong from start to finish. And there was yet more wrath to come. Sensing her husband's tightly harnessed fury, she could only follow him meekly back into the sitting room. She didn't want to look into his eyes and see the depth of his dismay and disappointment, but bravely she forced herself to meet his gaze.

To her surprise, his countenance softened, and he stepped close, cupping her cheek in his palm. "Sweetheart, you look frayed to threads."

She had expected anything but tenderness. Completely unprepared for it, her vision blurred with tears, and she reached out blindly for him.

He drew her close, rocking her in his arms. "It's much harder, is it not, when you have someone else to worry after?"

A chill tore through her. How could he possibly know about the child she was carrying? Easing back, she searched his face.

"From the look of you, my sister must have led you on quite the merry chase."

Immense relief surged through Prudence. "Yes. Quite."

"Well, dearest wife of mine," he said, scooping her up into his arms. "I want to hear every last detail. Even if—" His lips found her neck. "Even if it takes hours and hours. In fact," he breathed huskily against her ear, "I'd best have our supper sent to our room. It may take all night."

"And don't let them forget my bath," she whispered.

❧ ❧

One part of Morgan was delighted at having Prudence here with him, but that part warred with the rest. While she soaked off the layers of travel dust, she had related many alarming bits of news. Robby MacKinnon, dead! Chandler escorting Emily to Princeton. Young Chip Drummond now with Chan at the forefront of the colonial defense. The pieces tumbled over one another in Morgan's mind. But more often than not, anger at Evelyn surfaced to top them all. How dare that brat pull Prudence into danger, not once, but over and over?

Prudence rose from the tub and wrapped her shining, lithe body in a thick towel. After drying herself, she slipped into one of his long nightshirts, then took the seat opposite him at the small bedroom table.

Morgan noted the deep circles under her eyes. How much sleep had she lost chasing after Evie? As she ate with relish, he also wondered how many meals she had missed. Yet, his beautiful and beloved wife was here . . . not merely in the city of the enemy, but in the very house where three of them lodged!

"You're not eating," she said. "Aren't you hungry?"

Only now realizing that he hadn't touched his meal, Morgan picked up his fork and sampled the first bite. "Perhaps," he said after swallowing, "it's a good thing you stopped off at the Lyons' Den and met the good people who run it. Should anything ever happen to separate us here, I want you to go there at once."

Her light gray eyes clouded with alarm. "Not back to your family?"

He shook his head. "Nor to yours. Those are the first places the British would look. And make it a point to tell Evie not to mention a word about Princeton to anyone—especially Clay Raleigh. He's here, or didn't you know that?"

She smiled. "You don't think he would have left Evie without voicing loud objections to his father, do you?"

"I can well imagine," Morgan said scornfully. "He already puts on airs as if he's married into the family. I've been obliged to take several meals with the bloke."

"My, that is persistent of him, considering you can't abide the man."

"He hasn't seemed to notice," Morgan said with chagrin. "His presence, however, has created somewhat of a complication. Did I ever mention a Captain Long to you?"

Prudence frowned.

"An officer I first met in Boston. He had a very suspicious nature then, and has even more of one now . . . particularly when it comes to me. He's been prodding Raleigh for information about me. And there's this large gap of time, you see, between my departure from Boston and my arrival in Philadelphia."

Still frowning, Prudence tipped her head. "Does it matter?"

"It might to him. I've decided to tell him you and I took an extended—if unapproved—honeymoon to the Caribbean. One I'd just as soon my parents did not learn about."

"And you feel that will suffice."

Morgan shrugged. "Actually, now that you're here in the flesh, it'll be a miracle if he doesn't remember you from the night you were serving refreshments at that Christmas party instead of partaking of them as any pampered daughter of a Tory merchant should."

"He was there?" she asked in shock. "At the Clarkes' house?" Her fork hung suspended in the air. With a grimace, she filled it again. "I'm sure he wouldn't remember one serving girl from nearly two years past."

"I never forgot you," Morgan said softly. "Despite your plain attire, you were by far the most beautiful woman at the affair."

"And you, my dear husband," she said, covering his hand with hers, "are biased."

"Quite right." Standing, he pulled her up and slid his arms around her, relishing her fragrance, her touch, her essence. "And I'm madly in love. Have I told you, of late, how much I adore you?"

She circled his neck with her arms and smiled up at him. "You told me you loved my hair, when you were washing it, but the rest of me you left sorely in want."

"I did, did I? Well, we shall have to remedy that." He leaned forward for a kiss, but a knock on the door interrupted him.

"Morgan? Pru? Are you in there?"

"Go away," Morgan groaned.

Evie barged in anyway. "Sulk all you want. I have marvelous news for Prudence. See?" She whirled in place, billowing the skirt of an elegant gown.

Prudence moved out of his embrace and stepped toward her. "Where did you get that?"

She grinned from ear to ear. "There are three whole closets full. Come see."

Grabbing Prudence before she could follow, Morgan scowled. "What's going on here?"

"Clothes! Evie has found us some clothes." Pulling him along, she traipsed after the younger girl.

Entering the spacious, feminine chamber with three frilly

beds, Morgan saw an equal number of wardrobes . . . and each was full to bursting.

"I can't believe anyone would sail to England without taking everything they owned," Prudence uttered as she surveyed the closets.

Morgan nodded. "Seems I recall the young ladies bemoaning the fact that everything smelled of smoke. Their mother told them they could have all new if they'd be ready to sail before eventide. They departed the very day after the fire, sure the rebels were bent on the utter destruction of the city."

Prudence pulled a green frock from the closet and held it up.

"A tuck here and there," Evie cried, coming to fit it to her waist, "and it will do perfectly. Now we can go out in public at will . . . and this time I'm going to dance the night away. I've wasted so much time mooning over that worthless Jamie. I'm going to flirt with each and every dashing officer I see, while charming all their most important secrets right out of them."

Morgan remembered Prudence's explanation of Jamie Dodd's less than honorable departure from the army, and he also remembered that Evie had been utterly smitten. The lad had hurt her deeply, and now she was in a dangerous mood. He would have to keep a close watch on her.

"Speaking of information," Prudence said seriously, "we heard so many conflicting reports on our way here. How is the battle going? Do you know, sweetheart?"

"Actually, not too much has happened as yet. Washington was able to remove all his men from Manhattan without a hitch, except for the men he left at Fort Washington, overlooking the Hudson. Howe landed the bulk of his army on a neck across the East River, planning to cut off the patriot retreat. It was a perfect scheme. The British picket line already in place would hold the colonial troops to the upper half of the island, and the warships would stop them from crossing the Hudson. Howe's main force was to surround and capture them as they tried to flee across King's Bridge to

Westchester on the mainland. Simple. Deadly. But God intervened in his miraculous way once again."

"Well, sit down," Prudence pleaded, lowering herself to one of the beds. "Tell us the rest."

He complied with a broad grin. "Wait till you hear this. Howe's army is still on Throg's Neck, the peninsula where they landed two days ago. A mere handful of Pennsylvania Riflemen withstood an entire division of lobsterbacks for more than four hours, giving reinforcements time to move into position. The sharpshooters were hiding in a big pile of wood and couldn't be blown out, no matter what the British threw at them."

"That's right," Evie announced. "It was a huge pile. I saw it."

Morgan's mouth gaped. *"You saw it?"* He swung to Prudence. "Just how close to the shooting did the two of you get, may I ask?"

One look at his wife's guilty expression, and he concluded that she had left more than a few pertinent details out of her story.

32

"That appears to be everything." Emily dried her hands and hung up the dish towel. "The kitchen's finished for another day." She brushed a strand of damp hair behind her ear.

Mrs. Lyons sank to a chair. "And none too soon, either. These old feet of mine are killing me."

The twin girls Jasper had hired the previous week rushed to her and bobbed in a curtsy. "May we go, then, mum?" they asked almost in unison.

The innkeeper's wife raised an eyebrow as if doubting their enthusiasm. "I suppose."

"Oh, thank you!" The freckle-nosed redheads ran for the common-room door, wedging themselves through it together.

Emily smiled after them. "You're aware that the Branson boys are waiting outside for the girls, aren't you?"

Mrs. Lyons stretched out a slippered foot and wiggled her toes with a groan. "Not till now. Oh, to be that age again and have so much energy. And happy feet."

"Sounds like you could use a spot of tea. I'll fix us some." Emily poured the last of the hot water into the teapot, then refilled the kettle and suspended it over the fire again. "A pity for Sarah and Selina that the college is in recess for the war. Such fetching lasses should have more lads circling around them than they could shake a stick at."

"Well, it's only because classes are in recess that their pa decided to leave them here with us. When the fightin's over and he comes home, he expects his curlyheads to be returned to him as pure as when he went off."

"I'm sure Mr. Lyons and that squawky cockatoo of his will keep a sharp eye on them," Emily said, measuring aromatic leaves into a teaball and lowering it into the pot.

"Won't they, though," she said with a chuckle. "Not much gets by that pair. I'm purely glad the girls are such cheerful workers, though, and sweet, like you." With a gnarled hand, she patted the seat beside her. "Sit yourself down, love. It's time I told you what a good girl *you've* been."

"With those poor feet of yours needing attention, I think we can dispense with the flattery," Emily chided, too weary herself to be entirely serious. She got the tea fixings together and brought them to the table.

"It's not exactly flattery I had in mind a'tall. Just wanted to tell you how proud I've been of you these past four weeks. A good many women spend months, sometimes years, carryin' on when they lose their man. But you haven't been like that. Nobody knows better than I how much you loved your bonny Scotsman. And though your loss is no less than anybody else's, you've managed to let him go without fallin' all to pieces. I know you still have hurtin' times when you're by yourself . . . but you've been a real blessing to your wee ones. The rest of us, too."

"Well, don't put my name in for sainthood just yet," Emily teased. "I may have mouthed a lot of very brave things when I first came back, but every single day I have to remind myself that Robby's gone. I often find myself . . . resenting, if I might admit it . . . that he's with God instead of with me. Then comes the light of day, and I must spend half my time repenting of my sorry thoughts." With a melancholy smile, she poured some of the amber liquid into a cup for Mrs. Lyons, then filled another for herself.

"Well," the older woman said, her careworn face soft with understanding, "don't you fret overmuch about that. The

Good Lord gave us the capacity to love to the fullest and to ache with the loss. In his compassion for us, he understands."

They sipped in momentary silence, with Emily relishing the first rest they'd taken all day. Now that the mornings and evenings had grown chilly, hot tea was especially welcome and soothing whenever they had a chance to relax.

"Speaking of loved ones," Mrs. Lyons said, "I wish the stage wagons were still comin' in from New York and Philadelphia. Chip hasn't sent word home for ages . . . and the bits of news we hear aren't encouraging. I hope it's not true that our army's losing battle after battle, retreating deeper into the New York countryside."

"Christopher is with Robert," Emily reminded her. "He couldn't be in better hands."

The older woman frowned, wrinkling the skin beside her narrow hazel eyes. "Wasn't too long ago your Robby wrote to tell me he didn't think Robert Chandler cared a whit about livin' or dyin'."

Emily sighed. "I pray that isn't true anymore. But even if it is, I know he cares very deeply about his friends staying alive. He's a wonderful and thoughtful man." Catching Mrs. Lyons's odd look, Emily wondered if her words had been misread. But she had only expressed her honest feelings. Robert truly had been very thoughtful to her and the children. He *was* a wonderful person. Anyone who knew him had to admit it. If only he would return to the peace of the Lord, he could consider finding another nice Christian wife, one who'd bring out the best in him. He had been alone much too long. She took another drink, then heard the faint crunching of horseshoes on the gravel drive.

"Not another customer who'll be wantin' to be fed," Mrs. Lyons moaned.

Emily set down her cup. "I'll go see."

"No need, child. Jasper will let us know if a body wants something. We deserve a few quiet minutes to ourselves."

"Which don't come very often," Emily said with a light laugh, "since I arrived with my two children."

"Never you mind about them, love. Those babies are keepin' us old fogies young. Why, old Jasper's middle has trimmed down considerably from chasin' those kids around outside."

The door to the ordinary opened, and to Emily's joy, there stood her brother Ben. It had been months since he had delivered the silver bracelet from Robby.

"Ben!" She sprang up and ran to him.

"Hi, Sis. How've you been?"

"Best not ask her," Mrs. Lyons said, coming to her feet. "She's mostly too hard on herself. Anyway, these tired old bones need a good hug."

After he laughingly complied, she sat him down and dished up a plate of food. "Now I must see to that husband of mine. You two youngsters have a nice visit . . . and don't even think of leavin' tomorrow morning without a decent good-bye. Hear?"

"Wouldn't dream of it," Ben said with a wink.

Emily, so full of questions she couldn't think where to begin, eased down opposite him, waiting impatiently while he wolfed down a few bites.

"Sorry," he said, wiping his mouth. "I was starved. I haven't eaten since leaving Philadelphia. I wanted to catch you before you turned in."

"Philadelphia? You went down there without stopping here on your way?"

"Wasn't much point in it, not in the middle of the night. I was in too much of a hurry anyway. I had an important message to deliver to the Congress . . . and they dispatched me back to New York with the same urgency."

Emily gave a helpless shrug. "Riding back and forth that often, I can't believe you didn't stop to see me at least once during the month I've been here."

Swallowing the bite he had just taken, Ben shook his head. "That's what you thought? Sorry, but this is my first trip through New Jersey. I was sent north, to Fort Ticonderoga. The war up there is going about as bad as everywhere else.

The British have regained control of Lake Champlain, but not the fort . . . yet."

"What about Jane and Ted and the baby? Did you see them? Are they in danger?"

He shrugged. "So far the Crown seems happy just to have control of the waterway south from Canada. They don't have much of a force, and," he added with a chuckle, "I doubt they're too eager to take on those grizzly Green Mountain Boys. Speaking of danger, though, that's why I'm here. We'll be riding out of here at first light. Pack only four satchels. I'll take one of the youngsters with me on my horse, and you can take the other on yours."

"What?"

"I know Robby thought you'd be safer here than in Rhode Island. But as it turns out, you've ended up right in the path of the conflict. Washington has crossed the Hudson into New Jersey, and the British are hot on his heels. Rumor has it Howe wants to take Philadelphia before the first snow. Our forces will try to slow them up, make them turn back to New York for the winter. Whatever transpires though, baby sister, you are sitting smack in the middle between those two cities."

Emily blanched at the disturbing news. It wasn't at all what she had expected. "The war is going that badly?"

"That bad and worse. It seems Rhode Island was the safer place for you and your babes after all. When we reach Washington's army, I'll request a few days' leave and get you back home where you belong."

"Home . . . I'd like that." Leaving her family behind after Robby's death had been one of the hardest things she had ever done. She missed them so much but had not allowed herself to dwell on it. Now, with the prospect of returning to them, the ache she had managed to suppress came forth all the stronger. "Well, when we do reach the army, I must find Christopher and Robert, see how they are. It's only right I let Robert know that we're returning to the farm, and why. I owe him that . . . and so much more."

❦ ❧

Morgan stood beside Prudence at the entrance of the Dillard home as they greeted an arriving couple—a quartermaster at the division level and the man's sumptuously dressed, but rather homely, wife. "It's splendid that you were able to come this eve, Colonel Farrell, Mistress Farrell. It's such a pleasure to meet you both at last. May I introduce my lovely wife, Prudence?" He turned to her. "These are the Farrells, sweetheart."

"I'm so pleased to make your acquaintance," she said.

At her radiant smile, the tall, portly man lingered overlong above her hand after the perfunctory kiss, his expression revealing without words how taken he was by her exotic beauty.

Morgan swelled with pride. In bronze satin with ecru lace, her olive skin absolutely glowed. Prudence was always a joy to have nearby, but she was proving to be quite an asset, as well. For their first dinner party, he had chosen who would be included on the guest list with great care. The event was sure to be fruitful. Quartermasters and New York merchants. A perfect business gathering . . . and a perfect occasion for information gathering, as well.

From experience, Morgan knew that the high command made no move without conferring with their quartermasters. The merchants, of course, would be trying their zealous best to anticipate and provide the military's every need and desire.

Ah, yes, he said to himself as he greeted the next arrivals, a merchant and his wife. *A businessman would have so many questions to ask, so many answers to obtain.*

The tinkling sound of laughter—a little too cheerful—drifted from the staircase. As the New York couple moved on, Morgan was afforded an unbroken view of Evelyn coming down the steps, dressed to the nines and on the arm of Lieutenant Johnson, the one officer out of the three lodging at this residence who was not presently in pursuit of the Continental army with General Howe. Morgan was hard-pressed to concentrate on the next guests—one of General Clinton's quartermasters and his companion. Evie had managed to dazzle not only Johnson, but no less than a dozen other officers who had come to call within the past three weeks.

As Evie swept toward Morgan, her curls cascading from a ribbon in the same sage green as her velvet gown, he had to admit that she looked especially grown-up. If it weren't for the fact that she was his baby sister, and a contrary imp at that, he might even admit she was becoming a true beauty.

Stealing a swift glance at Prudence put Evie's appearance in proper perspective. He took a mental note of how uncommonly docile and agreeable his wife had been since her untimely arrival. He hoped it wasn't merely her way of smoothing over her most recent disobedience. After all, the harrowing experience had taught her a much-needed lesson. With his mind otherwise occupied, Morgan mouthed polite pleasantries to the quartermaster at hand.

Evelyn fluttered her lace handkerchief in a flippant wave at him as she and Lieutenant Johnson strolled to the music room, where refreshments were being lavished upon the guests. With the butler ill, Morgan found himself forced to remain at the door, which was especially harrowing this evening. Evelyn was becoming more and more impetuous, and he could not afford to leave her to her own devices.

As he was about to give in to the temptation to follow after her, he heard another carriage enter the drive. He grimaced and turned to Prudence. "Tonight we won't merely take turns overseeing Evie. We'll both make it a priority."

"But then you wouldn't be free to mingle," she replied. "Trust me, I won't let anything distract me from looking out for her."

He scowled. "Did you see that lowcut gown she chose for the evening? I'll take care of business and still watch her. Men are not above spiriting young misses off into hidden corners."

"And might I assume you speak from experience?" she asked, arching her slender brows high.

Morgan chose to ignore the question. "It's hard to believe my parents are so blind when it comes to Evelyn. In Mother's letter, instead of ordering the girl home, as any responsible parent would, she only encouraged Evie to be *devastatingly charming* to any *good prospects*. It's ridiculous. Completely ridiculous."

With a light laugh Prudence gazed up at him. "Your mother is every bit as astute at marriage prospects as your father is at the business ones."

For a few seconds Morgan lost himself in his wife's captivating smile. Dismissing his sister from his thoughts, he stole a quick kiss. When was the last time he had told Prudence how luscious and tantalizing her lips were? At the sound of footsteps outside, he reluctantly forced himself to release her. He opened the door.

"At last I get to meet the elusive Mistress Thomas."

Morgan felt the hairs on the back of his neck bristle. What in blazes was Captain Long doing here?

33

"I knew you wouldn't mind if I brought Captain Long with me," Prudence heard the other British officer say. So this was Captain Long, the very man Morgan had not wanted her to have any contact with whatsoever . . . and who now stared at her with such intensity. "My wife took to her bed with a chill this morning," the quartermaster went on.

"So sorry to hear that," Morgan said, and Prudence knew how seriously he meant it. He extended his hand to the interloper. "Marvelous that you could come in Mistress Buchanan's stead, Captain Long. As you said, you've yet to meet my beautiful wife."

The man's sly eyes roved up and down Prudence. "Ah, yes. Delighted, Mistress Thomas. And now that I've seen you, I'm convinced we've never met. You, my dear, couldn't possibly have been in Boston during my stay there. You'd have been the lone blossom among the weeds in that dreary town."

"Oh, aren't you the naughty one!" Prudence did her best to smile coyly even as she suppressed her anger at his pointed insult of her people. "Now, if you'll allow me to show you to the music room, Captain Long, I'll put your curiosity to rest."

She couldn't help but notice the color drain from Morgan's face as she reached for the officer's arm and accompanied him away. So courageous regarding himself, her husband seemed the complete opposite when it came to her. But after having rehearsed at least half a dozen times the story they had concocted, he must rely upon her ability to tell it convincingly. "I'll see that our latest arrivals get settled, sweetheart," she told him over her shoulder, "and then return directly."

"Yes, well, just don't linger," he said, his eyes speaking volumes. "There remain a few more guests I still wish to present to you."

Prudence walked slowly down the wide hall with the two officers. "I'm dreadfully sorry not to have been in Boston a sufficient time to relieve your boredom, Captain Long. But I'm afraid I, too, endure that same affliction whenever I visit my cousin's family there. Perhaps it's just as well they've all departed from the city now."

"And what family might that be?" he asked with barely veiled interest.

She was prepared for the question. "I presume you knew the Hutchinsons?" Casually, she eyed the exquisite Oriental vases on pedestals along the paneled hall.

"The governor?" His tone revealed mild surprise. "No, I didn't have the pleasure. Governor Hutchinson left the colony some time before I arrived."

"Oh, yes. He did depart rather suddenly, didn't he?" she said smoothly. "But he's once removed from the cousin I visited. There are quite a number of us, actually. But then, of course you've heard." She gave an artful titter. "One of the reasons the Bay Colony rabble wanted Cousin Thomas ousted was because he leaned so toward giving his family the best appointments and contracts."

"Yes. So I heard."

"The captain says that as if it's a crime," she said, turning with an elaborate show of dismay to the other officer. "If one may not express loyalty to one's own family, pray tell, what else might a person do?"

The quartermaster chuckled.

"Wars have been started for less cause," Captain Long returned. "But you say you're not from Boston. I assume, then, that you're from Philadelphia?"

"Oh, no. Baltimore." Morgan had already assured Prudence that with Clay Raleigh around, a close connection to Philadelphia could too easily be investigated.

Reaching the music-room door, the captain stopped and turned to Buchanan. "Why don't you go on in, Frederick? I'd like to chat with Mistress Thomas a moment more before joining you." When the man nodded and left, Long turned back to her, his pretense of mere curiosity a very thin veneer. "This is all quite confusing. Clayborne Raleigh informed me that you hailed from Boston."

"Clay said that?" Prudence elevated her brows innocently. "Well, that shouldn't surprise me. He's so smitten with my little sister-in-law, I do believe it's impaired his hearing—save for that desperately hoped-for word *yes*. The truth is, my husband was considered quite the catch in both Philadelphia and Baltimore circles. When I learned he'd gone to those cold and dull climes of the north, I knew—as you said yourself, Captain—a southern blossom is so much more noticeable among so many . . . weeds." She tittered again.

Enjoying her own embellishment of the story she and Morgan had fabricated, Prudence tilted her chin fetchingly and continued. "So, as one might term it, I set my cap for Morgan *and* very quickly succeeded where so many others before me had tried and failed." Having studied the way Evie unfolded her fan and peeked demurely from behind it, Prudence spread hers and gave a slow, ingenuous blink. "Of course, if you dare let word of this reach my handsome husband, I shall deny it to my very dying breath."

"Indeed." Amusement lightened the ruddiness of his face, and he patted her hand where it rested in the crook of his arm. "It was rumored he had returned home to his ill father, yet Mr. Raleigh said you'd only recently arrived."

Prudence knew he was baiting her, but she refused to stray from her fable. "Oh, yes. That. I do hope you didn't mention it to Clayborne. We led Morgan's family to believe he was still in Boston, caught in the trouble and unable to return home, while we went off on such a romantic adventure," she sighed.

"Married aboard ship, a glorious year strolling the isles of the Caribbean and on to his friend's plantation in North Carolina. But, alas, funds do not last forever. When they grew sparse, we could do naught but return to Philadelphia." She rolled her eyes the way she'd also seen Evelyn do. "Thus far, Captain, no one is the wiser."

He did not answer immediately. "I must confess, I find it rather strange that you would tell me, a veritable stranger."

"Yes, but you, my naughty man, have an unfortunate memory. I do hope you didn't leave Clayborne any the wiser." With a small smile, Prudence leaned closer. "Oh, well. Even so, this is not Philadelphia or Baltimore, now, is it? What possible harm could be done here?"

"Ah, my pretty. One never knows how soon you and I might find ourselves in either place." He picked a nonexistent piece of lint from his immaculate red sleeve. "And secrets can be such fun, don't you think?" Weasel eyes cut directly to her.

Morgan was right. The man was a scoundrel. The sooner she rid herself of him, the better. "That would, of course, depend," she allowed, preceding the captain into the music room.

"Upon what, my dear?" His smug expression all but turned her stomach.

"Upon whether one is the cat . . . or the mouse."

"Indeed." A low laugh rumbled from his chest. "Along that same line, I can't help feeling a great measure of gratification knowing that some of the most *vexing* mice in these colonies are about to be dealt with, and quite severely. General Howe is amassing a fleet even as we speak."

"Why, that is good news. And surely no more than the upstarts deserve."

"Quite. How I wish I could go along to watch them squeak and scurry for their holes. But, alas, duty forbids it."

"You're referring to Philadelphia, are you not?" Realizing that all pretense of small talk had fled her voice, Prudence quickly amended the question. "I do hope your loyal friends there will be given warning first. Morgan's mother, for one, is ever so terrified that, given the slightest excuse, the rebels will run amok and burn us out, as happened here in New York."

"Well, put your mind at rest, mistress." He took two drinks from a passing servant and handed one to her. "The 'City of Brotherly Love' is not our destination. *Yet*. We've chosen a far more prickly rebel camp. The Rhode Islanders have thumbed their noses at us for the last time. And in a matter of days, they'll rue their every lawless deed."

Rhode Island! A colony that considered smuggling an honorable profession, whose honest citizens had set fire to one of His Majesty's policing vessels, whose troops had taken the fort at the entrance of their bay from the British even *before* the battles at Lexington and Concord. Rhode Island—where the Haynes family lived. They must be warned!

It took supreme effort to remain calm and continue her game with the vile man. "Oh, who wants to discuss such tiresome matters at a party?" she asked, touching the tip of her fan to his chest. "Now that you know everything there is to know about me, I think it's only fair to tell me something about yourself. Where are you from? And in what capacity do you serve in our glorious military?"

As he opened his mouth and began rattling off inane nonsense about having a fleet of his own, Prudence only pretended interest while her mind wandered to Rhode Island's jeopardy.

". . . so I've been outfitting several empty vessels in the harbor to house the prisoners General Howe will soon be bringing me."

Prudence almost choked on a sip of punch as she swallowed too quickly. "You're expecting more prisoners?"

He sneered. "If the general will cease being so cautious."

Prudence latched onto her own opportunity to taunt. "From what I heard of the great slaughter at Boston's Bunker Hill, it would seem he's afraid to risk that sort of loss a second time—particularly against an army as ill-equipped as the rebels are reported to be."

The muscles in his jaw tensed. "And next, I suppose children in the street will also be talking about his cowardice," he snapped.

Prudence parted her lips in false shock. "Surely, sir, you didn't think I meant that."

Captain Long, with deliberate effort, managed to regain his composure. "You, dear lady, merely speak the truth. Four times within the past two months our commander has allowed the insurgents to slip from his very grasp . . . when he had only to close his hand!" He demonstrated the act with forceful ardor. "When the Crown learns of his ineptitude, I doubt he'll be in command much longer."

"Oh, dear, speaking of commanding generals," Prudence said, grasping at the chance to leave, "I'd better hurry back to mine. As much as I've enjoyed our little chat, Captain, I'm afraid I must excuse myself." With her brightest smile, she dipped her head and stepped out into the hall.

Word had to be sent to General Washington about Rhode Island's peril at once.

❧ ❧

The high midday sun warmed Emily's shoulders as she, Ben, and the children rode on horseback alongside the Hudson River Road, about twenty miles north of Manhattan Island. "That's probably Colonel Hand's camp," she told Ben at the sight of a huge assortment of makeshift canvas lean-tos and dugouts sprawling back into the trees along the high bank. "I told you it wouldn't take long to get here."

Ben, with Rusty nestled in front of him on Rebel's back, branded her with a brotherly scowl. "Half a day to Peekskill, *and* half a day back downriver. You know I can't be wasting entire days just to take you visiting."

"Oh, stop complaining. You were right beside me when I promised Mr. and Mrs. Lyons I'd find Christopher and tell him to write home. They need to know he's all right. If he's still . . ." Hesitant to suggest the alternative since Katie was riding with her, she just let the sentence dangle. "I should just be grateful you didn't have to obtain leave. Now, my patriot among patriots, you won't have to miss out on being in the middle of things for a single moment."

"Excuse me, but I'd call an entire day a little more than *a moment*. This pouch I picked up from Washington's headquarters was supposed to go directly to Rhode Island. Without delay, I might add."

Emily averted her eyes and shook her head. "I swear. I don't know how Abigail puts up with you."

"She manages quite nicely, thank you. Abby doesn't drag me forty miles out of my way on a whim."

As they reached the first clusters of tents, Ben nudged his mount ahead. Several unkempt and unshaven men stood around the various campfires, some warming their hands while others cooked the noon meal. The aroma from the boiling cauldrons was unidentifiable.

Emily's heart went out to the ragtag soldiers. Everyone they passed as they rode deeper into camp appeared equally beaten down, and she knew the nights could get quite cold this time of year. She couldn't help noticing that their little party was drawing considerable interest, as well. It was probably a rare event to have a woman with children casually drop in.

"We'll head for the banner sticking up over there," Ben announced, and reined his horse toward it. "Someone at the command tent should be able to tell us where Robert's group is positioned."

"We're here?" Katie asked in her high voice. "Hurry, Uncle Ben. I want to show Mr. Chandler my new shoes."

"And I'm hungry!" Rusty added, bouncing up and down in the saddle. "Hurry."

"Emily!" a familiar voice called. "Ben!"

Quickly scanning the area, Emily wasn't able to pick out a recognizable face.

"Over here."

Emily stared, puzzled, at the bearded fellow coming toward them. If he hadn't smiled, she never would have known him.

The whiskers made him appear much older than eighteen. "Christopher!"

"Uncle Chip!" Katie cried in delight.

The lad reached them, and Emily handed her daughter down to him. Then she quickly swung down herself and grabbed him in a hug. Her happiness made it hard to effect a look of reprimand. "A whole month has gone by, and not a word to the Lyonses. They're sick with worry, dear boy."

Slack jawed, the young man had the grace to look guilty.

"Mama," Katie asked. "Where's Mr. Chandler? You said he was with Uncle Chip."

Emily glanced around at the dozen or so men standing around the nearest fire. Robert was not among them. A fluttering in her chest surprised her as she whipped her gaze back to Christopher. "Where *is* Robert?"

34

"Don't fret, ma'am," one of the soldiers told Emily as he stepped from the campfire to join her and Ben. "The sergeant is around here somewheres. Probably just down the river washing up. He pays more attention to that sort of thing than some of the rest of us." He grinned sheepishly.

Christopher nodded. "We've been digging trenches near the bluff most of the morning. The sarge will be back any minute."

"Oh," she said with a nervous laugh. "You frightened me, Christopher."

"So," Ben remarked with a glance around. "You boys are spending your time here fortifying. That's good. But I don't think you'll have to worry about General Howe for some time. Being an express rider for Washington and Hancock, I get around. From the placement of Howe's men, he'll be going after Fort Washington on Manhattan Island next, and probably Fort Constitution across the river from it. No doubt he hopes to have the island completely out of our hands when he settles in for the winter. I'm sure if he had time, though, he'd love to blow our Continental Congress right out of Philadelphia. I'd say you're quite safe here, for now."

"Maybe," Christopher said thoughtfully. "But if the Canadian general takes Lake Champlain and Fort Ticonderoga before winter, he could sail down from the north quick enough. That's why we're here. To stop him."

"Whatever you say. But I just got back from the north, and believe me, Colonel Arnold put up one good fight, and against tremendous odds. He did lose the run of most of the lake, but not before doing plenty of damage to Carlton's fleet in the bargain. And I don't think Carlton will take Fort Ti, which guards the south end, any easier. Like I said, you're safe for the winter."

"Well, now," another soldier cut in. "Our officers at headquarters might be interested in hearin' that. Soon as we eat, I'll walk ya over."

Rusty squirmed in Ben's arms. "Eat. Goody."

"Come on, kid," Christopher said as the others laughed. "I'll dish up some for you."

"Me, too?" Katie asked, and latching onto Chip's hand, tagged happily along to the campfire.

Emily, hesitating, gazed toward the river. Robert still hadn't arrived. "Where's the trail down to the water?" she asked. "I'd like to wash some of this travel dust off."

"Right next to that split tree yonder, ma'am," another soldier answered with a knowing smile. "Just follow it, and you're bound to run into your sergeant."

A flush warmed her cheeks. Robert was not "her sergeant." Only a dear friend. People shouldn't be so quick to jump to the wrong conclusion. Turning quickly away, she started for the trail, then worked her way down the narrow pathway etched out of the bluff overlooking the river. Trees clung to the uneven ground with gnarled roots, stretching like old fingers across the trail, waiting to trip her. Jutting stones presented an equal hazard, but she continued on.

The swift-running river below looked like a black ribbon under the slate sky and dull November trees. She wondered if it might have been more prudent to have remained above with the men. There was no sight or sound of any wildlife or birds, nothing but the constant drone of the big river.

About halfway down, she could make out a man. Stripped to the waist, he was on his haunches, washing his upper body. Just imagining how icy the water must feel in such a chilly temperature gave her goosebumps. She couldn't deny that the fellow must be a stalwart sort. A few steps farther, and she realized it was Robert.

He'd given no sign that he had heard her coming. But then, considering how loud the current sounded, she wasn't surprised.

A tangle of vines and boulders blocked the path, and she had to climb over tumbled rocks to reach the bottom. She was only a few feet away now. He was still turned away from her as he picked up a piece of toweling and rose.

And then she saw them . . . angry red scars lacing his back. "Robert!" she gasped. "What happened to you?"

He spun around and stared. "Emily? How on earth did you get here?"

"Never mind me. Your back. What have they done to you?" When he did not reply, she drew her own conclusions, and her eyes burned with tears. She blinked them away. "It was because of us, wasn't it?" she whispered. "You were whipped for bringing Robby home. For taking me to Princeton." Aching inside, she tried to step around him for another look.

"Don't." He caught her arm. "Nothing I decide to do is ever your fault. Don't even think it."

"But—"

"No buts, Emily." As if suddenly remembering he was only half clothed, he grabbed his shirt from a nearby bush and shrugged into it, but he did not take his eyes from her. "You look . . . fine. Are you?"

"I'm managing. Everyone I know has been praying for the children and me, and that does a lot to get one through a sad time. It's . . . getting easier. And you?" she said with a thin smile. "How have you been? We haven't heard a word from you or Chip since that first week after you left. We've been worried."

"Sorry, I'll tell him to write more often."

"And will you, too? The children and I worry about your welfare every bit as much as we do his, you know."

At first it appeared as if Chan was about to say something.

But not a word passed his lips as his gaze remained fixed on her face. He reached for her hand and squeezed it lightly, encouragingly. "I think a lot about . . . Katie and Rusty, too. One of these days, perhaps . . ."

There was something in his expression she couldn't quite read, but new lines of care were already etching themselves into his forehead. She knew that he, too, must still be trying to get over Robby's death. They had been best friends. Or was it something else? The weight of more responsibility—he had been made a sergeant—or perhaps his obsession with Julia. "How about coming to see Katie and Rusty right now?" she asked brightly. "They're up above with Ben and Christopher. Probably eating your share of the food, too. They were quite hungry."

"They're here with you?" He broke into a smile, but it faded almost at once. "Tell me, why *are* you here?"

"Ben. He came by the inn and informed us that we were in the path the war is taking, so he felt the children and I should return to the farm for a while."

Robert shook his head gravely. "Being on the coast, Rhode Island is as vulnerable as it ever was, Emily. Promise me, if there's any hint of trouble—no matter how slight—you'll ride away from there at once." He placed his hands on her shoulders. "Promise. Don't take chances . . . with the children."

"Surely you know I wouldn't do that."

"Forgive me." Dropping his hands, he frowned and ran his fingers through his hair. "Of course you'll do your best for them. It's just that—I worry."

"Well, so do I," she said evenly, lowering her gaze. "Promise me you'll write me every week at my folks'. I need to know you're alive and well."

His lips narrowed, then relaxed. "I will, if you promise. We'll both keep our promises to each other, won't we." It was more a statement than a question.

Emily had to smile. "Yes, dear friend. Both of us. Well, come on, Katie and Rusty have been saving up hugs and kisses for you."

❦ ❦

The balmy Indian-summer day seemed a special treat to Prudence as she and Morgan, along with Evie and Clay and another pair of military officers the girl had charmed, took an afternoon horseback ride on Nassau Island.

"I'm ever so pleased you could get away from your business today, sweetheart," Prudence remarked. "Evie is certainly enjoying her new mare."

Even as she spoke, Evelyn raced up a rise with Clay Raleigh and Lieutenants Johnson and Kildare in close pursuit. A gust of wind caught the ends of her silk neck scarf, billowing out the long, emerald green strands like fronds of a fern against the clear blue sky.

Morgan grinned. "It was a capital idea of Lieutenant Johnson's, taking a ride here. With the unrest on Manhattan and the mainland so volatile right now, this is undoubtedly the safest place for my little sister to try out her new hunter."

The sound of Evie's merry laugh reached back to them as she disappeared from view over the hill, the others giving merry chase.

"I sometimes think she's wilder than I ever was," Morgan mused, shaking his head in wonder.

Prudence smiled. "Nevertheless, that matter with Jamie Dodd hurt her more than she will admit. I think she's bent on proving to herself that she's still desirable—even if it is with the enemy."

"I talked to her about it this morning over breakfast. Johnson hadn't come down yet, so it seemed the perfect time. I warned her again about the risk of holding too many tigers by the tail."

"How did she respond?"

"She didn't, actually."

Prudence had asked the question more out of relief than anything. She was thankful that he hadn't made an issue of her not joining them regularly at the early meal. Hesitant to confess the matter of her morning sickness, she had given the excuse of wanting to lose a few pounds . . . but from his reaction, she could tell he didn't quite accept it.

She really should tell him about the baby . . . but he would send her back to his domineering mother posthaste, no doubt about it, and Prudence couldn't bear the thought. What could it hurt for her to wait until after Christmas? Yet it was a subject she couldn't even pray about. The Lord would undoubtedly side with her husband. But she was being extremely cautious these days, doing absolutely nothing that would bring suspicion upon her or harm the baby. Even Morgan had praised her for finally finding her *good sense,* as he'd put it. Yes. Christmas. She would tell him at Christmas.

". . . I suppose she's right," Morgan was saying as they passed an abandoned farm. Having lost track of the conversation, Prudence hadn't the slightest idea whom or what he'd been talking about. "Evie says the competition only makes the men boast more, have looser tongues."

They came to the crown of the small hill and saw Evie and her admirers in a mad race across the stubbled wheat field below. Prudence had to smile at the sight of Clay Raleigh, whose bright peacock blue stood out in stark relief against the red of the officers' uniforms. "Poor Clayborne," she said, breaking into a giggle. "He must feel at such a disadvantage, not being in uniform. He gave Evie a very expensive brooch earlier this morning. I suppose he's hoping to buy her favor."

Morgan chuckled. "Ah, yes. The competition has become rather fierce. I'll wager Raleigh never dreamed he'd find himself vying for the affections of some mere colonial commoner."

"Of considerable wealth, my dear," Prudence finished.

"So be it. Did I tell you the idiot is even considering applying for a commission himself just so he, too, can strut around in a uniform? Not that anyone could parade more than Johnson or Kildare, since their army has taken the forts on the Hudson."

Prudence shook her head sadly. "And so many prisoners from Fort Washington. My heart goes out to them."

From the top of a distant hill, Evelyn waved.

The two returned the gesture as they watched her turn and disappear on the other side once more.

"I suppose there's one small thing that may come out of all of this in our favor," Morgan said. "Captain Long may be too busy with the prisoners to attend many of the social functions for some time. The cur's still making inquiries about me, like a bulldog chewing on a favorite bone."

"I really thought he had accepted my story." Prudence grimaced as their mounts plodded steadily onward. "And it's just dreadful, the thought of all those men cooped up on his ships. I'm just glad that Robert Chandler's battalion was not among them." Then another thought occurred to her. "Morgan, General Howe wouldn't ship our soldiers to England, would he? And leave them to rot in those horrid prisons?"

"I seriously doubt it. At least, not for a while. They're of much more value here—as bargaining chips for the return of any redcoats we acquire along the way."

"Then we must pray for a big victory. And soon." She urged gentle Lady to a faster gait.

"I'm afraid that won't happen unless our army can replace its losses," he answered, catching up. "I've hesitated to tell you this, but I've heard that Washington is down to about three thousand men. Too few to make any sort of stand. And Howe has a large force chasing after them across the New Jersey countryside. For now, all they can do is try their best to stay out of Howe's way until General Lee and his men from Fort Constitution can catch up. And Philadelphia has promised to send a couple of their militias."

Taken aback, Prudence glanced at him. "Where have all our thousands of men gone?"

He shrugged. "As their yearly enlistments are up, many are not renewing them. I know this is painful to accept, but short of a miracle, this war may well be over before the first snow."

"You don't mean that. Tell me you don't. How can so many simply walk away from our cause? our righteous cause?"

Morgan's helpless look was his only answer.

But it wasn't enough to quench Prudence's fervor. "If a miracle is what it will take, then that's what God will provide. He'll not forsake us." Spurring her horse into a gallop, she took the lead. "Race you to the top!"

His long-legged Thoroughbred easily caught up with her and beat her shorter Narragansett Pacer to the crest of the hill—just as she had known it would. But no matter. The challenge had put a grin on Morgan's handsome face, and it grew broader as he watched her drawing up to him. That in itself was more than worth the loss.

Abruptly his smile vanished.

Prudence followed his gaze. From this vantage point they could see the open sea, where upwards of thirty men-of-war were even now heading in a northerly course. The fleet Captain Long had spoken of was on its way to Rhode Island.

"Oh, Morgan. It's happening. It's truly happening."

He reached over and touched her cheek with his fingertips. "Washington may have lacked men to send to the aid of their militia, but because of you, my love, the people of Narragansett Bay won't be caught completely unaware."

35

Emily, astride a nineteen-month-old filly in the corral, breathed deeply of the crisp fall air as she put the animal through its paces. For several days the weather had been quite mild, but it was hinting at a chillier turn. She knew winter would be upon them soon, but she hoped it would be some time yet before the biting north wind made outdoor work miserable.

"Looking pretty good," her father commented from the next pen. He returned his attention to the foal he was teaching to walk on a lead.

Emily glanced over at him. It felt wonderful to be with her parents again, and even more, to be working outside with her father. Since their aged hired Negro, Elijah Moore, had taken to his bed with a bad case of rheumatism a few months ago, training of the foals and colts had fallen behind. With Mama, Abigail, and Elijah's wife, Tillie, occupied in readying the house and food stores for the season of bitter cold, neither Mama nor Papa had objected when Emily suggested taking on some of what were considered men's chores. In times such as these, rules had to be set aside. At least, that's what Mama planned to tell any neighborhood ladies who raised their eyebrows.

Emily pulled in on the reins and nudged the filly's flanks. "Back. Back."

For a few seconds Rosebud pranced nervously, then obeyed the command. "Did you see that, Papa?"

"I sure did. She's catching on quickly."

"She should be ready to sell in another week or so, don't you think?"

"Could be." He tugged his stubborn foal toward the fence that separated the corrals. "That'll make four. When you finish with her, I'll take her to Boston with the rest. One of the livery stables placed an order for two, and I shouldn't have a problem selling the others on market day. So many of the city's horses were slaughtered for food during the siege."

Emily sighed as he shook his head, the lines in his face deepening as his brow furrowed. The starvation that had taken place in the barricaded port would take years to forget. "The war's turning out to be longer and harder than anyone expected, isn't it?"

His brown eyes met hers. "I imagine they usually do, honey-girl. Let's just pray we've got what it takes to see it through."

Emily dismounted and pulled out a carrot to reward the young filly. "And let's pray this little one doesn't meet the same fate as Dan's poor horse. He told me taking dear old Flame to the butcher was the hardest thing he'd ever done." She watched her father's face cloud with sadness. He had also felt the loss of the faithful pacer, who had seen Dan through his days as postrider and courier. "I don't think I could have done it," she added softly.

"Well," Papa returned thoughtfully, "if they hadn't, they and many of their friends might have starved to death. One does what must be done for the good of all."

"I suppose you're right." Emily brushed a forelock from Rosebud's face. "But to look into those big velvet eyes and—"

A clatter of approaching hoofbeats interrupted her words.

Emily started for the fence. Papa unhooked the lead from the foal and went out the gate as Emily climbed the corral rails. Grady Lee, a cranberry farmer from down in the bogs near the bay, was coming down the lane.

"What's the big hurry, Lee?" Papa asked, coiling the rope. "Something afire?"

The craggy-faced man nodded. "The Brits are bombardin' the battery out on the island. A whole fleet of 'em." He paused to catch his breath. "Come to see if any of your young menfolk are at home."

"No." Papa moved closer. "But I've a musket and a brace of pistols. I'll fetch them and be right with you."

He held up a bony hand. "No, I gotta keep spreadin' the word. Folks are s'posed to meet down at the wharf in Providence." He wheeled his mount and galloped away.

Papa started for the house with long, fast strides, and Emily had to run to catch up. "Don't go. Please," she begged.

He slowed for barely a second. "I have to, Em. They're here. At the entrance to our bay."

"But-but what difference could one man make?" she asked, chasing after him again.

His steps did not slow, nor did he respond. When he reached the front steps, he turned. "I'll leave a pistol here. If the British make it into Providence harbor with a large enough force to take it while I'm gone, I want you to shoot the horses."

Emily stopped dead, stunned.

"Did you hear me?" he asked, his voice sounding hollow to her ears. "I'll not have my animals fall into English hands to be turned on our own people." Without further comment or delay, he slammed into the house.

Staring after him, Emily was unable to even consider obeying her father's order. She swung to gaze out over the serene pastures and the treasured herd of strawberry roans grazing placidly on the dry grasses. She could never do as he had asked. And the children . . . how would she ever explain such slaughter to her little ones, or to Abby's? No. The very idea was absurd.

She went inside, lingering beside the door to pull off her gloves. Her children and Abigail's were on a quilt on the floor before the parlor hearth, sharing a picnic lunch. The little girls chattered happily to one another. The boys were stuffing chunks of bread into cheeks already puffed. Emily smiled at the typical scene. Everything was as it should be. Until she knew more, she would concentrate on keeping things this way, concentrate on the children and the farm. Nothing else.

❦ ❦

In the dark of night, footsteps in the hall and hurried whispers roused Emily. Four tense days had passed since her father had left, and sleep had been hard to come by. He'd sent word to them just yesterday that it was unlikely that Newport, at the mouth of the bay, would be able to stand off the Crown forces much longer. Was it indeed lost? Had he come back?

Rising quickly, she threw on a wrapper and rushed out of the bedchamber. The hall was still dark. No one had lit a candle, but a strange light glowed from the window of Abigail's room across from hers, outlining her mother and sister-in-law huddled together. Papa was nowhere to be seen. "Is that the sun coming up?" Emily asked as she became aware of a drumming sound, distant and deep.

Mama turned. "It's Providence, Emily. It's under attack."

Newport had fallen. And now the British were within five miles of the farm!

Abigail turned slightly, the glow from the night sky glistening against her tearstained cheeks. "Ben told me to go to Worcester, to Caroline's, if the British came. I should have listened to him. I was such a fool. What if the redcoats have already landed troops?" She swallowed, and her voice rose in panic. "Emily, help me. Go saddle two horses while I wake my children."

"No, wait." Mother placed a hand on Abby's shoulder. "Cassie and Corbin will catch their death if you drag them out in this damp night air." She looked at Emily. "Ride to the hill and see if you can tell how bad it truly is. But be careful."

"But Mother Haynes," Abby cried. "Look. The whole sky is ablaze. I can't wait."

Emily, fighting her own fears, forced herself to speak calmly. "Listen, Abby. You and Mother get all the children up and dressed in good warm clothing. I'll go see what there is to see. If it looks really bad I can have horses saddled for you in no time at all." Then she hurried to her own room to change.

"What about you?" Abigail asked, following her.

"I can't know until I see what's happening. I'll decide then what has to be done."

Moments later, Emily galloped bareback out onto the road and up to the knoll. She couldn't even let herself consider the horror of destroying the herd. The concept had been so unthinkable that she hadn't mentioned it to her mother or Abby. They had been anxious enough in Papa's absence.

I cannot do it, she assured herself. *I could never do it.*

When she reached the rise, she could see beyond the hamlet of Pawtucket to Providence-Town. Her heart stopped. The constant glow of a burning city and flashes of cannon fire could no longer be denied.

Oh, Father in heaven, why is this happening? Only three months have passed since I laid my dear Robby to rest. I cannot bear it. No, she could not do as her father asked. Better to let the British have the animals.

But the picture of an enemy cavalry blazed across her mind, soldiers mounted on sorrel horses, riding deep into the countryside, pillaging, burning, murdering. . . . How would she justify that to her neighbors?

Her heart throbbed as she rode to the highest swell where her worst fears were realized. The bay was a bright orange reflection of the fires as smoke rose straight up into the night sky. Beyond, nearly thirty ships were strung out in Narragansett Bay, sailing onward toward Providence Bay. Longboats were already making for the shore on the south side, landing troops. Burning buildings blocked any view of the nearest warships, the ones even now bombarding the city. Providence was doomed.

A profound ache filled Emily. Where was the Continental

army? Surely such a huge fleet of English vessels couldn't have left New York unnoticed.

She had to drag her horrified gaze from the panorama below. *Dear Father, what am I to do? My children are in peril, and Abby's children. Mother. All of us. Everything.* Just before she turned away in hopelessness, another glow appeared on the horizon southeast of the carnage. The gathering dawn.

Straightening her shoulders, Emily turned her horse and raced for home.

When she reached the lane, she could make out a strange wagon and team parked in front of the house. The growing light revealed a haphazard load of household goods piled in the wagon bed. On the porch, a coarse-featured woman with children clinging to her skirts was talking to Mother.

Emily skidded the horse to a stop and dismounted, then ran up the steps. "What is it? What's happened?"

Her mother's bleak expression answered before she spoke the words. "Your father's been shot."

"Papa? He's—"

Mama rushed over, arms open, and hugged her. "No, dear. He's not dead. It's a leg wound. Mistress Lippet says he was taken to her house on the road to Providence."

"You're Emily?" the woman asked. "Your Pa says you know what to do. He's sorry he can't take care of things himself, but he's counting on you."

With each word, Emily felt herself sinking deeper into a chasm of hopelessness. Her blood was turning to ice.

"You young'uns get back up on the wagon," Mistress Lippet ordered. "We need to be getting along. The post road to Boston is already clogged with folks trying to escape, so I'm taking the Worcester road. I got kin in Brookfield. God be with you, Mistress Haynes."

"And with you, Maggie," Mama responded, embracing her.

"Wait," Emily said suddenly. "Please. Two minutes. Mother, hurry Abby and the children downstairs while I saddle their horses." She sought the stranger's face. "Mistress Lippet, my brother wants his wife and their little ones to go to Worcester, and I can't leave just yet. Would you be so kind as to allow her to travel with you?"

"Why, of course." Her smile was genuine. "Wouldn't mind the company a'tall. We womenfolk can look after each other."

Time did not allow for more than brief hugs and kisses those few moments later. Emily's sadness at the tearful good-bye was tinged with a measure of relief as she and her mother, arm in arm, dabbed at their eyes and waved after their precious threesome. Now at least Abby and her children were taken care of.

"Bye, Cassie," Katie called long after they were out of ear-shot. "Bye, Corbin."

Mother sighed. "I don't understand why you didn't go with them. I'm sure you could still catch up, if you hurry."

Emily turned to her children. "Katie, you and Rusty run upstairs and bring me all the blankets off your beds. Hear? And hurry."

Her daughter's eyes rounded, but without a word she grabbed her brother's hand and tugged him into the house. The two had been unnaturally quiet. Emily knew they must sense that something was very wrong.

She made herself look straight at her mother. "Papa wants me to shoot the horses."

"What?" Mama's hand flew to the neck of her night shift. "He couldn't."

"He doesn't want the British to get them." Emily swallowed a lump in her throat. "But I can't do it, Mama. I just can't."

"No, of course not. And neither could I." She frowned, her gaze flicking toward the barn and corrals. "We'll open the gates, turn them out. Then you can catch up to Abby."

Emily shook her head. "No. It wouldn't do any good. They'd only come back . . . unless . . ."

Her mother took her by the shoulders. "Emmy. Listen to me. Those horses have been our livelihood, but a hundred herds could never take the place of you or those dear little ones. Please, dear, do as I ask. I must go to your father now, this minute, so promise me."

"I-I will." Even as she uttered the oath, the echo of the vow she'd made to Robert Chandler not three weeks ago flew into her thoughts. "Help the children get their blankets and clothes downstairs, would you, Mama? I'll hitch a horse to the cart. That way you'll be able to move Papa to some safer place, if need be. Remember, the two of you are as precious to us as we are to you."

Her mother took Emily's chin with trembling hands and bent to kiss her forehead. Emily knew her mother's heart had to be pounding with the same intensity as her own. "If he can travel, I'll try to convince him to go to Caroline's, too." She made an attempt to smile. "I doubt he'll agree to abandon the farm he's worked so hard for, but I'll do my best."

For a moment Emily debated whether or not to voice her thoughts aloud. "Mama, what if I could get people along the road to help me drive the horses to Worcester?"

Already halfway inside, her mother stopped. "I don't even have the time to consider something so insane. Remember your first responsibility—the children. That's all I can say." She went into the house, and the door closed behind her.

"The horses are far more than our livelihood," Emily whispered. "They're our responsibility, too."

Working quickly, she hitched the cart for her mother, then saddled two of the horses. Two others she rigged for packing. As she led them to the house, her mother came out, one arm loaded with her own blankets, the other curled around Emily's valise.

She dropped the case and hurried to the cart parked at the end of the walkway. "Whatever happens, I'll contact you at Caroline's. The Lord will see us through." She threw the blankets inside, hugged Emily once again, then climbed aboard and snapped the reins. "God be with you." The horse took off at a fast pace.

Emily, knowing that her mother was even now headed straight toward the enemy, wanted with all her heart to call her back. But it wouldn't have stopped her, and there was no time to dwell on her own mounting fears. *I'll have to trust both of my parents to your care, dear God. Please surround them with your angels. Keep them safe. And help me do what I must.*

As quickly as she could, she got Katie and Rusty situated atop Papa's gentlest gelding. Then, with the pistol tucked into her saddlebag, she mounted their most valuable stallion. "Wait right here," she told the children with a firm look. Then, with another desperate prayer, she steeled herself to accomplish the impossible. She unhooked the first pasture gate and rode in to drive the horses out onto the lane, then did the same in the remaining corrals until all were empty.

The quarter-mile fenced lane to the road now held sixty horses and provided a central corral. But at the sight of the rambunctious animals, she wavered. The grand dream of rescuing the herd revealed itself for the staggering impossibility it truly was. There was no way on earth she would be able to see it through.

I can't do this, Lord. Not by myself. But neither can I shoot them all or leave them here to be confiscated by the British. You're going to have to be our shepherd. Take us to your green pastures and still waters.

36

"Yee-hah!" Emily yelled.

Many of the horses flicked their ears in her direction, but they continued to mill about.

She snatched her whip from around her pommel, let it uncoil as she nudged her mount forward, then cracked the lash overhead. "Yee-hah!"

Those at the rear bolted for the others. Most of the herd was now on the move.

With a surge of optimism, Emily turned and smiled reassuringly at Katie and Rusty on the gelding behind her mount, then gave the whip another sharp snap.

This time the horses at the front started to move, too.

"Turn right!" Emily shouted to those running out onto the road—as if they could understand her. "Turn right! *Right,* I said!"

But they barreled straight ahead. Crossing the road, they galloped into an open field, one that Emily knew ended at a tangle of brush and trees bordering the Blackstone River. Blast. Trapped at the rear, she could hardly get to them.

But this was no time to be disheartened. Once she was out in the open, she would be able to turn them. She had to.

Too soon she discovered how wrong that notion was. Most of the pacers headed right into the thicket. And try as she might for the next two hours, she had yet to make any progress with the unruly creatures. No sooner would she flush one group out of the brambles than another would move in to take their places—lured by a number of volunteer apple trees among the native vegetation. She blew a wisp of hair from her eyes in disgust. It was useless. This job required more than one person.

Emily glanced toward the children, playing contentedly a safe distance away beneath an oak where she had tied their gelding. The packhorses munched serenely on the surrounding weeds. But the smoky sky and the dropping ash were constant reminders that she couldn't delay much longer. With a last utterly frustrated glare at the wandering sorrels, she rode over to her son and daughter. "Grandma was right. I can't do this by myself."

"I can help, Mama," Katie said bravely, standing as tall as her three-and-a-half-year-old frame could stretch. "Let me help."

"Me, too," Rusty chimed in.

Emily attempted a tender expression. "That's very sweet of my two angels. I know you would really like to help, but I've been given very strict orders not to take any chances with you." Maneuvering her mount next to one of the packhorses, she unhooked a long coil of rope. "I'm going to string three or four brood mares together. With those we already have, we'll have six. That will have to do. And I'm already on the best stallion." Suddenly aware of the silence, she looked in the direction of Providence. The cannonade had stopped. A bad sign. "Stay here now, and be good. That's the most help I could ask. I'll try not to be long."

Perusing the scattered herd, she tried to recall which brood mares were the youngest. She spied one of them, some yards off, craning its neck to reach a shriveled apple still dangling from a leafless tree. Slowly she reined her mount toward it at a nonthreatening gait, fashioning a lasso from one end of the rope as she went. But when she neared the mare, it shied away and crashed into the thicket, still chomping on the apple.

Emily knew that that particular mare had birthed two sets of twins in the past four years, and she was not about to give up. She rode doggedly after it into a patch of briers. The woolen divided skirt Mother had fashioned for her, to be more "ladylike" than men's trousers, snagged on a sharp branch and made one more tear to go along with those she'd already acquired during the past couple of hours. Shrugging off the damage, Emily saw that the horse she was following now seemed more cooperative, especially with most of its interest centered on a bounty of fallen apples under another tree. Moving stealthily up on it, Emily managed to snag the valuable mare.

One down. Cutting off a length of the rope, she tied the animal to the tree, then headed out of the brush in search of another. Emerging from the thicket, she glanced toward her children to be certain they were still safe.

The spot where she'd left them was empty!

Her heart froze. Soldiers? She slapped the reins across her pacer's neck and charged toward the road, searching both directions as she went.

A piercing whistle came from behind her. Almost unable to breathe for the constriction in her chest, Emily swung in the saddle.

About a hundred yards away were two riders. Neither, thankfully, wore a red uniform. She could also make out Katie's royal blue coat and Rusty's brown one. Men on horseback must have found them wandering. *Thank you, Father. Oh, thank you!* And now if the Good Samaritans would help her get all the horses on the road and headed in the right direction, she might still be able to manage.

About halfway to the approaching riders, they began to look amazingly familiar—like Robert Chandler and Christopher Drummond. It had to be her imagination. But—how could it be?

It didn't matter. With a squeal of delight, she heeled her stallion into a gallop and raced toward Robert, who at the same time urged his horse to canter toward her. They came to an abrupt halt beside each other. She seized his outstretched hand—the only thing she could reach from the saddle. "I don't believe it. You're here. The army has come to save us after all!"

Robert's mouth curved into a smile. "You and the kids look really fine," he said, not releasing her hand. "Katie says you're on your way to Worcester?"

Laughter bubbled out of Emily. "Yes. That's right." She took in the children's beaming faces, then glanced down the road once more. "Where are the rest of the riflemen?"

Christopher, too, arrived and brought his horse into the little circle. "Well, Em," he said jokingly, "it would appear you're not quite the horse expert you led us all to believe."

Emily hiked her chin. "Say anything you like. But if the two of you—and any more of your men you can spare—would help me round up Papa's horses . . ." She frowned, searching the distance. "Where is everyone, anyway?"

Robert shrugged with chagrin. "I'm afraid, dear girl, we're all there is."

"Oh, of course," she said, apologetic. "They've gone on to Providence. I'm lucky they could part with you. Do you think they'll be able to stop the British?"

Robert and Christopher exchanged a glance, then Robert's eyes locked on hers. "The army isn't here, Emily. Only us."

"But-but how can that be?" she asked.

"A couple days ago," Christopher answered, "I overheard some lieutenants mention the fleet that had sailed for Rhode Island. There we were, in some backwash of the war, doing nothing, yet no one could be spared to aid the Rhode Islanders. They'd heard that the militia guarding the bay had been put only on special alert, nothing more. Headquarters didn't want the Rhode Islanders to panic."

"Panic?" Emily echoed in angry disbelief. "We're not given to panic, I can assure you."

"And neither are the Pennsylvania Riflemen," Chip returned. "We held the English at Throg's Neck for four days. If they'd have let our battalion come, I'll wager those lobsters wouldn't have sailed into Providence with such ease. Right, Chan?"

Robert nodded. "But four hundred men can do only so much, lad. All we would've done was exact a higher toll from the redcoats. Nonetheless, our Colonel Hand felt so bad about the matter, he gave us permission to come help you. I have to admit, though, I did exaggerate a mite, telling him that you, a woman, had been left to run an entire horse farm by yourself."

With a droll smile, Emily made a sweeping gesture with her arm. "Well, as you can see, it was no exaggeration. The minute Papa heard about the invasion, he left and hasn't returned. In fact, he's been shot in the leg. Mother has gone to him."

Robert's smile quickly faded. "I am so sorry, Emily. And I'm doubly glad your father was no more eager than you are to hand over your horses to the enemy."

Christopher's face had taken on a look of amusement as Robert talked. His smile broadened. "There's more to it than that. Chan made a deal with Colonel Hand. Promised that if he'd give us leave to come move the herd, Chan would accept a commission as an officer when we return."

"You did?" Emily asked in amazement. Was this the Robert Chandler who, according to Robby and Morgan, had shunned all responsibility from the day he left his family plantation to come north? And perhaps, she suspected, for even longer than that? She shook her head in amazement. "I'll be forever in your debt."

Robert's gaze slid away as if he was embarrassed to be the recipient of her undying gratitude, but he quickly recovered. The edge of his mouth twitched into a partial smile. "I wouldn't be so free with your indebtedness just yet. We've still got to flush these nags out of who knows how many acres of brush. Oh, and which way do we point them?"

"That way." Emily pointed north.

"Wait a minute. Isn't Worcester between Albany and Boston?"

"Yes."

"Surely you have somewhere else you can go. If the British do succeed in pushing south from Canada before the freeze, they just might send a force across to take Boston from the rear. You might be no better off there."

Emily's shoulders sagged.

"I know a good place to take them," Christopher interjected. "To Dan and Susannah. The war will never reach that far into the Pennsylvania mountains. The Wyoming Valley is too remote for the British to bother with."

"But that's hundreds of miles from here," Emily said, her hope dwindling further.

"Well, last time I visited my sister and her husband there," Christopher replied, "I dropped by Dan's, too. He figured it's only about 350 miles away. That's not so far. Wouldn't take more than a couple weeks at most. And then the herd would be safe, wouldn't it?"

The more Emily thought about the idea, the better it sounded. "He *is* the oldest son," she said. "They belong with him far more than they do in Worcester with our sister's husband."

Robert held up a hand. "Hold on, you two. Aside from the major undertaking this venture would be, considering there are only three of us—and two small children besides—every last head of these horses will have to be ferried across the Hudson."

No one spoke for a few seconds until Christopher broke the silence. "We could drive them farther upriver—to Peekskill, where our battalion is. We could get them across on some of those flatboats our men have been building. If we offer the colonel a few head, I bet he'd get us ferried over quick enough."

Robert glanced around at the scattered pacers, a thoughtful expression pinching his straight brows. "You could be right." He turned to Emily. "But it's already December and getting colder all the time. How will your little ones fare out in the open for who knows how long?"

She slowly exhaled. "If I keep them dressed warm during the daytime, we should be able to find folks along the way who'll put us up at night. They'll be fine. I only wish Papa were here to make the decision."

"Mama?" Katie said, her voice unnaturally high. "I heard you tell Grandma that Grandpa wants you to shoot all our horsies."

"I'm so sorry you heard me talking, angel. Grandpa was very sad when he told me to do that. He wasn't being mean. He just didn't want the king's army to take them away, and he knew I couldn't move them all by myself. You saw the mess I made when I tried."

She giggled.

"But come to think of it," Emily went on, "I know Grandpa would be very happy if they were all safe with Uncle Dan." She took another breath and smiled at Robert. "If you're willing, let's do it."

37

With an aggravated sigh, Prudence went to answer the door. Again. Entertaining every afternoon was becoming a tedious ritual. Evelyn had given half a dozen soldiers and some merchants' daughters a standing invitation for tea . . . and of course there was always Clayborne Raleigh forever underfoot.

Her hand on the latch, Prudence assumed a bright smile and opened the door, recognizing the beaming officer immediately. "Oh, good afternoon, Lieutenant Crider. Do come in. Evie is in the music room with a few friends."

"Thank you." The muscular young man with a pronounced underbite bowed politely over her hand, but it was not hard to see that his attention was on the merry chatter coming from the far end of the hall. No doubt his thoughts were already on the lovely Evelyn, who was fast becoming adept at using those extraordinary Thomas eyes to their very best advantage.

Ushering him to the small gathering, Prudence took note that there were now three officers, Raleigh, and the two Deerfield sisters present. She would inform the cook. With the household understaffed since so many of the servants had sailed to Britain with the Dillards, Prudence found herself doing whatever she could to help out.

"Mistress O'Malley," she said, entering the cluttered kitchen. "We'll need refreshments for seven."

"Aye, seven it is this time, is it?" the frazzled Irishwoman said, blotting her forehead with the long sleeve of her work dress. "I'll see what's in the pantry."

After watching the cook bustle away, Prudence took two silver trays from one of the shelves. She gathered the tea service and set it out on the first, then continued with the tea preparations.

"Ah, here we are, lass," Mistress O'Malley said, returning. "There were still currant scones left. They should do nicely." She covered the remaining tray with a crisp linen square and arranged the baked treats in a circular design. "I think that's adequate. And I dearly appreciate the extra pair of hands."

Prudence returned her grateful smile, and the two took the refreshments to the music room, where Evelyn was playing the pianoforte for a duet sung by Melanie and Priscilla Deerfield. Around the room in ornate French chairs, the young men sat in rapt attention. The scene brought back the memory of Prudence's own musical debut. It was with no small relief that she had now put considerable distance between herself and Mother Thomas's unyielding demands.

Prudence set the tray on one of the smaller tables, then began to serve the tea.

"How about this one, Melanie?" Evie asked, flipping through some song sheets. 'Tender Rose, Flower of Love' is all the rage back in Philadelphia."

As the girls tittered among themselves and then attempted the number, which was obviously new to them, Prudence served Clay his tea. He flicked a glance up at her, and she offered a sympathetic smile. Accepting his drink, he winked, as if the two of them shared a secret. Prudence wondered why the young man still bothered to visit, with Evie neglecting him more and more. But, then, the competition of other eligible bachelors increased the value of the prize.

Returning for the next cup and saucer, Prudence did her best to maintain proper posture. Her bouts of morning sickness had ceased now that she was three months along, but her dresses were starting to feel tight around her waist. Odd that Morgan hadn't mentioned the subtle changes in her figure as yet. Dared she hope she'd make it past Christmas before telling him about her condition?

She shook off the troubling thought and stirred sugar into the next cup.

Melanie Deerfield fluttered over to her and helped herself. "Dear Mistress Thomas, you are such a godsend. I'm about to perish from thirst." She fanned herself for effect with her free hand as she returned to the pianoforte carrying her tea.

Judging Melanie's age as hardly a year less than her own, Prudence stifled an inward grimace at being referred to as Mistress Thomas. It made her feel as old as Morgan's mother. But then, her function here was more to chaperon than to enter into the gathering.

Evelyn snatched a cup of plain tea and added her own sugar with a sly smile while the Deerfield girls took seats among the men. Then Evie sashayed back to the instrument and leaned artfully against it, sipping her drink. Prudence knew it was a bold command for attention.

"Where is your brother this afternoon?" Clay asked Evie.

She toyed innocently with one of the shiny brown ringlets dangling beside her ear and deferred to Prudence. "Sister?"

"He should be home shortly," she answered. "He went to see the harbor master, hoping to expedite a sailing permit for a vessel belonging to a Philadelphia merchant." *One of the prime reasons that the colonists revolted in the first place,* she restrained herself from adding.

"Oh, the business of shipping is so tiresome," Evie sighed with a wave of dismissal. "So many rules and regulations, endless forms one must fill out. . . ." She sauntered up to the nearest pair of soldiers. "Particularly when we could be celebrating our latest victories. Do tell us, Lieutenant Crider, is there any more news? Has our good General Howe crushed those nasty insurgents yet?"

Don't be so obvious, Evie, Prudence thought, watching her cozy up to the military man.

But Crider merely straightened his spine, densely unaware that he was being used. He even appeared honored at having been singled out. "I do have some news regarding the cowardly rebels that you might find interesting."

As he continued, Prudence's mind drifted to Captain Long. If Morgan had not managed to arrange their social functions to avoid the scrutiny of that overbearingly distrustful man, save for that one tense evening, she and Evie wouldn't be able to probe so freely.

"And that's another matter," another of the officers was saying as Prudence's thoughts returned to the present. "The blasted rebels refuse to stand and fight like men. They're naught but a crafty lot of cowards."

"Aye," Lieutenant Crider affirmed, not to be upstaged. "Snipers sneak close at night, picking off our lads. In the light of day, however, they manage to stay at least a day's march ahead of our troops. General Howe's force is chasing them all over New Jersey. I just wish I could be there when we catch the blokes, rather than being stuck here in New York."

"Oh, but, Lieutenant," Melanie cooed coyly. "We would be deprived of your most charming company." She fluttered her pale lashes.

As if he hadn't heard the smitten young woman's thinly veiled hint, Crider turned to Evelyn, but she was casting an interested glance at the slightly less outspoken Lieutenant White.

"I'm sure the general has a plan," White assured her, his smile little more than a slash in his painfully thin face. "He has not failed us thus far."

"Well, I do so hope it's a clever one," Evie gushed, drifting back to the pianoforte. As she took the stool and brushed her fingers lightly over the smooth, yellowing keys, Lieutenant Crider rose and followed, spewing forth his calculated guess regarding Howe's plans. The other girls and Lieutenant White weren't far behind him.

Prudence found it quite amazing the way Evie managed to draw them all to her at will. All except Clay Raleigh, that is, who came to join Prudence on the other side of the room. "I wouldn't concern myself about those young officers," she reassured him. "Evie is merely flattered by all their attention, nothing more."

He turned a disinterested glance at the group, then shrugged a shoulder. "Yes, she's still quite young. Rather impressionable, as well. When these buffoons leave, I'll simply show them for the fools they are by telling her what General Howe's actual plans happen to be."

Trying not to reveal her own interest in his statement, Prudence wondered if the Englishman truly did know something of value. Morgan had told her Clay socialized with the higher ranking officers fairly often—far more than the two of them were able to do, since they had to avoid Captain Long as much as possible. "Now you have intrigued me, Mr. Raleigh," she said, her voice casual.

He gave her a calculating smile. "You shall have to promise not to breathe a word. Those fools—" he indicated the military guests with a jut of his chin— "would undoubtedly blab it all over the city."

"My lips are sealed," Prudence murmured, placing her hand over her heart as if in oath. "And whom, pray tell, would I pass it on to anyway?"

Apparently satisfied by her sincerity, Raleigh bent closer. "The general is merely pretending to play the rebels' game of cat and mouse. Once they're all ensconced deep in New Jersey, he'll abandon the chase and march his men to Philadelphia before Washington can so much as get wind of it and set up a defense. And in the bargain, Howe will capture most of the Continental Congress." Thus said, he leaned back again with a conceited expression.

"Why, that's . . . brilliant," Prudence managed, stunned. "I only hope, for the sake of my in-laws, it will be a peaceful takeover."

"General Howe is a most civilized man. You needn't trouble yourself. And then the general will control the two major ports before the first snow. After all, your Boston is all but finished as a port already."

Prudence flashed a disarming smile and touched his arm.

"I can see why you've been sitting here with such confidence this afternoon. Evie will surely be impressed by the amount of trust the leaders place in you—a trust, it would seem, far beyond what they bestow upon their own junior officers."

With a tip of his head, Raleigh demurred slightly. "A trust enhanced by their appreciation of a good cigar."

At the sound of someone in the entry hall, Prudence hoped it was Morgan and not another guest. "If you'll excuse me, I believe someone's at the door."

Walking quickly out, she raised a hand to prevent Morgan from proceeding farther and placed a finger to her lips. Then, with a glance over her shoulder to make certain no one else had ventured out of the music room, she took his hand and led him upstairs.

This information was much too important to delay.

❧ ❧

Morgan didn't bother with the pretense of amenities as he eyed the barkeeper of the Dog's Head Tavern, on his way through the common room and out the back door. The information Prudence had related to him was crucial to Philadelphia and the Continental Congress. Everything was at stake. Messages had to be dispatched by land and by sea. No chances could be taken.

Behind the tavern, he paced impatiently, waiting in the chill December dusk. Tonight. The messages had to be sent tonight, even if he had to ride to Philadelphia himself.

What was keeping that bartender? Turning, Morgan tried to will the door to open. But to no avail.

If he did take upon himself the role of courier, Prudence and Evelyn would be left alone in New York. Perhaps the barkeep knew a trusted man who might be sent to look after them. One who could pretend to be an uncle from out of town or something.

Show your face, man!

Morgan hoped fervently that Prudence had followed his instructions, made whatever excuses it took to rid the house of all guests. He didn't want *anyone* to linger, not even for supper. She had to know the importance of—

The back door squeaked open, and the barkeeper emerged.

Morgan expelled a breath and gestured for the burly man to follow him behind the storage shed. With relief, he heard him comply.

"What's up?" the barkeep muttered.

"Washington is playing right into Howe's hand. General Howe will chase after our army only until they're deep enough into New Jersey, then he'll break away and make a beeline for Philadelphia. And, I'll wager, the fleet Howe sent to Rhode Island is on its way south as we speak."

"Why would you think that? Won't the Brits want to hold on to the city?"

"No doubt Howe will leave a policing force there, but his reason for going to Providence was more punitive than strategic."

"Yes. A great plan, that." The words came from out of the darkness!

Morgan wheeled. *Long!* The captain stood no more than a rod away in the fading light, a pistol in his hand.

The barkeep broke and bolted down the alley.

"After him, men!" Long shouted. His single-shot weapon remained fixed on Morgan.

At the sudden sound of more running feet, Morgan searched the growing darkness. "Tell Pru!" he yelled, hoping against hope that the barkeeper heard him. As he looked back at his captor's gloating sneer, Morgan prayed with everything in him that the barkeep would somehow elude his pursuers and reach Prudence—and that she would do exactly as she had been instructed in the event that they were exposed.

"So," Long said, the word taking on the menace in his hooded weasel eyes. "I see our Mr. Raleigh was kind enough to deliver my message. He's such a prattling fool. But then, I shouldn't have to tell you that, should I?" A vile grin of triumph spread across his swarthy face as he stepped closer. "And my war plan—quite ingenious, is it not? Ah, such a waste, a man as masterful as I, relegated to the lowly task of prison warden. Don't you agree?"

Had it been any other man, Morgan might have attempted to talk his way out, but with Long that would be futile. Staring at the cold barrel of the pistol, Morgan's duplicitous life unrolled like a scroll in his mind. He had utterly failed as a Christian. Reneged on a sacred vow. Corrupted his own wife and sister. Lied. Betrayed his parents. No amount of smooth talking would justify any of that tomorrow when he stood face-to-face with an altogether holy and righteous God. Acute guilt sent blood surging to his head as he stalled, collecting his thoughts. "No one ever suspected me. Not even my own family. Only you . . . from the first moment we met."

Long gazed into the distance, the action revealing his concern over whether or not his subordinates had caught the barkeeper. He slowly turned back. "Surely you didn't believe you could visit a known rebel in my Boston stockade, then show up as a houseguest of a prominent Loyalist without arousing my curiosity. And how quickly you disappeared once your attempt to bribe me into releasing that traitorous friend of yours failed. Any fool could see right through you."

The reality of imminent death settled on Morgan. He struggled to breathe, attempting an offhanded tone. "But regarding the prisoner Dan Haynes, the things I said and did concerning him were quite straightforward. No scheme, no plot." Even as Morgan spoke, the cruel irony of it all struck him. He almost laughed. "I've spied and plotted for the patriots for years and never once was suspected. But the one time I try to do an honest favor, that's when I'm foiled."

"Yes," Long said, "and you just foiled yourself again when you yelled for the tavern keeper to warn your wife. I wasn't sure she was involved . . . until that very second. I must thank you. And dare I say, your lovely bride will look extremely fetching . . . in a hangman's noose. It's sure to be a novel occasion. A double hanging."

38

Prudence heard a horse gallop up the drive. She laid aside her embroidery and went to the parlor window, but she saw no sign of Morgan.

"That brother of mine can never get home to you fast enough," Evie teased. "He must have gone around back, and in such a hurry."

The girl took nothing seriously, not even the impending attack on Philadelphia. An unexplained feeling of dread filled Prudence, and she cast an anxious look at Evelyn. The younger girl sprang to her feet, and together they hastened to the kitchen.

The servants were in the midst of evening meal preparations when the two entered the busy workroom. "There'll be only our family and our lodger for supper this eve," Prudence told the cook in passing.

"Very good, mistress," the Irishwoman replied with relief. Undoubtedly she'd never had so many extra mouths to feed before Evelyn began her daily invitations.

Prudence and Evie raced out the door, but it was not Morgan they saw when they reached the stable. An unfamiliar horseman, burly and grim faced, waited atop his mount in front of the stalls. "Mistress Thomas?"

"Yes." An icy dread raced through her at his expression.

"I'll help you saddle up." He swung down as he spoke. "Run

back inside, get whatever funds you can find, and grab your cloak."

Prudence frowned in confusion. "Who are you? What is this?"

"No time to gab, mistress. You must leave the island at once. There's five, maybe ten, minutes at most. I commandeered a horse on the way, or you wouldn't have that much time."

"Morgan!" she cried, panic gripping her. "Where's my husband?"

"He's been taken. It was a trap. Get a move on, will you?"

"But-but what do you mean, *taken*? Where is he?"

"He's been arrested. There's nothing you can do for him now but give him peace of mind." He turned and gave her a firm nudge toward the house. "Move! You must make it to King's Bridge before the sentries are alerted to watch for you."

"But *you* escaped. How can you be certain my husband didn't?"

"I'm *not* sure. What I do know is you'll be caught if you don't get outta here now!"

Prudence, trembling, felt as if she were being torn apart. "How can I go anywhere without knowing what's happened to Morgan?"

"You have to go. You must." He paused, and a look of understanding warmed his beefy features. "Look. As soon as I'm able to find anything out, anything at all, I'll get word to you. Now, is there someplace you can go? someplace safe?"

She couldn't think. Kneading her temples, she finally remembered where she was supposed to go. "Well, it's—it's quite far. But yes—Princeton." Hardly able to bear the thought of leaving so suddenly, and with Morgan in peril, Prudence had to consider, above all else, the tiny child who even now was growing within her. She raced to the house. "Evie," she called urgently, when the younger girl did not follow. "Come! Now!"

Evelyn shot forward like a flushed rabbit.

"You mean, you'll need *two* horses?" the rider called after them.

"Yes," Evie answered. "Two."

❦ ❦

A wisp of steam curled up from Robert's cocoa, the second cup kind Mrs. Cogswell had poured him just before she and Emily started washing the supper dishes. Still seated at the worn table, he glanced around the homey farmhouse where they had been offered lodging for the night. When his gaze reached the sideboard, Chan allowed it to linger, to wander over Emily's slender form as she worked with her back to him. All her movements, whether seeing to horses or tending her children or taking care of housework, were graceful. And he found more than a small measure of enjoyment in watching her. Robby must have, as well. . . . And *he* should have been here now, admiring his "bonny Emily."

She chatted pleasantly with their tiny hostess as she worked, but she kept her voice low in deference to Christopher and the little ones sound asleep near the hearth.

Not paying any mind to what was being said, Robert let her soothing tones flow over him. Such a part of her, that airy voice with its utter sincerity. Added with the other homey sounds here, it awakened memories of the years in North Carolina that he had taken for granted . . . and only now made him realize how very much of life he had lost by shutting people out. He had missed so many joys.

But he needed to corral his wayward thoughts. The winsome lass he was permitting his gaze to linger over was his best friend's widow—and her husband's death was partly Robert's own fault. It wasn't proper to entertain even the tiniest fantasies about her. It wasn't chivalrous. His responsibility toward her was to see her safely to her brother's place. Better to leave that part of him that had been dead and buried for the last six years as it was—sealed up, with a great wall around it built from the petrified ashes of his dreams.

He gulped some of his hot drink and looked at Emily again.

Flickering candlelight danced among the honeyed strands of her long, golden hair and glowed from those incredible green eyes whenever she turned to make a comment to the hostess. Her skin, so creamy and flawless, looked like satin. She was so beautiful. So gentle and kind, yet strong. The epitome of the faithful, loving wife. A woman of priceless worth. *And much too good for the likes of you,* he reminded himself. Downing the last of the cocoa, he rose and carried the empty cup to the women.

Emily took it with a smile, then placed a hand on the older woman's shoulder. "Mistress Cogswell, we're all but done here. We've imposed on your kindness enough for one night. Pasturing our herd, putting us up for the night. You've been so wonderfully generous. Please, go to bed, won't you? I'll finish up what little is left."

The mobcapped hostess looked from her to Robert and back, then nodded, drying work-reddened hands on her apron. "Truth is, I'd purely appreciate that. If you're sure you don't mind?"

"Of course not."

"Then I bid you both good night." Padding across the cozy main room of the house, she retreated into her bedroom just beyond it.

Robert remained near Emily while she washed his cup and set it on the drainboard. She picked up the dishpan and started for the door.

"Here, let me," he offered, taking it from her. His fingers brushed her damp, slightly soapy hands, sending a jolt of electricity through him.

She didn't seem to notice. "Thank you. At least let me unlatch the door."

He followed as he silently reminded himself of his commitment merely to look after her. Nothing more.

The icy breeze that rushed past them caught his breath. "Shut the door behind me," he said as he ventured outside in his shirtsleeves.

He gave the water a quick toss over the split-rail fence, then walked back toward the house. Overhead, the millions of stars blinking against the indigo darkness appeared almost close enough to touch. *God is sure in his glory tonight.*

Chan stopped short. When had he begun thinking of God so matter-of-factly again? Since the flogging, perhaps? Or since the battle at Throg's Neck, when he and Christopher had come away unscathed, despite impossible odds? Whenever it had started, this new truce with the Almighty had been a long time coming.

He gave the pan a last shake, then returned to the back door and entered quietly, in deference to the mostly sleeping household.

"Hang it on the nail above the drainboard," Emily said softly. Seated at the table, she was drinking the remains from her own cup.

This time as he crossed the room, Robert felt her eyes on him. He turned to face her.

"Join me for a moment?" she asked.

Robert knew it was absolutely the last thing he *should* do, but he ignored his conscience. Everyone was asleep, the two of them as good as alone.

"I think we've done quite well this past week," Emily said when he sat down. "And now that we've gotten the herd across the Hudson without some man-of-war sailing upstream and firing at us, we should make it the rest of the way just fine. Don't you think?"

Much as he hated to shatter her illusions, Chan could only be honest. "Emily, we know that Washington's forces have retreated as far as the Delaware while they wait for General Light-Horse Lee and his command to join them. And since the British routed Lee's men out of Fort Constitution, they've been on the run across New Jersey."

"Yes, but we can cut west from Princeton and avoid all that."

Her eyes searched his face, and Robert steeled himself against their guileless beauty. "First we must cross most of New Jersey. And like I said, who knows where Lee is—or the British troops chasing him, for that matter?"

"God will see us through," she said with a confident smile.

Robert stared at her for a long moment. "Yes, he probably will . . . for you."

"Oh, not just for me," she said airily, her friendly tone still casual. "Chip told me God has been taking care of the two of you, as well. Exceptional care, if I may say so."

"That, I'm sure, is for Christopher's sake, not mine."

Emily frowned and shook her head. "You remind me so much of Robby when we first met. It's strange." A wistful smile touched her lips. "Maybe it's a curiosity that goes along with the name Robert. Like you, there was a time when Robby was angry with the Lord. Did he ever tell you about it?"

"Robby?" Chan seriously doubted that.

She nodded. "I suppose he told you some of his past, how he and his father scrimped, did without for years just to send him to the New World. His poor father, rest his soul, knew it was the one legacy he could give his son . . . that and a firm belief in God."

Chandler, enjoying the sound of her voice, didn't interrupt.

"Robby was kidnapped right off the Bristol docks before he had a chance to book passage. Impressed into service aboard a royal ship, forced to labor on it for months while it plied our coastal waters, he felt as if God had not only betrayed him but was taunting him besides. He was so close to his dream, you see. So close. It was almost always within sight, yet he was never allowed to set foot on it. Of course, you know he eventually managed to jump ship—and in the nick of time."

The tale was almost as fascinating as her voice, Chan noted. He wanted to hear the rest. "And?"

"That's how we met. I helped him escape the redcoats. It wasn't until afterward, when he could look back on it all, that he realized God had neither betrayed nor forsaken him. Robby had forsaken the Lord, had forgotten to keep the faith. As the book of Hebrews says: 'Faith is the substance of things hoped for, the evidence of things not seen.'"

Mulling over those words, Chandler smiled. "Scriptures are a whole lot easier to quote than to live."

Emily smiled. "I know," she said cheerfully. "So isn't it marvelous that the Good Lord blessed us with his mercy for those times when we fail?"

Robert could see in Emily's eyes her sincerity and the abiding friendship he knew she held for him. It was more than he deserved.

Abruptly, she looked away. She picked up her cup, took another sip, then smiled rather tentatively at him again.

Her expressions were usually quite readable, but this one puzzled Chan.

With a glance across the room at the sleeping forms, she leaned closer. "There's something I've been wanting to ask you in private. Do you remember when Prudence and Morgan's younger sister, Evelyn, stopped to see you a month or so ago?"

Vastly disappointed at the shift of topic, but not about to dwell on the reason, Robert brought his reaction to her back into line as she continued.

"Well, Christopher has been asking me untold questions regarding Evie. How old she is, are there many beaus . . . that sort of thing. Am I to assume the lad is taken with her?"

Robert's amusement took over. "Odd that you would notice. He scarcely mentions the girl to me more than twenty or thirty times a day."

A lighthearted smile softened Emily's features. "I thought so. When Evelyn was younger, she was always as cute as a button-nosed doll. I wasn't the least surprised she turned out to be such a beauty."

Chandler grinned. "She couldn't have been half as cute as our little Katydid is."

Tilting her head to one side, Emily's eyes took on a lively shine. "As cute as *your* Katydid. My Katherine's head has been swelled to twice its size since you told her she was the cutest little girl in any church."

"You mean, she's not?" Robert challenged, entering into

the good-natured banter. He was immeasurably relieved he hadn't ruined it all. He had come frighteningly close, with his comment about *our* Katydid. It wouldn't happen again.

The door to the bedroom opened, and Mr. Cogswell hurried out, tucking his nightshirt into his breeches with one hand. His work boots were clutched in the other. "A rider's comin' fast."

Jumping up, Chan snatched a lantern, and he and Emily dashed out the front just as the horseman reined his mount to a sudden halt.

"That you, Clem?" Cogswell asked from the porch, tugging on his second boot.

"Aye. Thought I'd ride over and let your company know I had some of me own this eve. A patrol of British officers stopped by to water their mounts. Asked about all them horse tracks on the road. I said they were from a herd bein' driven to Staten Island. But just to be on the safe side, I'd be outta here before sunup, if I was you. And stay off the roads."

Robert stepped to shake the gloved hand. "You're a good man for coming. I thank you."

"Well, best I get back home now. Don't want the wife to worry." Wheeling his mount, Clem galloped back the way he'd come.

Emily was so near, Robert could feel her trembling as she hugged herself. It took all the strength he possessed not to wrap her in his arms and pull her close. "I think it might be best for you and the children to stay here," he told her. "Christopher and I can handle the herd by ourselves. Then I'll come back and get—"

"*No,*" Emily said emphatically. "If it's too risky for us, it's too risky for you. Besides, what's the worst thing that could happen? They'd just confiscate the horses."

He could see by the look in her eye that there was no reasoning with her. He had been down this road before since he had been caring for her. But he wasn't her husband. . . . He couldn't resort to forbidding her. Not that Emily would take kindly to such actions even if he *were* her husband.

Chan figured he might as well give in now and get it over with, save valuable time. "Very well. But whenever there's a stretch of open ground tomorrow, we're going to run the horses. We're getting across New Jersey as fast as humanly possible."

"Right after we stop by at the Lyons' Den," she said in all seriousness, placing her fingers on his arm. "We can't leave the colony without going there first."

Mr. Cogswell, standing slack-jawed to the side, stepped closer. "You'd do better to cut across the northern end to Easton, not get anywheres near the road to Philadelphia."

"Thanks for the advice, sir. I'm afraid Emily can be quite stubborn at times."

"Can't they all." Chuckling, he returned inside.

"That may very well be," Emily said, her tone flat. "But Princeton is a good ten miles this side of Trenton. Surely both armies will be well beyond by the time we get there. It would be such a shame to deprive the Lyonses of a short time with Christopher. It would mean so much to them . . . and to me. Who knows when I'll see them again? Please, Robert, couldn't we at least head in that direction?"

With her looking up at him so pleadingly, it was impossible to refuse—even though Chan knew he was right.

"Please, Robert, pray about it. If afterward you still feel we can't go that way, I'll abide by your wishes. I promise."

When she released his arm and walked toward the farmhouse, the warmth of her touch went with her. Yet Chandler remained rooted to that spot.

She wanted him to talk to God, to listen to him. To forgive. To plant again that small mustard seed of faith . . . and find embers of hope among the ashes of his life.

For Emily, he had to try. He lifted his gaze to the moon peeking through the branches of a leafless tree. For her.

And for himself.

39

"Emily."

A hand gently stroked her hair, its touch as soft as her whispered name. She opened her eyes.

Robert knelt beside her, his face gilded by the flickering fire glow. "Time to go," he said quietly.

It took a few seconds for her to recall in which farmhouse they had stayed overnight. She yawned and sat up, still dressed in yesterday's clothes, and tried to gather her wits. Robert set her shoes beside her. Noting how helpful and solicitous he was being, Emily suddenly realized she must look a sight. She smoothed her rumpled dress and finger-combed her hair the best she could.

Chandler began rolling his and Christopher's pallets. The lad was also up and dressed—and she had heard neither of them stir. Emily stifled another yawn and quickly slipped on her shoes. The little ones were still fast asleep, and their kind hosts, the Cogswells, remained in their bedroom.

Emily rose to her knees and rolled up her own blankets, then turned to the children.

Robert stopped her with his hand. "Let's wait for Chip to bring our mounts around. It's well below freezing out. I thought we'd just pick up the kids wrapped in their blankets and keep them with us till after sunup."

Emily nodded, even though she knew it would complicate herding the horses through the darkness with a sleeping bundle in her arms. But the children had been such troopers, she really didn't want to disturb their sleep. She would manage somehow.

She handed Chan her bedroll, and he helped her to her feet. There was something especially comforting about having a very capable man looking after her and the children. Emily found herself enjoying the attention . . . but this arrangement was only temporary at best, and a man like Robert Chandler would be considerate to anyone.

She retrieved her cloak and started for the door when she heard the clop of the horses.

"Just stay by the fire till I've tied the bedding to the saddles," Robert said, striding past her. "No sense going out in the cold any sooner than you have to."

"Thank you." As she watched him go, Emily realized that she had always considered herself a rather independent and capable person. She and Robby had been so young when they married. They had both had to do some fast growing up. And they had not only been husband and wife but best friends and comrades, as well. It was odd to feel safe and secure in these dangerous times, especially now that she was a widow with two small children and sixty horses to move across hostile territory. But Robert's concern had brought back some of that old security, and she appreciated it more than she could voice.

Spreading her fingers before the warmth of the banked fire, Emily wondered if Chan had actually discussed the situation with God last night. As much as she wanted to ask him, she knew she could not. Better to wait patiently and hope. But it would be a terrible loss if he wasn't able to find peace with God again.

The door opened, and both men came in. Christopher swept Katie into his arms while Robert picked up Rusty. "When you mount," Chan told her, "I'll hand Rusty up to you; then Christopher can give Katie to me on my horse."

Biting cold assaulted her as soon as she stepped out the door, and her breath rose in clouds of mist. The skies had been dreary for days, but so far the clouds had done nothing but threaten. Positioning herself on her stallion, Emily admired Robert's sureness of purpose, the trust he instilled in those around him. She could see why Colonel Hand wanted to make him an officer.

An entirely new curiosity surfaced within her. Had Chan's family been disappointed when he abandoned that natural bent toward leadership after Julia died? What were his parents like? She couldn't recall his ever having mentioned them. Had they been praying for his restoration to faith?

Once everyone was situated, they headed for the fenced pasture to round up the herd, and Emily realized that she still didn't know which direction they'd be traveling. Surely he wouldn't mind her asking just that. Nudging her pacer ahead, she rode to his side. "Which way are we going, Robert?"

In the murky darkness, she could not discern his face. "Both, actually."

"Both?"

"You cost me a good deal of sleep, you know," he added wryly, then softened with a small smile. "But I don't mind. It was way past time for me to straighten out a lot of things. I had forgotten how much easier life can be when we trust the Lord rather than ourselves. Last night, although I still didn't have the answer I sought regarding our route, I finally decided to trust God to direct us today."

"I'm so very, very pleased to hear that. But . . . why would the Lord tell you to go both ways? That I do not understand."

He chuckled. "To make a long story short, I mentioned our dilemma to Chip this morning. He just shrugged and told me there was no problem. He has a cousin with a farm a few miles north of the Raritan River on the way to Easton. Since we're starting so early, he thinks we can leave the pacers at his cousin's, then take fresh horses for the ride to Princeton. There should be time for at least a late visit this evening. Of course, should the British get close, the plan might very well change."

"Oh, I don't know," Emily said, smiling. "I think I'll just

trust God for this plan, if you don't mind. And thank you, Robert. Thank you."

"For what?"

She shrugged. What could she say? For listening . . . to her and to God? For being so thoughtful and kind? For being exactly what she needed? She merely smiled. "I guess for simply being you."

❧ ❧

It had been a long, hard day, with intermittent sprinkles of rain throughout, yet Emily felt good. They had made Christopher's cousin's farm well before dark and left the herd under Mr. White's care. On fresh, borrowed mounts, they were sure to reach the Lyons' Den not long after dark. Yes, it had been a wonderful day.

And added to all its other blessings was one more . . . there was something very right about knowing her dear friend was now taking his direction from the Lord.

Hugging Katie to her, Emily glanced across at Robert and Rusty, little more than silhouettes in the deepening dusk. She wished she could see Chan's face clearly. He had been wearing a smile every time she had looked at him today, more often in one day than in all the time she had known him. She was beginning to understand that Robert's being sent to care for her had been as much a part of God's plan for him as it was for her. He had made his peace with God. Perhaps now, at last, he could put Julia to rest.

It was amazing the difference a smile made in his countenance. It took away from his long chin, adding a bracket of laugh lines beside his mouth, and displayed teeth that were white and even. The spark in his dark blue eyes diminished the years that grief had added to his age . . . and along with that incredible smile, it was more than appealing.

Perhaps, in time, Robert would find someone to love again. He had much to give, and he deserved to be loved, especially after so much wasted time.

She, on the other hand, would never seek the same for

herself. Robby's love had been a once-in-a-lifetime blessing, and the special bond they had shared she could never imagine replacing. Her heart constricted as memories assailed her. Anyway, it was Robert she was concerned about. She slid a sidelong glance at him, trying to conjure up the sort of woman he might find appealing—a woman who would be incredibly wonderful, breathtakingly beautiful, adept at all domestic duties. . . .

Christopher's shout cut into her fancies. "This way! Through the trees." He veered his horse to the right and led them through a dormant field into a stand of trees.

Emily could discern some shadowy buildings in the drizzle ahead, and a few dots of light. They must truly be close now. The trees were likely the woods behind the Lyons' Den.

Within moments her hopes were confirmed. They broke from the grove near the barn at the rear of the inn.

Jasper charged out of the back door with lantern in hand as they came to a halt. With a scowl on his craggy face and his hair bushing about, he looked like the very devil himself.

"It's only us, Pa Lyons," Christopher called. He dismounted and went to help Katie down from Emily's horse.

"*Chip?*" He raised the lantern higher, and his fiery expression transformed to one of joy. "And Emily! Praise the Lord! You're here. Safe. But what are ya doing ridin' through New Jersey?"

"We're taking Emily's herd of horses up to the Wyoming Valley, to Dan and Susannah," Christopher explained.

Jasper looked incredulous. "Don't you know our countryside is teemin' with redcoats? A patrol stopped off here not more'n an hour ago."

"When?" Robert rode into the circle of light. "Which way did they go?"

"They rode off toward Trenton." Jasper lifted Rusty down from Chandler's saddle. "Never thought I'd see the day when I'd be forced to serve the enemy."

Robert swung to the ground. "Do you happen to know where the armies are? If they've engaged yet?"

The innkeeper grimaced. "Not from what the redcoats were saying. But they sure were braggin' on the capture of General Light-Horse Harry Lee. Never heard the likes of it."

"Lee?" Chan asked in dismay. "Aside from Washington, he's the best general we've got. His command—did they capture his command, too?"

"Nay. Him and his staff were stayin' in the comfort of Morristown with a guard of only about fifty. Oh, enough war talk. We need to get these kids in outta the rain."

The fireplace in the huge common room gave off a heavenly warmth, and the children ran to it, discarding coats and scarves and hats as they went. Emily followed at a more sedate pace, picking things up after them. She couldn't help noticing that the ordinary was empty of customers—unusual for the supper hour. Obviously the invasion of New Jersey was playing havoc with business.

Mr. Lyons regarded Robert. "I'm assumin' the army gave ya leave to help Emily this time." From his demeanor, Emily knew he was concerned for Christopher's sake.

"That's right," Chan answered good-naturedly. "This time we have permission."

The older man nodded in affirmation, then turned toward the kitchen. "Esther! Come out here! It's Chip and Emily."

One thing Emily could always count on was the lively sparkle in old Mrs. Lyons's eyes. She fairly burst into the room and rushed to give everyone a hug.

Then Emily noticed others coming to join them. Morgan's wife! And his sister! Even as her mouth gaped open, she saw Prudence fly into Robert's arms.

For a split second he looked stunned; then he enveloped her in a hug. "Well, this is a surprise," he said with a smile.

Emily felt an unaccountable stab of resentment. She averted her gaze from the embrace to see Christopher go to Evelyn, eyeing her in wonder. The girl allowed him to take her hands, then moved closer, her own expression as openly pleased as his.

Looking from him to Robert, Emily could not deny that

Robert seemed no less pleased to see raven-haired Prudence. A vague memory surfaced of one of Robby's letters mentioning how fond he *and Chan* were of Morgan's Puritan wife. Surely a man like Robert Chandler would not allow himself to entertain feelings for his friend's wife, she protested inwardly. Yet clearly Chan did care for Prudence—perhaps even he wasn't aware just how deeply his own feelings went.

"What are you doing, traveling through New Jersey at a time like this?" he asked her.

Prudence's luminous gray eyes swam with tears, which spilled over and ran down her cheeks. She opened her mouth, but not a word came out.

Jasper stepped up to rescue her. "Morgan has been taken by the British."

Emily was speechless. She had known Morgan most of her life. Her mother's family and his were friends of old standing.

"We don't know that for certain," Evelyn declared with an angry pout.

"Is this true?" Robert asked Prudence, cupping her chin.

She nodded, and her tears trickled over his hand as she swallowed hard. "The man who came to warn us said they'd captured him. And it's been days. *Days.*" Her breath caught on a sob. "If he had managed to escape, he would have come for us by now. Or at least sent word." She sniffed in misery.

Robert's eyes met Emily's, and she could see how worried he was. Spies were sent to the gallows almost immediately—made an example of. Chan drew the crying young woman close again.

"Prudence may be married to my brother," Evelyn announced in defiance, "but she obviously doesn't know him as well as I do. No two or three soldiers would be able to hold Morgan. There could be any number of reasons for him to be detained getting here." Then she, too, started to crumble. "All kinds." The last words came out garbled as she began to cry.

Christopher pulled her into a comforting hug, pressing her head against his shoulder. "She's right," he said, looking at

Prudence. "No mealymouthed lobsterback could outsmart Morgan Thomas."

A shuddering sigh came from Prudence as she remained in Robert's arms. "I only pray that's true."

Emily found the news of Morgan's capture unbelievable. He had always been so clever. But then, she wouldn't have believed that Robby would be shot, either.

Prudence rose on tiptoe and whispered something to Robert.

He stiffened. Taking her by the shoulders, he held her at arm's length. *"You never told him?"*

"Told whom?" Evelyn asked. "What?"

"I, um . . ." Prudence's face drained of color as she met her sister-in-law's gaze. "I'm . . . with child."

"Pru!" Evie gasped.

Jasper whacked a nearby table. "Well, that settles it. I'm not takin' any more chances with these lasses. We've been hiding them from lobstercoats every day for the past week. Day before yesterday, the leader of a patrol asked for 'em by name. Described 'em perfectly." He turned to Robert. "I'm sendin' these two on with you. I know you'll look after them, just as you have our Emmy."

Emily regarded Robert and Prudence, the two still clinging to one another as though they belonged together, and her spirits sank. Despite Prudence's suffering and her jeopardy, despite the fact that Emily knew inside that she had no designs on Robert herself, she still regretted having insisted upon coming here.

40

"No!" Prudence wrenched out of Chandler's grasp, tears streaming unchecked down her face. "I can't go anywhere." Warding off Robert and Jasper with her hands, she backed away. "Morgan told me to come to the Lyons' Den. No place else. I must wait here. I have to. Unless . . ." She rushed back to Robert and seized the front of his coat. "Please, take me back to New York. I can't bear the uncertainty, not knowing. *Please.*"

Emily witnessed the return of the old pain to Robert's eyes as he stared at the willowy, black-haired girl. It caught at her heart. Earlier today, for the first time since she'd known him, Chandler had seemed unburdened, happy. And now this. Why, oh, why, had she compelled him to come here?

He looked from Prudence to her and then back and slowly shook his head. "You'd be putting your unborn child at risk. You know that."

"I know." In anguish she flung herself against his chest. "I know."

"Jasper?" Robert asked. "Do you know anyone who might be willing to ride to New York? We would pay well for any information on Morgan."

"Yes!" Evie cried with renewed hope. "That's a wonderful idea. *Please.*"

The innkeeper scratched his head, causing further disorder to the straggly white strands. "I might be able to find somebody."

Chandler gave a grateful nod. "If so, the message will have to be carried on up to Dan Haynes. As you said earlier, it's too dangerous for Prudence and Evelyn to remain here."

"But—" Prudence's light gray eyes flared. "If Morgan should come—"

"Jasper knows where Dan and Susannah live. I'm sure he'd waste no time at all sending him on to the Wyoming Valley. In the meantime, come on to bed. You'd best get whatever sleep you can. We'll be leaving Princeton before dawn."

In misery, Emily watched them go . . . Chandler holding Prudence close as they climbed the stairs together. This was the woman Chan and Robby had taken under their wing, looking after her in Morgan's absence last year when the men were at Cambridge. Robby had mentioned her in so many of his letters, proclaiming to no end all her marvelous attributes. At times Emily had wondered if he had merely found her fascinating . . . or was there more to it? Had he grown to love her a little? And might Chandler have felt the same?

Her feelings made no sense, and Emily tried to rid herself of them, but still the unanswered questions gnawed at her. She clenched her teeth together as she cast another look toward the stairs. If Prudence was supposed to have such *strength of character,* as Robby had put it, such *unfailing trust in God,* what had become of those noble virtues?

Even as the scornful thoughts crept into her mind, Emily knew they were not only uncharitable but also unfair—and more than a little unchristian. Prudence was living in a very precarious state right now, her future completely unsettled. The poor woman had been left to wonder if her husband had been imprisoned or, more likely, already sent to the gallows. And she was with child.

A tug on her skirt drew Emily's attention downward. Katie and Rusty, each with a hand clutched on a fold of the navy wool, gazed up at her, their little faces filled with confusion and fear. She bent down and drew them into her embrace.

"Ah, now, methinks some cheerin' up is in order." Mrs. Lyons stepped forward and scooped Rusty into her arms. "I've got a special treat in the kitchen for my two favorite young'uns in this whole world. And now's the perfect time for it, too. Comin', Katie?" she asked, turning to go.

"Uh-huh!" A big smile broke forth as the child latched onto the older woman's hand and skipped along.

"Thank you," Emily murmured. "They haven't had anything hot to eat this whole long day."

"Now that you mention it," Christopher said, looking longingly toward the kitchen himself, "neither have I. I'm starved. How about you, Evie? Come sit with me while I eat?"

Evelyn cast a fleeting glance toward the stairwell, then shrugged, and the two of them left the room.

"Have the twins heat up some extra bricks to warm the beds," Jasper called after Esther as he started for the entrance. "I best get to findin' somebody who'll brave traveling the roads to New York. Can't imagine that little gal bein' willing to leave here unless she knows someone's already been dispatched." He plucked his greatcoat from a peg by the door on his way out.

Emily looked around and found herself utterly alone, with nothing breaking the silence but the occasional crackle of burning wood in the great hearth. Even Methuselah's cage had been covered. This empty room, this solitude, were not at all what she had anticipated when she'd had the brilliant idea of coming here. She exhaled a ragged sigh.

❦ ❦

A few huge, fluffy snowflakes drifted tentatively down from the leaden sky, promising the first real winter storm. Emily, riding at the rear of the herd not far from her children, found the dreary afternoon a perfect match for her mood. After leaving Princeton three days ago and crossing the Delaware, they had spent a good part of the last two days traveling up a river road that wound through mountainous country. When the trail finally meandered away from the river, they climbed toward a cut in a pine-covered ridge. The temperature was dropping as they went higher, and icy winds buffeted them mercilessly.

According to Christopher, they would reach the Wyoming Valley by evening, but Emily wasn't so certain. Robert was being extremely careful of Prudence, traveling in her delicate condition, and insisted that they all stop to rest every hour or so. He had yet to stray more than a few yards from the girl, Emily noted, as she watched them riding side by side. She tried to check her bitterness. After all, having lost his own wife late in her confinement, Robert would naturally take special care of a woman with child.

If this horrid uncertainty turned out to be a confirmed fact, and Morgan truly had been put to death, what then? She could not imagine Robert forsaking Prudence, leaving her completely on her own. If the rider dispatched by Mr. Lyons came to impart the dreaded news at Dan's, Prudence would have nowhere else to turn. Only to Robert.

Emily let all her breath out at once. Her sole consolation was that sometime tonight they would finally get to Dan and Susannah's. She and her children would be safe there at her brother's, and so would the horses. She would have to be contented with that.

Emily rebuked herself. This was pure self-pity, and it was time to stop wallowing in it. She had no reason to resent Robert Chandler's concern for Prudence and her child, and she had a great deal to be thankful for, after all. There had been no sight of any redcoats on this entire journey. And her children, despite being so very young, had been amazingly good along the way, riding double for hours with scarcely a complaint. Katie, especially, had thought of the whole thing as a grand adventure. For a little girl not even four, she had become quite adept at handling the gentle mare and could actually be of help riding at the rear of the herd.

The snow was beginning to increase now, coming down steadily. And so was the wind. Cold and sharp, it managed to cut through their layers of clothing and rub raw any exposed inch of skin. As Emily neared the youngsters, she saw with alarm that their cheeks were red and chapped. Rusty was shivering profusely but gave a proud grin as she came alongside. They needed to get out of the storm, to someplace warm. "Come to Mama, Rusty," she said, reaching for her son. She wrapped the blanket from behind her saddle around him and tucked him close, then smiled at Katie. "Think you can do Mama a favor, *Miss* Kate?"

Her daughter straightened in childish pride. "Uh-huh. What?"

"Stay right here and make sure the stragglers keep moving while I go ask Uncle Chip where the closest house is. Can you do that?"

"Yes, Mama."

"Good girl. I'll only be a few minutes." With a nod of confidence at her daughter, Emily smiled and urged her own mount to a gallop.

As Emily approached Evelyn and Christopher, she noticed that Evelyn was also shivering and windburned, her curls whipped by the wind beneath her heavy scarf. Emily doubted that this city-bred girl had ever been at the mercy of the elements before. With a sympathetic smile, she switched her attention to Chip. "We haven't passed a farmhouse lately. . . ."

"Because there aren't any," he answered flatly. Then at her obvious alarm, he elaborated further. "Now that we're out of the Lehigh River Valley, we won't see a home until we cross these ridges and come down into the Wyoming Valley."

Emily glanced at Evie for a sign of panic, but there was none. Obviously she had more grit and determination than Emily had given her credit for.

"We have to keep going, Em," Chip said. "Do our best to get across the last ridge before dark."

She stared at him for a long moment. "Well then, keep Rusty warm for me, will you? I need to talk to Robert." She handed him her little boy. "Try to make sure his hands and feet stay inside the blanket."

"I'll look after him, too," Evelyn offered, moving her horse closer to Chip's.

"Thanks. And keep your eyes open for any kind of shelter. Anything. A hunter's shack, a shed, anything that can keep out this wind." Emily wheeled her mount, smiling at the realization that Rusty provided the young couple with a legitimate reason to ride even closer to each other.

By the time she got back through the steadily falling snow to Katie, Robert was with her already, lifting the child onto his horse. It made Emily feel a few degrees warmer to think his obsession with Prudence hadn't completely negated the concern he had for her children. *I'm surprised,* she thought cynically, *that he didn't put Prudence on his lap instead.* Emily pushed aside her wayward thoughts and smiled gratefully at him as she approached. Tugging the other blanket from behind her saddle, she handed it to him to wrap around Katie.

"See, Mama," her daughter said, pointing a mittened hand. "I kept the horses moving."

"Yes, and you did a good job, too, Miss Kate. I'm proud of you."

"Did Chip tell you where the nearest home is?" Robert asked.

Emily sighed. "He says there aren't any until we cross the mountains. There'll be farmsteads on the other side."

"We can't risk it," Robert answered, looking down at Katie with an ominous shake of his head. "I'm going to ride over into that grove of trees yonder, see if I can find a place to build a shelter. Tell Chip to bunch the herd here on the road. I don't reckon they'll stray in the storm. I'll tell Prudence on my way."

The snow was coming down fast and hard, swirling about on the wind and beginning to stick to the ground. "Don't go far. You might not be able to find your way back."

He smiled, hugging Katie close to him. "We won't, will we, Katydid?" Then he took off into the pines.

Emily breathed a prayer for their safe return as the pack-horses were cut from the herd and the rest bunched up. When the chore was almost finished, she looked across the sorrel rumps of the huddled animals and saw Chandler and Katie emerge from the woods. "They're coming back," she called, then, trailing a packhorse behind her, went to meet them.

Robert's face was glowing from the cold, but he flashed a confident grin as Emily and the others rode up to him. "I've found a stone outcropping that will protect us from the north wind."

Half expecting Prudence to whine and play on his sympathy, Emily was again humbled when the hollow-eyed young woman sat in stoic silence on her mount.

The biting wind whipped at the treetops, whistling through the pine branches on the outer fringe of the woods, slapping icy snow against their skin. But within the forest growth, the storm was considerably less vicious. Chandler led the little troop into a cut that turned into a gully, beyond which a wall of stone reached up nearly as high as the tops of the pines. He dismounted with Katie, carried her to the wall, and set her down in the shelter.

"Take the saddles and packs off the horses," he said above the howling wind. "Stack them around the children. Prudence, you stay with the little ones and keep them warm while the rest of us build a shelter."

Emily felt her blood rush to her head. Was Prudence now even usurping care of her own children? Then, just as quickly, she recalled the dark-haired girl's condition, and she prayed silently for forgiveness. Of course the able-bodied would have to look after those more vulnerable.

"Emily," she heard Robert say firmly. "You and Evelyn look under all the trees for dry wood to build a fire. Find as much deadfall as you can. Chip, start cutting evergreen branches. I'll strip some poles and start making a frame."

Then, quieting, he went to kneel by the children with a gentle smile. "You'll keep much warmer if you share the blankets," he said softly. Tugging them from each, he placed the shivering tots with Prudence and wrapped them all together. "This is gonna be great fun. We're going to play

Indian as we build the lodge and get a good fire going. But we're all going to need Indian names. All of us. Can you think of good names for us?"

The children nodded in unison.

Emily's heart melted as she watched this tender interplay. Robert was so good for her little ones. Better than many fathers she had seen. And in many ways he was good for her, too. Unexpected tears threatened, and she had to fight hard to keep them from spilling over.

"Hey, what's everybody standing around for?" Robert asked, swinging around. "Get going. We've got to get a warm place for these kids."

41

While the storm raged outside, the temperature felt quite moderate within the rough, pine-bough shelter—or Indian lodge, as Chandler had termed it for the children's sake. Emily, taking her turn at watching the fire, huddled before the crackling flames, feeding a steady supply of kindling to keep it going. Robert had left a small hole at the top, and the interior of the makeshift haven was amazingly smoke-free. She couldn't help smiling at yet another example of his ingenuity. Of course, Chandler gave the credit to his experiences the previous winter, during the time he had been camped outside Boston. But all Emily knew was that she and the rest of the small group would have frozen, were it not for him.

"Katie," Rusty moaned restlessly in his sleep. "Don't." He rolled over.

Emily glanced at her son, lying between Christopher and Evelyn for warmth, and wondered what mischief was being attributed to his big sister in his dream.

Katie was sound asleep herself, with Prudence on one side of her and Robert on the other. Fleetingly, Emily thought her slumbering babies looked like bundling boards used to separate courting lovers. But she dismissed the idea as quickly as it had come. She had never been one to entertain uncharitable feelings toward others, and why she'd been doing so during the past several days remained a mystery to her. She hardly needed a reminder that Robert's sole reason for being here in this wilderness was to help her and the children. He didn't need to be repaid with bitter, unkind thoughts.

The howl of the wind began to abate, and within moments the sound died away completely. As she silently lifted her thanksgiving to God, she realized with stark clarity that she had been neglecting her prayer time of late. The fifth chapter of Galatians flitted across her mind. If she had been walking in the Spirit, as she should, she wouldn't have been trying to devour Prudence or anyone else. She had no cause to think ill of Morgan's beautiful wife—and it was time to go to the Lord and ask his forgiveness, to reclaim the indescribable peace God had given her since Robby's death.

In the stillness of the night, Emily bowed her head. *Dear heavenly Father, I don't have to tell you I've been wallowing in self-pity and resentment for days and days . . . and this after talking so much to Robert about trusting you. Our country is being torn asunder by the awfulness of war, and every day more men are dying. And here am I, but one of many widows, facing the loneliness of a lost loved one. Prudence, too, has most likely experienced the same kind of loss . . . and I, who should be the first to comfort her and lift her up in prayer, have instead been shunning her, looking for reasons to dislike her. I can't even fathom why I'm so consumed with this lack of charity! I ask you to forgive my sin and cleanse my heart. I must have become too used to the comfort of having this caring man around. But that is no excuse for my thoughtless disregard of another person in need. Please help me make it up to her.*

Emily stole a glance at Chandler, sleeping with his back to her, and traced the outline of his broad-shouldered form in the glow of the firelight. Yes, this very dear friend would make some fortunate young woman a wonderful husband one day. And when that time came, he would do his own choosing. She could only be thankful that she'd had such a mate herself not so long ago. She had loved Robby MacKinnon with every fiber of her being, and that love would never die. She could do no less than wish happiness for her husband's dearest friend . . . her own dearest friend.

She bowed her head once more and continued pouring out her heart to God.

I thank you so much for sending Robert Chandler to us. He's been so very wonderful to me and to the children. They love him deeply. And I . . . I will always treasure the memory of his kindness. Please, keep me conscious of the fact that I need to press more closely to you and seek your will. You are the one who knows the future. I can only ask that you remind me to stay faithful to you, and please show me your will, dear Lord. And, yes, I know . . . help me to be the friend Prudence needs right now. The uncertainties of carrying a first child are more than enough. But to lose her husband as well, how will she bear that? Fill me with the love I should have had for her all along. I ask all these things in the name of your dear Son, Jesus.

Even as she raised her head at the close of her prayer, Emily felt a heavy unchristian ugliness fall from her heart. In its place flowed a new love and tenderness, and a resurgence of that first blessed peace God had given her weeks ago. She gazed through a blur of joyous tears at the sleeping group. *Thank you, dear God. Thank you.*

Emily added a few more twigs to the fire, and the spicy tang of pine pervaded the confines of the shelter, adding a pleasing aroma to the comforting crackle of the flames. Hearing no more gusts of wind outside, she wondered how much snow had accumulated. It wouldn't hurt to go and see.

She gathered up her blanket, wrapped it securely around her shoulders, and rose. She eased quietly out of the opening and stepped out into half a foot of newfallen snow.

The heavy cloud bank had moved on, leaving behind a star-spangled sky, and a half-moon glowed in magnificent splendor over a pristine world of blue white. Long branches of evergreen drooped to touch the ground beneath the weight of their burden. The glorious sight filled Emily with awe. *And thank you for this, too, Father . . . the loveliest gift of all.*

Not too far from the shelter, their mounts and packhorses dozed peacefully, huddled together. Emily hoped the others had fared as well out in the open. She took several steps to check on them, but remembering the fire and the constant attention it required, thought better of leaving. With the clouds all but gone, the temperature would likely drop a bit more.

"Beautiful night."

Robert's low voice startled her. Emily fought to calm her racing pulse as she turned to him. "Yes. Almost makes up for our being caught in the storm."

"Almost." He chuckled, then quickly sobered. "I've been wanting to catch you alone. I need to talk to you about Prudence."

For the first time, Emily felt empathy for the young woman, and she nodded at him to go on.

"She's in a terrible way. Nothing I say seems to ease her suffering. I've tried to avoid asking this of you, so few months after your own loss, but I was wondering if tomorrow you'd spend some time with her. You always know the right thing to say."

"I'm profoundly sorry you had to ask," she said quietly. "I should have gone to her on my own, instead of leaving the entire burden on you."

He smiled and lightly brushed a clump of snow from her shoulder. "I'd say you already have your hands full."

Emily knew Robert was just too chivalrous to let her accept her rightful blame. "Not with you here to help." She paused. "I'll do what I can."

He nodded gratefully. "It's more than only her mourning for Morgan. She's carrying a great weight of guilt over the matter, and nothing I say seems to make any difference. Fact is, she really is guilty."

"Why would you say that?" Emily asked, trying to conceal her surprise at his curious remark. "I probably should know what I'm dealing with."

Glancing into the distance, Robert appeared to be gathering his thoughts. Then he lifted the blanket flap of the shelter and checked inside before replacing it and meeting Emily's eyes. "Prudence's entire life and upbringing centered upon what was righteous and what was not. Honesty was one of her most rigid standards . . . so much so that she even rejected Morgan at one time for having taken money from his father for false purposes during his earlier spying days."

"I already know all of this," Emily said evenly. "Robby told me the whole story."

"Well, all that she ever condemned Morgan for doing, she's done herself, and worse. She encouraged him to renege on a vow of truthfulness he had made to the Lord, just to go back into spying again, even though she knew he did not feel peace about it. Her reasoning was that it served the greater good of our freedom; therefore, it wasn't actually *sin.* But now, not only does she question that conviction, but she bears the burden of having committed a far worse sin against him. She never told him about their child."

Emily's lips parted in shock. *"But, why?"*

"She feared he would send her back to Philadelphia. As it was, she and Evie went to New York without his permission."

"Oh, my. I can understand why she's inconsolable."

"There's more. She was the one who relayed the false information to Morgan. She sent him into the trap. She is positive it is all her fault and that his capture was God's retribution for her sins."

Emily exhaled in a rush, her breath vaporizing in the wintry air. This was what poor Robert was having to deal with just when he was beginning to find his own peace with the Lord. And she had left him to cope with all of it alone. Had his fragile new faith been crushed before it had a chance to take root? She needed to know. "And what do you think, Robert? Do you believe our heavenly Father is heaping vengeance on his daughter?"

He pondered the question for a moment. "What I think," he finally said, "is that *she* is reaping what *she* sowed."

"And what about Morgan?"

"According to Prudence, he accepted Washington's request to spy again before thinking it through, much less praying about it first."

Recalling her own prayerful struggle mere moments ago,

Emily had to smile. "That is something perhaps all of us are guilty of, one time or another."

"Except you."

"Especially me. But isn't it wonderful that we only need to repent in order to receive forgiveness? I think perhaps Prudence has forgotten that."

A slow smile widened Chandler's lips as he took Emily's hand in both of his. "I knew you'd know just what to say to her. I do thank you."

"For what?" she asked, refusing to acknowledge a strange fluttering in her heart. Surely it was only a friendly gesture on his part to warm her fingers in the freezing weather. She only hoped her voice would come out normal. "Don't thank me yet. I haven't even talked to her."

He continued to smile. "As you said to me a few nights past, I'm thanking you just for being you."

❦ ❦

Travel the next day was a little slower as they trekked through snowdrifts and icy creeks, but Emily felt warmer and lighter. She knew there was absolutely no reason to make more of Robert's words than he had intended, yet they were immensely fortifying. She rode, as always, at the rear with Katie and Rusty nearby, while the pacers made steady progress, eating up the distance between them and Dan's place. Emily could hardly wait to see her oldest brother and his wife again, to say nothing of her nephew and niece.

Ahead and off to the left, she glimpsed Robert as he rode away from Prudence and fell back toward her at the end of the herd. Emily knew this would be her cue to go and have her talk with Prudence. She glanced at Christopher and Evelyn to ensure that they were keeping watch over the horses nearest them; then she nudged her mount into a canter.

Robert, riding toward Emily on his way to the children, graced her with a smile. "How!" he called with an upraised hand as he switched his attention to Katie and Rusty. "Eagle

Eyes comes bearing greetings from Black-Haired Woman for Running Bear and Little Fawn."

The children giggled. "How, Eagle Eyes."

"Time for a powwow," Robert went on.

"Powwow?" Katie asked. "What's that?"

"That's what we Indians say when we want to get together and talk."

"Well," Emily returned with a hopeful smile, "I shall go have a powwow of my own."

He gave a nod. "For her sake and the baby's."

On her way, Emily prayed for wisdom and for the proper words. As she neared Morgan's wife, she felt much greater shame for her lack of compassion on the previous days. And how had she missed the dark circles shadowing Prudence's light gray eyes? Small wonder Robert had felt so concerned. She reined her stallion alongside Prudence's mare. "Robert is back visiting with the children," she began tentatively. "Thought I'd come ride with you for a while."

The dark-haired girl glanced behind them with a thin smile. "He does relish their every word. He's forever relating one antic or another to me."

Emily found the news oddly gratifying but had no inkling why she should. But now she debated whether to start right in or wait for an opening. A few moments of silence lapsed. She drew a calming breath. "Being with Katie and Rusty is only part of the reason Robert went back there, Prudence. He wanted you and me to have an opportunity to talk. He's quite worried about you."

Prudence met Emily's gaze, then looked away. "I know. He doesn't want anything bad to befall Morgan's unborn child . . . no matter who the baby's mother is."

"Surely you know Robert is genuinely concerned about you, as well as your baby."

A pink flush rose on Prudence's high cheekbones. "Yes." She urged her mount to a quicker pace.

Following behind her for several minutes, Emily used the

time to pray again for wisdom, then heeled her pacer to catch up. "Prudence?" she asked gently.

Silver eyes turned toward her for a fleeting second.

"I know something of what you're suffering. Truly, I do."

Prudence's expression turned bleak, and she emitted a sigh. "Forgive me, but you couldn't."

"Yes, I could." Emily reached to touch the other girl's arm. "Robert told me . . . everything."

With a sharp intake of breath, Prudence sought a glimpse of Robert, then turned forward, her demeanor haunted.

Emily pressed on. "I know a little of the guilt you're feeling . . . and so does the Lord. He's always there waiting to extend mercy and forgiveness. That's one of our most precious promises."

With a slanted look at Emily, Prudence grimaced. "I know most of his promises by heart, Emily. I attended church my whole life. I know I have God's forgiveness for the asking. It's my own I cannot give or accept. Thanks to me, our unborn child may never know his own father. How can I forgive that?"

"You have to find a way. The baby will need a healthy mother to care for it. No matter how much punishment you feel you deserve, you must forget your past mistakes and forgive. You must go on for your baby. Live today for today's sake, and try to make each tomorrow a little better. You can do that with God's help."

Prudence didn't respond. A tear traced a glistening path down her olive skin.

"With winter setting in, we're going to be together for some time to come. I'd like to be your friend. If you ever need to talk, I'll be there for you. And so will my brother Dan."

"Once they know the truth, they'll hate me. Morgan was one of their closest friends."

Emily smiled gently. "Dan and Susannah are very understanding people. Nonetheless, I'll speak to Robert. Neither of us will tell them anything. We'll leave that to you."

Nearing the next crest, Emily hoped it would be the last before they could start the downward trek into the Wyoming

Valley. "Just a little farther," she murmured, "and we can all rest and begin to heal."

"That does sound good," Prudence admitted quietly, looking ahead with a hopeful expression. But when she settled back into her saddle, the look vanished. "You know, I was always a very rigid person in my younger days. Very judgmental. But now I doubt I'll ever view another's imperfections—any failing—with disdain again."

Emily gave her a small smile. "This trip has been one of much soul-searching. I've had to face some of my own ugly secrets. But look." They had reached the summit, and she pointed at the vast expanse of the shimmering, snow-covered valley as it came into view far below. "It's all downhill from here."

Prudence didn't appear overly comforted at the quip. "I don't see how. We've lost so much, and if we lose the war, it will all have been for nothing."

Emily reached for her hand and gave it an encouraging squeeze. "It's time for us to let go, Prudence. Let go of everything. Even the war. God will see us through somehow. I just know he will."

"It all seems so hopeless," she answered miserably.

Emily nodded. "But when times are darkest, that's when we need God most."

42

"We're getting close," Christopher yelled to Emily, and excitement coursed through her. As they drove the herd by the quiet settlement of Wilkes-Barre, along the Susquehanna River, folks they passed waved and shouted greetings.

"We're taking the horses to Dan Haynes," Christopher answered, veering closer to the nearest settlers. "All the way from Rhode Island."

Emily could tell from the expressions of amazement that it was highly unlikely anyone had ever driven a herd this size into the area before. In her concern over evading the British, she had almost lost track of the arduous undertaking herself. She lifted her arm in a joyous wave to the plainly dressed townsfolk, wondering how many of them might be part of Dan's congregation.

"Howdy," Katie called, sitting tall and proud on her docile mount. She and Rusty waved, grins on their bright faces.

Emily's attention drifted across to Robert and Prudence. He was grinning, also. He turned in his saddle and waved—but not to the strangers. His wave was directed at her!

Her heart leaped, and she returned the gesture. This beautiful day marked the end of a long, incredible journey. But a rush of sadness dampened her enthusiasm. Tomorrow, or the next day at the latest, Robert would leave to go back to his battalion. Emily knew she would more than miss him. And he would once more be part of the desperate attempt to drive the

British from the continent. She had spent so much time needlessly feeling jealous of Prudence that she had lost sight of that very present danger.

After about a mile, Christopher motioned to turn the herd eastward, and they drove the animals across cleared fields. The afternoon sun glistened over the melting snow, lending a breathtaking beauty to the long, wide valley.

When they came upon a rude log cabin, a column of gray smoke churned upward against the stark blueness of the sky in a welcoming spiral.

"Halloo the house!" Chip hollered.

The door flew open, and out came the smiling family of four. Though Dan had always tended toward leanness, Emily observed that neither he nor Susannah had regained much of the weight they had lost during the months of deprivation they had endured inside the closed port of Boston. Yet to her, they had never looked better. Her brother was growing more and more to resemble their father, and a twinge of homesickness overtook her for a moment.

Dan, however, fairly beamed as he administered enthusiastic handshakes and stout hugs. Four-year-old Miles, with hair the same shade as his mother's, stood straight and tall, his dark eyes alight as he got in line for all the handshakes.

Emily remained in her saddle for a moment to look upon two-year-old Julia Rose, the niece whose name now took on an entirely new meaning. No longer would Emily think of her merely as the namesake of Susannah's best friend but as that of Robert's great love. The fair-haired child clung to her mama's skirts, peering shyly around them with huge blue eyes.

When one of the pacers milling about meandered a little too close, Dan snatched the child up into his arms. "I don't believe it! What is all this, Em?" He came to her side, a smile of incredulity lighting his dark brown eyes.

Emily laughed lightly and slid to the ground, only to be grabbed into a crushing embrace by her brother along with his little Julia. "I decided I have much better things to do than nurse this scrawny herd," she said after finally catching her breath. "You've been footloose quite long enough, big brother. Time you took on some responsibility."

"Well, not that I mind, you understand," he returned, "but as you can see, I don't even have a fenced pasture."

Robert, still on horseback, threaded his way through the pacers to join them. "That grand stack of logs yonder from when you cleared your land would make a fine split-rail fence."

"Robert Chandler?" Dan exclaimed in surprise. "And Prudence Thomas, too? I'm thoroughly confused now. But you can explain later." He turned to Christopher. "Chip, ride back to town and round up as many men as you can, even Connecticut lads and our friend Jon. Together we'll have a corral built before the sun sets."

❦ ❦

At Robert's insistence, Prudence had immediately been ushered to the bedroom normally used by Felicia Curtis, Yancy's wife, who had gone to visit her father for the Christmas holiday. Hesitant to take chances, he carried a tray of food to her instead of having her rise for supper. The children, exhausted from the trip, had been put to bed in the loft with their cousins right after the meal. And the men, weary and sore from the hasty fence building, stretched their aching muscles and retired early in Dan and Susannah's room, leaving Emily and Susannah alone to linger over cups of hot spiced cider.

Taking a soothing sip, Emily reflected upon the reunion, a curious mixture of joy and sadness. Her brother and sister-in-law had received word of Robby's death some months ago, but news of the invasion of Rhode Island and Morgan's capture were hard blows, particularly coupled with learning that the British had overrun New Jersey.

Susannah replenished their beverages as they relaxed at the dark pine kitchen table. "You've been on our hearts and minds so much, of late," she said, her pleasant British accent soft and familiar. "Now I know why Dan and I have felt burdened to pray for you." The concern in her blue gray eyes was mirrored on her face as she retucked a tendril of tawny hair into a ribbon at the nape of her neck.

Emily willed herself not to cry while she relived her grief one more time, answering all the hard questions for Susannah's sympathetic ear. It was so much easier to be strong when, moments later, they finally got beyond that subject. "And all I could think of," she confessed, "was Papa's dream, his herd. Knowing that his lovely farm might soon be destroyed, and that he and Mama were in danger, it suddenly became imperative to save the horses—or, at the very least, to keep the redcoats from confiscating them. Perhaps one day soon we'll be able to return them."

"Yes, well, we can only hope and pray that's so. In the meantime, I know Dan will take wonderful care of them. It astounds me that you were able to get them across all the rivers and over those mountains. God's miracles seem more wonderful by the day."

The front door opened, and Christopher and Evelyn walked in from the cold. They didn't appear to notice the two women as they crossed the room to the door of the room where Evie would be spending the night. Their doleful expressions as they bid one another good night would have been comical had Emily not been aware that Chip would be going with Robert, leaving Evelyn with the uncertainty of ever seeing him again. With a soft sob, Evie sniffed and entered the bedchamber, then closed the door.

"Oh, the bittersweet pangs of young love," Susannah said softly. Then her smile faded. "Speaking of that, is it my imagination, or is Robert's concern for Morgan's wife somewhat deeper than that of one friend for another?"

Emily almost choked on her cider. Recovering, she set down the empty cup. "Well, they've known each other quite a long time. And she's with child, you know. . . . It brings back memories of Julia."

"Oh, of course. I hadn't thought of that." She peered into

her empty mug, then reached for the warming pot at her elbow. "Would you care for more?" Without waiting for an answer, she refilled both their mugs one more time. "I'm sure it must be good for him. When he visited us in Boston, I doubt I saw him smile more than once or twice all the time he was there. It's quite refreshing to see such big grins on that handsome face of his. Several times today I even heard him laugh out loud."

Emily smiled as she pictured Chan's amiable face with its strong, chiseled features, the compelling blue eyes that sparkled with laughter or caring. "Those smiles started before we picked up Prudence and Evelyn in Princeton. Robert has finally accepted his loss after years of blaming God. He's repented and returned to his faith."

"That *is* marvelous—another of my daily prayers answered. God has been so good."

"Robby and I always prayed for him, too," Emily murmured.

"You are positive you're all right?" Susannah asked, giving Emily's hand an empathetic squeeze. "You've been faring well?"

Emily could not hold back a sigh. "I miss Robby, of course. I always will. But I know he's with the Lord, and with his father. Robby was quite heartbroken when he heard his father had died alone in far-off Scotland. I try to think of the wonderful reunion they must have had. It helps quite a bit."

"A reunion somewhat like ours today."

"Yes, I'm sure it was."

Susannah lightly tapped the tiny cleft in her chin as her fine brows furrowed in thought. "But there's something else troubling you, isn't there? There's a sadness in your eyes that isn't about Robby."

Emily swallowed hard. It was true; there was a strange unrest in her spirit. But she wasn't completely sure it could be expressed . . . even if she could confide in Susannah. "Oh, I suppose it's the war," she said, hedging. "It's all but lost."

Susannah's intent gaze remained fixed on her. "And?"

She raised her chin. "There's nothing else. Really. Well, only something too petty to discuss, to actually put into words."

"Nothing that makes you sad is unimportant, Emmy."

"I . . . don't know where to begin." A new wave of tears threatened, and it was all Emily could do to quell them. She averted her attention to the confines of the cozy room, with its finely crafted furniture and the homey touches Susannah had fashioned for their little home.

"It pains me to see you like this, Emily," Susannah coaxed. "Please know that you can always talk to me."

"It's-it's Robert Chandler," she finally blurted, the confession astounding even her. "I hate to think of him going back to battle." Suddenly aware of how deeply she meant those words, Emily felt that she had to justify them, lest her sister-in-law get the wrong impression. "When Robby died and Chan came to take the children and me to Princeton, he was so good to us. I can't tell you what a comfort he was, what a mountain of understanding and strength. He . . . was punished quite severely for leaving his post to bring my husband home to me, but he had made Robby a promise, and nothing could stop him." Emily flicked a nervous glance to Susannah, but seeing only compassion, she continued.

"Then when the British invaded Rhode Island and Papa sent word back to me to shoot the horses, Chandler was there again, taking charge. If it weren't for him, you know, I never would have made it all this way. He was a godsend." Her mouth twitched with a smile, and words came much more easily. "He has a remarkable sense of humor, did you know that? And he's so good with the children—" Realizing that she was no longer whispering, but talking far more loudly than she had intended, Emily stopped short.

"And now," Susannah finished for her, "all that attention he gave you he's now giving to Prudence. And you're a bit jealous."

Jealous! Emily felt the warmth of a flush. "Well . . . I suppose so. But it doesn't make sense. He's never so much as hinted that there might be anything between us. Not that there is . . . or-or should be. Oh, I don't even know what I'm trying to say. He's always been a perfect gentleman. I want you to know that. But . . . I can't help it. I've prayed, truly I have, but it hurts. You must think I'm a disloyal, selfish—"

"I beg your pardon, I didn't mean to eavesdrop."

Swinging toward the sound of the voice, Emily saw to her dismay that Robert stood in the doorway. Her face burst into flame. Never mind Susannah . . . what must *he* think of her!

"I heard voices," he went on. "I thought something might be amiss with Prudence."

Complete humiliation engulfed Emily like a wave. She fixed her eyes on the table, unable—and unwilling—to meet his gaze. No one spoke for several seconds.

Then Robert broke the silence. "Susannah, would you mind leaving the two of us alone for just a few moments? We need to talk."

No! Emily wanted to shout. *Stay here! Please!*

"Of course." With a troubled glance at Emily, Susannah quietly withdrew to the bedchamber.

Mortified, Emily hunkered slightly into herself.

Robert came to her side and took her hands, drawing her gently to her feet. He did not let go.

Unable to meet his eyes, she glued her gaze to the middle button on his shirt. What must he think of her? What had he heard? For that matter, what had she actually *said*?

"Tell me you meant it," he said, his voice low but firm. "What you told Susannah."

Emily turned her head aside. To her recollection, she'd been babbling like a lovesick—

"These . . . feelings . . . you have for me, they go beyond those of a mere friend?"

"I—" Did that mean he *wanted* her to have them—or *didn't*? And *did* she? *Could* she, so soon after Robby? Was that possible? Her heart pounded almost painfully in her breast. "But-but what about Prudence . . . if Morgan doesn't return?" she asked lamely.

"What about Prudence? If the worst happens, we'll see her through the rough times, be there for her, of course. But that isn't what I asked."

Hesitantly, she looked up at him. From the intensity of his stare, Emily suspected he could see into her very soul, read what was there even if she didn't say the words. She could not look away. Nor could she deny feelings which only now she began to recognize. "It's . . . true."

He expelled a rush of breath. The beginnings of a smile touched the corners of his lips, and his fingers tightened around her upper arms. "Does that mean you'd allow me to court you?"

She searched his gaze, still unsure. "If . . . you would have me."

"*Have you*? Oh, Emily, Emily." He crushed her against his chest, and she realized the thundering of her own heart was no match for his.

Too soon he broke away, but he stroked her face as he talked. . . . "I can't believe someone so good, so perfect as you . . . would want someone like me."

"Robert." Emily eased back warily. "I am not perfect. You must never think that."

He tilted his head, studying her, then bent and kissed her nose. "For now, this moment, I choose to consider you perfect, my angel. After this war is over, God willing, we'll have a lifetime to discover one another's flaws."

"Only if you stay alive," she whispered, a mist of sudden tears blurring his face before her eyes. "Promise me you'll come back."

"How could I not? I love you, Emily Haynes MacKinnon. You brought me back to life. And I promise you, nothing in this world will keep me from coming back to you." He tugged her close again, into the security of his strong arms. "And I know you need time . . . more time to grieve, to heal. But I'll come back, and I'll wait—as long as it takes."

Emily's heart was near to bursting with joy, with fear. Robert loved her. And she knew he couldn't really promise to stay alive. She could only put him in God's hands, but she knew somehow she could trust him there. And right now, tonight, she felt loved again. "I'll be here waiting . . . when you return."

43

All was quiet in the big room. Assuming that everyone had gone outside at last, Prudence threw off the blankets and quilts and got out of bed. The smell of baking bread was too hard to resist.

Emily's and Evie's sleeping pallets had been straightened, she noticed as she padded across to the birch commode, and someone had brought fresh water in the china pitcher. Wanting to be alone rather than face questions regarding Morgan, Prudence had feigned sleep most of the morning, and she hadn't seen who had been so kind. Soon she hoped to have the luxury of a full bath, but for now washing up would have to do.

The cool water was both stimulating and refreshing, and when she finished she turned to retrieve her clothing. The costly gown she had worn on the journey, soiled by days of travel, was not where she had left it. In its place was a much simpler frock Prudence decided must be Susannah's. Mere months ago, in Boston, she herself had worn plain things, and Morgan had fallen in love with her—the simple, straightforward Puritan girl. So much had happened since those days. What had become of that girl?

She let out a soft sigh as she shrugged off her night dress and slipped into the indigo linen frock. Perhaps the devious side of her had always existed somewhere deep within, just waiting for the right excuse to allow it to surface. *Righteous excuse,* she amended with disdain. She didn't deserve this sort of kindness now. She should wear her own soiled clothing as penance for her willful stupidity. Morgan had tried to warn her about rushing into the foolhardy life of spying, but ever out to prove how equally capable she was in the art, she'd been too stubborn to listen. Too *proud.* And as it said in the Scriptures, *Pride goeth before destruction, and an haughty spirit before a fall.*

Sharp thuds echoed outside the house as she laced the bodice of the gown. Prudence moved to the window, where she saw Christopher hard at work splitting logs. Off to one side, Evie watched with adoring eyes as her hero's youthful muscles rippled with each swing. Prudence observed the touching scene for several minutes, noting the vast change that had come over Morgan's sister. Gone was the brittle gaiety she had displayed during her weeks in New York, and in its place was a wide-eyed innocence Prudence had barely glimpsed when they had first met. Still, for one who had known nothing save the comforts wealth could provide, was it possible to find true happiness in a life of hardship with a man of the people?

Prudence shrugged. She supposed they would just have to find out on their own, with time.

Beyond the two young people, a movement within the herd of Narragansett Pacers drew her attention. Dan, Robert, and Emily walked among them, running their hands down flanks and forelegs, checking hooves. Everything seemed so pastoral, so peaceful. It was hard to believe that just across the range of mountains the world was "turned upside down," as the British marching tune proclaimed. Her thoughts drifting, Prudence started to turn away from the window, but something caught her eye. Robert came up behind Emily and placed his hand on her waist . . . and Emily leaned back against his chest with a smile!

How could they? Prudence was appalled. Robby had been gone but a few short months. How could his own wife—and his best friend, no less—have forgotten him so quickly? She would *never* forget Morgan. *Never!*

She swung away, tears smarting her eyes as she made haste for the main room. A tantalizing cloud of baking aromas enveloped her when she opened the door. Golden loaves of bread and several varieties of scones and cookies lined the side counter. Susannah, swathed in an oversized work apron, was even now putting a large plucked bird into a Dutch oven, obviously preparing a feast.

After placing the lidded iron kettle on the glowing coals, Susannah turned and looked up. "Oh, good. Do come and sit down, dear, and I'll pour you some coffee."

Prudence waved her off. "No, finish what you're doing. I can wait on myself." She fetched a cup and filled it, while Susannah hefted a bulky sack to the table and took several good-sized turnips from it.

Susannah smiled pleasantly as she began peeling. "You're looking quite a bit better this morning. But then, you come from good, solid New England stock. I'm sure you'll be blessed with a fine healthy babe soon to carry on the—" Stopping abruptly, she blushed and stood up. "Let me cut you a slice of bread to go with that coffee."

Prudence needed no one to finish Susannah's sentence. *To carry on the Thomas name.* She touched her rounding abdomen. Morgan had been his father's only son. And this baby he had known nothing about would be the only tangible proof that he had ever lived. Everything depended on her safeguarding this priceless child of their love.

Susannah returned and placed a plate of bread before her. "Try to think more on the happy times, if you can," she said gently.

Prudence, knowing that Susannah meant well, tried to lighten her expression. "But there's so much that was left unresolved. How will I ever explain all of this to his parents—about Morgan, about Evie being a fugitive . . . the baby." Even if it had been safe for her to do so, she couldn't have returned to them.

Susannah gave Prudence's hand a comforting pat. "Dan will help you write a letter to Morgan's family. I'm sure he won't mind. And, Prudence, I know it's very difficult, but just take things one day at a time. We're celebrating Christmas today."

"Christmas? It can't be."

"Quite right. It's not actually December twenty-fifth. But Christopher and Robert have agreed to delay leaving for their battalion until tomorrow, so Chip and Evie rode over to his sister's early this morning. Mary Clare and Jonathan and their children will be coming soon with some pies and cider. We shall have our Christmas feast while we're all together. I truly believe, dear heart, we need to dwell on our blessings for a little while. So many sorrows have befallen us in the past few months. We must not allow them to overwhelm us."

Prudence had heard scarcely a word after the mention of Chip and Robert's departure. "They're leaving tomorrow? We have to talk them out of it. I couldn't help seeing Robert and Emily outside awhile ago. If she cares anything about him, how can she let him go back there?"

The front door opened just then, and Emily breezed in with a smile. "Is there anything I can do before Mary Clare and Jonathan arrive?"

"Yes," Prudence announced. "Convince Chan not to go back. The war is lost. We've sacrificed enough."

A look of compassion warmed Emily's rosy cheeks. "That's tomorrow, Prudence. Let tomorrow take care of itself. All of us want to set today aside simply to love and rejoice with one another." Emily stepped behind Prudence and began unplaiting her long black hair. "Today I just want to love you and your baby. Let me start with this, fixing your hair. After all, I'll be showing you off to Mary Clare and Jon. He and Morgan were best friends in college."

"I know," she said wistfully. "'The Lords of Dunce,' as I recall. Or so Mrs. Lyons dubbed them when they had to remain at school during spring recess. They had been so busy being pranksters they hadn't taken time to prepare for their orals." She paused. "Oh, Emily, they're going to hate me."

"Not today they're not." Emily gave a playful yank on the braid.

Miles and Katie burst inside, their faces glowing from the cold. "Mama," Miles cried. "They're here! Esther and Bethy!"

"Those are the children," Susannah said. She wiped her hands on her apron. "I must go greet everyone."

By the time Emily finished tying off Prudence's plait, the front room was bursting at the seams with smiling faces and running, laughing children. Prudence saw a ruddy-faced young man she assumed was Jonathan walk into the house with his arm around Robert, both men grinning broadly. She didn't really feel up to all this. Perhaps she could slip quietly away to the bedroom without being noticed.

Emily, with another slim blonde in tow, cut off her escape. "Prudence, I'd like you to meet Chip's older sister, Mary Clare. Mary, this is Prudence, Morgan's wife from Boston."

"I'm pleased to meet you," Prudence said politely.

Mary Clare ducked her head slightly and didn't quite meet her gaze as she bobbed into a curtsy. "And you, Mistress Thomas."

Prudence took the shy girl's hand with a reassuring smile. "Please, call me Prudence. Morgan has spoken so fondly of you and your husband."

"He has?" Her look of surprise was overtaken by a pleased one. "I knew he would choose someone like you. Pretty and sure of yourself. Someone who could stand right up to him."

What an odd thing to say, Prudence thought.

"Evelyn told us all about you this morning," Mary went on, "how smart you are and how brave. And . . ." Her gaze faltered briefly, then settled once more on Prudence. "I know Morgan will come out of his predicament just fine. He could always talk his way out of any mischief he got into, couldn't he, Emily?"

Robert stepped up behind Emily and put his hands on her

shoulders. "That's right. We're not about to give up now, are we?"

Emily turned and gazed lovingly up at him, and the look made Prudence want to cry from loneliness.

Jonathan then came to join his timid wife, casually draping an arm over her shoulders. He extended his other hand to Prudence. "I'm Jon. It's a real pleasure to meet you. Welcome to our valley."

His eyes, oddly mismatched, with one green and the other blue, provided just the distraction she needed to keep her from drowning in her emotions. "Thank you," she managed, then glanced around for a plausible excuse to extricate herself from the group before falling apart. Seeing Evie and Christopher at the fireplace, their heads close together in conversation, only made matters worse. The love in the room was enough to suffocate a person. "We . . . need water," she blurted, and seized the bucket.

❧ ❧

Robert watched Prudence flee, and his heart went out to her. He knew her excuse was only a pretense. "Think I'd better go talk to her," he murmured to Emily, reluctant to part from her for even a few minutes on this, their last day together.

"I'll miss you," she whispered back.

The look in her green eyes made it all the harder to go, but he knew he needed to do what he could to calm Prudence's spirit.

Outside, he found Prudence leaning against a tree with her back to him, the pail dangling aimlessly from her fingers. He approached as quietly as possible on the snow-covered ground and placed a hand on her shoulder. "We all love you, Prudence . . . enough to talk straight to you and not beat around the bush."

Her head drooped, but she said nothing.

He knew she was crying. "I've learned some very hard lessons of my own, dear friend, since this war started. One of them is that dying is easy. It's living that takes all a person's effort. Love Morgan's memory; miss him. . . . But whatever you do, don't shroud yourself in guilt and remorse the way I did. Don't waste the gift of life God gives you each and every day. Make the most of today and every tomorrow as it comes. Forgive yourself . . . or you'll end up a useless shell of a person, as I was for far too long. Your baby needs—*deserves*—more than that."

Prudence turned and raised her eyes to his, her face awash with tears. "Is this really you talking? You've changed so; you've come alive. I . . . saw you with Emily."

He smiled with chagrin. "I admit, I've finally crawled out of that black pit I dug for myself. What a waste of years. But thanks to her . . . and God . . ." His throat tightened. "Just don't turn your back on God's healing power, as I did. Trust him."

She reached to touch his cheek with a thin smile, but she didn't quite look at him. "Careful . . . you're beginning to sound like Robby MacKinnon."

"Wouldn't that be something!"

"But . . . how can Emily forget him so quickly?"

"She hasn't forgotten him. Nor have I. He'll always hold a very special part of both our hearts. But war has a way of compressing time, of making things happen more quickly than they might under ordinary circumstances. The Lord has taken Emily beyond the sadness, the mourning, and now she's able to go on. We're all different, Prudence, and we all handle grief in our own ways. But God knows what we need. Trust him to help you, Prudence. Lean on him . . . and on us." Robert took her hand. "Come back inside."

"Not just yet. But, thank you. The others have said practically the same thing to me. From you, though, who suffered for so long, it has far more meaning. I need to think for a while, to be by myself."

He stepped back to study her, noting the tenuous courage in the lift of her chin, the flicker of hope in her gray eyes. "Then, you're going to be all right?"

She nodded and favored him with a small smile. "Now go back to Emily. Your day is fast slipping away."

Robert lingered another moment, just to be sure she was being truthful, then took the bucket from her and returned to the house.

❦ ❦

Prudence watched after him, unable to mistake the new spring in his step, the new straightness in his stance. She was happy for Robert, that he had finally been able to come to terms with his loss. Only now could she understand the depth of such pain, how it would cause a person to want to give up. How tempting it would be to wrap her own sorrow around her like a burial shroud and close herself off from the world. But then she thought of Emily and how the Lord had taken her through the death of her husband in a matter of months. Prudence knew it was her choice—to turn from God and the love and strength with which he would sustain her in the lonely years ahead, or to place her hand in his and allow him to be all that she needed.

Not far away, a half-grown colt suckled its mother, its head ducked low. Prudence strolled toward the large pen the neighbors had come together to build despite their recent territorial disputes. Either the war or Dan and Susannah's ministry had brought a new unity to the Pennsylvania and Connecticut settlers. Boston had taken a toll on the Haynses, especially Dan's gently bred English wife, and this rustic way of living could prove even harder. But Susannah possessed a peaceful spirit that always shone through. Perhaps Morgan's pampered little sister would also adjust to the added rigors.

The countryside surrounding this small town was incredibly beautiful. There was much to be said for moving to virgin territory, carving out one's own place in the world. The Haynes land was rich and flat, with hills rising behind it, a small creek running off to one side, the river below. No doubt, with the herd and his ministerial work, they'd do very well here. It was a fine place for new beginnings.

The stock moved about in the corral. None of them looked particularly the worse for the hasty and difficult trip.

It still amazed Prudence to think of the horsewoman Emily had turned out to be. She was as capable as any man, yet she possessed such a sweet spirit. Emily . . . and Robert. The thought no longer brought disquiet. Now that she thought about it, that loving calm that seemed so much a part of Emily was probably exactly what Robert needed after so many years of spiritual unrest. The union would be good for Emily and her children, too. Robert would see that they had every advantage. He was the only male heir of a prosperous family . . . like Morgan.

She rested her hands on her blossoming belly. Had her duplicity cost her child his birthright?

That thought was discarded almost as soon as it came. Morgan's father and mother would welcome this grandchild with all the love they had, despite everything. Prudence knew she had judged her mother-in-law far more harshly than the woman had deserved. True, Mother Thomas was domineering, but she herself admitted as much . . . and everything she had insisted upon had been because she wanted the best for those she loved.

With a regretful sigh, Prudence propped her arms on the corral fence. The memory of her singing lessons surfaced in her mind . . . and her debut. A little smile broke free. Who would've thought Morgan could sing like that? Ah, what a champion he'd been that day! Despite herself, she laughed.

"What's so funny?"

Prudence's heart stopped. *Morgan?*

She whirled around. He truly was there, alive, and in the flesh. She flung herself at him, kissing him and crying and touching him to make sure she wasn't dreaming. "I thought you were . . . I thought they'd hanged you."

"I'm sure you did," he said gently, his lopsided grin sobering as he stroked tears from her cheek. His strong arms wrapped around her in a crushing embrace that stole her very breath. "When Jasper and Esther Lyons told me how upset you were, I rode straight through."

She reached to touch his unshaven cheek, taking in his mud-splattered clothing. "But—how did you manage to get away?" Prudence searched his cobalt eyes, still trying to convince herself it was not a dream. She lost herself in their rich depths.

"I was able to wrest the pistol from Captain Long. Shot him in the leg in the process, I'm afraid. Needless to say, he was less than pleased. He yelled all manner of unkind references to me *and* my mother as I ran off toward town. Then I doubled back and sneaked aboard the ship I had acquired the sailing permit for earlier that afternoon, and it sailed with the tide. The only problem was, when we reached open water there was no wind. Just a dead calm. It took six days to reach port. I can't tell you how sorry I am at being delayed."

Prudence, loving the sound of his deep voice, struggled to assimilate everything he was saying. "I was afraid even to hope you were still alive. I only knew I didn't deserve to ask God to keep you safe, not after all the horrid things I've done. I felt it would have been my just punishment if you were taken from me." Fresh tears trembled on her lashes.

"Shh." He drew her into his arms once more, rocking her gently until her shaking stopped.

Prudence relaxed into his comfort, and she never wanted to draw away. "When you reached Philadelphia, did you stop in to see your parents?"

He stiffened a bit. "By the time I reached them, soldiers had already been to the house. They were beside themselves with worry . . . and disillusionment. My spying days are through, Prudence. No cause can be so noble if it creates such grief. I can hardly bear to think about all my lies, the bad influence I've been for Evie."

"The blame is much more mine than yours. If I had been the kind of wife I should be . . . the kind of Christian I should be . . . none of this would ever have happened." She hesitated. "How was your mother when you left her?"

An odd expression clouded Morgan's rugged features, erasing most of the cockiness that normally resided there. "You know, I've only lately discovered how fragile she really is. She's always lived protected from the harsher realities. And Father actually does love her very much, despite his complaints to me about her overbearing ways. He was trying very tenderly to comfort her when I departed."

"I could use a little of that myself," she whispered.

A slow smile spread across his mouth, and he lowered his head, their breath intermingling for a sweet eternity before he covered her lips with his. She slipped her arms around his neck and pressed closer, deepening the kiss until it left them both breathless. Neither spoke as they stood in each other's embrace, their hearts beating as one.

Prudence eased back and looked up at him. "Someday we must make amends. I only pray the damage we've wrought can be undone."

"I quite agree. And to make matters worse, the whole city is in chaos with both armies heading there. As it turned out, Captain Long hadn't been that far off with his fabricated information. The Congress left and relocated in Baltimore. Anyway, when I reached Princeton, I sent a note to my parents letting them know that you and Evie were safely tucked away for the moment."

Prudence smiled. "Yes, we are. All three of us."

His thick brows drew together in a slight frown. "Oh, you mean Emily, too?"

She shook her head. "Not exactly. I mean Evie, me, and our baby."

"*Baby?* We're going to have a child? You and me, the two of us?"

Smiling, she nodded.

"Praise be!" He grabbed her exuberantly and swung her around in a circle, then caught his breath and stopped as suddenly. "Oh. Did I hurt you? And that long horseback ride—"

"I'm fine, truly I am. And more than fine, now that you're here. Just a little tired . . . which is quite normal."

"Well, you must stay put from now on. Here, where it's safe. Promise me you'll do that, Prudence. I won't rest until you do."

"Believe me, sweetheart, I'll never put our baby in jeopardy again. I now understand what it is to be totally responsible for another's life. I shall try never to worry you with my recklessness from this day forward."

He breathed a sigh of relief, and a trace of a cocky smile lifted one corner of his mouth. "It's about time you learned your place."

Prudence ignored the spark of mischief in his demeanor. "My *place*?" The very thought rankled her.

Morgan laughed and pulled her cloak more securely around her. "And right now, my love, your place is inside, out of this December cold."

"And yours," she teased, "is right beside me, hugging and kissing me at least once every minute for the rest of this day."

Desire darkened the blue of his eyes. "That's a rather tall order, but I'll give it my best shot. Starting now." He hauled her into his arms and kissed her again, an unspoken promise that made her blush, especially when accompanied by the knowing grin that followed.

Prudence struggled to regain her composure as he ushered her to the house. She nudged Morgan off to the side and put a finger to her lips. Then, opening the door, she paused on the threshold, gazing at the happy gathering, her own heart fairly overflowing with joy.

Emily, slicing carrots at the table, looked up. "Oh. We were getting worried. I was about to go looking for you."

"No need," Prudence answered, scarcely able to maintain a straight face. "I'm sorry for worrying you. But—I've found a Christmas gift that just might make up for it." Stepping aside, she made room for Morgan.

When he entered, a collective shout of joy rang the rafters, and the two of them were swallowed up by a jumble of hugs and laughter.

Dan finally raised a hand for calm. "I didn't think it was possible for one more blessing to fall upon us this day, but apparently the Lord saved the best for last. Let's join hands and thank God for his goodness."

Prudence slipped her hand into Morgan's much larger one and smiled across the ring at Robert and Emily. This truly was a place—and a time—for new beginnings. And she was beginning to like the thought. No matter what lay ahead for the dear folk in this gathering, the Lord would see them all through. She couldn't ask for more.